By Slanderous Tongues

By Slanderous Tongues

Mercedes Lackey
Roberta Gellis

By Slanderous Tongues

This is a work of fiction. All the characters and events portrayed in this book are fictional, and any resemblance to real people or incidents is purely coincidental.

A Baen Books Original

Baen Publishing Enterprises
P.O. Box 1403
Riverdale, NY 10471
www.baen.com

ISBN 10: 1-4165-2107-0
ISBN 13: 978-1-4165-2107-5

Cover art by Stephen Hickman

First printing, February 2007

Distributed by Simon & Schuster
1230 Avenue of the Americas
New York, NY 10020

Library of Congress Cataloging-in-Publication Data

Gellis, Roberta.
   By slanderous tongues / Roberta Gellis, Mercedes Lackey.
      p. cm.
   ISBN-13: 978-1-4165-2107-5
   ISBN-10: 1-4165-2107-0
   1. Great Britain—History—Edward VI, 1547–1553—Fiction. 2. Elizabeth I, Queen of England, 1533–1603—Fiction. 3. Great Britain—Kings and rulers—Succession—History—16th century—Fiction. I. Lackey, Mercedes. II. Title.

   PS3557.E42B9 2007
   813'.54—dc22

                                                      2006028453

10   9   8   7   6   5   4   3   2   1

Pages by Joy Freeman (www.pagesbyjoy.com)
Printed in the United States of America

By Slanderous Tongues

Prologue

The small glade was filled with a silvery light that had no source in sun or moon. It was bordered by giant trees, their leaves a dark mist fading into the seemingly star-studded sky, their smooth-barked trunks shining softly with reflected silver. Between the trees, walling off the outside world, were curtains of spider web, as beautifully patterned as the finest lace, with tiny beads of dew gleaming like jewels along the strands.

A male being, not a man, for he was fully and truly Other, lay at ease on a raised bed of soft, dry moss. The silver light gleamed on his white skin, picking out with subtle shadows, the powerful muscles of arm and thigh, the flat, faintly ribbed belly, the swelling pectorals. His eyes were so black that no pupils could be seen, but there was a living glow to them; his hair was black too, somewhat tumbled now but showing the deep peak from which it was ordinarily swept smoothly back in springy waves. Even abandoned to utter relaxation Oberon would have inspired awe had any been there to see him.

Beside him, equally relaxed, lay a vision of perfect beauty, golden hair spread wide over the moss pillow on which her head rested. Her eyes were green, brilliant, their oval pupils, like those of a cat, a sharp contrast to the glowing green. Her skin was alabaster white but somehow warm and living, touched on cheek and lip with a pale rose that darkened provocatively on the upstanding

1

nipples of her bare breasts. And, like alabaster, her whole body seemed almost translucent, lit from within. Titania at rest was an image to be fixed in the mind and cherished forever.

Titania turned slightly toward Oberon and sighed. "There has been more than usual energy and excitement coming from the mortal world this past week, but it will not last."

A very faint smile touched Oberon's beautifully shaped lips; he did not move his head, but his eyes shifted so he could see his queen. They showed a wary gleam.

"No, I fear we have some dull years coming," he said.

Titania sat up. "And worse to follow, much worse."

Oberon shrugged, his glance caressing Titania's perfect body. "It is all grist to our mill, whether joy or pain the mortal energy comes to feed us, to bring us power for our magic."

"Faugh! The sourness of horror and agony coats my mouth, slimes my throat, and roils my belly. I prefer the sweet energy of dancing and singing, of poetry of love and heroism, of rich tales of imagination mingled with joy and tragedy." She leaned forward, eyes intent, lips thinning. "I do not want the fires of the Inquisition in Logres!"

"Titania . . ." Although he had not moved, there was a tense warning in Oberon's voice. "I cannot deprive the Unseleighe Sidhe of their share. Something calls the energy of pain to them and so their power grows and they feel rich. Our power thins for a time, but only for a little while." He lifted a hand and touched her shoulder, then allowed his fingers to slide down her arm. "It ill befits you to be so greedy when the evil will last so few mortal years, barely an eyeblink to us. I am lord of both Seleighe and Unseleighe kind, whether the Morrigan admits it or no. That I linger among the Seleighe is my choice. That I favor the Seleighe is also my choice."

"So you say." But Titania's lips had pursed into a mulish pout. "But I would not see the promise of the great blossoming destroyed and there are threats gathering about the red-haired queen. It would be so easy . . . Mary is already ailing . . ."

Oberon rose so that he was facing Titania. "No! I will have no interference. A path is set. It must be trodden . . . even by such as you, my lady."

His head was well above hers and his shoulders half a body wider, but she faced him without flinching, power rising in her so that her flesh glowed faintly. "Why? There are strange things in the FarSeers' lens. Some Great Evil is stirring."

"I am no less aware than you," Oberon snapped. "When it moves, I will deal with it."

"Yes, I am sure you will, but then it may be too late. If that Great Evil touches Elizabeth, her spirit might be warped, bent into unreason and cruelty so that a blight falls over the blossoming." She was silent for a moment, then lifted her head defiantly. "If Mary does not provide a fertile ground to plant a seed . . ."

"No, I say!" A faint rumble as of far-off thunder disturbed the tranquil air.

"I will protect Elizabeth who will bring me my desire . . ." The thunder drew nearer; the air thickened and grew heavy. The light in the clearing darkened. For a moment the challenge between them threatened to erupt into violence, but then Titania cocked her head to one side and said, "I will offer a bargain."

"What bargain?" The thunder receded.

"I will not myself touch nor send any agent to touch Mary if Elizabeth is allowed free entrance and exit Underhill. Here I or her guardians can heal any hurt done her so that her spirit will remain strong and untrammeled until her fate comes upon her." She smiled in triumph as the faint light returned to the clearing, and air cleared.

The overt expression of Oberon's face and voice as he heard her was wariness, but beneath that was something that Titania could not read or was reluctant to read. Satisfaction? Had he known all along what she desired and was baiting her? Fury rose in Titania. More color touched her cheeks and made her breasts swell slightly so that the nipples were even more prominent and more rosy. She clenched her jaw. And suddenly Oberon leaned forward, touched her lips with his and brushed a fingertip over one rosy nipple.

"Done," he said, his lips moving sensuously against hers, and then, "You dazzle my eyes like the mortal sun when you are angry."

Anger collapsed again for the moment. She should have been angrier still . . . and she would be. She would rage . . . but after, after he had served her a new portion of delight.

Chapter 1

Elizabeth's world had fallen apart again. That morning a messenger had come to Katherine Ashley, Elizabeth's governess, from William Cecil, to say that a Dirge for King Henry would be sung and the bells rung in all churches that night. It was very kind of Master Cecil, who must be furiously busy. No one else seemed to have thought at all of what the loss of her father meant to Elizabeth.

A tear dripped down onto the book cover Elizabeth was embroidering, and she found her kerchief to blot her work and wipe her eyes. Across the hearth from her, Kat looked up. Kat had been with Elizabeth since she was three years old and Elizabeth knew Kat loved her as deeply as if she had birthed her. But she did not understand what the king's death meant. She did not understand that, fickle and often arbitrary as he had been, the king had been all that stood between Elizabeth and peril. She also did not understand that, fickle and arbitrary as he had been, Elizabeth had looked up to, and sometimes even worshipped her grand, glorious father, dazzling even in his ruin. The sun had left the sky, and what illuminated it now? A sad, sickly moon.

"What will become of me," Elizabeth murmured, her voice too low to carry to anyone but Kat.

"Nothing bad, love," Kat said soothingly. "You were very well provided for in King Henry's will. You will have lands and manors, and live just as you have always done."

"But who will tell me where to live and with whom? You know the king always decided which manor I should use and when I should share households with Edward, and now that is impossible. Edward is the king." She drew a sharp breath and tears flooded her eyes again. "Will *we* be allowed to choose in what manor to live?" Impossible, surely, and did she even want it? To decide things for herself—a prospect at this moment more frightening than attractive.

"I think perhaps you would be considered a little too young for that. You are only fourteen years old. You must give the Council time, Lady Elizabeth. There are so many things they must decide upon and they know you are safe here at Enfield with me and your household."

It was not the first time that Elizabeth had posed these questions to her governess since the king, her father, had died, and Kat looked anxiously at her charge. Elizabeth had her lower lip between her teeth, but she did not have that pallid, hollow-eyed look that Kat recognized as a sign of real physical illness.

The girl's cheeks were pale, but they always were because she had the white complexion that went with her red hair—except her skin was not so thin and delicate as some redheads and, thank God, she had no freckles. Her eyes were not her father's blue but her mother's brown. Fortunately, unlike Anne Boleyn's eyes, Elizabeth's were very light, almost golden when Elizabeth was happy. She was not beautiful but she was pretty enough to attract a man.

There was a prospect that had only just occurred to Kat of late . . . and not one she relished. Lady Elizabeth was still a valuable marriage pawn. Her disposition would be at the will of King Edward—or rather, King Edward's governors. Attracting men was not safe.

Kat bit her lip. Surely Elizabeth was too young to marry, but with her father, King Henry, dead, who knew what the Council would decide to do with the second in line for the throne. Doubtless the Councilors were fighting among themselves for power. Would one of them suddenly appear at Enfield and try to take possession of Elizabeth? The Lady Mary, Elizabeth's older sister, was the heir apparent, but she was a woman grown and had a much larger household to defend her.

What should I do, Kat wondered fearfully, *if a Councilor appears and demands that Elizabeth be in his charge?* Kat glanced toward the door, outside of which one of Elizabeth's four guardsmen stood. They were devoted and good fighters, but none of them was young and there were only four, although Dunstan, the Groom of the Chamber and the two stablemen, Ladbroke and Tolliver would fight too.

What if men coming to take Elizabeth had a legal writ signed by Edward? Then to resist them would be treason. But if they did not have a writ, then not resisting them would be treason. . . . And how could Kat tell a legal writ from one that was forged?

Oh, she was being ridiculous, Kat told herself, no one was going to try to seize Elizabeth. The young king, Edward, was whom they would be fighting over. And there would be much jockeying over which noble daughter he would wed, too. Young as he was, younger than Elizabeth, they would want him safely wed, and bedded to, if that were possible. But Kat wished Lord Denno would come. He would know what was going on in London; he would know what to do. Surely Lord Denno had not abandoned Elizabeth. She looked at Elizabeth again, but said nothing, returning her gaze to her own needlework.

Elizabeth, however, had been aware of the slightly tremulous quality in Kat's voice and of her anxious scrutiny. For a moment, her vision was too blurred to take another stitch, and she looked into the lively fire in the small hearth. The tears refracted her vision so that for one instant she thought she saw a little red salamander twisting and leaping with joy in the flames.

A single blink restored the fire to just orange and yellow light. Elizabeth sighed. Having her world fall apart was no new sensation for her. The first time it had happened she had been only three. That was when her mother had disappeared and no one would tell her where or why Anne Boleyn had gone. And suddenly she was no longer Princess Elizabeth but only Lady Elizabeth and instead of being cosseted and almost drowned in clothes and so many toys she had no time to play with them, there were no new toys at all and hardly enough clothing to keep her warm.

The world had slowly mended itself. Darling Kat had come to be her governess and a new household, much smaller but in some ways closer and warmer, had formed. And she had been taught to read and write—what a joy that was. She had hardly been conscious of what was happening outside her own small world, but her father had taken a new wife and had a son. That was very good because she was no longer a source of trouble for him. So now and then she had some notice from the king, her father, and his blessing. Henry had still been hale and hearty enough to be a modicum of the godlike, glorious "Bluff Hal" of his best years.

Only little Edward's mama had died. The next lady had not been to her father's taste, but she was willing to be divorced. So her father had been free to marry Catherine Howard, Elizabeth's own cousin. At first that had been all joy; Elizabeth had been invited to Court and made much of until the truth of Catherine's promiscuity was exposed . . . and Elizabeth's world had been shattered again.

Elizabeth swallowed, set down her embroidery, and chaffed her hands together to warm them. The memory of the black desolation that had seized her after Catherine's execution—a desolation laid upon her by a spell that nearly killed her—could still chill the very marrow of her bones. She knew it could never happen again; she had protection now. Defensively, staring into the fire, Elizabeth raised her shields both inner and outer, felt herself inviolate behind them, and was reassured.

Raising the shields in her mind and on her body reminded her that she had a few other tricks too. The corners of Elizabeth's lips quirked when she thought of the effects of tanglefoot and stickfast, and, in dire need, of *gwythio* and *cilgwythio*.

She lifted the embroidery and set another stitch, then frowned and looked at it more closely. "Kat," she said, "I have just bethought myself . . . Is this work grand enough? Do you think I should redo part of the embroidery using more gold and silver thread? Edward is no longer my dear little brother. He is king now."

Relieved to hear such a practical and reasonable doubt, instead of the repeated fears about what would happen to her, Kat leaned forward and took Elizabeth's work from her hands.

She looked over the design carefully and said, "Grace of God, I never thought of that. It is true that any pretty design was enough in the past. King Edward would have enjoyed it because *you* made it for him. He does love you dearly but . . . but as you say, he is king now."

The echo of Elizabeth's own words hammered home the meaning. Edward was king because her father was dead!

Cold swept over Elizabeth again and she shuddered. It did not seem possible that Henry VIII could be dead. He had always been there ruling England. He had always been larger than life, the one most important being in the world. He had always directed her fate. How could he be dead? How could ten-year-old Edward be king?

And, she swallowed hard, where did that leave her? What would be her place now? Would the provisions of her father's will be kept? Would she remain the second in line for the throne? What would happen to her?

Underhill. Elizabeth could barely think the word and her lips would not form it, even silently, but she knew it was there, a safe haven if all else failed. She clasped her hands tightly together in her lap and shuddered.

Was Underhill still there for her? Too vivid in her mind was the dreadful quarrel she had had with Underhill's king. How could she have been so foolish? Surely after dealing with her father, knowing that meekness and devotion were the only paths to winning any concession from him, she should have known better than to openly contest King Oberon's will. But it was for her Denno! She had nearly lost Lord Denno!

Nearly lost him more than one way, Elizabeth thought, but she did not feel like weeping over that memory. Although she was frightened by remembering, she was also warmed by recalling how Denno had leapt in front of her to shield her from any blow Oberon might have launched.

She was thrilled to see with her own eyes Denno's devotion. Still—she should have been more careful. Denno always said he would guard her to his death. This time it might have come to that. But Queen Titania had come just in time and snatched them out from under Oberon's power, sending them all whirling back to where they belonged.

Nonetheless, the last look she had had of King Oberon's face had not been reassuring. She had feared he would loose the blast he planned for her at his queen. But Denno had assured her that Queen Titania would not be hurt because King Oberon desired her above all else. Elizabeth was glad to hear that, but Denno looked . . . odd when he said it. His eyes had taken on a kind of glazed shine and his lips seemed to be fuller than usual. Suddenly Elizabeth wondered what it would be like to kiss those lips.

For a moment she was shocked at the thought. Lady Elizabeth, the king's daughter, the third highest lady in all of England, thinking of kissing a common merchant! Of course, he was a lord in his own world and she had kissed Lord Denno before, a peck on the cheek, when he had particularly pleased her, but . . . Elizabeth looked into the fire again, feeling warmer. This was different. She had not been thinking of a light peck of gratitude when she thought of Denno's lips.

Should she try . . . No! He would be so shocked. He thought of her only as a child and she was forever getting him into so much trouble. This last visit Underhill Oberon had threatened to strip Lord Denno of his powers and send a new guardian to watch over her. Elizabeth felt herself growing furious all over again. How dare Oberon make free with *her* people?

"Well," Kat's voice broke into Elizabeth's thoughts. "I believe if you just make all the centers of the flowers gold, and perhaps stitch a line of silver around most of the leaves that you will not have to unpick anything. Perhaps I can find a pearl or two to add to the bottom of the place marker."

Elizabeth agreed readily, took back the embroidery, and began to stitch at it again, smiling slightly. Yes, Denno was hers, yet it was true that Denno was also King Oberon's subject. Elizabeth sighed, but this time her fingers did not falter on her work. Her own father would have been no more accepting if a foreign person had claimed first right to one of his subject's services.

Yet, Elizabeth thought, she did come first. Denno had gone Underhill to find out whether King Oberon had truly been angry or only seeking information in his own devious way. Elizabeth had a sudden, vivid mental picture of Lord Denno, an image of courage and defiance, facing his king. Her heart squeezed tight in panic. She hoped he had not found more trouble trying to serve her. She wished he would come. He had been gone for several days.

Elizabeth's Lord Denno in his own place was Lord Denoriel Seincyn Macreth Silverhair, warrior and noble among the Seleighe Sidhe, rider with Koronos in the Wild Hunt . . . and chosen by the FarSeers of Avalon to guide and protect the red-haired woman who—if she came to the throne—would bring such glory and honor to England, much joy and power to the Seleighe Sidhe.

He had not willingly taken up the duty laid upon him by the FarSeers, among whom was his own twin sister, Aleneil. Denoriel, the warrior, had been appalled at being turned into a nursemaid. But he had found far more danger, interest, and excitement in the mortal world than ever touched him Underhill. Being a merchant was fascinating. He did not need the money, of course. He could ken gold to fill his coffers with little effort, but seeking merchandise and buying and selling to *earn* a profit...

Denoriel laughed aloud and stepped into the room in which he mostly lived, when—more and more rarely these days—he was in his apartments at Llachar Lle, the so-called Summer Palace in Elfhame Logres. Llachar Lle—Denoriel often remarked that he could not imagine why it was called the Summer Palace since the weather Underhill invariably suited itself to the being experiencing it and never changed. The thought flicked through his mind and he dismissed it. His twin sister Aleneil was already waiting, and Denoriel sat down in a cushioned chair opposite the sofa she had chosen.

He had long since accepted the fact that they no longer looked much like twins. Aleneil, like most Sidhe, showed no sign of ageing; her hair was spun gold, her eyes emerald green, their black long oval pupils enhancing the color. Her complexion was a flawless, lucent white with just enough rose in cheeks and lips to confirm her blooming health.

Familiar with his own image, because in the mortal world he often needed to look into a mirror to check that illusion covered his oval pupils and long, pointed ears, Denoriel knew he was the one who had changed. The battle with Vidal and his minions when Elizabeth was a baby had damaged him.

No, not actually the battle but his drinking the lightning that was the magic of the mortal world in order to fight when his own strength was gone. His hair was white now rather than gold, lines of pain creased the corners of his eyes and bracketed his mouth, and his skin was tanned and hardened by its exposure to the sun and changeable weather of the World Above. Fortunately no further damage had been done him in this last confrontation with Vidal. Whatever curse Vidal had cast on him that caused him such pain, Oberon had negated.

The changes were all to the good, of course. He would have had to remember to disguise himself with such changes as the years passed so that Elizabeth's human governess and household officers did not wonder why thirty years had left no mark on him. Now there was no need, only to remember to make the pupils of his eyes look round and hide the long pointed ears behind an illusion of human ones.

At least Aleneil no longer asked anxiously if he was well each time they met. She had grown accustomed to his new appearance.

"What a frown," Aleneil said, looking away from the scene of a meadow with a manor house fronting a small copse of trees that one saw through the window of Denoriel's parlor. There was now a glimpse of silver water off to the side of the trees; it was an enchanting illusion, all the more intriguing because it seemed to grow and change. Denoriel's skill with magic was continuing to increase, Aleneil thought approvingly.

"I was just thinking of Prince Vidal Dhu."

Aleneil made a face. "I agree, thought of Vidal is enough to make anyone frown. I try not to think of him at all."

Denoriel shook his head, and his frown deepened. "No, Aleneil, we must think of him. Elizabeth is now second in the succession and Vidal has recovered most of the cleverness and power—I can vouch for that; he nearly had me in that last fight—that he lost when we first fought over Elizabeth."

Now it was Aleneil who frowned. "Yes, but I worry less about Vidal himself than about the fact that he *is* Prince of Caer Mordwyn and he controls perhaps a score of Dark Sidhe, not to mention endless ogres and boggles and phookas and hags and Mother knows what else."

"Most of those are useless," Denoriel replied, dismissing the minions with a gesture. "He cannot, without bringing Oberon's anger down on him, send the monsters into the World Above and most of the Dark Sidhe are even more sensitive to the iron in the mortal world than the Seleighe are. But speaking of Oberon, I wonder what happened between him and Titania when she sent us all to our own places."

Aleneil laughed heartily. "Coward! I came to Llachar Lle as fast as I could Gate from Avalon, and you had already fled to the mortal world so you wouldn't be Underhill while Oberon and Titania settled their differences."

"I don't like earthquakes," Denoriel said dryly and added, "but they are settled?"

"Yes, abed as usual." Aleneil's lips twisted. "He cannot resist her—nor she him, especially when they are furious with each other." She rolled her eyes and flushed delicately. "Most fortunate. But their lust is so all-pervading and powerful that their reconciliations have a strong effect throughout the Seleighe Court."

"Then it is just as well that I was in the World Above," Denoriel said, somewhat sourly. "As I presently have no one on whom to vent such desires. I have been chaste as a Christian priest since I became entangled with the Tudors."

The last word cued something in his mind, and Denoriel had a sudden, vivid vision of Elizabeth, her flaming hair spread over the pillows of his bed, her white body . . . He cut off the thought and forcibly brought to mind Titania's perfection, but golden round-pupilled eyes, not green, gazed reproachfully at him.

"What *are* you thinking about," Aleneil said, grinning.

"That I am tired of being chaste," Denoriel replied, deciding hastily that he had better find a willing partner before he went back to the World Above.

"You may not have time to mend that condition," Aleneil said, suddenly serious. "Do you remember that we have been wondering whether the Visions in the great lens were predictions of a likely future or just future possibilities as usual?"

"Yes. I am no FarSeer, but it seemed to me that the lens was showing what would be this time—that Edward would rule, then Mary, and then Elizabeth."

Aleneil shook her head. "There is another Vision."

"Do not tell me the one of Elizabeth is gone!" Denoriel exclaimed, getting to his feet, a hand on his sword hilt.

"No, no. Mary's fires burn and Elizabeth's glories still appear, but there is another." Aleneil folded her hands in her lap, and her eyes clouded.

Denoriel sat down again, frowning. "A boy or man? Is there some male heir we have overlooked?" His lips thinned with impatience. "Then there is no certainty in what you have Seen. The Visions are still only possibilities."

"I suppose so, but it is not a male we see. It is another girl, younger she seems than Elizabeth, a small, thin creature that looks so sad it breaks my heart." Aleneil had been much taken with the poor waif she had seen in the Vision. Like all the Seleighe Sidhe, she loved children, even those of mortals, and it made her want to weep when one looked so tragic, so lost. "It was a very brief Vision, only of her weeping as someone—we do not recognize the man; his face is hidden—holds out a crown."

"A small, thin creature with sad looks?" Denoriel cast the net of his memory wide, and immediately snared a prospect. "I wonder if that could be Lady Jane Grey? She was in the group of girls that Queen Catherine Parr gathered to be schooled with Elizabeth, and was the only one small and thin and sad. This Jane was Elizabeth's only rival in her love of books and learning."

Aleneil blinked. "But why in the Mother's name should she appear in the lens?"

For a long moment Denoriel was silent. Then he said. "Jane Grey's mother, Frances Brandon, was named in King Henry's will. I have committed to memory every word of that will so that I will understand what pertains to Elizabeth."

Aleneil shook her head. "But who is Frances Brandon to be named in the late king's will?

"I was curious also. My friend Sir Anthony Denny explained. Frances Brandon is the daughter of Henry's sister, Mary—she who married her childhood love Charles Brandon after she became the widow of the king of France. Yes, Henry was determined that no Scot would ever rule England, so he cut out the heir of his aunt Margaret, the current king of Scotland. The succession was set to be Edward, Mary, Elizabeth, and if all else failed, Frances Brandon or her heirs."

"So we are Seeing the three possibilities according to the provisions of the late king's will."

"So it seems." Denoriel was silent for a moment and then he said slowly, "The old Visions of the queens look the same? I mean, neither Mary nor Elizabeth is old?" Aleneil nodded and Denoriel continued, frowning. "I cannot see what that can mean except that Edward, who is king already, will not reign long."

"I fear so," Aleneil said sadly. The loss of any child was a tragedy to the Sidhe who had so very few.

"So one of the three will reign after Edward?"

Aleneil took a deep breath. "Usually that is what Visions one virtually atop the other mean. But in this case, Eirianell does not think so. She said that she had once before Seen a like set of Visions. She now wonders whether what we have seen are not alternatives but what will be, that each of the heirs will, in turn, take the throne. Oddly, the new Vision did not disturb her at all—except that she warned more strongly than ever that a change in the lives of any of these women will alter the future that has been shown for all. And she feels that all of them will be threatened in some way."

Eirianell was the eldest and wisest of the FarSeers. She had gazed into the great lens and interpreted the Visions that rose in it since Atlantis had sunk beneath the waves. If she stated an opinion, Denoriel would not doubt her. He bit his lip.

"Vidal's FarSeers will have the same Vision," he said, forehead creasing into an even deeper frown. "A new Vision will likely set him to trying to remove both Jane Grey and Elizabeth. I cannot protect them both. I wish I knew how he interprets the Visions."

"I can find out," Aleneil said. "I can ask Rhoslyn."

"What?" Denoriel's voice rose with shock.

Rhoslyn Teleri Dagfael Silverhair and her twin brother, Pasgen Peblig Rodrig Silverhair, were to Denoriel's regret his and Aleneil's half brother and sister. Their common father, Kefni, had been caught in a powerful fertility spell woven by Rhoslyn's and Pasgen's mother Llanelli. Powerless to resist, Kefni had coupled with her and made her pregnant, but inwardly he was furious at the use made of him, so he had rushed home to his lifemate, Denoriel's and Aleneil's mother, and using the remains of the spell had impregnated her also.

Children were very rare among the Sidhe. When the Unseleighe learned of the two sets of twins, they raided the Seleighe domain during the celebration of their births and abducted all of them. Kefni, a great warrior, followed swiftly, caught the party that had Denoriel and Aleneil, killed two, and wrested the babies from them. Having returned the twins to safekeeping in Avalon, he set out to recover his other children.

Kefni was wounded and tired but he did find Rhoslyn and Pasgen. Unfortunately a still larger party of Unseleighe was on his heels. He sought to take refuge in a church, where he would be safe from most of the unholy creatures and would only need to fight off the Dark Sidhe, but he was denied the refuge by the priest, warding him away with Cold Iron. Kefni died and the children were carried back to Vidal Dhu's domain. Pasgen and Rhoslyn would have died too, if Llanelli had not followed them into painful and hateful exile.

Of course it was not Pasgen's and Rhoslyn's fault that they had been raised by the cruel and treacherous Unseleighe. But in Denoriel's opinion the trees had grown as the twigs had been trained.

"Rhoslyn is not a safe source of information about Elizabeth," he added to the exclamation of surprise.

"She is different now," Aleneil protested, her gaze earnest. "Since Elizabeth explained what happened to the changeling Rhoslyn had created, that you had not murdered it but it lived many years as Richey with Mwynwen, Rhoslyn has sworn she will do her best to smooth Elizabeth's way and to protect her."

"She is a liar!" Denoriel insisted stubbornly, memories of Rhoslyn's disguise as the false nun all too vivid in his mind. "Do not trust her, Aleneil."

Aleneil sighed, wishing she could make her brother see Rhoslyn as she had, and did. "Creating Richey changed Rhoslyn. That changeling could not have meant more to her than if he had been a child of her body. More than half her animosity toward Elizabeth was owing to her wish to hurt you as she had been hurt. Once she knew you had not murdered the little boy, that he had lived happily with Mwynwen for years, much longer than anyone could have expected—"

"Aleneil," Denoriel interrupted, "can you not see that her very conviction that I would kill a child—even a changeling child—marks something rotten in Rhoslyn?"

"No," Aleneil replied quietly. "I see that she has lived with cruelty and expects only that from others. But what she wrought with Richey—you did not know him as I did; you were busy with Harry—but Richey had the same sweetness and goodness as Harry. He was more childlike, as is to be expected, but he was—I would have said, he almost seemed to have a soul. I do not think, even with the miracle that Rhoslyn wrought, that a made thing could grow like a true mortal, and yet—Richey was so near as to convince me of his nature. And there was *nothing* evil in Richey."

"That is true," Denoriel murmured. "He was good all through, with the same generosity and self-sacrifice as are so much a part of Harry."

"How could she have done that and be black evil herself?" Aleneil insisted with a shake of her head. "I cannot believe it."

Suddenly Denoriel remembered the tears streaming down Rhoslyn's face when she accused him of murdering the poor changeling. And she had never taken any active part in threatening Elizabeth. Perhaps she was not all bad.

Then he shook his head. "Even if Rhoslyn is not evil, what of Pasgen? He tried to kill Elizabeth, not once but twice! And you must also remember that Rhoslyn is not her own mistress.

Vidal must have his hooks into her and might well force her into something she would not wish to do. Aleneil, do not trust her. Elizabeth is too precious. Vidal will do anything at all to prevent Elizabeth from coming to the throne. Who knows what pressure he can bring to bear on Rhoslyn?"

Aleneil sighed again. "Well, I will be careful, but I cannot see what the harm could be for me to ask whether she knows what Vidal's FarSeers have Seen and what she thinks it means. I will not tell her what Eirianell believes."

"How can you reach her?"

"That is easy enough in the mortal world. She attends on the Lady Mary as Rosamund Scott. I can simply write her a note, perhaps to say that Elizabeth wishes to send her sister Mary a mourning prayer or something of that sort. It would not be thought strange. Elizabeth and Mary do write to each other from time to time."

Reluctantly, Denoriel nodded his assent. "Very well, but not yet. My principal source of information at Court is in the Tower waiting beheading. And the friend I have made more recently, Sir Anthony Denny, is so overwhelmed with business that I dare not intrude on him. Also Sir Anthony is not young and not perfectly well. I need to find a new friend in the heart of the King's Council."

Aleneil pursed her lips. "Why not Edward Seymour . . . ah, earl of Hertford? He is the king's maternal uncle and likely to be close to the boy."

Again, Denoriel shook his head. These mortals and their wayward Gifts—they made things very difficult sometimes. "Not Hertford. I suspect he has a thread of Talent and is made most uneasy by any touch of magic. He has a strong distaste for me."

"Then avoid him, and above all stay away from Edward." She sighed heavily. "That poor child. What a misery his life will be." She sighed again. "Does Elizabeth need Lady Alana?" Aleneil asked, mentioning her mortal world alter ego.

Denoriel sensed that his sister had some private business she wished to pursue . . . perhaps connected with the flooding of Underhill with its rulers' lust. Had she found a male in whom she could feel a real interest? Denoriel sometimes worried that because he and Aleneil were so close she could not find a partner to whom she could bond.

"Not yet," he said. "She needs first and foremost to know whether the Council will honor the terms of her father's will so she can settle her mind to where and how she will live." Then Denoriel's expression lightened. "And I think I have just come up with an answer to that, and an answer that will make Elizabeth very happy."

"Elizabeth needs some time of happiness. I sense that— Oh, Good Mother, what a fool I am," Aleneil exclaimed, laughing. "I forgot the most important result of Oberon's and Titania's reconciliation. Titania demanded, and received in response to her promise to do nothing to trouble Mary, permission for Elizabeth to come Underhill and, of course, to return to the World Above."

Denoriel blinked. "But none of us ever thought of doing Mary any harm! Poor woman, I fear the fanatical faith she clings to will hurt her and all of England without any help from the Sidhe."

"Poor woman indeed!" But Aleneil's expression was shadowed by just a trace of fear. "There is something about her that makes me most uneasy. I fear she would welcome the Great Evil if it would promise to return England to the old faith."

Denoriel felt himself blanch. "Aleneil! For the Mother's sake do not say things like that!"

"Sorry," Aleneil muttered. "Mary was once sweet and kind. It annoys me to see her so much a dupe of her priests." She sighed impatiently, "But I do not wish her ill. She has had ill enough in her life."

Denoriel raised his brows and then chuckled, good humor swiftly returning. "Titania knew we never meant Mary harm. And I cannot believe that Oberon did not also know it." He grinned. "That means the king was willing all along for Elizabeth to come Underhill."

Aleneil smiled, with a hint of mischief. "Yes, Oberon is often devious, and I think sometimes he does things deliberately to infuriate Titania. But not this time. He was really angry at Elizabeth, yet Titania faced him down—over a mortal. She is determined to see Elizabeth come to the throne and bring in what she feels will be a golden age for the Seleighe Sidhe."

Denoriel nodded and chuckled again softly. "I have a feeling she intends to sample some of those joys for herself. Poor mortals. Well, better them than me. And now I must get back to the World Above and arrange for Elizabeth to be safe and happy."

He rose as he spoke the last few words and touched his sister's cheek.

But Aleneil frowned, holding his hand against her. "Be careful," she said. "I swear I felt an ice faery slide down my spine. I have just remembered Oberon's strict order to Vidal not to touch Elizabeth. It is true that Vidal might be afraid to harm her directly, but he must realize that if he is rid of those she loves—you, Kat, Blanche . . . was not an attempt made on Blanche already? So soon after her father's death to lose any of them . . . all stability and safety will be gone from Elizabeth's world. She is so close to the edge all the time, so prone to make herself ill with fear and worry, she could be utterly vulnerable to the most ordinary misfortunes."

Denoriel went very still, but then nodded. "I had not thought of that. I will be careful and warn Blanche—and you guard yourself also."

Chapter 2

The house that Pasgen and Rhoslyn had once called the empty house—and still did because they could not think of another name for it—was now actually very full. Both of them visited regularly to make sure that all was well with their mother, Llanelli, who now lived in a new wing of the house with a full complement of guards and servants.

The visits were not the penances they would once have been. Llanelli had finally accepted that her twin children had grown into fully functioning adults, that they no longer needed a mother's care.

She had not forgotten or given up her first purpose, which was to preserve Pasgen and Rhoslyn from sinking into the foulness of Unseleighe malice and cruelty. However she had learned that the way to keep them longing for Seleighe lightness and laughter and love of beauty was to be as Seleighe as possible herself. When Rhoslyn or Pasgen or both came to visit, she was bright and beautiful, she sang or played music, she spoke of art and the most interesting of the healings she had done.

Those healings were even more important than art and music and laughter. Llanelli had found a genuine purpose in life and her children could feel the change in her. She had discovered in herself the ability to heal and had developed the talent into a full art.

Pasgen had arranged for booths to be set up in the three great markets, the Goblin Market, the Elves' Faire, and the Bazaar of the

Bizarre. Rhoslyn had provided a construct for each booth that was able to describe what healings were available and where to find the Gate that would take a sufferer to the healer's place of business.

Both Pasgen and Rhoslyn were aware that allowing Llanelli to see patients was dangerous, but neither could condemn their mother to fading into nothing. Still, both knew the Unseleighe Sidhe were not trustworthy. Any of them might think it deeply amusing to seize a gentle healer and torture her or play other nasty tricks. Also the possibility existed that Prince Vidal would realize that the healer was Llanelli and try to seize her, although he had shown no interest in her for years. Still, the one way to ensure the twins' obedience would be to hold their mother, and as Prince Vidal's mind and powers returned to their former state, he might well remember that. Both had done their best to protect her.

The terminus of each Gate was staffed by one of Pasgen's constructs, a huge hulking creature that was almost impervious to magic and was incredibly strong, with a skin like stone. There really was not a great deal that anyone could do to hurt it. The construct was very stupid, but it could fight and could sense an overt intention to do evil, which would call forth a challenge. That usually sent most of those planning to wreak havoc back from where they came.

The paths from the Gate to the house were walled off by force fields so that no one could either damage the garden or hide in it. And at the entrance to the healer's wing of the house, the patient was greeted by two of Rhoslyn's "girls."

The girls were obviously constructs because they were perfectly identical, except for the colored ribbon tied in a little bow each wore around her neck. It was an innocent touch. Likely those who persisted either because of their need for healing or their cleverer concealment of the will to do evil felt a sense of relief and safety with the girls after the seemingly overt threat of the Gate guard and the imprisoning walls of force.

For those able to conceal their evil intentions from the Gate guard, the relief was a grave mistake. Although the girls looked like starveling children with huge eyes, small pursed lips, and sticklike arms and legs, they were as strong as the brute at the Gate and far cleverer. Their little pursed mouths could open almost to their ears and held teeth to rival a wolf's and their spider-leg fingers could slice flesh and grind through bone. There was one who came truly needing healing and shivered whenever he saw them. He had seen one of the girls slice up an ogre into finger-food lumps, and he never could be easy in their presence again. The girls, too, were almost impervious to magic and understood their purpose, their only purpose, was to protect Llanelli.

A final set of protections were the two seemingly mortal servant/nurses, who assisted Llanelli in her healings. Also constructs, they looked like smiling, plump country girls, one brown-haired and the other blonde, both blue-eyed and rosy cheeked. They were not particularly clever, but were very strong, very devoted to Llanelli, and were able to perceive her emotions. They knew at once if she were frightened. Without any sense of self at all, either or both were ready to interpose their own bodies between her and any threat and fight for her to the death.

So far the elaborate scheme of protection seemed more than was necessary. There had been two Dark Sidhe who had felt that the extended torment of a healer would be very amusing. One, whose mind was not befogged with drugs, had recognized from the presence of the Gate guard that Llanelli would be protected and abandoned his purpose. The second had not survived his meeting with Lliwglas, she of the blue ribbon.

The Sidhe who had fled had mentioned the healer's protections to another, who had commented on the foolishness of a healer setting up a practice in an Unseleighe domain, but then, later, seemed to have reconsidered the "foolishness" in light of the extraordinary precautions. And no less than the Seleighe, the Unseleighe were inveterate gossips. The word of the healer's protections spread from him to still others. Pasgen was pleased by that development. It served two purposes: it discouraged those who wished to prey on a helpless healer, and now only those desperate for healing and surcease from pain came to the empty house.

In the dead of night of what was the fifth of February, 1547 in the mortal world, Pasgen waited in the parlor of the empty house for Rhoslyn to arrive. The parlor was a compromise between Pasgen's desire for absolute plainness and order and Rhoslyn's need for warmth and decorative surroundings.

The walls were a soft cream color with rich, but unadorned, wood moldings. There were pictures on the walls, which provided splashes of color, but they were not scenes of beautiful landscapes like those that adorned the walls of Iach Hafn, Rhoslyn's home.

The pictures were portraits: one of Llanelli, nearly as disorderly as an untamed landscape with her flowing hair and diaphanous robes; one of Rhoslyn, dark and severe in her Wild Hunt costume with Talog, the claw-footed, wolf-toothed, flame-eyed not-horse behind her; one of Pasgen, sitting quietly at his stark black and white desk with a single open book before him and to his right a wisp of coiling mist.

The door opened to admit Rhoslyn in full Tudor court dress. Her black hair was parted in the center and partially covered by a French hood of black satin and velvet trimmed with jet, her throat was almost covered by the upstanding ruffle of the white chemise gathered at the neck. Below this a dull silver kirtle, with the most minimal embroidery all in black, was visible above the low, square neckline of her black velvet gown and where the gown parted in the center. The silver sleeves of the kirtle were also visible where the sleeve of the gown, which widened below the elbow, was folded back displaying silver-gray squirrel fur in a wide cuff. Her only ornament was a necklace of jet beads supporting a jet-trimmed pendant holding a miniature portrait of Henry VIII.

A single glance was all Pasgen needed to satisfy himself that Rhoslyn had suffered no serious anxieties since he had last seen her. "Well, well," he said with a broad grin, "did you dress specially to please me, all white and gray and black?"

Rhoslyn was examining him with great care, feeling—because she knew Pasgen would hide anything wrong from her if he could—for pain or strain. She did detect a little tension, but the kind that came with excitement rather than with anger or fear. His looks were totally normal: gold hair combed back smoothly from a high forehead, ear points well up toward the crown of his head, large green eyes wide open now and displaying his pleasure in her company. That was rather new.

She smiled warmly at him, shaking her head as she seated herself with care for her wide skirts. "No, I did not even think once of you. The black and gray colors are to please Lady Mary, who is in deep mourning for her father. You did know that Henry VIII died in the early morning of January twenty-seventh?"

"I knew he was dead although not when," Pasgen said, "because I heard Elizabeth say so, but only by the strangest accident. And by the same accident I learned a great deal about what is going on in the Seleighe Court."

"That sounds like a dangerous accident."

"Oh, it was. I could have been dead or mind-wiped in one moment—"

"Pasgen!" Rhoslyn protested.

He laughed. "I said it was an accident. I assure you I did not intrude on King Oberon's business apurpose."

"Oberon," Rhoslyn whispered.

"He must have known I was not there to interfere in any way. He must have read my surprise when Vidal arrived and began what amounted to a war against our dear half brother Denoriel and his friends. I felt his Thought pass over me and sweep up everything in my mind."

Rhoslyn shivered. "I cannot help it. I am afraid of him. Vidal at his best—or worst—is a helpless child compared to King Oberon."

"You need not apologize to me," Pasgen replied dryly. "I feel just as you do and I would have fled incontinent"—his lips twisted wryly—"and I mean that in all ways, if I had not been too afraid to move."

"Then how—"

"You know I have been living mostly in the Unformed or Chaos Lands and that I have discovered that they are by no means all the same. Many are simply raw material but there are a few others—well, you know I have found sports in the mist, that red stuff and the bit you found that seems almost intelligent."

"Have you not got rid of that red devourer yet?"

Pasgen raised his brows. "Tell me how."

Rhoslyn sighed, lifted a hand, and when one of the servants appeared, ordered wine and cakes. "Not too much of anything," she said, and then to Pasgen, "I hope you will stay and dine with us when Mother is free?"

"Yes. I like to hear who she is healing of what. Sometimes I can tell from that where Vidal is and what he is doing. But to get back to what I was saying, I came across what seemed like a whole domain of intelligent mist."

"What? Oh, Pasgen, are you sure you did not do something to the place? A whole domain of intelligent mist?" She shuddered. "Think what it could do if it became inimical?"

"I am not an idiot. That was the first thing I did think of and I have been very, very careful. Thus, you can imagine that I was not too thrilled when Denoriel and Aleneil with that damned clever Elizabeth and two Sidhe who should long have been dead or Dreaming popped out of a gate."

"Whenever something happens that disturbs her Denoriel brings Elizabeth Underhill. They take her all kinds of places and teach her magic—"

"You mean she can now *apurpose* use the force that flung me into the void?" Pasgen interrupted, wide-eyed.

"No. She can only do little things, like stickfast. The great power is somehow tied inside of her so that she cannot usually reach it, but if she gets very frightened or very angry . . . She flung one of Vidal's mages into the void with his whole body caved in because he was threatening to cast a spell at Denoriel. She melded another's feet into the earth."

"How did you know that?" Pasgen asked. "I saw it happen. That was the next part of my tale."

"Aleneil told me," Rhoslyn said softly. "I will explain in a moment, but first I wish to beg of you, Pasgen, down on my knees if you desire it, that you do not trouble Elizabeth, that you think kindly of her even though she hurt you."

For a long moment Pasgen was silent, staring at his sister, whose eyes were full of tears. "Since I was trying to kill her when she hurt me, I cannot really blame her for defending herself. But . . . but why, Rhoslyn?"

"Because she told me, and I have confirmed her tale with the healer Mwynwen in Elfhame Logres, that Denoriel did not kill my poor little changeling. He carried the child to Mwynwen and she . . . she made a spell to feed it power so that it lived for ten years longer. She *loved* it, as much . . . no, more, I think, than I did. She named it Richey . . ."

"You put too much into that changeling," Pasgen said, his voice tight and hard.

"Yes," Rhoslyn whispered. "I will never make another like that. There was a great bleeding hole in my heart over that . . . construct. And one reason I wish you to spare Elizabeth is that it was her idea to tell me that Richey had lived many happy years. She almost forced Aleneil to tell me of Richey's life and death—"

"He . . . it is dead now?"

"Yes." Tears streaked Rhoslyn's cheeks and she wiped them away impatiently. "Even the full power of several Seleighe healers could not hold poor Richey together forever, but I saw . . . I saw the man who would have been destroyed had I made the exchange and I thank whatever Powers That Be that I failed. Harry FitzRoy is . . ." She hesitated and then went on in a rush but in a voice so low that only Pasgen's Sidhe hearing made out the words. "The other reason . . . Pasgen, I long for what Elizabeth will bring to the mortal world. Is there no way we can free ourselves from Vidal and make new lives among the Seleighe?"

Again Pasgen was silent for a long moment; then he said, "There might be, but for what purpose, Rhoslyn? Do you imagine that we would be received with open arms, greeted as prodigal children? If you seek companionship, you will not find it in the Bright Court."

"I think I asked you once before how that would be different from what I have here?"

"The difference would be that you would desire friendship, recognition, from the Seleighe Sidhe. Here, you refuse welcomes offered." There was another silence during which Pasgen looked down at his own, long-fingered hands wound tightly together. "To be ignored, even actively rejected, by those you admire . . . that hurts, Rhoslyn."

She glanced at him quickly and then away. Beneath a fold of cloth above the breast in her elaborate gown the small construct, like a little furry snake, quivered in response to a distress that did not show in Pasgen's face or manner. So Pasgen had tried to make contact with some of the Seleighe Sidhe and had been thrust aside or ignored. Rhoslyn touched a finger to the lindys to show she had felt its message and it could now be still.

"So what is this story about Elizabeth that you started to tell me?" she asked.

Pasgen's jaw tightened, but his voice was smooth. "I told you that Denoriel brought her, Harry FitzRoy, Aleneil and two of the elders I thought were already slipped over into Dreaming—only now they are as bright-eyed and lively as new-made—to this Unformed land that I was studying and Vidal appeared at the Gate and challenged Denoriel. More of Vidal's creatures arrived and those with Denoriel engaged them, but one mage was aiming a spell at Denoriel who was barely defending himself against Vidal."

"That he could defend himself at all . . . He must have been studying magic."

"I think so, but he was hard pressed and could not have defended himself against the mage too. His shields were eroded. But Elizabeth used a baby spell"—he smiled—"*cilgwythio*, in fact, to push the mage away." The smile grew rigid. "Only she pushed so hard, she crushed him like a grape and flung him into the void."

"Oh dear," Rhoslyn said, feeling a pang. "I had better mention to Aleneil that Elizabeth should be told to add 'from whence you came' to her spells. If she keeps flinging people into the void she will draw unwanted attention. Of course, the mage was dead already, but still . . ."

"I do not think it was sending the mage to the void. It was the power of the spell itself that attracted Oberon."

"Ah."

"There is no 'ah' in it yet. He stopped the battle and saw me, although no one else had noticed." Pasgen frowned. "That mist is very strange. I wanted to stay hidden, and it thickened around me. It was . . ."

"Did you thank it?"

"What?"

"Aleneil said the reason they went to that Unformed land was that Elizabeth had *asked* the mist to make a lion . . . and it did . . . and she thanked it, as if it were a living being."

Pasgen stared at her. "Asked the mist to . . ." He shook his head. "I was pleased I was concealed. Perhaps it felt that." He hesitated, shook his head again. "No, let me finish this tale or it will never be done and I think you need to know. Elizabeth called Denoriel 'my Denno.' Oberon objected and she . . . she confronted him, threatened him. She said 'My Denno or no Sidhe will come into the mortal world' or some such words."

"She threatened Oberon?" Rhoslyn said faintly, paling, swallowed, and went on, "But I know she is alive and well. He did not blast her, then. What happened?"

Pasgen grinned. "Titania. She arrived in a pillar of white lightning, told Oberon that Elizabeth was hers, must not be bent or broken, and then vanished them all away."

"And then?" This was more and more interesting by the moment. Elizabeth, that pale mortal girl, challenging the ruler of all the Sidhe? Did she somehow think herself immune? Or was she only courageous to the point of recklessness?

"I have no idea. I felt at that point that discretion was far better than valor and fled."

"My darling Pasgen, I never thought I would hear such sensible words from you," a light and lilting voice said from the doorway.

"Mother." Pasgen got to his feet courteously, then repeated somewhat dubiously, "Mother?"

The last time he had seen Llanelli she had hair like silver cobwebs, the green of her eyes was soft and faded, and she was thin nearly to transparency. The Sidhe who faced him now was full-bodied, her eyes were a bright hazel, and her hair a thick and vibrant red. She was not pretending not to be Sidhe; the pupils of her eyes were oval and her ears long and pointed, but she was certainly not Sidhe of Logres, either Bright or Dark Court.

Rhoslyn turned her head and smiled. A chair that had been near the wall moved to settle between hers and Pasgen's. "You look tired, Mother."

"Well, I am," Llanelli admitted as she settled into the offered chair. "I had a very interesting case, in fact, a return because the spells I used had not held. A Dark Sidhe who had obviously seized something of iron, although he did not at first tell me the truth and I did not know it."

"Not very surprising," Rhoslyn remarked. "Likely he was in the mortal world without Vidal's permission."

Llanelli smiled. "But stupid when dealing with a healer. His hand was badly burnt and swollen. I had spells to shrink the swelling and to soothe the burn, so he went away satisfied. But, of course, those spells did nothing to remove the poison of the iron so when he should have been healed and the spells dissipated, the poison had moved up his arm and the hand just swelled up again."

"It would," Pasgen remarked dryly, then shook his head at her. "But, Mother, I almost did not recognize you, except that I know your voice so well."

"I thought it best to change my looks." Llanelli frowned. "I did not want the healer, who can be reached so easily, to be too closely connected to you and Rhoslyn."

"Very wise," Pasgen said approvingly, "and stupid of me not to think of a disguise."

Llanelli flushed slightly at Pasgen's praise, which was not lightly given or often forthcoming.

"But the client," Rhoslyn put in anxiously, "was he unpleasant? Did the girls protect you quickly enough?"

"Poor creature," Llanelli said sympathetically. "No, he offered no threats. He was in too much pain and too frightened. The flesh of his arm was beginning to blacken. To speak the truth, I was frightened too. I did not know what to do at first, so I . . . I made a guess and had him thrust his arm into that—you remember, Pasgen, that you gave me a decorative piece, a bit of mist from one of the Unformed lands that you had somehow confined. It was very pretty to watch, coiling and flowing."

Pasgen sat up alertly. "I remember. You used the mist?"

"Yes. I had him thrust his arm through the field that contained the mist and I . . . I willed it to drink up what was not Sidhe substance. And . . . and I hope it did. At least the flesh lost that black look. But the mist . . . died? Can mist die? It just disappeared and there was this fine dust—"

"Do you still have the container with the dust?" Pasgen interrupted eagerly.

"Oh, yes. I am so glad you are here. Would it be possible for you to give me some more mist?" She looked at him with eager eyes. "I can think of several ways that I might try to use it."

"Let me see what remains," Pasgen said, getting up.

Llanelli rose also and Rhoslyn followed them, saying as they crossed the entrance hall that she would meet them in the dining room and tell the servants what to provide for dinner. The wait was longer than Rhoslyn expected and she was considering going after them, just a little afraid that Pasgen had seen something that displeased him and was trying to alter it or was scolding Llanelli. But then they came in together and although Pasgen was looking very thoughtful, Llanelli was smiling happily.

"I have been thinking," she said, as she took small portions of each dish, "that I had better decide what to call the new bit of mist Pasgen promised to get for me. It would be better if my clients did not know what cured them. I think it is known among Vidal's people that you and Pasgen are particularly interested in the Chaos Lands and anything from there might easily be connected with you."

"Are you not locking the door after the house has been robbed?" Rhoslyn asked.

"I hope not," Llanelli responded. With a faint frown of worry. "I think the Sidhe I treated was too upset to notice more than a sort of cloudy box in which I told him to put his hand and arm. It is certainly not usual to be able to take the mists out of the Unformed lands. I have never known anyone except Pasgen who could do it."

"Yes," Rhoslyn agreed, "which is why it worries me."

"Oh, Pasgen," Llanelli said anxiously, "I hope I have not put you into any danger."

He looked up from the thick, bloody slices of meat on his plate and smiled. "Not to worry, Mother. I suspect rather than getting me into trouble, you may have solved a dangerous problem that I had created all by myself."

Llanelli smiled, although she had to bite her tongue not to ask "What problem?" She still looked worried, but took a small portion of poached fish onto her fork and lifted it to her mouth. When Pasgen saw her eating, he smiled again and turned toward Rhoslyn, at the same time giving some attention to his dinner. He cut a portion of meat and popped it into his mouth.

Around it, he said, "So, if King Henry is dead, who will be ruling England?"

"Edward Seymour, earl of Hertford—although I expect that he will be duke of something or other as soon as the Council gets around to business. Lady Mary was pleased, except that she worries that he is too fond of the reformed religion. She says he has the best right, being Edward's uncle and I know Mary is quite attached to Hertford's wife."

"So you think she will not try to overset young Edward? She is, after all, an adult and was the first born." Among the Sidhe, rule was a matter of power and right, not male and female. In fact, many of the most powerful rulers had been and were women.

Rhoslyn shook her head. "She is a woman and knows she would have little support . . . well, except perhaps from the ardent Catholics." She hesitated and then continued. "No, not even from them. If there were no other heir, Mary would come forward to claim her right. She will, if any ill befalls Edward, but so long as he lives, she fully accepts the terms of King Henry's will. Edward and his heirs first, she and her heirs to follow, and then Elizabeth."

Pasgen laughed. "That Elizabeth! The way she stood there as upright as a sword blade and confronted Oberon." He shook his head, then laughed again, somewhat louder. "I do not envy Denoriel his task in dealing with her."

Chapter 3

Very often Denoriel was so exasperated with his charge that he would have been glad even of Pasgen's sympathy. However, on the ninth of February as he waited to be summoned to the presence of the Dowager Queen Catherine Parr, Denoriel was very pleased with himself. He was, for once, certain that what he was putting in motion would please Elizabeth.

In the confusion and jockeying for power in the wake of King Henry's death, his widowed queen had been thrust aside and nearly forgotten. Although she had been richly provided for in material possessions by the king's will, no political place, not even with respect to the children she had so lovingly overseen during Henry's life, had been designated for her. It was as if she had never been queen at all.

Denoriel had noticed that he was the only person outside of the queen's own household waiting in the hall for an interview with the Dowager Queen, and he saw that the hall was rather empty, as if the household had been reduced. Catherine, Denoriel thought, was an intelligent and gentle woman, and she had been left as regent by her husband when he was abroad. For all her quiet nature, she was not particularly retiring. She was no fool politically and she must resent being cast aside so brusquely.

The situation was just as well for his purpose, Denoriel thought, repressing a smile. He suspected that Catherine would be more willing to listen to him, perhaps even willing to press the Council hard to give her governance of Elizabeth. Now he permitted the slight smile that satisfactory thought gave him to show when the chamberlain approached and gestured for him to follow. After all, why not? Elizabeth was only third in line by the rule of the will. Her value to the Crown mostly lay in being a valuable pawn in the marriage game. At least, that would be so far as the Council was concerned. . . .

How little they knew his Elizabeth.

To Denoriel's considerable satisfaction, the chamberlain did not pass through the hall to the door of the great room beyond. He led the way to a side door that opened into a parlor. It was a pretty room with a handsome bed, at the foot of which stood a large, high-backed armchair in which the Dowager Queen was sitting. A small table was beside her and the chair faced the east wall which held a comfortable hearth.

The chamberlain announced his name. Denoriel bowed and when Catherine gestured to him, advanced toward her, stepping around the small table and standing to the side so that he would not block the heat of the fire from her. The chamberlain remained near the door.

"Your Grace," he said, bowing again. "Permit me to offer my condolences. You, and the entire nation, have lost a very great man. There will be no other like King Henry."

Tears misted Queen Catherine's dark eyes. "He was a being completely out of the ordinary, was he not?"

"Indeed, madam, he was. I only met him in person once, many years ago, when I was chosen by the earl of Ormonde to act as the Master of Misrule at the Yule festivities—because I could do some silly magic tricks—but even the few words he spoke to me were overwhelming." That was nothing less than the truth. He had never met anyone, short of Oberon and Titania, with such presence.

"Yes." She sighed, but blinked away tears and smiled, saying more briskly, "Magic tricks? My dear Lord Denno, I can hardly believe a sober and successful merchant like yourself could do magic tricks."

Denoriel smiled. "It was when Harry FitzRoy—ah, I beg pardon, the late earl of Richmond—was a boy. To amuse him—"

"The late earl of Richmond," Catherine interrupted, frowning, her voice a trifle colder, "that was ten years ago. And now you often visit the Lady Elizabeth, do you not? You have been tied to the heirs to the throne for a long time."

"Not because they were or are heirs to the throne, madam. Harry—pardon, but he is dead now and I always called him Harry; I find it hard to remember to say His Grace. We met by accident when I rode with a friend to Windsor to do some business with the duke of Norfolk. Harry was so like my own little brother, the one the Turks had killed, so sweet, so good." Denoriel shrugged, apologetically, and allowed a hint of sorrow to cloud his features. "To ease a long pain, I made it my business to see him again. There was no harm in it."

"No harm?" Catherine knew the ways of royalty and those that surrounded royalty. "I am surprised the friendship was permitted when he was the only son the king then had."

"Those who oversaw him soon came to realize that I was politically indifferent and desired no favor, except the pleasure the boy's company gave me." He sighed. And that was certainly true, completely true. Also true was the fact that though "Lord Denno" had a bloodline sufficiently high to make him appropriate company for the young royals, it was a foreign bloodline, and he had no real standing among the native nobles of England, which made him nothing like a threat to anyone else's ambitions. "Frankly, madam, it is the same with Lady Elizabeth. I have no political interest, no party I wish to favor. I am rich enough to care little to grow richer. But she . . . Harry loved her so much, so very much. It was, when he died, as if he left her to me as a legacy. I desire only her happiness, nothing more—and it is on her account that I have presented myself to you today."

"I can do nothing for you," Catherine said sharply. "My husband did not see fit to name me among the guardians of his children and the Council obviously has no intention of seeking my advice."

He narrowed his eyes, and took on a thoughtful expression. "The more fools they. No one knows the king as well as you do, Your Grace. Poor child, poor child. You could give him some comfort in this time of sorrow."

The Dowager Queen's lips tightened. "There is no chance of that. Hertford desires no influence save his own to come near Edward."

Denoriel actually thought that perfectly reasonable, although he believed Hertford was going about sealing his control over Edward the wrong way. The earl would have done far better to have enlisted Queen Catherine's help. She would have been glad enough to sing his praises to Edward, who loved her dearly and would have believed her, had she been consulted on the boy's management. But Denoriel was far too wise to show any interest in Edward. He shrugged his shoulders again.

"King Edward is far above my touch and beyond my ken. Truth to tell, I wish only to protect the Lady Elizabeth, and to see her happy and well-disposed. She feels—" At a sharp glance from Catherine, he nodded. "Indeed yes, Your Grace, I have seen her; her servants know me well, and Mistress Ashley, disturbed by her lady's despondency, thought I might give her some ease. Lady Elizabeth feels as if the whole world has shattered around her and the very ground is trembling beneath her feet. She was told of her father's death . . . and nothing more. She has neither been sent for, nor sent to anyone."

"She is well provided for," Catherine said.

"But no one has told her what is truly to become of her and, truthfully, she feels in strong need of the guidance she had when the late king was alive." That was the proper tactic to take, to remind Catherine, not that Elizabeth was old enough to be a pawn in the marriage game, but that she was still young enough to require guidance. "She feels adrift, lost. She is not yet fifteen years of age and does not know who will direct her life, where she will live."

Catherine looked troubled. "I do not know either—I mean who will direct Elizabeth. Possibly she will live with Mary . . ."

Denoriel was horrified by the idea. He did not think Mary could convert Elizabeth to her own narrow and fanatical faith, but that in itself would be very dangerous to Elizabeth. If the Visions in the FarSeers' lens were true Seeing, Mary would come to rule before Elizabeth. If Mary believed that Elizabeth would not follow her as a good Catholic, subject to the pope . . . Elizabeth would not survive Mary's reign. And he would lose Elizabeth!

Doubtless it was forbidden to bespell the Dowager Queen, but Denoriel did not care. He could not permit Elizabeth to be placed in Mary's charge. He raised an image of Elizabeth turned totally away from the reformed religion, to which Catherine was so strongly inclined, totally accepting Mary's rigid Catholic fervor. He pushed into Catherine's mind all the worst corruption of the Church, the sale of indulgences, the foul practices of the pardoners.

"No," Catherine murmured more to herself than as if she were aware of Denoriel. "Mary is a good woman, but she was warped by her mother's fate. It would be very wrong for Elizabeth to hear four Masses a day, to be taught that the pope is supreme, and that a few shillings rather than a pure life and God's mercy can buy absolution from sin."

"But madam," he said, softening his tone. "Surely, Mary has been apart from her sister too long to make a good guide and companion. After all, it is you that Elizabeth loves, you who gave to her some of the happiest years of her life, who made her feel safe and cared for. And she misses your company, your guidance and wisdom so much . . ."

Catherine's eyes were shadowed with remorse. "Poor child. She must feel that I, too, have forgotten her."

"No, not that, Your Grace. She fears worse than that. She fears that you have been forbidden to come to her or bid her to come to you." Denoriel also feared that.

Catherine shook her head. "No, not at all. Alas, to my shame, I have been so taken up with my own grief and fears that I *have* all but forgotten her. I have not even written to her to condole with her on her loss . . . and mine."

Better and better. "A letter would be a great help, madam. A letter would assure her that you think of her. But it is your *company* she desires . . . no, needs. She has said to me that if she could live with you, madam, she would feel cherished and secure."

To know that the Dowager Queen had not been ordered to avoid Henry's heirs was a considerable relief, but Catherine's ignorance of Elizabeth's fate was not proof it was undecided. Still, as long as no one knew the decision it might be changed. He might as well, Denoriel thought, be hung for stealing a sheep as for stealing a lamb and he set into the Dowager Queen's mind the notion that she ask Sir Anthony Denny to urge the Council to give her charge of Elizabeth.

Denny still had some power. He had been with King Henry when he died. He had agreed to keep secret the fact of Henry's death for the time needed to forward Edward Seymour's plans to seize Edward so he could be named Protector. Also Denoriel knew that Denny was fond of Elizabeth and always respected Catherine. Beyond that, Denny regarded Denoriel as a good friend and would not try to prevent him from visiting Elizabeth and the queen. The scheme could not have been better for Denoriel's purposes.

"You truly believe that Elizabeth desires to live with me?" Catherine asked, coloring very slightly.

There was a little catch in her voice as the feeling that she had been cast aside like a worn-out, useless thing was eased. Someone wanted her. Someone needed her. Until his death was imminent Henry had needed and wanted her. Before that, he had gladly given into her hands the care of his children, even his precious heir.

Mary was a woman grown, and though she and Mary had been friends, Catherine knew Mary had no need of her. She knew, too, she would never be allowed any close association with the little king. But Elizabeth . . . Memories of Elizabeth, of her bright looks, of her wit and her eagerness in learning, of her openly expressed affection and deep respect for her stepmother, filled the emptiness in Catherine's heart. And they shared one other thing—a passion for the reformed religion that even Henry himself had not possessed. For Henry, the change in religion had been a tool to gain him what he most wanted. For Catherine and Elizabeth, it was the one true path.

"I know that to live with you would give Elizabeth joy and comfort, madam," Denoriel said, again thrusting the image of Sir Anthony Denny into her mind.

"Well, why not?" Catherine said. "She is too young to live alone and I think the Protector would not want her to come too much under Lady Mary's influence. Hmmm. Why do I not write to her now, Lord Denno? You can carry the letter and if I have from her a reply saying how frightened and lonely she is and requesting my protection . . . Yes. I could take such a letter to Sir Anthony Denny."

"That would be very wise, madam. Sir Anthony is on the Council and I know he is fond of Elizabeth and would wish to give her comfort."

The queen smiled up at Denoriel. "I thank you for letting me know. If you will wait—"

She rose to her feet. Denoriel stepped back, away from the chair near which he had stood while he and Catherine had been talking, and bowed. The chamberlain began to come forward, either to show Denoriel out or tell him where he could wait while Catherine wrote her letter . . . and the door to the room burst open.

Denoriel stepped back yet again to be out of the way, which took him beside the bed into the shadow of the bed curtains. A tall, broad-shouldered man came impetuously through the doorway, just jogging enough aside not to knock down the chamberlain.

"Your Grace," he said in a loud penetrating voice, "I have come to beg your pardon for failing to escort you to church when the Dirge was sung."

"It is just as well you did not, Sir Thomas," the queen said. "It was better that I attended the lament for my husband alone."

Her voice was steady, but there was not the smallest hint of reproof in it for the gentleman's unceremonious entrance and she was smiling brightly. Moreover, Denoriel's keen vision picked up a renewal of the heightened color in Catherine's cheeks. He looked with considerable interest at the visitor. Sir Thomas was certainly a very handsome man—by mortal standards. He had a luxuriant red beard, curling auburn hair, and bright blue eyes. His clothing, Denoriel noted, showed no sign of mourning drabness.

"Surely you cannot think anyone would be offended if I lent you the support of my arm in church," Sir Thomas protested and then, lowering his voice slightly, "I want to be with you, Catherine. You know I never so much as looked at you all the years you were Henry's wife. I would not for any reason put you into such danger as my attentions might—"

Denoriel cleared his throat, took a step forward, and bowed. His face was carefully expressionless. "I beg pardon, Your Grace. I will wait in the hall for the letter you wish me to carry, so please you, or come again for it when you tell me if that will better suit you."

Sir Thomas' eyes stared with surprise, his upper lip lifted in what Denoriel suspected was a snarl, and one of his hands twitched. If he had been a servant, Denoriel thought, that hand might have launched a blow, but Sir Thomas' glance had taken in the rich elegance of Denoriel's clothing and the gold-hilted sword by his side.

"Who the devil are you?" Sir Thomas snapped.

"My name is Lord Denno, Sir Thomas. I am what I suppose is called a merchant adventurer, and during his lifetime I was honored

to be called friend by the late duke of Richmond. I was also fortunate enough to be included on the list of allowed visitors to the
children being schooled in Hampton Court before the late king's
death. I had come to offer my condolences to Her Grace."

"Yes, and to remind me that poor Elizabeth feels very frightened and abandoned. It was cruel of me not to remember her
and offer her some comfort. Sit down, Sir Thomas, for just a
moment while I write a note to Elizabeth, which Lord Denno
has kindly offered to carry to her for me."

"As you like, madam," Sir Thomas said.

Denoriel thought the formal address was a bit like locking the
door of the stable after the horses had been stolen, but he only bowed
again. Queen Catherine went to a writing desk placed against the
wall, and Sir Thomas, without a by-your-leave, plumped himself
down in Catherine's chair. That did not, at the moment, have much
meaning for Denoriel, who was wondering about the odd expression
on Sir Thomas' face when he heard Elizabeth's name.

"So you are a merchant adventurer," Sir Thomas said. "And
what might that mean?"

"It means that I have a fleet of ships that travel far and wide
for valuable cargoes. After His Grace of Richmond died, I traveled with my ships for several years, but then I grew homesick
for England."

"You aren't English!"

Ignoring the contempt in Sir Thomas' voice, Denoriel smiled.
"True enough, Sir Thomas. I was a prince in Hungary before
the Turks overran my country. Fortunately for me, I was away
on a long voyage so I survived and was able to hold together
my family's trading business. But I have lived in England for so
long, that it is home to me."

"How does a merchant come to know Lady Elizabeth?"

Denoriel smiled more broadly, partly to hide the uneasiness
he felt. He did not catch a clear thought from Sir Thomas, but
there was a feeling of avarice that exuded from him when he
said Elizabeth's name.

"I am a very rich merchant," he said.

That woke a spark of interest in Sir Thomas. "I doubt Elizabeth will be of much use to you in decreasing tariffs or winning
contracts."

"Oh, none at all," Denoriel agreed lightly. "Merely I came to know her when she was a babe because her half brother the late duke of Richmond was deeply attached to her, and when I returned to England, I wished to see into what kind of child the babe had grown. A distant cousin of mine is one of Lady Elizabeth's maids of honor and gained me an introduction. Lady Elizabeth found me amusing; I found her enchanting and so from time to time we still meet."

"More than from time to time, Lord Denno," Catherine said over her shoulder, smiling. "You were a regular and frequent suitor, and Elizabeth always looked forward to your visits, I know. She said you were one of the few people who was willing to quarrel with her."

She turned back to her letter writing and Denoriel found himself smiling at her back. She came of no very high family, and once she was sure he was not pressing for favors or urging any political policy on Elizabeth, she had never enquired too closely about his visits. The pleasant memory was abruptly terminated.

"Enchanting, is it?"

Although he spoke much more quietly, there was a nasty snarl in Sir Thomas' voice. Denoriel was annoyed with himself for using that word, but it was the first that came to his mind when he thought of Elizabeth. He could do nothing more than curse himself and try to amend the mistake, so he shrugged and laughed. "Enchanting" was not a word you should use in describing a girl whose mother was accused of witchcraft. Nor was it a word you should use in describing the third in line to the throne, who was, at this moment, most valuable as a marriage prize.

"Yes, absolutely enchanting. She conquered me when she was three years old, lisping her Latin in a baby voice with the seriousness of a scholar ten times her age, and I have been her courtier ever since." Then he scowled. "However, Sir Thomas, you need not fear that I have ideas above my station. I am not a young man and I am not a fool. Merely, Sir Thomas, I have always loved children, specially those who, like Lady Elizabeth, are very clever. And I have no child of my own."

"Why, Lord Denno? You are rich, handsome, and vigorous despite your age."

Denoriel started slightly. Catherine had come up behind him, the folded and sealed letter in her hand, but she was looking at him with interest and sympathy.

"I . . ." Denoriel hesitated and then said quickly, "Perhaps because I am a coward. When the Turks overran my country, my whole family was destroyed. I did not wish, I think, to open myself to such pain again. But then I found Harry—" he shook his head and sighed "—and then Harry died . . ." He blinked as if to force back tears. "No, I have no inclination for a wife and children of my own. Not at such a cost. Lady Elizabeth is a very interesting person. It has been a wonder and a privilege to watch her grow."

"Ah, well," Catherine said, "I, too, have had my losses, but I still think to be a wife and mother would be worth all else." She smiled at Denoriel and held out the letter. "Here, this is for Elizabeth. I hope it will please her and save you a skinning."

Denoriel grinned as he bowed and took the letter from her. "How did you know Lady Elizabeth skinned me?"

Catherine laughed lightly. "Because she grieved to me over having done so. Do not despair, Lord Denno. She is really very fond of you."

"How touching," Sir Thomas said, and put a hand possessively on Queen Catherine's shoulder.

She did not show any sign of indignation, shake his hand loose, or step away but put her own hand over it.

So that was the way the wind blew. Denoriel did not think the man worthy of her, but that was none of his affair. Having his letter in hand, he simply bowed, said a polite farewell, and left them together. He had forgotten them both as he left the palace, his mind leaping ahead to the joy he was bringing to Elizabeth.

Because no one at Enfield would know when he left London and no one in London would know when he arrived at Enfield, Denoriel asked the elvensteed Miralys to take him to Elizabeth quickly. Miralys did spend about two minutes going sedately from the stableyard of the palace to a nearby narrow alley, but then he covered the near eleven miles to Enfield in less than ten minutes. The effort—if it was an effort for Miralys; although Miralys had been Denoriel's mount since he was four years old, he still did not know everything the elvensteed could do—was wasted.

"Where have you been?" Elizabeth snapped at Denoriel when he was shown into the parlor in which she sat.

Kat Ashley drew a sharp breath and leaned forward to put

a hand on Elizabeth's arm. Aleneil, who in her human guise of Lady Alana was noticeable most as a remarkably handsome suit of clothing, uttered a small protesting murmur. One of the three other ladies attendant on Elizabeth, who had remained with her mostly because their homes were even more crowded and less elegant, giggled. The sound made Elizabeth stiffen slightly. Her eyes flicked to Lord Denno's face, but he showed no consciousness of how improper her tone had been to someone who had done so much for her over so many years.

"As you can imagine, my lady," he said calmly, "there is considerable confusion in the Court and Sir Anthony Denny, who honors me with his friendship, is busy beyond belief. I am afraid I wasted two days in trying to get an appointment with him."

"That does not sound very friendly," Elizabeth said in a tone that showed she was not mollified. Her lips closed tight over the words; she had meant to sound as if this remark and the previous angry cry were jests. Everyone knew she often teased Lord Denno.

Denoriel stared hard at her. She was really shaken to bits to show her feelings so plainly, particularly when attended by women not in her inner circle, but there was nothing he could do to help.

He could only continue on as if she had been courteous rather than rude. "He knew I came merely to tender my condolences, that I had no business to transact. What he did was reasonable and just. I was at fault in imposing courtesies where serious matters were under consideration."

"I am not a serious matter?" The voice was somewhat tremulous this time.

"Elizabeth!" This time Kat Ashley spoke her protest and warning aloud.

Denoriel smiled. "Come, Lady Elizabeth. Even you must admit that ensuring your brother is safe and there are no threats to the smooth transition to his reign are matters that must first engage those appointed to the Council by your father's will."

"No threats?" Elizabeth's eyes widened, and she looked up anxiously into Denoriel's face. "Surely no one would wish to harm Edward or contest his right to the throne!"

He tried to tender a warning with his eyes. These were matters she knew, as any royal child would know. One or more of her women could be reporting back to—well, anyone on the Council. One did not speak openly of such things. "I do not think so, but the matter of who will be his principal advisor . . . who, in fact, will govern England because, after all, Edward is only ten, even if he is a brilliant boy . . . is a matter of preeminent importance."

"Yes, of course," Elizabeth said, her voice flat and her face composed. "I am sorry if I sounded angry and impatient. I find it uncomfortable to be so uncertain, not to know where and how I am to live."

The smile Denoriel was wearing broadened. "Ah," he said, "but I have not wasted all my time. I may have an answer to those questions."

Her eyes widened. "Oh, Lord Denno, have you?"

"Well, I do have here a letter from Queen Catherine." He took the folded sheet from an inner pocket and held it up under his chin. "And she said to me she was very sorry her distress had so overpowered her as to make her blind to the grief of others. I believe she asks an important question of you."

Elizabeth rose to her feet and held out her hand into which Denoriel put the letter. "If you will pardon me," she said glancing around at the ladies.

Aleneil immediately rose to her feet, gesturing to the other ladies. They also rose, although much more reluctantly and followed Aleneil out into the common hall. So few were now in Elizabeth's household, that Kat Ashley had given orders not to light the fires in the great room.

Only Kat, Blanche Parry, and Denoriel remained in the parlor. Elizabeth broke the seal and read the letter quickly.

"Live with her?" she breathed, and then louder to Kat and Denoriel, "Queen Catherine asks if I would like to live with her! Oh, is that possible? Is it? How can she ask? She must know that the happiest days of my life were when we all lived together at Hampton Court. Nothing would give me more joy than to live with the queen."

Denoriel laughed aloud. Elizabeth's eyes were all golden and a faint color had come into her cheeks. "I told her I was sure you would wish to live with her, and I do not think she doubts it. However, a letter from you, saying how sad and lonely you are and how much you miss her company and guidance and would like to be with her would certainly enhance the chances of approval of the plan when she proposes it."

"She will ask to have me live with her?" There was no trace of the young lady of dignity in Elizabeth now.

"Yes, and if you will write the letter, I will take it back to London—"

"At once," Elizabeth said, moving toward a writing desk set under a sconce fastened to the wall not far from the door. "Oh Kat, light the candles." She laid the letter on the desk and turned back toward Denoriel as Kat lit a spill in the fire and used it to set the candles in the sconce aflame. "And, dear Denno, will you ride back today—"

"Elizabeth!" Kat cried. "Lord Denno has just ridden over ten miles in this bitter weather. It will be cruel to send him out again before he even has a chance to eat a bite and warm himself."

"But it will be dark by then," Elizabeth whispered, tears standing in her eyes. "And the letter will have to wait until tomorrow."

"What a selfish, noxious brat you are," Denoriel said, laughing again. "It will be dark by the time I reach London anyway and, although I will certainly bring the letter to the queen, she might not even be awake by the time I arrive. Moreover, you cannot expect her to do anything with the letter in the middle of the night."

"Not do anything, no, but Catherine likes time to think over what she will do and say, so if she has the letter tonight, she can plan how best to use it tomorrow." All child now, she was impatient of waiting, and wanting it all settled *now*.

"Very well," Denoriel said, sighing, although he was more amused than put upon. "I will take your letter today."

"At least go and sit by the fire and warm yourself, Lord Denno," Kat said, and when Denoriel had bowed and walked over to a stool near the hearth, she turned to lean over Elizabeth who was already writing. "What is wrong with you?" she whispered. "How can you be so inconsiderate? Lord Denno is an old man. I know he seems still hale and hearty, but to demand that he ride again in this bitter weather . . . What if he took an inflamation of the lungs? Elizabeth, my dear, do not subject him to a chance of a dangerous chill."

Although he pretended to be staring into the fire and quite unaware, Denoriel would gladly have strangled the kind and well-intentioned Kat Ashley. He was utterly furious that she should speak of him as an old man, weak and frail. Of course

Elizabeth knew what he was, but his hair *was* white and his face was lined, as few Sidhe's faces were, with pain and anxiety. For the deception he lived in the mortal world, the white hair and lined face were valuable, but he did not want *Elizabeth* to think of him as old.

Why not? The idea, new to him, was startling. He was more than happy to have Kat and all the rest of Elizabeth's household think him old. It was safer that way, less likely to waken suspicion that his devotion to Elizabeth was other than fatherly. Hurriedly, Denoriel checked that line of thought, yet he could not wrench his mind away completely. He had to acknowledge that when anyone said to Elizabeth that he was old, he was infuriated. That Elizabeth should think him old caused a pain in his throat and a tightness in his chest.

Denoriel blinked his slightly dazzled eyes and closed their lids to shield them from the brightness of the fire. It would not dazzle a mortal, but his vision was tuned to the much dimmer light of Underhill.

Elizabeth had turned to Kat and said, "Don't be ridiculous. Denno is—" What she wanted to say was *Sidhe, hardly more than a babe in arms among his own people*, but she could not form those words. What she did say was "—younger than he looks. It is the white hair that fools you. But he swears his hair went white when he heard that Richmond was dead. And I know he's very strong."

She bent again to her writing, by habit making sure that every letter of every word was elegantly formed, as Roger Ascham had taught her. No carelessness must show any disrespect for the queen.

First she wrote formal thanks for the queen's letter of condolence. Then she mentioned her gratitude to Queen Catherine for all her past kindnesses. And then, allowing a single drop of water to fall from the flask for thinning her ink and carefully blotting it—as if a tear had fallen—she considered how to describe her fear of being alone and lost with no one to teach her or advise her. Last she had planned to write openly of her great longing to be again safe under the protection of the queen's watchful eye.

Until those last sentences, much of the letter was formula. While she scribed those parts, the rest of her mind was considering what she had said and done that so much disturbed Kat. She had made a mistake. She knew Denno was young and strong despite his looks, but she surely did not want anyone else to know it. God forbid that anyone should suspect how she felt about Denno . . . even Denno did not know.

Elizabeth's pen hesitated and she stared blindly down at the beautiful script. It was impossible anyway, utterly impossible that Denno who laughed at her and called her a noxious brat would ever see that she was no longer a brat, that she was growing into a woman. Her lips twitched as she thought that she might still be pretty noxious. Then tears filled her eyes and another small wet spot had to be blotted from the paper.

Now what should she do? She knew but did not like it. She must apologize and bid Denno eat and rest so Kat would not be reminded she had said he was younger than he looked. Elizabeth stared for a moment more at the wall, willing the tears not to fall. A moment longer and she could give her mind to her letter again, working out how to phrase what she must ask for. When the words were straight in her head, she wrote them, ending with the large and elaborate "Elizabeth," a signature that was already well known.

Kat was back near the fire, talking to Denno. He looked uncomfortable, Elizabeth saw as she approached them, holding out the folded and sealed letter. Denno rose as she neared and Kat straightened up and smiled meaningfully at her.

Elizabeth sighed again. "I've been rude and unreasonable, haven't I?" she asked as he took the letter from her. "Don't pay any mind to me, Denno dear. Find a place to stay and get warm and have a good meal. I know it can't matter whether Queen Catherine has the letter tonight or tomorrow."

"No, it can't," Denoriel said, tucking the letter away and taking her hand to kiss, "but I assure you—" Kat had turned away, looking satisfied at Elizabeth's capitulation, and Denoriel gave Elizabeth a large and deliberate wink "—she will have it as soon as possible."

Chapter 4

"She is second in line to the throne now," Aurilia nic Morrigan hissed. "How can we be rid of her? If she comes to rule, we of the Unseleighe will be reduced to pale nothings, to beggars and snatchers of shreds of power."

Vidal Dhu, prince of the domain of Caer Mordwyn, looked at his helpmeet. Her body was still lush, her golden hair spread over the black velvet pillows that propped her upright and glittered almost as if threads of the metal had been spun fine and attached to her head. His mouth twitched. Perhaps they were metal. He was not absolutely certain how much of Aurilia was Aurilia and how much illusion. Certainly there was just the faintest hint of decay under the lovely outer shell. She had been damaged in her battles with mortals, and only she knew how much of that damage was permanent. Vidal did not mind at all. That hint of decay tickled his appetite.

They were in the outer chamber of Vidal's private rooms. This day the ceiling was draped in swathes of black satin, which glittered back the light from floating bubbles of luminescence. The walls gave back no light. What covered them were drapes of black velvet—all except two cloth-of-gold panels that seemed to hide windows. Vidal's chair was a stark contrast, a bone-white structure that came by its color honestly, being built of human bones. Yesterday the place had been all red and black. Vidal thought he liked that better. The gold was too cheerful.

"When and how can we be rid of Elizabeth?" Aurilia repeated. "I thought to take her and break her to our purpose but she is too old now and too much trouble."

"We cannot go near her," Vidal said.

He restrained a shudder when he remembered how Oberon looked at him when he had ordered that Elizabeth was beyond the right of the Unseleighe prince to interfere with. Then he swallowed. Oberon was not the only danger. Vidal remembered the crushed body of the mage that Elizabeth had pushed into the void. She seemed to have virtually no magic, to be a perfectly ordinary mortal in that respect, but when she was angry or frightened, things—happened.

Aurilia had sniffed her disdain of his words. Vidal was tempted to unleash a lessoning on her, but he needed her to be clever right now and to bespell her might thrust her back into the near mindlessness that her confrontation with Elizabeth's maid had caused.

Slowly Vidal shook his head. "No. There is a better way. We will help her to destroy herself," he said. "I have been going about this wrong. I put myself into needless danger. She is as stupid and passionate as any other mortal, and for one in her position, that is deadly dangerous. Each time she has been brought to the brink of self-destruction, that accursed pair of guardians has brought her Underhill for healing and saved her. And that is all that saved her."

"Ah," Aurilia breathed. "And Oberon will not interfere in a private battle between Seleighe and Unseleighe."

Vidal Dhu smiled knowingly. "No, he will not. So if we remove Denoriel and Aleneil . . . Elizabeth is very headstrong and without their guidance and protection she has no others in her household that can curb her will. No, we need not touch her or her servants. Her place in the succession is dependent on her good behavior and especially on not marrying without the Council's approval."

"Marrying?" Aurilia's brow creased and her expression became slightly anxious. "But she is only a child . . ."

"Mortal time passes more swiftly than ours, my lady," Vidal said. "Elizabeth is more than fourteen years old. Mortals ripen faster too. She will be feeling the urges of her body and if we can be rid of her Sidhe guardians, she will tumble into bed or into marriage, either of which will remove her from the succession. Think what happened to Catherine Howard, her cousin—to Mary Boleyn, her aunt, even to her own mother! And they were all women grown. There is hot blood in her veins, and without a guide, it will make itself known."

Aurilia frowned again and reached over to the table near the sofa on which she lay. She took up a glass of cloudy, faintly blue liquid and sipped at it, the frown deepening.

"That is not sufficient. When Mary tries to turn this country again to her stupid Church, whatever Elizabeth has done wrong will be forgotten by those who support the Reformed faith. They will raise her up as a pretender—"

"Well, I have no objection to a lively civil war in England," Vidal said, showing his sharply pointed teeth in what was not a smile.

"Nor have I," Aurilia agreed impatiently. "Unless those who support Elizabeth win. It is too dangerous a chance. We need to be rid of her altogether."

"Yes, you are right." Vidal nodded. "But that is no problem. Once she is stripped of her right to succeed Mary, Oberon will no longer care what happens to her. Moreover she is no longer a child and the stupid Seleighe will forget all about her. The only ones who will care are those who have taken oath to protect her, and we have already decided that Denoriel and Aleneil must be destroyed first."

"Denoriel is no problem," Aurilia said. "He spends half his life Gating from Underhill to the mortal world and around the mortal world. Get that clever Pasgen to fix his Gates so that they deliver him somewhere fatal."

"Ah."

This time it was Vidal who breathed a sigh of satisfaction. Aurilia had, as she often did, solved a problem Vidal had been too close to. He could not trust the Dark Sidhe to remove Denoriel. That misbegotten fewmet of a sick ogre had never been an easy mark for violence. He had been foremost of the riders in Koronos' Wild Hunt and could withstand Cold Iron far better than any other Sidhe Vidal knew. Too many Unseleighe Sidhe had died in earlier attempts to finish off Denoriel.

Because he would not admit the fear, even to himself, Vidal found reasons not to take on Denoriel again in a duel of magic. He had discovered by his own dangerous depletion that Denoriel was armored against death magic and had some nasty tricks of his own. Vidal's next thought had been to order Pasgen to kill Denoriel, but he remembered that Pasgen had already tried and failed.

Or had he tried? Vidal's lips lifted in a snarl. He suspected that Pasgen was not really willing to attack his half brother. There was some stupid remnant of feeling about blood kin in Pasgen. But to redirect a Gate : . . Yes, Pasgen should be willing to do that much, especially if the terminus of the Gate would not seem to be fatal . . . as far as Pasgen knew. Vidal himself could arrange what followed.

"As for Aleneil," Aurilia said with a nasty smile, breaking into Vidal's thoughts, "life in the mortal world is so dangerous. You know where Denoriel's house is, I believe. I also believe he is known to be rich. A little gold should easily arrange that mortal thieves armed with mortal weapons attack the house . . . naturally when the woman is alone. They would be told of jewels in her chamber. A steel knife should finish her without any magic being involved."

"Very wise, my lady. Once those two are gone, and Elizabeth has been cast out of the line of succession, we will be free of Oberon's command not to meddle with the royal line." He nodded decisively. "We can then arrange to have Elizabeth killed without the smallest difficulty."

"Hmmm. Yes. I think that is, indeed, the best way to go about the business. We have *some* time. Edward will not fail too soon." She sipped from her glass again. Set it aside. "Still, it would be best to be rid of Elizabeth as soon as possible, before she becomes well known to the people. Her death should be of interest to no one."

"That is a wise point. I had better sharpen my tools in the mortal world. Unfortunately the one best broken to my need is no longer trusted by his fellow Councilors. I will need to set hooks into some new members of the Council." He snorted in disgust.

"Why trouble yourself? You may be needed for more important work. Is this not, my lord, just the sort of task for that upstart Pasgen?"

Vidal's eyes narrowed. "Upstart, yes. I do not trust Pasgen for more important schemes than altering the terminus of a Gate."

"Do you think his taste of ruling the Unseleighe has given him ideas above his powers? Will he confront you, my lord, and try to wrest the throne of Caer Mordwyn from you?"

Was there not as much eagerness as doubt in Aurilia's voice and manner? Interesting. So Pasgen was a temptation and Aurilia was notoriously weak in the face of temptation. Well, that was good to know. If he needed to be rid of her . . . rid of them both with one blow . . . Vidal carefully did not stare at Aurilia.

But there was no need to set any traps yet. Vidal had decided long ago that he must eventually be rid of Pasgen, but not immediately. The young Sidhe was powerful and inventive. If he could be cowed to obedience . . .

Not cowed, perhaps, Vidal thought, remembering Pasgen's carved-out-of-stone expression, but it should be possible to control him. The sister was not nearly as powerful as Pasgen. If he took her and held her . . . Would Pasgen even care? Vidal cast his mind's eye back on the twins. They stood together against him for defense, but he remembered that in most other things they were bitter rivals. But there was someone else even weaker than Rhoslyn . . . Yes! The mother!

That stupid simpering Seleighe Sidhe who had followed her children into his domain. Just as well, he supposed. The twins had been feeble, sickly creatures mostly unable to absorb the sharp and spicy power of pain and despair that was drawn into his domain. Likely they would not have survived if . . . what was her name? Llanelli, yes, he remembered that. If she had not cared for the twins they would have died.

Of course she had tried to subvert her children's induction into the beauties of pain and horror, but he had stopped that. It all came back to him with the memory of her name. Llanelli had hated the dark joys of his realm so much that she had eagerly taken the syrup of oleander which he promised would bring surcease. Oleander, virulent poison to humans, but a bit of oblivion mixed with febrile joy to Sidhe—a swift addiction to the sad.

In no time she would do anything for the drug. And when he said he had no more she *had* done everything, including going to the mortal world and selling her body to gross mortals, whoever would steep the essence of the plant for her. Vidal grinned, recalling how many of the men who tried to make syrup of oleander for her died of the poison and she grieved over them, which made her want the oleander more.

Whatever had happened to her? Likely she had drugged herself into Dreaming, which was just as well. For a moment he thought but he could not remember either of the twins ever mentioning her. Perhaps she was dead.

"And what are you grinning about?" Aurilia asked waspishly, reaching for her glass again.

"Oh, a memory of a Bright Court Sidhe who was not very happy here," he said, and then added, "Do you know how to contact Pasgen?"

"No more than you," Aurilia replied with a tartness that told Vidal she had tried. "One can leave a message at that house they are supposed to live in . . . except that they are never there."

Vidal nodded. "And there is no trail from that house to where they do live. I have set watchers on them, but none has ever followed to the end. Still, both come there from time to time. I will set watchers again, not to try to follow either of them but when one arrives, I will go myself and make sure of their obedience."

It took only a little time, however, once Vidal no longer had Aurilia to impress, for him to decide he would do better to confront Pasgen on his own ground. He also chose as a messenger a Sidhe with so little power that Pasgen would both scorn to attack and be subtly insulted.

That messenger's mouth opened in surprise and terror when a growling ogre rose from beside the Gate platform as he arrived. He desperately called up his shield—not that it was strong enough to protect him from an ogre, but . . . And then he saw the creature was not an ogre. The face was as bland as a baby's, the hands relaxed, not fisted to strike, the mouth closed, not half open to show an ogre's tearing fangs. It stared at him for another moment and then sank down beside the Gate platform again.

Catching his breath, the Dark Sidhe stepped off the platform and started down the well-marked path toward the house. As he went, he swallowed, glad that he was only bearing a message for Rhoslyn and Pasgen. He had realized within a few steps that the path was the only way he *could* go. The garden to either side was walled off by some powerful shield magic. He hesitated, bitterness welling up in him; he could not even imagine the strength of will it had taken to create those spells and power them to work.

Then he wondered whether Prince Vidal had ever sent a subject he wanted destroyed to this house with its mind full of death and destruction. He assumed that the made thing by the Gate—because it certainly was a construct; Rhoslyn he had heard was a genius with constructs—had the ability to sense danger to its maker and would attack those who meant harm. There would have been no escape. If the construct did not seize him and pull him to pieces right on the platform, it could have pursued him down this walled path.

The door of the house opened as he approached, and another construct asked tonelessly whom he wished to see.

"Mistress Rhoslyn and Master Pasgen. I carry a message from Prince Vidal."

The construct looked utterly blank, its mouth half open as if it were about to speak but had forgotten the words.

"She is here," the Dark Sidhe said angrily. "I know she is here. My master's watcher saw her arrive."

The construct's mouth closed and it stepped aside.

"Yes, I am here," Rhoslyn said, appearing in the doorway in the construct's stead. "But Pasgen is not. What does Prince Vidal want?"

For a long moment the Dark Sidhe stared at her in amazement. He never went to the mortal world because the Cold Iron permeating the works of humankind was terrible to him. Thus he had not seen Tudor court dress and was astonished.

Rhoslyn wore a kind of close fitting hood that hid all of her hair except the smooth parting and two bands to each side of her forehead. The hood was so heavily embroidered in a floral pattern in silver and varying shades of gray and pale blue that the original color of the cloth could not be distinguished. From the top rear of the hood, a dark veil flowed down over one shoulder.

That shoulder was nearly bare, as the gown she wore was open almost from armpit to armpit. Around her neck were several strands of jet beads, wound together almost into a collar. One strand, much longer than the others, hung down over her bosom and supported, in a black frame, a miniature portrait of a broad-faced man in a fancy hat.

The gown itself was of black velvet, embroidered in silver and from the waist it hung open above a silvery gray underdress, embroidered in black. The sleeves of the gown were slashed open from shoulder to wrist, and through the openings, which were fancy-hemmed in silver, puffs of a white chemise were pulled.

The Dark Sidhe, used to females in leggings and tunics or in beautifully flowing loose garments, gaped at the rigid figure.

"Well," Rhoslyn repeated, "what does Prince Vidal want?"

"How would I know that?" the Dark Sidhe said bitterly, shaking his head and blinking his eyes as if Rhoslyn's appearance stunned him. "The prince bid me bring you and your brother to Caer Mordwyn. When do you expect Pasgen?"

Rhoslyn sensed that the Sidhe confronting her was barely Sidhe, so weak were his powers. So he was no more than a messenger. She allowed the shield she had formed around herself to dissipate and stepped back to allow the messenger to enter if he wished. He could do no magical harm and her mental call had brought Cannaid, the "girl" with the white ribbon, silently into the corridor.

"I don't expect him at all," Rhoslyn said.

"I don't believe you. Your brother is trying to avoid his duty to Prince Vidal. I want to look through the house."

Rhoslyn frowned but stepped aside as the Dark Sidhe came up the three steps and entered the house. She was thinking furiously hard as she backed away and then, when her back was covered by Cannaid, led the Dark Sidhe toward the peristyle. The colonnaded center of the house enclosed a shallow pool of clear water in which brightly colored fish swam. Doors—some open, some closed—broke the smooth line of the marble walls sheltered by the colonnade.

Vidal must want Pasgen and her to do some dirty work in the mortal world during the confusion of the change of rulers. Rhoslyn was sure that Pasgen would refuse, and it seemed that Vidal knew Pasgen was unwilling. That was why the messenger had been told to look through the house.

No, that was stupid. A Sidhe with such weak powers would never find Pasgen if he did not want to be found. And Vidal wasn't stupid—likely the search was Vidal's unsubtle message that he was growing impatient with Pasgen's continued absence and would not give up or forget him. Possibly Vidal still thought that Pasgen feared him.

Rhoslyn suppressed her flash of indignation. That belief was very useful. And it would be just as useful for Vidal not to learn that the bond between her and Pasgen was deep and strong. She would go with the Dark Sidhe and pretend to tell everything she knew about Pasgen's whereabouts . . . no, she *would* tell everything she knew, no pretense about it. Rhoslyn smiled and touched the quiet lindys as the Dark Sidhe turned away to look at the closed doors around the peristyle. Of course she would tell everything; truly she knew nothing.

"So look," she said to the messenger, gesturing around at the doors and seating herself in a chair that faced the shallow pool under the open roof of the peristyle. "I assure you I have no intention of hiding my brother from Prince Vidal. Pasgen can't stick me with his problems. Let him take care of himself."

Her complete indifference to the messenger's search, which was unfeigned because Pasgen wasn't there, convinced the Dark Sidhe, who had a modicum of truth sense, that a real search would be useless. He made a casual survey of the rooms, so he could tell Vidal that he had looked, and then returned to tell Rhoslyn that since Pasgen was not there she must come to Vidal alone.

She made a weak protest and even whined a little, saying that she was doing all she could in the mortal world and that if Vidal asked more of her she might lose her place with Lady Mary.

Meanwhile she had ordered Cannaid to get Lliwglas and for the two to meet her outside the house. The Dark Sidhe glanced at them as they fell in behind Rhoslyn when he shepherded her out, but they looked so much like starving children, with their sticklike limbs, huge eyes, and pursed mouths that he did not object to their company.

He told Rhoslyn to set the Gate for Caer Mordwyn, but she looked at him as if he were mad and said that Pasgen had made the Gate and it went *only* to one of the three markets.

"That is not very convenient," the Dark Sidhe snarled.

Rhoslyn laughed. "If Prince Vidal was hoping that you would be able to see how to pattern Pasgen's Gate, he is doomed to disappointment. It has only the one path, to and from the Market. But it isn't inconvenient at all. From any of the markets, there are Gates that lead everywhere."

There were indeed Gates to everywhere; in fact before one entered the Market, set in the area in which transport waited, there were Gates that had one terminus to each of the other markets and four blank termini. Those could be patterned to any terminus at all, and that terminus would be erased as soon as those traveling by that Gate arrived. There was even one Gate that responded to a traveler's mental command. It was not much used, since the command needed to be clear and firm. If not, the traveler might emerge in an unexpected or unwanted place.

Rhoslyn almost headed for that Gate. She used it often and had never had trouble with it. However, she remembered in time that she was trying to act annoyed and bewildered, and stood looking uncertain until the Dark Sidhe chose a Gate. However, she did not wait for him to pattern one of the blank points; she willed the terminus at Caer Mordwyn herself.

For once they arrived at a simple black and red Gate platform reasonably close to the palace. Rhoslyn hesitated nonetheless; Vidal had a nasty habit of emplacing traps on and around his Gates. The Dark Sidhe, however, stepped off without triggering any disaster and so did Lliwglas. Rhoslyn then followed with Cannaid bringing up the rear.

The palace itself was also strangely nonhostile. The doors opened smoothly as their party approached; graceful curvilinear designs in gold eased the oppressive quality of the black marble corridor. No razor-edged, bloodsucking ribbons launched from the pillars; no tripwires rose from the corridor floor; nothing corrosive or simply nasty poured down from the ceiling.

The safe and quiet progress made Rhoslyn more and more uneasy. It was possible that the lack of attack might have been because the traps and devices sensed that Rhoslyn was covered with strong shields, but she did not think so. Vidal's mind was plainly elsewhere, planning something truly frightful. Rhoslyn began to be frightened—and then realized that was just the effect this strange peacefulness was designed to produce.

Nonetheless, Rhoslyn was wary and uneasy. She could feel the angry tension in the constructs who followed her, but was able to send a mental message for them to be calm when the first words out of Vidal's mouth were, "Where is Pasgen?"

"I have no idea," Rhoslyn said, not trying to hide her nervousness. "I saw him only a few days ago. We dined together. He did not say where he was going when he left."

Vidal turned his head and looked at Aurilia, who was sitting in a cushioned chair. Her ever-present glass of blue cloudy liquid stood ready on a small table by her side, and her brow was creased in a deep frown.

"Well?" Vidal said to her. "Is that true?"

"No, it is not strictly true, but it is not a lie either," Aurilia said.

Rhoslyn emitted an exasperated but slightly tremulous sigh. "All right. He said he was going into the Unformed lands—but that scarcely means I could know where he is now or guess how to find him."

Now Aurilia shrugged. "That is true."

Vidal snorted a generalized disbelief. "I cannot believe that he sleeps and eats in the Unformed lands. You must know how to get to where he truly lives."

"I did," Rhoslyn admitted.

She looked into herself and found a strong discontent with her life in the Unseleighe Court. She nourished it with all the resentment she felt against Vidal. Aurilia frowned, touched her temple, reached for her glass, and sipped.

"So?" Vidal urged.

Rhoslyn bit her lip and said, "He closed my way to him. Closed it, as if I would go to his house when I knew he was not there and steal from him."

Vidal had glanced at Aurilia again but only briefly before he said to Rhoslyn in a smooth sympathetic voice, "That seems unjustifiable. You have always been a loyal sister. Perhaps he has not closed the way. Perhaps you mistook one of the changes. Why do you not let me come with you and see if I can detect—"

"No," Rhoslyn interrupted. "Pasgen would murder me if he discovered I had shown you a way to reach his stronghold, even a way he had closed. Oh, no. Pasgen taught me my shields and he can get through them. You can do nothing to me that Pasgen cannot do worse."

There was enough truth in that not to tickle Aurilia's truth spell into warning. Pasgen had indeed taught Rhoslyn some shields. He probably could get through her shields; truthfully, Rhoslyn did not know any shields that would be proof against Pasgen if he had time enough to work on them. It was also true that Pasgen could probably do more terrible things to Rhoslyn than Vidal ever could . . . because Rhoslyn loved Pasgen and disliked and despised Vidal. Vidal could only hurt her body, not destroy her heart and mind.

"You are a fool. I am stronger than Pasgen," Vidal spat.

"Likely you are stronger," Rhoslyn agreed, "but if you struck out at me, likely you would destroy me." She shrugged. "Pasgen knows me all too well. He could wrench me apart bit by bit forever. And he would not like it if you hurt me, Prince Vidal. Pasgen regards me as his and would resent even a bruise on my body or mind."

Vidal did not respond to that directly nor did he even look

at Aurilia for confirmation. He was certain that Rhoslyn believed what she said. In fact, he believed it too. Instead of confirming or denying her threat, he shook his head at Rhoslyn, and said she was foolish to think he intended her harm, then added with poorly concealed avid interest, "What is he doing in the Unformed lands?"

Rhoslyn shrugged. "He told me he thought there was some source of power there." That was the perfect truth. Aurilia's truth spell would accept the statement.

"Well, of course there is." Vidal uttered a bark of laughter. "You know that yourself. You use that power in your creations, I suppose. But no one has ever found a way to separate the power from the chaos that is there."

"You asked me what he was doing," Rhoslyn said. "I told you what he told me. It may not have been the truth, but that is what he said to me."

"Never mind what he is looking for in the Chaos Lands," Aurilia suddenly put in. "Tell me instead what brought him to that house you use only for messages."

"Not only for messages," Rhoslyn said. "Since Pasgen does not want me in his stronghold and I do not want him in mine—to which, I must say that he has not yet found a way—we usually meet in the empty house. It really isn't empty, of course. It is fully furnished and has a staff of servants. We just never found a name for the place we could agree on."

"Yes, well, why did Pasgen call you there when you last met?" Vidal asked.

"Oh, he wanted to know what I was doing and whether I had spoken to you, Prince Vidal. And if I had, what you wanted."

"And what will you tell him when you next see him?"

Rhoslyn found a thin, nasty smile. "The truth, of course. I always tell Pasgen the truth. I will tell him that Prince Vidal asked for him and wishes to see him and that Lady Aurilia was most interested in what brought him to our house. Of course, if you have any messages for him, I will leave them at the house for him."

"You will not wait for him there and tell him directly?" Vidal asked.

"No, of course not. You know I cannot spend long Underhill."

"You cannot spend long Underhill?" Aurilia echoed.

Rhoslyn looked from her to Vidal and shrugged again. "Prince Vidal charged me mortal years ago to watch over Lady Mary and be sure that her faith remains strong and unchanged. I have faithfully performed that duty. Now that her father died so recently, Mary is given over almost completely to prayer. I am one of her mainstays and dare not be away from her for long." She made a wry face. "It is well that Sidhe do not need sleep so that I can come Underhill during the mortal night to refresh myself."

"So you are a trusted servant to Lady Mary," Aurilia said, her eyes brightening with avid speculation. "Can you not convince her to lend you to Elizabeth—"

"No!" Rhoslyn interrupted. "I dare not go anywhere near Lady Elizabeth. Do you not remember that she can see through illusion? Do you want her screaming that Lady Mary sent one of the Fair Folk to wait on her?"

"She would not be so foolish. No one else would see your eyes and ears. All would say she was mad."

"Unless she ordered one of her servants—they are fanatically devoted and would obey even an order that seemed mad—to seize me and *feel* my ears. Illusion will not hide their true shape. And perhaps that monster maid of hers would touch me with her Cold Iron crosses and my disguise might fail altogether."

Aurilia gasped at the mention of the necklace of crosses that Blanche Parry, Elizabeth's trusted maid wore. Twice those iron crosses had severely damaged Aurilia, once almost fatally, the second time robbing her of coherent thought and memory for some months. Her head still ached, although most of the pain was kept at bay by the potion her mortal healer prepared for her; however, the potion dulled her wits. She knew that and hated it, but could not endure the pain.

Rhoslyn pretended not to notice that Aurilia had almost drained her glass of cloudy blue liquid. She shuddered and went on, "Can you imagine what King Oberon would do to us all if we were exposed to the royal family in the mortal world?"

"Aurilia," Vidal said sharply, "forget Lady Elizabeth. We need to be free of Aleneil and Denoriel first. Then Elizabeth can ruin herself." He turned to Rhoslyn. "So, Rhoslyn, can you reach Aleneil? You are both servants to the late king's daughters. You should be able to find a reason to speak to Aleneil."

"So I might, if we were anywhere near each other. Lady Mary

has moved to Essex, and Lady Elizabeth is still—or was still; I am not sure—at Enfield, only about ten miles from London. Mortals do not Gate about you know. It would take me hours, perhaps a full day, to get to Aleneil."

"You are useless!" Aurilia spat. "And your brother is a traitor."

She lifted her hand to cast a spell at Rhoslyn, and Cannaid was in front of her maker, poised to leap, the fingers of her hands suddenly longer and gleaming with razor edges. Vidal gestured and the construct struck an invisible wall and rebounded. It did not, as most constructs would, claw uselessly at the wall of force; it crouched somewhat, its stick-thin legs now double thick with hard muscle, obviously intending to leap over the barrier.

"Cannaid, stop," Rhoslyn said, to protect her construct.

Although the creature was resistant to most magic, Vidal was surely strong enough to blast it or draw out its power so that it crumpled to nothing. She turned a shoulder angrily toward Aurilia.

To Vidal she said resentfully, "I will go now. I have no control over Pasgen and do not see why I should be threatened because of it. I will continue to watch and guide Lady Mary because her well-doing will be of benefit to me and I desire no quarrel with you, Prince Vidal." Every word was true and would so be marked by Aurilia's truth spell. Then Rhoslyn added, "But do not try me too far."

Chapter 5

Having delivered Elizabeth's letter to Queen Catherine, Denoriel was at a standstill. The queen had been deeply moved by Elizabeth's plea and had promptly sent a message to Sir Anthony Denny. Graciously, she allowed Denoriel to wait in the hall, and at mid-morning let him know that she had received a reply in which Sir Anthony had promised to visit her soon.

There was nothing more Denoriel could do. To try to see Denny and urge him to attend to Elizabeth's problems would be counterproductive. Sir Anthony liked him, but his suspicions would surely be aroused if both Queen Catherine and Lord Denno suddenly began to press him on Elizabeth's behalf.

Denoriel could have gone Underhill, but there was nothing there to hold his interest. He did remind himself that he should attend some festivities and seek out a willing lady, but the thought caused a decided discomfort in his stomach and a coldness where he should be feeling heat.

Exasperated with himself and the situation, Denoriel made his way to his London house where he was greeted with cautious enthusiasm by Joseph Clayborne, his man of business. Joseph actually ran Denoriel's business, keeping him in touch with the market and what other merchants were doing and saying. Denoriel then often arranged to get cargoes of what was most strongly desired through Seleighe contacts in domains all over Europe and even the Middle East.

Joseph was well aware that there was something very strange, uncanny even, about his master, but he had come to like Lord Denno. He was, moreover, no religious fanatic who felt that one should not suffer a witch to live. Joseph had never seen Lord Denno do any man any harm; contrariwise he had known Lord Denno to be generous and loyal even at some risk to himself.

"M'lord, do you have a moment?" Joseph asked, standing in the doorway of his handsomely appointed office.

"All the moments you want today, Joseph," Denoriel replied, smiling. "The Court is in such disarray with everyone scrambling for a new or better place that no one is willing to speak to me."

"Do you have *any* news?" Joseph asked. "It would help if I seemed to know what was going on."

"I think, since he holds the king, that Hertford, although I doubt he will be Hertford much longer, will come out atop in the Council. Right after the king died, Sir Anthony told me it was mostly Hertford's plan, although Paget agreed to it, to delay the announcement of the king's death until Hertford had secured Edward."

Joseph frowned. "To what purpose?"

Denoriel shrugged. "Henry was so strong a king that there never was another—at least not since Wolsey—to whom the nation could look. The new king is a child of ten. Someone had to seize the wheel and steer the ship of state."

"It is true," Joseph said. "I cannot think of anyone I would look to. I suppose Hertford is as good or better than another. At least he is the king's close kin without any claim at all to the throne."

Denoriel had not thought of that aspect of the kinship between Edward and Hertford. It was, now that Joseph had called it to his attention, another reason that the Council might be willing for Hertford to be first among them.

"Yes," he said, nodding thoughtfully, "Hertford is Edward's *maternal* uncle with no blood tie, no matter how distant to the king, and Queen Catherine does not come from a powerful family . . . nor one with overweening ambition."

Joseph stepped aside invitingly, and Denoriel walked into his chamber, dropping into a comfortable chair placed to the side of the table on which Joseph worked, where only those specially invited were likely to sit. Joseph went around the end of the table and sat in his own chair.

"So you assume Hertford will rule? Do you know him? How will this affect us?"

"Well, Hertford will not favor us with news or show my wares," Denno said with a rueful smile, "but I doubt he will trouble us either. I met him twice or thrice in Norfolk's company, and from what I learned from listening to him and from hearing Norfolk speak about him, it seems he is a strong man, certain of will, and with an unblemished honor. He was said to be fond of Edward too."

"You never pursued the acquaintance with Hertford?"

Denoriel laughed. "No. There was nothing to pursue. Hertford did not take to me at all. When I kissed his hand, he withdrew it as if my lips were coals. And it did not seem, at the time, worth the effort to win his trust, which shows how badly mistaken I can be. Truthfully Norfolk had survived so much—I mean two nieces executed for adultery, and one of them actually guilty of betraying the king. I thought the old man would last forever."

Joseph smiled in reply. "I think everyone expected the king to pardon Norfolk, but Henry was dying. And Norfolk is still in the Tower waiting execution. I fear there will be no quick release for him now . . . either way."

Denoriel sighed. It was hard to actually like Norfolk, who was the sort of man to use anyone or anything that came to hand, but one could certainly admire the shrewd old man. "Yes. I went again to the Tower and offered Norfolk what help I could give. He thanked me but said it did not matter that King Henry had died. King Edward was as welcome to his life as King Henry." Denoriel shook his head. "He is rich enough to be comfortable, for whatever thing he needs for his comfort, he can arrange to have, so there is really nothing more I can do."

Joseph frowned. "If you will pardon my saying so, you have done enough for the few favors the duke has shown you."

"We were not really friends . . . I doubt Norfolk could consider a foreign merchant a friend, but I rather—appreciated him. Now I suppose I must find another link to the top." Denoriel pondered his few options. "Sir Anthony is friendly enough and well trusted by the Council, but the king's death has sorely shaken him. I think if he had leave of his fellow Councilors that he would ask to retire."

"A link to the top," Joseph said thoughtfully. "Sir Anthony

Cooke is tutor to Edward and well beloved of him, from what I have heard."

Denoriel shook his head before Joseph could go further. "No, I do not want my name or anything about me known to the king or his close companions. That would only draw close scrutiny, and expose my long association with Elizabeth."

Joseph looked disappointed. "Even at a safe remove? I thought news might flow both ways through one of Cooke's daughters. All three were in the group that Queen Catherine gathered as company for the royal children when they were at Hampton Court and all seem to have been fond of Lady Elizabeth."

"Likely," Denoriel nodded, thinking it next to impossible for anyone who knew her to be less than fond of Elizabeth. "She spoke of them to me, saying that aside from Lady Jane Grey, the eldest Cooke daughter was the best scholar. That would be—" He pressed his memory. "Mildred. Of course, Mildred was some years older than the others, it is reasonable she should have been the best."

"Yes, Mistress Mildred," Clayborne said, nodding. "We have twice received messages from her, requesting a few bottles of a particular wine, which she had had at Lady Elizabeth's table. Apparently Lady Elizabeth told her that you had provided the wine."

"You mean I should scrape an acquaintance on the basis of the wine?" Denoriel said doubtfully, then shook his head. "It is too close, and anyway she will not be at Court any longer even if her father is with the king."

"She is not in the country. Mistress Mildred lives here in London. She married a man called William Cecil—"

"Cecil," Denoriel interrupted, eyes wide with surprise. "You are telling me that Mildred Cooke is William Cecil's wife?"

"Yes, but I assume she will still see her father—"

Now *here* was the sort of acquaintance he needed at Court! William Cecil, as clever as Cromwell but with honor and heart that Cromwell never had. He was going to go far and climb high, or Denoriel would be very much surprised. "Never mind her father, if she is Cecil's wife . . . How did you plan that I scrape an acquaintance with Mildred?"

"Who is William Cecil?" Joseph asked with great interest.

"Right now he is *custos brevium* in the court of common pleas, but he already had some notice from the king—I mean the late King Henry." Henry had been a good judge of men too. Never of women, but his ability to weigh the worth of a man was uncanny. "Cecil is a man with keen ears and sharp eyes, a man who knows when and how to hold his tongue. He will go very far, and more to the point, he already wishes to please Elizabeth. He has several times sent Mistress Ashley snippets of Court information that pertained to Elizabeth, and he is the one who wrote to inform her of the Dirge for her father. No one else thought to warn her—alas, not even I. Yes, indeed, Joseph, I would like to be called 'friend' by William Cecil."

"Very possible." Now Joseph was looking pleased. "I honored Mistress Mildred's requests for the wine that I mentioned, but I had a new request just yesterday, and we do not have any more of that wine. I was about to write to her and explain, but if you want an entree into the house, you could take her a substitute in person, and give her the explanation yourself. Since you seem to be interested in William Cecil, perhaps the lady would introduce you to her husband?"

"Yes, of course she would," Denoriel said; it would be the work of a moment to put the idea into her head. "Thank you, Joseph. As usual you have outdone my expectation in solving problems for me."

Clayborne laughed. "Only by accident this time, my lord." Then he added, "There is nothing else in a business way . . . and of course, the only thing you have received in the way of social invitations has been cancellations of events. I sent civil notes." Suddenly his brow furrowed. "But there was an oddity the other day. A gentleman . . . well, no, probably he was not a gentleman. Let me say it this way. A person clean and in good clothing—but I would say not accustomed to being well dressed, combed, and shaven—came to the door and asked Cropper for Lady Alana."

Odd. Very odd. "Asked for Lady Alana? But I did not think anyone except Lady Elizabeth's household knew that she often stayed with me when she was in London. And Alana is with Lady Elizabeth now, so no one from there would be looking for her here."

"Yes, m'lord. That was why I said it was an oddity. And even odder, when Cropper said she was not at home, he did not ask for you, but asked to speak to me . . . by name."

But there might be an explanation that Joseph shouldn't know. Joseph thought the person was not accustomed to good clothing or to being clean and shaven, but what if the person was not accustomed to *mortal* clothing and disguise as a human. What if the person was Sidhe? Denoriel had thought when he spoke to his sister in his apartment in Llachar Lle that Aleneil might have private affairs to see to Underhill. Perhaps affairs of romance. What if she had not been able to settle the matter?

If Aleneil had given a Sidhe the direction of the house on Bucklersbury, it was someone she wanted to see. Had they quarreled? Had she not made clear the time she wished to see him? Denoriel wondered if he should go Underhill . . . and do what? Start seeking Aleneil's lover? She would murder him. The safest action here was none at all.

"Why should that be so odd?" Denoriel said, seeking to cover his thoughts. "If he was not a gentleman, he might think he would get short shrift from me. As for your name, I would not be surprised if your name was better known than mine in this neighborhood." He smiled. "After all, I am in and out so often that I am almost a stranger in my own house."

"That might be true," Joseph said, but still frowning, as if the encounter had left him feeling distinctly uneasy.

Denoriel shrugged, only now he was suddenly doubtful of his previous reasoning. Aleneil was not likely to have chosen a fool. On the other hand, a Sidhe who disliked the mortal world and had never visited it, might well be awkward . . . if the man was Sidhe. Dark Sidhe? No, the Dark would surely not ask openly for Aleneil. Who among the Unseleighe would be foolish enough to venture here to look for her?

"I suppose Alana might have told someone that she could be reached through me," Denoriel temporized. "Did he leave a message? I could take it to her."

"That was the other oddity. No." Joseph shook his head. "He did not leave a message, said his matter was in his head and private and asked when Lady Alana was expected. I told him, of course, that I did not know, that it was her habit to send us a message on the day or a day before she was due to arrive. He then said he would come by again and left. Perhaps he did not think he had enough money to bribe me to tell him when Lady Alana was expected, but he offered to make it worth Cropper's while if Cropper would leave a message for him at the Broached Barrel when Lady Alana was due."

Denoriel grinned. "Cropper told you?"

"Indeed. He is not taking any chances on losing his place. He is very happy here." Joseph smirked—or at least, came as close to a smirk as he ever did.

"Happy enough not to ask questions about the other servants?" That was a pertinent question.

Joseph smiled at him. "He knows the other servants are . . . a little odd but has 'decided' that they are really foreign foreigners, not like Frenchies, who are almost human—anyhow that was how he described them to me. And he doesn't talk about what he sees, nor does his wife, so the children accept them as . . . ah . . . foreign foreigners."

"Joseph, if you ever threaten to leave me I will have to kill myself because I am afraid I really would not be able to live without you." Denoriel cast up his hands with a smile. "How did you manage to get someone who is not stupid as a stone to accept this household as ordinary?"

Clayborne met his eyes steadily. "The same way you bound me, my lord, by obligation. George Boleyn knew of my trouble, but it was you who offered me a way out."

"Nonsense, you have no obligation to me. You paid back my 'rescue' of your enterprise long ago." Nevertheless, Denoriel was touched. Loyalty—something no coin could buy, and was rarer than perfect pearls.

"True enough," Clayborne said, suddenly grinning, "but now I am yours through self-interest. I told you some time ago that I was growing rich in your employ. Your generosity in allowing me shares of your cargoes is hastening the filling of my purse." He shook his head. "I will not leave you, my lord, I promise, until and unless I train a substitute so well that you will not know a new man is in my place."

"I doubt that is possible," Denoriel said. "I have grown very fond of you, Joseph. George found you for me. How did you find Cropper?"

"Very easily. I went to the debtors' prisons. I looked for a family, but not too large. I spoke to the wife and then to the husband, and then I enquired of the officials about the details that caused the incarceration. I was lucky. There were three families that did not deserve their fate, but only Cropper was of a size and intelligence to make an adequate footman. I paid off his debt, found lodgings for him and the family in the back of a house in the Poultry, gave the family a few pence to get started . . . and now you have a most devoted servant."

"I think *you* have a most devoted servant," Denoriel said smiling, "but I am not complaining. I am sure the devotion runs over onto me." He stood up. "Since you have twice told me there was no business, I had better go away and leave you to deal with that pile of documents."

"Yes, my lord." Clayborne also stood. "So do you want me to write to Mistress Mildred Cecil about the wine—"

"No, of course not." He shook his head. "I will soon begin to forget my head on the days it is not screwed on tightly enough. I will go to see her myself. What kind of wine did she want?"

Without the slightest hesitation, Joseph picked a rather small sheet of heavy paper from the middle of a pile and handed it to him. "There is her letter. What I sent both times was rumney, but I think if you took her some claret, and perhaps some alicant, it will do. She will like the claret, what with the honey and spices in it; most women do, but in case her husband has more austere taste, the red should also suffice."

Denoriel nodded. Although he did not know what was kept in his warehouses, he actually did know the contents of the wine cellar in the house. There was a Gate there, behind a large tun, and Denoriel felt that examining and commenting upon the contents of the cellar was a good excuse for being in it so frequently.

"We have both in bottles," he said after a moment of thought. "And her direction?"

"In Cannon Row. Cropper will know the house. He took the rumney."

Joseph had risen while he spoke; he walked to the door of his office, opened it, and shouted for Cropper, who appeared in moments. Joseph told him what he should fetch from the cellar and that he would be carrying the wine to the house in the Strand.

Meanwhile, Denoriel had gone up to his bedchamber where he stood in front of the ruinously costly cheval glass to examine the illusion that made the pupils of his eyes round and gave him the appearance of small round ears. Then his eyes went to his clothing and he sighed heavily. How humans could torture themselves with such unwieldy and uncomfortable garments, he could not understand.

Over a spotlessly white shirt with full sleeves, the neck gathered into a low ruff, Denoriel was wearing a padded petticoat in lavender velvet; that was sensible in providing warmth in a world where the weather did not conform to the being's comfort. Over that was the doublet, in a rich silk brocade of silver and lavender, tight to the waist, with sleeves slashed at elbows and forearms so the white shirt could be pulled through. Long hose of dark gray tied up with points to the petticoat were covered with slops—heavy silk, striped in gray and lavender—which were in turn covered by the skirt attached to the doublet. And over all the gown, gray with lavender piping on all the seams.

And the mortals seemed to *enjoy* the torture of removing and replacing the garments several times a day at the slightest excuse.

Fortunately no one had spilled anything on Denoriel during his wait in the queen's hall, so that he did not *need* to change. For verisimilitude he had a wardrobe full of clothing in his bedchamber, but he rarely wore any of it. To dress in any of those garments, he would have to call one of the male servants to help him tie points and button buttons. And the Low Court Sidhe who cooked and cleaned the house all laughed so hard over the clothing that they weren't much help. It was far easier to Gate Underhill and magic the clothes onto his body than to dress here in the World Above. Since none of the servants spoke more than a word of English, they could not betray him. And today he had a good excuse; none of the clothes stored here was in suitable colors for the half mourning that a foreign noble would be expected to wear. Not the black of full mourning. That would be presumptuous.

Cropper was waiting in the corridor near the front door carrying Denoriel's fur-lined cloak. The basket of wine bottles rested on the table with the salver for cards. Cropper put Denoriel's cloak over his shoulders, opened the door for Denoriel, waited until his master had passed through, picked up the basket, and closed the door behind him. He waited for Denoriel to set out and followed him, a careful three steps to the rear.

A few feet down the street, Denoriel was aware that Cropper had hesitated and fallen back a few steps. Denoriel did not turn his head to look, assuming something was in the man's shoe, or a shoe had come loose. He did not want Cropper to feel he was being criticized, just slowed his pace a bit so the man could easily catch up.

When they reached Cannon Row, Denoriel became aware of the inconvenience of finding a place when the man who actually knew where they were going, was behind him. He stopped, gestured Cropper forward and said to him, "Go ahead and make sure it will be convenient for Mistress Cecil to receive me—or Master Cecil if the mistress is not at home and he is."

Pasgen was enjoying himself studying this Unformed land, but he stopped dead as he felt the lindys under the wide collar of his shirt stiffen. He was dressed only for comfort and some protection against odd outcroppings of rock or twigs and thorns in a white silk shirt with full sleeves, close-fitting black velvet trousers, and soft, unpolished, knee-high leather boots. And because one never knew what might have been loosed by some lunatic or mischievous Sidhe in an Unformed land, he wore both silver sword and long knife.

The lindys twitched. Pasgen tensed, hand raised to spell him to the Gate, although he realized that a spell in this place might be very dangerous. Nonetheless, if Rhoslyn was in trouble and needed him immediately any other danger was insignificant. But the lindys did not convulse. It did not even stiffen into rigidity, only lying still and tense. Pasgen dropped his hand, the slight glimmer of blue power fading from his fingers, and concentrated on sensing what information the lindys held.

Rhoslyn's construct could only warn her if he were in acute danger and help her Gate to wherever he was; he did not want to stress her with his tensions and anxieties. His lindys gave much more complete information. For a moment he closed his mind to the faint cries of fear and an only slightly louder roaring that had attracted his attention and concentrated on Rhoslyn. She was Gating, anxious but not threatened, ah, Vidal and Aurilia—Pasgen's nose wrinkled—Aurilia using a truth spell.

A thin smile stretched Pasgen's lips for a moment. Doubtless Vidal wanted to know where he was. Since Rhoslyn did not know, she could answer with perfect truth. Nonetheless Pasgen set off in the direction of the Gate. He wanted to be near enough to Gate immediately if Vidal did more than question Rhoslyn.

Pasgen could not see the Gate through the swirling mist, but when that little monster Elizabeth and her party had arrived he had felt her mark the Gate. Then he, too, had felt the difference of the power flow in the mist where the Gate was. Resentment flicked him because she, ignorant and untaught, had found magic that he, deep scholar of power, had never noticed.

Then he smiled again. He could not envy what was inborn. She was some little prodigy of art and nature, that Elizabeth. He was really pleased that he had promised Rhoslyn to do her no harm. A double benefit to that: he would be able to study the puzzle of her power and indirectly to frustrate Vidal at the same time.

A pleasant sensation of satisfaction rose in him as he neared the Gate, and he folded his legs and sat down on the invisible—ground? was it ground? The surface, anyway. He was now only a few long running steps from the Gate. He doubted Rhoslyn would need his support, but in case she did, he would not need to use magic to reach the Gate. And in this particular Unformed land he did not want to use magic unless it was a matter of life and death.

For as long as the lindys remained tense and unmoving, Pasgen concentrated on the telltale. Distantly, from time to time, he again heard some sounds and wondered whether it was merely the soughing of the movement of shifting power in this very strange place or whether something material was crying and roaring. Then the lindys relaxed; Pasgen could feel Rhoslyn's satisfaction and was himself also satisfied.

He made a mental note to visit the empty house to ask Rhoslyn what Vidal wanted as he rose to his feet, but the forefront of his attention was now given to his ears. Surely the sounds were real and separate. The timbre of the cries was very different from that of the roaring and surely there was occasionally a rhythm almost like speech in those cries. His head cocked to the side, listening, Pasgen began to walk toward the sounds.

In mere moments they were more distinct and he no longer felt any doubt. One set of sounds was cries—almost Elven, almost human, but not quite either in pitch. And it was a set, one a higher, the other a slightly lower voice. The voices shrieked in unison and the roar sounded almost atop the cries. Without thought Pasgen began to run. Something? someone? was in deep trouble. Weirdly, the mist seemed to thin before him as if it were making a path.

Ooof.

The cry was thin and terrified, but Pasgen felt the impact of a slight but firmly solid body. Before he could make any response, a scream of agony rang out followed by a near deafening animal roar. And through the mist he glimpsed a tawny coat, a ragged mane. Pasgen drew sword and knife just as the mist curled away and disclosed a very genuine-looking lion just about to spring atop a vaguely Elven form.

Pasgen shouted aloud.

The lion lifted its head from its prey. Whatever . . . whoever had hit him, brushed his shoulder, running back toward the lion. Pasgen thrust it away with the elbow of his knife hand, away behind him, away from the lion. He had no idea why. The thin voice cried out again, despairingly. If he had a brain in his head, Pasgen thought, he would let the lion eat his meal and slip away while the creature was busy. But that would leave the lion loose in the mist, perhaps to leap on him when he was unaware.

He remembered suddenly that Elizabeth had said she had asked the mist to create the lion to save her from some human abductors. She had thought it would frighten them, but it had killed them instead and then almost killed her. It was too dangerous, and she had brought with her help—Denoriel; that boy grown into a man now, that he and Rhoslyn had tried so often to abduct and Vidal had wanted so badly; and two Elven makers—all to try to destroy the lion. And he, all alone, was shouting to draw its attention.

He succeeded.

The lion tensed, its head lifting, quivering slightly as it prepared to leap at him. Pasgen's sword rose to point at the lion; words of a spell of dissolution trembled on his lips—and were swallowed back. The Great Allmother alone knew what would happen if he spoke that spell without warding in this place. And even if it worked, Pasgen knew that the mist would not like it.

Later, when he had caught his breath and had time to think, Pasgen wondered if he had gone utterly mad. At the time, he shouted again and leapt forward before the lion could. The creature reared up in surprise, exposing its throat and chest. Pasgen plunged forward another step and thrust his sword into the beast's throat.

The blade went in to almost half its length, but there was no blood and an absolutely unweakened roar followed. Pasgen withdrew his sword, backed a single step, and slashed. He knew the gesture was utterly futile and would be his last, but he was so enraged at the thought that his life would end under the claws of a senseless beast that he had to strike out. To his intense astonishment, the sword went through the thick neck . . . and then the whole animal began to ravel away.

He stood staring, watching the rich color fade from the fur, the coarse and tangled mane become wisps of colorless mist, the whole dissipate into a formless wave of motion.

"Did you wish to be rid of it, mist?" he whispered, standing still, listening with every sense he had.

Behind him there was an indrawn breath. Pasgen whirled around, sword ready, but there was nothing to fight. What stood behind him, protectively over the thing the lion had savaged, was weaponless, small and slight. It was not elven; it was not human, but . . . Pasgen swallowed. It had red hair, and though the body and features were those of an ill-made doll, it had a bright, inquisitive feeling about it.

Pasgen blinked. Mist couldn't have a will! Mist held power, but only as wood held fire. Had the mist been enchanted by Elizabeth as so many who dealt with her were? Had it made an Elizabeth for itself? Cold shimmied up and down his back. Was he going mad to have such a thought about a domain of unformed chaos?

He closed his mind to those questions and took a step toward the recumbent thing. The red-haired doll stood directly in his path, upright as a stave, its indistinct features nonetheless forming a mask of determination. He became aware of the naked sword and knife in his hands and sheathed them. The rigidity of the ill-formed figure relaxed somewhat, but when Pasgen stepped forward toward the thing on the ground, she—the long red hair made it, whatever it was, feminine—sidled around in front of him.

"I mean your . . . friend . . . no harm," he said.

After a further moment of indecision, she stepped aside. Pasgen went down on one knee and found himself stilled by shock. A Sidhe, as badly made as the red-haired doll, but that was human . . . sort of . . . and this was Sidhe. The hair was gold, the ears large and pointed, the other features as indistinct as those of the thing with red hair, but . . . Pasgen swallowed again . . . the thing was somehow familiar, chillingly familiar. An image created from a faulty memory of him? A mist with a memory?

Pasgen was shocked again when his glance moved from the face down to the body. It had been ripped open from chest to groin. The thing could not have survived! Almost, Pasgen laughed. Clearly it was not alive to begin with, how could he think in terms of survival? But the lion had dissipated after a much less fatal wound. And as he watched, the great hollow scooped out by the lion's claws was already filling. The mist, it seemed, did not want to lose this . . . whatever it was.

"Is there anything I can do to help?" Pasgen asked, rising to his feet and facing the red-haired doll.

After a long moment, as if, perhaps, the mist had to make sense of what he had said and pass it to her, she smiled. Well, there was some motion around the slit that must be her mouth that Pasgen took to be a smile.

"I will leave you then," he said. "I have business elsewhere."

That drew no response at all and to his own intense astonishment, Pasgen bowed. He would not allow himself to think at all as he walked back toward the Gate. In his mind he said over to himself the most complicated, and harmless, spell he knew, one he had devised to create a room full of furniture all at once. There was deep, deep fear in him now, he who feared so little. But this—this was new, was unheard of—and the potential for danger was so great he resolved he would not think of it until he was somewhere safer.

When he reached the Gate, his will called up the glowing field into which patterns could be fixed. There were several already set. His glance ran over them; then, suddenly, he closed his eyes and took into his mind the feel of this Gate, thoroughly, carefully, so that he would always have it, know it, and be able to return here. Quickly then he chose a pattern already fixed into the field for a destination and directed his will at it.

Blackness, falling, arrival. Pasgen barely glanced around. The Gate was handsome but not spectacular and what he could see of the domain was peaceful and beautiful but too irregular to soothe him—a stream there, bushes and trees scattered, their leaves all helter-skelter any way they wished to grow. And there were voices, thin and at the same time rough with age, off in the distance where a shimmering white cupola barely rose above a small copse of trees.

Hurriedly Pasgen called the pattern field. All three great markets were permanently infixed. Hardly noticing which one he selected, Pasgen willed himself to Gate. Arriving, he made haste into the market, found another Gate, and after five more transfers, he was in his own domain. There, where each leaf on each tree, each bush, was placed perfectly, where the soothing tinkle of crystal music smoothed away the memory of strange, discordant sound, he sat down on a small bench . . . and began to tremble.

Chapter 6

"She is arrogant and needs lessoning," Aurilia said, scowling at the door through which Rhoslyn had passed.

But Vidal, although he was also staring at the door, obviously was not listening. "Perhaps it is just as well that she thinks I only want to find Pasgen," he muttered to himself. "He is so resentful of my recovery and my taking back the rule of Caer Mordwyn that he would doubtless ruin whatever I set him to do."

Aurilia had lifted a finger, which brought one of the newtlike servants into the chamber. While Vidal mumbled to himself, she sent the servant to procure more of her potion. Then she turned her still-brilliant green eyes on her prince.

"You are likely right about that, my lord," she said. "And it is no loss. All you need do is wear his seeming when you leave the palace. Those who see you will believe that Pasgen has set out to do your bidding, and so their minds will report if Oberon ever searches for one who has displeased him."

"Now that is a clever thought, my lady," Vidal approved, smiling at her. "Any watcher will have reported that Rhoslyn was here."

Aurilia nodded. "All will be convinced that Pasgen was here also, even if he came by a different route, most especially if several see him leave the palace."

Vidal's sharp teeth showed briefly. "And it will be even more convincing as I will be going to the house in the mortal world that Pasgen established for his disguise as the wizard Fagildo Otstargi. Yes, yes." His teeth showed again. "With the king's death, my failing tool is sure to have begged for Otstargi's advice. He will be good for one more task."

Cropper briskly plied the knocker on the door of the modest house and when it opened, said, before the servant could protest his coming to the front door, "My master, Lord Denno Adjoran, would wait upon Mistress Mildred Cecil if it is convenient for her to receive him. He wishes to explain why her request for the rumney wine has not been fulfilled."

The servant, seeing Denoriel at the foot of the three wide, shallow steps leading to the house, took in the quality of his clothing with a quick glance and the quality of his servant's livery; he stepped back, opening the door wider. Denoriel promptly accepted that invitation, coming up the stairs. Cropper had stepped aside as Denoriel mounted the steps and followed him in.

"I will see if my lady is at home and can receive a visitor," the servant said. Then, he gestured to the side of the passage that led through the house, which was furnished, close to the outer door, with a small table holding a salver, and to each side of the table a handsome chair. "If you would be good enough, Lord Denno, to wait . . ."

Denoriel looked around as the servant passed about a third of the way down the hall and then went left through a door, presumably into a parlor. Usually the door to the right led to the hall and the stairway to the second level. The passage was wainscoted in a richly finished oak halfway up the wall. Above, a pleasantly patterned plaster of soft ivory color made a fine background for several sober portraits.

Just above the table was one Denoriel recognized, Sir Anthony Cooke, whom he had seen walking with the young prince when he visited Elizabeth at Hertford Palace some years ago. Beyond Cooke, not far from the door the servant had entered, was the portrait of a lady. Denoriel had taken two steps to look more closely at the picture, when the servant came out of the door, said the mistress would be happy to receive him, took Denoriel's cloak and led the way.

A fire was blazing in a very handsome fireplace across from the doorway, the warmth extending a seductive invitation to join the lady standing in front of a cushioned chair. Behind the standing young woman, two others were sitting. Denoriel stopped and bowed. The young lady smiled and stretched a hand toward him.

She was simply dressed, her gown of dark mulberry red over a kirtle of soft lavender. The square yolk, from which rose the slightly stiffened, tall collar, open at the throat of a white lawn chemise, was black velvet. The sleeves were not padded and slashed but puffed slightly at the shoulder and fitted to the wrist.

Her hair was dark, pulled back smoothly under a French cap, and her eyes were a clear and sparkling gray. Her forehead was broad and smooth, her nose not large but nondescript in shape, and her mouth a little pale and thin but mobile and just a trifle curved toward a smile. She was not beautiful, Denoriel thought, but her expression was so animated, her whole face so lively, that she was most attractive.

"You must be Lady Elizabeth's Lord Denno," she said.

"I am indeed Lord Denno Adjoran," Denoriel replied. "As to being Lady Elizabeth's Lord Denno . . . I suppose I am most sincerely her servant if only the least among them."

A very faint frown marred Mistress Cecil's smooth brow. "It is true enough that Lady Elizabeth very rarely spoke of you, but Mistress Ashley thinks the sun rises and sets by your wishes."

Denoriel smiled and shook his head. "Mistress Ashley is too kindhearted and too indulgent. She forgets that some things are easily available to a merchant adventurer and puts too great a value on some bolts of cloth and a few bottles of wine. But sometimes even a merchant adventurer does not have to hand everything he desires. I regret to have to tell you, Mistress Cecil, that I have no more of the rumney wine."

"But I see your servant carries a basket," Mistress Cecil said, smiling also.

"Yes. I thought some claret for you and, if Master Cecil has more austere tastes, some alicant for him would make up for the missing rumney."

"That is very kind, too kind really. I should not have made so bold as to ask for the rumney, but I did like it so much when Lady Elizabeth invited us to breakfast with her. She said, when I asked, that she had it from you and I did not know where else to ask for it. But, you know, I did not mean to ask it as a gift."

Denoriel gestured dismissively. "A few bottles of wine. You

gave such pleasure to Eliza . . . I beg pardon, to Lady Elizabeth by approving her opinion on the oration of Cicero she was reading, that I wished to thank you."

Mildred Cecil now had a self-satisfied smile. She had been sure that Lord Denno was a personal favorite of Lady Elizabeth and had been disappointed when he claimed only friendship with the governess. That, being no fool, she saw was only caution. Lord Denno was almost certainly a conduit to Elizabeth.

Denoriel, seeing the smile, cursed himself for his slip of the tongue. Until he knew who would hold the reins of Elizabeth's life, he wanted no rumors about her unsuitable friendship with a common merchant. He knew Mildred to be a fine scholar, but sometimes the ability to understand Latin did not assure the ability to understand people and life. He was about to point out that Elizabeth's position was at this time delicate, when the door was opened by the servant who had shown Denoriel in, and a medium-sized man in sober but rich clothing came into the room.

"Lord Denno," he said, holding out a hand to be clasped. "I am William Cecil. I am pleased to meet you. I have heard much good of you from many sources. And I wished to thank you in person for your generous response to my wife's requests."

"Nothing." Denoriel again gestured dismissively. "As I said, I was happy to be able to do some small thing for a friend of Lady Elizabeth. And, Master Cecil, I would gladly give you a tun of wine for your thoughtfulness in sending information about the Dirge to Mistress Ashley. To my great shame, I had myself forgotten what that would mean to Lady Elizabeth."

Cecil smiled. "You have my wife to thank. It was Mildred who reminded me that Lady Elizabeth would want to know."

"Then I am more than ever in Mistress Cecil's debt, not she in mine. Indeed. Lady Elizabeth held her father in the highest regard. She loved and respected him. He was, in many ways, the center of her whole world. She still finds it very difficult to believe that such a man could be dead."

Shaking his head, Cecil sighed. "He was so strong a king that he was the center of all our lives here in England. There is great uncertainty in the Court over the provisions of the king's will. So large a Council would make a most unwieldy governing body. What say the merchants, Lord Denno?"

Before Denoriel could answer, Cecil looked around and said,

"Why are we all standing? Let me make you known to my wife's sister, Anne, and a friend, Elizabeth Sands. And let us all sit down."

For a few minutes there was no further conversation. Denoriel bowed to both ladies and murmured the standard phrases of pleasure in the introduction while servants brought and placed chairs. He liked the look of both women; Anne he thought was prettier than her sister, but she had the same expression of eager alertness, and Mistress Sands had a peculiarly sweet expression, but without any look of foolish simpering.

When they were settled, Cecil repeated his question about the merchants, and Denoriel, recalling various things Joseph Clayborne had said, replied that what merchants all desired most was stability.

"We would rather," he said "that there be one clear master than that several powerful lords be in contention for who shall be the most powerful. Such contention can only lead to unrest, and unrest is bad for trade within the realm and makes foreign governments contemptuous of us."

To that William Cecil nodded. "And have you heard of any preferences among your fellow merchants?"

"To speak the truth I have only hearsay from my man of business, who is most astute, and he named no preference himself. Myself, I was trying to obtain an audience with Sir Anthony Denny, who in the past has favored me with his notice. He did not have time to speak to me. However, from what I heard, here and there, it was assumed that the earl of Hertford, who has the king in charge, would likely head the Council."

Cecil looked rather pleased at that remark and Denoriel judged that Cecil had some connection with Hertford. What Cecil said, indirectly confirmed that notion.

"Very likely." And after a very brief hesitation, he continued, "I am sorry to hear that you could not win an audience with Sir Anthony. Perhaps I could carry a message to him or to someone else at Court?"

Denoriel had not only been attending to what William Cecil said but peripherally to the three women. All were completely at ease, which spoke well for Cecil's relationship with his wife; that he had not sent her away when he intended to have a serious conversation with another man implied trust in her discretion. That her sister and a visitor should be both interested and yet relaxed was significant, implying that he liked and respected women.

Another point strongly in Cecil's favor was that he had admitted it was his wife who had prompted him to send London information to Elizabeth through Kat Ashley. Not only did he trust his wife's discretion, but he took her advice. And all Sir Anthony Cooke's clever daughters, Denoriel remembered from the halcyon days at Hampton Court under Queen Catherine Parr's tutelage, liked and admired Elizabeth, who was as earnest a student as any of them.

Last and least, but also significant, was that Cecil had introduced him to the other ladies in his household and gone further in offering to allow him, merchant and foreigner, to sit with them. It seemed to Denoriel that through his wife Cecil already knew about his relationship to Elizabeth and by implication approved of it.

"I thank you," Denoriel said, deciding it was safer to make a clean breast of what he had done than try to conceal it, only to have it revealed—likely by that loudmouth Thomas Seymour he had met in the queen's lodging. "Nor will I refuse your offer, but I must tell you that I have engaged another advocate of my cause."

"Your cause?"

For the first time Cecil looked surprised and somewhat uneasy. Denoriel smiled at him. "My cause was to speak to Sir Anthony Denny about arranging that Lady Elizabeth learn who was to be in charge of her—and, of course, to urge the choice of someone who would be kind and she could trust."

"Ah, you were acting for Lady Elizabeth." He glanced at his wife. "I have heard that you often interested yourself in her."

There was no disapproval at all in Cecil's voice or face. Denoriel did not permit himself to sigh with relief, but he could feel himself relax. Anne and Mildred both smiled at him.

So he told the story of his connection to Harry FitzRoy and how he felt, after Harry's death, that Elizabeth was a kind of legacy. He shrugged. "I am very rich. I have no kith or kin. I have watched her grow since the day she was born, and I must confess I am totally enslaved by her."

Mildred giggled. "Most men are, and not a few women. Lady Elizabeth is a most fascinating person. A fine scholar, yes, but as interested in people as in her books."

Denoriel nodded. "Yes, and just now she is frightened and

unhappy. She feels as if the ground was snatched out from under her feet when her father died and that she is falling without hope of a happy landing."

"Poor child," Cecil said. And he looked as if he truly meant those words, not that they were merely something to punctuate the conversation.

"I know Mistress Ashley has assured her over and over that all would be well, that she is well endowed in her father's will, and that provision would be made for her ... but ..."

"I am sorry. I had no idea that Lady Elizabeth was so distressed." Cecil bit his lip for a moment but then shook his head. "Lady Mary is sorely grieved by King Henry's death, but otherwise calm. And I do not know what I can do for Lady Elizabeth. There is still much uncertainty ..."

"Well, I have made a start. When I could not reach Sir Anthony, I began to think of who else might have Lady Elizabeth's interests at heart, and the first person that came to mind—who was not neck deep in the formation of a new government—was the queen. I sought an appointment with Queen Catherine, and she was most sympathetic."

"The very person!" Mildred cried.

"Yes, indeed," Anne added. "Queen Catherine always had a special sympathy and interest in Lady Elizabeth. She was truly motherly toward her. And their ... ah ... thoughts and interests were much in tune."

"She is a lovely woman," Elizabeth Sands murmured, "both kind and clever."

William Cecil was nodding but looking somewhat puzzled. "I agree with you all," he said, "but I do not see how I can raise this topic on my own. Although it is possible that I will have some control over requests ... ah ... a request must be made."

"That is in the working," Denoriel said, almost rising from his chair in his enthusiasm. "The queen kindly wrote to Lady Elizabeth, and Elizabeth wrote back, mentioning her fears and her loneliness and begging the queen, if it were possible and to the Council's liking, that Queen Catherine have charge of her and that she be allowed to live under the queen's guidance. Queen Catherine liked the notion so well that she wrote to Sir Anthony Denny, and he promised to visit her soon to speak of the matter."

"Oh, excellent," Cecil said. "Nothing is yet certain on any score, but such an arrangement is surely possible." He pursed his lips. "Another week should decide everything. King Henry will possibly be buried on the sixteenth—"

"Will Elizabeth be expected to attend?" Denoriel drew a sharp breath, appalled at having interrupted, but Cecil did not look offended and merely shook his head.

"None of the children will be summoned," he said. "Only the queen is expected to attend and the reason I mentioned the funeral is because Queen Catherine will not be able to take Lady Elizabeth into her home until after that event."

"I see. Thank you for telling me. Once Lady Elizabeth hears that she will be allowed to live with the queen, she will be . . . ah . . . impatient."

Mildred giggled again at the understatement, and Denoriel smiled at her.

"Yes. I will be very glad to have a reason to give her for any delay she perceives."

They spoke a little longer about the funeral, Mildred wondering aloud whether it would be more terrible for Lady Elizabeth to see her father's body committed to the earth or just to be told of the event. Despite the pain of seeing a loved one physically buried, it must give a sense of finality, Mistress Sand remarked gently, which would allow one to grieve and then accept and be comforted.

Denoriel did not contribute to the conversation although he listened closely. He could not himself imagine such a dreadful event. He had not, of course, attended Harry FitzRoy's funeral; it was believed that he was on a long trading voyage when he was really Underhill recovering from nearly killing himself defending Elizabeth. But even if he had gone, it was not Harry's body but Richey's that was going to putrefy and eventually turn to dust.

His silence was noted with considerate concern. "You have seen too much death, I fear," Cecil said. "Come, let us be more cheerful. Let us try some of the claret you have been so kind as to bring."

Denoriel glanced at the window that flanked the hearth to judge the angle of the sun. "As a stirrup cup, thank you," he said. "I am afraid I have long overstayed the time of a polite visit."

"Not in our pleasure in your company," Cecil said, rising and going to the door to tell the servant waiting there to take the bottles of wine Cropper was carrying and to open a bottle of claret and bring glasses.

They spoke about wine in general until the servant returned and then Mistress Cecil made clear her appreciation of the quality of the claret Denoriel had provided. He said what was polite, finished his own glass of wine, and then made his farewells. William Cecil set his glass down on the small table between Mildred and her sister and said he would see Denoriel to the door.

As soon as the door closed behind them, Cecil said, "I am grateful to you, Lord Denno, for mentioning to me that Lady Elizabeth would like to live with the queen and Queen Catherine would like to have her company. I have heard that the queen is distressed and feels she was thrust aside and denied the opportunity to support King Edward in his grief."

Denoriel shrugged. "I do not know the king, having seen him only a few times at a distance when I visited Lady Elizabeth, but the boy is no more than ten years old and his father has been taken from him. He must feel frightened and lonely. He loves the queen and is accustomed to her management. Her influence might be useful . . . if it were properly directed."

There was a slightly protracted silence. They had reached the door, but Cecil did not signal the servant to open it. Finally, frowning unhappily, he said, "It will not happen."

Not daring to press further for the idea that the queen should be involved in caring for the child king, Denoriel shrugged again and made no reply.

"How would one know how that influence might be directed?" Cecil said softly. "And some of the Councilors are strongly opposed to her religious views. Moreover if her influence should continue to grow . . ." Cecil hesitated, looking thoughtful, but then shook his head and said decisively, "It will be better for her to live retired and be pacified with control of Lady Elizabeth."

Thinking of Thomas Seymour, Denoriel wondered if it was wise to have the queen living "retired," but he immediately decided it was none of his business. As the thought passed his mind he felt uneasy, as if he should care, but he still said nothing, only bowing as Cecil stepped back and gestured and the servant opened the outer door. Cropper put his cloak over his shoulders. In parting, Denoriel said only that Cecil had his direction; if he could be of use he would be happy.

He returned home thinking that Cecil must already have more influence than appeared on the surface and satisfied with the warmth of his reception. It was a relationship he definitely wished to foster. Cropper had been following, his careful three steps behind, but darted ahead of Denoriel to wield the knocker on the door. Inside, he took Denoriel's cloak and disappeared.

It was now time for dinner. Denoriel knew he should go Underhill and see if there were news or he was needed for something. Instead, with a moue of dissatisfaction, he opened the door to Joseph's office and invited him to join him for dinner at one of the taverns nearby. Joseph rose with such alacrity that Denoriel asked, as they left the house, if he did not like the food the servants prepared.

"Oh yes," Joseph said, looking over his shoulder at the opposite side of the road as they started toward the Chepe. "Just now and then I have a yen for a good piece of steak or a pork pie."

"Do you expect someone?" Denoriel asked, noticing the over-the-shoulder glance. "If you planned to meet a friend—"

"No," Clayborne said quickly. "I thought I saw two men watching the house earlier today. I could swear one started forward when I went down the road toward the Chepe this morning, and then turned away. But they are not there now, so perhaps I was mistaken."

"Watching the house?" Denoriel repeated. Dark Sidhe, he wondered, but dismissed the thought. Most could not endure the iron in the mortal world. "Rumor says I am rich. In these uneasy times, you should wear a sword, Joseph." He shook his head. "Ah . . . I never asked if you can use a sword."

"Not like you, m'lord, but I can," Joseph said, smiling. "And I take Cropper with me, with a good cudgel to hand, if I am carrying any real sum."

"That is wise."

Clayborne laughed self-consciously. "The man may not have started toward me at all. It may be my imagination, m'lord. That person who came asking for Lady Alana made me uneasy. But I thought it wisest to tell you even if I am making much ado over nothing."

"I am glad you did tell me. A stupid thief might not realize there is not much in the house to steal. And if I am away, you are alone here because the servants do not sleep in." In fact, the servants all went back Underhill to renew themselves every night. Recalling what Aleneil had said about Vidal's new purpose, Denoriel added, "We must talk over what precautions can be taken to make the house safe."

"Yes, m'lord, specially since you may choose to be away from London for some days."

Denoriel frowned. "Leave London? But I have urgent business here—"

"Not for a few days, m'lord. Nothing will really be done except for the funeral and the coronation, and preparations for those are already under way. I have had pressing requests from mercers who will supply cloth and vestments and who know you can obtain really remarkable stuffs. If we can provide that cloth—much of it being rich brocades and elaborate embroidery—we will, to be crude, fill our pockets at the expense of others' vanity. And it will do your reputation no harm to be able to get such exotic goods so quickly."

About to protest that seeing Elizabeth settled was more important to him than filling his coffers, Denoriel swallowed down the words. There was bound to be a further delay while Catherine made her request and the Council considered it. He was already restless and was going to irritate someone—or betray himself—if he did not remove himself from London.

What Denoriel had been much tempted to do ever since he left Cecil's house was to ride Miralys to Enfield and tell Elizabeth of the various forces he had assembled to give her her heart's desire. The temptation to see her smile at him, to feel her take his hand or kiss his cheek in thanks, was inordinately strong.

Nonetheless, he knew it was the wrong thing to do. Elizabeth, knowing what she wanted was near to hand, would be impatient and nagging. And the best laid plans that he and the queen and Denny and even Cecil made, might be turned amiss by those who wished Elizabeth ill but could hide their purposes under what would seem like conservatism.

"Well, that is true," he said reluctantly. "But cloth? Is it not too late to start making garments?"

"Some bolts of brocade will be useful, but mostly we need special embroidered pieces for stomachers and trimmings. Fur, too, if you can get some from the Hanse."

They had reached the tavern and were recognized and led at

once to the parlor off the main room. The parlor was well filled, although a table near a window was found for them. Denoriel stretched his ears to hear what was being said, but it was nothing new, mostly speculation on what would happen once young Edward was crowned. On one subject all were agreed, however; the young king was universally regarded with hope and love as most promising.

Having assured himself that no new rumors which might lead to unrest were stirring, Denoriel gave his attention to the problem of securing the house on Bucklersbury.

Dinner came and they ate slabs of beef roasted only to blood-tinged rareness, steak and kidney pie, pork pasty, bowls of well-buttered turnips flavored with wild onion and garlic, dandelion greens cooked with salt and fat bacon, supported by loaves of new-baked dark bread, heavy and moist.

With most of his mind on Clayborne's suggestions for the kind of goods he most needed and his proposal to hire two night guards if, and only if, he saw more suspicious attention given to the house, Denoriel was hardly aware of what he was eating. It was, indeed, only when he and Joseph were walking back to the house that he realized his Elven spirit should have been horrified by the crudity of his meal. Only it wasn't.

Thinking back, the strong flavors were still appealing—more appealing than the subtle delicacy of food Underhill. Definitely, Denoriel thought, grinning internally as he parted from Joseph at the foot of the stair, he was being corrupted by his long sojourn in the mortal world. He was actually grinning when he reached his bedchamber, ostensibly to change his clothing for traveling, but really to Gate Underhill. He was no longer hungry, of course, but he was looking forward to future meals.

Chapter 7

Vidal Dhu was in a foul mood. The dismembered parts of a half-dozen imps strewed the floor of his workroom. Five had come to their well-deserved fate through their inability to find Pasgen even though Vidal had reproduced for them not only Pasgen's appearance but the essence of Pasgen's being . . . as closely as he could remember it. But the imps failed him, time and time again. All his efforts had been useless and fury and frustration had brought death and destruction. Now he could not get an imp to approach him.

Usually imps came to him willingly because they enjoyed the pain and misery his messages caused. What was even more delightful so far as they were concerned, Vidal never minded that they inflicted their own small tortures on those to whom they carried his commands—provided, of course that the beings in question were weaker than the imps, for imps were cowards at heart. Nor did they usually care when he injured or killed one of them, since those that survived were allowed to tear what was left of his victim apart and eat it.

Normally, that is. Only now, his fury was warning them away.

That, of course, made him even more furious. *Why am I so surrounded by incompetence?* It was certainly not his fault that the imps were stupid, and failed in anything more complicated than bearing a simple message. It was maddening that even when they brought him an answer to the message, it was only bad news. Of course he was furious! Any rational being would be!

That was what had befallen the sixth imp. It had brought bad news from the servant in Fagildo Otstargi's house in London. Vidal ground his teeth and kicked the pieces of imp around the room, stamping down on one torso that quivered although its legs and one arm were gone.

Why had not that stupid servant of Otstargi's warned him that Baron Wriothesley, the tool he had so carefully shaped and controlled, had been more damaged by King Henry's death than he expected? In his heart, Vidal knew why; the servant was so mind-blocked he was far beyond thinking—but Vidal did not want to acknowledge that. Acknowledging that a failure was his and his alone was not an option.

Idiot servant! Vidal told himself he would tear the stupid mortal apart . . . He drew a long breath. No, he would not. Mortal servants were not so easy to replace as imps. Grinding his teeth again, he Gated himself out of the hidden workroom into Fagildo Otstargi's house in London.

As he arrived, Vidal took on the appearance of Otstargi—not so much different from his own except for the round ears and eye pupils. As he checked the appearance briefly in the mirror in the bedchamber, his breath drew in sharply. Had Pasgen chosen Otstargi's appearance deliberately to look like him? Had Pasgen planned to blame *him* for any crimes committed against Oberon's laws? If so, he had another bone to pick with that overindulged Sidhe.

After one last, fuming glance into the mirror, Vidal went out the door. He walked down the stairs and into the chamber Otstargi used to see clients and rang the bell that sat on the table.

It was fortunate that the servant was so slow. In one way it irritated Vidal further; in another, however, it reminded him that the servant was scarcely more than half alive and gave him time to control his rage. Eventually the servant shambled into the chamber. He showed no surprise at his master's presence, although Vidal had not played Otstargi in months. Had Pasgen been there?

Vidal was not concerned that the servant would lie; he would have no chance to do so. With utter indifference to any further damage to the servant, Vidal stripped his mind of all that had happened since he was last there: First, Pasgen had not returned to the house at any time. Second, Baron Wriothesley had come twice in the past week to ask for Otstargi; the second time he had struck the servant for not being able to tell him when Otstargi would return. Third, four other messages were waiting.

Being told to do so, the servant brought the salver on which the messages lay. Vidal opened them swiftly and breathed out quietly, his mood somewhat improved. All except one of the messages had been written after King Henry's death had been announced. That was very good. No one would know how long he had really been absent. Otstargi could write to each of them, saying he had returned as quickly as he could when the news of the king's death came to him and offer appointments the next day.

The three clients, useful but not really molded tools so that their dependence on him was not great, would accept that excuse for his lack of response for a few days. From three of them he could garner valuable news . . . He made a sour moue. It was likely he would need it since he could not lay hands on Pasgen and was forced to deal with Henry's courtiers by himself.

The last message had been written very early in the morning of the twenty-eighth of January, although it had been delivered later in the day. Henry had died only hours before and the death had deliberately been concealed. Vidal noted the name with care: Richard Rich. Not previously a client. Vidal's lips curved. Where had Rich got Otstargi's name? No matter. It was clear to Vidal that Rich was a man whose own interests came first with him. Such a man was most easily bent, although likely he could not be broken. Vidal's lips twisted. Of course not. There was nothing in the man to break.

Vidal wrote carefully to Rich, saying he would be honored to meet him at any time Rich proposed. To Wriothesley his note was more abrupt, saying he had returned only that morning but if the chancellor needed so badly to talk to him, he could make time that evening. He was not really surprised to hear the bell and then the servant's slow steps less than an hour after the servant had dispatched various street boys with the message.

"That will be Baron Wriothesley," Vidal called to the servant as soon as he heard the front door open. To that stupid human it would sound as if Vidal had predicted his too-early arrival. Ironic, really, that Vidal did have arcane powers—they simply did not include FarSeeing.

"Where have you been, man?" Wriothesley gasped as he came in the door to Otstargi's closet. "King Henry died—"

"Yes, I knew when he died," Vidal interrupted, "but only when it actually happened. Three times before this he had trembled on the brink. Twice I started back to England, only to have him greeting ambassadors the next day, so I am afraid I discounted much of the news of his failing."

"What am I to do? That upstart Edward Seymour is trying to seize the whole government, just because he is the king's uncle. He is at heart a rabid reformer. He will drive us even further from the good old faith . . ."

After urging him to sit down, Vidal let Wriothesley talk. Let him speak with indignation about how Seymour and Paget had concealed the king's death until Seymour could get the new little king into his own hands. It was all news that Vidal could use and essentially he was in sympathy with Wriothesley. Vidal did not like Edward Seymour any better than Wriothesley did, though for entirely different reasons.

After Henry had married Jane Seymour and she had borne him a living son, Vidal had made a tentative approach to Edward Seymour. The Seymours were in fact upstarts, as Edward Seymour had only been ennobled as earl of Hertford, after his sister's marriage. Otstargi's approach should have been welcomed by one who had so few friends and connections in Court; instead it had been coldly rejected. Well, Vidal thought, Seymour would have to go.

Then Vidal jerked out of his own thoughts to full attention to what Wriothesley was saying. He had been bemoaning his opposition to Seymour and that he might lose his place as chancellor. But he had had a brilliant idea of how to redeem himself. He was formulating a proposal to the earl of Arran, the Scottish regent, and to Mary of Guise, the infant Scottish princess' mother, that he believed would get little Mary to be Edward's wife.

"You fool!" Vidal snarled. "What have you done?"

"I am not a fool!" Wriothesley snapped back. "Oh, yes, you can often see that this or that may happen, but it is *I* who again and again have arranged for the happening to take place. It will be best for this nation, and for Scotland too, that Princess Mary wed King Edward. The endless wars that drain our substance will be ended. By my plan, England will not interfere in the Scottish government and the Scots will be free to form their own Church, which will please the earl of Arran, but Mary will be raised Catholic, which will pacify her mother. God willing, Mary will draw her husband to the true faith, and who cares if the Scots go to Hell for . . ."

Wriothesley had got this far in his explanation because Vidal was speechless with rage. He actually had to clench his fists to curb the simmering power from blasting Wriothesley, but he dared not do that until he knew how far this proposal had gone. It was, he feared, something the earl of Arran would be happy to embrace. Mary of Guise less so, even if the baby princess was raised a Catholic. Still, if enough pressure was brought to bear on her, she might agree.

Mary would try to resist; she wished to tie Scotland even closer to France with a marriage of the princess into the French royal house. Vidal was an enthusiastic supporter of this idea, which would ensure the war between England and Scotland would continue, probably long into the future. There were French princes enough to spare, but Vidal had high hopes that Francis, the heir to the throne, would be chosen, that Scotland would thus be irrevocably tied to French policy, which was most often opposed to England.

"Whom have you told of this plan?" Vidal's voice grated.

"Paget for one and several others, who all thought very well of it," Wriothesley said resentfully.

Vidal barely refrained from spitting in Wriothesley's face. If Paget knew and approved of Wriothesley's plan, there was little hope that the plan would not be brought up in Council, which meant news of it would surely be carried to Scotland. And without him there, stiffening Arran's spine and urging Mary of Guise to stand her ground, who knew but that the Scottish government would agree to the marriage.

"Perhaps they did," Vidal snarled, "but it is not good for *you*. You have paid me to look out for *your* interests and I have done so. This plan, whatever its effect on England and Scotland—I have not considered that—will ruin you!"

"Nonsense," Wriothesley said. "If it is my plan and all think it good, how can it harm me?"

"Will Seymour be pleased that the other Councilors wish to follow your lead in this matter? And how long do you think it will remain *your* plan rather than Hertford's? He will be doubly eager to be rid of you to remove you from the memories of the other Councilors."

There was a silence while Wriothesley considered and then, weakly, he asked, "Then what am I to do?"

Vidal wanted desperately to tell the stupid peacock to get out of his sight and stay out of it, but if he did, his other clients would feel he was disloyal and abandon him. And if Wriothesley was out of the government, he would need news. After a moment of staring into nothing, he shook his head.

"I do not think it matters what you do now, Baron Wriothesley," Vidal said, at least getting some satisfaction from the expression of dismay on Wriothesley's face. He could not leave it there, however, or Wriothesley would rush off to tell all the people who knew he went to Otstargi that the soothsayer would desert them at the first difficulty. "I am sorry," he continued, "that you will likely lose your office—I can do nothing about that. However, I have this comfort for you. Hertford will not rule England for long"—if Wriothesley took that as a prediction, that was fine, since Vidal intended to see that Hertford did not rule long—"and if the other Councilors remember you opposed Hertford's policies you may well come back into office."

Wriothesley was silent for a moment and then looked down at his hands. "There is no way that I can hold my position?"

Swept with irritation, Vidal snarled, "Be glad I have Seen no blood flowing over your image. Do not tempt fate. For now I can only suggest that you be circumspect."

Wriothesley paled. "How circumspect? Should I go to the country?"

Ah, to be rid of this idiot. Vidal swallowed down his immediate and enthusiastic approval of that idea. He might still need the man, so he said, "I have no Seeing for that. You must do as good sense dictates. Do not make Hertford believe you are dangerous. Now first tell me of those closest to Hertford that I may look for them in my glass. He has a wife and children?"

"You should find the wife easily." Wriothesley made a face. "She is so proud that I have heard her complain because Lady Mary and Lady Elizabeth, the king's own daughters, have precedence over her. There is also his brother, Thomas Seymour, who is a bit of a madcap. I heard he suggested himself as a proper suitor for Lady Mary or Lady Elizabeth. His sons . . . those from his first wife are of no consequence and those of his second are too young to be important."

With some effort Vidal remained utterly expressionless, hardly hearing what Wriothesley said about Hertford's sons. He was fixed on the fact that Hertford's brother Thomas had already suggested himself as a suitor for Mary or Elizabeth. Thomas must be turned away from Mary; no scandal must touch her. Vidal wanted her on the throne. But Elizabeth . . . Yes, it was possible that Hertford's brother might have access to Elizabeth and use it. He would act foolishly and impulsively because it was plain that Thomas Seymour had more pride than sense. Wonderful.

It would take little effort to beglamour this fool to woo Elizabeth openly. She was only fourteen. She would be flattered if the brother of the man who would soon be king in all but name courted her. Perhaps, Vidal thought, if this Thomas is as much a fool as Wriothesley's remark hints, I can convince him that he should marry the girl quickly, before anyone can say him nay, and that the sin would soon be forgiven.

"This brother, Thomas," Vidal said, cutting off some inessential nonsense that Wriothesley was spouting, "I would like to meet him. It seems to me that he might be the doorway to his brother's destruction."

Wriothesley, about to take offense at being interrupted, instead looked thoughtful. "True enough, he is a man of large ambition and too much belief in his own good fortune. But Hertford is not one to listen to foolish bombast. Still . . . I will do what I can to urge him to come to consult you. And now, I have taken up enough of your time."

On the words, Wriothesley rose and left the room. Vidal was too glad to be rid of him so easily. He was very much wrapped up in his own plans, and too concerned about whether it would be safe to ensorcel the man—once Wriothesley convinced Thomas Seymour to visit him—to give much thought to a tool that was now broken and near useless. Would Thomas Seymour be too close to the hand ruling England that Oberon would deem ensorcelling him dangerous? Hertford was definitely of the "thou shalt not suffer a witch to live" kind. If he suspected magic, he would pursue it relentlessly. Enough to bring Oberon's wrath upon him?

✧   ✧   ✧

Vidal was not happy, and the interviews he had with his three other clients the next day made him even less happy. Wriothesley's scheme had found favor with much of the Council. All agreed that it was the purpose of their late monarch to have little Princess Mary as wife to King Edward. King Henry had made war for that purpose, but if the Scots could be cajoled into sending the princess to England, they would not be violating the late king's will.

Other news was little better but no worse. From what was hinted, it seemed that Hertford would rule . . . and so Vidal said he would. That he said so and thus inclined the three men who visited him to support Hertford now guaranteed that outcome. To Rich, whom he saw last, he hinted that Hertford must be watched and if his pride offended the other Councilors that Rich should somewhat withdraw himself.

He gestured while he spoke, and soon Rich's eyes became just a little glazed. He did not seem to notice when Vidal took his hand, slipped off his seal ring, and under it slid a narrow gold band. The inside was inscribed with words that Rich would not be able to read—if he ever noticed the ring. For now the spell the ring carried would have little effect; Rich's thinking and behavior would be perfectly natural. Bit by bit, however, the man would grow dependent on Fagildo Otstargi.

One aim Vidal did not accomplish was to gain admittance to Thomas Seymour. He sent a message. It was ignored. He tweaked Wriothesley's chain and the chancellor—he had not yet been deprived of office—sent Thomas a message. That too was ignored. Vidal went himself to Seymour Place, Thomas Seymour's house, wearing the Don't-see-me spell—and it was a waste of power that nearly drained him dry in the mortal world. Thomas was not at home and he could not discover from the servants' talk where Thomas was, only that everyone knew the place and did not need to name it.

Dangerously weakened, both from use of power in the mortal world and from the excess of Cold Iron weapons and locks and decorative grills in Seymour Place, Vidal decided to deal with Thomas Seymour at some other time and Gated back to Caer Mordwyn. His workroom had been restored to order. The pieces of imp had been removed, probably eaten by the cleaners. The twisted agony of the figures hung on the walls and from the roof beams was soothing, but they offered no advice.

Vidal Gated again, this time to Aurilia's living quarters in Caer Mordwyn. Fortunately she was there, lying on a long, opulently padded chair with a high back and arms that supported her. The ever-present glass of cloudy blue liquid was on a small table beside her, but the glass was full. Her eyes were bright, she did not start or wince at the magic when Vidal appeared, and her brows lifted in easy question.

"My own creature," he burst out, "has gone mad and is planning to bring about peace between England and Scotland."

"Ah," Aurilia breathed. "I see why you are angry. You cannot permit peace with Scotland. We have been strong and well fed by the war that King Henry waged." She looked toward the glass of cloudy blue liquid but she did not lift it to sip from it. "Your creature? How did you let your creature get so out of hand?"

Vidal snarled and flung himself down on a sofa opposite Aurilia. "I was sure Wriothesley would follow the path he had pursued as long as Henry lived. But the king's death seems to have broken him loose from all common sense. He had always been so clever at following the main chance. How was I to guess he would of a sudden be afflicted with conscience over his stupid faith? All the years he was the king's servant he followed Henry's will in such matters without a qualm. And all because of a *form* of worship. Mind, it is the same god, just how to worship him that he sticks at—and because of that he will lose his place as chancellor."

"So?" Aurilia drawled the word. "Forge a new tool."

"I have already set that in motion," Vidal snapped back. "But meanwhile, that madman has presented a plan to the Council to end the war and get the little Scottish princess for Edward's wife."

Now Aurilia frowned and swung her legs off the long chair to sit more upright. Her back was to her glass of cloudy liquid and she did not glance at it.

"But that is just what the Scots do not want," she said. "They fear to be swallowed up by England and will fight forever to escape that."

"Except that Wriothesley's plan—and it seems he has already presented it to Paget and others on the Council and they think well of it—offers the Scots autonomy in politics and religion."

"No!" Aurilia exclaimed, leaning forward in her anxiety. "They might believe it but in the end it would mean the two lands would be one. We will starve! You must stop Mary of Guise from agreeing."

"Yes, but I cannot do so without returning to Scotland, and that would mean that I would not be able to watch the English court."

Aurilia relaxed again and tapped her fingers on the arm of her chair thoughtfully. "I see that," she said after a moment, "but I do not see why it is important. Let the government be formed while you stiffen the Scots' resistance. When you return you will be able to fasten your hooks firmly into your new tool and through him push the Council in the direction of a new war with Scotland."

"And what of my plans for Elizabeth? And Denoriel and Aleneil?"

"I will take care of that."

Vidal snorted. "As you took care of the death of that maid? You do not know the mortal world, Aurilia."

"No." She smiled. "But I now have a most faithful servant who does. Who *is* mortal." There was a moment of silence while Vidal stared suspiciously at Aurilia. She laughed musically. "You ordered him brought to me yourself."

A spasm of anxiety so brief that Vidal hoped Aurilia had not noticed touched him, but she had. She laughed again.

"No, your memory is not at fault," she said. "It was a matter of such small importance to you that you did not bother to remember. It is the human healer that you bid Pasgen find for me."

He frowned. It seemed a mighty frail support to hang their hopes on. "A healer? What good is a healer for my purpose?"

"Oh, Albertus will do nothing himself, but he can serve as my conduit to instruct and hire those who kill for money. Although he is happy here, I think Albertus would like to visit the mortal world. There are things he misses."

"Visit the mortal world?" Vidal repeated. "And boast of what he has seen and done Underhill?"

"I do not think he will do that," Aurilia said calmly. "He is no fool and must realize that no one would believe him. Moreover, he knows I will set watchers on him and that if he speaks he will never be allowed to come back here—and that his life in the mortal world will not be long."

Ah. Better.

"And I can furnish him with a handsome gold chain for his neck that will tighten if he speaks of Underhill or of magic and will strangle him if he persists." Vidal nodded.

"Oh, no, my lord," Aurilia protested. "He is too valuable to me.

Let it cause him great pain but not kill. I want him back." She gestured behind her at the potion.

Vidal looked at the full glass. "You do not seem to need it anymore, but perhaps a tame mortal healer is useful." Then he frowned and shook his head. "Yes, a healer? How would a healer know those who kill for money?"

Aurilia smiled. "He is quite taken with me and is more than willing to linger in my company. Thus he has told me much about himself—" she laughed aloud "—it was true, too. I had him bespelled to speak only the truth."

"So what is the truth?"

"Common enough among mortals, where strength and cleverness often go without reward. Albertus was a good healer, but never grew rich enough, fast enough in his own opinion. Thus he did many things that are against the stupid mortal laws. He was found out by a clever rival, accused, and would have been burnt alive."

Vidal laughed. "No wonder he was so willing to come here with Pasgen."

"No, that was years ago. He was eager to come Underhill because he is growing old. But when he fled, he was so nearly caught he could not take money enough to go abroad. All he could do was hide in the worst parts of the city where what they call the Watch does not go. The mortals—" she laughed again "—call it the underworld. There he still practiced as a healer . . . healing criminals and providing drugs and means for murder."

Vidal sat for a few moments considering. Finally he said, "Good enough. I see that he might well know such as would serve our purpose. Do you set your spies on him. I will bespell the neck chain and send it to you."

"Send it?"

"Yes. I will not return here from my workroom. I will Gate to Scotland and pretend I have just come there from France. Now, to get your Albertus to London . . . Yes, why not. I will also provide an amulet that will permit him to Gate to Otstargi's house. The servant there is so dull of mind that he will not interfere and probably will obey any order given him. But you had better warn your Albertus that he is not to meet with his hirelings there. Otstargi is still useful. I do not want him associated with any other crime than fortune telling."

Aurilia looked sidelong at Vidal. She did not really like the way he had repeated "your Albertus," but she did not wish to argue with him either. The amulet that would permit the healer to Gate to the mortal world would work for anyone, giving her an easy way there. Slowly she leaned forward again and stretched so she could touch Vidal's knee with one finger.

"I will see that Albertus commits no offense, my lord," Aurilia said softly, "but you are angry and your mind is troubled—no mood in which to cajole those stupid, stubborn Scots. Surely there is no need for you to make such haste to Scotland. You can bend the time to make your arrival earlier. Linger here with me a while to drink a cup of wine and perhaps rest . . . or not rest . . . in my bed for a few hours."

When she was sure Vidal was gone, Aurilia rose from her bed and went to look at herself in the long mirror that was fastened to the wall between two windows in her bedchamber. The light was wan. A gesture caused it to brighten. Aurilia hissed lightly between her teeth and then smiled. She was bruised all over and one of her breasts was torn and bleeding.

A gesture brought a troubling of the air that resolved into a squat, black, winged creature, which squalled as it was caught and suspended. Another caused a door at the far side of the room to open. In a moment a bent and wizened figure clad in filthy rags, with hair in tangled ropes and a long, twisted nose sporting several black and hairy warts appeared in the doorway.

"Quickly," Aurilia said. "Mend the damage."

The crone hobbled forward, almost seeming eager if one had not glimpsed the hatred shining from her eyes. Aurilia had, but she only laughed, and when the crone reached her and placed a hand over the savagely bitten breast, she glanced up at the black imp hanging impotently in the air. Although she winced slightly as her flesh was drawn together, her attention was on the imp, which she directed to bring Albertus.

"And mind, none of your tricks with Albertus. Tell him *politely* that I want him, or you will have no wings and be walking on sore feet for a long time."

The breast was healed. Now blood showed on the crone's rags but her nose was almost normal in size and appearance. The bruises began to fade on Aurilia's body and the crone whimpered slightly as the pain was transferred to her. At the same time, some of the lines smoothed from her face and her lips filled as teeth returned to her jaws.

"Enough!" Aurilia said. "And do not think you can pray for me to be hurt again so that you can regain your youth and strength by healing my hurts. I will know, and worse will befall you. But you are learning. When you are thoroughly obedient . . . who knows."

A gesture sent the old woman hobbling from the room, and another closed and locked the door behind her. Aurilia looked in the mirror again, muttered a few words. The faint remnants of the bruises that still showed on her body disappeared, her lips reddened and became fuller, her hair thickened and glowed a richer gold, her eyes became more luminous.

A last gesture brought two female Sidhe through the main door of the room. Both showed the too-fine hair and faded eyes of the aged, but they were not reluctant to serve Aurilia. They went at once to the east side of the bed where the wall seemed to be made of elaborately carved panels. Each placed a hand into a half-hidden slot and gently pulled. The carved panels withdrew, showing within a fabulous wardrobe.

On racks on the floor were shoes, some leather, some satin, some fur. All had gilded or silvered heels and soles; all were inset with precious stones. Above were gowns of heavy, shining, slubbed silk and of diaphanous veiling. The colors began on the left with silver and slowly intensified from pale to brilliant, from brilliant to deeply rich and on, at last, to black.

"Cerise, I think," she said.

One of the Sidhe lifted a heavy silken gown from where it hung and carried it tenderly toward her mistress. The other removed a tunic of the same color, but of fabric so fine it looked more like mist than woven stuff, coupled with full flowing trousers of just a slightly thicker weave.

"This will cling like a second skin to your body," the Sidhe with the silken gown said. "Not to the eyes, but to the senses will you be naked, thus exciting without offering any compromise of yourself."

"This," the second Sidhe lifted the tunic, which floated upward, "is invitation as well as temptation. Which will you have, madam?"

"The human is old and needs more blatant stimulation," Aurilia said, pointing to the tunic and trousers.

The first Sidhe went to hang the silk gown in the wardrobe and shut the doors while the second gestured down her mistress's body where undergarments appeared. Aurilia bade the first Sidhe wait in her sitting room for the healer and then stepped into the trousers. The tunic went over her head.

A last glance in the mirror showed her hair in place, her eyes glowing, her lips full, red, and inviting. She smiled at herself and went into the adjoining chamber where, on the table beside the glass of cloudy liquid, lay a thick and intricately woven gold chain. She leaned over to touch it, felt the hum of power, nodded, and lay down on the sofa.

The mistlike fabric of the tunic did nothing to hide the protuberant, dark nipples of her breasts. One of her legs negligently trailed toward the floor; the other was slightly raised at the knee. Through the diaphanous tunic and the scarcely more solid pants, a glint of gold showed where her thighs met.

She did not need to hold the pose long. The outer door opened; the first Sidhe said, "The healer Albertus, madam."

Aurilia gestured and Albertus entered. He bowed at the door, his eyes going at once to the full glass of cloudy blue liquid standing on the table. As he came upright, his brows were raised in query and then creased in worry.

"There is something wrong with the potion, madam?"

"Not at all but I find that I need it less and less."

The worried frown deepened. "Are you warning me that I am to be cast out? Discarded?"

"Oh, no! Not at all. Do come closer, Albertus. There is no need for us to shout across the width of the room."

As he drew closer, bowing again about halfway into the room, Aurilia examined him. He had claimed to be old and in fear of death when Pasgen—and where in the seven levels of Hell *was* Pasgen—brought him to her. Well his hair was white, but it was still plentiful; he was only a little stooped; she had given him back his teeth so his mouth was not sunken and while his nose was sharpened with age it did not yet hook toward his chin.

"I was only trying to explain why I feel comfortable parting with you for a few days," Aurilia said. "Would you not like to visit the mortal world for a little while?"

Aurilia's legs spread just a little farther apart as she pushed herself more upright. She saw Albertus' eyes flicker from her crotch to her breast and back to her crotch. She knew that none of the female Sidhe had been willing to bed Albertus, and she had not provided him with a construct that any sane man would want in his bed.

"I am sure there are things and people that you miss in the World Above," Aurilia went on, smiling. "And I have a small piece of mischief that would be best accomplished by a mortal in the mortal world. Thus, we each will gain—you a chance to satisfy any desires that are not fulfilled Underhill and I to be rid of a pair of nuisances that are interfering with fulfillment of *my* desires."

"Madam . . ."

He bowed again. Aurilia thought as much to hide his face and give him time for thought as out of fear and respect. She wondered why she had not in the past used mortals for any purpose other than torment. Well treated they were far more loyal servants than the Dark Sidhe.

"You know I wish to serve you as best as I can," Albertus continued, eyes on the floor now, as if he realized what he had betrayed about himself in his hungry glances at her breasts and crotch. "But to do that I must admit that I was nothing and no one. I had no riches and was no lord of great power to order men to do my bidding. I fear if I . . . ah . . . rid you of the nuisances you mention that I would be caught and punished."

"Riches are no problem. You will be well supplied with gold. Nor do I wish you in your own person to have any dealings with these nuisances. Surely there are those who would rob a house and do violence to those within or attack a man on the street if they were paid to do so?"

Albertus' eyes gleamed. "If I had the means to pay, yes indeed, my lady. There are those who know how to enter a house to steal and would not hesitate to quiet anyone within so there would be no alarm. And there are those who make their living by taking from careless folk in the street, who occasionally die of their carelessness."

"I am glad to hear that you think you can serve me in this."

"Only there is one problem, madam. How am I to explain where I have been all this time . . . however long it has been?"

"You will not need to explain unless you wish to do so. I can put a seeming on you so that no one will know you. But wherever you say from where you come, this place must not be mentioned. There will be watchers to make sure that no hint of your present place or duty escapes you."

She reached behind her as she spoke and picked up the gold chain. "You will wear this," she said, and he took it readily and clasped it around his throat, thinking, she was sure, that it was some kind of listening device. As he fastened the clasp, it disappeared and the chain shortened. He frowned, fear showing on his face, his fingers now trying to pull the chain away from his throat.

"Let it lie," Aurilia snapped. "It will do you no harm . . . so long as you do not mention, even in a hint, that such a place as Underhill exists. If you do . . . the chain will choke you. For a slight hint, it will merely tighten. For trying to continue to speak of our world here . . . it will strangle you."

"But an accidental mention . . ."

"You will choke. You will cough. You will change the subject. An accident will call forth only a reminder . . . unless the accident is repeated too often."

He seemed about to protest again; she frowned at him and he remained silent and bowed once more.

Aurilia nodded her satisfaction and went on briskly, "Now the nuisances. In London on what I believe is a street called Bucklersbury is the house of Lord Denno." Hidden by the coils of the gold chain had been the amulet for Gating to London. Now she picked it up. "This amulet will take you from any Gate in Caer Mordwyn to the house of a fortune-teller and magician called Fagildo Otstargi. Otstargi is away at present and his servant will not interfere with you. You may stay in that house for a day or two while you find another lodging, but do no business from there."

With obvious reluctance, Albertus took the amulet. He looked relieved when it just lay in his hand, and after a moment he tucked it into a pouch supported by his belt.

"You are to rid me of both Lord Denno and his distant cousin, Lady Alana, who occasionally stays in the house. I have no other direction for her."

"If this Lady Alana comes only occasionally, it may take me some time . . ."

"For now time is not an urgent matter. I admit I know little of the mortal world. I am leaving to you and trusting you to accomplish my purpose without more help than the gold I promised and the new face and body. And I must warn you that the man will be no easy target. He can use a sword. Be sure you send enough men against him. Do not think to spare the gold and keep it for yourself."

Albertus was silent, staring into the reflecting surface that had appeared before him. He was younger, but not a young man so that he still had the authority of age; his hair was grizzled, his eyes black instead of faded blue, his nose was shorter and broader and he had a short, pointed beard, also grizzled. His eyes shifted to Aurilia and he bowed almost double.

"No, indeed, madam. Why should I be tempted to steal your gold? As long as I am assured I am to come back here to Caer Mordwyn, for what do I need gold?"

Chapter 8

If Joseph Clayborne had not been well drilled in decent manners, he would literally have drooled over the goods that Lord Denno showed him in a locked back room of the warehouse in the alley off Thames Street. Bales of fur—lush silvery fox pelts, white ermine, sleek mink—bolts of rich brocades in every color gleaming and glinting with the gold and silver thread in the weavings, and separate packets wrapped in thick silk, which could itself be sold, that held ribbons and panels of delicate embroidery set with tiny pearls and precious stones.

Denno laughed. Joseph sighed. Even though it was the dead of night and Denoriel and Clayborne were alone in the back room with a locked door between them and the one guard standing near the outer door, Joseph made no mention of the fact that what he was seeing was impossible. Lord Denno had been gone only three days. There was nowhere, not even from his supposed sources in north Germany, France, and Spain that he could have shipped such goods in so short a time. It was another of the many mysteries of Lord Denno. It did make him curious though . . . if Lord Denno could somehow magically conjure all this, why did he not simply magic up gold and avoid all the tedium and risk of being a merchant-adventurer?

Perhaps he simply had some magical way of moving goods themselves. Surely that must be it. What was here would not fill a corner of a ship, so of course, for great cargoes, Lord Denno would still need his ships. Perhaps, as in the song about the Boys of Bedlam, Lord Denno could conjure a "horse of air."

Well, useless to speculate, and really, better not. Better just to pretend that he thought Lord Denno had all this hidden away somewhere, like a motley conjuror's false-bottomed box.

"May you live a thousand years, m'lord—as I understand they say when they mention the emperor in China," Joseph said, grinning. "I have more than half of this already sold, so much did I trust in you, but I cannot deny I spent a few uneasy nights wondering how I would explain selling what I did not have and leaving some very highborn ladies and gentlemen without proper trimmings for their new clothing."

"The dates for the funeral and coronation are now set?" Denoriel could not fathom these mortal ways of delaying such things until the poor corpse had to be buried in sealed coffins to avoid prostrating the bereaved with stench.

"Yes, m'lord. The funeral for the sixteenth as was proposed all along. There is to be much ceremony on the following day also. The young king is to be knighted and"—Joseph's lips twisted cynically— "those who have well served the kingdom will be rewarded. It is said that Hertford will have a dukedom and Dudley will be made an earl." He gestured toward the carefully laid-out goods. "I will hire extra men and attend to the distribution myself."

"All except these," Denoriel said, taking up four of the silver fox pelts and a tied bundle of the ermine. "These are for Lady Elizabeth and, hmmm," he also picked up several gleaming mink skins, "these, I think for Queen Catherine. I hope I am not taking what you have already promised?"

"Well, the ermine. Everyone was asking for ermine, but thank God I did not accept payment . . . except from Hertford's lady. I did not wish to annoy her. She is . . . ah . . ."

"Proud and spiteful," Denoriel said. That was an understatement. For someone whose husband was so recently jumped-up, she had the manner of one whose blood had come direct from Adam.

Joseph nodded. "Well, I doubt she will see Lady Elizabeth so she will not know the little lady is so well supplied. But I do not think that any of the royal ladies will be invited. From something in Lady Hertford's remarks to Lady Dorset—I cannot imagine why she thinks I become stone deaf the moment she does not address me directly—Hertford will be named Protector, and she does not take it well that Queen Catherine and Lady Mary and Lady Elizabeth will still have precedence over her."

"Truly if I were only sure that Queen Catherine will have charge of Elizabeth, I would be happy enough that neither of them should come to Court—at least until the striving for political place is finished." He shook his head. This was a bad business all around, what with spite, posturing, political maneuvering both subtle and unsubtle, added to all the usual court intriguing.

"There are times," Joseph said, "when I am very happy to be no more than a common merchant. And times when I could wish you were not such a successful one." He sighed. "Go home, m'lord, and get what rest you can. You look tired. I will send the guard out for more men." He reached out and took a rough cloth from a shelf on the wall and wrapped the furs Denoriel had chosen in it. "How thieves discover where goods of special value are, I have no idea. Sometimes I think that they use the mice and rats as spies."

Denoriel laughed heartily over that, knowing that such creatures— or what looked like them—could be used that way by the Sidhe, but not to find furs or silks and jewels which could be too easily come by Underhill. Then he shook his head over Joseph's suggestion that he wait for the extra men to come and take one or two to escort him home.

"It would take a very desperate thief to be out this late on so cold a night. Certainly it is not likely that there would be a large group out just to get a cloak." He patted his sword hilt. "And one or two I do not fear."

Nor was there anything to fear as he made his way to Thames Street, along it the short way to Dowgate, and then north, across Watling to the narrow, curving way that led to Bucklersbury. What might have been dangerously dark to humans was twilight to Denoriel. In fact he saw nothing at all moving—it was bitterly cold, even for him—and felt no threat until he stopped to fumble for the keys to his own door.

As he held the large key poised, he thought he heard the click of a doorlatch, and he turned swiftly, the key now in his left hand, sword half drawn in his right. Perhaps a shadow moved in the deeper dark of the doorway across the road, but his own door opened before the threat, if there was one, could materialize. Light spilled out of the open doorway, and Cropper's voice spoke a cheerful welcome.

"Been watching for you, m'lord. Master Clayborne said he thought you'd meet him at the warehouse. Welcome home."

Denoriel walked in, glancing over his shoulder, but there was no movement now in the opposite doorway, not even a shifting of shadow. Cropper also looked around Denoriel's shoulder at the house across the street, but he didn't say anything, merely shut the door, took Denoriel's cloak, and set the package Denoriel had thrust under his left arm on the small table.

"I thought you went home to your wife and child at night, Cropper," Denoriel said.

"Yes, m'lord. In the usual way, I do." The massive footman nodded. He was a most ordinary-looking man—most footmen were large and strongly built—but there was something about him that reminded Denoriel of a mastiff. Not in looks, but in attitude, perhaps. Friendly, good with children, but if the master was threatened—it would not go well for the one doing the threatening. "But since Master Clayborne saw those men watching the house—and I thought we were followed when we went to bring the wine to Mistress Cecil—I been staying if Master Clayborne goes out. He don't want to leave the house all empty and I don't mind, m'lord. It's an extra shilling, which I can surely use. Kept the fire going in the parlor, m'lord, and started one in your bedroom when Master Clayborne said you might be coming home. What do you want done with the parcel, m'lord?"

For one moment, Denoriel could not remember what was in the parcel he had carried. Although Clayborne had remarked he looked tired, he had no idea just how tired his master was. Even in the power-rich atmosphere Underhill, it took enormous effort to correctly ken such intricate and elaborate items as furs and brocades. Denoriel looked blankly at Cropper, then shook his head and told Cropper he hadn't decided and that he would take the package up with him to his chamber.

This he did, and when he had the door closed safely behind him, he began to gesture at his clothing. His overstrained power channels burned and he cursed softly, stopped his attempt to remove his clothing by magic, and started to struggle out of his garments one by one. It took forever, but eventually the gown and doublet, the jacquet and shirt, the upperstocks and hose were in a pile on the floor. Then, Sidhe did not sleep, but Denoriel lay down on the thick featherbed, pulled over himself the down coverlet and went blank and empty.

He was roused by Clayborne's voice calling at the door and opened his eyes to dull and rosy light. Apparently he had been resting all of what remained of the night and nearly all the next day. From the look of the light it was now evening.

"Come," he called.

"I am sorry to disturb you, m'lord," Joseph said, "but there was a messenger from the queen. He brought a note and I was sure you would want to have it as soon as possible."

Denoriel levered himself up, sat against the pillows, and held out his hand. He wasted no time in breaking the seal and unfolding the letter, which was brief enough to take in in one glance.

After the suitable salutation, there were only a few lines. *I have happy news and I have writ a letter to Lady Elizabeth explaining all. If you will come to Chelsea as soon as you may, and if you are willing to be my messenger, you may carry my letter to her.*

"I must go to Chelsea Palace at once," he said.

"Can it not wait until morning, m'lord?" Joseph asked. "Chelsea is a long way and it is very cold. And I must speak to you about the sales from the warehouse from where I have just returned." Denoriel shook his head, repeating Chelsea, and Joseph sighed and turned toward the wardrobe, asking, "Court dress?"

Denoriel groaned. "Since I am going to the palace, I suppose so. A curse on the formality . . . Oh, send one of the men up to help me dress."

"Yes, m'lord. Will you have the midnight blue lined with vair or the maroon trimmed with sable?"

"Blue." Denoriel watched Joseph pull garments from the wardrobe and lay them on the foot of the bed.

"And I will have a sup and a bite ready for you," Joseph said. "You've had nothing since last night and though the queen might offer you refreshment, by the time you reach Chelsea it would likely be only a glass of warmed wine."

About to protest about the waste of time, Denoriel was forestalled by his own belly, which rumbled audibly at the notion of food. Both he and Clayborne laughed.

"Yes, all right," Denoriel said, getting out of bed. "I would hate to have my stomach inserting comments into the conversation if the queen should wish to talk."

As Joseph went out, Denoriel noticed that the heap of clothing he had left on the floor was gone, the room was warm, the fire burning brightly. Someone had come in to pick up the discarded garments and lay fresh logs on the fire. No doubt one of the Low Court Sidhe that acted as servants in the house. They could move silently enough not to disturb his rest, and he would have sensed Sidhe in the chamber and not felt the alarm that a human intrusion would cause.

He turned toward the clothes Joseph had set out on the bed and stared. They assembled themselves on his body. Since he was not creating anything, very little power was involved. Nonetheless a faint ache along the power channels warned him that he would need to be cautious about using magic for some time longer. When the servant came in, Denoriel set him to making the bed while he took the mink pelts from the package, leaving only the fox and ermine for Elizabeth.

"They are to be a gift," he told the Sidhe in the Elven tongue. "Use some pretty cloth and ribbon to wrap them. When you are done, bring the gift to me in the small dining parlor."

Although Miralys took no more than a quarter hour to carry Denoriel from Bucklersbury to Chelsea, he was very glad he had taken Clayborne's advice and had a meal. He was not, to his surprise, expected. Fortunately he had carried Catherine's letter with him and her seal opened the gate. Nonetheless it was at least another half hour before he settled Miralys in the stable, removed his package from his saddlebag, and got back to the house. And then, although the servant who greeted him *did* seem to expect him, he was not at once shown into Queen Catherine's parlor.

The servant showed him instead into a reception room, saying that the queen had an unexpected visitor and that he would need to wait until she was free. Denoriel made no protest; in the mortal world he was, after all, no more than a common merchant—if uncommonly rich—and this might be Court business. However, he was soon sorry he had not asked the servant at least to tell Queen Catherine that he had arrived because he was left to wait longer than he expected.

The full dark of a winter's night had closed in before Thomas Seymour walked into the reception room, strolled up to the chair in which Denoriel was sitting, and smiled condescendingly down at Denoriel.

"Queen Catherine will see you now," he said. "I told the servant to send you in."

So it was this popinjay who had been the cause of the delay—not business. Denoriel rose to his full height and in turn stared down at Seymour, who was a tall man among his fellows but still at least a half head shorter than the Sidhe. The smile on Seymour's face faded and he stepped back a pace. Denoriel smiled.

"Thank you, Sir Thomas," he said softly.

Seymour backed another pace, then stiffened as he realized what he had done. His mouth opened . . . and the servant came around him, looked up at him, and then beckoned to Denoriel, saying, "This way, my lord."

A moment later Denoriel had scooped up his package and was in the queen's private parlor where Catherine was standing up, her hands clasped before her and an anxious frown on her face. "Oh, my dear Lord Denno," she cried, as soon as the door closed behind him. "That *stupid* servant! I had no idea you had arrived. Sir Thomas and I were only playing a silly card game. Who could imagine the fool servant would not announce you?"

Sir Thomas, eh, Denoriel thought, suddenly remembering how the servant had looked up at Seymour before he asked Denoriel to follow him. *I will see to you, you puffed up pile of . . .* He bowed and smiled at Catherine.

"It does not matter, madam. Even if you had seen me at once, I could not have ridden to Enfield tonight. Aside from the dark and the cold, I would have arrived so late that I could not have seen Lady Elizabeth."

"Ridden to Enfield tonight? But I sent the message to your house before dinner! Why did it take so long to come to you?"

"I—"

About to tell Catherine that Seymour had paid her servant to delay the message until it seemed as if Denoriel were unwilling to go to Elizabeth, he swallowed the words. He did not know that was true, did not want to be caught in a lie, and, in addition, from the way she blushed whenever she said Seymour's name, she would be angry at Denoriel over the accusation, not at Sir Thomas over the crime.

Denoriel sighed and said, "I'm afraid the fault for that is mine. I was asleep all the day. I had just returned from a most exhausting journey to bring to England some goods I had stored in foreign warehouses." He smiled apologetically. "But I believe the effort was well worthwhile." He held out the gaily wrapped package. "Do you look, madam, and tell me you forgive my tardiness."

It was common enough for those who intended to ask favors to gift the giver of those favors. Catherine suspected that the favor she would be asked was to allow Lord Denno to visit Elizabeth. Since she had already done so while the girl was in her care, she was perfectly willing to agree. She did not stop to think that the situation was different. Elizabeth was now second in line for the throne and Catherine was now solely responsible for her, not a mere caretaker under her father's direction.

Thus she undid the rich ribbon and opened the shining cloth. She had expected that there would be several layers of the same cloth, which was a pleasant but not extravagant gift, and so she gasped when the mink pelts were exposed.

"Oh, Lord Denno," she sighed, lifting the furs and touching them gently to her cheek. "Oh, this is too much. I cannot..."

"Indeed, you can, madam. Let me assure you that these are only a small sample, a bare token. I was very lucky in my purchase and have sufficient reward in seeing your pleasure, and in hoping you will allow me to give a similar token to Lady Elizabeth..."

She laughed aloud and stepped aside to lay the furs carefully on a table, then turned to face him. "So, I am to be bribed to allow you to court Elizabeth—"

"No!" Denoriel exclaimed, eyes widening with shock. "No, madam. I am far too old..."

Catherine laughed again. "Oh, Lord Denno, no. I only meant to court her favor. I know you have no evil intent toward the child."

Did he not, Denoriel wondered. The way his heart leapt when the queen said he would court Elizabeth was...wrong. She was a child. Fourteen years old. But Denoriel knew that many mortal girls were married at fourteen. Sometimes it was a marriage in name only, but sometimes...There were very young mothers. But he had no need to fear that. Mortal and Sidhe could couple but not breed. He could feel the heat of color staining his cheeks and running up the long peaks of his ears. By God's grace Catherine could not see that!

Concerned at having distressed him, Catherine came forward and put her hand lightly on his arm. "So, I see that you suffer from servants as stupid as my own," she said, changing the subject, "and they had not sense enough to wake you when a message came. Truly, I am glad of that, for you still look somewhat worn."

"It is not so much that my servants are stupid but that they do not speak or understand English. And Clayborne, my man of business, was in the warehouse with my one English footman. The message was left for Clayborne. He woke me as soon as he arrived at the house, but it was almost evening."

"I see." Catherine smiled. "A coincidence of errors. When no one came to announce you, I thought that you were not able to ride to Enfield. I must admit was annoyed that you had not sent a message to that effect, but Sir Thomas offered to send his man with the letter."

Denoriel froze, then forced a smile. "Did you give him the letter?" *If she had, Seymour would soon have lost it and maybe a little blood too.*

Catherine laughed aloud. "A further coincidence of errors. I am afraid we were so absorbed in that silly game that we both forgot. See, the letter is there on my writing desk."

"Then no harm at all is done," Denoriel said. "I promise that Elizabeth will have it when she sits down to break her fast in the morning."

Now Catherine looked concerned, but not for Elizabeth. "There is no need for that. You would have to start before dawn. I know you said you slept almost the whole day, but you still look tired, Lord Denno, and as you said yourself, you are not a young man. It does not matter if Elizabeth receives my news a few hours later. I can send the letter to Sir Thomas—"

The queen was not a cruel woman, but to her a few hours of anxiety for Elizabeth were a minor thing. Denoriel could see, in his minds' eye, Elizabeth at her most anxious, see her pacing and wringing her hands as she was wont to do when distressed. A strange twisting pain, as if his heart were writhing, made Denoriel draw a sharp breath.

"No, madam, I beg you to let me take it. Children have little sense of time. To me an hour is brief indeed. I know whatever my pain, if it is only for an hour it will soon end. But to a child an hour can stretch into an infinity of misery."

Catherine shook her head. "You spoil her dreadfully."

"I spoiled Harry too . . . but not enough for his short time. To me, it seems that every moment Lady Elizabeth is unhappy is a year too long." He allowed his voice to falter. "Because . . . one never knows . . ."

Catherine sighed. "Well, if you are sure that the ride will not be too much for you . . . Yes, I will be glad to know that Elizabeth begins her day with happiness."

He took the letter quickly and kept his farewell so short it was hardly decent, excusing himself with the need to go early to bed in preparation of his early rising. Catherine was content with that and hurried him on his way. Miralys was waiting at the door for him. Denoriel mounted with a word of thanks. He hoped the ostler would believe that he had come for the horse and not raise an outcry about a stolen beast, but it was too cold to want to have walked to the stable.

Miralys held to a decorous pace on the road that led to the palace gate as he had when they had arrived. It was less likely that the guards would see him virtually disappear in the dark, but they might be puzzled if they did not hear the sound of shod hooves on the frozen-hard earth of the road.

The road turned sharply left to avoid a small building by a private wharf. They were now out of sight and sound of the palace. Denoriel said "Home," felt Miralys tense to leap ahead, and a sharp *whirr* went right by his face. He had jerked his head back an instant before the arrow passed, warned by the aura of sickening cold that preceded the iron head.

Denoriel flung himself out of the saddle, shouting *"Cerdded! Rhedeg!"* The violent order to *Go! Run!* would catapult Miralys into his full speed. Without the command the elvensteed might have taken a moment to be sure of what his partner wanted, and that moment might have been too long if an iron-headed arrow, already launched, should touch him. Denoriel was not concerned for himself. He was a much smaller target than Miralys and he could use the Don't-see-me spell and become totally invisible.

He knew he could have escaped by staying in the saddle, but he was so furious, so wildly enraged by the attack, which could have wounded or killed Miralys, that he intended to lesson the perpetrators so that they would never attack anyone again. That he knew Miralys was not the target, that the arrow had been aimed high, at him, made no difference to his rage. He was small; Miralys was large. Miralys had been endangered.

"Gone! The friggin' 'orse disappeared!"

Denoriel had landed in a crouch near the hedge that lined the far side of the road. His sword was out in his hand and, his head turned in the direction from which the arrow had come, he saw the man standing in the shadow of the small building. Had he been looking in that direction, he could have seen him before he loosed the arrow, but he had been looking at the road in case there were deep holes.

The shout that the horse had disappeared drew Denoriel's eyes to the side of the road on which he was. He saw another man, spent bow in hand. He must have shot an arrow too, although Denoriel had not been aware of it. For a moment the second man's remark made Denoriel think that the purpose of the attack had been to steal Miralys, but the next instant confirmed that he was the object.

"Shut yer maw!" The man near the building had run across the road. His voice was tense but low, apparently he feared that sounds would carry to the palace guards. "'E fell off when t'orse jumped. Saw that. Where'd 'e land?"

"'Ope 'e broke 'is neck, yellin' like that and scarin' t'orse. Good 'orse it were. Like t'ave it."

"Where'd 'e fall, you fool? Need to finish 'im. 'Nyhow, think 'is friggin' 'ighness 'ud let us keep t'orse?"

"'Ood tell 'im?"

Denoriel watched them, mentally shaking his head, though he made no move that might alert his attackers. In a thin layer over his continued outrage at the threat to Miralys, he was almost amused by their foolishness. True, they believed he had fallen off and possibly been rendered unconscious, but if he had been stirring, their talk would have covered any sound he made.

"Shurrup!" the second man snarled. "Let's find 'im. We can talk about t'orse arter we slit 'is throat."

And then Denoriel made a mistake, engendered by his contempt. He strolled out into the middle of the road, which to him in the moonlight was as bright as day, and said, "I don't think I'd like that, and I certainly wouldn't like you to have my horse. I don't like being attacked—"

The men leapt apart, drawing swords and knives, and Denoriel realized that they were trained and practiced fighters despite their carelessness in making sure of their victim. He too drew his knife, watching the man on his left, which was usually a fighter's weaker side, advance. He was waving his sword in threat to attract Denoriel's attention; the one on his right backed away almost as if he had been surprised by Denoriel's remark and approach, and was about to run away.

Their contempt for someone they thought of as an effete dilettante saved Denoriel from his own error. The attacker advancing expected Denoriel to back away, right into the sword or knife of the second man. Instead, Denoriel leapt forward and beat aside the sword of the man advancing on him. It was not all gain. Denoriel gasped as the shock of close contact with steel ran up his sword into his hand. He was hardly in time to parry the knife stroke from the man's left hand. Another shock rocked him as steel blade met silver.

The pain and weakness of meeting steel reminded him that he could not afford to fence with these killers. Setting his teeth, he disengaged his weapon from the attacker's, drew back with elven swiftness, and plunged his sword forward again just to the left of the attacker's breastbone. The man screamed, his voice thin and high. Denoriel flung himself to his right, raising his knife and twisting as he tried to pull his sword from the man he had skewered.

The weapon came free just as a blow struck his shoulder from behind. Another thrill of pain and weakness passed through him from the nearness of the steel, but the heavy layers of clothing, the gown and doublet, jacquet and silk shirt, protected him from any direct touch. Still he shuddered and for a moment was physically unsure. Striving to find space to turn and face his second attacker, his foot caught against the spasming body and he fell forward crying out.

All he could do was to roll further right and bring up knife and sword. But the fall was lucky; the second man was near blind in the dark and the thrust aimed at the sound of Denoriel's cry pierced the fallen man, who screamed again. Shock at hearing his companion's shriek jerked the second attacker upright and half a step backward. Denoriel needed no more advantage. He leapt to his feet, now clear of the dying body. Nor did he wait for the second man's shock to abate or for him to decide whether to continue the fight or run.

He said, "You could not have mastered the horse anyway," stepped forward and ran him through the heart.

For a long moment Denoriel stood looking down at the second body, remembering how one of them had said "'is 'ighness" wouldn't let them keep the horse. Then he knelt and wiped his sword carefully on the dead man's doublet. When it was clean, he sheathed it and used his knife to cut away the purse hanging from the belt. Briefly he ran his hands down the front of the doublet, shuddering a little as he deliberately wrinkled the cloth and blood slimed his fingers. There was no sound of rustling as might be made from a hidden paper or parchment.

Then Denoriel's head came up sharply and he could feel his long ears cup forward. Voices. Footsteps pounding fast along the road. In the quiet of the night, the palace guards must have heard the cries. Denoriel hurried to the first body, cut the purse and again felt around the doublet for any concealed letters or messages. The voices were closer.

Although it would do Lord Denno's reputation no harm to have fought off two street thugs, it would certainly do it no good to be found with the thugs' purses and blood on his hands. Denoriel thought of vanishing the stains or covering them with illusion and realized he was trembling with weariness. No, let the palace guards think what they would. To have had a killing so close should make them more alert. With a shrug, Denoriel melted into the shadows of the hedge and hurried away, silent as a wraith.

He was now alert for any sound or movement along the road, both ahead of him, which he could see as twilight, or on the open road, which was bright and clear. Now that he had almost been killed by a steel arrowhead and that two men were dead, of course there was nothing to be seen. When the road had curved again and hidden both sight and sound of the guards, Denoriel stepped across the dead grass of the verge and silently called for Miralys.

Chapter 9

The door between the passage to the stable and the house was locked. Denoriel stared at it stupidly, aware of a fine trembling in his limbs and a hollowness in his gut that spoke of power drain and exhaustion. Had the house been attacked at the same time he had been? By whom? Why? What had happened to Joseph Clayborne?

He remembered at last that he had a key. The same key that opened the front door opened this one. He fumbled in his purse, inserted the key somewhat uncertainly after scraping it around the lock because his hand was shaking. Before he could turn it, the door was flung open and he was confronted by Joseph with a sword in his hand. Behind him, cudgel ready, stood Cropper.

Denoriel's mouth opened, but no sound emerged. Joseph, apparently, had decided to take over the business, and when the street thugs failed him . . .

"M'lord! M'lord, are you hurt?"

Joseph's voice was high with anxiety, the sword hastily sheathed. Cropper dropped his cudgel and rushed forward, hands extended to support his master.

Denoriel blinked. "Hurt? No, not at all."

"But you are all over blood, m'lord!" Joseph exclaimed.

"Yes, but not mine." Denoriel laughed shakily. "I was attacked on the way home from Chelsea. There are two dead men on the road—but I did not wait until the palace guard came to explain. When the door was locked and you opened it sword in hand . . ." He shook his head. "I began to wonder if you wanted to take over the business."

Now Joseph also laughed. "Not until I learn how to produce in three days a cargo such as was in the warehouse." He stepped back. "Come in, m'lord, do. Forgive me but you look terrible."

"I forgive you readily. I *feel* terrible." Denoriel went past Joseph and Cropper, who had flattened himself against the wall to make room. "But why are you armed for war? Are you expecting an invasion?" he asked as he entered the parlor and dropped into a chair by the hearth.

Joseph followed him into the parlor. "You said two men attacked you, m'lord? Could they have been the same two who have been watching the house? They are gone from the house across the road."

"Are they?"

"Yes. You wanted to know whether we feared an invasion." He shook his head. "You are a good deal richer tonight than you were last night, m'lord. I have never had a day for selling like today in my whole life. By midday I knew I would have no time to do any accounting and would need to bring the money home, so I sent for Cuthbert and Petrus to walk home with me. I do not like to walk from the warehouse to home carrying bulging satchels."

"Very wise."

"And toward evening, I bethought myself as to whether those men in the house across the road had just been waiting for a day of exceptional business, so I sent Cuthbert and Petrus to see if they could get rid of them."

"But they were gone?"

"Yes, m'lord, so I brought the money home. And no one bothered us. But later, after Cuthbert and Petrus were gone, I began to wonder . . . There is *so much* money. I began to wonder if those men had gone to get reinforcements, so Cropper and I armed, and when I heard what I felt were stealthy sounds on the side door . . ."

Denoriel smiled. "So you met me prepared for defense. I see. I wonder if the watchers were the ones who lay in wait for me at the palace? That would mean they had been watching all this while to see me go out alone."

"Could they have known about the cargo and meant to hold you for ransom?"

Denoriel shook his head. "The men who lay in wait for me at Chelsea meant death. It was only by chance that I did not get an arrow through my head. There is no ransoming a dead man."

"An enemy from your past?"

Denoriel shrugged. "From Hungary? I have been gone from there for over twenty years. A fellow merchant who envies my trading? What good would my death do him? Who else might think me worth the danger and expense?"

As he said the words Denoriel recalled the malevolent look on Thomas Seymour's face when he himself had stepped out of the shadows near the queen's bed. Yet this evening Sir Thomas had looked . . . contemptuous, as if Denoriel was no longer a threat. How the devil was he to deal with Seymour? Then Denoriel remembered his conversation with Aleneil when she warned him that Vidal might wish to destroy those whom Elizabeth loved.

An odd fluttering started right under Denoriel's breastbone at the thought that Elizabeth might love him. He suppressed it. But, he thought, even if she did not *love* him, Elizabeth surely relied upon him and hearing of his death so soon after that of her father would shake her to the core and make her vulnerable.

Vidal? Could Vidal have sent the assassins? For a moment Denoriel almost felt relief. Knowing who was trying to be rid of him would be half the battle won by knowing where to look for more trouble. Better Vidal, whom he could fight openly, than Sir Thomas. A chill passed through him as he remembered that the men who attacked him were not Sidhe. They were using steel arrowheads and steel swords.

"The truth is, m'lord, that I cannot think of anyone in the community of merchants that even dislikes you. A few envy you, but none believe they could take over your trade routes, so where would be the benefit . . ." Joseph shrugged.

Denoriel hardly heard him. He was thinking about whether he could still hope the attack could have been arranged by Vidal. But he could not speak of that to Joseph, so he turned the subject to the goods he had kenned and Gated to the warehouse.

Joseph waxed almost lyrical about the prices he had obtained and the fact that they were nearly sold out of everything.

Denoriel slapped his hand on the arm of the chair. "Grace of

God," he groaned, "I meant to tell you to hold back some lesser items. I have what I want for Lady Elizabeth, but I should have tokens for the maids of honor and for Kat."

A broad, self-satisfied grin spread over Joseph's face. "Aha! I have just what you need. A parcel of vair, good furs but too ordinary for a coronation, and a pair of marten skins. Somehow they fell behind the vair and no one noticed them. The vair will do well for the maids; Mistress Ashley will enjoy the martens."

"As I have said more than once, you are a wonder and a marvel, Joseph."

The man of business laughed. "Not so wonderful and marvelous as you are, m'lord. I can sell and I have learned to think about how to please people, so I remembered that you were likely to go to Enfield tomorrow and brought home the extra furs, but I could not produce such a cargo . . ." His voice drifted away; he hesitated but then turned away. "A glass of wine would do you good before you go up, m'lord. Shall I bring you the malmsey or claret?"

"Claret, I think."

Denoriel stared at nothing while Joseph went for the wine, thinking that Joseph surely knew he was not human and had decided not to pry or speak of it, even to Denoriel himself. Would it help if Joseph knew about the threat from Sir Thomas or Vidal? No. He already knew an attempt to kill had been made. Specifics were too dangerous.

He drank his wine when Joseph brought it, although alcohol had little effect on Sidhe, nodded his thanks when Joseph said he would have the extra furs wrapped and disposed in a saddlebag, and finally made his way up the stairs to his bed. Leaving his soiled clothing in a heap on the floor to be cleaned or disposed of, he lay down, but not for long.

If the Dark Sidhe were behind the attempt on his life, might they also try to attack Aleneil? He must warn her. Although he was shaking with fatigue, Denoriel drew on a bedrobe, stepped behind his cheval glass (which looked as if it were too close to the wall to permit anything behind it), and Gated to Llachar Lle. He felt better at once as the healing power of Underhill flowed into him.

Denoriel and Aleneil spent a long night discussing the chances that it was Vidal who had set the ambush for him and what to do about it if it was. Nonetheless Denoriel was as good as his word to Queen Catherine and did arrive with her letter just before Elizabeth came from her bedchamber to break her fast.

Kat Ashley had not been best pleased when Dunstan told her that Lord Denno had arrived so early; however, when he explained that Lord Denno had a letter for Elizabeth from Queen Catherine and that he was all smiles about it, she bade Dunstan bring him in at once.

It was perhaps unfortunate that Elizabeth entered one door just as Denoriel came in the other. He had the letter out in his hand to give to Kat, but after a single look at his expression, Elizabeth shrieked with joy and flew across the room to take the letter from his hand. Breath held, she broke the seal and devoured the first few lines.

"Oh, Denno," she cried, "I am to go to Chelsea and live with Queen Catherine."

"Yes, indeed, that much I know already because the queen was kind enough to tell me, but—"

"Oh, you promised I would!" Elizabeth breathed. "You promised and I didn't believe you because I wanted it so much." She flung her arms around his neck and kissed him, not on the cheek but full on the lips.

Denoriel froze, one arm was raised as if his hand still held the letter. The impact of her body with his as she flung herself forward to kiss him jerked that arm against her. For one instant it folded around her, and held her close.

"Lady Elizabeth!" Kat exclaimed.

"No, it must be there," Lady Alana's calm voice came from the bedchamber doorway. "Do look, all of you."

A sigh of relief caught in Denoriel's throat when he realized that Aleneil had prevented Elizabeth's "ladies" from seeing the embrace. The girls were still in the bedchamber looking for something.

"I beg your pardon," Elizabeth said, but her eyes were all golden and laughing, and her complexion showed not the faintest tinge of embarrassed pink.

She and Denoriel had both withdrawn a step so there was a distance between them. He stepped back again and swallowed. "I was about to say, my lady, that I knew you were to live with the queen, but I could not help but wonder about your household. I guessed from the weight of the packet that it was a long letter and probably contained such information."

"Well, my part of the letter doesn't." She laughed, her eyes on his long, pointed ears, which only she could see through the illusion of human round ears. "The letter to me only says I am to come to her in Chelsea and sets the time for the day after my father's—" her voice checked abruptly, amusement gone. Then she clearly forced herself to continue "—after my father's funeral, which she is to attend." Elizabeth bit her lip. "But I am not," she went on, her voice harder.

Denoriel had gritted his teeth when Elizabeth's eyes fixed on his ears and he felt them get warmer and warmer. He was sure they had become red and hot enough to light a candle. Worse was that, despite knowing he could not really have felt the touch of her body against his through all the clothing, he still had a distinct impression of her high, young breasts pressed against his chest.

"Oh, there it is." A young girl's voice came from beyond the doorway.

"Thank you, my dear," came in Lady Alana's soothing coo, and Aleneil stepped into the parlor followed by the three girls who were Elizabeth's maids of honor.

"And thank you, Lady Alana," Elizabeth said, holding out her hand into which Aleneil put a kerchief.

Embarrassment and desire had both vanished when Elizabeth's voice trembled over mention of Henry's death and grew thin and angry over her exclusion from the obsequies. Both emotions were further diminished by Aleneil's arrival with the maids of honor. Denoriel wondered whether Elizabeth had left the kerchief in her bedchamber. It had seemed to him that Aleneil had manufactured something to look for to keep the girls busy, but if so Elizabeth's smooth reception of the square of silk showed a remarkable ability at deception.

Aleneil dropped a brief curtsey and Elizabeth turned back to Denoriel to say, "I cannot see why I was not invited to see my father buried . . . to weep and say goodbye . . ."

"Nor is King Edward, nor Lady Mary invited to attend," Denoriel said hastily, and then with some deliberation, "I think that was meant as a kindness, not to exclude you but to shield you from so sharp a reminder of your loss."

"Perhaps," Elizabeth said, and her eyes glittered. "But I will remember who managed these matters."

She turned then to Kat Ashley, who had come close, and

handed her the several folded leaves that had made up the bulk of the packet. A single glance had shown Elizabeth that the folded sheets had not been written by Catherine herself but were in a secretary's hand. They were, as she suspected, instructions about when to move and how many of her household to take with her. Kat would tell her later.

Elizabeth saw the wary, anxious look on Denno's face and she recalled her last words and tone of voice. With a shock she realized she had sounded as if she expected soon to have power to do something about being offended; she restrained a shiver. That was dangerous. Her brother, the king, was alive and well. Her sister, who would succeed him if any tragedy should end his reign, was also alive and well. Only a violent conspiracy that removed them both would bring her to power. In her joy over living with Catherine, she had forgotten caution. No wonder Denno looked anxious. Elizabeth touched her lips with the kerchief Alana had handed to her.

"Have you broken your fast?" she asked Denoriel with lady-like civility.

The use of the kerchief reminded Denoriel of Elizabeth's eyes on his brightly glowing ears and he told himself that he would be a fool to linger and leave himself open to more of her mischief. But she had been so quiet, so oppressed since King Henry's death, it was a delight even to be the butt of her lightheartedness; however she did not look lighthearted now; her expression was bland, but her eyes pleaded.

"Yes," he admitted, smiling, "but that was a long time ago. It was scarcely dawn when I set out for Enfield."

"Then come and join us," Elizabeth said, gesturing toward a table covered with a cloth and arranged with one tall chair with back and arms in the center, two short benches at each end, and three stools each to the left and to the right of the chair.

Elizabeth went toward the chair, which Dunstan, appearing suddenly from an inconspicuous position against an inner wall, pulled out for her. As she sat she beckoned to Denoriel to take the stool immediately on her left. The stool on her right remained unoccupied as Aleneil sat down on the next stool, and the three young women distributed themselves on the benches and remaining stools.

Dunstan had moved Elizabeth's chair back to the table and was about to disappear again when Denoriel signaled discreetly for him to bring in the packages that had been left with him. Elizabeth had asked Denoriel politely whether it had been very cold when he started and he had begun to reply when Dunstan returned and laid the parcels on the table.

He broke off that answer to say, "One of my ships had just come in before I received Queen Catherine's message, so I was able to bring her a small token. And then, when her majesty gave me the good news that the Council had agreed you should live with her, I thought we should all celebrate."

He opened the largest parcel and handed two skins of vair to each of the girls who cooed and murmured with delight. The two marten skins, he laid near the vacant stool, on which he was sure Mistress Ashley would be seated. Elizabeth watched, her eyes brilliant, until he opened the last package and placed it before her. She caught her breath with delight.

"Ermine! Oh, Denno! And the silver fox! Oh!" She stared for a moment and then smoothed the fox furs with gentle fingers. "Oh, thank you! You do spoil me!"

"Not often," he said, smiling at her. "It is not often that my ships carry any item in which you might take delight. But the furs were appropriate to the weather, and I thought you might need new clothing, or at least trimmings, because you would be living with the queen."

There was now a general murmur of agreement and then each girl uttered personal thanks and excitedly told the "old merchant," who was by now so familiar as to be accepted as a confidant, what she planned to do with his gift. By then, Dunstan had reappeared at the head of several servants bearing platters of food, bowls for porridge, and trenchers of stale bread to hold meat.

Kat Ashley now left the queen's instructions on Elizabeth's writing table and came to the table to seat herself. She hesitated at sight of the shining marten skins, but then after a glance at Elizabeth's plunder and the gift each maid of honor had, sighed with resignation. There would be no way of wresting ermine and silver fox skins from Elizabeth and to demand refusal of the vair, to the maids of honor from financially straitened families, would be real cruelty. She sighed again.

"You are too generous, Lord Denno," she said, stroking the furs laid by her place. "We will all be in trouble if you continue to shower us with gifts."

Denoriel laughed. "*I* will be in trouble if I continue to shower you with gifts like these. I assure you, Mistress Ashley, this is a one-time thing. A special and rather unexpected cargo, and the news from the queen made me feel . . . ah . . . expansive."

Kat sighed once more. "Yes, you always have good reasons for your generosity, but I am sure I am supposed to prevent the presentation of such rich gifts, which might lead to the assertion of undue influence—"

Elizabeth's sharp giggle cut off Kat's speech. "When," the girl asked, "have you ever known Lord Denno to try to exert even the smallest influence on me? Have you ever heard him ask a favor? Or urge me to think about a particular subject or say or do anything special for him or another?"

"No, no," Kat agreed hastily. "*I* know Lord Denno is the soul of discretion, but if gossip about such gifts is spread to the Court, others might wonder what he expected in return for them. The queen—"

"Had her own token from my cargo," Denoriel said, grinning.

Kat laughed. "I should have known. Well, I am glad that we will not need to hide our new riches. We would not have had much time to do so. Queen Catherine, from what her secretary writes, desires us to arrive at Chelsea on the seventeenth. She intends to go directly from Westminster Abbey to Chelsea Palace on the sixteenth after the funeral, and has put all in train for Lady Elizabeth's apartments to be ready."

"The sooner the better," Elizabeth said. "I am starving for some rational conversation."

"Elizabeth!" Kat exclaimed, flushing.

Elizabeth flushed also. "Oh, forgive me," she said, looking around the table. "I do not mean that what we talk about is not interesting, only that the queen is older and wiser and has had so much experience in the world at large. She also owes me nothing and can instruct me with freedom."

"That is very true," Alana said softly and then chuckled gently, "and besides I do not think any of us will have much time for conversation before we leave Enfield. The queen's instructions say that the apartment will be ready, but what does that mean? Is it furnished? What are we to bring with us? Beds? Chairs? Tables? Only clothing?"

Kat nodded at her. "Lady Alana is always a fount of good sense. So, by the Grace of God, is the queen. The secretary writes that beds will be needed and that there will be room for any favorite item of furniture, but that there are tables and some chairs ready in the rooms."

"There are never enough chairs," one of the girls said. "The queen is used to seeing all her ladies and gentlemen standing."

"And that is quite proper," another girl said; she was sweet-faced but of considerable girth. "But we do not need to stand in our own private rooms. Besides that, what is left behind is often worn and not very sturdy."

"Also they never seem to leave small tables that can be set by a chair for a drink or a book," the last maid pointed out.

"But if we take chairs and tables and beds, we will need several wains," Kat Ashley protested. "To buy wains when, if we move again, it is likely to be within the queen's party is foolish."

"Yes, indeed, since I can supply wains," Denoriel said. "Just tell me how many, where they should be and at what day and hour, and you will have them."

"You are always my savior," Kat said, and laughed.

"Yes, and you, Kat, are growing quite adroit at voicing problems in the right way at just the right moment. We could, I am sure, have rented wains." Elizabeth laughed too.

"Which Mistress Ashley knows would be ridiculous when I already own many such. And *she* is polite enough not to ask me outright, which might be awkward for me if the wains were in use or not in London on the seventeenth. Thus if use of my wains would be difficult for me, I simply did not need to offer."

Elizabeth sniffed. "But you would have offered anyway," she murmured, leaning close so her voice would not carry to the others at the table. "I come first, do I not, my Denno?"

"You were a noxious brat when you were three, but adorable . . . and nothing has changed." Denoriel sighed. "Yes, my lady, you come first."

Rhoslyn sat with one hand touching the pendant portrait of King Henry that hung from her necklace and the other open on her lap. Her eyes were lowered, her face sad. Lady Mary was reading from one of the Fathers on the subject of life after death. Rhoslyn was really tempted to cast a spell that would strike Mary mute for an hour or two. That would cause some excitement.

These readings, or the reading of prayers for the dead, or

attending extra masses, had been constant since Mary had news of her father's death. She was, Rhoslyn guessed, trying to save his soul. She had written to the pope and to every conservative bishop she knew to beg that prayers be said for Henry. She had pinched her household to wring a few extra coins to send as offerings with requests for prayers. Rhoslyn had gained even more favor by presenting her mistress with a pouch of gold as an offering for the late king's salvation.

Behind her modestly downcast eyes and her sad expression, Rhoslyn wondered, not for the first time, whether she should receive a message from her fictitious brother requesting her company. Hearing that her brother had had one of his spells and needed her would save her from death by boredom. On the other hand, leaving Mary would deprive her of the opportunity to learn whether the political settlement would affect Elizabeth.

It was not likely to be a final settlement, she thought, trying to soothe her conscience so she could escape. And if Hertford took control, as looked to be likely, his wife was a good friend to Mary and would surely incline her husband in Mary's favor. There would be some weeks, possibly even some months of quiet and possibly by the time she returned, Mary would have had her fill of praying. But . . .

The lindys on Rhoslyn's breast, clinging just below the miniature portrait of the late king gave a convulsive shiver. Rhoslyn uttered an involuntary cry of alarm and pressed her hand over the little construct. Pasgen was hurt or frightened or in danger! Rhoslyn half rose from her seat. The women on either side turned their heads to look at her. Rhoslyn sank back in her chair and clutched the lindys gently. Her lightly clenched hand seemed to rest over her heart.

Whatever happened to Mary or Elizabeth or to England, Rhoslyn had to go to Pasgen immediately. In the moment she had to think—provided by all the ladies moving to look at her—she determined to use what had already happened. She cried out softly again and bent forward. So far the lindys had not convulsed again, as it would if Pasgen's fear or danger had increased, but it did not relax either. Under her fingers the construct remained stiff, indicating a steady anxiety or discomfort. Rhoslyn moaned softly, but not so softly that Mary did not hear. She looked up, peered forward with her short-sighted eyes.

"Rosamund! What ails you?"

"I do not know," Rhoslyn gasped. "A pain. Here." Her fingers arched over the lindys.

"I will summon my physician," Mary cried.

"No. No." Rhoslyn pleaded. "No physician. I am too familiar with physicians. I have a tonic that will take away the pain. But it makes me sleep, my lady."

"Oh, my dear Rosamund, you are excused all service until you are fully recovered. Jane, Susan, help Rosamund to her chamber and call her maid to her."

Rhoslyn was shaking with anxiety and eagerness to be gone, but she did not dare run to hide herself, pulling two of Mary's ladies with her. The lindys was quiet, although still very tense. Rhoslyn could not restrain herself from uttering a soft sob.

"Rosamund, do let me summon the physician," Jane Dormer urged. "Our lady need not know."

"No, this has happened many times before," Rhoslyn said. "I know what to do. I only need to be alone and quiet and it will pass."

"I will run for a footman," Susan said. "We cannot get you up two flights of stairs."

"Oh, yes," Rhoslyn breathed, with real gratitude, "thank you. And if you will send for my maid . . ."

In fewer moments than Rhoslyn had hoped, a tall and sturdy footman arrived. With a murmur of apology, he swept Rhoslyn up in his arms, hurried to the stair in the north wing, and carried her up to her tiny chamber under the gable. There was only a narrow bed with a tiny table beside it, a chest, and one chair, armless but with a back. Still this was luxury when Mary's other ladies were packed four to a room not much larger than Rhoslyn's.

The footman laid Rhoslyn on the bed. She fumbled in the purse hung from her belt and pressed a coin into his hand. He bowed and backed away but did not leave, standing near the door and watching her, in case she should faint or need help. Moments later, Jane arrived, panting slightly from the climb and urging Rhoslyn's maid before her.

The girl uttered a faint cry and raised her hands to her head as Rhoslyn violently thrust instructions into her mind. Jane and Susan looked approving, assuming the cry signaled distress at seeing her mistress prostrate. Then the instructions so forcibly inserted into her mind caused the maid to seek in the chest and take out a hard leathern case. She then closed the chest, set the case atop it, and withdrew from it a small bottle. This she brought to the bed, set on the table, and helped Rhoslyn to sit up against her pillows.

Rhoslyn removed the cork and set the bottle to her lips. Having taken a small draught, she sealed the bottle again, handed it to her maid, and smiled wanly at Jane and Susan.

"Thank you," she whispered. "Thank you so much. You need not stay. Nell knows what to do for me and I will very soon sleep, deeply and long. Tomorrow I will be quite myself. Please thank Lady Mary for her concern and tell her that I hope to attend her as usual . . . tomorrow."

"Do not seek to do too much too soon," Jane said. "I will wait on you tomorrow morning. If you are not completely well, I am sure Lady Mary will excuse you for another day."

"Thank you," Rhoslyn said again, as Nell approached and unclasped the heavy necklace that supported the late King Henry's portrait.

She did not smile, although if the lindys had not still been rigid she would have felt like doing so. Jane Dormer would be only too glad if Rosamund Scott did not feel well enough to attend Lady Mary the next day or any day. Jane was devoted to Mary and rather jealous of Rosamund, who, Jane believed with resentment, had divided loyalties. Rosamund too often would leave Lady Mary to attend on her brother yet remained a great favorite with Mary because she seemed to have an inexhaustible supply of gold.

Susan promptly took the hint that Nell would like to undress her mistress and stepped out of the room. A moment later, Jane had said, "Rest well," and followed Susan. As soon as the door closed, Rhoslyn raised her hand; the maid froze, then went to sit in a comfortable cushioned chair not far from the bed. She closed her eyes.

Rhoslyn slipped from the bed, drew two pillows from the mass supporting her and used them to simulate a body. A pass of the hands, three words, and a simulacrum of herself lay under the rich, furred coverlet. She turned to the maid, set a hand on each temple; her lips thinned with effort and the maid's face twisted with pain. Rhoslyn drew a deep breath, hoping to still the inner quaking that resulted from the draining of her power.

That did not matter now. If anyone came to inquire about her, her maid would open the door just enough to provide a glimpse of the body in the bed. She would say that her lady was asleep and that her color was good and her pulse quiet. The maid would request that the visitor not enter as to disturb her mistress' sleep might be dangerous. If no one came, the maid would get up and walk about every hour or so to keep herself flexible. Her memory would record her vigil accurately, only failing to notice that her mistress never moved at all.

It was the best Rhoslyn could do so quickly and she did not really care. She needed more urgently to get to Pasgen than to maintain her position with Mary. Behind the chair in which the maid sat was a tiny Gate, hardly large enough for her, but it took her to the Goblin Market. From there she wove the tortuous course that would take her to Pasgen's domain.

She found him still seated limply where he had dropped when he arrived and she sank down to her knees, taking his hands in hers. "What is wrong?" she whispered. "Are you hurt? Bespelled?"

"No." But instead of pushing her away, he gripped her hands and, after a moment, almost smiled. "I am frightened."

"Frightened?" Rhoslyn's voice shook. "Do we need fighters to defend us? I will go to an Unformed land—"

"No!" Pasgen exclaimed. And he told her about his adventures in the Unformed land, shuddering as he added, "What if there is some communication among the Chaos Lands? What if the land you work in should also wake? That thing . . . That thing it made was a travesty of . . . of *me*." He shuddered again. "It let me go, but I think only because it did not yet know how to stop me. I feel as if it is waiting for me, that it wants something from me. I—I feel it reaching for me."

Rhoslyn shivered too, then got to her feet, tugging at his hands. "Get up, Pasgen. Let's go inside. The wards on the house are stronger than those out here."

She did not doubt his word. Although Rhoslyn felt nothing untoward in the atmosphere of the domain, the description of those incomplete doll-like constructs was chilling. And the idea that the Unformed land itself had created them was mind-boggling.

Inside the house Pasgen sank into the hard-looking but surprisingly comfortable white sofa. After a moment he drew a long breath and shook his head. "I do not know," he murmured. "I cannot believe that anything can come through my wards. Yet I still feel a drawing on me."

"Are you *sure* those things were mist-made?" Rhoslyn asked.

"You said Vidal was in that Unformed land. Is it possible that he left someone there, someone who was not an expert in creation, and that person made them?"

He thought for a while and then slowly shook his head. "I have no proof of who made the things, but when the lion tore the . . . the male thing, the mist healed it. And that lion was no half-formed blob. Likely that was because Elizabeth had an image of the lion in her mind and must have projected it at the mist. So if someone wanted to create a construct of Elizabeth . . . or me . . . the image would have been much more real. I can only believe that the mist was working without a mind to direct it."

"You think it wants *you* to direct it?" Rhoslyn's voice was thin. She sank down before him again and took one of his hands. "Don't go back there, Pasgen. Don't."

"No, I won't. At least—" he swallowed hard "—not if I can help it. There is a . . . a pull on me . . . a kind of horrible curiosity about whether what I saw was real, a desire to see those things again, just to be sure. But I *am* sure! So why do I want to look again? Is that something the mist set on me?"

Rhoslyn tightened her grip on his hand. "You still feel an urge to go back there?"

"Yes. My infernal curiosity. I always want to know and this is such an enormous mystery. Perhaps what is driving me is within myself and nothing to do with that accursed mist."

"You need to be busy. You need to be busy about something entirely different." She spoke quickly, panic pushing the words out almost in a tumble.

"I am not sure I could be sufficiently interested in something entirely different. I . . . even as we talk, I am wondering . . ."

"You need to be where the mist cannot reach you!"

The note of panic was stronger in Rhoslyn's voice, which made Pasgen lean forward and put an arm around her shoulders. "I will try, but if it can draw me here, in the midst of my own domain and my strongest protections—"

"The mortal world," Rhoslyn interrupted. "Their life-force drains down to us, but nothing from Underhill reaches into the mortal world. If you go there, if you try to find out what mischief Vidal plans against Elizabeth, that should keep you occupied."

"The mortal world," Pasgen repeated. "I do not like the mortal world."

But even as he spoke his head turned away, outward toward the Gate which could take him back. Rhoslyn released his hand and took hold of his face, turning it toward her.

"Don't go there, Pasgen," she cried. "You will be trapped. Don't leave me alone!"

Chapter 10

Partly because he did not have anywhere else to go and half his mind kept toying with visiting some Unformed land, Pasgen Gated to the house of Fagildo Otstargi. Automatically he assumed the appearance of the mortal magician, cast a quick glance in the mirror to be sure he was unremarkable, and went downstairs. From the office, he rang for the servant who showed not the slightest surprise at seeing him.

Since he had not been back to the mortal world in years, the lack of response was unexpected, even in this dull creature. Pasgen touched his mind, found it wide open and scarred by cruel and indifferent handling. That annoyed him. He was not tenderhearted, but to damage a useful tool when it was unnecessary was stupid.

Pasgen was gentler but just as thorough and was soon learning everything the servant knew. He was uninterested in Vidal's dealings with Wriothesley. It must be Vidal, he thought, although of course the person the servant imaged was the Otstargi disguise; however, Pasgen did not think there were any other Dark Sidhe capable of withstanding the overall malaise caused by the iron everywhere in the mortal world.

Idly Pasgen wondered whether Wriothesley had retained his position, but knew even as the thought crossed his mind that it was irrelevant. He had no intention of mixing himself into Court politics. His ignorance about who would rule as regent for the child king was only equaled by his lack of interest in the subject. For a moment he found himself wondering why Rhoslyn thought being in the mortal world could distract him from the lure of the possibly intelligent Chaos Land. No, if it was intelligent he could no longer name it a Chaos, could he?

He was aware that thinking about those unfinished-looking constructs was dangerous; they grew less chilling and more intriguing each time he thought of them—and suddenly his attention was fixed by a name that now was dominating the servant's thoughts. Albertus. But the image in the servant's mind was not the elderly mortal healer. It was a person of late middle age and much different appearance. But Albertus? In Otstargi's house? Had Aurilia cast him out?

No, Pasgen realized, concentrating again on the servant's mind. From the way Albertus had suddenly appeared in the house, not coming to the door and entering in the ordinary way, the mortal healer had been Gated in. Pasgen bit his lip. Did that mean that Vidal had used Pasgen's own Gate? That was something that merited strict examination. True, the Gate to this house was from the Bazaar of the Bizarre, but how had Vidal found it? And could he somehow trace the path from it to Pasgen's domain?

There was no way to investigate that through the dull and damaged mind of the servant. Pasgen continued to follow the creature's thoughts and soon enough discovered that Albertus was currently in the house and had ordered a nuncheon of cold meat and salad. Pasgen dismissed the servant to serve the meal and went softly up the stairs to Otstargi's bedchamber.

He was aware immediately of the feel of a Gate, which he had not noticed when his own delivered him to this chamber. Now that he felt for it, he could feel its power. Pasgen wrinkled his nose. It was Vidal's work, no doubt of that, and he suspected from the amount of power that it was directly connected to Caer Mordwyn. He started to reach into it and checked himself with a slight snort.

Vidal would know from the servant that an Otstargi who was not himself had been in the house. Pasgen knew that if he touched the Gate, Vidal would be able to detect his touch; if he did not, however, Vidal would be left wondering whether Pasgen had been clever enough to leave some trap in the Gate while concealing his meddling. He found his own Gate as he had left it, quiescent, barely noticeable.

A wry smile twisted Pasgen's lips as he fell prey to the very doubts he had anticipated for Vidal, wondering whether the Gate had escaped Vidal's notice or had been subtly altered. It was true that he had just used the Gate to come to the mortal world from Underhill—but the trap would not be on the mortal side. Pasgen racked his memories for ways to detect meddling, but a sound drew his attention. Albertus had left his room.

Pasgen glanced in the mirror and frowned. Should he retain the Otstargi disguise? Likely Vidal would know he had been in the house when the servant's mind showed Otstargi at a time when Vidal knew he had not been Otstargi. Then Pasgen grinned. Why not add confusion to doubt. If he now were seen by the servant as himself, would not Vidal be wondering who the other Otstargi was? The next moment showed Pasgen in his own form, long ears, oval pupils, golden hair and elegant elven dress.

He stepped out of Otstargi's bedchamber and, seeing the man the servant's mind had imaged about to step off the stairs, called, "Oh, Albertus, there you are."

The man started slightly and turned. He frowned when he saw Pasgen but not as if he were puzzled about who had called him by name. "I am not doing any business from this house," he said defensively. "Lady Aurilia should know I would not disobey her. There was no reason for her to send you to oversee me. Merely I eat and sleep here." He made a disgusted grimace. "The accommodations where I must go to hire men for the task she set me are beyond reason repulsive."

So Aurilia, not Vidal, had put the disguise on Albertus. The voice was that of the mortal healer. Just to make sure, Pasgen said, "Yet that was where I found you."

Whereupon the man confirmed his identity by his immediate understanding of Pasgen's remark.

"And that was why I leapt so eagerly at your offer," Albertus said. "Nor have I regretted it for one moment. I came here only because my lady ordered it, and you can go back and tell her that I will obey her implicitly."

Pasgen laughed. "I am glad that you are so satisfied with the bargain you made with me. No, Lady Aurilia does not distrust you. I did not come to oversee you. I came to discover how you progress and whether I can do anything to help speed matters along. I will join you for your nuncheon and we can talk."

He had no idea what task Aurilia had set the mortal healer, and he did not dare touch Albertus' mind; Aurilia would know that at once. But if Albertus assumed that Pasgen was also Aurilia's servant—as might seem reasonable since he was the one who had found Albertus and brought him Underhill to Aurilia—it should be easy enough to learn what Albertus was about.

Albertus hesitated at the door of the parlor, where a table had been set up with one chair and one place setting. Then he waved Pasgen ahead of him and told the servant to bring another chair and another plate. It was apparent to Pasgen that Albertus was not sure of their relative status in the hierarchy. Since Pasgen wished to establish his right to ask questions and receive answers, he strode forward as a superior would and seated himself in the chair.

Neither spoke again until Albertus was seated and the platters of cold meat, cheese, and bread were set on the table. Pasgen helped himself first and nodded to Albertus.

"I am sorry if Lady Aurilia feels I am moving too slowly," Albertus said apologetically. "When she told me what I was to do, I thought it would be easy. All I had to do was hire a few bravos."

"But now that is not enough?" Pasgen invited further explanation.

"No. Something has made the household wary against attack. I am reasonably sure that there are men watching the house from across the road, at least at night."

"Obviously not your men. Did you find out who had hired the watchers?"

"No. My men never thought to be secret and try to take them. All they cared about was driving the others away. That was when I still believed four or five strong thugs could break in and do the business. In any case the others slipped away as soon as my men approached, as if secrecy was very important, but it was too late. The household was alert. And did you know that the servants are all Low Court—" Albertus suddenly coughed and raised a hand to his throat where a gold chain glittered.

Pasgen realized immediately that the chain was bespelled to prevent the mortal healer from speaking about Underhill, thus understood that the house Albertus had been ordered to invade must be Denoriel's. Only Denoriel could be using Low Court Sidhe as servants. What did Aurilia want in the house?

"Are they?" Pasgen said. "How interesting."

"Yes, well, there is no bribing such servants and they can speak little or no English so it is impossible to learn anything from them." He went on to explain what he had learned about Denoriel's household from discreet inquiries in the neighborhood, ending with "And the doors are not only locked and bolted but barred. That much I learned from going to the house myself. Once I waited in the entryway for a parcel and once I came begging to the kitchen door."

"Such devotion!" Pasgen smiled slightly. "I will tell Lady Aurilia how devoted you are to her service."

"I am also eager to get back Und—"

This time when Albertus' voice was cut off, he made a gargling sound, and began gaping, eyes bulging, mouth open. After another few minutes he was able to breathe again and, shivering, seized his mug of ale and drank.

"Perhaps you had better just tell me what you have done here and now and how this will affect your task."

Albertus nodded, trying to insert his fingers between the chain and his neck, but what he said was, "When I saw the difficulties, I realized that I needed men with brains and skill, not just strength and indifference to blood. And the ones who have brains . . . if they know how to get into a house so closely guarded, they are too clever to kill."

Kill! The word lay heavy in Pasgen's mind. He had been thinking that Albertus was to steal something or arrange for something to be found in Denoriel's house that would disgrace Elizabeth. Some token to betray her connection to a common merchant, even if he were very rich and claimed to be a foreign nobleman, would create a scandal. Vidal's and Aurilia's purpose was to prevent Elizabeth from coming to the throne. Denoriel's death could not advance that purpose.

"It means," Albertus was continuing, "that I must choose the men very carefully indeed and find some way to control them lest they decide they can profit more by betraying me before they have blood on their hands."

"I can see your difficulty," Pasgen said slowly, trying to calm himself by thinking that Denoriel would be very hard to kill. "Since you cannot ensure discretion by such means as that." He gestured toward the gold chain.

"This is the first time!" Albertus exclaimed bitterly. "You are one of us. I thought I could speak openly to you. With others I am more careful."

Pasgen shrugged. "It is not possible to explain fine differences to inanimate objects," he said blandly, but he was allowing a frown to grow on his face, and then he shook his head and sighed. "I am not at all certain I agree with Lady Aurilia about having Lord Denno killed. He has close connections with the Court and a great outcry will be made."

"I do not care for that," Albertus said, lips thinned. "I intend to carry out Lady Aurilia's order. And beside, I have already planned a way to avoid exposure. I will invite the men to a celebratory drink when I pay them—a drink laced with a slow-acting poison. It will take them several days to die and they will have their full wage, so there will be no trail leading back to me."

"You do not think you might want them again?"

"There are plenty more where these will come from. I have another more serious problem. I discovered this Lord Denno and the woman—he claims she is his cousin, Lady Alana—are seldom in the house at the same time."

So Aurilia planned to have Aleneil killed too! Rage flickered in Pasgen. He did not love Denoriel and Aleneil; he would not hesitate to play some nasty and embarrassing, possibly even painful, tricks on them but . . . but they were blood of his blood, his father's get! They were not meat for such as Aurilia to dispose of.

But why did Aurilia want them dead? He did not dare ask Albertus, who was only forthcoming with his plans because he believed Pasgen already knew everything. Pasgen realized he would have to find and talk to Rhoslyn but meanwhile he had to delay Albertus. He blinked and shook his head.

"You will not succeed in having the house invaded more than once no matter how clever and skilled your hirelings are. And if *all* those who did a task for you are soon dead, you may have difficulty in finding other *clever* men." Pasgen chewed his lips gently to appear to be thinking hard. Finally he said, "It really would be better if the whole business were completed at once. I will go home and explain to Lady Aurilia the need to some-how get Lord Denno and Lady Alana in the house at the same time—and ask her advice about how to proceed. She will not blame you for the delay."

Albertus' face showed relief. "Ah, thank you, Lord Pasgen. That will make my task easier and more certain of a happy conclusion."

Happy! Pasgen thought. He pushed away the remains of his meal and rose from the table with a word of parting. He had considered killing Albertus where he sat, but instead he went quietly into the corridor and up the stairs. Killing Albertus when the servant's mind could be stripped of his presence in the house would accomplish nothing—except to expose him to Vidal and Aurilia as an open enemy.

That would only increase the danger to Denoriel and Aleneil. Vidal and Aurilia would merely find another tool to accomplish their purpose and doubtless take good care to hide that tool from him. Pasgen slammed the door to Otstargi's bedchamber, but he did not go to either his Gate or Vidal's. He sat quiet, listening. In a short while he heard Albertus' voice and the servant's mumbled reply. Somewhat later he heard the door of the house open and close.

All the while he had waited for Albertus to leave, the back of his mind had been wondering what to do. There was no way he could stop Albertus without bringing more danger on his half sister and brother. Yes, sister and brother by blood. He knew them only slightly, but they were all the family he and Rhoslyn had . . . Llanelli had lost her mother, and her father too, in the fall of Alhambra and she had never had siblings. It had been the loss of her parents that made her so desperate to have a child that she violated Sidhe law and custom, forcing human and Sidhe mages to work the Life-for-life spell that created fertility in her and in Kefni.

Pasgen shivered. His father had saved Aleneil and Denoriel but left him and Rhoslyn to be raised by the Unseleighe . . . left them to misery and pain . . . No. That was unfair. That was what Llanelli said, but Llanelli had never forgiven Kefni for leaving her and using the remnant of the spell to impregnate his lifemate.

But no. No, he had learned better since. Kefni had not left him and Rhoslyn willingly. He had *died* with them in his arms when he was overtaken by the Unseleighe who were pursuing him. Pasgen realized, although Llanelli and Vidal never admitted it, that Kefni had been trying to bring Rhoslyn and him into Seleighe lands.

It was not really strange or unnatural that their father had gone for the babies of his lifemate first, Pasgen thought. Llanelli always spoke bitterly of the choice Kefni had made, and Pasgen realized he had absorbed that bitterness and painted Denoriel and Aleneil with it. Perhaps they were self-righteous prigs, but they were still his sister and brother and he did not intend to see them die for some idiot whim of Aurilia's or Vidal's.

Only how was he to save them? He could not stop Albertus from hiring henchmen. To frighten, drive away, or even destroy those whom Albertus chose would merely expose his attempt to save Denoriel and Aleneil. He needed to know what Albertus planned and must seem to help, not hinder him. Then he had to work from the other end. He had to protect Aleneil and Denoriel.

At that point Pasgen laughed. He could imagine how his brother and sister would react if he suddenly appeared as a protector. Even if they did not attack him and drive him off on sight, they would never believe him. They would be sure his warning was some kind of a trap. But warn them he must. Pasgen shivered again. If they should die . . .

He would not be able to live with that in his mind, with the guilt that would choke his senses. And if Rhoslyn learned . . . He remembered the intensity—the hidden longing—with which she had spoken to him of the Bright Court and her meetings with Aleneil. Rhoslyn had forgiven him his attack on the child Elizabeth because it had not succeeded and because Elizabeth had hurt him, but she would not forgive him Aleneil's death.

First he must deliver a warning. It seemed from what Albertus said that Denoriel's household had already faced some problems. Those could not have been of Albertus' making; he had not yet made any attempt. An attack that failed by Vidal's or Aurilia's forces? Possibly. It did not matter except for influencing just how Pasgen should deliver his warning.

As himself, he decided. Denoriel would not attack him physically in his own house, even less with magic—not that he feared Denoriel's magic. Denoriel had a man of business who lived in the house and merchants came and went doing business. It was too public a place to use magic or even for an open attack on a stranger.

Pasgen's eyes narrowed. Perhaps—perhaps the best arrow in his quiver was the clear, unvarnished truth. He could say that he was doing a favor for Rhoslyn, who was grateful for Denoriel's kindness to her changeling. He would simply tell Denoriel about Albertus' hiring of mortal henchmen and leave. He frowned a moment trying to decide whether to attempt to answer any question that Denoriel asked or simply say what he had to say and go. Either way Denoriel would not believe him; Pasgen smiled bitterly. Denoriel's doubts about Pasgen's purpose would increase his alertness, which would probably be enough.

Having decided, Pasgen went to the mirror and cast only the most necessary illusions—round ears, round-pupiled eyes, and simple, sober clothing. Then he went out and walked to Bucklersbury, his steps slowing as he neared. In the end, he went right by the house, feeling heat in his face as he contemplated rejection, perhaps ignominious expulsion. He had no profit or pleasure ever from Denoriel and Aleneil; why should he open himself to shame, likely to derisive laughter? Would Underhill be so much damaged by their loss?

At the corner of the street, he stopped and looked down into the dirty gutter. Not Underhill. Underhill, Oberon's creation, would continue without noting the loss of two, or two hundred, or two thousand Sidhe. Underhill was truly eternal. But he . . . Pasgen did not like to contemplate being laughed at or rejected, but he would be like the gutter, full of slow-moving filth if he issued no warning.

For his own sake, Pasgen went back down the street and knocked briskly on Denoriel's door. There was a small brass plate affixed. It said ADJORAN and below that MERCER AND FACTOR nothing more. The door opened before Pasgen could have second thoughts, and a tall, muscular manservant stepped back to invite him in.

"Whom shall I say, sir?"

So briefly he hoped the manservant, being human, would not notice, Pasgen hesitated. The one thing he had forgotten when deciding to go as himself was that he might have to give a name. Well, it would be stupid to try to hide that.

"Pasgen Silverhair," he said. "I would like to speak to Den . . . ah . . . Lord Denno Adjoran."

"A moment," the servant said. "May I take your cloak?"

"It is not necessary. I do not expect to be here long."

"Yes, sir."

The servant bowed and took only a few steps along the corridor. He scratched at the first door on the left and went in without waiting, closing the door behind him. Pasgen could not help but grin, imagining the expression on Denoriel's face when he heard the name and preparing to wait some time while Denoriel made up his mind whether to have him thrown out or to receive him. But the door opened almost as soon at it closed. The servant stepped out, holding the door open.

"Please, sir." He gestured for Pasgen to enter.

That was too quick, entirely unexpected. Before he thought, as he stepped forward, Pasgen raised his shields. Then, stopping himself from shrugging, he walked inside—where, just inside the door he checked abruptly.

A man—certainly not Denoriel, totally human, Pasgen's senses told him—had risen from behind a table littered with papers, cloth samples and a myriad of other oddments. Behind him were shelves on which thick ledgers stood and beyond them books, bound in leather and buckram. A quick glance around showed a surprisingly luxurious room. The floor was covered by a thick, intricately woven carpet. To the right, a hearth with a lively fire was flanked by two cushioned chairs; to the left were two windows facing the street with a handsome writing desk between them.

The man himself was soberly dressed, but Pasgen took in the rich, if discreet embroidery across the yolk of the doublet, the points of a heavy silk shirt peeping above the doublet's neck, the general high quality of all the fabric. This man of business was doing very well for himself . . . and did not need to hide that success from his master.

"I beg your pardon, Master Silverhair," the man who had stood to greet him said, "but Lord Denno is not here. My name is Joseph Clayborne and I am Lord Denno's man of business."

"I really need to speak to Lord Denno himself," Pasgen said. "I know he is a busy man, but I am . . . ah . . . a fellow country-man of his. I think if you send my name to him that he will be willing to see me."

"No, truly, sir," Clayborne said, "Lord Denno is not in the house. In fact, I think he is not in London." He smiled slightly, then sighed. "Lord Denno is seldom here, but I am fully empowered to do any business you might have."

"It is not a matter of business," Pasgen said. "It is a personal matter. Is . . . is Lady Alana here?"

"No, sir." Clayborne looked surprised. "She does stay here from time to time, but not often and she has sent no message that we were to expect her."

Pasgen frowned. "It really is important that I see either Lord Denno or Lady Alana—"

"Sir, neither of them is particularly exclusive or proud. I assure you that I have no instructions, not even to ask if a visitor could see them personally. And I believe that if either were here they would be willing to speak to you." Clayborne sighed. "I do not even know when Lord Denno will return. I wish I did."

Very gently, very carefully, Pasgen pushed into the man's mind and discovered immediately that he was not lying. He did not know for certain where Denoriel was, but believed he was with Lady Elizabeth, who was moving from Enfield to Chelsea that day or the next. Just as carefully, just as gently, Pasgen withdrew. Clayborne had frozen for the moment that Pasgen invaded him but his expression had not changed. Clearly Denoriel made no habit of stripping the mind of his man of business. Pasgen hoped Denoriel would not notice *his* assault on such an obviously favored servant.

A wave of frustration flooded him, and he clenched his fist under the sleeve of his gown to prevent himself from raising his hand and blasting Clayborne simply for relief. In the next moment he almost began to laugh. Albertus was seeking bravos in London and had been working out how to get into the house. So, as long as Denoriel and Aleneil were not in the house or, at least, not in London, they were safe.

"May I write Lord Denno a note then?" he asked.

It would be safe enough to state his warning clearly. Even if the man of business were empowered to open Denoriel's letters, which seemed to be the case from a pile of opened documents on the table, he would learn nothing since Pasgen intended to write in Elven.

"Certainly, sir." Clayborne came out from behind the table to lead Pasgen to the writing desk between the windows. "Paper," he pointed to a drawer. "Pen and ink." He bowed and withdrew, returning to his table where he bent his head over a pile of papers compressed by an odd-looking stone.

Pasgen glanced at the stone as he opened the drawer of the writing desk and then bent his perception on it more fully. When he concentrated, the aura of the stone came clear. It was from Underhill!—a sovereign remedy against poison and bespelling. A favored servant indeed.

Withdrawing a sheet of heavy paper from the drawer, Pasgen seated himself, dipped quill in ink, and began without salutation: *Because Rhoslyn is grateful to you for the kindness you showed to her changeling, she asked me to pass to you a warning. For some reason unknown to me or to Rhoslyn, both Prince Vidal and his lady desire not only you dead but Aleneil also. Vidal is gone from Caer Mordwyn, I know not where, but Aurilia has ordered a mortal servant to arrange for your death. I came upon him by accident and he, thinking me in Aurilia's confidence, told me that he is hiring men whom he believes will be capable of invading your house despite your precautions and murdering you and Aleneil. Believe me or not as you choose. Pasgen Peblig Rodrig Silverhair.*

Chapter 11

In mercy, the sun was shining, the sky was a clear, pale blue, and the wind, though chill, held a hint of spring. Denoriel could only be humbly grateful to the Powers That Be because Elizabeth would have insisted on leaving for Chelsea even if it had been pouring rain. She was as excited and light-spirited now as she had been downhearted before she learned she was to live with Queen Catherine. Yet she was going into much greater danger than she had been in years.

Elizabeth would need to be cautious, to be circumspect. She should have shown herself modest and obedient and ridden in the traveling wagon Queen Catherine had sent. Possibly she would have been willing to ride in the wagon if it had poured rain. Possibly.

Denoriel doubted it. He had not even suggested the idea, although he knew he needed to alert her to guard herself. He hated to dim the glow of her golden eyes; he wanted her to be happy. But the reliance she put on the queen to protect her was probably unfounded and dangerous. And Aleneil would not even be with her.

Denoriel's jaw set hard, but he relaxed it. He had not thought to tell Aleneil to stay with Elizabeth and it seemed she had business of her own. As Lady Alana she had asked for and been granted a leave of absence and Denoriel had no idea where she had gone. She was not in her own house in Avalon. He had left a message with her servants, but even if she got it, she could not immediately go back to Elizabeth. The silly maids of honor would be surprised and gossip.

What he had done was to suggest that Elizabeth include Blanche among the young noblewomen. He knew that giving Blanche a place in that vehicle would draw some angry looks from the maids of honor and possibly a protest from Kat. But when Elizabeth glanced at him with widened eyes, he only whispered that she order Blanche to carry her jewels, which would provide a reason for Blanche not to go with the other servants. Elizabeth, bless her, had not asked why, only gave her orders and ended the noble maidens' incipient protests with a peremptory gesture.

Now he glanced sidelong at Elizabeth who sat her mare as firmly as if she had been nailed to the saddle. The animal was full of energy, curveting from side to side and tossing her lovely head. Elizabeth had been too downhearted over the past weeks to want to ride, and the mare needed exercise.

Ahead of them rode Gerrit and Shaylor. Just behind were the other two guards, Nyle and Dickson, and behind them Dunstan, followed by Ladbroke and Reeve Tolliver leading Elizabeth's extra horses. Denoriel glanced back along the road. First came the traveling cart, then three wains loaded with clothing and such furniture, paintings, dishes, and decorations as Kat and Elizabeth had decided they could not do without. And lastly a fourth wain fitted with benches and some pillows for the servants.

Elizabeth also looked back. He saw her nod; they were now out of sight of Enfield and it was safe for her to lean confidentially closer to him. "Denno, why did you want Blanche to travel with my maids of honor? Surely they are not important enough to draw—" her voice stopped, her lips quivered; she could not form what she had intended to say. "No one would care to hurt my maids," she finished. Her eyes sparked gold with—Denoriel almost groaned—what he greatly feared was anticipation. "Will we be attacked?"

"Not you," Denoriel said. "After what Oberon said—" Oberon was a name much used in poetry and betrayed nothing; moreover, there was no prohibition about *him* speaking of Underhill, though if it were reported he might be stripped of his power or even killed, "—I think you, personally, are safe from any attack. Mistress Ashley, though . . ."

"Kat!" Elizabeth breathed, looking stricken now. "No! It would be because of me. I could not bear it if Kat were hurt."

"Yes, my dear," Denoriel said. "I know that you would be wounded to the heart if any ill befell Mistress Ashley. That is just why I fear she might be a target, just as Blanche was last year. You must be watchful, and not only for what only you can see but for mortal attack also."

"But why did you not warn me sooner? I never thought of any danger to her. I did not watch at all . . ."

"There was little danger in Enfield. Your household was so much reduced and there were no diplomatic visits nor any interaction with the Court. Any stranger would have been noticed at once. And Blanche is always watchful for . . . ah . . . other dangers."

"I see." Elizabeth bit her lip gently. "Chelsea is much larger and it will be full of people I do not know."

"Yes, and Mistress Ashley must deal with the officers of the queen's household and their servants, particularly for the few weeks immediately after your arrival to arrange where, when, and how your households will combine."

"What can I do?" Elizabeth breathed. "Can I send one of the guardsmen with her? Will she allow it? Will she not ask why I have ordered such a thing?"

"Not a guardsman, no. However, could you not suggest that she take Dunstan with her? Much of what she will decide with the queen's household officers will be what he will be responsible for. You can hint it would be better if he heard his duties and responsibilities directly from them rather than have her need to make notes and repeat what was decided. And Dunstan is handy both with the sword and with a knife."

"Yes. Yes, he is. I have seen him practice with the guardsmen." She smiled, although her eyes were not quite as bright now. "Thank you, Denno. God's Grace, what would I do without you?"

"You are very welcome," he said soberly, "but likely it would be better if you did not make any point of how useful I am to you. It will be construed as a common merchant exerting undue influence on a lady of importance and power."

They rode in silence for a little while. Denoriel thought Elizabeth looked delicious with the tip of her nose and her cheeks unusually pink because of the cold and her excitement.

Suddenly she turned on him and said, "You did that apurpose! You did not want me to be so happy and carefree."

Denoriel opened his mouth, but nothing came out. He was

silenced by a terrible pang of guilt. Was it possible that he did *not* want her to be happy and carefree because then she would not need him? It was an ugly thought.

Possibly true too, but it did not matter. Elizabeth was one step nearer the throne now than she had been during her father's reign, and both threats and temptations would surround her. During the upheaval right after Henry's death, everything had been too uncertain to allow her to be a target, and her own fears and depression insulated her. In Catherine's household, she would not be so safe.

"I always want you to be happy," Denoriel said. He had to say it whether it was true or not, but he added soberly, "But it is true that I did not wish you to think that you were coming into a new stage of life in which there would be no dangers and dark places."

"Surely the queen does not wish me harm!"

"No. No, indeed," Denoriel assured her hastily. "Queen Catherine, I believe, loves you dearly and only wishes you the best of everything. However, you must remember that she is no longer your father's wife. She . . . she has her freedom and much wealth. There will be many . . . ah . . . visitors to Chelsea."

"Denno, speak plainly! What are you saying to me?" Elizabeth's red brows contracted into an angry frown.

"That Queen Catherine will be courted. She might even marry again."

"Marry again? After being my father's wife?" There was indignation in Elizabeth's voice.

That was dangerous. If Elizabeth showed disapproval of what Denoriel guessed would be Thomas Seymour's courtship, Catherine might well decide that having Elizabeth in her household was inconvenient. And, since Elizabeth was still too young to live alone and since Catherine had always liked Mary, the odds were that Catherine would suggest Elizabeth join her elder sister. That, Denoriel had already decided, would be utter disaster.

"Elizabeth!"

Denoriel's voice was so sharp that Elizabeth jerked her mare's rein and the animal jibbed. He reached out to grasp the mare's headstall, but Elizabeth already had her under control. She stared at him now, her mouth a sullen line.

"You loved your father, most rightly, and to you he was like the sun, a great and glorious being. But think of him for a husband. Think of the physical man, not the king."

Her gaze, which had been fixed challengingly on him as soon as the mare was docile, first looked away, then dropped.

"Did you know, Elizabeth, that your father was Queen Catherine's *third* old husband, that she was married when not quite fifteen to a sick man old enough to be her grandfather? In fact Lord Borough's son was suitably married to a woman who was seventeen years older than Catherine."

Elizabeth made a soft, horrified sound. She was nearly fifteen and knew that for diplomatic purposes she could easily be married to a king old enough to be her grandfather. Perhaps for once her mind's eye recalled her father as he was that last year of his life—too grossly fat to walk, always stinking slightly from the unhealing sores on his leg.

Denoriel was sorry to spoil her memory of the perfect being who had been king, but he continued inexorably, "Catherine was a perfect wife to Lord Borough, as she was to your father, and when the old man died, he left her rich. But in a way he died too soon. She was less than seventeen and her guardian—her mother had died the same year as Lord Borough—chose Lord Latimer for her second husband. He was not quite as old as Borough, but already ailing. She was his *third* wife."

Elizabeth had not raised her eyes again. She was looking down at her gloved fingers holding the reins.

"Again Catherine was a good wife and the kindest and most loving of stepmothers to Latimer's two children."

"As she was to us," Elizabeth murmured. "It was no pretense. She really cared for us."

"Yes, indeed. You may well meet Latimer's children. I am sure they will visit Queen Catherine now that she is no longer so hedged in with ceremony. They still love her dearly. Latimer loved her too. When he died, he left her even richer. And she was no longer a minor. She was old enough to make her own choice. As you can imagine, she was courted by a number of strong and handsome young men. I have heard rumors that she had almost decided among them, but then the king asked her to be his bride."

Elizabeth was silent again, but she looked at Denoriel and then looked away. He knew she was thinking, *another sick old man.*

"She was young enough still to have children," Denoriel said. "She is *still* young enough to have children, Elizabeth. And she loves children so much. Would you deny her the right to have her own child . . . because she was married to your father? Has she not waited long enough, been dutiful enough, to marry once for love?"

Elizabeth did not reply, and Denoriel said no more, content to leave her to her own thoughts. Elizabeth did love Catherine; she would be—because of her personal fears of what she might be forced to accept—sympathetic to the queen and come to accept courtship and marriage for Catherine.

Denoriel was not very happy about inclining Elizabeth in Thomas Seymour's favor. Because of his suspicions it was Seymour who had tried to have him killed, once he was reasonably sure that Catherine would invite Elizabeth to live with her, Denoriel had taken some time to discover what he could about Sir Thomas. He was very dissatisfied with what he learned. He sincerely wished that Catherine had not chosen so ill, that she had sought out worth rather than a beautiful body and flashy good looks. However, Denny had told him that it was Thomas Seymour the king had displaced and it was all too natural for Catherine to turn to the man she had loved once again.

If that was true, Catherine would take Seymour. What could be more flattering than that he had waited for her, not endangering her with his attentions while she was Henry's wife, but rushing forward to court her again as soon as she was free? Denoriel wondered if there were some way to let Catherine know that Seymour had proposed himself for both Mary and Elizabeth before he at last turned to her.

Could Elizabeth drop that information—as if she had been warned that Seymour had asked for her and that he was not suitable? No! She was little more than a child, just over fourteen. But girl children, who knew they must some day marry, were fanciful. If Elizabeth knew that Seymour had asked for her, would she be flattered? Inclined to look at him as a suitor?

Better to tell Elizabeth about Seymour's earlier aborted court-ship of Catherine, which would fix him in her mind as belonging to Catherine. Denoriel just prevented himself from wrinkling his nose as if he smelled something foul. Unfortunately that tale might also paint him to Elizabeth as noble and chivalrous, which was far from the truth. He was only greedy (Catherine was rich and Elizabeth well endowed) and ambitious, seeking to lift himself up to his wife's position.

"I suppose," he said, "since I have said this much, I had better give you the rest of the rumors."

"Rumors? About Queen Catherine? Who dared . . ."

"It was before she was queen, when the king first approached her. There was some anxious talk about whether his majesty was going to be cuckolded again because Mistress Parr had a lover already."

"A lover?" Elizabeth's voice rose in protest.

Denoriel reached over and patted her arm. "More was rumored than was true."

"Then why did you listen to such scurrilous talk?" she asked, hotly accusatory.

"Elizabeth! Not for any dislike of the queen. She is and always was a woman I greatly admired. But, as you can imagine, I was concerned—particularly when I also heard of how good a stepmother she had been to Latimer's children. I was afraid she would make you love her, and if she too were discovered to be unfaithful—"

"Never! Never once did Queen Catherine show favor to any man or meet with any man except in public rooms in the presence of the entire Court. She never even entertained the officers of her household in her private withdrawing rooms."

"A wise and virtuous woman."

"Yes! She is! And, thinking back, no man sought her favor either. I think the rumors you heard were just mean-spirited gossip, made up to sully Her Highness."

"No, Elizabeth. The rumors were true enough. Oh, not that she had a lover but that many men courted her after Lord Latimer's death and that she had all but decided on one of her suitors when your father intervened."

"She did not!" Elizabeth cried, tears standing in her eyes. "I tell you there was no man." She uttered a sob and then said loudly, "I watched! I *did* watch this time in case . . . I would have warned her."

"There was no need for warning. The gentleman was clever in the ways of power."

Denoriel hesitated, wondering if he should tell Elizabeth that

Seymour loved Catherine's rich estates far more than her person, and that he suffered only a check to his greed not a wrenching of the heart when he gave her up. Swiftly, he decided against that kind of criticism. In fact he did not know Thomas did not care for Catherine. Considering Catherine Howard's fate—and that of her lovers—Thomas' restraint might have been to protect himself as well as a lady for whom he cared.

"When he knew the king intended to make the lady an offer," Denoriel continued when Elizabeth looked an inquiry at him, "he went away. And he never approached her in all the time she was your father's wife. But after King Henry died, he came swiftly to offer the . . . the consolation of his condolences and his service."

"Oh." There was a little silence in which Elizabeth looked straight ahead and blinked twice. Then in a small voice she asked, "Who?"

"Sir Thomas Seymour."

For a little while she did not respond at all. Then she cocked her head to the side and said, "The king's uncle . . . the younger uncle. Yes, I've seen him." Her lips began to curve. "Yes. A tall man and well made. Not so tall and well made as you, my Denno, but still an impressive figure. And handsome too. A thick curling head of hair and an auburn beard to match, although I think I prefer you smooth shaven."

Denoriel was considerably startled by Elizabeth's use of him as a model against which Seymour did not quite match up. He found himself warm and flattered . . . too warm! She was only a child! But before he could think what to say, she had glanced sidelong at him, eyes glinting.

She paused as if to think and then giggled. "How would you look with a white beard?"

"Like an old man," Denoriel said somewhat bitterly, owing to the sudden bursting of his bubble of pleased surprise over her praise.

"Oh, no." The sharpness and mischief were completely gone from her voice. "You will never be old, my Denno."

The tone in which those last words were spoken sent a new pulse of warmth—no, think the truth—desire through him, but the words themselves were enough to add pain and chill to Denoriel's desire. Within Elizabeth's life-span, he would never be old. She would age while he would not.

He remembered the many warnings given him when he began to love Harry FitzRoy, that Harry's life compared with his was like the blooming of a flower, sweet and beautiful, but gone to brown death in a day. That did not matter. In the end he had not lost Harry, who was alive and well and making merry mischief Underhill.

Only Elizabeth was not a little boy. She was female and from the tone of her voice not immune to him. Because he was the only male who had ever been so close to her? And she was, although high young breasts now shaped her riding dress and her narrow waist flared into broadening hips, still a child. His hurt in her short life was irrelevant; her hurt if he bound her love to him was wrong, dangerous to her.

He would deliver her safe to the queen's care and take himself Underhill. He would join Harry's pursuit of the evils that had made El Dorado and Alhambra uninhabitable to the Sidhe . . . and he would strangle his unnatural desire.

Rhoslyn returned to Lady Mary's residence only an hour or two before dawn of the next day. She replaced the pillows in their usual position, gestured to remove her clothing, got into bed and released the maid. The girl blinked, yawned as if she had been asleep, which she believed she had been, and peered anxiously at her mistress. Assured that Rhoslyn was breathing quietly, she then clucked softly at her own carelessness and occupied herself with putting away the clothing Rhoslyn had left in a heap on the floor.

When the maid came to look at her again, sometime later in the morning, Rhoslyn stirred and pretended to wake. She had spent the quiet hours between releasing the maid and this wakening thinking about Pasgen, and she had decided that she did not dare leave him all on his own. He would doubtless come to the mortal world as he promised, but if he did not discover anything to hold his interest, he would be consumed by curiosity and God alone knew what he then would do. Rhoslyn shook her head at herself for calling on the human God who meant nothing to her.

Yes. She had spent far too much time listening to prayer and discourses on the human soul. She was not human and, she hoped sincerely, had no soul. It was enough to live for a few thousand years. There was no need to be greedy and desire immortality, particularly if one was threatened with unending torment for not adhering to the ridiculous patterns of righteousness demanded by the humans' God. Rhoslyn had been amused at that thought, but she suddenly shivered. Was that not what she had lived in all of her life, a place of unending torment?

She tore her thoughts away and concentrated on choosing clothing, deliberately selecting a pale yellow shift gathered at the throat to make a small frill and a dark green gown. The combination made her dark skin sallow and she drew her hair back under her green and yellow headdress.

The effect of her choice was immediately apparent when Susan Clarencieux, another favorite of Lady Mary, scratched and was admitted. "Oh," she said softly, "Mistress Rosamund, I see you are still not well. You should not have dressed."

Rhoslyn sighed. "I felt it necessary. You are very right, Mistress Susan, I am not so much recovered as I hoped. I fear I must ask Lady Mary to give me a leave of absence until I am stronger and I wished—during this sad time—to ask her in person, rather than just write a note."

"Lady Mary is free now, Mistress Rosamund, and sent me to ask about your well-doing. Let me give you my arm and bring you to her."

Mary was so kind and so concerned that Rhoslyn almost felt guilty for diminishing her already thinned entourage. Rhoslyn suspected that she was not the only lady or gentleman who had had enough of prayers for the dead. Moreover, Pasgen was more important than Mary, actually more important than England. Whatever happened would be over and done with in little more than an eyeblink compared with Pasgen's lifetime. Pasgen must be protected against himself.

On the other hand this really was a good time to be away. Nothing at all of political importance was likely to happen for a few weeks. Rhoslyn knew she could not leave her post permanently. Mary was now the heir apparent to the throne and as soon as those who would control the government felt they were secure, they would begin to apply pressure to Mary to bend her one way or another. Until they were sure, however, Mary would be courteously left alone.

Rhoslyn did not anticipate and did not have any trouble in

winning her freedom. Lady Mary had taken her hands as soon as Rhoslyn was close enough to be seen. She urged Rhoslyn to sit down, exclaiming that she was sorry to see Mistress Rosamund still so pale. And Rhoslyn had hardly mentioned her desire to retire to her brother's house, when her request was approved. Her only problem thereafter was how to escape Lady Mary's anxious attempts to assist her in every way possible.

She succeeded only partially at last only by allowing Mary to provide for her transportation into London, where she said a message to her brother would bring his servants. That agreement at least saved her from another reading from the Fathers on the higher value to be placed on the comfort of the soul than that of the body because it was important to leave as soon as possible.

Even so, she raged inwardly as the clumsy vehicle—the most luxurious available but still slow and uncomfortable—crawled toward London. She was terrified that Pasgen would find some way around the promises he had made to her. She could too easily imagine him being drawn to examine more closely those ill-formed constructs and being swallowed up by the malevolent Chaos Land.

A few moments after Mary's vehicle deposited Rhoslyn in an elegant inn, she was out of the place by a back door. She made her way to Pasgen's Gate just north of Westminster Abbey, transferring from the terminus at the Goblin Market to the Gate that took her to the empty house. There the worst of her fears was assuaged, for she found Pasgen himself writing a message, purportedly from her imaginary brother's servant, asking her to attend on her brother.

"But I could not for the life of me think of a way of getting the message to you soon enough," Pasgen said.

Rhoslyn's eyes widened with alarm. "Soon enough for what? You are not going back to that dreadful place!"

Pasgen frowned. "I will have to go back, Rhoslyn," he said slowly. "I cannot leave what may be a real danger to the whole of Underhill without finding out if it *is* a danger, and if it is, without doing *something.*"

She felt rising panic. "You need do nothing, certainly not go back to that hellish place! I will go to Oberon and report what you saw—only, of course, I will say that I saw it, that I had chosen an Unformed land at random to create a few constructs—"

"Rhoslyn." Suddenly Pasgen started to laugh. "I am the one who was always wiping up the messes you had left with your spells—"

"Yes," Rhoslyn interrupted forcefully, "and it is about time that I paid back all your favors. No, seriously, Pasgen, Oberon will not question my appeal to him. I am known for my creation of constructs and if anyone were to induce a mist to imitate creation, it is logical that it was me."

"But it was not you . . . and, Rhoslyn, it was not me either. The mist did not learn creation from me. I was not creating anything, only studying its properties. It was Elizabeth. She did not know how to create so she made a picture in her mind and begged the mist to create it."

"I will not tell Oberon about Elizabeth," Rhoslyn said quickly. "The less he thinks about her the safer she is. I will just tell him about the strangeness of the mist in that Unformed land."

For a moment Pasgen frowned thoughtfully at her, then he nodded. "Telling Oberon is not at all a bad idea, but not until I have a chance to test that mist again."

"Pasgen! You promised!"

"I know, but my curiosity is eating me up alive. I will be careful, Rhoslyn. I will stay right by the Gate . . ."

She shivered and caught at his hand. "Please, Pasgen!"

He laughed and turned his hand in hers so that he could squeeze it comfortingly. "Well, it is not something you need to worry about right now. I was not writing to say that I was off to the Unformed land. Why in the world would I send a note to the mortal world to tell you that?"

"So that I would be at hand Underhill to try to rescue you?" Her voice was tart with irony.

He pressed her hand again. "Would you, Rhoslyn?" Then he bent his head and sighed. "Yes, I know you would. And that is the thing most likely to keep me out of that Chaos Land." He gave her hand a last squeeze and said more briskly, "No, I was not planning to attack that problem just yet. We have another."

Rhoslyn let out a long breath. "Whatever it is, I welcome it if it has distracted you from that malevolent mist."

But he was shaking his head. "No, Rhoslyn. I do not believe the mist is at all malevolent. To me it seemed merely curious."

She bit her lip, and looked him in the eyes. "That an Unformed land can have become self-aware enough to be curious is dreadful and frightening enough. What is this other problem?"

His mouth thinned into a grim line. "It seems that plans are being made to arrange the deaths of Denoriel and Aleneil in the mortal world."

Her eyes widened, but what he had just told her seemed to make no sense. "Aleneil and Denoriel? That is ridiculous! How did you learn of this?"

"The first thing I decided to do when I Gated to the mortal world was to check on Fagildo Otstargi's house," he said, with a deep anger smoldering in his eyes. "The servant, to my amazement, was not in the least surprised to see me come down from the bedchamber. Now I chose him for his stupidity, but not to have noticed that I had been gone for several years seemed stupid beyond what was possible."

"To me also," Rhoslyn agreed, frowning.

He smiled, but without a trace of humor. "It seems that 'I' had not, after all been gone for years. 'I' have appeared irregularly from time to time."

"Vidal," Rhoslyn breathed.

"Yes, Vidal."

She clasped her hands together in distress. "He is trying to do something forbidden in the mortal world that will bring Oberon to attack you!"

"That was my first thought," Pasgen agreed. "But then I learned by looking into the servant's mind that Albertus, Aurilia's servant, was living in Otstargi's house and that his purpose was to arrange the deaths of Aleneil and Denoriel."

Rhoslyn's eyes opened wider still. "What profit can Aurilia gain by their deaths? Aleneil is a FarSeer, but only the youngest and least powerful of those in the Bright Court. You said that you chose Otstargi's servant to be very stupid. Could he have misunderstood what he heard?"

Pasgen grimaced. "I did not learn it from him, but from Albertus himself." And he went on to describe to Rhoslyn his whole conversation with Albertus.

"So there can be no mistake." Rhoslyn nodded, and felt a shadow of the same anger Pasgen was feeling. "But I still cannot understand why Aurilia should want to harm Aleneil and Denoriel."

"At first I was puzzled also," Pasgen admitted, "But when I gave the matter some thought, I understood that there was a simple and obvious answer. Aurilia is as power-hungry as Vidal. What is the greatest threat to the power of the Unseleighe in the near future?"

"Not Denoriel and Aleneil," Rhoslyn said with a laugh. "By Danu! They are minor cogs indeed in the clockwork of the Bright Court."

"No, you are right," Pasgen said, then leaned forward to emphasize his point. "But who depends on them? Who needs them?"

Enlightenment showed in Rhoslyn's dark eyes. "Elizabeth. It is Elizabeth Aurilia wishes to destroy, but surely there are more certain ways . . ." She paused, and narrowed her eyes. "No. Vidal and Aurilia will not attack Elizabeth directly, not after the warning you told me that Oberon gave to Vidal. Yet Elizabeth must be the target."

Pasgen raised his brows. "I cannot think of anything else that would make Aurilia part with Albertus. He is the healer who mixes that bluish drink she is forever sipping."

Rhoslyn did not look as if she heard his remark. She mused a moment more and then said, "I see. For all her high courage, Elizabeth is a tense and fearful creature. Vidal and Aurilia think that if Denoriel and Aleneil die and their support is withdrawn, Elizabeth will . . . break apart." After a moment, Rhoslyn shook her head. "But she will not."

"Do not be so sure," Pasgen said. "I saw how she acted when Oberon denied her claim that Denoriel was *her* Denno. She is closer tied to him than you think." Pasgen's lips thinned. "That does not matter. I do not wish Denoriel and Aleneil to be killed by common, mortal thugs so that Vidal and Aurilia will have more power."

"I agree most heartily with you, brother," Rhoslyn replied, nodding decisively. "But I see that we cannot ourselves be too direct in our actions. If you remove Albertus or interfere with his servants, you will then become the first target. I think Vidal would be glad of the excuse to attack you. However, neither Denoriel nor Aleneil is helpless. If we warn them—"

Pasgen gave a disgusted snort. "I tried."

"You mean they would not even give you a hearing—"

"No." Pasgen laughed at her indignation. "They were not at the house on Bucklersbury and were not expected there. I did leave a note for Denoriel with his man of business, but what if Aleneil comes to the house before Denoriel does?"

"Yes. The man of business would not give her your note if you addressed it to Denoriel. Hmmm." She looked down and then raised her eyes and tears glittered in the lower lids. "Aleneil does not have the defenses Denoriel does. I do not want Aleneil to be hurt or killed. She has been kind to me and . . . she is my sister."

She was his sister too, Pasgen thought, and a gentle spirit, if she had been kind and welcoming to Rhoslyn. Perhaps . . . just perhaps if Aleneil would support her, Rhoslyn might achieve her dream of some acceptance in the Bright Court. The thought left him with a hollow feeling. He did not think the toleration would be extended to him. Would he lose Rhoslyn? Not completely. Never completely, but . . .

"I think," Pasgen said hastily, "that I will go back to Otstargi's house and see if there is anything I can do to 'help' with Albertus' plans."

"Yes." Rhoslyn smiled at him gratefully. "And I will go to the house on Bucklersbury and ask to see Lady Alana. As Mary's maid of honor I could well have a message to pass to Elizabeth through Lady Alana, and I have asked for leave from Mary to rest, so I have a reason to be in London."

Chapter 12

Denoriel, as he had promised himself, did go Underhill after he had seen Elizabeth settled into the queen's care. At the time he and Elizabeth arrived, Thomas Seymour was not in evidence and Queen Catherine was clearly very, very happy to welcome her stepdaughter. They were so absorbed in each other that both had been barely courteous to Lord Denno.

Plainly Denoriel was in the way of the ladies making enthusiastic plans for the future. Thus, he had taken his leave, telling himself he was grateful that neither Elizabeth nor Catherine seemed to realize it was almost dark and asked him if he had a place to stay. He did stop by the stable to remind Ladbroke of his direction in London and that a message sent to the house on Bucklersbury would soon reach him.

Miralys made no more than a few moments' work of returning to London, and Denoriel Gated home to Llachar Lle from the Gate in the basement of the Bucklersbury house without ever going into the house at all. He did not bother going to his apartment in the palace either, but Gated to Avalon from where Miralys took him to Aleneil's house. Before he could lose himself in Harry's attempts to clear the evil from the abandoned domains, he had to make sure Aleneil would return to guard Elizabeth.

He had a few choice words to say—not to Aleneil's servants; they were blameless—when he learned that Aleneil had already

165

returned to her house, received his message, and gone to meet him in the house on Bucklersbury. If he had not been so impatient and had walked into the house, Joseph would have told him Aleneil was there, or he would have encountered Aleneil herself.

Mumbling dissatisfaction under his breath, Denoriel bade Miralys take him back to the Avalon Gate, from where he Gated to Llachar Lle, and then Gated again from his apartment to the house on Bucklersbury. By the time he arrived, he was aware that he was power-drained, not severely, but he was definitely not full. He thought for a moment of Gating back to his rooms in Llachar Lle again and resting until his full power was restored, but decided it would be foolish to do so. Since he would not need to protect Elizabeth, it was unlikely he would need to use any magic before he returned Underhill.

As he came up the cellar steps, Joseph came out of his room and said, "Ah, Lord Denno. How nice that you have come. Lady Alana is here—in your office—and I have a message—"

"From Lady Elizabeth or Queen Catherine?" Denoriel asked, although he was fairly certain there had not been time for a message to come from Chelsea. Still, he found himself wishing that Elizabeth would remember she had hardly said farewell to him.

"No, my lord, from a gentleman who said he was a fellow countryman of yours."

Denoriel made a face. There had been more than one over the years who claimed to be exiles from Hungary. Most were cony-catchers who thought they could extract money from his sympathy for those fleeing the Turks. Those did not even speak Hungarian. Not that Denoriel was fit to be an orator in that tongue, but Jenci Moricz of Elfhame Csetate-Boli in Hungary had drilled enough of the language into Denoriel's mind so he should not be betrayed by ignorance if someone from Hungary should appear in the English Court. A few who approached him had actually been displaced Hungarians. Denoriel had found work for them in his trading enterprises . . . outside of England.

"Likely another appeal for money." Denoriel made an impatient gesture.

Joseph frowned. "He did not seem that kind to me."

"Oh well, whatever it is can wait until I speak to Lady Alana. Hungary is twenty-five years behind me. It cannot be anyone I know. Will you have the servants bring us a meal?"

"Yes, m'lord, but I did not expect you today . . . nor Lady Alana, and since we have seen no more of watchers in or near the house across the road and all the money is safely deposited with your goldsmith, I took the liberty of making a . . . a personal appointment."

Denoriel noted the faint extra color in his man of business' face and, though he was very tempted to chortle knowingly, made himself expressionless. "Ah. You intended to be out of the house this evening?"

"Yes, m'lord, but Cropper can stay if you like."

He made a dismissive gesture. "The men who attacked me are dead. I doubt there is any further threat. There is no reason why you should not go out. Cropper can go at his usual time. I will be here to guard the house and provide company for Lady Alana. If necessary, I can ask Cropper's wife to come in to serve us. But I do not think it will be necessary." He grinned. "Maids of honor often must do things like warming wine and putting hot bricks into their ladies' beds. Lady Alana and I will manage."

Joseph breathed an obvious sigh of relief and Denoriel was again tempted to laugh and again restrained himself.

"Thank you, m'lord. Oh, and if you should want the note the fellow countryman left for you, it is right in the middle of my table, atop two invitations that I thought you would like to see."

"Thank you, Joseph," Denoriel said and turned away.

He entered his own office with so broad a grin on his face that Aleneil, sitting by the fire, laughed in response.

"Oh you!" she said. "Don't you ever give a hint of why you want me? I thought it was surely bad news."

"The news is not what I was smiling about," Denoriel said, sobering, but then he smiled again and sat down across from her. "I couldn't help laughing because Joseph obviously has an assignation for tonight. He was much distressed, poor man, because we both showed up here without giving him any warning and he was afraid I would want him to stay in."

She tilted her head to the side, her eyes warm with welcome. "Why should you? And I don't see what there is to laugh about in a man wanting to go out once in a while."

"Why he thought I might want him to stay? I will tell you that later. It is part of the bad news." He shook his head. "But the real reason Joseph feels he must be here whenever I am is because he is not sure I can pour wine for myself and he is absolutely certain I cannot heat water to make tea." Denoriel was grinning again. "But I never knew that Joseph *had* a private life or was the least bit interested in anything beyond trading."

"More shame on you! He has worked for you for . . . what? Fifteen years. And you did not know he was . . . ah . . . human?"

Denoriel sighed. "You are right, Aleneil. And I *like* Joseph, truly. But I am so tangled up with Elizabeth that I hardly notice anything else."

She regarded him with a chiding look. "Begin to try to notice now. It is not for greed alone that Joseph has been with you so long. Do not let him feel that you do not care about him."

"No. I do care." That stung a little. He valued Joseph! He told the man often enough! "And he—he knows I am not human, or at least, no ordinary human, and has decided not to ask. I will pay closer attention to him."

She nodded decisively. "And so you should. Now, why am I here instead of attending a very tempting ball?"

After what Aleneil had made him see about Thomas, the question gave Denoriel a terrible pang of guilt. He was putting Elizabeth before Aleneil's comfort too. The FarSeers had Seen that he must protect Elizabeth to bring in the golden age the whole Seleighe realm desired, but the dullest part of that duty had been dropped on Aleneil. It was she who had taken on the plain looks of Lady Alana to serve as lady in waiting or maid of honor.

Before he could answer, the servants brought in the meal Denoriel had ordered. He and Aleneil moved to the table, and he said, "I am very sorry, Alana my love, but—but I feel I must ask you to go back into service with Elizabeth. I would do it instead of you if I could, but this will need someone right in her household."

Clearly Aleneil was not pleased. "Elizabeth cannot be in any danger! After the warning Oberon gave Vidal, I cannot believe he would dare—"

"Not that kind of danger." He sighed, and reluctantly continued his explanation. "I agree that Vidal will make no direct attack on Elizabeth. But have you never thought, Aleneil, that there are more ways of making sure Elizabeth never comes to the throne than by ending her life? For example if she were to be in some way disgraced, she could be made unfit in the Council's opinion to be in the succession—say, caught in a love affair or married. Henry's will forbade marriage without the permission of the Council."

Aleneil's frown deepened. "Elizabeth knows the terms of her father's will."

"Yes, but she is not quite fifteen." He shook his head. "Remember what happened to Catherine Howard, raised in that ill-organized household where she was fostered! I grant you that the queen is unlikely to leave Elizabeth so ruinously unsupervised, but young girls can find ways to do what they wish, and Elizabeth is head-strong. Catherine is no longer Henry's wife and men will begin to gather around her full purse like flies around dead meat. There will be an—an atmosphere of courtship. Young girls are romantic, and Vidal has at least one servant at Court, mayhap more, who will spread rumors or raise questions about Elizabeth's lascivious nature—saying she is like her mother." He sighed. "And then it only takes one man to turn her head."

Aleneil chewed meditatively and then sighed. "Yes, I see the danger. Not that Elizabeth would agree to marriage, but she might well agree to a kiss or two."

Or more than a kiss or two ... Though kisses alone could be dangerous. "And Catherine will not really be guarding Elizabeth as she should. Catherine will be too busy with her own love affair. Her mind is made up already."

Aleneil's eyes widened. "Already? Henry is not yet a month dead!"

"The man courted her before Henry asked her to be his wife, and was back at her feet ... I would guess the day the announce-ment of the king's death was made." He tried not to show his distaste for what should have been a genuine display of fidelity. Or actually, it was a genuine display of fidelity—to Catherine's wealth. "So faithful a lover—one she had all but accepted in the past. They are agreed by now, I am sure. Both times that I went to see her at the palace, he was already there. And he did not like ..." Denoriel's voice faded and he put down his fork, his expression grim, remembering his suspicion that it was by Thomas Seymour's orders that he had been attacked.

"Who is it?" Aleneil demanded, then changed her question. "No, tell me first what is wrong."

He began to eat again. "The two things are connected. The man is Thomas Seymour, Hertford's younger brother. The first time I met him I had gone to the queen to tell her of Elizabeth's misery and to ask if she would be willing to take Elizabeth into her keeping. Seymour just burst into her chamber, plowing past Catherine's servant . . . and she did not remonstrate with him. He took offense at my being there."

"Took offense at your being there?" Aleneil echoed.

"He is, I fear, a confirmed womanizer and suspects everyone else of similar propensities." Truly, the more he thought about Thomas Seymour, the less he liked the man. "Certainly he wishes to diminish my credit with Queen Catherine. I am certain he suborned one of Catherine's servants so that a note she sent to me before midday asking me to call upon her was not delivered until late afternoon."

"Why? Since the note *was* delivered what was the point of the delay?" He could see Aleneil's thoughts racing down a multiplicity of paths.

"I think . . ." He hesitated. "This is all guessing, understand. And understand, too, that I do not like the man and may think ill of him out of prejudice, but after our first meeting two men appeared in the house across the road watching this house. I think they were watching for me to go out alone. But as you know I almost never do go out alone because I Gate from here."

"I do not like the sound of that at all," Aleneil said, pushing away her plate. "But I do not see how it is connected with delaying the queen's note to you."

Denoriel also put aside his near empty plate. "I think there was a dual purpose to that delay. First to make it seem as if I were indifferent to Catherine's summons. She has been hurt by the way that the Council and Hertford have thrust her aside, and she tends to see offense where there is none. Secondly, I believe, although I have no real evidence because the men are dead, that Seymour used that delay in my coming to call those two henchmen from watching this house and set them on the road from Chelsea to ambush me."

"Oh, dear Mother," Aleneil breathed. "Were you hurt?"

"No," Denoriel said sourly. "I just told you that the men were dead. At the time I thought . . . no, I did not think at all. They shot at me—I was riding Miralys—and I flew into such a rage at the thought that an iron arrow might have touched my elven-steed that I set out to kill them . . . and I did. So then, of course, there was no way to discover with any certainty who had set the ambush."

His twin shook her head in bewilderment. "But—but to seek to kill you because Queen Catherine spoke to you and used you as a messenger . . . that is mad. Quite mad."

"Seymour is a man who thinks the world should turn only as he directs it," Denoriel said sourly. Bad enough that he was entangled in a covert Underhill conflict, but to be caught up in mortal machinations was outside the pale. "He may have uttered some criticism of me to the queen—hinted she should not demean herself by associating with a common merchant. Then, likely, she tried to defend herself by telling him I was no *common* merchant, that I was an exiled prince, and that I was as rich as Croesus. It is possible that her praise made me seem in some way dangerous to his hold on her."

"Still to set men to kill you—"

Aleneil stopped speaking as the sound of the knocker from the front door came faintly into the room. She glanced out and saw that though the sun had set, the narrow alley alongside the house was still quite light. The knocker sounded again. Denoriel got to his feet.

Denoriel frowned. "I thought Cropper was still here. He does not usually go home until dark, but I had better see who that is. Thomas would not like it if I turned away a customer desperate enough to come at this hour."

But the knocker did not sound again. Denoriel shrugged, thinking whoever had been at the door had given up. He moved away from the table, about to join Aleneil who had gone back to the fire, when there was a scratch at his office door.

"Ah," Denoriel said softly to Aleneil, "Cropper was still here, just a bit slow to answer the door." And then raising his voice he said, "Come."

Cropper opened the door. "M'lord," he said "there is a lady askin' for ye, but—"

A frantic voice on the other side of Cropper's massive voice called out. "Aleneil! Aleneil, I can feel you. Tell Denoriel to let me in."

"Rhoslyn!" Aleneil cried, jumping to her feet and running to the door.

Cropper flattened himself against the door to be out of the

way, and as Aleneil passed him, slipped out into the corridor. Denoriel came to the door himself, watching the dark-haired, dark-eyed young woman as she reached a hand toward Aleneil. He put his hand on his sword hilt.

But Rhoslyn spared no more than a glance at the sword, and returned her pleading gaze to Aleneil. "Please! I mean no harm. I come to warn you of danger. Please listen to me."

Aleneil flashed a repressive look at Denoriel, took Rhoslyn's hand, and drew her forward into the room. She led her to the chair in which she had been sitting and gestured for her to seat herself.

"What are you doing here, Rhoslyn?" Aleneil asked. "I thought you were with Lady Mary."

About to shut the door, instead Denoriel stepped aside so the servants could come in and clear the table.

"Pasgen was afraid Denoriel would not get his warning or that he would dismiss it and not tell you about it." Rhoslyn fairly radiated alarm and sincerity. This—was certainly new.

"Denoriel had no warning from Pasgen." Aleneil turned her head to look at her brother. The servants went out and closed the door. "Did you get a warning that you dismissed?"

"After what I told you happened on the road from Chelsea? No, I certainly would not have dismissed it. I got no . . . Oh. Grace of God! That must have been the letter from my 'countryman' that Joseph told me about." Denoriel laughed and shook his head. "I thought he meant someone pretending to be an exiled Hungarian. I will go—no, we will all go together into Joseph's office, and I will get the note."

"You cannot fetch a letter from your man of business' desk alone?" Aleneil asked in some surprise.

"No, I cannot leave you alone here with Rhoslyn."

"Rhoslyn will do me no harm!" Aleneil said sharply, seeing the sudden glisten of tears in the dark Sidhe's eyes. "And if she wished to, I am a woman full grown and can defend myself."

Denoriel's mouth opened, then when Aleneil's brows rose in affronted inquiry, he closed it and went out. The light, even though Joseph's room had windows on both the wall in the front of the house and on the side alley, was definitely dimmer. Had Denoriel been human, he would have had to light one of the candelabra on the desk to see, but it was bright enough for

Sidhe eyes. He picked up the sealed note on the top of the pile and hurried back.

Aleneil had taken a seat in the corner of the sofa closest to Rhoslyn's chair and was listening to Rhoslyn describe life in Mary's household.

"I could not see that I was the least necessary. She has been reading prayers for the dead and lessons on the immortal soul since the day Henry's death was announced." Rhoslyn looked exasperated. As well she might. Even by the standards of a pious mortal, Mary's state of mourning was excessive. "She was not invited to the funeral or Edward's coronation—and I think that very wrong. She is the heir apparent. Should she not bear witness to her brother's—" Rhoslyn stopped abruptly as Denoriel came in and closed the door behind him.

As Aleneil and Rhoslyn watched, Denoriel cracked the wax seal and opened the note. "Ah, definitely from Pasgen," he said. "It is written in Elven." His eyes traveled over the short note. "And it is definitely a warning." Denoriel looked at Aleneil. "Apparently my guesses about Queen Catherine's suitor were wrong. I assumed that Vidal would have no way to hire mortal assassins, but it seems that Aurilia's pet mortal healer has the connections necessary."

Aleneil frowned. "I do not know whether I am more relieved that you have no mortal enemy so close as Queen Catherine's household or more distressed over Aurilia's mixing herself into this business. She was the one who wished to be rid of Elizabeth's maid. Perhaps that failure scared her away from attempts on Elizabeth's servants, but if she is now threatening you . . ."

Denoriel shrugged. "I will be careful not to travel alone in the future and raise shields if I must." He laid the letter on the small table beside the chair in which he had been sitting and turned to Rhoslyn, his lips curved in what was not a smile. "Please thank Pasgen for his warning, which was conveniently delivered nearly a week too late."

"Too late?" Rhoslyn cried. "That is impossible. Pasgen only learned of this yesterday, and that was when he came here to tell you. A week too late? What can you mean?"

"I mean that an ambush was set for me on the road between Chelsea and London four days ago."

"Four days ago? How can that be? Yesterday when Pasgen

left that letter for you Albertus had not yet chosen the men he intended to employ. He said he was on his way to do so when Pasgen came here to warn you. Unless Albertus lied?" Rhoslyn wrung her hands and her shoulders drooped with defeat. "If it is so, I am sorry. Pasgen did not dare touch Albertus' mind because then Aurilia would know and the plans would be changed. He thought it would be safer if we knew what Albertus intended."

"So this Albertus was not discouraged by the loss of two of his men? I killed the two who attacked me near Chelsea."

"Chelsea?" Rhoslyn repeated, frowning. "You mean the attack on you was near Chelsea? That cannot have been Albertus' work. Did I not hear you say before that you suspected some mortal of instigating that attack?"

"Yes," Aleneil said. "A suitor of Queen Catherine's has taken a strong dislike to her association with a common merchant like Denoriel."

She was going to explain further when there was a scratch on the door. When Denoriel called "Come," Cropper entered, carrying a lamp. He looked around the dark room and shook his head gently as if the failure to light the candles was no more than he expected. Nonetheless he asked politely if he should do so. Aleneil hastily agreed, and when he had used a spill, ignited at the lamp he carried, to set aflame the candles in the candelabra on the mantelpiece and on the long table near the inner wall, he picked up the lamp and bowed.

"Is there anything further I can do, m'lord? Bring up some more wine? Make tea for the ladies?"

"No, thank you, Cropper, we will manage on our own."

"Yes, m'lord," Cropper said, but he looked doubtful and then added uncertainly, "The other servants, they're gone, m'lord. Do you want me to stay?"

Denoriel shook his head gravely. "No. Go home and have your evening meal, Cropper. You are just across the garden. If I need you or Mistress Cropper I can just step out back and give you a call."

The man looked troubled but said, "Very well, m'lord. The front door is only locked, m'lord, not barred, so that Master Clayborne can let himself in. I'll go out that way so you won't have to replace the bar on the back door, but if you want me wife, you'll have to walk around the house, or take down the bar on the back door . . ."

"All right, Cropper," Denoriel said. "You can go now."

Still looking anxious, the man bowed himself out, closing the door behind him.

Meanwhile Rhoslyn had been thinking hard, putting aside the shock that had all but numbed her when Denoriel said Pasgen's warning had come too late, that he had already been attacked. She sat up straighter.

"I do not wish to add to your troubles Denoriel"—the very faint curve of the corners of her mouth implied the words were not completely sincere—"but I think you will be safer if you accept the fact that you have two enemies, not one. Albertus' plans did not include an ambush on the road between here and Chelsea. He told Pasgen that he had a way to get into this house to attack as soon as you and Aleneil—"

"Aleneil!" Denoriel repeated. "Who would threaten Aleneil? You are making this up for some crazy purpose—"

"I do not think so," Aleneil interrupted. "Do you not remember that we talked about Vidal trying to strip Elizabeth of all support, all stability? How better to do that than to remove *both* of us. Aurilia's servant must be trying to accomplish Vidal's purpose. Think how vulnerable Elizabeth would be to a lover who offered support and comfort if you and I were both dead."

"Yes," Rhoslyn put in. "And how better to be rid of both of you than to attack you with iron and steel weapons when a mortal would think you were asleep in your beds? That is what he told Pasgen he planned. And Aurilia believes Oberon would not punish her or Vidal if *you* were destroyed, especially by mortal means." Her sober expression gave him pause.

"How could this Albertus know when Aleneil and I were here and asleep in our beds? Those men who watched the house . . . But they have been gone for days. The servants cannot speak enough English to send a message . . ." Denoriel hesitated, then looked at Aleneil and said, his voice flat with pain, "Joseph? Was that why he went out?"

"If you think a message went to this Albertus from one of your servants," Aleneil said quickly, "it is more likely Cropper than Joseph. But I doubt either one is involved. Far more likely, if he is conversant with the underbelly of London, Albertus has set beggars or children to watch the house. No one pays them any mind."

Denoriel brightened immediately. "You are right. Children run by all day long, and I've seen beggars at the corner where Mercery meets Poultry. With a little care, the beggar could look down Bucklersbury and see this house very well. So we may assume that Albertus knows we are both here. Will he act at once? Should we perhaps put out the lights and pretend we have gone up to bed? But what are we to do with Rhoslyn?"

"I would do what I could to help," Rhoslyn said hesitantly, "but I am afraid I do not well endure Cold Iron. I fear I might fail at some critical moment."

Denoriel's lips parted to say he had been considering how to restrain her, not whether they should enlist her help, but Aleneil forestalled him.

"I do not want to put you into danger, Rhoslyn," his sister said warmly. "Not only from the weapons these men will carry but from the chance that one of them will escape. If he should tell Albertus that another woman was here and describe you . . . Word might get back to Aurilia and from her to Vidal."

Rhoslyn shuddered slightly and then said very softly, "I would not care. I am so tired of the Dark ways. I am ready to . . . But I do not know what Pasgen wants to do. And I could not—cannot be separated from Pasgen."

Aleneil leaned forward and took her hand. "Then go and tell him you have warned us and we are on our guard."

Chapter 13

Joseph Clayborne was uncomfortable. Of course he had never been completely at ease with the lady who had so incomprehensibly approached him and invited his attentions, but this pressing invitation for tonight had been entirely unexpected. She said her usual visitor could not come and she was suddenly free and without company. Would he not join her so she would not languish in loneliness.

By all rights, this lady should have been far above his touch. Not that Joseph underestimated himself. In fact, now that he felt himself to be firmly established with Adjoran, Mercer and Factor, not only as the man of business but as a small trader in his own right, Joseph had begun a negotiation for the hand of a lovely and very clever young woman from a well-established family of apothecaries. That had nothing whatever to do with this present arrangement.

He had never been completely comfortable, but he had enjoyed the lady's company enormously. She was witty and pretty and had quite a remarkable repertoire of sexual twists and styles. What made him uncomfortable was that, aside from the substantial fee she graciously accepted as a gift, she had made no demands on him. In his limited experience . . . that was unusual.

When she first approached him, Joseph had assumed she had been assigned by a more consequential lover to drain him of what he knew about Adjoran, Mercer and Factor. It seemed a logical reason for a lady of her type to bother with so simple a man as himself. He was prepared to give her some inconsequential information or to put her off. That, he expected, would be the end of their relationship.

Still, he could enjoy her while it lasted. But she never had questioned him about Lord Denno. On his earlier visits, there had been little pretense about the purpose of their meeting. They had talked about light, inconsequential things, shared a few cups of wine, and hopped into bed. He had been finely wrung out each time, but as soon as he was ready to depart the lady was glad enough to see him go.

Tonight was different. She had plied him with wine and really put herself out to divert him with talk. If he had not been quite clever in getting rid of some of the wine and refusing more, he would have been roaring drunk—or asleep like the dead. And she was very interested in the arrival of Lady Alana.

Through the slight haze in his thinking caused by the wine he had not been able to avoid, Joseph wondered how she knew about Lady Alana's arrival. Lady Alana had come on horseback without any fanfare, escorted by two of Lady Elizabeth's men, who had returned to Enfield as soon as Lady Alana was safely in the house.

The questions about Lady Alana, the insistent offer of more wine after he had refused and said if he drank more he would be incapable of achieving his primary purpose, and the repeated delay—teasing and titillating but nonetheless deliberate delay—in coming to that primary purpose, drove Joseph from mild unease into active discomfort.

"Come, let us to bed," he said firmly, and when the lady laughed and remarked that he would be well rewarded for just a little more patience, he stood up and reached for his gown, adding, "Then I will go. I have been patient long enough. I want to be home before morning."

"Why?" the lady asked, rising also. She pulled his hand away from his gown and flung her arms around his neck. "The house is not empty and will be quite safe. I do not expect any other company. Why do you not plan to stay the night?"

Joseph was drunk enough to be strongly aroused by the lush body pressed against his—and just barely sober enough to know there was something wrong about the lady's manner and the offer she was making. The combination of the haze of wine and the sharp struggle against that haze made him more duplicitous than he usually was (outside of business). He agreed at once to stay the night, unhooked his sword from his belt, and began to remove his clothing; then he helped the lady remove her clothing, at a rate somewhat faster than she had intended.

Naked, he plastered his lips to hers, preventing her from protesting, and bore her backward onto her bed. In the past, with an eye ahead to an innocent young bride, Joseph had been more than willing to make love slowly and learn from an expert what would stimulate a woman; tonight he plunged ahead, driving to his own climax without regard to whether he was giving equal satisfaction to his partner. And then he rolled off the bed, rose to his feet, and began to drag on his clothing, ignoring the lady's cries of protest.

If his suspicions were unfounded, if he arrived at home and found all quiet and serene, he would send the lady a lavish gift. He would apologize for his boorishness, blaming his unaccustomed overindulgence in wine. If she were innocent of any particular purpose in delaying him tonight, likely she would forgive him and nothing would be lost.

But now that he had slammed the door on her protests and curses over his sudden departure, that seemed less and less likely. If, as he now feared, she had been paid in one way or another to seek him out and offer him her favors just so she could draw him out of the house on Bucklersbury tonight, he would never see her again. Unless—Joseph's teeth set hard—if harm had come to his master or his master's cousin, he would see to it that she was never able to play such games again!

He shook his head as he hurried along the street. No, he realized, she had guarded against that. He doubted, now that he stopped to think about it, that the lady lived in the rooms in which she had entertained him. They were well furnished and even elegant, but there had been no more than a dressing gown and a few extra garments, nothing like the wardrobe such a lady would have. And the name she had given him, only the Christian name, of course, was undoubtedly false as well.

As he careened along the street, Joseph felt in his pocket for the key to the house. When he was sure it was there, he breathed a sigh of relief followed by a black frown. Had he ever missed it when he was with that lady? He did not think so, but he loosened the sword he carried in its scabbard.

Rhoslyn walked westward quickly until she came to Soper Lane and turned left. That was one of the many ways she could have gone to the Gate near Westminster or Otstargi's house. However, as soon as she knew she was out of sight and almost certainly out of sensing distance, her steps slowed. She shrank into the shadow of a recessed doorway—the street was silent and empty but she did not want to draw attention if someone should peer out of a window or if a cutpurse were in hiding to take a lone walker. She had to decide what to do.

She was annoyed by Denoriel's distrust, but had not much cared. What hurt her was that Aleneil, too, did not trust her enough to ask for her help. What Pasgen had said was true. Tears filled her eyes. Even if Elizabeth did come to the throne, the outpouring of creation, of the energy of life, love, art, would not bring light to her life. She would not be welcome among the Bright Court; she would still be alone, cut off from the explosion of joy.

Pasgen, too. Although he never admitted his desire to join the *lios-alfar*, she knew he must have made some attempt and been rejected. She lifted a hand to wipe away the few tears that had wet her cheeks. At least she had Pasgen and he had her. She had better go tell him that she had warned Denoriel and Aleneil and Denoriel had read his note.

Slowly Rhoslyn began to walk toward Otstargi's house, but it was a very long walk. She felt a fool. She could have asked Aleneil to Gate her to one of the markets. From there she could Gate to Otstargi's house where Pasgen should be. She stood still, again irresolute. Would Aleneil be willing to expose Denoriel's Gate to her?

Again she began to walk south, again hesitated. She felt the lindys under the bosom of her gown begin to tremble as her resentment and sense of abandonment grew, and she patted it, hoping to quiet it despite the heavy cloak. She did not want to alarm Pasgen. Thought of him started a cold sense of alarm that again stopped her motion.

Where was Pasgen? Had that trembling of the lindys been a reflection of her emotion or the beginning of a warning that Pasgen was in trouble? What if Pasgen had come upon Albertus while he was with the bravos he was hiring? What if Albertus had turned those bravos on Pasgen? Rhoslyn turned and began to hurry back the way she had come. She would demand the use of a Gate!

The house was completely dark when she arrived and her sense of panic had diminished. As she realized how silly she had been, the lindys, which had been shaking and twisting, quieted so that she was assured it was her emotion to which it had been responding, not to any need of Pasgen's. Still, by now she was nearly exhausted. The thought of beginning a long trek to Westminster or Otstargi's house held no charm.

Rhoslyn climbed two of the steps to the door, and stopped. She remembered suddenly that Denoriel employed Low Court servants but that Cropper had said they had all gone. Gone where? Back to their trees or groves, of course. The beings of the Low Court loved to come to the mortal world. She was sure that Denoriel's servants wandered the shops and markets of London spending gold he kenned for them, but they could not long be separated from their life-sustaining ties Underhill. So they must have a Gate.

Breathing a sigh of relief, Rhoslyn went down the steps and around toward the side of the building. She was sure she would be able to sense a Gate. And a Gate that allowed a gaggle of Low Court elves to pass would certainly accept her. A step at a time she paced the alley but there was no resonance that thrummed Gate to her. It was not in the alley then. She sighed but with resignation. She had not really expected it to be in the alley.

One terminus must be in the house, but she had hoped the one used by the servants would be outside. Yet it must be in some kind of shelter so that people passing the alley or even walking through it would not see the servants disappear. The stable, of course. She walked more quickly to where the alley ended in a pair of rough double doors.

What a fool she was, she thought again. If she could find the servants' Gate, that would be fine, but if she could not, she would just borrow the man of business' horse. She hoped he had not taken the horse that night. She did not think he had from what the footman said.

The lock that held together the doors of the small building was a simple one. She magicked it open without any difficulty. The horse, as she hoped, was there; it whickered softly when she approached the stall and moved readily to the side when she slapped it gently. She rubbed its cheek and muzzle and then stepped out of the stall to feel for a Gate.

No Gate. Even closed, this close to it she should feel some resonance and she did not. But something came and went in that stable by no mortal means. Rhoslyn stood still, extending her sense for detecting magic. Not elven magic, yet . . . She passed behind the horse to the second stall, which was empty. Empty? But Denoriel was in the house. Oh. His elvensteed. Of course it would not remain in a mortal stable. When Denoriel needed it, the elvensteed would simply be there.

For a long moment she was racked with envy. She had given the not-horses a kind of life, even a kind of beauty; she had given them strength and endurance, but there was no way she could give them magic. For a moment longer, she stood in the empty stall thinking of the power and magic of the elvensteeds—and in that moment her ears cupped without her volition, responding to a sound, a soft secretive sound . . . a voice, a man's voice, in a harsh whisper, a light scratching as on a closed door . . .

Rhoslyn froze, then came swiftly but silently to the stable door and inched it open. It was full dark. Even Sidhe eyes could not see with perfect clarity, but once the door was open she heard more. Stealthy movement, a foot scuffing on a gravel path, scratching again. Rhoslyn slipped out of the stable, crossed the alley and crept along the side of the house to the back wall.

Counting on the relative night-blindness of humans, she peered around the corner. Her breath caught as her sensitive ears heard the scraping of the bars of the back door being lifted, the snick of the lock being turned. Who could be the traitor? Could the man of business have hidden himself instead of leaving? The footman, Cropper, did he just pretend to go to his own home so he could open the back door for these murderers? Was that why Cropper made a point of the front not being barred? So that Denoriel and Aleneil would watch the front if they watched at all?

A shadow shifted and then disappeared. Rhoslyn bit her lip. What should she do? A second shadow shifted and slipped inside the door. If she called out, would Denoriel or Aleneil hear her? If she called out, would not those men with their steel weapons turn on her? She shuddered and whimpered. What good would her death, such a horrible death, do? She had no weapon. She could do nothing to help. Surely Aleneil and Denoriel, having been warned, were on their guard.

A third and fourth shadow disappeared into the house. And then a fifth and sixth came out of the dimness near the back fence and moved forward. No. However strong a swordsman Denoriel was, he could not withstand the steel weapons of six against him. And Aleneil had no weapon at all! She had been wearing mortal court dress, carrying not even a little eating knife.

Without deliberate intention, because she could not help herself, Rhoslyn moved around the edge of the house, pressing herself into the deeper shadow against the wall. The intruders, intent on their own business, paid her no attention. She saw the fifth man slide in through the open door and suddenly a fear even more horrible than that for Aleneil and Denoriel took hold of her mind.

If Pasgen had not found Albertus at Otstargi's house, he might come to meet her here. Gate-master that he was, he would surely come by Gate, and Denoriel's Gate was inside the house! That would expose Pasgen to fools who could not tell one Sidhe from another.

Her lindys thrashed frantically against her bosom adding to her terror even as her hand clamped hard against it. Stupid! Stupid to allow herself to be so moved. Now it was too late! Pasgen would think she was in danger. Even if he had no intention of coming before she fell prey to imaginary terrors, now he would come to her.

Before any thought of what she would do came into her mind, Rhoslyn had cast the Don't-see-me spell and leapt forward as she saw the sixth man step toward the open door. She was on his heels, so close that she almost cried out against the terrible ache the weapons he carried awoke in her. Worse, he felt the movement of the air around him and spun around. Rhoslyn had to leap again, away to the side.

She almost slammed into the large table used for preparing food. She caught herself, teetering dangerously, but found her balance. Impact with the table would have exposed her to the thugs. Don't-see-me did not bestow invisibility; it only made eyes slip away, refusing to register what was bespelled. Touch and sound remained. If she hit the table, it might have shifted or the thud of her impact might have drawn close enough attention to her that the spell would be disrupted and she would become visible.

She froze where she had come to rest, back against the counter where pots and pans, long forks and carving knives, were laid ready for the next day's work. Fearing her violent movement might have betrayed her, she did not stir again. Breath held, moving only her eyes, she gazed around, but none of the men had turned in her direction. All were as still as she, looking toward the door into the dining room. Behind them, the back door began to close.

At first Rhoslyn's breath caught again when she thought it was being closed by magic; a mage would surely find her. Then she saw small, pale hands pushing against it. A child! Of course, the Low Court Sidhe who were Denoriel's servants would let in a child. They would be delighted to feed it and let it warm itself against the winter cold. If the child hid, they would lightly forget it or think it had run out again.

Bitterness rose in Rhoslyn's throat. She had not understood until this moment, when she realized that neither of Denoriel's servants had deliberately betrayed him, how much she envied him their obvious, open affection. Her constructs would die for her—because they did not know what life was, because they were bespelled to obey and protect, not because they cared for her.

Before the door closed all the way, the child slipped out, the movement drawing Rhoslyn's attention. One of the men, cursing under his breath, came to close the door, which he secured only with the latch. Carefully Rhoslyn slid away from him to reduce the pain his weapons caused. And then she blinked down at the counter where the tools and vessels for eating and drinking lay.

Even in the dark of the unlit chamber those tools and vessels were bright. Far brighter than any iron would shine . . . Rhoslyn had to bite her lip to keep from laughing. Of course! Since the servants in Denoriel's house were Low Court Sidhe, there could be no iron. Every tool and vessel in the house was made of pure silver or the special alloy of silver, tin, and brass that was harder than steel.

The men had been all clumped together near the door that opened into the dining chamber at the front of the house, opposite Clayborne's office. Now the one who had closed the door went to the banked hearth. A moment later, a spill woke into flame and from it, flame touched the candle in a small lantern. The light was abruptly cut off when the door of the dark lantern was closed, but another was lit and then muffled.

Rhoslyn could see one of the lanterns being passed forward,

then the man closest to the door lifted the latch. A lantern was uncovered. Rhoslyn could see the men filing through the door and she snatched up two of the longest knives from the counter. One she held with practiced ease; the other she thrust though her belt. If she could, she would give it to Aleneil; if she could not, she would have an extra weapon if the first were torn away.

Silently, her heart pounding in her throat, she followed the men through the dining room. The man with the lantern had opened one of the double doors to the corridor. He touched another of the men, who unshielded the second lantern and stepped out of the door. Over the shoulder of the first man with the lantern, she saw the second turn toward the stairs; two men followed him. All tread carefully near the wall so that if a stair was loose it would not squeak.

Again Rhoslyn was racked with indecision. The house was utterly silent. The little light cast by the lantern, barely enough for the humans to see their way up the stairs, gave light enough for Rhoslyn to make out two closed doors in the upper corridor. But why had not her half sister and brother burst out of the door of Denoriel's chamber and attacked the intruders? Could Aleneil and Denoriel have dismissed the warning she and Pasgen had given? Should she shout a new warning? Should she stab the man closest to her and kill him?

Even as the thought came to her and she stepped closer, intending to reduce her half siblings' enemies by at least one, pain grew in her. It seemed to echo through her body, as if that body were empty and she realized that the hand that held the knife was trembling. The Don't-see-me spell was draining her and in the mortal world there was no way to renew her power. If she struck and the spell died . . . if she shouted . . . the three men still in the room would be upon her.

In the moment that she stood paralyzed between fear and fear, her need to decide was gone. The second group of three men went out into the corridor and began to mount the stairs. The first three were on the landing, bunched together, and suddenly one of the closed doors burst open. A gleaming blue levin bolt struck the man with the lantern. He screamed and fell.

Rhoslyn leapt forward, seized the hair of the last man, pulled his head back, and slit his throat. She had not realized how sharp the knife she carried was. The throat was slit far more thoroughly than she intended so that the man's head came loose and he fell forward, fountaining blood and striking the man ahead of him. That man shouted and turned, thrusting instinctively with the sword he carried.

Fortunately Rhoslyn was already staggering backward because a second levin bolt flew down the stairs. It was a shimmering silver, not a hard, glowing blue like the first. The man attacking Rhoslyn screamed and staggered but did not fall, somehow twisting to face where the blow had come from. That was just as well because, between shock and pain, Rhoslyn's spell failed and she lay in the corridor momentarily exposed and defenseless.

Pasgen had not found Albertus at Otstargi's house. The mind of the servant told him, however, that Albertus had been there and that he nearly always returned just about sunset when he sent the servant out to buy food and sometimes drink. Pasgen decided to wait. He occupied himself pleasantly enough with some of the books he had purchased years before to give verisimilitude to Otstargi's study. Some of the human misconceptions about magic recorded in those books were amusing, and here and there he had found a spell or a concept that was new and of value.

As the light dimmed, Pasgen became aware of the tension in his lindys. He put the book down and concentrated. Ah, Rhoslyn had found Denoriel and Aleneil together. He tensed, starting to grow angry at the thought they might expel her without a hearing, but then the lindys grew calmer, although not in its full resting state. Apparently they, or at least Aleneil, were listening to what Rhoslyn had to say.

Pasgen went back to his book, although half his attention was now on the lindys, but it was quiet, no more than mildly tense, as it would be if Rhoslyn was talking to those with whom she was not perfectly comfortable. Eventually, however, he set the book aside and frowned.

He had been distracted by fearing for Rhoslyn's hurt, but now the fact that Denoriel and Aleneil were together in the house on Bucklersbury reminded him that that was what Albertus was waiting for. And Pasgen knew it was not common. Likely one or both would be gone on the morrow and it might be long before they were again together in the house.

Pasgen glanced out the window. He had been reading for longer than he thought. It was past sunset. Mortals would consider it dark, and Albertus had not come back to Otstargi's house, which according to the servant had been his custom. The break in Albertus' habitual behavior indicated a strong probability that he had seized his chance and sent out the men he had hired that very night. Pasgen stood up, irresolute. Had Albertus gone with his hired killers to the house on Bucklersbury or was he waiting in whatever place he had used for hiring them to hear of their success?

Should *he* go to Bucklersbury? Pasgen's lips thinned. If he showed himself in the middle of an attack, Denoriel would be most likely to spit him before asking why he was there. But— Then the lindys under his collar convulsed. Pasgen ran to the door and was halfway up the stairs to the Gate in the bedchamber before he realized the creature was quiet again. He stopped on the stair and concentrated.

Dark. Ahead of him an open road, empty and silent. Rhoslyn was no longer in the house with Aleneil and Denoriel. What could have caused that spurt of fear? He tried to "see" through the senses he had bespelled into the lindys, but there did not seem to be anything to see and the intense fear was gone. Rhoslyn was uneasy, but not from any threat to her.

He stood on the stair, half turned to go down and pick up his book again. He was aware that Rhoslyn had decided something; she was in movement. He went down two steps, shook his head, and looked upward. He thought that Rhoslyn was on her way back to the house on Bucklersbury. What a fool she was! Had they not already turned away her offer of help?

He and Rhoslyn had done their best and tried to give warning. If those high-nosed Seleighe Sidhe would not listen, their hurt was on their own heads. But if there were an attack and Rhoslyn mixed herself into it . . . Pasgen spat an oath and began to run up the stairs.

Rhoslyn could create, but she had long ago lost her taste for pain. She had not even ridden in the Wild Hunt for years. She was no warrior. He had better be ready to go to her defense . . . and the Gate in the house on Bucklersbury had been designed by Treowth.

Pasgen spit another obscenity as he closed Otstargi's bedchamber door behind him. He had once tried to divert the termini of one of Treowth's Gates to the holding cell in his domain and had been finely scorched for his temerity. Would he be able—not to change anything; he would not try that again—to convince the Gate to let him pass through it? His body resonances were much like those of Denoriel, half brothers as they were.

He had to find the Gate first, Pasgen thought. He began carefully, bringing up the pattern-taker in his own Gate and searching through it for the feel of Treowth's work. He found a flicker, but it was very faint, something far distant. He tried again, felt a shiver of response which then slipped away.

Had he not been specially attuned to Gates he would not have caught it at all. Now more slowly he felt for a pattern, felt, sensed . . . And it was there, so clear, so sharp, and yet so very, very narrow that in his surprise at finding it so strong, he lost it again.

It was easier to find the second time, although it nearly slipped away from him again as he took a breath. Carefully, he touched it, seeking its resonance. And it was gone again! His sense of it had slid to one side or the other. Marshaling his patience, because haste and anger would lose the thread entirely, he scanned once more.

Knowing for what he was looking brought him to the band of magic more quickly. He found it, seized it. Listened . . . And his lindys went mad!

He could not concentrate on the lindys to see what was wrong with Rhoslyn and hold the Gate at the same time. Cursing, he fixed his mind on his sister, saw her watching shadows slipping into an opened door. Pasgen uttered a few more choice words. She did not fear for herself but for those Seleighe idiots. At the moment Rhoslyn was in no danger.

Now he would need to begin searching for that thread of a Gate all over again. But it was not at all difficult this time. It was as if the Gate was coming to know, to accept his touch. The lindys while not convulsing was highly agitated. Pasgen set his teeth and ignored it, striving to bring the pattern of Denoriel's Gate into the pattern-taker of his own Gate so that he would have a sure and permanent entry.

A flare of heat. Pasgen released the Gate pattern immediately. For a brief moment before he steadied them, his lips trembled. Treowth's work was so far beyond his own. He had no idea what protections the Magus Major had put upon Denoriel's Gate. And when Pasgen had applied to study with him, Treowth had refused him. He had said that to teach an Unseleighe Sidhe with Pasgen's talent more magic was an invitation to catastrophe.

No oath Pasgen had offered to swear had changed Treowth's mind. Pasgen had found himself, quite suddenly, back in his own domain. How Treowth had been able to place him there, Pasgen had no idea. Even Rhoslyn did not actually know where his domain was, only a path that would take her there.

The movement of the lindys was growing more and more violent. Pasgen spared a moment to look again. Saw Rhoslyn take up two knives and begin to follow on the heels of the invaders. No! Pasgen shouted mentally, cursing himself for not bespelling Rhoslyn's lindys as completely as his own.

He swallowed hard and pushed away his sense of what Rhoslyn was doing to feel again for the pattern of Treowth's Gate. This time he found it immediately, just as the lindys almost pulled itself free of its tether to his tunic. He had one searing vision from it of Rhoslyn fallen, of a body spewing blood nearly at her feet, of a man with a sword twisting above her . . .

Pasgen threw himself into his own Gate, holding the resonance of Treowth's Gate fiercely in his mind. He fell through darkness but not into light. He was lost in the Between! He was dead! No, not yet. Holding with all his strength to the pattern of Treowth's Gate, he forced himself physically forward in the darkness and slammed into something hard that fell with a loud crash.

Chapter 14

The collapse and shattering of Denoriel's very costly cheval glass startled the three men who had driven him back against the wall of the upper corridor. Denoriel himself was too far gone in pain and exhaustion to be startled. His mind was fixed on the only thing that could save him—if the destruction of his ability to do magic could be called salvation. But it was not only his own life that power could save. Aleneil was rapidly failing before the attack of the fourth thug.

In that one moment of distracted attention of the three men menacing him, Denoriel reached for the thin white line of power within the diffuse cloud of energy that was the exhalation of mortal life. He drew it in, crying out as the power seared through the channels in his body. The desperate dragging weakness that had been growing worse with each parry to ward away the steel weapons of his attackers, was suddenly gone. The sword, which had begun to feel as heavy and unwieldy as a full-grown tree, was again light and lithe, an extension of the hand that held it like a long, deadly finger.

Denoriel beat away the most immediate threat, that of the man to his left. He scored on the hand that held the sword, but not deeply enough to make the man drop the weapon. And he was desperately aware that the man to his right was about to thrust with the hand in which he held his dagger. If the steel touched

Denoriel's body, he would be lost. Then, incredibly, the door of his bedchamber flew open and a blue bolt struck the attacker, who did not even have time to scream before he fell.

Pasgen uttered a foul oath. He had not meant that levin bolt to save Denoriel; he had meant it for the man turning away from Aleneil to menace Rhoslyn, who, shaking with pain and weakness, was nonetheless climbing the stairs, knife in hand. But Pasgen was disoriented. He had thought himself lost in the Between that linked Gate to Gate. He had given himself up to a most horrible death, until he was aware of pushing physically against the solid wall of darkness that imprisoned him.

Physically? One could not move physically when traveling by Gate. The crash Pasgen generated when he overturned the cheval glass, had jerked his eyes open. He had not realized that he had closed them in his fear of invading Treowth's Gate. The utter blackness he had thought was Between, lightened at once into a dim bedchamber. With his last image of a man, sword in hand, turning on Rhoslyn, Pasgen drew lavishly on his inner strength to form a levin bolt. And when he burst out of the door of Denoriel's bedchamber, he loosed that bolt at the first sword wielder he saw.

The wrong man! Denoriel had been driven to the left along the passage almost into the corner. The stairway, rising along the wall of the kitchen, was more central. The man turning to menace Rhoslyn was to Pasgen's right. Pasgen drew a hard breath, already aching with the closeness of all that bared steel, and found he had not sufficient power to form another bolt. Yet Denoriel, who had been at his last gasp of energy, was now fighting his two remaining opponents like a demon. What had renewed him?

At that moment, Rhoslyn cried out with pain as she managed to block the attacker's sword thrust with the long knife she carried. But though the weapon did not touch her, it had some inimical effect. She staggered down a step, still clinging to the rail, but her hand was already loosening its grip. Pasgen reached for his sword—and realized that he had not worn it, since he did not fear Albertus. He had no weapon and the steel sword was drawn back to thrust at Rhoslyn again.

Desperately Pasgen cast the feeble amount of energy he had dredged up and then almost fell to his knees. He had never been so drained, so empty of power. The man, struck by the stinging but essentially harmless flickers of energy, howled and swung around . . .

And the front door burst open, admitting a furious-looking mortal, sword in hand, who rushed up the stairs, shoving past Rhoslyn, to engage the thug.

"I knew it! I knew it!" the mortal cried, slamming aside the attacker's sword, and driving his own weapon into the man's chest with such ferocity that the point jammed on some bone.

Cursing violently, the mortal pushed the wounded man to the floor, put his foot on the screaming thug, and yanked his sword free. Without a second glance, he left the shrieking man lying on the floor while he rushed toward Denoriel, who was still engaged with two opponents.

Meanwhile Pasgen had gathered enough strength to stagger to the stairs. He found Rhoslyn still clinging to the banister and trying valiantly to crawl upward.

"Knife," she whispered, her eyes running tears of pain and weakness. "Give Aleneil the knife."

She thrust the thing into Pasgen's hand, which had started to shrink away. But even as the knife touched him he realized that it could not be a steel weapon or Rhoslyn could not have held it.

"Hold your weapon," he said. "I—"

"I have another," she said, her voice a little stronger; her hand went to her belt. "Save Aleneil."

Knife in hand, Pasgen stood. Aleneil, although barely able to keep erect, was in no immediate danger—no danger at all, really, as Denoriel had just thrust his sword through one attacker's throat, releasing a river of blood. Pasgen could see his half brother grimace as a spray of the blood hit him, but he did not wince away, holding himself ready to support the mortal who had come to his aid.

It did not look to Pasgen as if the mortal would need support, but the one he had left on the floor was now only groaning and had begun to fumble for his sword. It occurred to Pasgen that it would be much better if none of the thugs survived. Questioned, they would set a trail to Albertus and through Albertus to Otstargi's house. He took two steps, turned his back so Rhoslyn could not see, and thrust the knife he carried through the thug's eye into his brain. All sound and motion ceased.

Almost simultaneously the mortal fighting against Denoriel's second opponent thrust into the attacker's chest as he had before. This time his aim was better. The thug only had time for a single gasp before the sword pierced his heart and stilled it. By the time Denoriel's swordsman had pulled his weapon free, his opponent was dead.

"God's Grace, Joseph," Denoriel said, "you come most timely. I—"

His voice checked abruptly as he saw Pasgen, with the bloody knife in his hand. His sword rose slightly, then dropped when his eyes went to the man Pasgen's levin bolt had killed. Then his eyes passed Pasgen to Aleneil, wilting but intact against the wall and to Rhoslyn limp on the stairs.

"Aleneil! Rhoslyn! Are you all right?"

"In a moment." Aleneil's voice was shaky, but not faint. "See to Rhoslyn . . . and . . . and Pasgen. They saved us."

"Why are you still standing, Denoriel?" Pasgen asked.

He had backed down the stairs, away from the steel sword and knife that lay near the dead man.

"M'lord!" the mortal's voice was loud and very angry. "If you would take your—your guests into your study, I'll get Cropper and we'll take care of this trash."

"Good God, how?" Denoriel asked.

"Mostly by calling the watch and telling the truth, that these men got in and attacked us. They'll get the constable and he'll have the bodies taken away." Clayborne grimaced suddenly and his hand clenched on the sword he still held. "Tell me, m'lord, how did they get in?" he asked intensely. "Was it through the front door, which wasn't barred?"

"I don't know," Denoriel admitted.

"They came in through the back," Rhoslyn said faintly. "There was a child who unbarred and unlocked the door."

"A child?" Aleneil echoed.

"Pfui!" Clayborne exclaimed. "Those 'foreign' servants of yours are perfect cods-heads where children are concerned, m'lord. They are forever taking in every child beggar and feeding it and giving it any coin they can come by. Really, m'lord, they must harden their hearts . . ." His voice faded and then came again, loud and angry. "But what did they want? It does not take six armed men to rob a house, and—and there is little here. . . ."

Denoriel shook his head. "I fear it is to do with Lady Elizabeth,

Joseph. But I would prefer that you did not use that reason to the authorities. Blame it on that exceptional sale we had last week."

"Yes, m'lord. I know what to say."

While they had been speaking, Joseph had wiped his sword on one of the victim's clothing and sheathed it. Now he came down the corridor, shooing Denoriel before him, and offering his arm to support Aleneil. Denoriel barely glanced at Pasgen as he passed, but paused to help Rhoslyn to her feet and to support her down the remainder of the steps.

As soon as they had entered Denoriel's study and Joseph had closed the door behind them, all the Sidhe began to recover from the pain and weakness the steel caused. There was no iron in Denoriel's chamber. What metal had been used was silver or silver alloy and the plaster and lathe walls kept out the noxious influence from Clayborne's room.

The four stood for a moment just staring at each other, then Denoriel led Rhoslyn to the sofa and seated her in one corner. Without invitation, Pasgen sat in the other corner. Aleneil sank into one of the tall-backed chairs, and Denoriel went to throw some new logs on the fire, which was burning very low. Pasgen, who was pressing his hands against his thighs to still their trembling, watched.

"Thank you," Aleneil said. "I do not understand, but I will ask no questions. Just, thank you. Denoriel and I are alive by your mercy."

"Whatever our differences, you are blood of our blood." Pasgen's voice was harsh. "I would not see you ended for a whim of our . . . ah . . . gracious prince."

"I thank you also." Denoriel did not sound as warmly grateful as Aleneil had, but his voice acknowledged debt. "Can I bring you some refreshment? I have only mortal fluids here, but the claret is sweet and pleasant."

He gestured toward the table at the back of the room where stoppered flasks stood behind an array of glasses.

But Pasgen was staring at him in a kind of greedy wonder. "You do not need to sit down," he said, "yet when I came out of the bedchamber door you were nigh fainting. Where have you found power to resist the steel weapons?"

"I am not so sensitive to the effects of iron as most," Denoriel said.

But even as he spoke, his face took on a puzzled expression and he looked down at himself, almost as if he expected to see something changed or different about his body. He brushed ineffectually at the blood stains on his clothing, then frowned, concern over something taking the place of puzzlement.

Pasgen leaned forward eagerly. "Have you found a way to store power in an amulet or some other . . ."

"No," Denoriel said, for a moment looking even more undecided, and then obviously coming to a conclusion. "There is plenty of power in the mortal world. If you look with your inner eyes you will see a mist or miasma of power. I do not know why we Sidhe cannot draw on it."

"I know about that mist," Pasgen said impatiently. "I tried to draw it in years ago when I came into the mortal world, and could not. I suspect that is what seeps down Underhill. Something in the transit from one world to another makes it usable to us." His eyes widened, his face showing a strange mixture of desire and rejection. "Are you telling me that *you* have found a way to draw power from the mists when I could not?"

"Not from the mists," Denoriel said, and hesitated as if undecided again. But then he looked at Rhoslyn, at the blood still staining Pasgen's hands, and continued, "If you look you will see . . . I do not know quite how to describe it, like clots in the mist, some formed into threads and sometimes even ropes. Do not touch the ropes! They are very dangerous. Power beyond a thousand levin bolts flows in them. I could sense it from a distance when I needed strength, but the Mother kept me from seeking therein. However, the very thinnest threads . . . It is like drinking lightning."

"Is that what you did?" Pasgen asked.

Simultaneously, Aleneil cried, "Oh, Denoriel, you said you never would again!"

Denoriel smiled at her. "And that is what I intended, believe me." He looked from her to Pasgen. "Yes, I drank lightning when I was guarding Harry FitzRoy. I did not know then what a danger it was and I came near to burning out my power channels when I used the mortal power to withstand Vidal in Elizabeth's bedchamber. I could not so much as light a candle or pass through a Gate for near four years."

"Yet you did 'drink lightning' while fighting." Pasgen's voice was utterly neutral as if a conflict between admiration and rejection had brought complete cancellation of emotion.

"Denoriel!"

He laughed gently, coming to bend over Aleneil and kiss her forehead. "When I saw that the choice was between burning away my ability to do magic and death—with your death and Rhoslyn's added in—the loss of magic did not seem so terrible."

Aleneil stood up, holding onto the chair. She was still shaky but determined. "Come. Let us go home. Mwynwen will mend you. Come. Quickly."

Denoriel shook his head and urged her to sit again, going to sit himself in the other chair. "I do not know why, Aleneil, but I do not need mending. I am not in pain, although when I took in that thread it was like a blast of fire and ice together through every vein. But then the pain was gone, and look—" He held out his hand and light glittered along the tips of his fingers.

"Are you sure?" Aleneil asked anxiously.

"It is not something I would be foolhardy about," he assured her and then, looking at Pasgen's rapt expression, "In the Mother's name, Pasgen, if you wish to try that game, be careful. Seek out the smallest, thinnest thread . . . and do not play the game when you are alone."

"A healer mended the damage you took?" Pasgen asked.

"Lady Mwynwen had much experience with power. She had a changeling child that she kept alive for many years—"

"Richey," Rhoslyn breathed.

"Yes," Denoriel said gently. "He was a very happy child, until near the end when feeding him power caused him pain. Perhaps that is why she knew what to do for me."

"But she would not treat one of the Unseleighe?"

"Yes, she would!" Rhoslyn and Denoriel said together.

"She is a true healer," Denoriel added. "I do not think she *can* turn away anyone in need."

Pasgen seemed about to ask another question, but there was a heavy thump in the corridor outside the door. They listened then, aware that there had been voices and heavy footsteps for some time. Pasgen shook his head.

"What have you done to those men that they serve you with such devotion even without orders?" he asked Denoriel, his voice tinged with bitterness and raw envy.

Denoriel laughed softly. "I have lived so long in the mortal world that I think and feel like a mortal. To the men I have done nothing at all, except treat them as a good human master would and put them in the way of bettering themselves. Joseph is honest by nature, and I have made that honesty more profitable to him than trying to steal from me. He feels my trust and gives his in return. As for Cropper, I think his devotion is to Joseph, who rescued him from debtor's prison."

"A little kindness and consideration seem a small price to pay for such loyal service," Rhoslyn murmured.

"In a way, yes. In a way, no." Denoriel sighed. "When you must be considerate, you must think about the person. And when you think about people, you find yourself as bound to them as they are to you."

Aleneil laughed suddenly. "I see you did not need that lecture I gave you, love."

"Again yes and no," Denoriel said, smiling at her. "You reminded me that I must show that I think about them. Mortals cannot read feelings very well."

There had been new noises going on in the background during the conversation. Heads turned to listen as the front door opened and slammed shut and conversation died at the sound of several coarse men's voices loud with shock, more talk, the front door opening and closing again. Finally came a quick scratch on the study door. Denoriel went over and opened it at once.

Joseph Clayborne came in, shut the door behind him, and said softly, "There's only five bodies, m'lord. I thought it would be too hard to explain the man whose throat was slit. Cropper got rid of him while I tapped the two who didn't seem to have any reason to die on the head with his cudgel. A broken skull is good enough reason for furnishing worm's meat. Then I caught the watch and they sent a man off to fetch the constable. Cropper and I are waiting for the constable now, and likely you'll have to answer questions, but they won't be hard ones."

So it proved when the constable, half asleep from being roused from his bed, arrived. He listened to Joseph's tale about the large sum of money he had been forced to carry home and his fear that the house had been watched. He shook his head over Joseph's mistaken assumption that the danger was past so that he and Cropper were alone after he dismissed the extra guards. Cropper agreed to every word Joseph said, and the constable said he could go to bed. Cropper left.

Next it was Denoriel's turn, and he had a most sympathetic listener to his confirmation of Joseph's information. Denoriel then explained about his having met in a nearby inn his cousin's good friend, Mistress Rosamund Scott, a maid of honor to Lady Mary. The constable bowed in respect to the name. Clearly the heir to the throne's maid of honor must not be embarrassed, nor her escort, the Honorable Pasgen Silverhair, harassed.

Thus, Denoriel said, he had unexpectedly returned home to entertain his guests. The constable made shocked noises over their terrible surprise at discovering the invaders and being attacked.

In the end the constable was rather apologetic over the invasion of Lord Denno Adjoran's household, and he admitted that he knew one of the corpses as a clever rogue, who had managed to escape prison. In no time at all, he had ordered the watch to remove the bodies and he had promised a report that would absolve of any blame Lord Denno, his servants, and his friend the Honorable Pasgen Silverhair. It was an odd name, but odd names did come out of Scotland and Wales. He nodded assurance at the picture of a proper English gentleman of good family (except for the odd name and the blood on his hands) with his blond hair and guileless green eyes.

The ladies, though mentioned, were not required to appear. Denoriel begged the indulgence, confessing that his cousin Lady Alana and her friend had been so overcome by the blood and violence that they had needed to be carried up to bed. The constable gave rapid assurance that he would not dream of troubling maids of honor to Lady Mary and Lady Elizabeth and bowed himself out. Everything put him at ease; even if the gentlemen and the servants had killed five men, well they were *gentlemen,* these were common thieves, and they had spared the Crown the expense of a hanging.

The thieves deserved their fate; the handsome house, the nameplate by the door, with which he was familiar, assured him he could find these people again if he had any further questions. He was quite sure he would find that the other corpses were known offenders and he would have no further questions. And that was assuming that his superiors did not tell him to mind his business and let his betters mind theirs.

Peace restored, Pasgen went upstairs to join Rhoslyn and Aleneil and clean the blood off his clothing and person. Denoriel was about to follow when Joseph asked for a word with him, and drew him into his own office. There he proceeded to confess the whole tale of the woman he had been seeing and his suspicion that her purpose had been to keep him away so that Lord Denno and Lady Alana would be without any support or protection.

Denoriel patted him on the shoulder comfortingly and assured him that he had no need to blame himself since it was not his key that had admitted the assassins but the foolishness of Denoriel's own servants. If the lady's only purpose had been to keep him out of the house—that had failed, since Joseph had come just in time to save the groats.

Obviously still shaken by what he felt was dereliction of duty, Joseph burst out, "It will not happen again. I am seeking the hand of Jane Standish, the apothecary's daughter, and if I am successful, I will be busy in my own bed at night in the future."

"My very best wishes!" Denoriel exclaimed, exhaustion making him more amused than, perhaps, the circumstances warranted. "From what you say about sleeping in your own bed, may I hope that you intend to bring Mistress Clayborne here to live? There is that extra room near your bedchamber that could be easily changed into a parlor for your lady. It would be very pleasant for me to have a lady always in the house."

Joseph flushed bright red. "My dear Lord Denno," he said, somewhat breathlessly "I—I did not mean to presume in such a way. Of course, I did think that to live here after I was married would be a great advantage to me, but—but to assume . . . without even asking you . . . That . . . I am ashamed. And I am not even *sure* my suit will be successful."

Denoriel laughed. "I think it will be, and it would be a considerable advantage to me also for you to continue living in the house as I am so much away. But I will not press you, and I will understand if the lady wants a house of her own." He put a hand on Joseph's shoulder. "Your marriage will not change your place here with me, I assure you."

"Thank you, m'lord," Joseph sighed. "I am all shaken to bits tonight. I cannot think of what possessed me to make a statement like that . . . so presumptuous."

Denoriel tightened his grip slightly. "Not presumptuous between friends, as I hope we are. But you are right that we are all shaken to bits. Let us talk over your happy news at a calmer time. Go to bed now, Joseph. I will see to my guests. Mistress Scott has lodgings very close."

There was more in Denoriel's grip and order for Joseph to go to bed than simple words. He had not before used Sidhe compulsion on Joseph, but the man's eagerness to help was a hindrance right now. In fact, Joseph would remember seeing Mistress Rosamund Scott and the Honorable Pasgen Silverhair leaving in Denoriel's company and Denoriel promising him that he would have servants from Mistress Scott's lodging to light him home.

Actually all four Sidhe were gathered in Denoriel's bedchamber. Having rid themselves of any vestiges of the fight, Denoriel offered to Gate them anywhere they wished to go. Pasgen and Rhoslyn immediately opted for any one of the great markets and Aleneil decided to accompany them because she badly needed to restore her drained power. Without any discussion or hesitation, Denoriel chose the Bazaar of the Bizarre. Even if someone knew Pasgen and Rhoslyn were Dark Court while Aleneil and Denoriel were Bright, nothing was really strange in the Bazaar of the Bizarre. In fact, on the rare occasions that Dark and Bright Court Sidhe met in amity, it was there.

On arrival, though, they stood looking at each other somewhat awkwardly, not quite knowing how to part. They had met before but only briefly and then in an attitude of angry contention. The whole business, from Pasgen's warning to Denoriel and then his and Rhoslyn's rushing to Denoriel's and Aleneil's defense was so strange. Yet all four had felt somehow more complete, and now found themselves reluctant to part.

Suddenly Pasgen said, "Oh, let's have a drink and some food at the nearest inn. I have just remembered that I have something important to tell you."

Sighing with exhaustion, but no longer shaking, the four divided at the huge sign that said NO SPELLS, NO DRAWN WEAPONS, NO VIOLENCE on one line and below that ON PAIN OF PERMANENT REMOVAL. They remained parted to pass the next warning: YMOGELYD PRYNWR, which warned any buyer to beware on his or her own account. The market offered no guarantees. Since they were already on their own feet, they did not bother to read the smaller print: "If you can't walk, hop, crawl, roll, slither, or whatever it takes to move you on your own, you can't come in."

Beyond the signs, they came together again, each wondering a little about why, but not daring to speak of what seemed so natural. Without a word, they followed the first air spirit that called out promise of entertainment and refreshment at an inn only a few steps off the main thoroughfare.

Tafarn Caredig Chewerthin—Inn of Kindly Laughter; Denoriel almost laughed aloud even before entering when he found himself translating the name into English—had wide open doors on an interior made brighter by elf-lights than the soft outdoor twilight. The patrons were the usual odds and sods that came to the Bazaar of the Bizarre, some things that did not seem flesh and blood at all, some weird and wonderful creatures of colors for which no one on Earth had a name, beings tentacled and clawed, Dark Sidhe and Bright, gnomes, kitsune, even toward the back wall, a large, jeweled carapace from under which peered two bright orange eyes.

The variety of patrons was not at all remarkable in the Bazaar of the Bizarre. What was remarkable was the quiet. Everyone was talking, but softly. The only sound that rose above the low hum of quiet conversation was an occasional shout of laughter.

The four Sidhe exchanged glances. The Bazaar had magic, of course, to enforce Removal when necessary, and for some reason there was an unusual abundance of ambient power in all the markets, which was why the depleted Sidhe had chosen the destination. It seemed, however, that the Inn of Kindly Laughter had its own special spells and that those were condoned by whatever power governed the market.

Aleneil smiled and stepped over the threshold, Rhoslyn followed immediately, and somewhat to Denoriel's surprise, Pasgen was right on her heels. Denoriel did not hesitate, but he wondered as he stepped in if the ambient good will was going to interfere with good sense.

The thought slipped from his mind as he made his way in his companions' wake to an empty table. As soon as they settled, a kitsune server, dark eyes bright in her fox face, came to ask what they wanted. A pitcher of nectar was agreed upon. Denoriel poured for them all when it arrived as the others, although slowly recovering their strength, might not have yet been able to hold the pitcher steady.

There was another silence as all sipped and swallowed. Denoriel wondered, with a small spark of pleasure that he had not expected to feel, whether Pasgen's remark about needing to tell him something had been an excuse for them to stay together. But before he could find a topic of conversation that was not too trivial but would support remaining in company, Pasgen frowned and set his goblet on the table, although he retained his grip on it.

"Do you remember the Unformed land where you fought Vidal and Elizabeth confronted Oberon?" Pasgen asked rather harshly. "The place where you came to kill the lion that Elizabeth created?"

Denoriel shuddered. "How could I forget it? But how did you know about Elizabeth and Oberon?"

"I was there," Pasgen admitted. "And no," he added hastily, seeing the change in Denoriel's expression, "I had nothing to do with Vidal following you there. I was there before any of you arrived and had been for some time. That Unformed land attracted me."

He hesitated, looking out over their heads. Rhoslyn put a hand on his arm and said his name in a gentle warning. Pasgen shook his head as if to clear it.

"I have for some years," he continued, "been studying the Chaos Lands. The mists are not all the same."

"That is true," Rhoslyn said. "I found out long ago that some Unformed lands are suitable for creation. In others I am less successful—my creations fail or are ill-formed."

"Yes," Pasgen said, clenched his jaw and then relaxed it deliberately. "But that one—" his hand gripped the goblet tighter. "Tell your friends not to go there," he said grimly, "not to use those mists for creation. They . . . in that domain they are . . . I fear they are growing sentient. There is a purpose in them, and a kind of intelligence."

Denoriel could see that Pasgen's hand was white with the pressure he was exerting on his goblet. It was clear to him that some powerful emotion had gripped his half brother. Yet it seemed impossible to Denoriel that an Unformed land, a mass of formless mist, could possibly become anything at all without direction.

"Careful," he said to Pasgen, tapping his fingers, "you will shatter that goblet." And then, "But—"

His voice checked as Pasgen took a large gulp of his drink and set the goblet down. Denoriel had remembered that Elizabeth had said the *mist* had made the lion, that she did not know how to make it and had "asked" the mist. The memory eliminated his first reaction, which was to suggest that Pasgen had been indulging in some mind-altering drug, and his second, which was to wonder what evil Pasgen had set up in that domain that he wished to hide.

"Sentient," Denoriel repeated. "That is hard to believe."

"It was not easy for me either," Pasgen snapped, "and I will admit, which is also not easy, that I was so frightened when I was forced to believe I came near to fouling myself."

"What happened?" Aleneil asked, reaching out to touch Pasgen's hand which was clenched tight and very cold.

"The place was strange when I first came to it," Pasgen said. "The mists seemed to respond to my thoughts, and that troubled me, but not at first because of any doubt about the mists. I was worried about my own reactions, wondering whether I was exerting my will without real intention . . . which can be dangerous."

"Yes, indeed," Aleneil murmured.

"But the oddity and my self-examination kept me there. I decided to stay for a while and made a chamber for myself. Considering that I am no maker, like Rhoslyn, it was surprisingly easy. I suppose I should have suspected then that this domain was no ordinary place, but I was still thinking mostly about myself, about my seeming inability to be aware of willing or stop myself from willing." He looked at Denoriel. "And then your party arrived."

Denoriel nodded. "King Henry had just died, and we were trying to distract Elizabeth from her grief. We knew she would think unfitting a ball or a trip to one of the markets but then she remembered the lion she had . . . ah . . . asked the mist to create and said it was dangerous, that it had killed two men and almost killed her, so we went to hunt it down."

"It is gone now," Pasgen said, took a deep breath, and described the attack of the lion, the two ill-made figures that seemed an attempt to mimic Elizabeth and himself, and the whole incredible sequence of events, ending with a confession of the terrible desire he felt to return to the domain.

No one made a sound while he spoke and when he was finished, the silence continued. No one disputed the tale. Aleneil covered her face with her hands and shivered. Denoriel looked grim as death. Rhoslyn took Pasgen's hand, which was trembling slightly. After a moment he pulled his hand away from her, straightened in his chair, and tried to sound nonchalant.

"I told you because I felt Elidir and Mechain should be warned against using that domain for their makings." His pose faltered and his voice was tired.

"Merciful Mother, you are so right." Denoriel shook himself as if he could throw off the cloak of fear Pasgen had woven. "I will tell Harry. Thank you." He hesitated and then said, "But can we leave that place as a possible trap for the unwary? We have to do *something.*"

"I agree," Pasgen sighed. "But what?"

Chapter 15

They had come to no conclusion when the four finally parted. Pasgen offered, (rather too willingly, Denoriel thought) to go back to that Unformed land and see what he could see. Rhoslyn objected. Pasgen promised not to leave the Gate but just stand there and examine the mist and anything the mist chose to show him. He could depart on the instant if he saw or felt anything threatening.

"No," Rhoslyn said. "Or maybe, yes—if you will let me pattern the Gate and stand ready to snatch us out of there as soon as I feel threatened."

He frowned, but only slightly. "You will feel threatened at the first swirl forward of the mist."

"I am not new to making," she replied, with a little tartness, but only a touch.

What surprised Denoriel was the amiability of the exchange. He wondered again if something in the Inn of Kindly Laughter should be held suspect, but Rhoslyn and Pasgen were brother and sister and often together. He and Aleneil often disagreed amiably too.

"Pasgen," Aleneil put in, "Rhoslyn is right. I don't think you should trust yourself. You will see something that will make you curious and follow it, perhaps into terrible danger. On the other hand, Rhoslyn, someone should take another look at this place. And I think, if it is as you said, Pasgen, that we had better take this problem to Oberon and let him decide what to do." She paused, and added, "He is, after all the High King of us all, Bright Court and Dark."

All four fell silent, looked at each other, then looked at the table. After another moment Denoriel said, "Elidir and Mechain are old and experienced makers. Perhaps they should be the ones to look and . . . ah . . . take the news to Oberon if they do not know what to do."

"No!" Pasgen's voice was tight and almost sounded as if it were forcing a way through a solid obstruction. "I do not want the mist hurt. It did nothing to harm me. It did not try to save the vicious lion. It did not try to imprison me. If it—if it is learning to live, how can we dare kill it?"

There was another silence, as Denoriel tried to take in all the implications of what Pasgen had just said. Denoriel thought that a very strange sentiment for the notoriously cruel and wanton Dark Sidhe, but he said nothing. Rhoslyn looked appalled, holding tight to her brother's hand. Aleneil looked very troubled, plainly thinking over what Pasgen had said and possibly wishing to save the mist.

Denoriel shook his head. "I think we can trust Elidir and Mechain not to take any precipitous action. They need not fear any inimical beasts because Harry can use his steel gun if it is necessary. I will go with them also. When they come to a decision—if they come to a decision—I promise that we will do nothing until we discuss the matter with you. Would you be willing to make such a compromise, since Rhoslyn seems to fear danger for you if you go yourself to that place?"

Pasgen thought it over, biting his lower lip. Finally he nodded, slowly, reluctantly, and sighed. "I will agree, not because I think I would be in any danger if I went there, but because . . . because I want to go too much."

"Thank you, brother," Rhoslyn breathed.

"Now, how will I be able to let you know what Elidir and Mechain have discovered?" Denoriel asked.

A brief, awkward silence ensued. Denoriel knew that Pasgen and Rhoslyn knew where he lived, but neither wanted to come into Seleighe lands without being accompanied. Aleneil had taken Rhoslyn to Mwynwen's house so that Rhoslyn could ask about

Richey. Rhoslyn had met Harry there and, oddly, that seemed to comfort her more even than the tale of Richey's mostly happy life. And neither Pasgen nor Rhoslyn was prepared to provide direction to their own domains.

"Ah," Pasgen said. "You could leave a message for us in the empty house. Not that the house is really empty, but neither Rhoslyn nor I live there. Likely neither of us will be there, but the servants are designed for taking messages and will not make any mistakes in transmitting them. You can suggest a place and time to meet. And if we cannot come then, Rhoslyn will send an air spirit to make a new arrangement where and when we should meet."

"All of us," Aleneil said quietly.

"Yes, all of us," Rhoslyn repeated.

That promise seemed to ease the awkwardness all had felt about parting. Denoriel raised a hand to call the kitsune server to them and signed he would cover the cost for all. Pasgen and Rhoslyn nodded thanks and left the inn. Denoriel had gold coins in his hand, but the server shook her head.

"What can you supply to us?" the kitsune asked.

"Mortal goods," Denoriel replied promptly, then his eyes sought the bejeweled carapace and orange eyes, which were still in the back of the room. He remembered Elizabeth's bargain with the crab person of Carcinus Maenas and laughed. "How about a cask of fish, real mortal fish, fresh or salt."

"Done," the server said, and dropped a thin wooden amulet in Denoriel's hand. "Put that on the cask in any Gate and the fish will get to us."

Denoriel took Aleneil's arm as they left the inn to offer support. She smiled at him when they stepped up on the Gate. "Pattern me home, love," she said with a sigh. "I am better, but still very weary and I need to rest. Mother Goddess, that iron hurts. It seems to draw the very life out of me, and every time that beast thrust at me, my shields became so eroded that I had to build them anew. I was drained to the dregs. Pasgen and Rhoslyn were both trying to come to my assistance, but they were even worse hurt by the man's steel. If Joseph had not come when he did . . ."

In Avalon where the Gate set them, the blank-faced guards nodded in recognition. Ystwyth was there, waiting, her large brown eyes turned anxiously on her friend. Denoriel boosted Aleneil into the saddle so the elvensteed would not need to kneel, and they were gone. Miralys, after a glance at Denoriel, simply stepped up on the Gate platform and allowed Denoriel to whisk them both away to Elfhame Logres. As the steed started toward the palace at an ordinary horse's trot rather than the space-eating gait he could use, Denoriel told the elvensteed what had happened.

Without instruction, Miralys then changed direction and carried Denoriel, not home, but to Mwynwen's house at the far end of the elfhame. Denoriel was not certain whether Miralys was bringing him to the healer to be examined for any ill effect of drinking lightning or because Harry lived with Mwynwen; however, Denoriel did not care which was true.

If Harry was not at home, Denoriel thought, he would try the Elfhame Elder-Elf, although these days—Denoriel grinned broadly—it would be better called the Busybodies' Elfhame. A very few of those who had taken refuge there had slipped away into Dreaming before Harry arrived. Afterward, one by one he found challenges for them that shook them out of boredom and often thoroughly terrified them so that they came alive.

Harry had arrived at the Elfhame Elder-Elf by accident, not being very experienced with patterning Gates. Wandering, lost, through the beautiful domain, he had found two drooping beings, white haired, rather limp, who had looked at him kindly but with eyes misted with age. Not knowing how to reorient himself, he had asked them for help and noticed that both became more animated as they explained what he had done wrong.

That they were puzzled by his ineptitude was clear and Harry never minded making himself the butt of a joke. By the time he had told them the whole tale of how he came Underhill, that he was Prince Denoriel's ward and Lady Mwynwen's lover and patient, both suggested that they go with him to his intended destination, the Elves' Faire. Young, pretty mortals, they said, were in some danger of being enticed by strange promises, seduced out of the market, and snatched away and sold.

Harry had been to the market with Denoriel many times and was in no danger of being seduced by false temptations. Moreover, as the illegitimate son of the King of England, who for some years could not seem to breed another boy, there had been no temptation, no inducement, that had not been offered him so he would whisper things in his father's ear. Harry knew how to refuse temptation, but he did not say that. He saw how the old Sidhes' bodies had straightened, how their faces lost the slackness of total boredom when they offered to guard him from harm.

He did not pretend he did not know they were old. He asked them questions about the past, and eventually one of them told him about the danger mortals held for Underhill. As examples, they described the cursing of Alhambra and El Dorado by the priests of the Inquisition and the evil that still lived there.

Harry's eyes widened and his fair skin flushed with anger. "What revenge had been taken for such insult?" he cried. And when Elidir and Mechain looked at him blankly—the Sidhe were mostly shallow creatures who did not feel deeply about anything—Harry asked if they had no pride.

Pride the Sidhe had. When Harry put the case in that light, that it was an insult that a Sidhe domain should be given over to human evil, both frowned in displeasure. Harry nodded agreement and asserted firmly that it was time, then, to clean out the cesspools.

They sighed, slumping again, and told him they did not think they could raise an army sufficient to attack the cities. Harry laughed aloud. Elidir and Mechain were puzzled. The places had been lost by battle; the Sidhe could not imagine any other way to regain them. But Harry had been well taught in every form of political chicanery and covert military maneuver. "Let me see the cities," he said, "and I will find a way that we three, with perhaps a few friends, can destroy or drive out the evil."

First they had to find the cities, so long lost from the known places of Underhill. Elidir and Mechain had to rediscover ways to search through ancient forms of patterning. Magic skills long disused were awakened. Fighting skills, too, because both of the Sidhe felt responsible for the hapless mortal and believed they would need to defend him.

Two of the elder elves were soon as bright as new buttons. And when they took Harry to Alhambra and they were attacked, their defensive magic—and Harry's well-wielded sword were barely enough to bring them away safe. All three were furious and resolved one way or another to be rid of the disgusting menaces in the breathtakingly beautiful hame. They went to a market to eat and drink and make plans.

From that time to this, Elidir and Mechain, and a half dozen others strong in magic had no time to be bored. They had been laboring, often in great danger, to clean the lost elfhames from evil. Other problems cropped up from time to time and came to Harry's ears or Mwynwen's. Harry promptly brought the problems—and an inventive solution—to the Elfhame Elder-Elf. Denoriel now enjoyed a visit to a place that had once been full of sorrow—but the path of this endeavor must take him to Mwynwen's house first.

Mwynwen greeted Denoriel pleasantly, as she had no urgent patient, and was plainly interested when he told her about his lack of reaction to taking in mortal magic. She examined him closely and agreed that he seemed unharmed. Perhaps the scarring of his power channels had made them more resistant, but she urged him to be very careful; resistant channels might also be more brittle. A tear would be a disaster.

He attended to her advice seriously, and readily assured her that only dire necessity would drive him to touch mortal power. The spell that drew power to him Underhill was more than enough. When he asked for Harry, however, she showed some signs of irritation.

"Not here," she said. "When *is* he here?"

"Every sleep time for him, I am sure," Denoriel replied, laughing.

"Oh, yes," Mwynwen said, not laughing in response. "He is strong and eager enough in making love, but he does not really need me anymore. The elf-shot poison is gone. I have not needed to drain him for a year. And he seems so sure of himself. He has learned to read and write Elven and he never asks my advice . . . well, now and again when he is not sure of Sidhe protocol. But if I suggest something to him—"

Denoriel laughed again. "He is a grown man now, Mwynwen, and mostly knows his own mind. If you wished to share his adventures, I am sure he would welcome you."

"I do not! Killing and trapping!" She shuddered. "I know the things he and his old Sidhe take and destroy are evil, but for me—" She shivered again.

Denoriel shrugged. He did not, of course, agree with or even understand her response even though Aleneil reacted similarly. He had been a member of Koronos' Wild Hunt for more than a hundred years, and their purpose was much the same—to destroy evil that otherwise would escape.

He managed to say something polite, and then said, "I will try the Elfhame Elder-Elf then, but if I should miss Harry and he should come in, would you tell him to come to my apartment in Llachar Lle?"

She shook her head and sighed, but agreed to pass on the message, and Denoriel went out to remount Miralys. Elder-Elf's Elfhame could be patterned directly from the Logres Gate, and everyone there knew Harry. Someone had seen him and waved vaguely in the direction of Sawel's house, warning Denoriel that he should approach with care as there were frequent explosions. Denoriel chuckled. They were trying to do something with holy water, possibly to disguise it so the black entities in Alhambra would not recognize it, could be doused with it, and destroyed. Whatever it was Sawel was trying, the holy water did not approve!

As Miralys carried him in that direction, moving again no faster than a mortal horse lest he run down a busy and absent-minded elder, Denoriel suddenly "reheard" what Mwynwen had said about Harry. Miralys stopped and Denoriel patted his silken shoulder in appreciation.

"Right," he said to the elvensteed, "I'll walk. I need time to think."

But he didn't walk. A gesture brought a bench when Miralys had disappeared, and Denoriel sat down on it. He had always known, although with typical Sidhe avoidance of the unpleasant he had refused to think about it, that Mwynwen had never cared for Harry as a human woman would care for her lover. At first it was irrelevant, as Harry's primary need was for healing. And even when he saw that Harry was enamored, what could he do?

Mwynwen had lost the "child" she had been raising for ten years. Richey, as she had named him, was not a living child but a changeling, which Mwynwen had kept "alive" with a spell that constantly fed it power so that it would not fall apart. The changeling's body had grown, except for its expressions, which retained much of the sweet innocence of the ten-year-old it had been when it came into Mwynwen's keeping.

Physically Richey continued to closely resemble Henry FitzRoy. At seventeen, both were dying, Richey because its made body could no longer absorb the power it needed to stay intact; Harry from the poison of an elf-shot wound taken in defending Elizabeth from capture by Vidal Dhu. It had been possible, at Richey's request, to exchange the young men so that Richey could die in peace and Harry be healed, although Harry was permanently exiled to Underhill because he was dead and buried in the mortal world.

Mwynwen, heartsick with grief over losing her child, which was about the only strong emotion most Sidhe could feel, agreed to cure Harry, whom she called "Richey's gift." He, too, was her "child," sick, needing constant care, and totally ignorant of the manners and mores, the customs and history of Underhill.

So for many years Mwynwen had another "child" to raise and was content, even more than she had been with Richey because as soon as Harry was well enough he began to crave her body. Mwynwen offered it, as she would offer a new toy to a frail child, and was surprised and rewarded when the toy was as delightful to her as to Harry.

But Harry was mortal, and as his body was cured and his ignorance corrected by education, he grew from a child into a man. He developed interests of his own, closer to those of Denoriel than to those of Mwynwen; he hunted, fought any invasion of Dark Sidhe or their creatures, rode in the Wild Hunt, explored strange domains. Mwynwen was quite correct, Denoriel thought. Harry did not need her anymore, at least, not as a child needs a mother. Denoriel shifted on the bench.

The question now rose of whether Harry *needed* Mwynwen as a lover. Denoriel knew that some humans were as light in love as Sidhe; however, some tended to be much more faithful. Those would marry and live together all of their lives, sharing their joys and griefs and leaning on each other for comfort and support.

Sidhe lived too long. There were a few who life-mated and clung to each other for the thousands of years that they survived. Most drifted in and out of love, if one could call it that. Before he brought Richey to Mwynwen, Denoriel had been Mwynwen's lover. They had drifted apart easily when his attention was fixed on Harry and hers on Richey.

Denoriel stared sightlessly at the smooth green turf between his feet. If Harry had formed a lasting human passion for Mwynwen, he was about to be hurt when Mwynwen withdrew herself. Should he try to warn Harry, Denoriel wondered? How? What should he say? Should he tell Harry he had better pay more attention to Mwynwen, offer to do what she would like best? Should he try to introduce Harry to a few Sidhe ladies who were curious about him and would gladly—for a little while—take a human lover? Would that make Mwynwen jealous or simply give her an excuse to break the relationship?

Denoriel sighed. He had no idea how Harry would react to such a suggestion. He stood up abruptly. He said he loved Harry, but he realized that for some time he had been so busy with Elizabeth that he was not sure he knew Harry very well anymore. Well, Elizabeth needed some weeks or even months to settle into her new household. He would give that time to Harry and see what he could do . . . if anything.

He had barely set out toward Sawel's house again—it was set well away from the main building and clustered cottages of the other Sidhe—when the warned-of explosion came. With Harry firmly in mind again, Denoriel rushed forward to help, but found everyone unharmed. They were prepared for explosions now, it seemed. At first they were all too absorbed in what they had been working on to do more than greet him in an absent way, but when they had thrashed out the reasons for the unwelcome, if not unexpected, results and worked out a new refinement, Harry came over and hugged Denoriel. His two most constant companions, Elidir and Mechain, followed close behind him.

"We are trying to find a way to entice the Great Evil out so we can somehow thrust it into the Void," Harry said. "It cannot be destroyed, but it must not be loosed either. Do you think the Void will hold it?"

"You will need the opinions of better mages than myself," Denoriel said, "but I have a new and possibly even more dangerous problem to describe to you."

"More dangerous than the Great Evil?" Mechain said. "Or is this a ruse to keep Harry away from this work?"

"And where is our adorable Elizabeth?" Elidir asked. "You have not brought her Underhill in far too long. I did hear that Oberon had consented to allow her to visit again."

"Harry is a man grown and I hope knows how to judge his own danger," Denoriel said, and then laughed. "Of course I wish to keep him out of danger, but this new business . . . Can we go somewhere where we can sit and talk in comfort? The stink—what *is* that unsavory odor?—around here invites our swift absence."

"Your place," Harry said to Denoriel. "Elidir and Mechain's cottage is really too small and besides—" he grinned broadly "—I still love to be waited on by your invisible servants."

Before they had taken ten steps toward the Gate, five elven-steeds were somehow beside, ahead, and behind them. They all mounted, arrived at the Gate in what seemed like three strides, Gated through, and were at the broad marble steps of the palace in three more strides.

With wine and cakes and small savory tidbits readily to hand, Denoriel repeated what Pasgen had told him. He expected argument and denial. Instead Elidir and Mechain exchanged long glances. Elidir rubbed his long-fingered hands together nervously; Mechain shuddered.

"I knew there was something wrong in that Unformed land, I knew it," Elidir said. "You remember," he said to Mechain, "that one time we were there when there was grass near the Gate for the elvensteeds to graze—and neither of us had made grass there."

"We thought the elvensteeds had done it," Mechain said. "I never knew them to make before, but who knows what they can do? I have never reached the bottom of what Phylyr can do." She hesitated and then near whispered, "But sentient?"

"So far it does not seem dangerous," Denoriel said, "but my half brother—"

"The Dark Sidhe?" Harry asked. "Do you trust him? He tried several times to kill me, I remember. Could he have set some kind of trap in that Unformed land?"

That question caused a digression into Rhoslyn's changing attitude and her influence on her brother. Finally Denoriel shrugged. "It isn't something we can just ignore," he said. "I think we have to go and look at the place and see if we can feel anything there. And since we will all be alert for danger, I think all of us together can deal with any trap Pasgen left, if he did leave one."

"Yes, we must go," Elidir agreed. "We have not been back to that place since we took Elizabeth there and fought that battle against Prince Vidal. But even before then, Mechain and I had decided not to use that Unformed land anymore."

"Yes," Mechain said. "It was too easy to make there."

Harry said only, "Wait for me. I must get my sword and pistol from Mwynwen's house. Lady Aeron will take me. I will only be a few moments."

That was true enough. Denoriel had barely enough time to absorb the fact that Harry had said, "Mwynwen's house" instead of "home." Very interesting. It was as if Harry had become more guest than lover. But before Denoriel had a chance to examine the idea more carefully, Harry was back and they were all on their way.

Both Elidir and Mechain knew the pattern for that Unformed land as well as they knew the one for Elfhame Elder-Elf. They agreed to ask the elvensteeds to remain behind as they did not intend to get off the Gate platform. All were ready to repel attack as they dropped through the darkness of Between and arrived at their goal.

No attack. Nothing that Denoriel could feel, although both Mechain and Elidir drew in sharp breaths. Harry drew his sword and loosened the catch on his pistol. He would not draw that except in dire need because it would be harmful to his companions. Denoriel did not draw, although his hand rested on his sword hilt. Then he, too, drew in a sharp breath.

There was nothing to see. The mists coiled and then streamed away, puffed here and there, blew right and left and around, as the mists in any Chaos Land did. Elidir stretched out a hand.

"Rest," he said. "You have done enough. We will ask no more of you."

"We thank you," Mechain added, "for all you have done for us. Now rest."

There was a stirring in the mist not far from the Gate platform and a glint of gold and bright red where the hair of a man and a small woman might be. Together Elidir and Mechain willed the Gate to take them back to Elfhame Logres and to their elvensteeds who waited. No one said a word as they mounted, and they were still silent as they took the seats in Denoriel's parlor they had vacated so short a time earlier.

"I fear that what your half brother told you is true," Elidir said, when he had swallowed the nectar an invisible hand had poured into his cup.

"It welcomed me," Mechain whispered, but not so softly that all did not hear her.

Elidir nodded agreement. "Me also, as if I were an old friend returned after an absence."

"And me it questioned," Denoriel said, "wanting to know who I was. I had a quick, muddy image of Pasgen—that is my half brother's name—and a feeling of doubt." He shivered. "We differ enough in the set of our minds—he is much more mage than I, and I can bear the mortal world and its burden of iron better than he. But . . . but that a *mist* should feel this?"

He looked from face to face. Harry looked slightly regretful, as if he knew that mortal without Talent as he was, he alone would not be touched by this wonder . . . or horror. But he was not too regretful; his immunity to magical influence of his thoughts had saved his party in the stricken elfhames more than once. Elidir and Mechain wore similar expressions of distress mingled with confusion.

"But there was no threat to me. No feeling of threat at all," Mechain said unhappily.

"No, nor even to me," Denoriel admitted, "when it realized . . . I cannot believe I am saying this, that a mist *realized* I was not Pasgen. But my half brother, who was frightened near out of his wits when he realized that the mist was making on its own, also felt no threat and . . . and when I had suggested that we bring the problem to Oberon"—he hesitated while all the others stared at him with widened eyes—"he begged me not to. He said—mind you, he is of the Unseleighe kind—but he asked whether we had the right to kill what was coming to life."

"Are we certain that Oberon would kill it?" Mechain asked.

"Who can know what Oberon will do?" Denoriel sighed. "What he does will be beyond us once the matter is in his hand, so the decision, and we must consider it to be death or life, is ours."

Elidir nodded acknowledgment of Denoriel's statement of responsibility, but when he asked, "So what do we do?" he looked at Harry, not Denoriel.

"We watch, or rather, you watch, since I was not aware of anything," Harry said promptly. "If there's anyone more sensitive than you . . . yes, yes, set the burden on Gaenor. Later, or tomorrow, we can explain to her what we fear and take her there. We can introduce her as a—as a maker who has been so long away from making that she does not well know it anymore. See whether she feels any response from the mist."

"And if she does?"

"Then Elidir had better come back alone or, or with Mechain, of course, and tell the mist to sleep again. After leaving it quiet for some time—you can suggest to Gaenor that she try to find some spells to deactivate a made thing, and that she had better be ready to flee as soon as she casts the spell because the mist might not want to be deactivated."

Mechain blinked at Harry and breathed out a whistling breath. "Well, that should wake Gaenor up smartly."

Elidir chuckled.

"And she can keep going back for . . . oh, a full season. But if the mist is still awake, if it is doing new things, or if it starts to threaten Gaenor, I think we will need to take this trouble to Oberon. God knows, *I* cannot think of a way to deal with a *mist.*"

"And we had this new burst of creatures in El Dorado," Elidir said, the good humor gone from his face. "They are almost impervious to magic, but they need killing. It is interesting that they are smaller and weaker than the last plague that was produced."

Denoriel gestured and the air was troubled. "Will you all dine with me?" he asked. "It is some hours since we have all eaten and I would like to hear your plans. Elizabeth has just moved into a new household; she is to be under the dowager queen's care. She will be too busy to come Underhill or even to see me for a few weeks, perhaps as long as a month. Thus, I will be free of my duty to her and would like to come with you and help clear the plague from El Dorado."

Chapter 16

Pasgen and Rhoslyn sat together in the parlor of the empty house. Both were somewhat revived. Pasgen had taken Rhoslyn to the Chaos Land where he most often found the sweet and restorative mists. He had breathed/drunk some down and she had tried, although with less success. Now she blinked back tears and lowered her head.

"It is only in the Seleighe domains that power comes to me softly and sweetly. When Aleneil took me to visit Mwynwen, I was warm all over and so strong when I left."

"Then visit her again," Pasgen said. "It may not be only the Seleighe domain that fills you with power. Mwynwen is a healer; she may have a spell on the house that brings in extra power."

Rhoslyn blinked and cocked her head. "Hmmm. Aleneil would Gate me in if I asked her and I could tell Mwynwen that I had come to ask after the boy. She was pleased enough to show him off when Aleneil brought me, and he was then mending but not yet well. Yes, that was a wise thought, Pasgen. The way I feel now it will take me months to draw enough power and I do not have months. I need to get back to Mary."

Pasgen sighed. "And I have to get back to Otstargi's house and discover what Albertus plans when none of his men return to him." A moment later his eyes brightened with interest. "While I am dealing with him I can look about for those strings of power Denoriel mentioned."

"Pasgen, no! Denoriel warned you not to play with that power."

"Denoriel!" Their mother's voice came from the doorway. "What have you to do with Denoriel? He is unreasonable. He hates you for what is no fault of yours. Has he suggested something dangerous to you?"

"With great reluctance," Pasgen said impatiently. "And he warned me not to try to seek that source of power."

"Pasgen—" Llanelli came forward and took his hand in hers. "Does it not occur to you that he might know your curiosity about all forms of power, that he might seem to be reluctant so you would not guess he was setting a trap for you?"

"Denoriel is not the trap-setting kind," Pasgen replied, his lips thin. "I am the trap-setting kind. Denoriel might attempt to damage me, but he would do it with his knife or his sword..." He hesitated. "Or even with a spell these days. But it would be an open direct attack. He is not devious."

"Has he not spent much time in the mortal world with that boy and the girl the Seleighe hope will be queen?" Llanelli bit her lip. "Mortals are devious. Sidhe learn from those with whom they company."

Ironic, that. Considering that the most devious of mortals could not even begin to challenge the least devious of Unseleighe.

Pasgen laughed. "Mother, you have spent all our lives telling us how much better it is to live Seleighe. Is not the best chance we have of finding a welcome there through our half brother and sister?"

"Oh..." Llanelli looked around for the chair that Rhoslyn ordinarily brought to her. It was not there, and Rhoslyn was lying back in her own chair, eyes closed. "Rhoslyn!" she exclaimed, forgetting or dismissing what she had been about to say to Pasgen. "What is wrong? Are you hurt? Ill?"

"I am just drained, Mother," Rhoslyn said, opening her eyes. "Pasgen discovered a plot to kill Denoriel and Aleneil. We tried to defend them."

"Defend them?" Llanelli stiffened. "Why should you defend them? They are misbegotten! A remnant stolen from the spell that I found and sacrificed mages to cast. Your stupid father did not stay with me, as I devised. No. He had to go rushing back to that . . . that pallid nothing with whom he claimed a life bond. Underhill would be better off without—"

"No, Mother," Rhoslyn interrupted firmly. "Aleneil has been very kind to me and Denoriel at least courteous. They are our sibs, and I will not see them wasted for no more than Vidal Dhu's whim."

Llanelli's eyes flashed and her lips thinned, but she did not pursue that thread any further. "But what did you do? Why are you so diminished?"

The brother and sister exchanged glances, but it seemed best to tell her enough to satisfy her rather than leaving her curious and anxious. Pasgen told most of the story and at last Llanelli sighed and shook her head.

"I wish you had not. If Vidal hears of this, he will be furious. You will be endangered . . . and I dare say that you will not see Denoriel or Aleneil coming to *your* rescue."

"They might." Pasgen smiled. "Well, Denoriel might just for the pure joy of fighting. Aleneil is no fighter—"

"Not so," Rhoslyn said also with a faint smile. "She does not like fighting, but when she must she is no weakling. She held me off finely that night in Elizabeth's chamber."

"Yes." Pasgen nodded. "And she was holding her own against two or three phookas before Oberon stopped the battle with Vidal's creatures in that Unformed land." As he said the words, his head turned.

Rhoslyn leaned forward and put her hand on his arm, saying warningly, "Pasgen . . ."

"What is it?" Llanelli asked.

But the possibility of a sentient Chaos Land was not something either was willing to mention to their mother, and Pasgen said quickly, "Rhoslyn and I must go back to the mortal world."

"For what?" Llanelli asked sharply. "To again endanger yourselves on behalf of the misbegotten twins?"

"More to make sure that Albertus has no idea that I was involved in the failure of his plans," Pasgen said. "I am not looking for any open conflict with Vidal."

To that, Llanelli agreed vehemently, her eyes widened with fear. Her soul was scarred with the terrors and torments Vidal had inflicted on her when she was trying to save her babies and the

further agonies she had suffered when he had addicted her to oleander and periodically withdrawn it to ensure her obedience to him.

Although Pasgen had assured her that he could stand against
Vidal and she had nothing to fear any longer from that dark
prince, she did not believe him. Pasgen was, after all, her child.
In her heart he was still small and helpless. It did not seem possible, no matter what he said, that his primary reason for avoiding
a conflict with Vidal was that he did not wish to be ordered by
Oberon to rule the Unseleighe.

"As for me," Rhoslyn said, "I must return to my service with
Lady Mary. If Aurilia or Vidal learns that I am no longer watching her, they may find a less pleasant duty to force upon me."
She sighed. "I just wish I was not so drained. Perhaps I will stay
here for some time and try to Gate back in time—"

Pasgen shook his head. "A few hours or a day does not matter,
but if you leap back more time than that, a few of the sensitive
mortals will be made uncomfortable."

"Oh," Llanelli said, smiling. "I can mend the draining. I have
learned some things as a healer, you know. You are better off
doing what Vidal wants so he will have no complaints."

Aleneil was on legitimate leave from her duties with Lady
Elizabeth and she took full advantage of the total absence of
iron in her home and environs. At first she simply rested, mostly
sitting in her garden with Ystwyth beside her. As power began
to renew her and she felt more alive, she began to look through
the invitations that had come to her.

She went to a small party to decide whether further embel-
lishment should be designed for the Avalon Gate. She accepted
a dinner invitation by a Sidhe who led a party that advocated
total separation from the mortal world. She enjoyed the lively
arguments she stirred up by remarking that the notion, however
attractive, was not very practical.

Did they wish to starve the *lios-alfar* of creative energy, Aleneil
asked? And to the riposte that the mortals gave that off whether
they would or no, she pointed out that the energy came in sweet
and bitter, and if they did not guard the provider of the sweet,
they would need to sustain themselves on the bitter.

"Why should the bitter win?" her host asked haughtily.

"Because," Aleneil replied with lifted brows, "we can abjure the mortals, but we have no way of forcing the Unseleighe to do the same. Since they desire the bitter energy of pain and misery, they will somehow destroy those who bring out the new, the wonderful, in music and art and writing. Only the bitter will be left."

There was more argument, but it was soon led to other less controversial topics by the host. However, when Aleneil had said her thanks for a stimulating evening, she found she had company. One of the Sidhe, who had been quiet but very interested in the discussion, followed her close when she left. Before Aleneil could feel frightened, because she knew she was depleted and could not well defend herself, he said his name was Ilar, and asked if he could accompany her.

His eyes were clear and the almost-blue green of the best emerald; his hair was pulled back from his ears and face by a diamond clasp so his face was well-exposed. He looked, Aleneil thought, younger than most, his expression full of life and curiosity. She gave him her smile and her hand.

They spent some time in Aleneil's home talking about the mortal world. He said he knew his host hated it, but was at least interested; most Sidhe were not only uninterested but also ignorant. Aleneil was neither. She warned him first of the ever-present ache and drain of the ubiquitous iron in mortal buildings and tools. Unwilling yet to divulge how deeply she was mixed into mortal affairs, she told him only that FarSeeing duty sent her to the mortal world. There she became depleted and had come Underhill to restore herself.

"I must dare the danger of iron before I know if I can endure," Ilar said, "but to dare, I must know how to live, how to act, what I need to carry with me."

Aleneil suggested several brief trials to test himself and, if he could endure, to begin to establish a persona in the mortal world. She did not think he was serious about the attempt; she suspected he was more interested in bedding her than in the mortal world and was just using that to make his way with her. She did not mind in the least; he was bright and fresh and was at least willing to talk about something aside from dress and gossip.

They did lie together and found the experience pleasant. Some days later Ilar invited her to his home in Caer Cymry. When they arrived they were just in time for a "human tournament." Aleneil agreed to go, although she was not very happy about the word tournament, envisioning blood and death. And, in fact, it was a contest where mortal servants strove against each other for prizes, but there was very little blood and no death. A few fought, wrestling or with fists, but most danced or displayed feats of strength and agility.

Part of the pleasure, Aleneil realized, was that the mortals enjoyed the tournament as much as the Sidhe; in fact a mortal had conceived the idea to mitigate his boredom. The games were of considerable benefit to all; the mortals could win freedom from servitude. A great deal of energy was given off by the mortal striving; exuded Underhill, it was no longer completely mortal energy and the Sidhe could use it. Aleneil began to feel less exhausted.

Altogether she was delighted with Caer Cymry. Ilar introduced her to the Sidhe who were also delighted to meet one of the Far-Seers of Avalon. Cymry enjoyed a different lifestyle than Avalon, with less magic and more mortal servants. Yet the Cymry Sidhe knew little about the mortal world; their servants were mostly purchased or bred Underhill.

Aleneil began to worry that Ilar intended to visit the mortal world to abduct mortals for the Cymry Sidhe. He shrugged, saying that was not his first purpose, that he was looking for adventure, but he admitted he might take a neglected child or other miserable mortal—only for their own sake. Their own mortals bred very well, he assured her, and the Cymry were not in need.

Having seen enough of the mortal world to understand that many mortals would be better off Underhill, Aleneil did no more than warn Ilar about the intensity and duration of mortal affection and urge him not to separate those who loved. He laughed at that and turned the subject to loving her, promising to prove his devotion by obeying her warnings. Aleneil would have worried more except that it was apparent the Cymry Sidhe only wanted willing mortals. They were mostly too kind and too lazy to break them.

Ilar was good company and Aleneil found it pleasant to have a companion, who was also a good lover. Eventually, however, she found herself completely restored and began to feel bored by the balls and musical events, even in Ilar's company. What was Elizabeth doing, she wondered? Surely she was settled by now and, being Elizabeth, trouble might have found her.

She told Ilar she must return to her duty and, as she expected, he made no objection. However, to her surprise, he asked whether it would be possible for him to meet her in the mortal world if he were comfortable there.

"Not while I am actually doing my FarSeer's duty," she said, and then went on to explain that she did get leave and how he could leave a message for her in Denoriel's house on Bucklersbury. They had a last time of loving in Aleneil's house and parted contented with each other and looking forward to meeting again.

No hearts were broken; no tears were shed. When Ilar was gone, Aleneil stood in front of her long mirror and made sure that her clothing was all in the height of style and perfectly enchanting and that Lady Alana's face was so plain and ordinary that one could hardly see it. She was humming happily when she dismounted from Ystwyth in the stable by the house on Bucklersbury.

There she learned that all had been quiet with no further sign of watchers across the road or attempts to invade. The servants had been told of how a child opened the door and made them vulnerable to attack and warned not to let anyone in; they could feed the beggars but only outside the house. Nonetheless both Joseph and Cropper examined the house, specially the kitchen area, with care and double-checked locks and bars before they went to bed.

A message was sent off to Elizabeth to say that Lady Alana was ready to return to duty. That was not, of course, the norm; usually maids of honor had stated periods of service and came and went according to a schedule. But Elizabeth knew who and what Alana truly was, and Mistress Ashley understood that Lady Alana was very wealthy and had business of her own. Since she served without support and was most sensible and useful, Kat was glad to see her whenever she came.

Thus Aleneil received a gratifyingly rapid reply written in Elizabeth's own beautiful hand. The "come as soon as you can, dear Lady Alana" that closed the formal acceptance of service was the first small indication that trouble might be looming on the horizon. Aleneil told herself that Elizabeth was probably just suffering from a reaction to her feverish excitement when she was given permission to live with Queen Catherine and was now feeling sad and bored. However, she told Joseph she wished to leave as soon as possible.

The next morning Joseph sent for Cuthbert and Petrus, two men he regularly employed as guards. They brought with them two pack-horses to be loaded with the bulging bags and baskets filled with Lady Alana's wardrobe. The party left for Chelsea immediately after an early dinner and arrived well in time for the evening meal.

Lady Alana hardly needed to wait at all to be received by Queen Catherine, and she was greeted warmly—more warmly than she expected. Of course the dowager queen knew Lady Alana from her service to Elizabeth when they all lived together at Hampton Court, but Aleneil was worried by Catherine's eagerness, concerned that Elizabeth was unhappy.

That fear was put to rest as soon as Elizabeth was summoned. Her eyes were wide and bright gold, her usually pale cheeks just barely touched with rose. She looked healthy and lively. Whatever made Elizabeth urge her to come quickly and made Queen Catherine welcome her so eagerly was not frightening to Elizabeth.

By now, there was no time to change Lady Alana's traveling dress, and Catherine graciously gave permission for her to take her evening meal with the household as she was. Elizabeth sat at the table with Catherine, in a lower chair but on the dais. The tables for the two sets of maids of honor were just below.

Aleneil was welcomed to Elizabeth's maids' table with little cries of pleasure and with a kiss on the cheek from Katherine Ashley. That renewed Aleneil's trepidation somewhat but the gossip among Elizabeth's attendants, who were all eager to tell the ever-sympathetic Lady Alana all the news, was mostly innocent. Snippets about what Master Grindal had set as lessons, the charms of the new teacher of dance and the misfortune of his being not only foreign but low-born, the trials of serving a lady so quick at languages as Elizabeth when she demanded all conversation be in French for a whole morning.

The talk, sanctioned with nods and smiles by Mistress Ashley, implied that there had been no alarms or perceived dangers and should have set Aleneil's mind at rest. However, Aleneil detected something held in reserve by Mistress Ashley, something of which the maids of honor were not aware but Kat Ashley was, and which she was of two minds about mentioning.

Kat was given no choice, however. When the meal was over, Elizabeth was dismissed with surprising promptness by Queen Catherine. To Aleneil's surprise, Elizabeth did not stiffen up with resentment; she seemed to take the hurried dismissal as a matter of course and came quickly down from the table on the dais. Abruptly, without even a glance at Kat, Elizabeth gestured Lady Alana to follow her to her own quarters.

There as soon as Naylor had closed the door behind her, she

caught at Aleneil's hand. "Will you sleep in my chamber, Lady Alana? Will you, please?" Elizabeth begged.

Aleneil opened her eyes wide in astonishment. Elizabeth knew that Lady Alana always had a chamber to herself—it was necessary so that Aleneil could Gate Underhill to restore the power that living in the mortal world drained. Her privacy had been maintained, even in the most crowded situations, and there was plenty of room at Chelsea. However as the request was coupled with an upsurge of the suppressed excitement in Elizabeth's manner, Aleneil did not feel that she should seek an excuse to refuse.

"Of course, Lady Elizabeth—"

The door opened and one of the maids of honor came in, voices in the corridor betrayed the imminent arrival of others. Elizabeth uttered a brief hiss of irritation and her lips thinned to a straight line. Plainly she had hoped to have more time to talk to Aleneil alone, but there was no fear in her face or her manner, just frustration.

"If you feel my company can provide you with comfort," Aleneil continued smoothly, "I will be glad to sleep in your chamber until you are completely at ease in this new place."

"Oh, thank you, Lady Alana." Elizabeth glanced sidelong at the maids of honor clustering together, uncertain of whether they should approach their mistress when she was talking with a long-time favorite. "I would have sent for you to come back to me sooner," Elizabeth added, seeming to become aware that they were scarcely new arrivals and she had had plenty of time to grow accustomed to Chelsea. "But Kat said you had neglected your own interests too long when I was grieving and that I must not demand more of you."

And now that she looked closer at Elizabeth, Aleneil could see that the girl's eyelids were heavy and that shadows of sleeplessness lay below her eyes. Yet there were no other marks of fear or anxiety. Indeed, Aleneil would have said from voice, stance, and expression that Elizabeth was in high spirits and brimming with mischief.

"That was very kind of Mistress Ashley," Aleneil said, not knowing whether she should be worried that Kat would not notice a real emergency or whether this was a case of Elizabeth being self-indulgent. "I am glad," she continued to be on the safe side, "that your need for me was not urgent. But if it ever is, you must not be concerned about my affairs. If you need me," she lowered her voice a little "or Denno, you must send for us"—she glanced up toward the air spirit bouncing gently near a window—"at once."

"No," Elizabeth murmured, "it was not that"—she also glanced upward at the window—"kind of need. Just—"

"Now, Lady Elizabeth," Kat Ashley said, shepherding the last of Elizabeth's ladies into the chamber, and coming to join her charge and Aleneil. "You know that Lady Alana has just arrived after a long ride. You must allow her to rest and to settle herself."

"She is going to stay with me," Elizabeth said eagerly. "Until I am . . . am less uneasy. Would you please have a servant tell Blanche to bring what Lady Alana will need to my chamber and have a bed made up for her there?"

Kat looked troubled for a moment but then sighed and nodded. As she went off to send a servant for Blanche, the other girls came forward to join Lady Elizabeth and Aleneil. There were five now: the three that had remained with Elizabeth during the sad period after her father's death had been augmented by two even younger girls whose terms of service were beginning.

One of those asked, "Will we wait for Lady Jane? Will she join us for the evening lesson?"

A very slight shade passed over Elizabeth's face but was instantly banished. Had Aleneil's perception been less quick than a Sidhe's she would not have seen it. Having seen it she still forebore to smile. Elizabeth in some ways was indeed the noxious brat Denoriel called her. Her scholarship was prodigious, but it was little better, sometimes not quite as perfect as that of Lady Jane Grey. For that reason, and possibly because Lady Jane was *so* well behaved, so polite, so self-effacing, Elizabeth had never really liked her. Likely Queen Catherine knew it because Lady Jane was not among Elizabeth's ladies. She must be directly in the queen's care.

Blanche Parry came in at that moment, carrying Aleneil's bags. Her head turned at once up toward the window, and her step hesitated. She sniffed, almost as if she were a scenting hound, and then crossed the chamber toward the door in the far wall.

Another servant might have sidled around the room to keep as clear as possible of the "gentry," but Blanche had been with Elizabeth since a few days after her birth. Although a mortal, Blanche had some Talent—not as much as Elizabeth, who could see through Sidhe illusion. Still, Blanche could sense the presence of otherworldly beings, like the air spirit, and she could use Cold Iron to drive off inimical Sidhe. Not surprisingly, Elizabeth prized her above any other servant, except Dunstan and Ladbroke.

Without any expression now, Elizabeth said, "Of course we will wait for Lady Jane. She enjoys Bible reading so much. She just loves to translate the Greek so we can understand." She then turned toward Aleneil and smiled somewhat stiffly, possibly a little ashamed that Aleneil had witnessed her waspishness. "You may go and rest, Lady Alana. I will speak to you later."

With only Blanche in the bedchamber, and the additional safety of a screen before the hearth behind which she could dress, Aleneil shed her traveling garments and put on court dress with a few waves of her hand. The garments she removed undid themselves and reappeared on Blanche's outstretched arm, and a new set of garments slid from the packed bags without causing tangles and fixed themselves on her body.

"Blanche, what is going on?" Aleneil asked softly. "Do I need to try to find Denno and get him here?"

"Oh, no," Blanche said with a grin. "It isn't anything dangerous—" she paused and frowned. "No, I can't see how it could be dangerous to my lady." Then she smiled again. "But I'm not going to say a word more because she's been waiting and waiting to talk this over with you and if you know ahead of time it will spoil her fun."

Aleneil sighed. "Then it isn't something in which Elizabeth herself is involved?"

"That's right m'lady. My baby's just watching." The frown reappeared and Blanche sighed. "Just hope she isn't learning too much. I would have kept it from her if I could, but she was out walking with only the guards. They turned away, but she saw what she saw and then she set out to watch apurpose."

Although she was puzzled, the matter certainly did not seem urgent. Aleneil dismissed it from her mind and occupied herself with becoming familiar with the area of the palace assigned to Elizabeth. Cloaked in the Don't-see-me spell, she examined the small apartment Kat shared with her husband, Thomas Parry's office/bedchamber, the two crowded rooms the maids shared, and the two rooms assigned to the grooms of the chamber and Elizabeth's tutor.

That was as far as she had gotten when the air spirit appeared and beckoned and Aleneil returned to Elizabeth's bedchamber, where she rose from a chair as if she had been asleep. Blanche came in as if to help Elizabeth undress for bed, but Elizabeth waved her away and said, "Get my cloak and Lady Alana's. We will walk for a few minutes in the garden."

"It is only the beginning of March, Lady Elizabeth," Aleneil said. "Evening walks are better saved for later in the spring."

Elizabeth giggled. "There is a nice sheltered shed and we will not need to stay long." Her nose wrinkled. "We may not need to stay at all, if Lady Jane spent so much time on the lesson that they are gone."

"Who?" Aleneil asked, but Elizabeth only giggled and shook her head.

Blanche returned with their cloaks and Elizabeth hurried Aleneil out through the servant's door to avoid her guards. Aleneil bit her lip. No matter how innocent the matter that enthralled Elizabeth, this escape of those provided to protect her was not good. She would have to talk to Elizabeth about that, but now was not the time.

Fortunately they did not go far. A path led through the garden in which herbs and some vegetables were grown for the kitchen. The path had numerous narrow branches which divided the plant beds. Aleneil had begun to ask a question, but Elizabeth put her finger firmly over Aleneil's lips and she was clearly taking care to step softly.

About halfway down the path, Aleneil's dark-seeing eyes noticed that there was a wall ahead broken by a low wrought-iron gate. Two people stood by the gate, which was closed, leaning toward each other. It was too dark for the human eyes of those standing by the gate to have seen her or Elizabeth, and she did not think that Elizabeth had seen them either.

Aleneil's long ears twitched forward, but before she could hear what they were saying, Elizabeth had turned left to draw her into a side path and then after about ten or fifteen steps right again into another narrow path but this one parallel to the main path. Aleneil could see where she was going, of course, but Elizabeth did not stumble, as if she had walked this way before. They did not go much farther.

Aleneil saw a dark bulk ahead—ah, the shed Elizabeth had mentioned. Elizabeth slowed and put her hands out. When her fingertips touched the shed, she began to sidle around it toward the left, then along the side. At the edge she stopped and just poked her head around. Aleneil took a step to the side onto a narrow strip of unkempt land, too close to the shed to plant or bother mowing. She crouched down. It would be impossible to see her from the gate in the wall, but she could see the man and woman there.

The woman was Catherine. The man—Aleneil doubted that Elizabeth could make out his features, but she could see him clearly enough to know that it was Thomas Seymour. He was objecting to something Catherine had said, saying it was too long, far too long.

"I cannot wait, I cannot," he said. "I am in agony, fearing every moment that you will be snatched away from me again. You do not know what I suffered, thinking of you in another man's arms. Let me in! You cannot feel anything for me if you will not even let me in."

The gate clicked open. Elizabeth withdrew her head and then seeing how Aleneil was crouched down, knelt beside her. Aleneil had heard Seymour so clearly that she suspected Elizabeth could hear also.

"You must trust me," Catherine said. "I promise I will take no other husband. You know I could not withstand the king, nor did I wish to. If I brought him comfort in the last years, then I am well rewarded for my sacrifice. I did a duty with a glad heart for the good of the realm." She raised a hand and stroked his cheek. "Tom, he is not cold in his grave yet, and he was a great man, a great king. I cannot act as if he were nothing and marry again so soon. Only two short years."

"Those years will not be short for me." The man's voice was petulant. "And I will need to watch you being courted by every fortune hunter in the country."

Catherine laughed softly. "You cannot fear I will be seduced by a man who cares more for my lands than for me! Not when I have so faithful a lover."

Seymour had passed through the gate and now drew Catherine aside, bending over her and leaning down to put his lips to the side of her jaw. She drew in a breath, sharply enough for Aleneil to hear, and beside Aleneil, Elizabeth shivered. Seymour kissed all along Catherine's jaw and then her chin, forcing her head up slightly so he could press his lips to her throat. Catherine's breath was coming quick and hard . . . and so was Elizabeth's.

"Tom, stop!" The queen's voice was shaking, pleading.

"I cannot bear it, I tell you! I need you. I want you."

His lips had found their way down to the pulse in the hollow where the collar bones met. Catherine's hands came up and cupped his face, lifting it, but he turned his head in her hands and began to nibble on her ear.

"Have I been too faithful? Belike you are so sure of me that I am a dull thing—"

"No, no. I always favored you above all others. You must know that the other time I was free my mind was bent to marry you above any other man I had ever met."

"Then why must we wait? Catherine, you know my brother will not favor this union. If we do not seal it before the Church and with consummation, I fear he will find some other duty for you. Perhaps he will try to use you to bind the Empire to us, or to make peace with France. You are a great prize and he will tear you away from me."

"No one thinks me of any value. You have seen how the men in the government avoid me. No one will care that I wish to marry you, but the whole world will scorn me if I do not observe a decent mourning. Do not tease me so, Tom. I will be yours, I swear it. Perhaps we could become betrothed . . ."

He began to kiss her again—her lips, her throat, her ears; Catherine was sobbing very softly but clinging to him. Suddenly Elizabeth shifted uneasily and then also made a very soft sound.

Aleneil started. She had almost forgotten the girl beside her. The caresses exchanged by the humans had no effect on her. She had been thinking about what Denoriel had told her about Seymour. Apparently Denoriel had judged him correctly. He was a selfish lout; she sensed the insincerity of his passion. He was using lust to force poor Catherine, who had been starved all her life for a strong, young man's desire, into an action that would profit him greatly. It might not profit her. She might be open to considerable criticism if she married so soon after King Henry's death.

That was not important, Aleneil knew. Catherine was not her duty and must manage her own affairs. Elizabeth, however . . . When she felt Elizabeth shiver, heard that low, breathy sound she had realized that the girl had been unfortunately aroused by Seymour's caresses. Aleneil was annoyed with herself. She must stop thinking of Elizabeth as a child. Mortals ripened fast, and a girl of nearly fifteen years of age was likely more vulnerable, more likely to be affected and inflamed by the stench of human lust.

Chapter 17

Rhoslyn held a missal in her lap, her eyes seemingly bent on the pages, her lips moving occasionally, as if she repeated some words to herself. It was a safe occupation in Mary's chamber and saved Rhoslyn from trying to embroider and join the gossip, which was the way most of the ladies in Mary's service spent their time.

She had been welcomed back by Lady Mary with warmth and some concern, but had assured her lady that the rest she had taken had restored her. She looked well, her hair springy and shining, her dark eyes bright, a faint color warming her olive complexion.

Llanelli had indeed restored Rhoslyn, transferring power from her own body to Rhoslyn's. When she realized what her mother had done, Rhoslyn cried out in protest, but it was too late. Llanelli was again drooping and faded, her hair no more than a white mist, her skin transparent, and her eyes clouded. But she had laughed softly and assured Rhoslyn that as she knew how to feed power to others, she knew how to draw it into herself. With that, Rhoslyn had to be satisfied, since she had no way to return what Llanelli had given her.

She had spent three mortal weeks in her own domain, renewing the energy of her constructs—although she was very careful to sense for anything unusual in the Unformed lands she used—and making the landscape around her home more gentle and beautiful. When she returned to the mortal world the worst of the winter was over and, to her unspoken pleasure, Lady Mary had stopped reading prayers for the dead.

Life had returned to its normal tempo, except that Rhoslyn detected a kind of tension under the placid exterior. The earl of Hertford was now duke of Somerset and Mary heard from her good friend—her Good Nan and Dear Gossip, Ann Stanhope, Somerset's wife—that Somerset would soon be appointed Protector officially. Mary knew that Somerset leaned toward the reformed religion, but in the past he had ignored her Catholic rites. Naturally Mary hoped he would continue to do so, but she was slightly uneasy.

Rhoslyn turned a page of the missal, her long ears cupped forward. Mary was sitting with two of her Spanish chaplains and was again lamenting to them the strongly reformist character of Somerset's Council. This was nothing new and she and the chaplains could go on for hours, pointing out to each other how the lack of a universal mass and the dismissal of good works would bring anarchy and disaster.

Rhoslyn relaxed and actually read a line or two of the missal, just in case one of the women asked what had been holding her attention. Then her head lifted, started to turn; she caught herself and uttered a small, false cough. None of the other women had yet heard anything.

In the next moment a groom of the chamber entered the room and carried a letter to Lady Mary. She lifted it high to her near-sighted eyes and her body became a little tense and alert, not as if to brace herself against a blow but as if she was puzzled. Rhoslyn heard the very faint crackle as the wax of a seal was broken and the rustle as heavy parchment was unfolded.

A few minutes later she heard Mary gasp and exclaim softly with dismay, "How dare he!"

Rhoslyn laid the missal down in her lap and looked toward Lady Mary. She allowed a look of concern to wrinkle her brow, but did not rise and go to her. Rhoslyn was liked and trusted by Lady Mary but not quite as much as long-time and confidential servants like Jane Dormer, Eleanor Kempe, or Susan Clarencieux. Jane Dormer and Eleanor Kempe were not in the chamber. It was Lady Susan who put aside her embroidery, rose, and hurried to her mistress.

"What is wrong, my lady?"

"This!" Mary thrust the now crumpled parchment toward her lady but did not release it. "This letter is an abomination! How dare he?" She signed for the chaplains to leave.

"Who, madam?" Susan urged, as the two men bowed and went out. "Who has insulted you? I am sure that His Grace of Somerset would put a quick end to any offense against you."

"From his own brother?" Mary cried. And a moment later because she was a fair and honest person, "He did not insult me, precisely." Then color rose in her cheeks. "What he asks is an insult to honor and propriety. He has the—the effrontery to ask me to write in his favor to the dowager queen."

Susan looked puzzled. "Write in his favor to Queen Catherine? His favor for what purpose?"

Mary stood up, crushing the letter further between her hands. "He wants to marry her! My father is not two months dead and Thomas Seymour has the gall to ask me to urge Queen Catherine to forget who her husband was and marry this—this no one from a family created noble only because their sister was fecund."

"It is a disgusting presumption," Lady Susan agreed, breathing quick with her anger. "Write and tell him so."

Since none of the voices had been lowered, Rhoslyn could assume there was no secret in the matter. She rose, set aside her book and came toward Susan and Lady Mary, who had just raised a hand to summon a servant.

"Forgive me," Rhoslyn said softly, "but I could not help but hear. I agree, of course, with everything both of you have said, but I beg you, my lady, do not answer yet. You are overset. To reply so soon is to grant too much importance to this upstart. Let him wait on your answer. What he asks is almost comical—would be comical if his brother were not likely to be the ruler of this realm."

For a moment Mary looked as if she would push by Rhoslyn but fortunately Jane Dormer and Eleanor Kempe came in. Both saw at once that Lady Mary was greatly disturbed and they hurried forward at her gesture. They were informed by Mary in a furious voice of Seymour's letter. Jane and Eleanor asked at once if they would be permitted to read the letter lest Seymour's poor writing (not, of course, Mary's faulty vision) might have made some words seem what they were not.

"It is outrageous, yes," Eleanor Kempe said, smoothing the

parchment and folding it neatly, "but to refuse too quickly or with insult, my lady, might enrage Seymour and draw Somerset's attention to us."

Mary had calmed somewhat. "Surely Somerset cannot know of this," she said. "Surely he cannot desire his brother to gain so rich a prize both in Queen Catherine's wealth and in the love of the people for her."

"There might be reasons for Somerset's approval," Jane Dormer said thoughtfully. "Could he hope the young king, who loves Queen Catherine dearly, would be angered and repulsed by her marrying again before King Henry was cold in his grave? And the queen's casting off her mourning so swiftly might also turn the people away from her. Moreover the use of Queen Catherine's purse might reduce Seymour's demands on Somerset for more lands and appointments."

Mary peered from one face to another. "I do not know. I suppose it is possible." She hesitated and then added, "Rosamund agrees with Eleanor that I should *not* answer him at once and not say openly how disgusting I find his proposal."

"Mistress Rosamund is wise in this." Eleanor Kempe nodded. "He writes with such foolish certainty, as if merely to ask you to do something would oblige you to obey. And Jane's notions must be considered. Wait a few days, as if taking advice before you answer. I feel, like you, that Somerset is not likely to favor a marriage between Queen Catherine and his brother. Waiting cannot hurt."

"There is an aspect of this that none of us have considered, my lady," Jane Dormer said, looking anxious. "The letter says he has already asked the queen to be his wife. Does this not mean that he has been at Chelsea often? I mean, one does not come on one visit to a lady like Queen Catherine and say you wish to marry her."

Everyone looked at Jane, and she shrugged. "One must woo such a lady at length. That means that Lady Elizabeth has also been in Seymour's company. Should you not discover if you can what is happening and if Seymour is too often there, write to your sister and offer her a refuge? It might be that Lady Elizabeth finds her position awkward. It might even be that Queen Catherine would be glad to be rid of her."

Rhoslyn blinked. Jane Dormer was the youngest of Queen Mary's ladies, little more than a girl, but she was clever and as passionately devoted to the Catholic rite as Mary herself. Rhoslyn wondered whether Jane was as worried about contamination by Seymour as she was about contamination by Queen Catherine's reformist leanings.

Doubtless Jane meant well in wishing to bring Elizabeth under Mary's influence. She would think of it as saving Elizabeth's soul. But it would be terribly dangerous. Rhoslyn did not think it possible that Elizabeth would eagerly espouse the Catholic rite, which did not matter, but the girl was only fourteen. Far too likely, she would not dissemble and show Mary that she could not be bent in that direction.

The FarSeers' scrying pool showed as one possible future that Mary did come to the throne. In that case, Elizabeth would be killed. Mary would not allow her heir to favor the reform religion and reject the authority of the pope. If Mary had Elizabeth executed, the burgeoning life, the beauty, the richness that Elizabeth's reign might bring to England would never happen.

A discussion about the pros and cons of inviting Elizabeth to join the household went on around Rhoslyn, but she could think of nothing to say. To oppose the idea without compelling reason would not help Elizabeth and might damage her own position with Mary, which, if Elizabeth came into Mary's household, would be more essential than ever. The sound of her mortal name drew her attention.

"Rosamund," Mary said, "you know one of Elizabeth's ladies, Lady . . . ah . . . Alana. The one who dresses so well that one cannot see what she looks like."

"I cannot say I *know* her, my lady. We were thrown together when Lady Elizabeth came to speak to you but you were too unwell. It was some years ago and Lady Elizabeth wanted permission to walk in your private garden. I took it upon myself to say I knew you would be willing, but I went with them—Lady Elizabeth was attended by Lady Alana—to be sure Lady Elizabeth had no mischief in mind. She felt at that time, that Edward preferred you and I feared was jealous."

Mary frowned. "But you have spoken to Lady Alana since then, have you not?"

"Oh, yes, whenever our paths cross. She is a most civil individual and always greets me and asks how you do. In fact, I met her in London when I was there to see my physician. She had taken a brief leave of absence from her duties to Lady Elizabeth while they moved from Enfield to Chelsea and was staying with Lord Denno, a wealthy merchant."

"A merchant!" Susan Clarencieux was shocked.

Rhoslyn smiled. "He is rich as Croesus and quite a favorite with Mistress Ashley, Lady Elizabeth's governess."

"Perhaps another reason for Lady Elizabeth to live here with our lady," Jane said. "I think Mistress Ashley is not careful enough of her charge and should be overseen."

"How does a merchant come to call himself Lord Denno?" Mary asked, frowning.

"As I heard it, rightfully enough," Rhoslyn replied. "It is not an English title, of course. Before the Turks overran Hungary, his family was of the royal line there. The lands are poor and unprofitable in Hungary and so most of the nobility were merchants of one kind or another."

Mary was still frowning. "How does Lady Alana, a maid of honor to Lady Elizabeth, come to live in a merchant's house? Can she afford no better lodging?"

"She can afford what she likes. Her clothes and jewels are lavish. You know, madam, that my brother is most generous to me, but I could not match her spending. As to her staying with Lord Denno . . . It is for comfort, I believe, for a house always ready, for well-trained servants that she need not oversee. Moreover she and Lord Denno are distant—very distant—relations, and call each other 'cousin.' I think her great-grandmother, or perhaps her great-great-grandmother, married some ancestor of his. They also know each other from her service to Lady Elizabeth and his frequent visits there."

Mary had cocked her head to the side quizzically and her brows were up. The other three ladies were staring at Rhoslyn in some surprise.

"For someone who does not *know* Lady Alana," Mary said, "you seem to know a great deal about her."

"Oh," Rhoslyn said and looked down at her toes. "When I first arrived in London, I was so weak and so bored—"

"London? Why did you not go to your brother's house where you would be carefully tended?" Eleanor Kempe's voice was flat.

"Let my brother see me ill?" Rhoslyn rounded her eyes in pretended horror. "Never! It might kill him. Certainly it would bring on a most severe attack of his nervous condition. I am all he has. He must not know I also have my troubles. He must never fear he will be left alone."

"But surely if you stay at your brother's house in London the servants must gossip to those in his country seat."

"I stay at the Golden Bull in London. My brother sold his house there when it became clear that he could not endure the city."

"Ladies." Mary held up a hand and her quiet voice quelled all other questions. "I know all about Rosamund, but not how she came to know so much about Lady Alana."

Rhoslyn smiled. When she first came to serve Mary, she had inserted into Mary's mind a whole history for Rosamund Scott and impressed upon her that all this must be kept secret because both Rosamund and her brother were very sensitive about his illness, which some could call madness. Mary *thought* she knew all about Rosamund and would protect her from too much curiosity from her other ladies.

"I could not do much when I first came to London," Rhoslyn admitted, "but I wished to find something for you, my lady, a token of thanks for your kindness to me. Since I could not shop from merchant to merchant, the landlord of the Bull suggested I go to Adjoran, Mercer and Factor. It was not far. I could be carried there by litter. It was not a shop either, so noisy and exhausting, but Lord Denno's home where his man of business showed me samples he had in the house. I found that black lace shawl—" Rhoslyn laughed softly. "It was so lovely I near to nothing kept it for myself."

"It *is* lovely," Mary said, smiling. "I felt quite guilty when I took it and saw your eyes linger on it."

"Oh, no. It was always meant for you, my lady, but the pattern is quite enchanting. However, Lady Alana came in just as I was looking at it closely and startled me so that I had another pain in my chest and came over faint. Lady Alana saw me to my rooms. She did not wish to leave me to the mercy of the inn servants—although really they are very good and attentive—and she stayed until I was recovered. She came again, the next day, bringing the shawl and . . . and bless her, she *does* talk."

"Does she?" Mary sounded quite interested. "Could you find some excuse—Chelsea is very close to London—to invite Lady Alana to dinner or for some other small entertainment, now that you are well and strong again, to give thanks for her kind care of you?"

Rhoslyn only allowed herself to look surprised although she was utterly delighted. She had been wondering how she could get leave again to warn Aleneil about Mary's intention of asking Elizabeth to live with her.

"I suppose I could. It *was* very good of her."

Mary nodded. "Yes, it was. And I am sure when you seek a subject of conversation, since she has already told you all about herself, it would be natural for you to ask about Queen Catherine's household."

"Ah!" Rhoslyn widened her eyes into an expression of enlightenment. "Yes, of course. Likely Lord Denno's man of business will know how to reach Lady Alana."

"Exactly," Mary said. "And it would also seem natural that you would be very interested to hear all about Lady Elizabeth, how she is overseen, what she does, who serves as chaplain in the household, and . . . how much time she spends in Thomas Seymour's company."

Joseph Clayborne made no difficulty about sending a messenger with a note for Aleneil to Chelsea, and that very night Rhoslyn met Aleneil in the Inn of Kindly Laughter.

"Mary isn't the only one worried about Elizabeth," Aleneil said, after Rhoslyn had told her about Seymour's letter and Mary's reaction. In turn, she described Seymour's clandestine courtship. Sighing, she added, "And it is very exciting for Elizabeth. She is just at that age when mortal girls begin to dream about men. She is just burning with curiosity. I fear she will be casting her eyes on any man she finds attractive."

"She mustn't," Rhoslyn said. "There must be no scandal. Mary cannot decide what she feels about Elizabeth. She hates her still because she is Anne Boleyn's daughter, but she remembers tenderly the little girl who ran to her with love and joy. She remembers the baby kisses with which her little gifts were received because then Elizabeth had nothing. Other times she thinks of the too-clever girl who welcomed all the questions about the Catholic rite posed by the reformers and for whom little King Edward has a stronger affection and more respect than he has for her. If she could do that girl an injury she would."

Aleneil sighed. "And there was that stupid business about Elizabeth meeting a man in the garden at Hampton Court. Nothing was proved because the man was Harry FitzRoy and he had an amulet with the Don't-see-me spell. But still Mary made a huge fuss, and then no one would believe her and nothing came of it. Doubtless that rankles."

"Gentle Mother, if any scandal should remind Mary of that! She still speaks of it and is convinced that Elizabeth is as promiscuous as her mother—"

"Who was not promiscuous at all!" Aleneil said sharply. "Only Henry, because he needed to be rid of Anne, and Mary because she wanted to believe it, ever thought Anne was promiscuous."

"That may be true, but the memory that remains of Anne is that she was a whore. Any whisper of Elizabeth and a man and Mary will believe it fact, and Mary has a direct line to Somerset through his wife to whom she writes as Dearest Nan and my Good Gossip. Almost, it would be better for Elizabeth to accept the invitation to live with Mary—"

"No. That would be a catastrophe, and not only because of the religious problems. Although ordinarily Elizabeth is very cautious about Mary, and I think she would really return Mary's love if it were proffered, she already knows she has Catherine's love. She is very happy living with Catherine. It is a merry, lively household. To force Elizabeth into Mary's dismal care would only make Elizabeth so resentful that she might lose all her caution in her attempts to free herself. And Elizabeth can have a tongue like a honed dagger."

Rhoslyn bit her lip, then said, "Yes. I can see that Elizabeth living with Mary is impossible. When I report to Mary, I will do my best to make Catherine's household sound unexceptional; however, because of Seymour, whatever I say, Mary will invite Elizabeth to come to her. Make sure Elizabeth's refusal is very gentle."

"That presents no problem. Elizabeth *will* be grateful for Mary's care, and will say so. She will doubtless also say her obligations to Catherine are too great for her to leave."

"But you still have the other problem, that of Seymour's behavior with Catherine awakening Elizabeth's body. Someone must satisfy that need in sufficient secret that there is no chance of discovery—" Rhoslyn's voice checked abruptly and she frowned. "Sidhe," she said. "A Sidhe could never be caught with her because he could vanish in an instant." Then she uttered a low laugh. "And we have a Sidhe ready to hand who can endure the iron of the mortal world and who is already intimate with the household . . . Denoriel."

Aleneil drew in a sharp breath. "But Denoriel thinks of Elizabeth as a little girl. And likely Elizabeth thinks of him as a rich old uncle. Both would be horrified by the thought of sex between them."

"Are you so sure?" Rhoslyn asked. "What Pasgen told me about Elizabeth's confrontation with Oberon over Denoriel seemed to me more . . . ah . . . *intense* than feelings for an old uncle. 'My Denno' Pasgen said she called him, and threatened to close the mortal world to Sidhe if she were deprived of him. And as for Denoriel's feelings, once his conscience is soothed, he will be happy enough to have a fresh, young lover."

Aleneil sat silent thinking back over Elizabeth's behavior to Denoriel. She *did* flirt with him. The way she looked up at him under her lashes, all the bickering that only led up to her sweetest smiles even when he did not yield to her will. And Denoriel . . . hmmm. Recently Denoriel seemed to feel some constraint about being in Elizabeth's company, especially since her figure had begun to form.

"I will see what I can do," Aleneil said.

However, it turned out that at first there was very little Aleneil could do about inducing Denoriel to make love to Elizabeth. Denoriel was not to be found. He, Harry, and half the residents of Elfhame Elder-Elf had disappeared into the terrifying precincts of Alhambra.

On the other hand, Lady Alana had made decisive strides in calming Elizabeth. The expeditions to watch avidly while Seymour caressed Catherine were at an end. Closeted alone with Elizabeth, Lady Alana had made clear the impropriety of what Elizabeth had done. Crude and vulgar were not words ordinarily applied to Elizabeth, but Lady Alana applied them now and said how shocked she was to find Elizabeth spying on a woman who had done so much for her and was herself doing no wrong.

Lady Alana rehearsed the same arguments Lord Denno had provided. The tale of Catherine's long dutiful behavior as wife to aged and unlovable men; her right to seize, while she still could, some joy and the chance of motherhood. Elizabeth readily agreed; she had overcome her jealousy on her father's behalf.

To make more certain that Elizabeth would see Seymour as

Catherine's "reward" for duty nobly done, Lady Alana pointed out that King Henry was dead; he could not feel betrayed. Had he not set restrictions on Elizabeth's marriage and Mary's and set none on Catherine's? Was that not almost permission for her to take a younger, more appealing husband?

Finally, Lady Alana pointed out, if Elizabeth were caught, what would Queen Catherine feel? Would she not believe she had been betrayed by a person to whom she had always offered kindness? Might she not send Elizabeth away?

Curbed so sharply by one who had always been supportive, Elizabeth agreed she would watch no longer. And just in time it seemed, for Dunstan, fearing an adverse reaction from Elizabeth to news of Catherine being courted, reported to Lady Alana that rumors were rife among the servants about the dowager queen's late night excursions and her meetings with a man. Doubtless Catherine's maids had noticed her absences and murmured to others. This one and that one had bumped into each other lurking in the kitchen garden. The gossip was that Seymour had won his point. There would be no two-year wait for marriage.

The delay did not even last two months. Sometime late in April, Thomas Seymour and Catherine were secretly married. The truth was not kept secret from Elizabeth; it came from Catherine herself, stiff with anxiety. But Elizabeth only kissed her and wished her well. Elizabeth was sworn to silence, Catherine confessing that she feared the Lord Protector would not be pleased and that she wished to gain the king's consent before the marriage was made public.

Elizabeth kept her word to Catherine, not mentioning the wedding even to Lady Alana. However in quiet times, as she embroidered or practiced on her virginal, the scenes in the garden came back to her and her eyes glistened as she thought about Seymour's caresses now free to wander all over Catherine's body. At those times Elizabeth would look up from her work or her music and ask Lady Alana where Lord Denno was and why he had not been near her in almost a month.

On a voyage, Lady Alana said, but Elizabeth caught the concern in the cat-pupilled bright green eyes she saw under the thin-lashed, mud-colored illusion. Her Denno was doing something dangerous, she guessed. There was no way that she could ask what it was, and when she said sharply that Lady Alana should send him a message, she was answered not in Lady Alana's coo but in Aleneil's sharper tone that she had already done so.

Elizabeth was frightened. She knew she did not need Denno. She was busy and happy, pleased with her new tutor, Master Grindal, enchanted by Catherine's glowing joy, free to ride out even into London with her guards and grooms, not even pressed for money because Catherine covered many of her expenses.

Still, there was a large hole inside of her. If she did not *need* Denno, Elizabeth acknowledged that she wanted him, wanted his firm, warm hand holding hers, the sound of his voice—even opposing her will—the brush of his warm lips against her hand and once or twice against her cheek. Why had she never turned her face so that their lips met? Would she know then what made Catherine sigh and glow as if lit from within?

Chapter 18

Pasgen had, as he said he would, gone back to Otstargi's house after he left Rhoslyn. He was there, seemingly idle and relaxed by the parlor fire, to witness Albertus' return after it was certain that all of his men had been killed without accomplishing their purpose.

Totally distraught, Albertus poured out the details of the disaster to Pasgen. Only the child who had opened the door for the men and fled had survived, crouching outside the house in the alley and watching. The child had seen Cropper carry out one corpse, had seen the arrival of the watch and the sheriff, had seen the removal of the other five bodies. Worse than the failure, the child had escaped before Albertus could seize him and might describe the fiasco to others, making it impossible for Albertus to hire more men.

"I do not think it matters. You cannot hope to play the same game again," Pasgen said mildly, as if he had no interest in the subject. "It will be impossible to get anyone else into that house. They will watch closely for intruders and likely they will hire extra guards."

"What can I do?" Albertus' voice trembled. "You know my lady can . . . ah . . . be harsh to those who fail her."

Pasgen shrugged indifferently. "I have no idea of what happened in the house and you say the men did get inside. The best I can do for you is to tell Lady Aurilia that your plan worked but that together Aleneil and Denoriel were too strong even though you sent six men against them. I will make as good a case for you as I can."

Not that Pasgen had any intention of going anywhere near Aurilia. But since she did not know an attempt had been made and had failed, she might not yet be impatient for results. Pasgen could only hope that Albertus had made sufficient of that blue potion Aurilia was forever sipping so that she did not call the healer back Underhill.

Albertus had thanked Pasgen fulsomely for his help and took heart, saying that he realized he would have to pick off Aleneil and Denoriel separately. Pasgen listened with an approving expression. Why not? Both Aleneil and Denoriel were Underhill now where Albertus could not touch them and did not plan to return to the mortal world for some time.

Aleneil would be safe even when she did return. She would be in Elizabeth's household where no one Albertus could hire could penetrate. As for Denoriel, Pasgen would give another warning but Denoriel could take care of himself. For now, whatever his plans, Albertus had been rendered impotent.

In due course, Pasgen Gated Underhill to seem to be going to report to Aurilia. As soon as he arrived, he felt the pull of that cursed Unformed land. At first he resisted, idling in his own domain, making sure that the force field around the red mist was sound and strong, that the container of iron filings was well shielded but ready to hand. Pasgen looked at it and sighed. He knew he should empty the iron into the red mist, but he still could not bring himself to do it. He spent time, too, with the wisp of partly responsive mist. Sometimes he thought it was learning, sometimes not.

His resistance did not last very long. In the back of his mind, even as he examined the doings of the mist that used to fascinate him, was the urge to return. His curiosity about the red-haired and gold-haired dolls was eating him alive. Had they dissipated? Had they become more real? Had the mist made more figures?

After a brief struggle with himself, which he pacified by vowing he would not, as he had promised Rhoslyn, leave the Gate, he yielded. When he stepped into his most private Gate, in a warded chamber of his own house, the pattern of the sentient Unformed land leapt into his mind . . . and he was there before he could suppress it. He had barely had time to look around, had not had time to send out a testing tendril into the mist, when the Gate thrummed and a second Sidhe appeared, a levin bolt already burning in her hand.

"What do you here?" she cried, raising the hand in which the levin bolt glared.

Pasgen backed a step, calling up his shields, although he knew it was useless. If she loosed that bolt this close, it would burn through even his shields. "I am Pasgen," he gasped. "I was the one who gave warning about this land."

Slowly the levin bolt began to fade, not dispersed but drawn back into the Sidhe. Despite the lingering threat, Pasgen wondered how she had done that, wondered if it might possibly be through some forgotten magic. That she was very old was immediately apparent. Her hair was white spun mist, so thin, so short that it floated, barely held back from her face by a plain leather thong; her eyes were the palest green Pasgen had ever seen, the color of shallow seawater above white sand. But those eyes were sparkling bright, her expression was alert and interested, and that levin bolt had nothing of weakness or uncertainty about it.

"Ah," the tenseness that told Pasgen she was still on guard decreased and she nodded. "You look like . . . who?"

Pasgen's moue of distaste was more habit than expressive of real feeling now. "Denoriel," he said. "We are half brothers."

The old Sidhe nodded satisfaction. "He spoke of you when he warned the Elders about this domain. I am Gaenor. Once I was a great maker. I know mist. I have been set the task of watching here. When I felt the Gate in use, I was concerned."

Pasgen grimaced. "As I was when I felt you coming. Watching, are you? What have you found here?"

Her face took on a thoughtful expression. "Mostly a feeling . . ."

"A calling? A drawing? I will confess the place draws me. You should have been warned against that. I told Denoriel, I am sure."

But as he spoke, Pasgen found himself looking out into the mist rather than at Gaenor's face. Was that a flash of gold near a ruddy spot? He almost stepped off the Gate platform, but Gaenor had a grip on his arm and drew him back.

"Did you see that?" he asked urgently. "Is that red hair near golden? Have you ever seen the . . . the . . . I do not know what to call them."

"The mist's creatures?" Gaenor's voice was calm. "Not clearly."

"Do you not think it . . . strange? That we can talk about the makings of a mist?" He uttered an uneasy laugh.

She smiled slightly. "When you are as old as I, you will find very few things strange. I come here often and watch. I send no thoughts out into the mist . . . ah . . . you did and there is an answer . . ."

It did seem that the mist was thicker and more curling, that it was coming closer to the Gate platform, that behind the roiling mass were two more substantial clots, one topped in red, the other in gold.

Pasgen shuddered. No mist in any Unformed domain had ever invaded a Gate as far as Pasgen knew, but here— Pasgen took a deep breath, racking his brains for some way to set up a force field that would hold back the mist. But the Gate might disrupt any field he tried or, worse yet, the field might damage the Gate, stranding them—

"Rest!" The voice was command, but honeyed with good will. The mist billowed uncertainly. "You have done enough. No aid is called for here. Rest."

Only, the hand that gripped Pasgen's arm was trembling, the desperation in the hold in total variance to the calm of the voice and the blankness of the mind.

"Rest," Gaenor repeated. "I am called elsewhere but I will come again soon to be with you."

On the last word, they dropped into blackness and emerged in the unadorned Gate on the peaceful, perfect lawn of Elfhame Elder-Elf. Gaenor stepped off the platform, her hand still tight on Pasgen's arm and turned her nearly colorless eyes on him.

"The mist knows you. It was coming to you."

Wordless, Pasgen nodded.

"You must *not* go to that Unformed land again."

"It was not threatening me," Pasgen said. "I felt no anger, no evil at all."

"That is not to the point," Gaenor snapped. "If I felt any evil in it, I would have gone to Oberon. But innocence and ignorance can cause evil. I have never known any mist to approach a Gate and I made in many Unformed lands. The mists are always drawn back at least enough for someone to step off the platform. Do *you* know what would happen if the mist entered a Gate?"

"No," Pasgen admitted. "Do you?"

"It is not something I want to find out." Gaenor's mouth twisted wryly. "What if it were possible for the mist to pour through a Gate? What would happen to the domains we have built if they were covered in chaos mist?"

"I have no idea," Pasgen said, his eyes brightening with speculation. "But I could—"

"No you could not!" Gaenor exclaimed. "Not with any of the mist from *that* land." She took him by one of his long ears and shook him. "Child, your mind is too strong. You are not a maker, but you . . . you spew thoughts of such power that it is possible they become almost like made things."

"Gentle Mother," Pasgen breathed, in a pacifying tone he had rarely used with anyone. "I was studying that Unformed land because it had been used by many makers and because I had heard that a mortal child, Talented but mortal, had 'asked' the mist to make a lion and the creature was made. That was before I ever came there, I am sure of that. Surely it is not *I* that has caused this thing!"

Gaenor released his ear and shook her head, frowning and uneasy. "If it made the lion for this mortal child, it was already able to take from the child's mind what 'lion' was. But you said there were other creatures that no one asked for and you had been 'studying' the mist. Did it learn from you to think? to desire?"

"I do not know," Pasgen replied, slowly, and after much thought. "I have been studying Chaos Lands for . . . for a long time. I think I had better go to all those I remember, all those I have been in more than once, and see if they are different."

The ancient elf nodded. "A good thought, child. I hope you find nothing amiss, but whatever draws you, you must resist. You must not go to that land again."

Her alarm actually truncated his own longing to return. "No. No, I will not."

The anxiety Gaenor had caused Pasgen to feel about his investigations had the good effect of almost eliminating the pull on him of that strange place. From Elfhame Elder-Elf he Gated home, not directly, of course, but eventually. He ate and rested and then got out his notes about the many Chaos Lands he had visited and also the empty and sometimes partly formed domains. The empty places, finished or unfinished, always made him sad because they told so clear a tale of the diminishing population of Sidhe.

Then he set out to retrace the steps he had taken when he began to study the mist in the Chaos Lands. He went first to those places he visited most frequently, where he could somehow draw power from the mist into himself. To his relief he found nothing at all strange in those places. They were Unformed lands, nothing more. He stood quietly in each place, open and waiting, but he felt only the formless, undirected, silent hum of power and the usual, faint movement of the mist, which was only strange because there was no breeze to move it.

Somewhat calmed by the lack of any feeling in the places from which he had drawn power most often, he then traveled systematically to each Unformed land he had ever touched. In two he did find something like the almost self-willed mist he had captured to study, and he formed force fields around the new wisps and removed them to his workroom lest they grow and contaminate the whole domain. Then he returned to those places and sought for more or for any sensation of loss.

Pasgen was very thorough in his examinations. He did not hurry. He was essentially unaware of the passing of mortal days, then weeks. Twice he went to Elfhame Elder-Elf and spoke to Gaenor, but she had nothing to tell him. She thought she might have glimpsed the two mist-made constructs, but if she had, it was no more than a glimpse. They did not approach her, and neither did the mist create anything new for her.

As his anxiety ebbed and he became even more aware of the shades of difference in the mists of each Unformed land, Pasgen shook off the feeling of being drawn. He was deep in his attempt to discover why there were differences in the mists when the lindys he never failed to wear convulsed and then leapt madly against the restraint that held it to his clothing.

Cursing himself for nearly forgetting his sister, Pasgen ran for the Gate and actually entered the pattern of the empty house rather than going first to one of the markets.

There was no guard on the Gate. Pasgen did not look for the remains of the construct that was set to guard it. He knew it had to have been destroyed. He ran full tilt for the house itself, pulling up shields and forming levin bolts as he ran. At least the lindys was quieting and still telling him that Rhoslyn was here at the empty house.

He stopped in the doorway, staring, appalled, the power of the levin bolts trickling away. He was too late to fight. The house was silent; there was no battle now, but the entire entrance hall was a shambles. Pieces of goblin lay leaking on the floor and splatters and gobbets of their green-gray flesh and blood stained the walls.

An ogre's arm twitched near the door to the parlor; the head was not far away. But under the huge torso was the crushed body of one of Rhoslyn's girls, her head twisted right around to stare over her back.

"Mother," Pasgen breathed and rushed toward the back of the house and the passage to Llanelli's wing.

Once inside the passage, he heard a sound, a woman sobbing, but he could go no faster. He kept slipping and tripping over the goblin parts that covered the floor. There must have been a hundred of them, he thought, as he staggered through the open door to the reception room of the healer's suite.

There, unhurt, Rhoslyn sat amid the carnage, holding a blue ribbon in her hand and weeping.

"Mother?" Pasgen cried. "Where is mother?"

"Safe," Rhoslyn sighed. "At the Elves' Faire. We had a meal together and then I came here to leave a message for you and saw . . ." She shivered. "I sent an air spirit to tell her to stay there." She held up the ribbon and tears ran down her face. "It was all I could find. They tore my girl to pieces."

"Not before she tore a lot of them to pieces," Pasgen said. Then, very quietly, he asked, "Who did this? Why?"

"I don't know." Rhoslyn took the hand Pasgen held out to her and got to her feet. "But it must be Vidal. No one else could have sent such an army of goblins, and there were ogres too."

"But Vidal is in Scotland," Pasgen said. "Dealing with the Scots is like herding cats. No sooner do they agree to something than a new cause of insult arises among those who were allies, and all the parties change sides again. He is so busy making sure that no party grows strong enough to force an agreement with the English, that he left mortal affairs in England in Aurilia's hands and she—"

"That was over two months ago, Pasgen," Rhoslyn pointed out.

"Oh."

He drew Rhoslyn closer and guided her to the front door entrance to the separate wing. He had to force the outer door open. Another ogre lay there, its head hanging sideways by a flap of skin in the back, its bowels laid open so that the guts hung out. Two of Pasgen's hulking guards also lay destroyed; one with a crushed head, the other with its chest caved in, the ogre's foot still embedded.

Rhoslyn sighed. "I will have to ask leave of Lady Mary again. It will take me weeks to make more guards and girls."

Pasgen walked out into the garden, the force fields that sealed off the path opening for him and Rhoslyn. When the house was hidden by the shrubbery, he "called" a bench and sat down beside her.

"How did you happen to come here today?" he asked.

"I always have dinner with Mother on Tuesday," Rhoslyn replied, looking surprised. "Soon as Mary's household is asleep, I lock my chamber door and Gate to the Elves' Faire to meet Mother. Usually I just Gate back to Essex, but Mother was beginning to worry about you because she has not seen you in so long, so I came here to leave a message for you."

"You always have dinner with Mother on Tuesday," Pasgen repeated. "So anyone could have known—"

He stopped as both of them became aware that the Gate had been activated. Both stood up. The Gate was used again. Together they rushed out into the path, which they found clogged with Vidal's creatures, giggling and growling. There were only a few goblins but there were at least a dozen *bwgwl,* two black annises, four trolls, a mass of boggles, a flurry of hags, and a host of trows.

At the head of the clot of evil was a Dark Sidhe, who glanced at the house and giggled to himself. Rhoslyn recognized him as the nearly disminded oleander eater, who was often left to "greet" and infuriate those who came to speak to Vidal.

"With Prince Vidal's compliments," the Sidhe said when he noticed them. "The prince finds that you do not respond to his summons left with servants at this house." He giggled again. "He told me to make sure you would obey any future order he sent." He pouted. "Your guards were too effective so we did not finish. Now stand aside."

He gestured at the horde behind him and they began to run, hop, glide, slither forward. Rhoslyn gasped and raised her hands, blue fire limning her fingers. Before she could act, Pasgen had drawn power from everywhere. The force fields that shielded the garden collapsed, Rhoslyn felt cold and empty and the light died from her hands, the horde shrieked and wailed as their life-force was drawn. Pasgen pointed.

"Stay," he said. The whole group froze in place. And then he said, "*Burn!*"

That was when the screaming started.

Vidal Dhu spat an ugly oath when Pasgen and Rhoslyn appeared on the path in front of the creatures he had allowed that drugged fool to take with him. Vidal had not expected anyone to be in the house but the helpless constructs that took and relayed messages.

He had sent two ogres and an army of goblins to kill as cruelly as they could all the servants except one, who would be left with his message, and then to ruin the garden, tear down what they could of the house, and cover what they could not destroy with urine and feces. He had not expected that there would be fighting constructs in the house. Rhoslyn's girls and guards had cost him almost a quarter of his court. That had added fuel to the rage that unexpected events had set afire.

When Vidal had returned to England he had been in high good humor, having convinced both Scottish parties to agree on one thing. Both now had the same absolute determination to "save" their princess from the degradation of being married to the English king. He was even mildly pleased by Aurilia's plan to have Denoriel and Aleneil killed. He doubted that such a plan would be successful, but it could in no way be traced back to Underhill. And if it should work, that cursed girl Elizabeth would be left bereft and unprotected, easy prey to a most unsuitable marriage with Thomas Seymour.

Such a marriage would call for a public and immediate removal of Elizabeth from the line of succession. The Protector—he had heard in Scotland about Somerset being elevated from head of the Council to Protector—was not likely to permit his brother to have so much influence on the government or to be in line to rule as a queen's consort.

A silly girl would not think of that. She would be easy prey, easily convinced that she needed Seymour when she had lost those so dear to her. She would be desperate for love, for comfort—and Thomas Seymour would provide it.

Grinning, Vidal explained . . . and his whole beautiful plan collapsed around him because Aurilia laughed and told him Seymour was already married, and not to one easy to put aside. His wife was the dowager queen, Catherine.

He slapped her face and called her a liar. All trace of languid relaxation disappeared as Aurilia shrieked and leapt to her feet, mouth agape to bite, hands extended with elongated nails ready to claw. Vidal launched another blow but she caught it and jumped at him. Her weight, considerably more than one would expect from her seemingly slender body, drove him backward. She caught at him, overbalanced; they fell to the floor snapping and snatching.

Aurilia's claws caught in Vidal's trews and she ripped them open. Her gown had not been much more than a few wisps to start out with and was now barely shreds. Vidal heaved and rolled, bringing Aurilia beneath him. She snapped at his face. He put a hand under her chin and slammed her mouth closed right on her tongue. As she howled, muted by the hand that gagged her, he heaved up and thrust down.

It should have been impossible for him to impale her, but the violence and pain had the same effect on her as on him. She curved her lower body up toward him, her legs going around his hips; heaving up as he thrust down. Now it was his turn to howl, as he missed his target and was crushed against her pelvic bone. However his next thrust went home.

Twice. Thrice. Scoring each other with nails and teeth. Sucking, soothed, by the faintly metallic taste of blood. On the fourth thrust Vidal found completion. He ground himself against Aurilia until the last spasm passed and then pushed her aside.

"You stupid fool," he snarled, curling around and levering himself to his feet. "You cretin! You brain damaged half-wit, wasting your time trying to kill one of the strongest fighters in the Seleighe domain with a few mortal bullies. Why did you not prevent Seymour from marrying?"

"Do not call me brain-damaged," Aurilia howled, virtually springing to her feet. "You are the idiot, the cretin! Did you tell me a word of this? Yes, you said Elizabeth must be disgraced and it would be easier if Denoriel and Aleneil were dead, but not a word did you say about Seymour."

"I did!" Vidal bellowed.

"You did not!" Aurilia screamed.

They exchanged the useless accusations several times but their rage was fading and finally, only glaring, not threatening, Vidal asked, "Do you even know where Elizabeth is?"

"Fool! Fool!" Aurilia snarled over her shoulder as she moved to the table that held her blue potion. "If you had only told me that you meant Seymour for Elizabeth, to be rid of her by disgrace! When I knew Seymour was courting the queen, I paid no more attention to him. Why should I think his marriage to Elizabeth would disgrace her? He was the Protector's brother! I assumed the Protector would approve his marriage to bring more power into his hands." Aurilia lifted the glass and swallowed the contents, then shrugged. "She is right there in the palace with them."

The last sentence made no sense to Vidal for a moment; then he asked, "Elizabeth is living with Catherine and Seymour?" The voice in which that question was posed was thoughtful and calm, Vidal's expression interested rather than furious.

"Yes, she is." Aurilia had also calmed; she returned the glass to the table without trying to drain the last drops.

Vidal smiled. "Ahhhh. Perhaps it is just as well that you did not interfere in Seymour's marriage. Had he married Elizabeth and the disapproval of the Council of that marriage removed her from the succession, well, marriage to someone only slightly unsuitable is not such a dishonor. If there were need, she could be restored to her place as an heir. But if Elizabeth were to take Seymour as a lover . . . Oh yes, a married man, married no less to her stepmother . . . If *that* was discovered . . ." Vidal's smile broadened. "No, they could not restore a whore to the succession."

He approached Aurilia and lifted her face with a hand under her chin. "I am sorry I grew so angry. I should have thought first. All in all, you have done very well. Now I must obtain an amulet—"

Suddenly Aurilia pushed him away and rushed by him. He drew breath between his teeth, whirling around, clawed hand out to seize her. However he stopped short when he saw her standing quite still and looking down at the scrying bowl he had abandoned when he saw Pasgen and Rhoslyn come out onto the path to confront the Sidhe he had sent to finish the destruction of their house.

Aurilia's eyes were as wide as they could get and her mouth hung just a little open with mingled pleasure and fear. "I think you have just lost another quarter of your servants," she said, shivering but licking her lips.

Pasgen watched the burning horde for a moment—the squat, broad rectangles of flame that were the trolls; the wavering, twirling pillars that were the hags and annises; the bouncing, squirming

bags that were the *bwgwl* and boggles; the little flitting convul-
sions that were the trows—then he smiled.

They were still screaming and writhing when he drew Rhoslyn
around them, through the garden, and to the Gate. He pressed
a token into her hand. "Go home and then to my house—the
token will open it—bring your servants and mine to clean up
the mess in this place."

Rhoslyn could scarcely hear him for the screaming. "Enough,
Pasgen," she cried. "Enough. Finish them."

He looked at her for a long moment, then said, "Very well. It
is their nature. I am sure Vidal was scrying what was happening
and I wanted to be sure that he would see what befalls those he
sends against us. But he would not care. He might enjoy it." He
turned his back on her and looked at the agony on the path,
gestured and said, "Ashes."

And there was silence, and nothing on the path except ashes.
He turned back to face the Gate and started to step up on it.
Rhoslyn caught at his arm.

"Where are you going?"

Pasgen frowned. "I think it is time to remove Vidal. He has
always annoyed me, but this . . . insult went too far."

"No!" Rhoslyn exclaimed, clinging to his arm, which was hard
as silver alloy under her hand. "No! I cannot leave you behind. I
cannot lose you! But if you kill Vidal, Oberon will order you to
rule the Dark Court. No, Pasgen. Please. Do not permit yourself
to be bound here forever. At least let me *dream* that some day I
can escape from Dark to Bright."

He looked back down the path where the faint breeze that
murmured through this domain was beginning to sweep the ashes
away. The white-hot fury that had scalded him inside began to
cool under the chill of his memory of ruling the Dark Court
while Vidal was recovering from the injuries dealt him in the
battle to seize Elizabeth.

At the time, Pasgen had actually undertaken the role Oberon
had given him with some enthusiasm. Neither he nor anyone else
had expected Vidal to survive the wound he had received from
Harry FitzRoy's iron bolt. Pasgen assumed he would hold Caer
Mordwyn forever.

He had some notion that he would be able to instill order
and rationality into Vidal's servants and creations. He was not

then certain what he would do with them when he brought them under his control, but he had some nebulous dreams of a kingdom where those who were feared and hated, despised and unwanted everywhere else, could live in peace and plenty and find companionship among each other.

Pasgen had credited much of the evil in the Unseleighe creatures to Vidal, who had urged them to greater disorder and cruelty, laughing at their killing and maiming of each other and their depredations in the mortal world. Pasgen had soon discovered he was wrong about that. Vidal *enjoyed* what his creatures were and did, but he was not the main cause of their behavior.

Many were inherently evil and could take no pleasure unless they were causing pain. Nor did they care whether that pain was inflicted on outsiders who scorned them or on their fellow creatures. Many were not intelligent enough to know good from bad, nor was there any way to teach them. Some he could have saved—the mischief makers who did no real harm—but most were beyond anything but destruction.

Because he was stronger than they were and destroyed the very worst of them, Pasgen had gained control. He had stopped the excesses that had enraged Oberon and might have led to human invasion Underhill. However, the moment he was occupied with something else, the creatures violated every rule they had sworn to. Pasgen had learned to despair of ever bringing Vidal's realm to some permanent kind of order. He knew that he could only stop the worst excesses of Vidal's creatures by constantly exerting his power over them.

It had been horrible. He had never been so miserable in all his life, not even when Vidal had seized him to teach him the beauties of pain. With Rhoslyn's help he had escaped Vidal, but there would be no escape from Oberon's geas once it was set on him.

Hot rage and ice-cold memory struggled in him and came to a compromise of chilly, controllable anger. Pasgen looked down at his sister's hand, desperately gripping his arm. He brought his own hand up, covered hers, and patted it.

"Clever Rhoslyn to remind me of what it meant to be ruler of Caer Mordwyn. You know I can take Vidal now, that I have no need to fear him."

"Oh, yes, I know that." She did not look back at the path where a thin layer of ash was still drifting.

"Then you will not be afraid, although I still must go and deal with Vidal. However, I promise I will not kill him nor even injure him in any serious way."

"Why? Turn your back on him, Pasgen. Ignore him. He's lost . . . I don't know how many servants. Even Vidal must realize that it is too expensive to attack us."

"I doubt he cares about that," Pasgen said, a muscle in his jaw jumping. "And what if Mother had been here when that horde of Vidal's arrived?"

Rhoslyn's hand gripped Pasgen's arm tighter. "We can abandon this place—"

"No, we really cannot." Pasgen patted Rhoslyn's hand again. "Not without taking from Mother what has returned a life to her. If we built a new place we would have to forbid her to Heal. If we allowed her to bring patients there, how long would it remain undiscovered?"

A small smile softened Rhoslyn's tense mouth. Pasgen always tried to pretend he did not care about Llanelli, but *he* was the one who had realized what this attack might mean to her. Rhoslyn had not given her mother a thought. She sighed.

"I hate when you confront Vidal," she said, but the remark was no longer either an argument or a plea to stop him. "I am always afraid that you will go too far. Vidal we can outwit or avoid . . . not Oberon."

"I know that," Pasgen assured her with passionate sincerity. "No confrontation. I will simply go and tell Vidal that I and mine are outside of his limits and that I will serve him no longer. Unless—do you want me to say you, too, will no longer serve his purposes?"

"No. As long as he mainly desires me to watch and protect Mary, I want to seem to be his obedient servant." She frowned. "But if he was scrying the attack on the empty house, he must have seen us together."

"And seen you make me stop the burning and try to stop me from going to confront him." He pursed his lips a moment, then smiled. "I know what to say. I will tell him that you are mine and must not be hurt or frightened even though we have quarreled because you wish to remain his servant."

"Very good! I need to remain with Mary and if he thinks I am no longer obedient to him, he will do something cruel or disgusting to make her dismiss me. She is a good woman. I do not want to add to her troubles a fear that she cannot trust her judgment of people. And I hope I will be able to soften her attitude toward Elizabeth too."

Pasgen tightened his grip on Rhoslyn's hand for just a moment, then pulled his hand forcefully from hers as if he were angry. He even pushed her slightly backward, as if to prevent her from following him into the Gate, jumped onto the platform, and activated it.

The last bit of play-acting, in case Vidal was still watching, was wasted. Aurilia's half-frightened, half-voluptuous remark about the loss of his servants had drawn Vidal's attention to the scrying bowl. When he saw the whole mass of his creatures aflame, he had bellowed with rage and slammed the bowl from its stand.

That had caused another argument with Aurilia, who screamed at him for destroying the image. He shouted back that he was not her panderer, to gratify her lower forms of amusement in watching people burn.

"Fool! Fool! I can set afire anyone I want for the fun of seeing someone burn. You destroyed the image and now we do not know what happened. Did the flames go out before they accomplished anything? That would have told us that Pasgen's power is limited. Did they destroy? Was Rhoslyn adding to Pasgen's strength? Was she trying to stop him?"

Vidal was too angry to concede the importance of her questions and merely shouted back, and after a few more basically meaningless exchanges she stormed out of his reception chamber. By the time the door slammed behind her, Vidal had spit out most of his spleen. His first fury over Pasgen's response to his attack was fading into a decided feeling of alarm. Now he, too, regretted destroying his scrying image and the questions Aurilia had raised seemed strongly pertinent.

One thing he was sure of: he would not need to wait long to have those questions answered. If Pasgen had the power to utterly destroy the force he had sent, he would be roaring out of a Gate in Caer Mordwyn very soon. If Rhoslyn had been helping her brother, she would appear with him breathing fire. Vidal began to gather power and build shields.

Power he found in plenty. The anxiety over King Henry's death and whether war would break out between the Catholic supporters of Mary, who was eldest, and Edward, who was male, had gripped not only the nobles but all of the people. The tense energy of fearful expectation oozed out of all and soaked down Underhill, draining away from the warmth and light of the Seleighe domains to those of the Unseleighe.

With shields, Vidal was less successful. He was so strong that he had seldom bothered with shields, depending on swift and deadly attack to confound any who opposed him. He raised shields by habit and did so now, not even considering that they were ragged things with here and there a rough spot, a crack, a hole, rather than smooth mirrors. But Vidal only thought of them as a minor delaying tactic while he launched blows.

He thought, too, of summoning assistance, but the memory of the pack of creatures burning on the path leading to the empty house made him decide against it. If Pasgen saw a host arrayed against him, he was more likely to try to set fire to the whole mass, as he had done before. Vidal was not really afraid of Pasgen's fire; the creatures he had burnt were weak nothings and the Dark Sidhe so addled with oleander as to be useless. He was sure his attack would weaken Pasgen's control and he could quench any flames that reached him.

Perhaps, he thought, reaching mentally to the Gates of his domain, Pasgen would not even reach the palace. If he caught him at a Gate, he could twist . . .

But then the whole palace rang like a giant bell, and Vidal sensed that the place the clapper struck was right outside his door. He spat an obscenity. He had forgotten that Pasgen was a genius with Gates. That accursed, misborn creature had forced a Gate right into the palace. Why, oh why had he ever thought of seizing those babies? He had brought a serpent into his very house.

Vidal gathered his power, formed it into a bright lance, thick and strong. He did not thrust it through the door, which was protected with warding spells, because he did not wish to weaken its force. And if Pasgen had second thoughts and did not enter so much the better. The quarrel would be more easily settled when Pasgen was less angry. But the door opened. Pasgen did enter, and Vidal launched that lance, feeling a mingling of satisfaction and regret that he would be soon rid of a growing nuisance.

The lance struck—and shattered into a thousand glowing shards, each still so powerful that where they fell drapes and furniture charred or began to smolder. Furious, Vidal sent a shower of knives glowing with the poison that made elf-shot fatal. Most, to Vidal's rising rage and terror, slid around Pasgen; the few that struck also shattered.

He called into being a shining net in which each knot held a thread that would pierce whatever the net enfolded and grow into the body. Taking its sustenance from the flesh it invaded, it would send out more and more threads until there was nothing in the net but the eater itself. But before Vidal launched the net, he became aware of an odd tugging, a sense of loosening, just as he also realized that Pasgen had not attempted any counterstroke.

They stood staring at each other for a brief tense moment, until Pasgen said, "You no longer have any shield. I have drawn the power into myself."

And then Vidal shrieked and cast the net because he felt his own power being drained. But though the net fell true, it just lay atop and around Pasgen without touching him. Vidal bellowed curses invoking the Great Evil to swallow Pasgen whole because in a way he knew that he, himself, had given Pasgen this invulnerability. Pasgen had learned shields thoroughly. Before he could do almost any other magic, he had raised and perfected shields to protect himself from Vidal's torments.

Vidal drew power, but as fast as he drew it, Pasgen drained it. He staggered back and back again, feeling his limbs trembling. He had never been so hollow and empty. He could make no defense; his attempt to raise another weapon made him unable to support himself. He sank into his throne as if into a shelter, though the sense of shelter was illusory and he knew it. But the worst of the draining stopped.

"I have not come to suck you dry, Prince Vidal, despite the insult and offense you have offered me," Pasgen said quietly. "I know that you are most fit to rule Caer Mordwyn and I wish you to rule it as you have ever done. However, I *am* insulted and offended. Thus, I hereby renounce all ties, all loyalty to you. I will answer no summons from you nor do you any service."

"And all protection from me?"

A new painful draw of energy made Vidal gasp. Pasgen's mouth quivered, and with a mixture of rage and fear Vidal wondered if the young Sidhe had restrained a sneer.

"Yes," Pasgen said, "I renounce your protection also, but only for myself. My sister, fool that she is, does not agree. She still wishes to be your servant—likely because she is as eager as you are to see Mary come to the throne. But she is still my sister and I warn you—"

Vidal screamed faintly and nearly lost consciousness as a horrible sucking seemed almost to be drawing the blood from his body.

"I warn you that if harm of any kind befalls Rhoslyn, if she is even frightened or threatened, or more damage is done to my property, I will return and not only suck you dry but draw the power from Caer Mordwyn so that the whole domain falls to dust."

Chapter 19

It was the middle of June before one of the many air spirits that Aleneil had sent in search of Denoriel found him and convinced him to return to Llachar Lle to meet his sister. Part of the reason he was so slow to respond was that Aleneil had not provided any real reason for him to hurry home. Elizabeth was fine, although she was growing irritable over her Denno's long absence. Life at Chelsea and Hanworth, another of Catherine's properties farther away from London and mostly out of reach of casual visitors, was pleasant for everyone.

Aleneil could not put her finger on why she felt so uneasy. But with all her heart she wanted Elizabeth to be distracted from her growing liking for Thomas Seymour. To Aleneil, the man was rank and unwholesome, although she could not say why. True, he flirted with Elizabeth, but he flirted in exactly the same way with all the attendant ladies, Catherine's as well as Elizabeth's . . . except her. Aleneil wondered guiltily whether that was why she disliked him so much. Was it merely offended vanity? Underhill Aleneil was beautiful; the mortal Lady Alana had not enough character or expression on her face even to be called plain.

When one of the air spirits finally popped into Elizabeth's parlor, circled Aleneil's head and cried into her mind that Denoriel was in his apartment in Llachar Lle, Lady Alana got suddenly to her feet, pressed a hand to her forehead, and pleaded a headache.

Elizabeth had almost dropped her embroidery when the air spirit arrived, and her lips parted but before Elizabeth could give or deny leave, Lady Alana withdrew from the group.

All the girls looked at her in surprise, but Aleneil simply curtsied and backed out of the chamber. She did not even go to her room, but hurried to the sheltered side of the stable where Ystwyth was waiting. Her anxiety that Denoriel would simply leave again when he did not find her waiting for him was such that Ystwyth leapt up into the air and broke the barriers between the worlds.

The elvensteed came to rest at the portico of Llachar Lle, and Aleneil rushed up the stairs and through the corridor to virtually burst into Denoriel's apartment. He had felt the strong disturbance that Ystwyth's arrival made in the usually quiet power flow of Elfhame Logres and had gotten to his feet, his hand going to his sword hilt when Aleneil almost leapt through the doorway.

"Don't you dare leave!" she cried, raising a hand palm out toward him as if to hold him back.

"Leave? I've only just arrived. What is wrong? Why are you so breathless?" He looked toward the door, hand tightening on his sword hilt as if he expected her to be pursued.

Aleneil sighed and sank down onto the sofa facing the fireplace. Denoriel had been away so long that the tiny spell which kept the multicolored flames playing over crystal logs had lost power and dissipated.

"Do you realize that it has taken me over two months to get sight or speech of you?" Aleneil was exasperated and did not try to hide it. "Where have you been? What have you been doing?"

He grinned. "Having a wonderful time," he said, teasing because of her displeasure. Then, more soberly. "I told you I was going with Harry to the abandoned elfhames. He and his friends from Elfhame Elder-Elf had cleared out all the magical curses that those Churchly lunatics put on the cities, but they could not touch the Great Evil that had taken root there."

"You were fighting the Great Evil?" Aleneil breathed, eyes wide.

"No not that. It summoned—or perhaps just its presence brought—a host of *things* from the lower planes. We were busy getting rid of them and sealing the doors through which they came. Harry, the eternal optimist, hoped that the Great Evil would retreat with those that escaped us as we sealed the doors, but that did not happen. It is again isolated, and Harry has withdrawn his party partly to avoid tempting it to further action, partly to take time to search out a new route to it. He is as inventive as a—" Denoriel broke into a laugh. "I was about to say he is as inventive as a mortal."

Aleneil snorted. "Well, you look wonderful, so I suppose all that fighting did you good, but Denoriel, ridding Alhambra and El Dorado of the evil that was set into them is not *your* purpose. You know what the FarSeers have Seen. You are tied to Elizabeth and to her rule."

"Is something wrong with Elizabeth?"

He was half out of his chair and Aleneil waved him down. "Except for growing more and more impatient over your absence, one would think there is nothing wrong . . ." Then her voice faltered and she wrung her hands. "But there is! I have no clear Vision, I have seen and heard nothing real, but I *feel* something bad is coming, and it is all to do with Thomas Seymour."

Denoriel frowned blackly over the name. "He has got the queen, I suppose. Poor woman. She deserves better."

Aleneil sighed with agreement. "Yes, but you could not convince her of that and would not have been able to do so even if there had been as much difficulty over the marriage as Seymour expected."

"Marriage?" Denoriel repeated, frowning even more angrily. "I thought after the first flush of infatuation she could be shown what he truly was. The queen planned on a wait of two years, a full year of mourning and another year to show her great respect—"

"Maybe her head planned on a wait of two years," Aleneil interrupted with a wry twist to her lips, "but her nether parts decided that two months was more than long enough."

She went on to tell him about the clandestine courtship and the effect it had on Elizabeth.

Denoriel sort of drew back in his chair and said, "Impossible. Ridiculous. Elizabeth is only a little girl!"

"Denoriel, she is *not* a little girl. She is a mortal of near fifteen years of age—a mortal and ripening fast. She has a fine bosom and nice broad hips, and she fair panted when she watched Seymour kiss Catherine's throat and ears out in the garden."

Denoriel flushed. "But you said they married. They must have a more private place for their caresses now."

"Oh yes," Aleneil's lips twisted, "Queen Catherine and Seymour were married sometime about the end of April, but they feared that his brother, who is now Protector, would interfere, so they still met secretly. Only after the wedding, Seymour came in the early morning and they kissed and fondled all the way into the entry of the house nearest her bedchamber with all the servants and half the ladies in waiting goggling out of their windows." She hesitated and then said, "And I will tell you plain, Denoriel, that I do not like the way Elizabeth looks at Seymour."

"What the devil do you mean?" Denoriel said, his skin darkening further. "Surely now that Seymour and the queen are married she looks at him no longer."

"Yes she does." Aleneil's lips thinned with distaste. "She is only fourteen years old. Her body is ripe and it is waking to urges she hardly understands. But those urges must not be connected to Seymour!"

Denoriel had looked away. Aleneil could see that his jaw was set hard.

"The worst of the trouble," she continued, "is that he looks back! Oh, not only at Elizabeth. At every woman in the place. And Catherine thinks his flirting is charming. But the others do not matter. Denoriel, Elizabeth must be given something else to look at."

"No!" The objection burst out of Denoriel with the force of violent jealousy. He swallowed hard, started to compel himself to agree, and then, relieved, shook his head. "No," he repeated more calmly. "Elizabeth must look at no one, must show no favor to any man. She is forbidden to marry except with the Council's approval. There is the shadow of her mother's execution for adultery over her. One slip and she will be named a whore and removed from the succession."

"I am so glad you see that, and I think Elizabeth sees it too. But she wants what Catherine has, what Catherine's foolish desire has been holding under her nose for weeks. Her young body is driving her, that *and* the knowledge that she might, for political reasons, be forced into marriage with a graybeard or a drooling idiot. She wants to know what Catherine feels, to taste desire. She wants to believe that a kiss or two in a corner would do no harm."

Denoriel stiffened and finally said. "No again. What if she were caught? No, you must tell her—"

"Idiot!" Aleneil interrupted sharply. "I *have* been telling her! What do you think has saved her so far. But I cannot hold her much longer. She needs a lover."

"No!"

"Yes." Suddenly Aleneil smiled. "What if she could never be caught? What if the lover could disappear? And what if there could be no danger at all of her getting with child?"

"Aleneil, what are you saying? She is still a child herself."

"The legal age for marriage set by the Church is twelve for females. Plenty of girls have *borne children* at fourteen, so do not talk like a fool. You know Elizabeth's will. She knows she cannot marry, but if she makes up her mind to taste the sweetness of love . . ."

"No."

"Oh, stop saying 'no' as if what you say can have any effect. You must *do* something."

Denoriel squared his shoulders. "To that I agree. I will talk to her. I will explain to her—"

"Dannae forfend!" Aleneil exclaimed, with an expression of horror. "You fool! When you next see her, you will tell her that she has ripened into a woman, in your eyes a beautiful woman. You will find a private place while I delay her maidens, and you will kiss her!"

Color again rose in Denoriel's cheeks, the pupils of his eyes widened, then shrank again, and his lips, a little fuller than usual, parted to take a deeper breath. A moment later, he stiffened and shook his head violently.

"Do not bother to say 'no' again," Aleneil snapped. "Who else can disappear so that Elizabeth can never be found with a lover? Who else has been Elizabeth's friend for so many years that no one really sees him anymore? Who else has the white hair of the aged and infirm, and cannot, no matter how passionate their embraces, make Elizabeth pregnant?"

Denoriel sat looking at his sister as if she had hit him on the back of the head with a board. "Me?" his voice squeaked.

"Unless you are willing to suggest another Sidhe to fill the role, and I—"

"No." That time it was Denoriel who interrupted and quite

forcefully. "Another Sidhe might become bored and leave her. She would be hurt."

"Hurt? Mere mortal heartache? That would be the least of our worries. You know Elizabeth. She could turn vindictive against all Sidhe, and if she comes to rule, as we all hope she will, she could close the mortal world, at least of England and Wales, to us."

"That's my Elizabeth." Denoriel sighed.

"So it must be you who courts her and loves her. Only you will have the care of her that she will need. Only you can be trusted with her."

For one moment an expression of avid desire made Denoriel's eyes glitter and his lips fill. In the next moment the light in his eyes died and he shrugged. "For the reasons you gave, it might seem so, but she will never have me. You have given all the reasons for that, too. She regards me as an old uncle, to be teased, to do her favors, to amuse her."

There was such pain in his voice that Aleneil reached out and took his hand. "I don't think so," she said and eased her voice into softness. "Did you not hear her say 'my Denno' to Oberon himself? Did you not hear her say if you were not *her* Denno that she would close the mortal world to Sidhe?"

"But that could have been a child's demand for a favorite toy. Dannae knows, Elizabeth is willful."

Aleneil smiled. So, there was desire on Denoriel's part as well. All the better. "Oh, no. Elizabeth knows and respects, even fears, authority. Oberon *exudes* authority. He is king and none can mistake that. Nonetheless, Elizabeth defied him—for you. She would not have gone so far for an old friend or an old uncle. Not even, I think, for her Da now that she is sure he is alive and well. But for the love of her life?"

When Aleneil mentioned Da, which was what Elizabeth called Harry FitzRoy, Denoriel's memory suddenly brought up one of the many quarrels he had had with her. She had been demanding that he bring Harry to the mortal world to visit her, saying she needed to be *sure* it was Harry and not some simulacrum or some Sidhe beglamoured to look like Harry. She had asked passionately whether she was never to touch her Da's hand or feel him hug her.

Denoriel had then pulled her closer and asked if his hugs would not do. To his pained surprise, she had drawn away from him.

When, shocked, he asked if she did not like him, she had assured him that she liked him, liked him very much, *but not that way.* He remembered now that, without bothering to try to understand what she meant, he had been delighted her affection for him was far different from her affection for her half brother.

"I do not know," he said uncertainly. "What if she is disgusted by my attempt on her or frightened by it? What if I am no longer welcome to her?"

Aleneil shook her head. "Are you planning to leap on her and commit rape? She would have time enough to warn you away if she does not desire you in such a way that your friendship would not be damaged. But surely after all these years you know how to approach Elizabeth." Now she laughed, and looked at him sideways. "Have you never wooed a lady?"

Despite feeling he would be torn apart by the maelstrom of emotions in him—a hot and eager desire, an icy terror that the desire might be rejected, a sick trembling of doubt over desiring a child—Denoriel could not help grinning at his sister's question.

"Actually, no," he said. "Mostly they woo me."

For some time after Pasgen left his reception room, Vidal simply sat, breathing and drawing in power to restore what Pasgen had drained from him. His first thought, when thought was possible, was gratitude for the quarrel with Aurilia that had left him alone when Pasgen arrived. The last thing he needed was a witness to—

His thoughts checked. What *had* Pasgen done? By a fierce exertion of his will, Vidal did not shudder. A Gate. A Gate right into the palace itself, right outside his very door so that he had no warning that Pasgen was coming. He knew Pasgen was an expert with Gates, but not that he was so powerful he could override the warding on Caer Mordwyn. That, Vidal told himself, was something he must not forget; he would need warding of a different kind, warding that would disrupt a Gate, anyone's Gate, and send the traveler into the void.

His tense pose eased slightly. Surely if he had the warning he had expected to get, he would have been able to deal with that young upstart. But Vidal's mind was clearing more and more and lying to himself was less easy. He thought of the shields against which his worst attacks shattered and his hand formed a tight fist. He should have expected that. He knew Pasgen was expert with shields, so why had he been so surprised when the shields held against him?

Vidal's eyes closed and foul words trickled in a steady stream from his lips. He was surprised because the last times Pasgen and Rhoslyn had attended court, some of Vidal's teasing little torments had got through Pasgen's shield. The obscenities came quicker, louder, as he realized that either the shields had been deliberately imperfect or Pasgen and Rhoslyn had only been pretending to be hurt.

Rhoslyn, she was nothing. He would . . . The obscenities died on his lips. And then the memory he had tried to avoid came, wrenching his pride, tearing his confidence, generating . . . terror. He would do nothing because Pasgen had said that if Rhoslyn were hurt or even frightened, he would return, drain Vidal to true death, and turn Caer Mordwyn to dust.

How? How had Pasgen drawn power out of him? Vidal knew that healers and others could infuse power into another, but draw it out? His brow furrowed. Surely he had heard rumors—no, ridiculous. Those were only tales of horror . . . or were they? Had he not felt his shields ravel away and then a growing weakness and then—he shuddered again—that feeling as if the blood was being drawn out of his body.

The terror slowly faded away. Doubtless Pasgen, who was something of a scholar, had found evidence proving that tales of power-sucking creatures were true. So he had found them or found records that explained what they were and how they worked. What Pasgen had found, Vidal was sure he could find also. There were a few among the Dark Sidhe who would enjoy seeking such information.

Vidal jerked upright in his chair, much of his energy restored by the shock of fear that had hit him when his thinking process caught up with his plans. There was no Dark Sidhe, no living or nonliving creature, that he would trust with such a seeking. It was danger and threat enough that Pasgen knew how to draw power; he might as well cut his own throat with a dull knife as to allow anyone else to know it could be done.

But Pasgen already knew and had nearly killed him. He must find a counter to Pasgen's magic, which meant he must himself seek the records from which Pasgen had learned how to manage power. A low growl like that of a frustrated animal worked its way out of Vidal's chest. He had no time for tearing libraries from healers and mages and struggling through obscure texts in search of that secret.

Obtaining the information from Pasgen himself was out of the question. While Pasgen could drain power from an enemy, Vidal was no longer fool enough to confront him. Could he find and steal Pasgen's spell? Vidal growled again.

In all the years he had sought—mostly idly, it was true, but sometimes intensely—he had never found Pasgen's home domain. He could institute another search . . . but if Pasgen noticed . . . Vidal did not finish that thought. What he told himself was that it was unlikely Pasgen would keep his deepest secrets in his own home in any case. So finding the draining spell would mean a minute study of his own library and then of others . . . No, now was not the time. He had other more immediate problems.

His FarSeers had warned him that a new Vision was intruding on those of Mary and Elizabeth, which had been stable for so long. Yet another female had been offered the crown, one he did not recognize and now, of course, he could not get Rhoslyn and Pasgen to identify her. But more significant than that was that the image of Edward as king was growing soft and wavering and sometimes failed to appear.

If Edward's reign was not going to be long, Vidal thought, he would need to be sure Elizabeth was removed from the succession soon. Otherwise she could be presented as a rival to Mary by those who wished to keep the reformed religion. Since the Vision of Elizabeth's reign, curse her, remained strong and constant, Vidal had no intention of taking the chance that Elizabeth and her party would win.

Even before seeking the secret of drawing power—as long as he avoided Pasgen he did not need that ability or the means to counter it—he must arrange to reach Thomas Seymour and bespell him to believe that if he made Elizabeth his whore, he would eventually rule at her side.

Vidal had intended to get Pasgen to deal with Seymour. Pasgen had a knack with amulets as well as with Gates. But he was not sure he would trust Pasgen, even if there were some way to control him. Vidal paused on the thought. Something was tickling the back of his mind. As he regained strength and his mind cleared, Vidal had become aware that his memory was not perfect.

Rhoslyn . . . No, Vidal dismissed the idea of using her as a hostage. Pasgen would be keeping a watch on his sister. He would know at once if anyone tried to seize her. Before he could control the movement, Vidal shivered. But the odd sensation at the back of his mind—a feeling he hated because it meant he had forgotten something large and important—kept nagging at him.

He would not think about it and it would come back to him. Meanwhile, Vidal decided, he would see if he could pacify Aurilia; she was good with amulets too. He snapped his fingers for an imp, gave it a mental picture of one of the mortals seized in a raid in Scotland, and bade it bring the man. While he waited, Vidal looked around the chamber to be sure that there was no sign of the conflict with Pasgen. Much of his normal power had been restored and he gestured away the few scorch marks on walls and drapes.

He looked over the blank-faced but large-thewed young man when he arrived led by a newt servant and nodded. Aurilia would appreciate this kind of unspoken apology. And then, looking into the empty eyes, he remembered.

Pasgen and Rhoslyn had a mother! Although he had originally been willing to leave the babies with her—he had suspected she was right and that they would not survive in the care of the Dark Sidhe—she had later annoyed him by keeping her children from fully embracing the Unseleighe way. Such deception and rebellion required punishment. Vidal smiled.

First he had used her, enjoying to the full her hatred of him and her self-hatred when she could not resist him. Then, to fully enslave her, he had made her—he remembered now, Llanelli was her name—an eater of oleander. He snorted his contempt, remembering more clearly. Once beautiful, she had become a pallid nothing. Her wailing and pleading and even her attempts at seduction to get the drug had become annoying.

But Pasgen and Rhoslyn still felt bound to her even in that state. Then they were still weak in power and learning; they had pleaded with him to let them tend to her. Vidal paused momentarily to savor the memory of Pasgen begging a favor. He shook his head. What fools they were. Did they not know better than to beg?

If they wanted Llanelli, they should have seized her. So what if the spells with which he had bound her, because of her silly attempts to escape, would cause her excruciating pain? It would have been her pain, not theirs; they could have enjoyed it.

Begging! Fools! To teach them just how powerless they were against him, he refused. But he had not wanted the nuisance of any attempt to abduct her nor the nuisance of having her in Caer Mordwyn, so instead of giving Llanelli to them, he had let them know he had cast her out. He had had her dropped in one of the great markets, expecting she would kill herself or turn to whoring to get more of the drug—enough perhaps to send her to Dreaming. If they found her, what a revolting thing she would have been.

He frowned, trying to recall whether he had heard anything more about her, but nothing came back to him. Pasgen and Rhoslyn had never mentioned her again. It was possible she was dead or that they had been so disgusted they had simply turned away and left her, put her out of their minds.

Now he regretted throwing away a useful tool. He raised a hand to summon another imp. Finding Llanelli, if she was still alive, was a task he could leave to the Sidhe of his court while he attended to getting Elizabeth disgraced. He could not believe that Pasgen would keep a watch on his mother like that he kept on his beloved sister. But once Llanelli was in his hands, Pasgen's blood tie would oblige him to protect her. So, if his Sidhe could find Llanelli, even if she were Dreaming and as good as dead, he could use her to control Pasgen.

One last glance around his apartment, which now looked just as he liked it—walls draped in black velvet with red hems, like thin streams of blood on the floor, edges bound in gold, enough to look rich but not so much as to lighten the atmosphere. He gestured to the newt servant who prodded the bespelled mortal from his room to Aurilia's and through the door when it opened. If there were a trap in that seeming welcome, the prisoner would be caught in it.

If the bribe he was offering was not enough . . . However, Aurilia was easier to pacify than he had expected. She looked from him to the ensorcelled young man of heroic proportions and very little brain and nodded at the peace offering.

"What do you want?" she asked pleasantly enough.

"An amulet. An amulet that will draw Thomas Seymour to visit the magician Otstargi and fall into the magician's power—an amulet that will make the man believe that Otstargi has the true key to his fortune and advancement."

That produced a smile and a gracious nod. She even suggested he take a seat in her parlor and offered wine and sweet, sugary little cakes. Vidal did not hesitate to accept her offer; he only bespelled both the goblet of wine and the plate of cakes to be sure they were not poisoned. Aurilia did not seem to mind. She giggled.

That did not make Vidal as happy as it should. He had to wonder, as he saw another empty glass on the table near her chair, whether she had drunk too much of that potion her mortal healer provided. However, when he began to give her details about the amulet and what it must do, her questions and suggestions were solid and sensible.

Finally she said, "I cannot promise that one amulet will be able to do both tasks. In two days I can have ready one that will draw this Thomas Seymour to Otstargi. You can send an imp to touch him with it and then put it in his pocket. Once he is in your presence you can surely find some excuse to give him the other amulet."

Vidal nodded. The less complicated the spells the better chance they would work. "For how long will the spell last?"

"Not very long, a week or two, but if your advice brings him success of one kind or another, he will believe without any further spelling. Or if you need another spell—" she glanced at the blankly staring young giant and smiled "—I will furnish it."

"True enough." Vidal's lips pulled back so that his long sharp teeth showed. "And if what I advise is what this fool Seymour will enjoy and would have done anyway, he will not need a spell to coerce him and will believe in me even more fervently. How long did you say before the amulet will be ready?"

"Two days."

Chapter 20

"Where the devil have you been?" Elizabeth glared at Denoriel, the amber of her eyes seeming to be touched with red, but her voice was too low to be heard by the ladies that followed along the path behind her. In a swift, careful glance over his shoulder, Denoriel saw Lady Alana drop something, cry out softly, and gather the three young women closer to help her pick up the oddments that had somehow fallen out of the purse which had mysteriously come loose from her belt.

"You know where I was," Denoriel replied, equally softly, but walking on swiftly. And in case some vagrant oddity along the path threw his voice back to the women, he added, "I was on a voyage, attending to my business."

"And no doubt attending to some pretty foreign ladies, too," Elizabeth muttered angrily.

Denoriel's mouth opened, but nothing came out for a moment. His heart had leapt right into his throat, choking him. Was Elizabeth jealous? Did she want him to pay court to her or was her anger just because a possession of hers had not been where she wanted it when she wanted it? No, it could not be simple possessiveness. If she were just annoyed by his absence, she would have said something to imply she was more important than his business. Instead she had mentioned pretty ladies. But he had not the courage to put his hope to the test and have it destroyed.

"No," he got out. "It was business." Another glance behind showed the ladies still in sight but certainly out of earshot. "I was . . . I was with Harry. You can ask him."

"And when am I ever likely to see him again?"

Denoriel chuckled. "Whenever you are ready and you promise to stop biting off my head."

"Oh," Elizabeth said. She looked away, also glancing behind to make sure she would not be overheard. Then her eyes came back to him and her lips thinned. "Do you not deserve to have your head bitten off when you have so neglected me? You have been away nearly two months. On business, perhaps, but I am sure you made time for pleasure too and foreign women must be more attractive than plain English girls."

For one moment Denoriel simply stared at her, his eyes wide. Elizabeth had seen elven women, had seen his bedchamber and knew that Sidhe did not sleep; she knew what the bed was for. The geas Titania had put on her prevented her from speaking of Underhill or anything in it. Foreign women was the closest she could come. He called his time Underhill foreign voyages. But in the past Elizabeth had never seemed to care whether he played with women. Aleneil was right; she was changing. It must be jealousy that had honed her tongue.

"There is no woman more attractive to me than you, my lady," Denoriel breathed.

She hissed a little with anger and snarled at him, "I do not like it when you lie to me, Lord Denno."

"I *never* lie to you, Lady Elizabeth," he snapped back. "*Never.* There are things I do not say and things I cannot say, but I have never told you a lie."

Elizabeth blinked at him, her firm lips beginning to soften and tremble. Then she lowered her head and glanced at him sidelong from under her lashes. "Well, but it cannot be the truth that no woman is more attractive to you than I. Surely there are more beautiful women with . . . ah . . . with better shaped bodies."

"Yes, indeed." Denoriel grinned down at her, laughing at the shock and fury on her face over his ready agreement. "I have certainly seen women with more beautiful faces and bodies than yours." He paused and added, "So what? What I said is still true. Those women are not nearly as attractive to me as your ladyship."

"You mean as a friend."

Her head was down again. Denoriel glanced back. The women were once more following them, but at a greater distance and they were fully engaged in a lively conversation. Denoriel raised a hand and lifted Elizabeth's chin.

"I am afraid to offend, my lady, being what I am and you what you are, but no, not as a friend, although I value you for that friendship also. To me you are the most beautiful and desirable lady in all the worlds. Indeed, you are the only lady for me, there is no room in my heart for any other—no matter how beautiful or how shapely."

A faint color touched Elizabeth's cheeks and she looked away from him again. "But in your own land, you were a prince," she said softly. "So you need not fear to offend by . . . by saying you favor me."

As if by an accident of the path Denoriel swayed closer so he could take her hand and in the shelter of their bodies kiss it. The color in her cheeks rose. A burst of laughter came from behind. Hastily Denoriel released Elizabeth's hand.

"I wish I could take you on a voyage with me very soon," he murmured.

Elizabeth's eyes lit to bright gold. "It would have to be a short one," she responded. "I do not wish to alarm Queen Catherine by taking to my bed. I do not wish to do anything to diminish her happiness. She glows with joy."

"Yes, I saw. I was required to gain her approval to visit you." Denoriel paused and then added dryly, "I hope she remains happy."

Elizabeth looked surprised. "Why should she not? At last, after three marriages to old men she has a young and vigorous husband. Thomas—" Her voice, which had been full of lively enthusiasm checked, and she went on with more restraint, "I mean Baron Seymour of Sudeley, but that is such a mouthful and he is so good-humored and not one to stand at all on ceremony. We have all begun to call him Thomas."

"Have you?" Denoriel asked flatly. "All of your maidens and Catherine's women call Seymour Thomas?"

"My maidens do," she said defensively, and then with reluctant honesty, "Some of Catherine's women are more formal." She hesitated, aware of Denoriel's disapproval, and frowned back at him. "I cannot see what has put your nose out of joint. Was it not you who told me that Catherine had a right to some joy after her dutiful behavior as wife to three old men? Now she has a lively man who enjoys lighthearted amusement. Why do you dislike Thomas?"

Denoriel was tempted to tell her the man was a flirt and a lecher and add what else he knew about Seymour. But some of it—like the fact that Seymour had tried to get Elizabeth herself for his wife before he returned to Catherine—was better she did not know. It might prove that Seymour was not the faithful lover he pretended to be, but it might make Elizabeth more vulnerable to him by indicating that he wanted her more than Catherine.

About to say something about Seymour's boisterous manner, which he felt was unseemly, Denoriel suddenly saw a reason for dislike that was not only true but would advance his purpose of fixing Elizabeth's mind on himself.

"I do not like any man who has your favor," he said harshly, and abruptly drew her into a side path bounded by high hedges that led into a "wilderness."

Surprise made her stumble against him, and he pulled her tight. That made her look up. Denoriel dropped his head and touched his lips to hers. She stood absolutely still, but rigid, as if turned to stone. Denoriel was too close to see her face. She could have been frightened or disgusted or simply surprised again, but he suddenly remembered Aleneil laughing and saying that surely he did not intend to leap on her and commit rape. Appalled, Denoriel was about to release her, but then her free arm began to slide up his back, holding them close.

A cry came from the path and then another voice asking, "Where did they go?"

Denoriel lifted his head. His eyes blazed like emeralds in the sunlight as he looked down into her face, but his voice was just as usual when he called, "Here, in the path to the right. Lady Elizabeth thought she saw a fox, but it was nothing but a rabbit."

Still staring into his face, Elizabeth ran the tip of her tongue over her lips, but her voice, too, was natural, a little high and touched with irritation. "It *was* a fox. I could not mistake that shade of red." Then she laughed. "But if you saw a rabbit, Lord Denno, then let us forget the fox. It will do more good than harm in the garden if it takes the rabbit."

For just a moment their eyes locked. "Tonight," he said. "Tell Blanche."

✧   ✧   ✧

In the first week of July, actually while Elizabeth and Denoriel were walking in the garden, Thomas Seymour was staring down at a letter bearing a most interesting seal. The letter on a salver had been carried in by a footman who begged pardon for disturbing his master but said he was told it was most important.

Seymour did not notice the man's slack expression or that he should never have been carrying messages at all, his duty being to guard and open the door. Seymour rubbed the seal. It looked flat, but his fingers felt a definite thickness. He rubbed it again, aware of a subtle but pleasant sensation.

Well, he thought, this was telling him nothing, and he broke the seal. It resisted his pressure momentarily, confirming his feeling that the seal was thicker than it looked. And when it broke, one could see that it was not a thin, flat round of wax. Curious, he ran his fingers over the broken ends, but then grew impatient with the silly thing. After all, it was the letter that was important.

The message was from a Fagildo Otstargi, but the direction impressed Seymour favorably, being a house near the Strand where Seymour's own Somerset House stood. Then Seymour remembered the name Otstargi. Wriothesley had sworn by the man, saying he had saved his position, even his life more than once. He had tried, Seymour also remembered, to induce him to consult the conjuror, but he had been too busy and Wriothesley had been eased away from power.

So the charlatan had not saved Wriothesley's position as chancellor. The contemptuous notion was replaced in his mind by the fact that Otstargi had warned Wriothesley in time to retire gracefully . . . and with a handsome title and all his ill-gotten gains. Resentment pushed out any memory of the word charlatan. No common barony for Wriothesley, as had been passed off on him, making him a mere Baron Seymour of Sudeley; Wriothesley was earl of Southampton.

I deserve more, Thomas thought; I am the king's uncle just as much as my damned brother. But Edward was now a *duke* no less. Thomas had thought he was clever enough, what with Catherine's influence with the young king, to win himself more than the pittance he had received. True the king had supported his marriage to Catherine, but nothing since then. Perhaps a little help from Otstargi, who certainly had raised Wriothesley from knight to earl, would not be amiss.

The letter from Otstargi was simple enough. It apologized for intruding on so busy and important a person but claimed that this Otstargi had learned some facts he felt would be of interest and profit to Baron Seymour of Sudeley, who had been appointed Lord High Admiral of the English fleet. Vaguely Seymour had a feeling he had had a similar letter in the past, but it did not seem important. Why should he not see the man?

It happened that the rest of Seymour's morning was free. John Fowler, a confidential servant who slept in Edward's room and had been handsomely bribed to help make Thomas the king's favorite uncle, had sent a hasty message that Edward had the sniffles and would not be walking out; the planned meeting between uncle and nephew would need to be postponed. So why not use the morning to discover what this Otstargi thought would be of interest and profit? Nothing could make him take the man's advice if he did not like it. Without realizing what he was doing, Seymour pulled on the halves of the broken seal, which readily came off the paper and dropped them in his pocket.

He left no message with his servants as to where he was going. Somerset would have a fit if he heard his brother was about to consult a magician. The thought gave Thomas a certain amount of pleasure he walked the short distance between his great house and Otstargi's smaller one.

It was, however, a respectable house, large enough to show the owner was prosperous, and the door was opened by a respectable servant, although he was so expressionless as to look like a waxwork. Moreover Thomas was not kept waiting. Only a few moments after the servant carried in his name, the door reopened and he was invited in.

Master Otstargi was standing behind the table at which he had been working. He was a swarthy man, his dark skin hinting at travel in southern climes, his hair and eyes also dark. He bowed, not obsequiously low, but with politeness as if he knew his own worth. For once that did not annoy Seymour. He told himself that a man so sure of his value might actually have some value.

"Please sit, my lord," Otstargi said, gesturing toward a substantial chair opposite his own at the table.

Thomas did not bother considering any particular approach. The man might be nothing more than a common charlatan. "What did your letter mean, that you had made discoveries of interest and profit to me?" he asked directly.

Vidal, in the guise of Otstargi, was no more loath to be direct. "You have been shabbily treated, my lord," he said. "The king has two uncles and the power his office confers should have been shared equally. There can be no doubt that your brother, the duke of Somerset, is most fitted to control the petty details of managing the kingdom. Contrariwise, your warmth of heart and liveliness of nature should have been devoted to managing the king himself. You would win from him by love and laughter every benefit Somerset wrings out by command. That practice with a boy of the king's age, only generates resentment and will, in the near future, breed disaster."

Thomas' mouth opened, but he did not speak. Otstargi had seemingly divined his plans, to split the power in the realm by dividing the duties just as Otstargi described. Thomas knew that for once he had not discussed these plans with anyone, not even with Catherine. Fowler knew, of course, that he was striving to make Edward his friend, but Fowler believed that was to make Edward support his marriage.

Finally Seymour asked sharply, "From whom did you hear this?"

Otstargi laughed. "I have my own methods for getting information and they do not involve bribing servants. You would be best advised, my lord, just to believe what I tell you, and act on it."

Seymour had drawn an indignant breath over the almost contemptuous tone in which the charlatan spoke, but with the words, Otstargi spun across the table a brilliant crystal. Seymour grabbed for it instinctively, and when his hand stopped the stone, his indignation fled. It was a ruby, a deep glowing red with a design he could not quite make out carved into its surface.

For a moment as he picked up the stone to examine it more closely, a wave of dizziness swept over him and an unexpected roiling in his belly. He forgot both sensations, absorbed by the beauty of the ruby, and then he closed his hand over it.

"Beautiful," he said. "Are you selling it?"

"No, it is not for sale, but you might have it as a gift with my goodwill."

Thomas opened his hand and looked down at the ruby, which glowed like pulsing blood in his hand. He knew men did not give such "gifts" without large expectations of return favors, but his hand closed over the stone again.

"That is an expensive gift," he remarked. "I suppose I am in a position to do you a substantial favor."

Otstargi smiled. "And profit yourself richly as well," he said. "You were appointed Lord High Admiral when you were made a baron? Yes?"

"Yes." Thomas's mouth twisted wryly. "A singularly useless appointment. The navy is so starved that it is almost impossible to make any profit from it. The supplies are inadequate. Trying to pinch them only brings complaints from the captains for which the Council blames me."

"Ah, but I can suggest to you an easy way to profit and to save your captains for more important military action . . . for which they will be needed in the future."

"Military action?" Seymour repeated, frowning. "When?"

"That I cannot say with any certainty, my lord, although I think not soon enough to interfere with your profits."

"*My* profits?"

"This is the beginning of the high season for trade, and thus the high season for piracy."

"Piracy."

Thomas shook his head impatiently, annoyed at sounding like an echo at this third repetition. As Lord High Admiral, part of his duty was to eliminate the pirates that preyed on the shipping coming out of the Mediterranean Sea, along the coasts of Spain and France and even into the Channel. Admittedly he had not exerted himself over that duty, but surely this Otstargi would not gift him with a rich ruby to encourage him to hunt pirates.

Otstargi tented his hands on the table and rested his long chin on the tips of his fingers. "Yes, piracy. A very frustrating charge for you, as it is a large ocean and your few ships cannot be everywhere."

"That's true enough!" Thomas exclaimed angrily. He had been taken to task by a few gentlemen of the court over his lack of success at stemming the piracy.

"It might be arranged for your ships to take some of the pirates with relative ease."

"You have informers who will tell you where and when—"

Otstargi lifted his head and held up a finger; Thomas, his hand tight over the inscribed ruby, fell silent. It felt quite natural to him, and he had no sense of how unusual it was for him to obey such a gesture. Otstargi smiled broadly.

"It does not matter how I know where and when a ship will fall into your power. What does matter is that while your ships are engaged in capturing or sinking those pirates, others—with rather more valuable cargoes—will slip away to a safe haven, in the Scilly Islands, for example."

"There's nothing in the Scillys, except sheep and cows."

"And a deep harbor or two or three. But you are right about the Scilly Islands. They would not be considered a good market for pirated goods, which is why pirates would be safe there."

Slowly Seymour shook his head. "No, because there would need to be a way for buyers to move the cargoes, which means more ships. The fleet sails right by those islands. Some bright and noble captain is sure to notice that there are more ships than usual in the ports and insist on investigating." His mouth twisted with distaste. "Honorable idiots."

"Surely it is within your power to assign the honorable idiots to . . . say . . . the east coast to guard against the French sending men or supplies to the Scots?"

Though he was acting as Otstargi, Vidal had not lost sight of another purpose. When the English attacked the Scots, he did not want help from the French to reach them. The English could not gain a decisive victory, and even if they could, the Scots—with his assistance—would not keep any treaty they made. But if the Scots, with French help, pushed the English back, that might stop the fighting for some time, and that was the last thing Vidal wanted.

"You are right about that, Master Otstargi." Thomas grinned. "And the honorable idiots will be so pleased at being sent to guard against the French that they will bless my name."

Vidal cocked his head. "Then that is agreed?"

"Why not? No one will lose by it. We never seem to catch up with the pirates anyway, so the few we take will redound to the credit of the fleet, and those who . . . ah . . . are not sighted would have done what they did with or without my assistance."

"True, very true. But the trouble is that what you will get from the pirates, although a nice addition to your income, will not be near enough for you to buy support in the Council to give you charge of the king's person."

"I am counting on the king's own preference for me to sway the Council."

Slowly Vidal shook his head. "I am quite sure the king will not be allowed to state his preference unless the Council is somehow encouraged to ask him for it. That will take money, real money."

"My wife is very rich—"

"No. The last thing you should do is strip Queen Catherine's estate, specially so soon after you are married. Even if your wife understands and agrees, there will be—if not outcries of outrage—nasty whispers and rumors from her kin and those who consider themselves her friends. Nor will you be able to defend yourself and show that the spending now will benefit her in the future, not without warning your brother of your plans, which might be fatal. I have a better suggestion to offer you."

Rolling the ruby gently between his hands, Thomas now regretted that he had not sooner taken Wriothesley's advice and consulted Master Otstargi. "Yes?" he asked, eager to hear this new suggestion.

It was very much to Thomas' taste. There was a Sir William Sharington, vice-treasurer of the Bristol Mint who was buying up and minting considerable quantities of Church plate. If Seymour would offer protection to this scheme, Sharington would readily share his huge profits. Thomas quickly agreed to travel to Bristol to settle the matter personally with Sharington, while making calculations about the cost each month of supporting ten thousand men. Enough money would permit him to challenge the Protector openly.

"You will lose that stone, if you keep rolling it about," Otstargi said, a smile in his voice. "You should have it set into a ring."

"I may well do that," Seymour said, tucking the stone carefully into his purse. "Well, I thank you for your good advice," he added, preparing to rise.

"One moment more, my lord," Otstargi said, pretending to appear uncertain. "I have Seen something very strange in my glass and I think I had better tell you about it, although I am not at all sure of its meaning."

"If it does not concern me—" Thomas began, uneasy at the open mention of crystal-gazing and fortune-telling. Both were condemned by the Church and by the law also.

Otstargi shook his head. "But it does concern you, my lord,

too closely for me to ignore what I have Seen. More certainly because I cannot understand what I See and have Seen repeatedly. I know you are most happily married to a lovely lady, but I See you always in company with a different lady, much younger, pale with red hair."

"What?"

Seymour's exclamation did not imply that he had not heard what Vidal said but that it had some startling significance to him. This was just what Vidal wanted; knowing Seymour to be something of a lecher, he had been concerned that the man would not immediately identify the pale, red-haired girl with Elizabeth.

"Yes, a young girl, pretty but thin, with very red hair. And there are several images, always in succession. First of playful contacts, a quick caress, a kiss, often in the presence of others. Then images of you two alone in far deeper intimacy. And last—the girl is older in the last image—you and she seated in high chairs under cloths of state in the richest apparel, all trimmed in ermine."

"Seated under cloths of state and wearing ermine?" Seymour's voice was carefully neutral but Vidal was most satisfied with the gleam in his eyes.

He kept his own voice mildly puzzled. "That is the image, I do not understand it at all. The king, God bless him, is alive and well and you are married most happily to a woman with dark hair. But there is no sense of time in these images. The first, likely is now or in the near future. The last may be years away."

Thomas made no reply at first and he had lowered his gaze to the polished surface of the table between him and Master Otstargi. After a long moment he raised his eyes from the tabletop to the magician's face, his expression now thoughtful.

"The first image could be of me fixing my favor with the red-haired girl. The second a natural progression." Thomas smiled complacently; he had brought a number of doubting females to bed. "The last—"

"I beg you will not speak of that. Perhaps I should not have told you of it, but I felt you needed to be warned."

Vidal spoke sharply, thrusting a needle of compulsion at Seymour. The man was a blabbermouth. If he "confided" to anyone his hope of marrying Elizabeth and ruling as consort by her side, he would be hung for treason before he could actually disqualify her for the throne.

"I am not a fool, Master Otstargi," Thomas said, getting to his feet and speaking louder and more assertively than he had since he tucked the ruby into his pouch.

Vidal did not reply nor did he try any further spells. Sometimes spells could conflict and cancel or damage each other's effect. He was also concerned that the spell on Aurilia's amulet was not as effective as it should be unless the amulet was actually in Seymour's hand, and as he saw Seymour to the door he remarked that he hoped the ruby could be set and worn as a ring to remind Seymour of the profits to be gained by their bargain.

The grunted reply was not reassuring, but there was little more Vidal could do. To bind the man securely enough to ensure utter compliance would change his behavior so much that his intimates and servants would know there was something wrong with him. Better to set a watcher on him and see what he would do.

Chapter 21

Elizabeth and Denoriel were surrounded by young women, all asking in high voices where was the fox? the rabbit? before Denoriel could say what would happen tonight and about what Elizabeth should warn Blanche. If she could have stunned every one of those encroaching idiots, Elizabeth would have done so.

Laughing heartily, as if he were glad to see the intruders, Lord Denno pointed out that both fox and rabbit would have been frightened altogether out of the garden and the wilderness by the noise they made. He flashed a glance at Elizabeth, but she was staring purposefully down the path and somewhat too intently invited the girls to accompany her on a search. She drew a sharp breath when they all agreed Lord Denno was right, they should have been quieter.

"Nonetheless," she began, hoping she could manage to lose the whole party for at least a few minutes in the wilderness, but she was interrupted by the sound of church bells chiming Nones.

"Too late," Lady Alana said. "We really must return now. Remember, Elizabeth, that the music master is appointed to come to you."

"Bother the music master!" Elizabeth muttered under her breath, and then somewhat louder, "I have hardly had a chance to hear about Lord Denno's latest voyage, which I gather was exciting and profitable."

"Tales of my voyage will keep," Lord Denno said, laughing again. "They would perhaps be better told at a time when there are fewer distractions by wild beasts."

"Not if I have to wait two months for them," Elizabeth complained, her voice just a trifle tremulous.

"No, no." Denoriel smiled at her, his eyes peculiarly intent. "I am done voyaging and will see you again very soon. But I hope you will pardon me for parting here, since we are much closer to the stable and your excuse will save my poor old legs from double the distance."

Elizabeth was quite startled. In the past Denno never mentioned his age, never asked any relief from any physical task, always insisted he was well and very strong, which, indeed, he was. Stronger, in fact, than any other man she knew. Quite unreasonably, Elizabeth could feel the warmth of his lips gently clinging to hers. It occurred to her that he would want her attendants to think of him as old. She could take greater liberties with an old man . . . like kissing him.

She drew her lips into what she hoped looked like a pitying smile and said, "You will never be old, Lord Denno. I—I will not permit it." Then she sighed and shrugged. "But I will give you permission to leave us now."

As she said the words, she suddenly felt resentful. Denno had always clung to her company for every minute he could eke out. She was quite sure he had not begged leave to save himself the walk back to the palace. Perhaps he was eager to get back to the business he had mentioned when she asked where he had been.

She had a sudden vision of the elven women she had seen in the market places, of Mwynwen's exquisite face. But he had sworn she was the woman he desired, and swore too that he had never lied to her. Well, that was true, as far as she knew. And he had said "Tonight" just before her maidens had caught up with them. What could he mean by "Tonight"? Certainly he would not dare try to visit again? But perhaps he would. Perhaps he would claim to have forgotten something in her apartment when he left from the garden.

That seemed a reasonable idea, and Elizabeth's mind was so occupied with ways to find some privacy so she could again touch Denno's lips that her music lesson was less than a success. She apologized and promised to practice more, but she was thinking

of Denno's brief kiss. She had kissed many other men in greeting and parting, but she had never felt anything—except disgust
sometimes when the lips were wet and slobbery. She must see
if the little feeling of warmth in her breasts, the little frisson of
tickling that was not tickling between her legs would come again
when Denno kissed her.

All her plans to get Denno off into a private corner, however,
were in vain. He never came.

As the evening wore on, Elizabeth became quite waspish, so
much so that Catherine asked her whether her visitor had tired
her. At least she was able to answer honestly that he had frustrated
her—but that it was all her own fault, which was, of course, she
said with a laugh, what put her so much out of temper. She had
spent so much time quarreling with him about not warning her
in advance he would be away, that she had had no opportunity
to hear about the strange and wonderful places he had seen on
his voyage.

Catherine laughed at her kindly and promised to allow another
visit, even to write and *invite* Lord Denno to visit. They would
all enjoy hearing about his foreign voyages, so perhaps she would
ask him to join them for dinner and an evening. Then she sighed
and shook her head.

"I am afraid I am looking to fill time with a safe and harmless
visitor. Tom will be away longer than he thought. It seems he
must travel into the west about these stupid pirates and assign
some ships to watch the east coast to keep the French from sup-
plying the Scots."

All of the ladies, including Elizabeth, expressed their sympathy
over her husband's absence. They all—all except for Lady Alana
who, as she often did, held her peace—said, with perfect sincerity
that they would miss him. His loud voice and boisterous suggestions for games such as hoodman-blind, where smacking kisses
were exchanged when a victim was caught, enlivened the quiet
days and evenings at Chelsea.

Like all the other young women, Elizabeth had been somewhat
excited by those smacking kisses, and the way Seymour's hands
ran over her body as he claimed to be trying to identify her. It
was perfectly safe, of course, with Catherine playing with them
and laughing as heartily as anyone else over Tom's antics.

That kiss of Denno's—that had not been at all safe, and was all the more exciting. Elizabeth's tongue peeped out to touch her lips. But then the lips set hard. He had said "Tonight," but he had not come. Elizabeth's needle stabbed so hard into the book cover she was embroidering that it went quite through the cloth, and she barely repressed some pungent words as she worked it out again.

By the time she had recovered the needle, Catherine had put down her own needlework and was gesturing all the ladies to come together for evening prayers. Elizabeth's heart felt oddly heavy, but in one way it was a relief. She need not suffer expectation any longer. It was far too late for Denno to come. What had he meant? Had she misheard the low, hasty words? "Tonight. Tell Blanche." Tell Blanche what?

The answer to that question became apparent when Blanche almost drove Elizabeth into her dressing room as soon as she arrived at her apartment. However, instead of hastily beginning to remove Elizabeth's clothing and make her ready for bed, the maid turned her and pointed.

"Look, my lady," Blanche murmured, softly enough not to be heard if one of the maids of honor should step into the bechamber.

She gestured to a pretty porcelain oval lying just atop Elizabeth's jewel box. The trinket was about as long as Elizabeth's thumb and was painted with a delicate scene of a doorway surrounded by climbing flowers.

"I don't remember having anything like that," Elizabeth said, her own voice a murmur in sympathy with Blanche's desire not to be overheard. She bent over the trinket, all at once soothed, beginning to smile, a hand rising to pick it up. "Where did it come from?"

"*Something* brought it," Blanche said with a tremor in her voice. "Something laid it down on the box—right in front of my eyes. I haven't touched it."

Elizabeth drew back, catching at the maid's hand. "Something evil?" she breathed.

She remembered all too well having been driven nearly to ending her own life by a spell of dissolution transmitted by a jewel embedded in the cover—of all things—of a Bible. But that, she remembered, had made her feel uneasy, drawn to touch it, but slightly sick and unwilling. This, this also carried a temptation to touch but it made her smile.

"Oh no," Blanche assured her, her worried look easing. "It . . . what I felt was like that little thing I could never see that used to stay near you after you were sick that time and then again last year. No, it didn't feel good or bad but . . . I felt it was a happy thing. The reason I wouldn't touch it was because of the crosses. I was afraid I would spoil it."

Air spirit, Elizabeth thought but could not say. Air spirits often carried news or brief messages Underhill, but they did not ordinarily come into the mortal world unless they were sent. Elizabeth eyed the porcelain oval with a momentary doubt and then suddenly knew what her Denno had meant when he said, "Tonight. Tell Blanche."

She remembered the time when he had brought her Da back to the mortal world. They had needed a Gate and Denno had given her a token carrying a spell that would call the Gate to it. Elizabeth drew a deep happy breath. He would come tonight to take her Underhill and, of course, he had meant to warn Blanche not to touch the token for fear that the necklace of Cold Iron crosses she wore as a defense against Unseleighe attack would destroy the magic Denno had spelled into the token.

"Where shall we put it?" she asked Blanche, looking around the dressing room.

It was a small chamber, cluttered with Elizabeth's hanging dresses, chests of undergarments, a small table with a mirror, and several stools. Remembering the last time she had used Denno's token to draw a Gate, Elizabeth giggled. Forgetting that Denno would have to step forward out of the Gate, she had laid the token on a garden bench at the center of the maze and poor Denno had fallen off the bench right into a bed of dead flowers.

He had been surprisingly understanding, but once was more than enough for that kind of stupidity. "Not in here," she said to Blanche.

"And not in your bedchamber," Blanche said at once. "That is too dangerous. No matter what I say to those girls, they *will* poke their heads inside the door—to see if they would be disturbing you or if you are asleep and a scratch would wake you." Blanche sighed with exasperation. "And, of course, Mistress Ashley cannot be kept out. We cannot take the chance that someone will step in or look in just at the moment Lord Denno takes you away or brings you back."

"Your chamber?" Elizabeth asked hesitantly.

That was the best choice because it was just the other side of the dressing room, but Elizabeth hated to ask Blanche to permit a man into her room. The maid was very particular about her reputation and even met old fellow servants like Dunstan and Ladbroke in the corridor outside of her room rather than within it.

But Blanche nodded without reluctance. "No one will see him. If a maid pops in by accident, I know he can disappear. Besides, I have the very place. I guessed that thing appearing as it did meant *he* would be coming." She drew Elizabeth behind her through the dressing room and into her own small, dark chamber.

There, between two wardrobes stood a figure molded of pasteboard—actually Elizabeth's form, which allowed her maid to mend and adjust her clothing. If that figure was pulled forward, and perhaps dressed, in the dim room the space behind it would be mostly invisible.

"Very good!" Elizabeth exclaimed, eyes bright, turning toward the dressing room. "Now, what should I wear?"

"Your nightdress," Blanche said.

"But I wanted . . ." she sighed and then giggled.

What was she thinking? The clothing that Lady Alana could produce Underhill far outshone anything in her own wardrobe, to be truthful, anything in the queen's wardrobe . . . or that of the Protector's wife, who really put on most unsuitable airs.

"And you have a very pretty nightdress," Blanche reminded her. "I made up that last packet of silk and lace Lord Denno brought when you were so worried about where you were going to live. You hardly looked at it, my lady, but it is quite beautiful. You know Lord Denno never skimps you."

No he did not, Elizabeth thought, pulling her Cold Iron cross out of the bosom of her gown and slipping it into the heavy pouch of silk that would shield Denno's token from its influence. She went into the dressing room then, and picked up the pretty porcelain oval, smiling as she realized that the door design was a clever message.

Blanche had already moved the pasteboard form and Elizabeth laid the token on the floor, not too close to the back wall. She wondered about how Denno would know they were ready, but could not guess since she could not sense any air spirit. Just in case some word was necessary to activate the guide, she touched the oval and said *"Fiat,"* which keyed most of her own spells.

Then she pressed a hand to her lips and rushed back to the

dressing room. If Denno responded to the call of the token and came at once, she would not be ready. He would see her undressing. With lips parted to urge Blanche to hurry, Elizabeth suddenly smiled and swallowed the words. If Denno should see her undressed by accident...

Thoughts wavering now between hope and shame, she stood still while Blanche began to remove her sleeves and then unfasten the points of her skirt. As the heavy fabric slid down, she stepped out of it. The elaborate brocade was another gift from Denno and made her recall Blanche's remark.

It was true, Denno would never skimp her in any way. Not in the gifts he brought...nor in the touch of his lips. That was right, somehow; it was thrilling, it woke odd exciting sensations in her body. How wonderful that Denno was not human! What she did with him or felt about him had nothing to do with her life in the mortal world. Elizabeth hoped she would never need to marry, but if political necessity forced her into that state, human to human she would be a virgin still.

Human to human made her think of Thomas. When he touched her and kissed her, she felt hot and fluttery...and uneasy and ashamed. She knew that even though Catherine was with them and even joined in the games, Thomas should not be so handling her innocent maidens—or a king's daughter. Catherine was too much in love, Elizabeth thought. She could not bear to deny her husband any pleasure.

The soft slither of silk down her body, simultaneous with the click of a door latch, drew her lips into a brief pout. It was too late for Denno to catch a glimpse of her clothed in nothing but her hair. But in the next moment she realized it was not the door to Blanche's room that had opened, that had been left open, but the door to her parlor.

Elizabeth uttered a small, exasperated sigh. She had been glad when she came to Chelsea that Catherine had told her the door to her apartment need no longer be guarded. Not that she had dismissed Gerrit, Nyle, Shaylor, and Dickson. They still guarded her when she went riding or down the river to London. And they stood guard on the palace as a whole with Catherine's men, but she would never have escaped such long-time, devoted servants when she crept out to watch Catherine meeting Thomas. They would have clumped along behind her...Elizabeth giggled at the image, then sighed. Tonight a guard at the door would have been useful to keep out intruders.

Likely the unwelcome arrival was Eleanor Fitzalan, a sweet child, but far too prone to wish to be helpful. Forever creeping into her bedchamber to ask if she wanted a drink or to have her candle trimmed or some other service. Elizabeth frowned. How was she going to make sure that none of those silly girls discovered she was absent from her bed?

Blanche had already stepped around her to send away whoever had come in, but she stopped and Elizabeth heard her sigh with relief. In a moment she herself smiled as she understood. Lady Alana had just stepped through the dressing room door.

"With a tongue as sharp as yours is, Lady Elizabeth, I cannot imagine how you inspire such devotion. No less than three of your ladies were on their way to discover if they could do anything to amuse you and soothe your irritation. I did manage to send them back to their own beds, but it was not easy."

"Likely my sharp tongue *is* the reason." Elizabeth said, grinning. "They think if they divert me, I will be less sharp tomorrow. You would think that experience would teach them better. However, it is very likely that I will be mild as milk tomorrow *without* their attentions. I wish I could hope that would start a precedent. Are you coming with me?"

"Yes." Aleneil smiled and turned to Blanche. "No need for you to look so worried, Blanche. The door to the parlor is stuck and will not open until I return. Go to bed and get a good night's sleep for a change."

"I don't sleep easy when my lady is . . . is away," Blanche said, frowning.

Elizabeth embraced her. "There's no need to worry. Lady Alana and Lord Denno will both be with me and for once I am not grieving and distracted." Suddenly a smile like sunshine lit her face; over Blanche's shoulder she had seen Denno standing in the doorway. "Sleep well, Blanche," she said but without looking at her maid, and walked past her into her Denno's arms.

He drew her with him so quickly to a black gaping between the wardrobes that at first Elizabeth did not take in what she saw. Even as the blackness and falling that was Gating passed over her, however, she realized that the other end of the Gate opened into the bedchamber she used in Denno's house. Had Lady Alana been left behind? Elizabeth stiffened slightly. Did Denno intend to . . . to take her to bed now? Without even asking her? She had responded to his kiss, yes. But . . .

But his mouth was on hers even as they touched the bedchamber floor and the half-frightened, half-resentful thoughts puffed away, evaporated by the warmth that coursed from his lips to hers. Only for a moment, though, as the kiss was broken and both of them pushed forward by the arrival of another body.

"I am so sorry," Alana said, chuckling, "but the Gate was so small and narrow, and already starting to close, that I had no choice."

She did not sound particularly sorry, and the voice was not Lady Alana's coo but Aleneil's sweet, brisk tones. Elizabeth did not care; she had no attention to give to Alana/Aleneil. She was staring at Denno. He had looked just as he always did when he came to the door of Blanche's room, his hair white, his face browned and lined by exposure to mortal weather. Now he looked . . . young. His hair was gold, his skin pale and smooth as cream. His eyes had not changed, except that they were sparkling, emeralds touched by a beam of sunlight. The points of his ears though were pink.

"Denno?" Elizabeth asked uncertainly.

"Yes."

He studied her face and Elizabeth wondered what it showed. She herself was uncertain of what she felt. Now that the first shock of seeing him young again had passed, her remaining surprise was largely owing to the fact that his appearance was not strange but utterly familiar. She realized suddenly that was how Denno had looked when she was little more than a babe, when he had come with Da to play with her—and he looked utterly familiar because it was how her mind had "seen" him all these years, why to her Denno would never grow old.

Gently she raised a hand and touched his cheek, then slid the hand around behind his head so she could pull his mouth down to hers. Aleneil's voice made Elizabeth start back and Denno lift his head.

"If you two intend to stand there staring at each other much longer, I wish you would tell me so I can think of some excuse to carry to Queen Titania. You did agree to go to this ball, didn't you, Denoriel? And Ilar will think I am not coming if I don't get there soon."

"Ball?" Elizabeth repeated, staring now at Aleneil, who was dressed in the most fantastic creation Elizabeth had ever seen.

She had to call it a creation because there was not enough of it to be called a gown. It was made completely of golden ribbons, one over a handspan wide went around the back of Aleneil's neck, crossed over her breasts barely hiding them, and then went around her narrow waist, fastening with a golden rose seemingly carved out of a giant topaz. The top of the skirt did manage to hide her private parts, being made of rosettes of the same ribbon in strategic places. But below her hips the skirt was all ribbons, showing a long length of white and shapely leg when Aleneil moved.

"Yes," Denno replied, "one of the great balls given by Oberon and Titania twice a year. It is open to all Sidhe, Dark Court and Bright alike."

Elizabeth started slightly, having almost forgotten the question in her voice when she repeated the word "ball." Then she blinked. "Dark Sidhe are also invited? But are they not evil and dangerous?"

"Not at the ball," Denno said, laughing. "There is a truce during the ball, all differences being set aside until a full mortal day after the ball ends."

"Truce?" Elizabeth's doubt showed in her voice.

Denno laughed again. "Oberon's truce is somewhat different from those of the mortal world. One *cannot* do any violence or even utter threats during Oberon's truce. Poisons are made harmless; even fingernails become too soft to scratch. Do you remember how he froze us all when Vidal attacked us? An impulse to violence or a threat has the same effect on any Sidhe who dares violate the truce. And it does make one look *very* silly to be frozen until Oberon decides to release one."

"You will be quite safe," Aleneil assured Elizabeth, twirling around so that all her ribbons floated up and gave glimpses of her legs. "Now, what would you like to wear? You can, of course, have the gown with the fur sleeves, but there is a great deal of dancing, quite lively dancing, and I think that gown would restrict you."

"I couldn't," Elizabeth said hesitantly, staring at Aleneil's dress.

"Oh, nothing like this," Aleneil assured her. "Just something soft and flowing that will let you feel free."

Elizabeth considered for a moment and then asked hesitantly, "If I don't feel comfortable in what you make for me, could I change into my other gown?"

"Of course you could, love." Aleneil cocked her head at Denoriel who was still looking at Elizabeth with a rather bemused expression. "Denoriel, go change your own clothing while I devise something Elizabeth will like." And when he did not move, she walked over and pushed him gently toward the door. "Go. Dress."

When she had closed the door behind him, she stared intently at Elizabeth for a moment. Now, as had happened the first time Elizabeth visited Underhill, her nightdress appeared on the bed and she could feel soft undergarments against the skin of her body. A moment later another soft, silken weight on her body—although nothing near the weight of a full Court dress—told her she was dressed, except that her left arm felt bare. Slowly Elizabeth turned to look in the full-length cheval glass.

"Oh, my," she breathed.

The dress, of a heavy amber silk, was softly fitted to her body from her left shoulder to the gentle rounded curve of her hips. From there, the thick and shining silk flowed smoothly to her ankles where a band of gleaming black fur made a hem and then spiraled up her body, past her waist, to form the edge of a huge sleeve/cloak that could be drawn up to cover her bare right shoulder.

There was no left sleeve either; the long armhole was decorated by an incredibly complex embroidery of gold around ovals of jet. The edge of the sleeve/cloak was also embroidered in gold around jet. A choker of brilliant topazes circled her neck and a broad bracelet to match covered her left wrist. Her head was free of any cap, but the hair in front of her ears had been plaited into several thin braids and then wound into a kind of crown at the top of her head fastened in place by a tiara of topaz.

Elizabeth stared at the coronet, flashing in the bright red of her hair. In the mortal world she would never dare wear such an ornament; she was a king's daughter and in the royal succession but by her father's decree not a princess.

"Well, love, can you wear that?"

Elizabeth looked at the smooth, white skin of her left arm; it almost seemed to glow against the amber silk and dark fur. She pulled the cloak/sleeve up a little higher on her right shoulder;

the silk draped gracefully against her neck, and the fur border lay against her hand without slipping. She could dance in that gown, Elizabeth thought, even a great galloping dance without feeling as if she might be tripped or toppled by its weight.

"Yes, oh yes. That is ... if you and I will not be the ... the barest people in the room."

Aleneil laughed again. "No, you need not fear that. We may be the best covered. Of course some will wear gowns that cover them from neck to instep, except that the fabric will be nearly transparent. Last ball one of the ladies wore nothing but a web of pearls. All sorts of things peeped out here and there."

Elizabeth took a few steps to one side and then turned quickly so that the hem of the gown, weighted as it was by the fur, flared around her legs. "It's light as a feather," she said, then sighed. "I do love my Court dresses, but they are not light . . ."

Her voice trailed away as Denoriel came to the door. He wore a silver jacket piped in black with a stand-up collar. It was fastened with jet buttons slantwise along his left shoulder and then down the side. Under the silver jacket were close-fitting black silk trews, piped in silver. His sword belt was black, the scabbard and hilt of his sword silver, the hilt of his long knife silver topped with a coruscating opal. Shining silver half boots covered his legs to the calf.

"Do you approve? Will you dance with me, my lady?"

"Every dance," Elizabeth said, moving forward to take his hand.

"Oh, no," Aleneil put in giggling. "There will be many others who wish to dance with the mortal princess, Elizabeth, and they will be quite cross with poor Denoriel if you cling too close to him. Besides, I think Harry will be coming. Will you not want to give your Da at least one dance?"

"Da will be invited?" Elizabeth's expression grew radiant.

"Everyone is invited," Denoriel said, frowning suddenly. "Which reminds me. You must be very circumspect in what you say, Elizabeth. Although violence and threats are forbidden, promises made at the ball are still promises. You must not even say things like 'I will see you again soon.' You may say 'I am glad to meet you' and other meaningless phrases, but nothing that can be taken as a promise."

"I will be careful," Elizabeth said solemnly.

"Then let us go," Aleneil urged, shooing them toward the door. "Ilar will have given me up as lost."

The elvensteeds were waiting at the foot of the stair, Ystwyth black as night with a golden mane and tail, Miralys a deep blue with silver mane and tail. Denoriel mounted, then leaned down and lifted Elizabeth to the smaller saddle behind his own. Elizabeth was not surprised when the skirt of her gown, which had not been so full, simply widened to allow her to sit astride. For a moment she felt annoyed again by the easy accommodations magic permitted, then she smiled.

Underhill was a game, a dream, a place where the forbidden and impossible could happen. It was a momentary escape from real life and should be enjoyed as such. Yet Elizabeth did not have the smallest desire to live in the dream for more than a short time. Longer, it would bore her to death.

Sliding an arm around Denno's waist to balance herself, Elizabeth offered up a small prayer of thanks to the real God for allowing her this delightful distraction. That thought sent a chill and then a flush of warmth through her. She knew, although even here Underhill she did not dare articulate the idea clearly, that this had been given her to support her in a time when duty and responsibility would grow so heavy as to crush her if some relief were not offered.

A flash of gold broke her thoughts and drew her attention to Aleneil, who floated up into Ystwyth's saddle. The ribbons glittered, even in the moonless, sunless twilight, shining, rising up and then drifting down around her. Magic. Elizabeth grinned, watching as the ribbons fell in such a way that Aleneil's legs were not completely exposed, only a tempting glimpse of white skin being revealed now and again.

The usual few strides of the elvensteeds brought them the seemingly long distance from the Summer Palace to the Gate of Logres. Ystwyth mounted the white, blue-veined marble under the high dome of opal lace supported on the pillars of chalcedony and promptly disappeared. Miralys followed. Elizabeth was a trifle surprised when they did not even pause a moment for Denoriel to visualize his destination, but then dismissed the puzzlement. Likely Oberon had bespelled every pattern holder in Underhill to bring Sidhe to the site of the ball.

That they had arrived where they should was immediately

apparent. Before them stretched an enormous field of the soft moss starred with small white flowers that seemed to cover the ground in Logres and Avalon. Far ahead Elizabeth saw the darkness of a large building, but it was too distant to make out any details. She looked down at where Ystwyth preceded them, noting with some amusement that the moss, soft as it looked and felt, never bruised or broke no matter the weight that compressed it.

Suddenly very happy over this very minor example of the silly dreamlike quality of Underhill, Elizabeth rubbed her face against Denno's back, and he turned his head and kissed her forehead. Elizabeth started to raise her face to bring their lips together, but they had come close enough for her to see the building and the garden in front of it and she could not help drawing in an awed breath.

The palace, for it could be nothing else, was no more than three stories high but seemed to stretch a mile on each side of the huge, open double doors. It glowed a pale gold, lighted by thousands and thousands of small lights. On each end were four towers, topped by onion-shaped domes and in the center was a single structure, rising another five levels, surrounded by four smaller towers, each topped with an onion dome. The front of the building was protected by a dozen pillars connected by wide arches, which supported the overhanging third story of the building.

There were details that Elizabeth could see as they drew closer which were well worthy of examination, but her attention was drawn to the people, strolling in the garden, walking up the broad stairs to enter the building while others came down. In a sense it was not much of a garden. Mostly it was more of the ubiquitous moss with only a few beds of flowers around a handsome but not spectacular fountain.

The fountain was a boundary of some kind for Miralys stopped there and Denno helped Elizabeth down and then dismounted. Off in the distance to right and left Elizabeth could see many other elvensteeds, and Miralys and Ystwyth, from whom Aleneil had dismounted, started off to join their fellow creatures.

"Good," Aleneil said, "the musicians haven't set up yet so we are early. I said I'd meet Ilar at the fountain—"

"Have you been here before?" Denoriel asked, sounding surprised.

"Of course not. You know Oberon creates a different palace and garden for each ball, but—" she giggled "—there is *always* a fountain."

"So there is," a new voice said.

It was a pleasant tenor, lighter than Denno's strong baritone, and the Sidhe who had spoken was somewhat shorter and more slender. His hair was a paler gold, his eyes also a lighter green than Denno's vivid emerald, but his smile was very sweet and a more than usually warm expression made his face attractive.

He held out his hand to Aleneil and said, "Magnificent. Exquisite. I have never seen the like of that gown." He then kissed the hand Aleneil had placed in his.

"This," Aleneil said, "is Ilar from Elfhame Cymry."

As Aleneil introduced him, he turned his head to look at Elizabeth. "What a lovely mortal child. Wherever did you find her?"

"This is the Lady Elizabeth, the late King Henry of England's daughter. By permission of Queen Titania she is welcome to visit Underhill when it pleases her." Denoriel's voice was cold and hard and his hand came down firmly on Elizabeth's shoulder.

"Ah," Ilar said, dropping the hand he had raised as if to take hold of Elizabeth. "She is yours, Prince Denoriel."

"She is her own," Elizabeth said sharply. Although she was startled by hearing the new Sidhe name Denno a prince, she had a more important point to make. "Prince Denoriel is my friend and my protector, for which I am sometimes grateful—" she glanced sidelong at Denno "—and sometimes not. But I belong to no one except myself."

Ilar looked startled but took his cue from Aleneil's slight laugh and Denoriel's resigned sigh, both forms of acceptance of Elizabeth's words, and shrugged slightly. Then dismissing an awkward subject, he gestured widely around the grounds and toward the glowing palace.

"I think King Oberon has outdone himself this time. Shall we go in and see what marvels he has made for us to wonder at?"

All the rest murmured agreement and Denoriel stepped to the side and placed Elizabeth's hand on his arm. However they had hardly taken five steps to go around the fountain toward the palace, when the sound of hooves made them draw together. An elvensteed stopped almost too close to their group and someone leapt down, crying, "Bess."

Elizabeth promptly turned away from Denoriel. "Da!"

"Oh, my love," Harry FitzRoy exclaimed, "you are a woman, a fine lady. Where is my little girl gone?"

"She is still right here," Elizabeth said, rushing into FitzRoy's outstretched arms. "I will never be too grown up for a cuddle from my Da."

Ilar was staring at Harry with disbelief as Lady Aeron nudged him gently. He turned, with an arm still around Elizabeth, to put a kiss on the elvensteed's muzzle and stroke his cheek down hers. Lady Aeron, now seemingly satisfied, loped off in the direction Miralys and Ystwyth had taken.

"Another mortal?" Ilar murmured to Aleneil. "A mortal with an elvensteed? I did not think that was possible."

"Elvensteeds do as they like. Lady Aeron has always been Harry's from when Denoriel was forced to bring him Underhill to save his life when he was a child. Harry is also King Henry's get, but outside of the mortal custom of marriage."

Denoriel had joined Harry and Elizabeth and Harry was laughing and shaking his head about something Denoriel said. The movement disarranged his hair, and Oberon's blue star shone clear on his forehead. Ilar's eyes widened again.

"You of Logres are well entangled with King Henry's children." But before Aleneil could answer, Ilar nodded. "Yes. I remember. One of our FarSeers Saw that three of that king's children would rule."

"All three?" Aleneil asked eagerly.

Ilar shook his head. "I think so, but it matters very little to us in Cymry who rules in Logres so I am afraid I did not pay attention. I will ask, if you would like me to, when I return home." He stiffened and turned his head. "Ah, the musicians are tuning their instruments. There will be dancing soon."

The sounds preliminary to music drew the attention of the other three, and Denoriel stepped over to Ilar and Aleneil to tell them to go ahead as he, Harry, and Elizabeth were waiting for Mwynwen who had been delayed by a last-minute patient. However, they had hardly started toward the palace again when the healer arrived. When she had dismounted and shaken out the many layers of filmy gauze that made up her gown, the first strains of a galliard were floating over the garden. Couples were forming. Harry took Mwynwen's hand and bowed over it.

"Lady, will you dance?" he asked.

"Why not?" Mwynwen replied.

The tone of her voice drew Denoriel's eyes to her face. It was pleasant and indulgent—a friend accepting a pleasant offer from a friend. There was none of the delight, the faint excitement that colored an exchange by lovers. Afraid to look at Harry and see pain or incomprehension in his face, Denoriel turned to Elizabeth and took her hand.

"And you, my lady?" he asked.

Her eyes were bright gold and a very faint color tinged her normally pale cheeks. The delight, the excitement—a lover's welcome to his question—were there. Denoriel raised her hand to his lips.

"Yes," Elizabeth said, "yes I will, thank you."

Chapter 22

A broad set of steps of some gleaming gold-colored marble under each broad arch led to a wide portico on which guests could stroll to the open doors of the palace. On one of the sets of steps, Vidal and Aurilia stood with three of the cleverest and most vicious Dark Sidhe.

Vidal had abandoned his usual dark-haired and dark-eyed visage—even he recognized he would be a travesty in Oberon's presence. He was presently indistinguishable from any of the hundreds of male Sidhe at the ball. His hair was blond, his eyes green, his ears moderately large and pointed.

Aurilia, who also did not want to draw attention to herself, had damped down the spectacular beauty she most often wore. She was beautiful, of course; all Sidhe were beautiful, but there was nothing exceptional about her appearance or that of their three companions.

All of the Dark Sidhe, who had been informed about Elizabeth and her likely companions, were watching as Elizabeth danced down the columns of pairs, now partnered by Ilar while Denoriel danced with Mwynwen and Aleneil with Harry. They circled, whirled round, and then bowed, all gasping slightly with effort. The galliard started slowly and with great dignity, but the musicians steadily increased the tempo of their music and after a time the dance turned nearly into a rout.

The last circling would have brought a new change of partners, but Denoriel nipped Elizabeth out of the line and held her away from the new forming set, laughing and saying that if she were not exhausted she should be. Aleneil and Ilar also stepped to the side and Mwynwen, breathing hard, leaned on the arm Harry had extended to her.

"Them," Vidal said. "All of them, but specially the man with the human girl. I almost did not recognize him. He has made himself look younger and removed the marks of his living in the mortal world. He is the Denoriel of whom I told you and his death is worth a domain of your own with servants to care for it."

"Perhaps the prize would not be worth the doing," Piteka, the tallest of the Dark Sidhe said, his mouth twisting. "He is in some strongly warded company. One wears Oberon's own mark."

"Piteka, I am not asking you to try to kill FitzRoy," Vidal snarled. "No one cares about FitzRoy anymore anyhow. He is dead in the mortal world and cannot help that accursed Elizabeth to the throne. Denoriel is only an ordinary member of the Bright Court with no special protections."

"From what I hear," Goeel, the skeletally thin Sidhe next to Aurilia, said, "he has protection enough without any help. He was the foremost rider in Koronos' Hunt, always sent to face the mortals with iron weapons."

Vidal laughed harshly. "His resistance to iron will not help him Underhill. He has not hunted for years, even with Koronos' tame pack. I doubt he has drawn a sword since then, too. He is, as you can see, duty bound to the mortal girl and spends all his time in the mortal world as a merchant watching over her. Merchants are not known for feats of arms."

Chenga, the one other female Dark Sidhe with them, shuddered. "I will not go into the mortal world. Not even for a domain."

"No one is asking you to go there," Vidal snapped.

"Who is Aleneil with?" Aurilia asked before any of the others could speak.

Vidal frowned as he studied Aleneil's companion. "From his looks I would say he is Cymry. I think the clothing is handmade rather than kenned. The Cymry are letting their magic slip more and more, keeping hordes of mortals to act as servants and artisans and, I suppose, playthings."

"Ohhh?" Aurilia drew out the word. "Weak in magic, are they?

It might be easy enough to visit Elfhame Cymry without saying exactly from where one comes. Do you think Aleneil might go there with her Cymry friend? We need her dead also."

Chenga now made a wordless, interested noise. "I would not mind going to Cymry," she said. "If this Aleneil comes there, an accident might befall her among all those clumsy human folk, and the blame would fall on the Cymry."

"An excellent notion," Vidal said, sounding pleased, "but do not be rid of her too soon. I told you that Aleneil is Denoriel's twin sister. See if you can befriend her."

"I need a reason."

Aurilia grinned, showing her sharpened teeth. "Tell her you have a hunger for her brother. Try to get her to bring Denoriel to Cymry. We could set a magic trap for them both. Likely the Cymry would never notice it."

Chenga looked after Denoriel. The whole party had started up the stairs under a different arch and were plainly going into the palace to seek refreshment or to join a new set of dancers.

"Perhaps," she said, leering slightly, "I will go and introduce myself to him now. It cannot take much to win him away from that scrawny mortal. There is nothing to her except the red hair."

"I do not think you will succeed," Aurilia said with a sidelong glance at Chenga.

Actually she didn't think that Denoriel would be interested in the Dark Sidhe's rather tattered charms, but to speak her doubt would act as a challenge. Chenga refused to accept the fact of her fading attraction. When Denoriel did not respond she would be angered and better motivated to see him dead.

"I know how to draw a Sidhe," Chenga snapped. "That little mortal cannot hold much interest for him. Vidal said before that she was his duty and he is dutiful—" she wrinkled her nose as if over a bad smell "—but I will convince him that by bending time a little he will have his pleasure and not violate his duty."

Aurilia shrugged. "You have good binding spells, but you cannot cast them here. Perhaps if you can get him to dance with you and whisper to him that you have heard of some threat to his charge, he would come to meet you. Elfhame Cymry will seem safe enough to him."

"Yes. Even if you cannot speak to Denoriel, you should go to Cymry," Vidal said suddenly. "See if you can find a place to live among them, but you must be careful and not harm their mortals—"

"Not harm the mortals!" Chenga interrupted furiously. "You know I cannot draw power from the Bright ways any longer. If I cannot draw from the pain and misery of their horde of mortals, where will I find strength to live?"

"You do not need to live there," Vidal said, smiling now. "You need only bind the mortals in your living place to watch and listen. When they learn of Aleneil or Denoriel coming—and most especially if they bring with them the mortal Elizabeth, they must dispatch a messenger to you. I will provide the messengers. Then we can go to Cymry. They are very insular in that elfhame and do not often come to Oberon's attention. He will not know of the watch you keep."

"And will not know that the Dark Court is in any way involved," Aurilia remarked with enthusiasm. "But we must try to get them all together. One accident is . . . an accident. If there were any blame, it would fall upon those of Elfhame Cymry. Two accidents will not be overlooked. So hold your hand until you are sure. If we succeed, I will give you some spells that will make you utterly irresistible to any creature."

Chenga glanced at Aurilia without either gratitude or trust, but she did not reply to her. Instead she held out her hand to the tall Sidhe. "Come, Piteka, let us go inside and see what our quarry is doing."

Rhoslyn had also come to the ball. She had tried to get Pasgen to accompany her, but he would not. He was still worried about the "sentient" Unformed land, although he had decided that it was not the land itself that was drawing him to it but his own insatiable curiosity. He had been able to assuage that somewhat by making several visits to Elfhame Elder-Elf where he had met with Gaenor. She, he found, had a curiosity at least equal to his own but better controlled by the eons she had lived. Still, she was willing, even eager, to accompany him in his testing of the Unformed lands and in capturing any wisps of mist that seemed different.

Although she was not happy about appearing all alone at a ball she knew would be populated mostly by Bright Court Sidhe, she could not resist the lure of the beauty she knew she would see, of the music she would hear, of the laughter and light spirits. She could be quiet, she thought, and watch from the sidelines. Perhaps she would see Mwynwen or Aleneil, who would be willing to exchange a few words with her.

She did not at first see anyone she knew, and shrank against an elaborately carved pillar in view of the doorway. Beyond her, the pillars, all glowing with lights set into the leaves that made up the top of the shafts, marched in a triple column all the way around the huge room. They supported an intricate vaulted ceiling from which hung more lights. And each of the pillars, Rhoslyn realized, looking as far as she could see and knowing they continued farther, was individually carved with birds and beasts and plants and Sidhe, and everything beautiful and monstrous, that lived Underhill.

The carvings were so fascinating that Rhoslyn forgot she was supposed to be keeping herself unnoticed. She stepped out from her shelter and was about to move to the next pillar, when a particularly willowy Sidhe glided up to her and touched her hand.

"Dark. How lovely. One does get so tired of golden hair and green eyes. The musicians are tuning their instruments. Will you dance with me?"

Dance. When was the last time Rhoslyn had seen anyone dance, except the leaping and writhing of agony? Could she dance? She had some memory of Llanelli teaching them some steps... And he had called her "dark" without knowing that she was truly Dark Court. He thought it was an affectation, which, of course, it was; there was no rule that Dark Court Sidhe should be dark of hair and eye. Most remained blond.

Tremulously, Rhoslyn smiled. She wanted so much to dance and to take pleasure in music and laughter, but she was afraid that if this Sidhe touched her he would know what she was, and she was afraid that her awkwardness, her lack of knowledge of the dance would betray her.

"I—I was supposed to be waiting until my friends came," she said hesitantly. "And I am not from Avalon or Logres so I do not know the dances of these hames."

The Sidhe smiled at her. "Listen to the music," he said. "They are playing for the mortal galliard."

"Oh, I know that!" Rhoslyn exclaimed, and put out her hand before she thought.

She certainly did know the galliard, and most of the other human dances too. Mary loved to dance, and though there were not often many men in her household, the ladies danced together with considerable enjoyment. They even did the wilder reels and voltes, since they were private; no one from the Court would see them to criticize and speak of impropriety.

Beyond the pillars there was a huge central open space in which several columns of dancing pairs had formed. At the end of the open area, opposite the doors, was a dais upon which a half dozen musicians sat. How the sweet sounds they made filled the whole room, Rhoslyn had no idea and did not care. She danced down the column with her attendant Sidhe, laughing with delight and hardly suffered a qualm when he handed her off to the male of the next couple to dance up the column again.

Dancing and keeping up her shields was draining Rhoslyn, but her heart leapt within her and though her legs felt like jelly she reached for a third partner's hand. They made it as far as the top of the column, when the Sidhe she was dancing with faltered.

"I am sorry," he said, drawing her out of the column toward the pillars.

"No, I thank you," Rhoslyn sighed. She was shaking all over and her partner propped her against one of the pillars nearest the dancing floor. "I should never have continued when you first became my partner, but as I told the gentle Sidhe who asked me to dance, I have not done so in a great while and I . . . I could not resist."

"I, too." The Sidhe laughed lightly. "I am not so young as I once was, but when the music catches me, I forget. Shall I bring you something to eat and drink?"

"No, I thank you. I have not been to one of King Oberon's balls in a long time and I cannot resist looking over the table he is offering."

"Ah, Aidan, there you are!" A lady of ripe and visible charms in a glittering and swirling net of silk and gems came through the pillars toward them. "I should have known," she said, laughing, "that you would be among the dancers and looked there instead of where you said we should meet."

"Oh, Shaliar, I am so sorry, but I could not resist." He glanced apologetically at Rhoslyn.

Before he could offer either an invitation to join them, which would have, Rhoslyn was sure, annoyed his lady friend, or make an apology for leaving, she waved a hand at him. "No, go, please. And thank you for the dance. I, too, was supposed to meet friends and was seduced away from our meeting place by the music. I will go back where I should be as soon as my knees stop quaking."

He bowed and left with considerable promptness, for which Rhoslyn was grateful because she felt more hollow and weak by the moment. She needed power or she would fall! Then everyone would notice her and see she was Unseleighe because she could not draw power from the Bright ways. Panic seized her for a moment as she realized she would have to drop her shields to draw that power. But if no one was near, perhaps the miasma that betrayed the Unseleighe to the Seleighe would be lost in the immense magic of Oberon's creation.

She slipped around the pillar until she would be hidden from the dancing floor, dismissed her shields and, as her vision dimmed, desperately opened herself to the energy that filled the Bright ways. Her teeth were set hard to restrain any cry of pain, her body tensed to resist the agony and burning she had always been told would come if she tried to draw the power of the Seleighe Sidhe.

There was no pain, no heat of burning. Only a gentle warmth filled her. Her vision cleared, her trembling stopped, but she clutched at the deep carvings on the pillar with a grip that, had her nails not been rendered useless by Oberon's magic, would have scored the stone. Lies. All lies. Everything she had been told all her life was lies. She *could* live in the Bright Court and draw on the energy of love and laughter.

Rhoslyn leaned on the pillar, weak and trembling again because she was torn among a mingling of rage, joy, and relief. Her hand went up to touch the lindys buried in the shining folds of her gown. She must tell Pasgen. She must explain to him that she could use the power of the Bright ways, that the tale it would destroy the Unseleighe was a lie.

Then she remembered that one of the Dark Sidhe Vidal had sent to spy on some doing of the Bright Court had stayed too long, had been detected, and had drawn Bright power in his need to escape. He *had* been burned, had been screaming in agony until the Healers carried him away. Rhoslyn thought back but she could not remember seeing him again.

Was it only she who could live Bright or Dark? Why? Oh.

Perhaps because she had been born Seleighe. Her eyes narrowed and she stared across the rows of pillars not seeing the elaborate carving. She had had to be trained to use the Dark power she remembered. Yes. She had heard tales of what an unpleasant child she had been, crying and crying, always hungry for power that she would not take.

But Pasgen had more easily accepted the Dark power of pain and misery. Perhaps he would not now be able to draw from the Bright ways. Could she— The thought was broken by the sound of voices, one she recognized readily. Elizabeth. Aleneil and Denoriel had brought Elizabeth to Oberon's ball. For a moment Rhoslyn could not decide whether to step out and greet the party or flee . . . and then it was too late.

"Rhoslyn!" Elizabeth cried. "Are you enjoying the ball? We were on our way to the refreshment tables, but then I saw the pillars. Are they not wonderful? There must be hundreds, and I swear that each one is different."

"I have not seen two the same," Rhoslyn agreed, smiling at Elizabeth but taking a quick glance at the large party with her.

Aleneil was smiling a welcome. Denoriel—Rhoslyn almost had not recognized him, looking so young; she was puzzled at the illusion for a moment because Denoriel had never seemed to her to be vain. Then she saw the way Elizabeth clung to his arm. Had Mary feared the wrong influence on her sister? But before she could follow that thought, Harry FitzRoy had come forward and taken her hand.

"I remember you, lovely lady," he said. "You came once to Mwynwen's house to ask about my brother Richey—I guess he was my brother."

"He was as close as I could make him," Rhoslyn said, looking into the brownish eyes, so different from the clear, bright—and too often empty—eyes of the Sidhe. "But he could not really grow up. And I think you have done so."

"I'm afraid I have," Harry said rather wryly, with a glance at Mwynwen. "Do you mind?"

But Mwynwen did not return the glance. She was looking out into the dancing space, scanning the many Sidhe there.

Rhoslyn laughed. "Not at all. I am glad and grateful that poor Richey had so much joy in his life. That eased a deep pain, a knowledge of wrong done to him by making him alive and knowing. I had never hoped that he would be loved. I am equally glad and grateful that my purpose was never fulfilled and that you were not captured for the Dark Court. You have grown up into a complete man and a good one, I think."

Harry bowed his head briefly. "For the good opinion, I thank you. But I see you have no companion. Will you not come with us to taste what delights Oberon has provided to eat?"

Rhoslyn looked around at the others in the group. The delicate Sidhe beside Aleneil had a courteous if indifferent smile; Aleneil nodded at her; Mwynwen gave her an absent but not unwelcoming glance; and Denoriel was looking down at Elizabeth who was also smiling and nodding. Harry still held her hand.

"I do not wish to intrude," Rhoslyn said still doubtful although she was very eager to join them.

"It is no intrusion," Harry said firmly, and drew her hand into the crook of his arm.

He offered his other arm to Mwynwen, but she patted it kindly and shook her head. "If you have company, Harry, I see an old friend that I would like to greet. I or we will join you later."

Elizabeth was surprised. She watched Mwynwen walk away toward the dancers, recalling that only a few years past Mwynwen was so jealous of her Da's affection that she had hidden him from her. She also remembered all the tales of Sidhe lovers and how they broke the hearts of any mortal unwise enough to yield to them.

Her Denno? She raised her eyes to his. He was not looking at her and his long lashes half hid his eyes. Uncertain now, she could not read them, but the hand he laid over hers on his arm was possessive, comforting. Only Mwynwen had also been possessive of her Da, and now . . .

She saw that Denno was watching her Da, and she saw the faint frown, the downturn of the lips that meant concern. Denno's love for Harry had not changed or lessened in twenty years. Surely that was constancy enough. She tightened her grip on his arm, and he smiled down at her as they walked around the rows of pillars to another open area.

This area was smaller than the dancing floor and was taken up with tables arranged in the shape of a great C, all draped in spotless white cloths. That was as it should be and no more or less than what was proper for any great man's entertainment.

However, instead of silver all the dishes were gold. Elizabeth knew it probably did not matter to Oberon whether he made silver dishes or gold, but she could not help wrinkling her nose at the ostentation.

"And what do you disapprove of now, my dear lady?" Denno asked, chuckling.

"Do you not think that gold dishes are a bit more than is necessary to state Oberon's power?" she asked.

Denno laughed aloud. "But, my sweet, Oberon is not trying to impress his courtiers as a mortal king might. True, none of us—not even a whole group acting together—could create this palace and its gardens, but any one of us could create a gold service of dishes. They are gold, love, because iron is deadly poison to the Sidhe, but silver is as deadly a poison to many of the other creatures Underhill. Gold is harmless to all."

"Oh." Elizabeth blushed. "I suppose I should know more before I judge anything." But she noticed that Denno was looking at Harry again, and she whispered. "Do you think Mwynwen has hurt my Da?"

He glanced down at her, a false smile beginning to bend his lips, but they lost their curve as he took in her expression. Without speaking, he steered her to a table and put out his hand. An empty platter, clear glass, appeared in it. Denno began to fork various tidbits, none of which Elizabeth could name, onto the dish. When it was modestly filled, he handed it to her and another platter appeared in his hand.

"We will talk about it later," he said, frowning now. "You may understand better than I. Enjoy the food now, love."

"I am sort of afraid of it," Elizabeth confessed. "I do not recognize anything."

A soft laugh to her left drew her head to Ilar, who was standing beside her with Aleneil—who had a well-filled plate in her hand and was just gathering in a three-tined fork. Elizabeth watched with interest as she used it to stab what looked like a tiny yellow bird. It did seem that the three prongs held the food more firmly than two.

"You won't find anything unpleasant," Ilar assured her as he filled his own plate. "The fanciful shapes are only that. What Aleneil has taken is only a cooked egg molded into the shape of a bird."

"And this?" Elizabeth asked, pointing the fork that Denoriel had just put into her hand at something white wrapped in a brownish shell.

"I would say some kind of shell fish in a rind of bacon." Ilar replied. "It is very tasty if that is what it is and if it is, it is something that His Majesty has stolen from our mortal cooks."

"You actually have your food cooked?" Elizabeth asked, the morsel she had speared suspended just in front of her mouth. "Denno's just appears by magic."

Ilar laughed again. "And it is always the same dull dishes each time, is it not?"

"Well, not dull to me," Elizabeth replied defensively. Whatever she thought of having food appear by magic, she was not going to agree with some outsider who was criticizing her Denno. "It is all very well cooked and tasty."

But Ilar only laughed once more and said, "Well cooked, tasty, and the same thing all the time. Well enough for you, who visit Underhill only now and again and so find the dishes to be various, but think of poor me, who would need to eat them each day."

Aleneil put her fork into her plate and playfully punched Ilar in the shoulder. "Oh, you sybarite. All you can think of is a variety of pleasures."

"And what is wrong with that?" he asked, smiling. "If it makes everyone happy. So, yes, Lady Elizabeth, in Elfhame Cymry we do have our food cooked by our mortals. This way we get a great variety of dishes. All the mortals compete with each other to produce new wonders for us."

But Elizabeth did not smile back. "That must be a great deal of work for the poor mortals. And what happens to them if they cannot produce a new wonder for each meal?"

"Ah." Ilar set down his plate and patted Elizabeth's arm gently. "No, no. You must not think us cruel or our mortals overburdened. They enjoy the challenges new creations pose; it keeps them from being bored. Mortals are so easily bored. They are mostly happy, and when they are not, mostly their sorrows are of their own making." He sighed and picked up the plate again. "I can see that you do not really believe me. Well, I have an answer to that. Let Lady Aleneil bring you to Elfhame Cymry, and we will allow you to wander where you will and speak to any you wish."

That reassured Elizabeth so that she smiled and looked up at

Denoriel, who smiled back at her. "On another visit," he said. And then to Ilar, "I am curious to see Elfhame Cymry myself, but this is my lady's first ball and I think she should enjoy it to the full."

Ilar laughed. "I did not mean now." He reached out and ran a hand caressingly down Aleneil's ribbon-clad arm. "I think my lady intends to dance until the music ends."

"Perhaps not quite that long," Aleneil said, also laughing and pulling gently on Ilar's long earlobe.

It was such a sensuous gesture that Elizabeth immediately glanced at Denno's ears and then, wondering if he had noticed, she felt warmth and probably color rise up her throat. Unwilling to meet his eyes, she looked away, only to see her Da and Rhoslyn laughing together.

A little pang of jealousy went through her, because her Da was so interested in a person other than herself, but a broad shoulder nudged her and Denno, grinning in a private kind of way that hinted he had noticed the way she looked at his ears and blushed, told her there were seats and tables where they could eat.

She smiled up at him. There was an intentness in his eyes that was exciting and comforting all at once. He had not made a jest of her blush and spared her further blushes. She knew she was first with Denno; he had promised she would be first with him all the days of her life—and despite her suspicions and her doubts, Denno had never lied to her. The whole party moved toward the tables.

From the shadows among the rows of pillars, eyes watched. Chenga's nails dug into Piteka's arm. "So, your listening spell did work and I am now sure that the girl will come to Cymry." She flashed a sidelong glance at him. "Very well, I owe you. Still, it is I who must ingratiate myself with the Cymry Sidhe, so remember, the greater part of the reward for being rid of her will be mine."

"We will bargain again when you are successful," Piteka hissed softly. Then he laughed. "If you are there to bargain. She has her own defenses, that harmless-looking mortal. Do not forget the mage she sent into the void, crushed like an eggshell."

Chenga did remember. She swallowed and her gaze shifted to Denoriel and then to Aleneil. "They will all be going to Cymry and they are likely to be all together. I wonder if some domestic disaster—the mortals actually cook and serve; could there be an explosion? a fire?—could take them all at once? If the Sidhe died with the mortal, would that not be less suspicious?"

Piteka's eyes brightened. "If you could arrange that, I think the reward offered will be more than enough to share between us."

"Then you should be ready to accept what I am willing to yield. It is I who will need to coddle the mortals and see how I can arrange the accident. It will not be a moment's work, and remember, too, that I will be tormented by not sucking dry those pampered pets."

"Perhaps you could make away with one or two here and there," Piteka suggested, not meeting her eyes.

"And be discovered and cast out. No, I thank you."

"The last thing I want is for you to be discovered." The lie sounded convincing, until he said, "If you are unmasked, no other Dark Sidhe will be able to settle among them and try again."

"Which is just what you would like," Chenga snarled. "No doubt you have another plan. Forget it. I warn you that if you foul my arrangement or betray me in some way, I will make it very clear to Prince Vidal that you assisted the escape of those he wishes to be victims. It was the prince who urged me to go to Cymry."

Piteka smiled, his pointed teeth shining in the shadows. In fact he did have another plan, but it had nothing to do with Elizabeth. Oberon had forbidden meddling with Elizabeth and Piteka was not going to get caught in that trap. Vidal would lay the blame on whoever harmed her and come away clear while Oberon—internally Piteka shuddered thinking of what Oberon was capable. No, his plan had nothing to do with that forbidden fruit.

Vidal wanted to lay hands on Llanelli, Rhoslyn's and Pasgen's Bright Court mother, and had sent watchers to discover her. Doubtless Vidal wished to use the mother to control the children. Piteka did not care about that, only that Vidal wanted her and would reward the finder. The watchers had found nothing, but by accident Piteka had discovered that Llanelli was working as a healer and living in the place Rhoslyn and Pasgen called the empty house.

Piteka's only doubt was whether to take Llanelli prisoner at once and claim his reward immediately or wait until Chenga acted. Then, in the unlikely event that she was successful, he could claim part of her reward before he brought Llanelli to Vidal. He put the indecision aside and replied calmly to her threat.

"And so you will, so you will. I will not interfere. It will be no fault of mine if you cannot make a simple plan work."

Chenga dug her nails into his arm. She could not attack him or leave him if she wanted to listen further to what those in Elizabeth's party said because he had cast the listening spell. But he only laughed again at her fury, and they both followed, still hidden in the shadows.

The pillars did not encircle the area where the tables were set; that was open to the dancing floor with the serving tables between the pillars and the tables arranged for eating. After a brief consultation, Chenga and Piteka came out into the open. They did not approach Elizabeth's party but settled well away from them.

The spell held, but the effort was wasted because the group was saying nothing that could forward their cause. Mostly Aleneil and Ilar were playfully arguing the pros and cons of mortals Underhill and the varied uses of magic with amused comments from both Denoriel and Elizabeth.

One subject of interest to Piteka did come up; the mortal with the blue star on his forehead was telling Rhoslyn about the elfhames he and his friends were trying to rid of evil. That was something Prince Vidal would be interested to hear. If the multitude of curses and small poisonous plagues were gone with only the Great Evil clinging there, El Dorado and Alhambra could be used by the Dark Sidhe again, Piteka was sure.

In his interest in the subject, Piteka forgot to watch the dancing while he listened and turned his head to look at the mortal with the blue star. Rhoslyn had been hanging almost breathlessly on his words, but she felt Piteka's attention, turned to see who was watching them . . . and recognized him.

Her expression changed to such enmity that Piteka was startled. He had always thought of Rhoslyn as a shadow of Pasgen, unlikely to do much on her own, but here she was, having wormed her way right into the company of those Vidal wanted eliminated. Piteka could think of no reason for her looking daggers at him but that she had some plan of her own that she feared he would spoil or preempt.

He did not fear Rhoslyn—well, not much—but to be on the safe side, he seized Chenga's hand and drew her to her feet. "Let us dance," he said.

"Harry," Rhoslyn said, leaning forward to whisper into his ear. "There were a pair of Vidal's favorite Dark Sidhe on the far side of the tables. When Piteka noticed I had seen him, he took Chenga onto the dancing floor."

Harry promptly pushed away his nearly empty plate and got up. Aloud, he said, "I thought I saw Mwynwen go by alone, Denno. If I can catch up, I'll ask her to join us. Will you come with me, Rhoslyn, and second the invitation?"

"Of course," Rhoslyn said, and as they passed out of hearing, added, "I think Vidal's servants joined the end of the second set of dancers. I will point them out to you and you can tell Prince Denoriel."

Aleneil and Ilar looked after Harry and Rhoslyn. "If that is a reel the musicians are starting to play, they will never catch Mwynwen," she said.

"Innocent," Ilar remarked with a smile, putting his arm around Aleneil and pulling her to her feet. "I think your Harry just wants a little time alone with his Rhoslyn."

"In a reel?" Aleneil asked, laughing as she yielded to his pull.

"Shall I show you how?" Ilar suggested, drawing her toward the dancing.

The mostly empty plates promptly disappeared, except for those of Elizabeth and Denoriel, who put his hand over them. Elizabeth looked toward the dancing couples, but Denoriel said, "Later," in an odd, throaty purr.

His eyes were intent, his gaze slipping from her lips to the curve of the very top of her right breast, which had been bared when she pushed aside the sleeve/cloak to eat. Although his hands were still, Elizabeth could almost feel his fingers caressing the curve of her breast, her throat, running up her cheek. She felt a tide of heat rise up her neck and burn in her cheeks, and she looked down.

"Eat something, love," he murmured.

Elizabeth opened her mouth . . . she was not sure for what purpose: to protest, to beg to dance, to say anything at all just to break the tension she felt—and Denno put a tidbit between her lips. Instinctively, not wanting to spit it out, Elizabeth began to chew and saw Denno watch her lips as she chewed and swallowed. Elizabeth stared at him as he offered another bite.

He might as well have been kissing her. Elizabeth began to tremble inside, but whether from fear or some other emotion she did not know. Denno held another bit toward her, but did not actually put it between her lips. She leaned forward to take it. The food was warm, moist, and delicious. She chewed that too, slowly, leaning even further forward, until their lips met.

The sensation of kissing and chewing was very strange. There was a pulse low in Elizabeth's belly that beat in the same rhythm as her jaws. Her thighs and the private parts between them felt like the food, warm and moist. Then she swallowed.

With part of the table between them, their lips just barely met, and slipped apart, and met again. The sleeve/cloak no longer covered her shoulder and Denno's hands slid over her bare skin. His hands were warm and hard-callused but as gentle as the kiss they still shared. Under his touch, Elizabeth's skin tingled; smooth as was the silk of her undergarments, she could feel her nipples rubbing as they rose and thrust out. The sensation was unbearably exciting.

"Let us go home," Elizabeth breathed.

Chapter 23

On the morning after Lord Denno's visit, Elizabeth's maidens were confronted by a new problem. The door to her private parlor would not open. They pushed and pulled, but the door was immovable, and one of them finally ran off to tell Mistress Ashley that Elizabeth's door was locked. First Kat said it was impossible; Elizabeth never locked her outer door and rarely the inner one. However, she brought the key.

This was of no use. It would not turn to unlock the door, but turned readily to lock it. Kat could hear the tumblers of the lock fall into place. She unlocked the door again, and told Eleanor Fitzalan to hold the knob so that the latch would stay open. Then she pushed at the door. When it did not stir, she told Eleanor to continue holding the latch but to stand aside, and she put her shoulder to it. But it did not move a whit. Finally, growing frightened, she called aloud for Elizabeth.

Elizabeth had stirred sleepily in her bed when the girls had first tried the door, but all she did was bury her face in Denno's bare shoulder. That had been a ball to end all balls, she thought, even though she had done far less dancing than she expected. Nonetheless after some highly informative hours spent in Denno's bed, she had complained about being deprived of dancing to Denno, leaning over him provocatively so that he lifted his head and kissed her pink nipples.

There would be other balls, he promised, pulling her down atop him, when they would dance every dance. His hands were busy on her body, and she only murmured that she liked this dance better as she straddled him and came down on him, and then became incapable of speaking at all.

After they had caught their breath, though, Denno had urged her to put on her nightdress. They had to return to the mortal world soon, he had said . . . and stopped to draw her to him and kiss her again. But then he pulled away, sighing that if he twisted time too much it would leave her exhausted and confused and make everyone worried about her.

She had laughed and said she was already exhausted; however, weary and sated, she did not object to being taken back to Chelsea. Only when they arrived at the narrow Gate between the wardrobes in her dressing room, she clung to him. It was still dark, she whispered, and her bed would be so cold; he should come with her. He did not need much urging.

They tiptoed through the dressing room to the bedchamber and Denoriel shed his clothes and carried her with him to the bed. They cuddled together at first between the chilly sheets and then as they warmed, stretched out, still touching for comfort, for companionship . . . and fell asleep. It did not matter, Elizabeth told herself as she drifted off. Alana had not yet returned and until she did, the door would not open.

Elizabeth's nuzzling on his shoulder when she heard her maidens at the door woke Denoriel. He gasped with shock when he realized he had fallen asleep in Elizabeth's bed and there was now light behind the curtains. He looked at her, and she lifted her head and smiled.

"That was a—most remarkable ball," she whispered.

"There will be many others," he promised, equally low-voiced, as he began to slide out of the bed.

Elizabeth sat up abruptly. "But only with me!" she exclaimed, still softly but with an intensity like a shout.

Denoriel laughed silently. "You need not fear for that. You are . . . something very special. Fresh and new and with an appetite that is not worn out and jaded. Bess, my love, I have not been so drained out in . . . in . . . I cannot remember when if ever. I need no one but you."

There had been a cessation of sound from outside the outer

door while this soft exchange had taken place, but Denno was listening. He spelled his clothing on him, and cocked his head as he heard voices anew.

"I had better go."

"No!" Elizabeth exclaimed and shook her head impatiently when she could see he was going to scold her for being incautious. "Alana—" she could not say the word *bespelled* and had to settle for "—did something to the door. They will never be able to open it."

"And she is not here," Denoriel said. He grinned briefly then shrugged. "I am glad she is having a good time, but she should have remembered that she had fixed the door." Suddenly, he disappeared. "Let me see if I can sense her spell and undo it."

Elizabeth was still wearing her nightdress and she padded into the parlor after him. Now she could hear the maidens' voices as they greeted Kat. Then she heard the tumblers of the lock close and open. She bit her lip. If Denno could not undo the spell (she could think "spell" although not say it), they would have to break the door. Could they even do that if it was bespelled? Then she heard Kat crying her name.

"I'm here. I'm fine," she called in reply. "I overslept. I don't know why the door is stuck. Send someone for Dunstan and a couple of the guardsmen."

Denoriel appeared suddenly and whispered in her ear, "I can't do it, but I'm going Underhill and I'll send an air spirit to find—ah, I just felt the Gate. There she is."

On the words Aleneil, fully dressed in Tudor garments, came rushing into the parlor, looking quite distraught.

"I'm sorry," she whispered.

"Never mind." Elizabeth giggled. "I understand completely." And then she blushed hotly as she realized what she had said. Aleneil did not seem to notice; she was looking at the door. She lifted a hand, and Elizabeth caught it. "No, not yet. Let the men come and push it. Then release it."

That worked so well that Dunstan came staggering into the room when he pushed on the door, which had flown open. He averted his face hastily from Elizabeth in her bedgown and went out almost as fast as he had come in. Alana equally hastily drew Elizabeth with her back into the bedchamber. Kat followed them and Blanche came rushing in through the dressing room door.

"What did you do to the door?" Kat asked, looking quite cross.

"Nothing," Elizabeth said, wide-eyed with sincerity. It was true enough. "I never touched it."

"And I only closed it, Mistress Ashley. I didn't slam it or anything," Aleneil said. That was true too.

Kat frowned. "It is dangerous for Lady Elizabeth to be locked in her chamber with only one lady."

"But Lady Elizabeth wasn't locked in, madam," Blanche put in. "Through the dressing room is my bedchamber and that has a door to the corridor."

"That is even worse," Kat said sharply. "Heaven knows what accusations could be made against you, Lady Elizabeth. I do not want that door locked again."

"But it wasn't locked," Elizabeth said, as her head came through the shift Blanche had put on her. "You know it wasn't. You couldn't unlock it with the key, but it did lock and then unlock, and all the maids of honor saw you—"

"How do you know that?" Kat asked.

Elizabeth blinked, remembering that she had stood and listened while Denno worked on the spell just reveling in being near him, but she could not say that. A small wave of coldness passed over her as she reminded herself that she could never admit how sweet every moment with Denno was. As soon as she showed him more favor than she ever had or a single glance exposed her hunger for him, he would be torn away from her. He was male and she was no longer a child.

"Oh," she said, looking at her clasped fingers, "I heard the key turn and turn again just as I came into the room."

"By God's sweet Grace, you stood there and listened to us struggling to open the door and never said a word?"

Desperately Elizabeth thrust all thought of Denno out of her mind. "Well, of course I didn't," she said indignantly. "I didn't know who was there or for what purpose. I wondered when I heard the door lock, but when it unlocked I was all ready to run back into my bedchamber and scream for Blanche until you called out, Kat. I did answer you right away."

Kat sighed deeply and shook her head. "So you did, love. So you did. I am sorry to be scolding. It was all no fault of yours, but if those girls caught a whiff of a locked door, doubtless the whole palace would know before time for a noon meal. They do not mean any harm; I think they love you well, but they do not think either."

Elizabeth said she understood and that she would tell Queen Catherine what had happened and ask her to give an order to have the door examined. Kat approved heartily and Lady Alana said she would certainly tell the queen that it was she who had closed the door, not Elizabeth. By the time the conversation ended Elizabeth was fully dressed and ready to join the ladies in the parlor.

There Dunstan was kneeling on the floor, examining the edge of the door and the door frame quarter-inch by quarter-inch. He came and bowed to Elizabeth and then slightly to Kat.

"I've no idea, my lady," he said. "I've been over the door and the door frame, top and bottom and both sides. There's no stickiness, no roughness as if something was stuck and torn loose. The wood is smooth and sound, the lock is in perfect order."

"Magic," Elizabeth said, and laughed. "I would even believe it if there were any purpose to it." Then she sighed. "I believe you, Dunstan, but I will have to tell Queen Catherine, and I'm certain she will also have someone look at the door. Please do not think I do not trust you, but if the tale came to her as gossip, she would doubtless wonder."

"Know that, my lady. I just had a look to be sure that when you went out you wouldn't find yourself locked out. I've opened and closed the door about twenty times, too, and had Gerrit slam it really hard. It still didn't stick."

"Thank you." Elizabeth smiled at Gerrit, who was waiting near the door, and told him he might go.

She asked Dunstan to wait while she wrote a note to Queen Catherine and asked to speak to her as soon as was convenient. When he left with the note all the girls burst into speech at once. They all marveled at how and why the door had stuck; they all commiserated with Elizabeth on the fright she must have had; virtually the whole discussion was repeated while servants brought breakfast and the meal was consumed.

Through it all, Elizabeth did not once lose her temper, although sometimes her answers were slightly at random. Kat watched her with a slightly troubled frown and noted that seemingly for no reason at all her color rose and then, when her attention was demanded, subsided. The meal ended at last and Elizabeth sent Alice Finch for her Plato, since her tutor would arrive later in the morning. However, before she could open the book, one of the queen's servants came with a message that Elizabeth would be welcome to Catherine at any time. Elizabeth almost jumped to her feet.

"I am sure," Kat said soothingly, "that the queen will not assume any ill cause for the sticking door."

"No," Elizabeth agreed, her color rising again as she remembered Denno lying naked beside her in her bed, "but I confess that I am glad Sir Thomas is away. He would likely make a merry jest of a locked door and what might be taking place behind it."

Kat did not like the blush when Elizabeth mentioned Queen Catherine's husband. "I think I will go with you and explain that the door was stuck, not locked."

"And I," Lady Alana put in, "to say that Lady Elizabeth never touched the door at all. I was the one who closed it."

Elizabeth sighed. "In truth, likely we will never know why the door would not open, and I do not care. Perhaps Queen Catherine's carpenters will discover the cause. If not and if it should happen again, I will have the door removed and replaced."

Queen Catherine, however, made nothing of the tale. She agreed to dispatch her carpenter to look over the door, but only laughed when Kat apologized for putting unhealthy ideas into a young girl's mind.

"Do you have unhealthy ideas, dear Elizabeth?" the queen asked.

Elizabeth clapped a hand to her lips as a giggle rose in her throat and then escaped. She had intended to look wide-eyed and innocently puzzled, but the giggle would not permit that escape.

"Oh, I do," Elizabeth admitted, "but nothing that would require a locked door. Do you remember, madam, the furs that Lord Denno brought for us in the late winter? I have been wondering whether I could extract a few more fox furs from my poor Denno. Really the fox fur is too long to make good trimming. Just a few more and I could have a lovely short cape for the autumn."

"Poor Lord Denno indeed," Catherine said. "And I suppose I am supposed to invite him to dinner so that you can plunder his warehouse again? For shame! He is far too generous to you. Likely

I should not permit . . . Ah, but I have sinned that way myself, have I not? I also accepted the furs he presented to me."

"Yes," Elizabeth said, blushing again, "I would like you to invite him."

"You are a shocking child," Catherine said, leaning forward and stretching a hand to Elizabeth. "You should not accept so many favors."

"He asks for nothing in return," Elizabeth said quickly, and then swallowed hard as she remembered what she had paid in return for Denno's long loving.

"I know." Catherine sighed. "That seems unnatural in a common merchant, even if he does claim foreign nobility. It worries me, a little."

"But he has always been that way," Kat Ashley put in. Her shaky finances had been shored up too often by Lord Denno for her to contemplate his company being forbidden. "From the time Lady Elizabeth was only a baby, and I know that he was just as devoted to the late duke of Richmond. In all those years he has never asked a favor or any kind of preferential treatment in tariffs or such matters."

"He is too rich to care," Lady Alana said, smiling. "I think he continues to trade as an amusement; he has a most astute man of business to do the dog work. And he continues to cosset Lady Elizabeth, because he has nothing else to love in his life."

"Why did he never buy land? Marry? Could he not have made a new life?" Queen Catherine asked doubtfully.

Lady Alana sighed. "He lost too much. His entire family. Everything except the business. He survived because he was on a trading voyage when the Turks overran Hungary. Years ago the pain was too fresh. He could not marry and have children for fear of more loss. Now, he is too old, I think. I suppose he could have bought land, but he has no one to whom to leave it. He had rather have Lady Elizabeth to care for and spend his goods on."

"How sad," the queen said with ready sympathy. "Well, of course I will invite him to a private dinner." She could not invite a merchant to mingle with her noble friends; then she thought of another problem, hesitated, and asked doubtfully, "About what will he talk? Trade?"

Elizabeth and Alana laughed together, and Kat smiled. "Most likely," Kat said, "about gardens. He is very fond of flowers and this is a good season for them. But he is a most courteous gentleman. He knows I do not care much for a garden except to walk in it, so if he sees the subject is dull for you, he will find others. To me, he talks about music and masques and even the newest plays."

"Then I will certainly invite him. I will sit down and write a note right now."

"But not religion," Elizabeth remarked, wishing to warn Catherine away from her favorite subject. "He will listen but never approve, disapprove, or argue any point."

Catherine laughed ruefully. "He will get along very well with my dearling Tom then. He always has the best of reasons to disappear as soon as one of the chaplains or scholars begins to speak."

The dinner to which Catherine invited Lord Denno was a resounding success. They sat only six to the table in the small dining parlor: Catherine herself, Elizabeth, and Kat Ashley; Lord Denno, William Grindal—Elizabeth's tutor—and John Whitney, a gentleman-in-waiting. They were very merry, with Lord Denno telling tales of his travels and holding his own on every subject, including disputation about a Latin term and a lively discussion of swordplay from horseback.

When on another occasion Sir Anthony Denny arrived unexpectedly on some Court business and had to be invited to dine, Catherine was forced to mention with some embarrassment that she had also invited the merchant Lord Denno. But Sir Anthony was delighted. Lord Denno was an old friend, he told her. He had been so busy that he had not seen him recently, but it would be his pleasure to meet Lord Denno again.

Thus when, two weeks later, Sir Thomas had returned home and Catherine sensed he was growing restless in the quiet of Chelsea, she thought Lord Denno would be a safe diversion. Catherine was not yet ready to have any of Tom's political cronies taking up his attention and possibly drawing him away from her, but Denno might provide variety. Denno could talk horses and dogs and even engage in some practice swordplay with Tom, and Catherine thought Lord Denno's courtesies to Elizabeth would amuse Tom—she so young; Denno so old. Surely no man as handsome and virile as Tom could find Lord Denno a threat.

Unfortunately Catherine had forgotten the men had met before.

She only recalled, when Tom stiffened up upon Lord Denno's arrival, that Tom had resented Denno's presence in her chamber when Denno had come to tell her of Elizabeth's need for a home. Tom was contemptuous of a mere merchant. After the first rude slight, Lord Denno fell silent, although he looked more amused than insulted. Elizabeth, however, burst into tears and left the table. Catherine signaled her servants to curtail the meal and the discomfort soon ended.

Afterward Tom delivered a tirade about the unwisdom of his wife engaging in such an unnatural friendship. Catherine was about to point out that Sir Anthony Denny had found Lord Denno acceptable company and that Denno was Elizabeth's friend and had been Elizabeth's friend all of Elizabeth's life. However, before she could defend herself, Tom roared that he did not want any rich, old men running tame around his wife. Catherine blushed with delight and forgot everything except that Tom was jealous of her. Without another thought for Elizabeth she readily promised never to invite Lord Denno to her house again.

The next day when Tom had gone out, Catherine felt guilty about depriving Elizabeth of her friend but could not bear to cross her beloved and delightfully jealous husband. She decided to break the news that Lord Denno must be forbidden the house at once to give Elizabeth time to recover from her disappointment. She did not want Elizabeth to show an angry or tear-stained face to Tom, or indeed to give him the sharp edge of her tongue. That might give Tom a distaste for Elizabeth, which could make difficulties.

To Catherine's surprise, Elizabeth only sighed and said with perfect calm that it did not matter. Later in the day, after a dinner about which Catherine had strong anxieties but which turned out to be especially pleasant because Elizabeth was particularly lively and amusing, enlightenment dawned.

Catherine knew how tenacious Elizabeth could be and she realized the girl's calm acceptance of forbidding Denno's visits could only mean that Elizabeth had no intention of giving up his company. Elizabeth rode out with only her own guards and grooms to accompany her three or four times a week. Doubtless she would meet Lord Denno then and perhaps in public places like the markets of London. She had been constrained when she met him in company. Likely she would be more free with only her household, who knew him well, as witnesses.

Frowning down at her needlework, Catherine wondered whether she should even try to do anything about it. She glanced quickly at Elizabeth, seated across from her near an open window. The light turned the girl's hair to flame, lent a glow to her pale cheek, and marked the faint upward curve of her lips into what was nearly a smile.

Elizabeth also seemed absorbed in needlework, but she was clearly thinking about something pleasant. Catherine sighed softly and dismissed the idea of trying to prevent Elizabeth from meeting Lord Denno. Elizabeth was her guest, not her prisoner. To try to control her would only drive her away and likely into trouble. The girl would come to no harm in Lord Denno's company and, Catherine reminded herself, she had only promised Tom not to invite Lord Denno to the house. It was herself Tom wanted separated from Denno; he did not care about Elizabeth being in his company.

Elizabeth was indeed smiling at her thoughts, which were mostly centered on Denno's coming, as soon as everyone was asleep, and taking her Underhill. He had done so every night since their first coupling, even when her courses were on her and they could not make love. She discovered that the physical act hardly mattered when they knew they could take that pleasure at any time. It was enough to lie together in Denno's bed to kiss and cuddle and talk.

The sigh she had uttered when Catherine told her that Tom did not think a merchant a suitable friend for Henry VIII's daughter had been one of pure relief. If Denno was forbidden to come to Chelsea, Kat and her maids of honor would not think it strange that he did not visit and she would not need to meet her dearling in their company again.

She had felt, when she asked Catherine to invite Denno to dinner, that she could not bear to be parted from him for an extra moment. She had not realized she would not dare fling herself into his arms, touch him, kiss his smooth skin, stare at him as if she was about to eat him whole. She hardly dared address a word to him, lest her voice betray her love and her longing. That first dinner had been pure torture.

The second dinner had not been so bad. They had been lovers for more than a week and she was growing to believe her joy would be lasting. The bursting rapture of their lovemaking was no longer so new and so overwhelming. She had had time to absorb and accept that the pleasure was no one-time thing but infinitely renewable.

She had been able to speak to Denno at that second dinner, even give him a smile without betraying how their relationship had changed. Of course, Sir Anthony Denny took up nearly all of Denno's attention, but she was able to bear that also, sure now that Denno was all hers. In all other ways than being her lover, her Denno was still her Denno, as indulgent in some things and as inflexible in others.

The smile on her lips deepened a little. She had been shocked when she asked him to cast a glamour on her so that she could go with him to a particularly bawdy new masque she wanted very much to see. Denno had flatly refused. It seemed a betrayal for him to be able to resist her in anything, now that she had given him the joy of her body. She had allowed her eyes to fill with tears and said tragically that he could not love her if he refused to satisfy her desire for a little amusement. And he had replied, as he had throughout the years, that no matter how much he loved her he would always refuse to give her what would do her harm.

"I am the one person in this world or any other," Denno had said, "who cares more for your good than for any other thing. It was my duty and is now the dearest joy of my heart also. I will always stop you from doing anything that would hurt you no matter how much you resent it. And I will always tell you that you are doing wrong when you *are* doing wrong."

At the time she had been furious. She had jumped out of bed and threatened never to couple with him again. And when he did not respond with instant submission, she had demanded to be taken back to Chelsea at once. Without a word he had banished the illusion that brought back his youth, had called clothing to his body, and had Gated them both back into her dressing chamber.

He did not say he would come again the next night so she could deny him furiously; he did not even ask when he should come again. He saw her to the door of her bedchamber and lifted his hand to banish the sleep spell he had laid on Frances Dodd, who was the maiden on duty that night and slept in the truckle bed beside Elizabeth's.

But Elizabeth had had time to recognize the Denno who, so many years ago, had disagreed with her about changing her garden because he knew her willful notion was wrong. A flicker of Foreseeing touched her, of a future in which his steadying good sense in resisting her desires would keep her from grave error. Elizabeth caught his hand and then threw her arms around his neck. He was rigid as granite.

"No, don't let her wake," she had whispered. "Take me back. But you must explain why it is wrong for me to go to that masque."

He had refused at first, and Elizabeth had realized she had really hurt him. But then he yielded, and once again Elizabeth was assured that his words were utterly true. He only ever refused what she asked when it could do her harm. The needle flew in her fingers and the pattern of tiny fairies flitting around a climbing vine of golden flowers took shape.

It was a particularly lovely piece, which Elizabeth had designed herself: tiny, fantastic creatures on a very narrow ribbon on which Denno could hang keys or a pomander. She knew that he could make far more valuable things, chains of gold or platinum studded with jewels, but she thought he would prize this because it was her handiwork.

Chapter 24

When Sir Thomas Seymour had traveled west, he had still been very unsure about the advice the charlatan Otstargi had given him. He had brought with him a substantial force to take and punish the pirate Thomessin, who had seized on the Scilly Isles and was using them as a base for his piracy. He found, however, just as Otstargi had suggested, that Thomessin was very ready to share his spoils and to influence others in Sir Thomas' favor.

Sir Thomas had then occupied Lundy Isle, which he made available to other pirates on the same terms he had given Thomessin, ignoring the protests of the French ambassador. That was a mistake because the ambassador had brought his protests to Sir Thomas' brother, the Protector. Somerset had written Thomas a furious letter, but Thomas had faced him down, writing back that the pirates were too elusive and that the French ambassador was maligning him apurpose to make trouble between them.

There was some reason for Somerset to believe that. His dealings with Scotland were becoming more and more difficult and he had received evidence that the French were supporting the Scots in their resistance to marrying their infant princess, Mary, to King Edward. It seemed quite mad to Somerset that the Scots should resist so simple a solution to the long years of war between the two nations.

By May, when Thomas returned to Chelsea, Somerset was already beginning to plan his campaign against Scotland to take the princess by force of arms if he could not have her by diplomacy. The French were certainly urging the Scots to remain intransigent so their ambassador's tale of Thomas' dealings with the pirates had become less convincing. When Thomas came to pay his respects to the Protector, Somerset did not chide him about the privateering in the narrow sea.

That plus the substantial sums Thomas had carried east from the isles and from his share of the clipping and other devices William Sharington was using to bilk the Bristol Mint made Thomas believe that possibly Otstargi was more than a charlatan. And every time Thomas looked at the glowing ruby Otstargi had given him, he felt a strong urge to consult the man again, charlatan or not. Certainly Otstargi had given him profitable advice. Thus, Sir Thomas sent a message to London informing Otstargi when he had arrived in Chelsea.

He was annoyed when he did not at once receive a deferential reply begging to know when it would be convenient to him for Otstargi to make an appointment. He was even more annoyed when the answer finally came. In addition to simply stating that Otstargi would be willing to receive him in a week's time, the note said, "Make sure that the person known as Lord Denno is no longer welcome in your house. He is a great danger to the success of your most important enterprise."

The fortune-teller had overreached himself, Thomas thought, tossing the note aside. Although the name sounded familiar, there was no Lord Denno in the household. However, only a few days later his wife mentioned that Lord Denno had been invited to dinner. Then Thomas recalled that the man was a rich merchant who had made a valuable gift of furs to Catherine and been entertained alone with her in her parlor.

At that time such gifts could have reduced his influence with Catherine. Thomas remembered he had decided to be rid of Denno, who was of no importance. He had set a watch on him and when he learned Denno was coming to the palace again, had directed two of his men to remove him. Those men had been found dead the next day. Thomas remembered the chill he had felt when he had the news, but no harm had come of his too-casual order. Denno had taken the warning and not again tried to reach Catherine, and Thomas had been glad to let the matter drop.

I should not have done so, Thomas thought, when he saw Catherine greet the man with the warmth of an old friend. He had been hoodwinked, Thomas decided; the encroaching commoner had somehow continued to see Catherine. But Thomas was no longer a suitor hoping for favor. Now that Catherine was his wife he needed no subtleties. As a husband, he could simply give an order to cut Denno's acquaintance and be obeyed. Nonetheless, his respect for Otstargi, who had foreseen or learned of Denno's intrusion into the household, increased.

He went to his appointment with Otstargi with rather more interest than he had felt on his first visit. Nor was he disappointed; after they had discussed the success of the ventures with the pirates and with Sharington, Otstargi told him to decline the offer to command the army that was to be sent by sea to support the Protector's invasion of Scotland.

Thomas frowned. "I will be called a coward."

"Oh, no. Suggest instead that the Protector make you lieutenant-general of the south to guard against any French invasion. Somerset will be very glad to do it, since it will keep you from dimming his glory."

"I am not so sure I want him to reap too much glory in Scotland."

Otstargi laughed. "He will win a battle but lose the war. He will not get the princess, and meanwhile you will have a chance to make yourself pleasant to the landowners, most of whom your brother has managed to offend. You might even put the coin you have gathered to good use and collect arms and men—you can say they will be sent north if the Protector needs them, but they will be *your* men."

Thomas' eyes glittered. "That sounds like good advice."

"All my advice is good. So, have you yet discovered who is the young girl with red hair who seems always to be in my images with you?" Vidal/Otstargi knew perfectly well that the red-haired girl was Elizabeth, but because he could not set watchers on her or, indeed, anywhere in Catherine's household lest she or Blanche sense them, he needed Thomas to tell him what was going on.

The question startled Thomas, who had after considerable thought decided to put aside the notions Otstargi had given him.

That image of him and Elizabeth seated together under cloths of state . . . perhaps Otstargi had somehow picked up that idea from him, from an inadvertent comment about his hopes, before his brother had told him he would sooner see Thomas hanged than Elizabeth's husband.

"You are still seeing me connected with that girl with red hair?"

"Yes. More than ever, but mostly I see her as still very young playing games with you, being teased and petted by you, and becoming more and more fond of you. Do you yet know who she is? I think she must be some great man's daughter . . ."

"Great, indeed," Thomas said. "She is Lady Elizabeth, the late King Henry's daughter, and she is my wife's guest. Are you suggesting that I court her . . . in my wife's presence?"

Otstargi laughed again. "What could be safer? Surely no one will think ill of you or of her if your games include your wife?"

"Perhaps not, but what can be the point of attaching Lady Elizabeth? I am married already. Your vision of Elizabeth and myself seated under cloths of state must be false."

Vidal/Otstargi almost gave away his satisfaction over the way that idea had fixed itself in Thomas Seymour's rather limited mind. He said pointedly, "Images are neither true nor false. They depend on the actions of those who are imaged. I can tell you that that particular image will certainly be false if you do not fix yourself immovably in Lady Elizabeth's affections. The road to my Vision will not be quick or smooth, but if she is bound hard enough to you . . ."

Now Thomas smiled slowly. "I am not inexperienced with women, and she is young. I think it should be possible for me to make her love me."

"That would be very wise, and remember that the farther along that path you draw her, the harder she will fight to have you."

"I am already married," Thomas pointed out.

Vidal/Otstargi shrugged. "Now," he replied. "Accidents happen—"

"No! I will not, nor will you harm my wife!"

"I will not, certainly," Vidal agreed easily—and why not agree. Catherine was useful at this moment as hostess to Elizabeth, which gave Thomas free access to her. If later he felt Thomas needed to be free to seduce Elizabeth into marriage, he certainly would not be bound by anything he said to the fool.

"Besides," Thomas added, "my brother says Elizabeth is beyond my touch. In fact he said he would sooner see me hanged than married to her."

Otstargi/Vidal smiled with genuine pleasure at this confirmation that Elizabeth would be permanently disgraced by any relationship with Thomas.

"I would not take his words too seriously," he said. "I agree that he would stop you from winning her regard if he could, but what he does not know, what is sheltered by your wife's presence and approval . . ."

Thomas made an inarticulate sound and started to rise.

Otstargi held up a hand and said, "Wait." He hesitated, frowned, and then added, "I feel I must warn you that I will not be here to help you further. It will be useless for you to write to me or come here. I must leave England for some time. However, I have told you already all I have seen that is of importance to you. Stay out of the coming war with Scotland and bind to you Lady Elizabeth."

Vidal didn't want Sir Thomas or any other client coming to Otstargi's house. He had to be in Scotland very soon and would likely have to remain there for some time. A war was brewing and he needed to make sure the Scots yielded nothing to the English so the war would continue. But he had to warn his clients away because he had discovered that Pasgen had been in the house.

That had been a terrible shock. To learn what had happened in his absence, Vidal had stripped the servant's mind as soon as he arrived. He nearly burst with rage when he discovered that Pasgen had been in the house several times. His fury was such that his mind blast had almost killed the servant, who dropped unconscious to the floor. Vidal had raised a hand with every intention of incinerating the useless hulk, but bethought himself of the nuisance of getting a new servant and wiping its mind, and kicked the prone body instead of killing it.

When his rage subsided enough for him to think, Vidal realized that he would have to warn away Otstargi's clients and he had done so; Seymour was the last. He did not want Pasgen meddling with those under his influence. But even as that thought came to mind, he recalled the image the servant had given him. Pasgen had not disguised himself as Otstargi. He had retained his natural form and had spent his time talking to Albertus, Aurilia's mortal healer.

Why? Pasgen was never interested in mortals. Why had he spent so much time with the healer Aurilia had sent to arrange the deaths of Denoriel and Aleneil? Vidal kicked the body near his feet again out of impotent fury as he guessed that Rhoslyn had convinced her indulgent brother to save their half brother and sister. Rhoslyn was softhearted and not too clever. Vidal ground his teeth.

Hearing the servant, who had taken two days to recover, return from seeing Seymour out recalled to Vidal the events of that first day back in London. Now he was angry again. Stupid mortal! Vidal regretted having sent Aurilia's mortal healer back to her. He should have torn Albertus limb from limb. Doubtless the fool had told Pasgen his plans; likely enough that was why Albertus' plans had miscarried.

Vidal stared into nothing across Otstargi's table and vowed he would master Pasgen. He would! There must be some way . . . Then his tense body relaxed. Yes, there was. One of the cleverest and least trustworthy of his Dark Sidhe, Piteka, had questioned him on what reward he could have for finding Llanelli. Such a question meant that Piteka must have some information about her. Vidal nodded. It would be very useful to have that idiot Llanelli in his hands. Both Pasgen and Rhoslyn would dance to his tune when their mother would suffer for their intransigence.

For a moment more Vidal remained seated behind the table thinking about the taking of Llanelli. Then he rose and climbed the stairs to Otstargi's bedchamber from where he Gated back to Caer Mordwyn.

Arrived in his own bedchamber in the palace, Vidal shook his head. He would need to warn Piteka that Llanelli must be kept in close confinement but not seriously harmed. Piteka could torment her and sup off her misery, but Piteka was often too enthusiastic about wringing life-force from his victims. And, Vidal thought, he would speak to Chenga too and remind her . . .

Vidal ground his teeth again. Reminding Chenga that she must pass as Bright Court Sidhe would be useless. Chenga was a weak reed on whom to rest a deception. She had done well to discover that Elizabeth would visit Elfhame Cymry, but Chenga loose in an elfhame full of fat and pampered mortals was an invitation to disaster. Vidal knew she would not be able to resist seizing and tormenting a few of the mortals, exposing herself as unfitted to live in Cymry. Likely she would not only be expelled but marked so she could not return.

Nor could he send his imp watchers to Cymry. They would be detected and driven out or killed. Yet Cymry was his best hope of being rid of Elizabeth. They held full many mortal balls and tournaments during which many non-Cymry Sidhe mingled. And they had little magic so Denoriel would be less watchful.

A fireball formed on Vidal's fingers and burned a table near his hand. That Denoriel was sly as a kitsune and his mortal friend, who carried iron weapons, was fearless. When Vidal learned that Denoriel was bringing Elizabeth Underhill almost every mortal day, he thought one of his Sidhe would be able to touch her with poison or strike her with a levin bolt, but Denoriel's movements were too erratic. Goeel had found them in Fur Hold but could not get near Elizabeth.

A flicker of black. Vidal howled and raised his fist over an arriving imp, but his lifted arm was caught and held midair. He broke the spell. Before he could smash the imp to relieve his frustration, he heard Aurilia say lazily, "Oh, there you are. Don't squash that imp. I find it useful."

Vidal turned on her, black/violet light flickered for a moment on the tips of his fingers. Aurilia sent two little forked lights, one of which touched each of Vidal's hands. He hissed and shook them, but the threatening light on his fingers died.

"And what has put you into such a fine humor?" Aurilia asked. "I thought you were only going to see that loud-mouth human who is only too eager to do what you suggest."

"It is nothing to do with him; he is less than nothing. He will try and he might even succeed in making Elizabeth his mistress. Then I need only expose her. She will be disgraced and removed from the succession, but it is not sure enough. She must be dead."

"Why?" Aurilia asked, lifting her brows. "Titania has a particular liking for the creature, and I am not too eager to incite Titania's displeasure."

Vidal shrugged. "Fortunately Titania is inconstant in her favor. We must take the chance. Elizabeth must be dead! As long as she is alive, she can be as easily restored to the succession as she was removed from it. Edward will die in a few years. The poison of the thorn that touched him is slowly eating at him. Then Mary should come to the throne. And we would have the Inquisition and the burnings. But those who rule for Edward will not want Mary to succeed Edward and bring back the old religion. They will restore Elizabeth and try to enthrone her to keep the new religion."

"Yes," Aurilia agreed, but she looked puzzled, "but Mary's supporters will not yield tamely. A little civil war . . . that would be delicious. There will be looting and burning and rape. Let them fight, my lord. It will be a rich soup of pain and misery for us to feed upon."

"Unless Elizabeth's supporters win!" Vidal spat. "No, she must be dead. But as you say, she is Titania's pet. She needs to die by accident in a Bright Court elfhame and if possible by a mortal mistake. I know she intends to visit Elfhame Cymry." He explained why Elizabeth would be specially vulnerable in Cymry and then clenched his fist. "But I have no way of learning when she will be there."

"I thought Chenga—"

Vidal shook his head vigorously and explained his thoughts about Chenga.

Aurilia nodded slowly; then her eyes grew intent. "Let Chenga go anyway," she said, "and we will send Albertus with her. When she hurts their mortals, Cymry will drive her out. Then Albertus will beg sanctuary among them and be received with sympathy. Relying as they do upon mortals, they will be delighted to get a good healer. In a short time, he will be trusted and not watched."

"But he cannot Gate. How will he bring us news?"

"Oh, my lord, an amulet will let him Gate, and will make sure he Gates only to where we wish him to go." She smiled, showing her sharp pointed teeth. "Mortals do get ideas of their own."

Considering the profit Otstargi's past advice had provided for him, Thomas thought it only sensible to follow the advice about Elizabeth also. After all, since she was a member of Catherine's household, he would not need to make his courtship of her obvious by visiting her openly. And whether or not that vision of him and Elizabeth under cloths of state came true, it could only do him good to have her in love with him. Catherine would only be amused by Elizabeth's childish devotion.

He intended to show his particularity at once, but Elizabeth was out riding when he returned to Chelsea. He did ask Catherine where she had gone, but Catherine only replied that Elizabeth was safe, accompanied by two guardsmen and two well-armed grooms. She carefully did not mention that Lord Denno was probably also of the party. Thomas did not ask further; of a jealous nature himself, he did not want Catherine to suspect he was too interested in Elizabeth.

The next afternoon was too hot for riding and moreover threatened rain to end the sultriness. At dinner, Elizabeth and Catherine had a discussion about the morals in Plato's work and how they proved that modern Christian teaching was eternal truth. Thomas was very bored and suggested that perhaps Elizabeth should take her lessons in the afternoon rather than the morning. That would leave the mornings, which were cooler for her expeditions ahorse.

"No, no," Elizabeth protested, laughing. "Master Grindal would be most displeased if I came to him tired from riding and eating. As it is, even in the morning I can barely absorb the weighty subjects with which Plato deals."

"And why should so lovely a young lady care for Plato's weighty subjects?" Thomas asked archly.

"Well, for one reason, so that her mind should be as lovely as her face," Catherine said with a laugh. "I have often regretted that my tutors did not press me to learn more than I did."

"I am not sorry," Thomas said, quick to catch the slight acidity in his wife's voice. "You are perfect as you are."

Catherine blushed with pleasure, but Thomas, not being completely a fool, did not again compliment Elizabeth's beauty in Catherine's hearing. He did, however, engage all the younger ladies of the household—of whom he insisted his wife was one—in a game of hide and seek.

Thomas was loud in comment and protest when he was tagged and made them all merry. But when he found Elizabeth he made just a moment to whisper a compliment on her figure and to pat her behind as he prodded her out of her hiding place. Catherine, he kissed for his tag. Catherine was as happy and merry as the youngest of the girls.

Thomas spent more time at Chelsea than usual and most of that time with the ladies of the household. Elizabeth was part amused, part flattered, and part irritated by Tom's boisterous playfulness.

One day he actually enlisted Catherine's help to hold Elizabeth still, while he cut away her gown bit by bit.

Catherine thought it very funny, adding to the excitement by tickling Elizabeth. But although the fact that a man other than her Denno was removing her dress excited her, it also annoyed her. She knew she would not dare ask Catherine to pay for the gown—it would seem mean and selfish after all the teasing and laughter—but that meant she would herself have to pay for a new gown. Still she did not fight Thomas off, and it did send a thrill through her when her underdress exposed her to his eyes.

This time, however, Kat, who had watched the other games indulgently, scolded Elizabeth for allowing her gown to be cut up in public. That annoyed Elizabeth even more. Would it have been better to allow Thomas to undress her in private? She suspected that was what he intended to suggest—silly man. Denno did not roar with laughter at his own jests or poke her to bring his cleverness to her attention. Denno trusted her to be clever enough to understand his sly humor and made undressing a sensuous delight instead of a coarse joke.

All Elizabeth could say in her defense was that she could not stop Thomas because Queen Catherine was holding her, and she dared not wrench herself away. Nor could she long remain annoyed with Thomas. Compared with Denno, Thomas seemed to her like a very large, clumsy puppy who was trying to amuse her. She just accepted his advances and smiled brilliantly on him whenever they met.

Once in a while it occurred to Elizabeth that he was deliberately trying to arouse her but she dismissed the idea. He was Catherine's husband and was only trying to keep Catherine's guest happy in the only way he knew to make a female happy, by flirting with her. The proof of that to her was that he flirted with all the other ladies in the household too. She could not spend much thought on Thomas. Her other life, of which he knew nothing, was currently too sweet.

Most nights Denno took her Underhill. Sometimes they explored the markets or places like Fur Hold, where she had danced on a platform to Denno playing the lute for an audience impossible to describe. Da was with them that day and had fended off a rude Sidhe who had grabbed at her. They thought it was because of her dancing; Elizabeth dismissed it and forgot it when Da told her that he had performed on the same platform, recalling when he and Denno had arrived there by accident and he had sung "Maiden in the Moor."

Sometimes with Da who was on rare occasions accompanied by Rhoslyn, sometimes with Aleneil and Ilar, but most often just she and Denno explored the safe holds and hames of Underhill. They ate in wonderful places, and Elizabeth wore costumes of such beauty and magnificence that they took her breath away. But best of all, wherever they went, they came home to Denno's rooms in Llachar Lle and to his wide bed and the ever-increasing pleasures he gave and took from her body.

Elizabeth felt that she was living two entirely separate lives. She did manage to concentrate on her lessons so that her tutor, Master Grindal, was satisfied with her progress, but Denno and Underhill held most of her attention.

She was aware only vaguely that whenever Thomas came to stay with Catherine, whether it was at Chelsea or at Hanworth out in the country, or in Seymour Place in London, he paid her more and more particular attention. She did not tell Denno; it was not important to her and likely Denno would tell her she must discourage Thomas. That would upset Catherine so Elizabeth kept Thomas' behavior as a little amusing guilty secret. Perhaps she should have been colder, but she was flattered . . . and Catherine was always there.

Besides it was hard to think of how to stop it. The flirting always started innocently with Thomas amusing the whole company, mostly with physical games—hoodman-blind on a day that it rained too hard to go out; catch-as-catch-can on a day in autumn when running was welcome to warm the blood.

Moreover Thomas held every feminine captive against him in hoodman-blind, and touched her to make sure of her identity, not only Elizabeth. She thought he took a trace longer with her and often pressed a small kiss to her neck as he sniffed for her perfume. But she could not help being flattered, and she was sure Catherine never noticed.

Even when they played catch-as-catch-can, which was too wild for long fondling, Thomas would manage to seize her shoulder and, his body blocking Catherine's view, was able to stroke her breast where it bulged above her gown and pinch the nipple. He was very crude compared with Denno, and that amused Elizabeth even when a guilty thrill went though her.

Elizabeth was just beginning to wonder if Thomas was growing too particular in his attentions when, one morning, he and Catherine burst into her chamber to catch her in bed before she woke. Denno was in bed with her. He often lay with her for a while when he brought her back to the mortal world, talking idly or drowsing if their lovemaking had been particularly energetic. It was a kind of bridge between one life and the other.

Denno's keen ears caught the footfalls coming across the parlor; he muttered the Don't-see-me spell and disappeared. However, he could not hide the upheaval of the bedclothes as he left the bed. Elizabeth could only try to seem so startled as almost to convulse, shaking her arms and legs and lifting the bedclothes all around her body. She cried out, too, and tossed her head from side to side so that the pillows beside her place had a reason to be dented as well as her own.

She was utterly terrified and must have looked it so that Catherine came well forward and assured her that all was well, that she and Tom had only wanted to surprise her. Realizing that Catherine and Thomas had no suspicion that Denno had been abed with her permitted Elizabeth to begin to laugh when they tickled her feet and threatened to pull the blankets off her. But she was really angry because she knew that the sweet bridge between mortal world and Underhill was lost. After the incident with the door being stuck, she could not use that device again. She and Denno would never again dare to share her bed.

Elizabeth hoped that her reaction, which was certainly not all pleasure, would end any future playful invasions. But only a few days later, Thomas came to her chamber alone. Elizabeth leapt from her bed and fled behind the bedcurtains, calling her maidens to her. All of them hid behind the bedcurtains. They all laughed and Elizabeth pretended to do so, but she would not come out, no matter how long Thomas waited, calling out teasing threats.

By then, Blanche had run out the back door and brought Kat, who was not amused. She waylaid Thomas in the gallery outside Elizabeth's bedchamber and told him that what he was doing had already become a matter of unpleasant gossip and that he must stop or evil would be spoken about Elizabeth.

Thomas defended himself, saying he meant no ill, but Kat was frightened; she had heard that married or not he had an eye for women. That was not so terrible, many men were like that, but Elizabeth was not "any girl." Kat went to the queen and spoke her fears. Catherine only laughed at what she called Thomas' antics, but she did promise Kat that she herself would come with Thomas in the future.

So she did and the early morning visits tapered off and stopped. Elizabeth thought Thomas was annoyed; he cast some speaking glances at her. That was flattering too, but she replied to the invitation in his looks only with a smile.

Currently Elizabeth had something far more interesting to think about and plan for. She had been invited to Court by her brother. She took part in no more romping games for she was too busy with her wardrobe and an embroidered handkerchief for Edward. She had heard that the usual New Year's gifts were forbidden by the Protector, but she hoped to slip the handkerchief to her brother when no one was watching.

She was very excited. It had been almost a year since she had last seen Edward—when they wept together over the news of their father's death. In fact, she was so excited that she had forgotten entirely that it would be impossible for Denno to see her while she was at Court. That information came to her as a terrible shock one night. She had slipped out of bed and was waiting languidly for Denno to magic her clothing onto her; instead he snapped at her angrily.

"Do you not care at all?"

Elizabeth blinked. "Care? Care about what, love?"

"That we will not see each other, touch each other, for weeks?"

"What?" Elizabeth said stupidly. "Why? Why should we be parted? Are you angry with me?"

"You are going to Court," Denoriel said, staring at her.

"Yes!" Elizabeth smiled brightly. "It will be so wonderful to see Edward. I know I will have to bow to him and I will not be able to hug him and be familiar as we were, but we will be able to talk about his lessons and mine and—"

"And I am forbidden to go anywhere near your Court!" Denoriel interrupted.

"Oh!" Elizabeth breathed. "Oh! I had forgotten that." Her eyes were a muddy brown when she lifted them to him. "But when I was at Hampton Court with Catherine, we met in the maze or in the wilderness and when I rode out."

"Yes, and do you remember all the trouble you fell into when Lady Mary saw Harry in the garden? If we are seen ..."

"We will be more careful," Elizabeth said, her voice tremulous. "You do not need to appear at all. I can get out and meet you somewhere and you can make a Gate and take me Underhill." In the mortal world she could not have said the words Gate or Underhill, but in Llachar Lle she could.

But now the black anger had faded from Denoriel's face. He realized that Elizabeth was not indifferent to their parting, that she was so accustomed to his building a Gate wherever she was and taking her away that she had not thought about the dangers and difficulties of meeting in the overcrowded and gossip-ridden Court. His use of magic at Court could also call down Oberon's wrath for greatly increasing the danger of exposing the existence of the Sidhe.

He got out of bed himself and gestured their clothing onto their bodies. At that sign that her time Underhill was over, she did not know for how long, Elizabeth uttered a small cry of distress and reached out toward him. Denoriel took her hand and then drew her into his arms. He had been thinking that she was as shallow in her affection as the Sidhe, that she had used him while she was bored with her staid life with Catherine and now that a better amusement was offered would cast him aside.

That was clearly not true. Her beautiful, long-fingered hands were fastened tight into his doublet, and her expression was full of distress. Denoriel regretted his abrupt disclosure now. He had been hurt and stupidly wanted to hurt her in return. Of a sudden he remembered that she was only fourteen years old; to salve his conscience he always thought of her as a woman. And in many ways she was fully adult—but now he realized she was still a child in the delight she took in Court life, which had simply wiped every other consideration out of her mind.

"Careful cannot be enough, Elizabeth," Denoriel said gently, unfastening her fingers from his doublet and kissing them. "The Court will be so overcrowded that I do not dare come into any chamber there. Blanche will not have a chamber of her own but be crammed in with many other maids, and likely you will not have your own dressing room but need to share with your maidens. Out of doors is impossible. It is December."

Elizabeth swallowed hard. "I do not care for that. All know I love to ride. I will say I do not mind the cold. Mayhap there will be warmer days. If you leave an air spirit with me, I can send it for you—"

"Little love, that will not do. You are the king's sister. If you say you want to ride, a party will form. Can you imagine what will be said of you if you deny them and say you want to ride alone?"

"Then I will find some place where we can meet at night. I will . . . I will beg Elidir or Mechain to teach me a sleep spell. I will put sleep upon those in my chamber—"

"Elizabeth! Do you think the corridors and antechambers are *ever* empty when the full Court is present? No, love, it would be a disaster if you are discovered creeping out alone. It would be far worse than when you were eleven years old. Even then Mary called you a whore. What would she call you now if you were seen creeping out in the middle of the night?"

She stared at him for a moment, eyes wide and desolate, but Denoriel felt relieved because she had obviously accepted that sneaking away at night would ruin her. Then she drew a sharp breath and smiled.

"You are a merchant," she said. "And everyone knows I have received beautiful cloth and furs from you. Surely I could come to your house or your place of business to look over what you have. I need a fine New Year's gift for Catherine."

He smiled at her. "First of all, if you think you will be able to come alone, you are mad. Half the Court buys from me and will think I will give them special consideration if they come in your company. How do you propose to disappear from their midst? And secondly, you can come once, perhaps twice if I say I do not have what you request but will obtain it for you, but no more than that, Elizabeth."

"I know." Her eyes were still dark and troubled. "But I miss you so much. I cannot bear to think of not seeing you, not speaking to you at all for so long."

Now Denoriel laughed. "It will not seem so long to you. You will be constantly engaged. But let me remind you that you should make time to talk with William Cecil. He is already the Protector's secretary and might be able to do you much good. And give a good greeting to his wife, Mildred Coke, she was."

Elizabeth shook her head at him. "I do not need that reminder. I have not forgotten that Cecil has often sent me valuable news. And as far as Mildred . . . Do not be so silly. Mildred has been a good friend since I was with the group at Hampton Court.

Of course I will greet her, and ask her to join me if she has no other company."

Denoriel sighed. "You will enjoy yourself so much, I hope you will not forget me entirely."

"Denno!" Elizabeth glanced significantly at the tumbled bed. "How many lovers do you think I have?" Then she sighed. "You were angry because you said I did not care, but now it seems that you do not care!"

He stroked her hair. "I care," he said, feeling his own heart sink again, for though the time they would be parted was not long by Sidhe standards, it would still be too long. "Trust me, my heart. I care."

Chapter 25

There was no sign at all in the grounds or the empty house of the carnage and destruction Vidal's minions had created. The guard at the Gate was even stronger and less subject to spells. The paths through the garden were again warded by force fields and were immaculate, totally free of any sign of the host that had burned there at Pasgen's command. The house itself was shining and spotless; new constructs received and transmitted messages for Pasgen and Rhoslyn, new servants were ready to provide any comfort required, and a new set of guards and girls, stronger and more deadly than ever, was ready to protect the place.

This Tuesday evening Rhoslyn had suggested to Llanelli that they dine at the empty house instead of at an inn in the Elves' Faire. It seemed to Rhoslyn that Llanelli did not look as bright and vibrant since Vidal's minions had destroyed the empty house and its constructs. She thought that if Llanelli saw that the empty house was returned to normal, she would be less uneasy.

However, Llanelli had been less than pleased with the idea of returning there. Rhoslyn had assured her that there was no residue of the destruction, but Llanelli was still reluctant. "That the place has been cleaned and new servants installed is not the point," she said to Rhoslyn. "It would be better to abandon that domain altogether and make a new empty house."

"But what of all your patients, who are accustomed to coming to that place for your healing?"

"No more. Thank the Mother I had no patients coming to the empty house that day and that no one tried to see me without an appointment. The constructs in all my market booths tell any who ask for me I no longer treat patients there." Llanelli shivered and then controlled the trembling.

"I had no idea you had taken such a dislike to the place," Rhoslyn said. "I wanted to abandon it myself. It has bad memories for me, although of course there is a new blue-ribbon Lliwglas now. But when I suggested that to Pasgen, he did not want to interfere with your work."

"I do not heal there any longer."

"Come and talk to him about it," Rhoslyn urged. "He is going to meet me there, which is why I wanted you to come so you could join us for dinner." Rhoslyn was a little surprised by the flash of fear she saw in her mother's eyes, but it was gone in the next moment.

"Pasgen will be there?" Llanelli asked.

"Yes. I had a message to meet him there. And the empty house is convenient. As you know we have Gates that go there from all the markets. It is safe now, Mother. Pasgen . . . ah . . . spoke to Vidal after the attack and assured me that Vidal would never attack the place again. And indeed, there has been no trouble there."

"Pasgen should stay away from Vidal." Llanelli's voice trembled. "Pasgen is too sure of himself. He always thought he was stronger than Vidal . . . and suffered terribly for it. And you did, too. Burned and cut and bruised . . ."

"Mother, that was only when we were children. Pasgen and I soon learned to shield ourselves."

Llanelli did not seem to hear her, her memory was fixed in a horrible past where she could not protect her children from their tormentor. "I tried to warn him," she whispered. "But he would not listen."

"Pasgen *is* stronger now. Do not fear for him." Rhoslyn was less sure than she sounded, but it seemed to her that Llanelli's rich coloring was faded, her hands restless, betraying uneasiness, and she wished to reassure her.

"So you say. You always thought Pasgen was near a god. Anyway it is not a matter of strength alone. Vidal is so sly, so clever . . . Pasgen doesn't take Vidal seriously enough." Llanelli bit her lip then drew a deep determined breath. "Very well," she agreed. "I will come with you. Perhaps I can convince Pasgen to abandon that domain."

However, when she and Rhoslyn reached the empty house, Llanelli said that since she was there, she would gather up some supplies that she had left behind. Lliwglas could carry them to the lodging she had hired in the Elves' Faire. Rhoslyn nodded and went in the main entrance as Llanelli walked around the corner of the house to go in through her own door.

As she lifted her hand to wave the door open, Rhoslyn paused, her head cocked, listening intently. Had she heard a faint exclamation? The sound was not repeated, and after another moment, Rhoslyn went in. Lliwglas was there and would protect Llanelli from any harm.

Then she forgot the sound she had heard. Pasgen was waiting, a delicate glass of pale wine in his hand, his legs stretched out and crossed at the ankle. Rhoslyn smiled. She had not seen her brother look so relaxed in a long time.

"Well," she said, sitting down in a chair at right angles to his, "you look comfortable."

"Wouldn't Mother come with you?" he asked, setting the wine down on a small table that appeared at his elbow.

Rhoslyn lifted a finger and a servant appeared. She pointed to the wine. In another moment a goblet like Pasgen's appeared on a table beside her chair. She picked it up and sipped, shrugged her shoulders.

"Yes, she did come, but not very willingly. You know, Pasgen, she still fears Vidal and I cannot convince her that you can protect her. No matter what I say, she still thinks of us as children, not strong enough to resist him. She wants you to destroy this domain and build a new one."

Pasgen frowned. "The trouble is, Rhoslyn, that in any domain I cannot protect her if she is so afraid of him. That is half his battle won for him, the fear of his victims."

"Think about some way to convince her. She is beginning to look worn again. She says she has given notice to all of her clients that she no longer heals at this house. She has chambers for healing at all three markets now and lodging at the Elves' Faire. If she does not need this house any longer, maybe we *should* destroy it."

"No." Pasgen's voice was sharp, his expression hard. "It makes no sense to abandon this place. It is a lodestone for trouble." His frown darkened. "Also, to destroy it would make Vidal feel that he had won, had driven us away."

"I suppose you are right about that." Rhoslyn sighed and let herself slump into the cushions. Then she straightened, put down her goblet, and said in a determined voice, "I don't care! I don't care what Vidal thinks! Pasgen, I want to join the Bright Court."

She hesitated, expecting Pasgen to tell her again that she would be worse off trying to join the Seleighe Sidhe, but he only lifted his own wine and sipped at it, then looked thoughtfully into the near-transparent liquid.

Recalling Pasgen's previous warnings, Rhoslyn continued, "I don't care if most of the Seleighe Sidhe ignore me. I do have a few friends among them. I went to Oberon's ball—"

"Many Dark Court Sidhe go to Oberon's ball. It is his purpose that the Seleighe and Unseleighe mingle in peace at the balls." He put down the wine again.

"Yes, and I admit I went shielded—oh, I have something important to tell you about that, but I want to finish about the ball first. But it did not matter that I was shielded. Harry FitzRoy saw me—you remember, the one I made the changeling for. He knew I was Dark Court, but he still asked me to dance. And Aleneil was there with a Sidhe called Ilar from Elfhame Cymry. Aleneil knew who I was too. They were all friendly. Even Denoriel was friendly and danced with me. He had brought Elizabeth."

Rhoslyn had got that all out very fast, expecting that Pasgen would tell her that Harry FitzRoy was a mortal and did not understand Sidhe protocols or that Aleneil and Denoriel were just conforming to the rules of the ball. However, he did not interrupt her or argue, only looked down at his hands, clasped in his lap.

"Pasgen?" she said doubtfully.

"I also have a friend . . . well, more than one friend, from the Bright Court," Pasgen said in a low voice. "She—"

"She!" Rhoslyn interrupted, putting down her wine and clasping her hands. "Oh, Pasgen, is there finally someone—"

He laughed. "Gaenor is old enough to be my great, great, great, great—I do not know how many greats—granddam."

Perhaps there was a tinge of bitterness in the laugh, Rhoslyn thought, but there was also pleasure and amusement. Her heart leapt with hope. If Pasgen had found sympathetic friends among the Seleighe Sidhe, surely he would be willing to appeal for acceptance into the Bright Court.

Her hopes rose higher as she heard Pasgen continue, "But she knows the mists and the Unformed lands as well or better than I." He glanced at his sister sidelong, almost as if he were shy, and reached for his wine again. "She has taught me a thing or two—" he laughed and Rhoslyn saw that his usually pale cheeks had a flush of color "—or maybe three or four." He turned and looked Rhoslyn in the eye. "She was once a very great maker. You would like her, Rhoslyn."

"I'm sure I would," Rhoslyn agreed warmly. "You must arrange a meeting for us soon, and that will be easy because of the other important thing I learned at the ball. Between keeping up my shields and dancing—that Harry just loves to dance—I was drained to the dregs. I was afraid I would faint and so I braced myself against hurt and drew in the Bright Court power. Only, Pasgen"—she reached across the space between the chairs and grasped his arm—"there was no pain, no hurt. That was all another lie Vidal told us and some trickery he worked on us. The power was sweet and warm and it restored me more fully than the mists of misery." She drew a deep breath. "I *can* live in the Seleighe domains. I can."

Pasgen shrugged. "I can too. Even if Bright Court power is beyond me, and I do not think it will be, I have the power of the mists."

"Then let us beg audience from Oberon and declare that we wish to be recognized as Seleighe."

Pasgen drained the wine from his goblet and put it down gently. "Yes, Rhoslyn, we can go, but our mother cannot."

"Our mother . . ." Rhoslyn repeated and suddenly shuddered and put a hand to her lips.

She had forgotten that in order to become pregnant, Llanelli had committed several unforgivable crimes. Vidal had made sure that she and Pasgen had the whole story in the ugliest terms he could find in which to tell it. Vidal felt it was a good counter to the sweetness and light Llanelli continually preached to them. She was, he said, for all she aped Bright ways, as Dark as any Sidhe in his Court.

Llanelli wanted what she wanted and decided she wanted a child and Kefni Silverhair for its father. She had forced Sidhe and mortal mages to create spells of such power that the mages were drained to death. She had induced a male and female virgin to couple, and sacrificed them while in the act of copulation. She had put a spell of compulsion on Kefni Silverhair, who was committed in a life-bond to Seren Teifi, to forget his bonded and couple with her.

Kefni, strong in magic himself, soon broke Llanelli's compulsion and fled back to Seren. But the spell of fertility was strong with the spirits of the dead binding it. When Kefni coupled with his bonded, she, too, got with child.

At first Llanelli had not known. She had sent news of her conceiving to Kefni, hoping—perhaps even expecting—that he would leave Seren and come to her to have his child. However, he did not come to her, only sent a message that if she had needs, she should send him word and he would see that the needs were fulfilled.

Llanelli was angry but told herself that she had been mistaken in Kefni, who had even less heart than most Sidhe, who at least loved children. But when Denoriel and Aleneil were born and doubled the rejoicing that her twins had inspired in the Bright Court, she realized what had happened—that Seren had also conceived. Llanelli seethed with rage and spite and finally thought of a way to revenge herself.

Rhoslyn shivered, remembering . . . remembering the pain that had stabbed her when Vidal Dhu, prince of the Dark Court revealed the black inside her mother's bright exterior. Though Llanelli cursed Kefni Silverhair for abandoning her children to the Dark Court, Vidal told them it was Llanelli herself who had sent him news of the multiple births and urged him to seize Seren's twins. He had, of course, taken hers too. Vidal was Vidal.

"It has been so long," Rhoslyn breathed, her eyes filled with tears, "and she has suffered so much. Surely if she begs pardon, offers atonement, she will be forgiven."

"Will she?" Pasgen asked. "What atonement can she offer? Kefni Silverhair is dead. Seren Teifi also. She had no will to live after her bond-mate's death. As soon as her children were old enough, Seren slipped into Dreaming and from Dreaming to death. They were favorites, Kefni and Seren, of Titania, who found their mutual devotion fascinating. Titania's memory is long and her quarrels with Oberon do not affect the influence she has on him." He sighed. "No, there is no way back to the Bright Court for our mother."

There was a silence. Then Rhoslyn said, "I see." Her voice was flat.

Pasgen reached blindly for his wine, his gesture stiff and clumsy. The glass, struck by his fingertips instead of being caught in his hand, tipped, spilling wine. He did not catch it or wave a hand to remove the spilled wine. He was staring into the distance, clearly seeing nothing.

"They will accept you gladly, Rhoslyn," he said. "According to Gaenor, there are now no great makers in the Bright Court. You will be happier when you have found a place there. And Oberon and Titania will not object to your protecting Mary. They do not look forward to her becoming queen, but all mortal events are like a short dream to them."

"It does not matter. I cannot leave our mother alone here, Pasgen."

"You would not be leaving her alone. I will be here and I will make sure that I have reminders to see her at least once a mortal week to make sure all is well with her."

"No!" The protest was instant. "Become Seleighe without you? I will not. I could not."

"Of course you could," Pasgen said, but he did not look at her. "We could still meet—"

"No!" Rhoslyn was even more emphatic. "Meet where? I could not go to your domain. Someone would surely report on my attachment to members of the Dark Court. And even if we met in the markets—"

Rhoslyn broke off, suddenly aware of Lliwglas standing silently near her. When she looked at her, the construct bowed. "Lady Llanelli says she will come to this house no longer, mistress. Shall I stay with her in her lodging in the market, return and remain here, or wait here and return with you to your own domain?"

"Hmmm." Rhoslyn narrowed her eyes. "Has Lady Llanelli suggested what she would like you to do?"

"No, mistress."

"Where is Lady Llanelli?"

The construct turned immediately and looked out into the entryway.

"I'm here," Llanelli said from near the stairway, as if she had just come down from her apartment on the second floor.

Rhoslyn noted that Lliwglas' brows were drawn slightly together, as if she did not understand something. But what was there to puzzle her? By then, Llanelli had come into the parlor. Rhoslyn thought she looked pale and haunted.

"What happened, Mother? I thought I heard you say something just as I came into the house, but I thought you were talking to Lliwglas. Did you call out for me?"

"No." Llanelli shook her head. "I really, really do not like coming to this house anymore. There was a shadow on the lawn, and my heart virtually leapt into my throat before I realized it was only a shadow. And then when Lliwglas opened the door—just about as that shadow startled me—her shadow fell across me and frightened me even further."

"There is nothing of which to be afraid, Mother," Pasgen said. "I promise you. Vidal will not come himself nor send any of his creatures here. To be safe from Prince Vidal's mischiefs, this is the best place in all Underhill."

"If you say so, Pasgen," Llanelli said, but her voice shook. "Maybe your reasons will convince my head, but my heart leaps up and down and does not care what my head thinks. I am not happy here, so I will not come . . . and you need not bargain with Vidal about this house for my sake."

"But surely this is more comfortable and safer for you than a booth in one of the markets," Rhoslyn said, looking very troubled. "Perhaps if I give you a route to—"

"No!" Llanelli cried. "No. I do not want to know where you or Pasgen have your true homes. I am not strong. It would not take much before I told what I knew."

This was no more than the truth, as both Pasgen and Rhoslyn knew, for soon after they had rescued her from where Vidal had dumped her, Llanelli had escaped from Rhoslyn's keeping and, to obtain oleander, had betrayed the route to Rhoslyn's original domain. Having what he wanted, Vidal had dumped her again drugged out of her wits. Pasgen had found her and taken her to his home, where he kept her much more strictly until she had conquered her addiction to oleander. Warned that she had told Vidal how to find her private domain, Rhoslyn had destroyed it and built a new domain—one she liked much better than the old one.

Unfortunately, after her confession of weakness, Llanelli went on to beg Pasgen not to overestimate himself and underestimate Vidal. Pasgen sighed, but patiently explained that he was not such a fool as to do so, that his shields and his spells had been tested.

Far from comforting Llanelli, this only seemed to frighten her more. Finally when Llanelli was wiping her eyes and did not notice, Rhoslyn leaned over, caught Pasgen's arm, and shook her head at him. He took a deep irritated breath, but after that he allowed his mother to utter her warnings and only spoke to assure her he would be very, very careful.

That Llanelli did not believe Pasgen's assurances was so clear and that Pasgen might well lose his temper and be unkind if she did not stop her useless warnings drove Rhoslyn to intervene. She seized a pause while Pasgen was swallowing what he wanted to say, rose to her feet, and suggested they go into the dining parlor. As they took their accustomed places, she began to talk brightly about Lady Mary—a subject about which neither Pasgen nor her mother cared much.

The servants brought in a most piquantly seasoned pale fish as an appetizer. Pasgen ate with stolid indifference to the delicate flavor; Llanelli pushed the slice of fish around on her plate after one small bite.

Hastily Rhoslyn said, "You remember I told you that Lady Mary had invited Elizabeth to come and live with her when she learned that Sir Thomas Seymour was suing for Queen Catherine's hand in marriage."

"I remember," Llanelli said indifferently, her eyes fixed on Pasgen.

The servants removed the appetizer and replaced it with bowls of soup. Rhoslyn unwisely took a spoonful; she expected Pasgen to carry on the conversation and deflect Llanelli, but he did not make any reply to her last statement. He was looking down into his soup plate as if a scrying image was forming there.

Into the silence Llanelli said, "Pasgen, you must promise me—"

Pasgen drew a sharp breath and looked up, his brows bent together into an angry frown.

Before he could speak, Rhoslyn said, as if she had not heard her mother, "Lady Mary was hurt when Elizabeth refused her offer of hospitality, which has made Mary unhealthily interested in news about Queen Catherine's household."

"Unhealthily?" Pasgen repeated, pulling the bowl of soup closer. He was still frowning, but the expression was one of curiosity rather than irritation. "Why unhealthily?"

"I fear Mary is looking for some reason to complain of Lady Elizabeth's behavior to the Protector. Mary has a direct line to his ear because she is a great favorite with the Protector's wife. It seems odd because Lady Somerset is a strong advocate of the reformed religion and Mary will not abate a jot of her Catholicism, but they write to each other and, I suppose, avoid mention of religion."

"But why is Mary looking for a reason for complaint?"

Rhoslyn sighed. "Partly because she simply hates Elizabeth for being Anne Boleyn's daughter and also," Rhoslyn smiled faintly, "I think because Elizabeth looks so much like her father. Mary has always maintained that Anne was a whore and Elizabeth a bastard. It is a hard position to maintain when, take away the fat, Elizabeth looks so much like Henry."

"Yes," Pasgen agreed. "The hair. The complexion. Those hands. And her manner. But her eyes are dark."

"Another thing," Rhoslyn said, "I think Mary is becoming anxious about being allowed to continue to practice the Catholic rite. I know she has received letters hinting that she must soon conform. She wishes, I fear, to direct Somerset's attention to Elizabeth's misdoings so he will let her hear her Mass in peace."

"I see," Pasgen said, scraping the last spoonful of soup out of his bowl and pushing it aside.

At which point, it dawned on Rhoslyn that Pasgen was really listening to her, not to avoid needing to listen to Llanelli but because he was interested. She cocked her head at him questioningly.

"Why are you so interested in Mary?"

"I am not the least bit interested in Mary," he replied, "but I am very interested in Elizabeth eventually ascending the throne of England."

Rhoslyn blinked. "You are? Why? Oh, I know that if Elizabeth comes to reign, the Bright Court will be rich with power and the strength that comes from mortal creation. But you do not care about that. You have your mists."

"Well, I do care." Pasgen looked aside. "Gaenor and the others will all profit from that rich flow of power." Then he laughed, a sharp crack of sound with little mirth in it. "But my real reason is not so altruistic. I want Elizabeth to come to the throne simply because Vidal Dhu is so determined to prevent her from becoming queen. I want to see the Dark Court lean and weak instead of battening on others' misery."

"Vidal," Rhoslyn said, suddenly thoughtful. "I never thought of him, I wonder if Vidal can have anything to do with Seymour's behavior, because, if the rumors coming out of Queen Catherine's household are true, Seymour is quite mad."

"What rumors?"

Rhoslyn sighed. "That Seymour is paying particular attention to Elizabeth. He caught her in the garden of Chelsea last summer and cut her dress to pieces while his wife held her. And while they were in Seymour Place in London, where the servants mix and mingle with the servants of other high households, it was whispered that he invaded the girl's bedchamber while she was still abed."

Pasgen shook his head. "It seems to me that Lady Mary already must have all the information she needs to blacken Elizabeth."

"Well, no, because Catherine was always there. Even Mary cannot make a scandal about Elizabeth's behavior when Seymour's wife was helping him and most of Elizabeth's maidens and Catherine's ladies were taking part in the games."

"Is that true?" Pasgen asked.

"I have no idea what is true," Rhoslyn said irritably while the soup bowls were removed—Llanelli's still almost full—and a roast goose and a roast haunch of lamb placed on the table. "And I cannot meet with Aleneil to find out. We were seen the last time and Mary asked me what I was doing with one of Elizabeth's ladies. I could not even ask Aleneil at the ball because Elizabeth was there and Harry . . . if the smallest hint that Elizabeth is not perfect reaches Harry, he flies into a rage. I wish you could find out whether Seymour really is pursuing Elizabeth and stop him if he is."

Llanelli chose a slice of the goose and settled back in her chair with some satisfaction. Pasgen was filling his plate with meat and vegetables, but his attention was on Rhoslyn and he was clearly interested in stopping Seymour's activities. His eyes were bright and intent as he questioned Rhoslyn about where Seymour was likely to be found away from Elizabeth and bemoaning his mistake in attacking Elizabeth some years before. It was no use, he said, to wear any disguise since Elizabeth could see through illusion in the mortal world.

If Pasgen were busy in the mortal world, Llanelli thought, he would not be confronting Vidal. She did not actually eat much of the goose because she was so terribly afraid. Pasgen said Vidal would not come or send servants to the empty house, but he was wrong. It had not been a shadow that frightened her; it had been one of Vidal's henchmen. She even knew him; Goeel, holding out a pouch of oleander, calling softly that he had a gift for her.

When she had not moved toward him, he had started to rush forward likely to seize her, but Lliwglas had opened the door and he had withdrawn into the shadows. She did not dare tell Pasgen about Goeel; he would react like an angry child who had not got his way. Pasgen was a fool to think he could attack Vidal and win. Was not Goeel's presence proof that Pasgen could not protect the place? Vidal was the stronger.

It would be best if Rhoslyn and Pasgen found admittance to the Bright Court. Then they would have Oberon's protection and Vidal would not dare harm them. She must find a way to convince Pasgen that she did not need him or Rhoslyn. She put a piece of the goose in her mouth and chewed and chewed and chewed; the lump in her throat made it impossible to swallow.

Chapter 26

Elizabeth was chagrined to discover that her dearling Denno was right—as he so often and so insufferably was—about her time at Court. She did not suffer agonies of missing him. It was not that she ever forgot him. He was in her mind every moment, but her thoughts were happy, warm, and comfortable. She remembered past pleasure and the passionate praise of her lover, which armored her against the suggestive flirtations of self-seeking courtiers who then turned to others. And she thought of all the news she and Denno would have to discuss when they were curled together in his bed.

There were puzzles, too, she thought with satisfaction, that her Denno would be able to explain. She already had reasons to be grateful to him for keeping her abreast of the shifting of power and position in the Court. Most of his information came from William Cecil, and Elizabeth made sure to seek Cecil out and to thank him for his courtesies to her. He had risen in the world of power and was now personal secretary to the Protector.

Most important to Elizabeth and one thing that made her separation from her Denno worthwhile was her meetings with Edward. The sweet, shown in their very first meeting, was that Edward still loved her. He was not awesome in person as her father had been, but for a little boy of eleven, he had great dignity.

Elizabeth responded full willingly. She had curtsied right to the ground when she approached him, bending her knee every few steps as she came closer. On the fifth curtsey, Edward had come forward to take her hand, lift her to her feet, and invite her to sit on a bench—for which he ordered a cushion and signed to be drawn close to his great chair.

He had leaned forward to kiss her cheek, glancing sidelong at the Protector, who was standing near, and murmured, "I can do no more, dearest of sisters."

It seemed quite mad to Elizabeth that Somerset should object to her affection for Edward and his for her, but that was one of the puzzles she hoped Denno could explain. And as for her and Edward, she was experienced in Court life and knew just what to do and say.

After launching into the required questions about her brother's health and replying to his questions about hers, she said, "I like my new tutor very much, but I do miss Master Coke, although he was dreadfully strict."

When she mentioned Coke's name, Edward cast an anxious glance over toward Somerset but at the last words, she saw relief in the boy's eyes. Apparently the Protector did not want Edward to be fond of anyone, perhaps except himself. If so, Elizabeth thought, he was going about winning Edward's affection in the wrong way.

"Yes," the king said, "we are reading Cato, who is not very entertaining. He was a stoic, you know."

"No, not entertaining, but a good teacher of moral conduct."

She then quoted in Latin some lines about truth and honor, casting a quick glance at the Protector, who had turned toward them with a slight frown, which showed, Elizabeth thought, that he did not understand. Doubtless Somerset had learned Latin, but it was years behind him.

Edward promptly added a tag that was so well known that everyone who had studied Latin would know it. Elizabeth came back with another tag, also popular . . . and Somerset's frown cleared. Then he looked away.

In Latin, Edward then said softly, "He has even sent Barnaby away. I have now no one."

"I wish I could be with you," Elizabeth murmured. "We had such pleasure learning together. But you are king now, Your Majesty. Being alone is one of the burdens of that state." Tears filled her eyes but she blinked them back.

"But being poor is not," Edward hissed. "I am kept poorer than a street beggar. I cannot even give a shilling to someone who does a service for me. I should have a decent purse to spend."

"Indeed, you should," Elizabeth agreed, and seeing Somerset look at her over his shoulder, smiled and clapped her hands together softly, as if admiring a riposte by Edward.

He saw where she had looked, also smiled, and clapped as if satisfied with some success, his expression not directed so much at Elizabeth as at what they were saying. That seemed to reassure the Protector. At that moment William Cecil came across the room and bowed to Somerset, to whom he said something very softly. Both men moved away.

Edward took a quick breath and went back to English. "You must know the Protector's brother, Sir Thomas, who is Queen Catherine's husband. Through my servant, John Fowler, Sir Thomas has offered to augment my purse. He laughs and says he remembers being young far better than Somerset."

"I have no doubt of that," Elizabeth replied somewhat dryly. "For a grown man, he is very childish." She remembered some of the things Denno had told her about Thomas, things he could not have said out of jealousy because she had never told him about Thomas' flirtations. "Seymour certainly likes to get his own way and I have heard"—she lowered her voice even more—"he is not altogether honest."

A rather mulish set firmed Edward's mouth. "Twice I have needed to borrow from my servants and then needed to beg Somerset for a little money with which to repay them."

"He gave it to you, did he not?"

"A king should not need to beg."

Elizabeth heard the hurt pride and the irritation. It would do no good for Edward to be angry at her also. "Oh, no," she said. "That is true. Only if you take money from Sir Thomas, be on your guard. I think he is not so careless and innocent as he pretends. Even in his own household, mostly he wants a return when he gives a gift."

"I have already done him a favor in supporting his marriage to Queen Catherine," Edward said resentfully.

"Yes." Elizabeth saw Somerset coming toward them with a man she did not know and said hastily, "But that will only whet his appetite for more favors, since he found you willing once."

"Ah," Edward said. "You are a good and careful sister."

"I love you and wish only your good in all things."

And then Somerset was bowing and presenting the French ambassador who had, he said, a message from his master for King Edward. Elizabeth took the hint and rose to her feet, dropping another curtsey and backing away. Kat Ashley, who had been waiting at a little distance, came to join her.

"Sir Thomas was looking for you," Kat said. "They are dancing in the farther apartment. But when I said you were talking to the king, he went away. Will you go to join him in the dancing or do you hope to be recalled by King Edward?"

"No, the king will not summon me again," Elizabeth said, knowing it would be most unwise for him to do so while Somerset was there. "Let us go and watch the dancing."

Kat laughed. "You will not watch long. All the young men want to dance with you."

That was true enough and Elizabeth did not spend much time by Kat's side. Robert Dudley was the first to reach her and she accepted his invitation gladly. She knew him slightly because he had been one of the young men who attended the "school" Catherine had formed in Hampton Court. Elizabeth remembered him as being quick and clever but not much interested in classical learning. Still, Dudley was among the most amusing of the young men and she could easily have been more than safely attracted to him if her mind and heart had not been full of a green-eyed, long-eared lover who was quicker, cleverer, and far, far more elegant.

Dudley would gladly have kept her as his partner longer, but Lord Strange came right onto the dance floor to claim her hand for the next set. And so it went, one partner claiming her from another. Somewhere during a laughing exchange, Thomas was there and took her hand, leaving Henry Brandon, who thought he was about to lead her into the set, astonished and annoyed.

"I thought you were going to save all your dances for me," Thomas said, frowning down at her. "Did we not agree to that in Seymour Place?"

Elizabeth remembered the teasing conversation. "But that was in jest," she said, raising her brows. "How should I wait only for you?" She laughed again, but uneasily. "I would have been left standing by the wall for set after set while you danced with Queen Catherine."

"And is that not only right and proper?" Thomas asked archly, with a smirk.

The expression made Elizabeth even more uneasy. Could he believe that she was jealous of his attentions to his wife? Had she been wrong in enjoying his rough playfulness, even encouraging it? She should not have done that, she thought now, but it was very hard to reject him in any way he would understand when Catherine was watching. Elizabeth could feel heat rising in her face and knew that she was blushing, which made her blush even more.

"That you should dance first and most often with your wife is of course right and proper," she said, and was aware that her voice was low and choked.

The smug satisfaction on Thomas' face was awful, as if her anger and embarrassment was a confession. Fortunately the movement of the dance parted them so that Elizabeth was able to regain some of her composure. However when they had gone down the aisle and came together again, he pulled her closer, almost breast to breast.

"But would I not have been worth the wait?" Thomas murmured, breathing in her ear.

Elizabeth was shocked and enraged by the self-assurance. What was wrong with the man? He was married. Did he think himself so irresistible that she would forget her place in the world and her obligation to Queen Catherine for so great a multitude of kindnesses as to play love-games with Catherine's husband? Fury and shame choked her and she could think of no clever retort before the figure of the dance separated them again.

In the next movement they changed partners and Elizabeth noted that Thomas was murmuring, probably sweet words, into the next lady's ear. He pulled her close in the *pas de deux* too, and she laughed and pretended to push him away. Elizabeth was greatly relieved. She had been taking too seriously what was just Thomas' way. Nonetheless, she resolved, as Henry Brandon finally claimed her for the next set, snatching her away from Thomas' outstretched hand—stretched out but almost carelessly, as if he expected her to set her hand in his instead of Brandon's—that she would use more caution in responding to Thomas when they were *en famille* again.

That thought lost its sharp anxiety over the next week and grew even less insistent when Elizabeth asked and was given permission to extend her visit to Court over Christmas and the New Year. Because she knew her request had irritated the Protector, she was not sure she had done the right thing, but she had no one to ask for sound advice. Kat could only see that there was no impropriety and that the request had given the king pleasure, and Denno was out of reach. As he had warned her, it was impossible to find a moment's privacy when she made an excuse to visit his house to ask his advice. At least a dozen highborn ladies, including the duchess of Somerset, who watched her like a hawk, had insisted on accompanying her.

However, when she had come to take her leave of the king, Edward had looked so lost, his face frozen into the proper expression, his eyes dark and glittering with unshed tears, that instead of taking leave, she had gone down on her knees and begged to be allowed to stay with him through the holidays. Fear had warred with desire for an instant on the young king's face, and then he had said in a loud, if rather tremulous, voice that he would enjoy above all other things having his sister's company for some weeks longer.

He said it loud and clear if shakily. A concourse of gentlemen, among them Sir Anthony Denny, Lord Russell, the marquess of Dorset, and the earl of Warwick were standing close by. All of them smiled at this mark of innocent filial affection. Most had been witness during Elizabeth's visit to the conversation between the children. All had been impressed by the learning of each, of the serious discussion of the classical texts and of religion, of the respect of the girl and the dignity of the boy. Elizabeth had asked no favors and the young king had said not one word that the Council would not have approved.

The chancellor, Sir Richard Rich, and the Protector did not smile, but even the Protector was not comfortable about denying what everyone else felt was so harmless a pleasure. But now and again during any time she spent with Edward, Elizabeth was aware of Somerset's eyes on her and his gaze was not kind. Nonetheless, in the face of Somerset's decree that there be no giving of New Year's gifts, she managed to pass the fancifully embroidered handkerchief to Edward and saw him tuck it quickly away, and when the young king asked for a portrait of her, she looked to Somerset, and when he shrugged, not too graciously, she quickly agreed.

Perhaps comforted by the thought of having her picture, Edward parted from Elizabeth almost cheerfully. And having been parted from Denno for near a month, she was so eager to feel his arms around her again that she felt little regret, even about leaving the gaieties and formalities of the Court, which she loved.

She was waiting in Blanche's bedchamber near the Gate between the wardrobes when Denno came through the very day she arrived in Chelsea. Joy burst like fireworks within her when she saw him, and she cast herself into his arms, kissing his neck and chin again and again as she hugged him.

"I do not think I need to ask whether you missed me," he said, between returning her kisses on any part of her he could reach.

"Shhhh," she responded in a low murmur, "Eleanor is asleep, but not sleep-spelled, and a man's voice . . ."

He nodded, disengaged them from each other, and went out, crossing the dressing room and just barely opening the door into the bedchamber. Through the narrow slit, he pointed a finger at Eleanor, who was sleeping peacefully in the truckle bed at the foot of Elizabeth's high four-poster. Denoriel whispered the spell. As he spoke, the girl relaxed utterly into a sleep that almost nothing could break.

An arm snaked around his waist and he was turned, his head pulled down so Elizabeth could kiss his mouth hungrily. "Yes," she said. "I missed you. Oh, not so much at first, but more and more as the days passed."

Denoriel's eyes glowed, but he did not answer, only rushed her back through the dressing room where Blanche sat sewing, smiling too, past Blanche's bed and through the Gate. When he swept her off the platform, her nightdress was a day gown. Miralys was waiting, but Denoriel did not mount.

"I've taken you to Elfhame Elder-Elf," he murmured, bending his head toward her waiting lips; his expression was absent, his attention on her face, but the words that came out of his mouth were those he had been planning to say. "You wanted to learn a sleep spell, and Mechain and Elidir have been asking for you, Harry says . . ." He hesitated, tasted her lips again, and then said, his voice husky, "But perhaps we should go back to Llachar Lle first."

The pressure of his body against hers and the memory of their shared passion was enough to arouse her. She stroked the arm that embraced her, lifted her mouth to him again.

"Yes." Elizabeth's eyes were slightly glazed, but a moment later she had turned her head so that their lips did not meet and said, "No. You can't twist time here." She sighed and stepped away from him just enough so they did not touch. "They would know when we used the Gate, and I would be thinking about Da and the others waiting for us instead of just feeling you touch me. I couldn't properly enjoy myself."

"I could send an air spirit—" Denoriel began, and then shook his head and laughed.

"Yes?" Elizabeth laughed too, if a trifle shakily. "And what would you have it say? That my lord and my lady were too busy . . . ah . . . futtering to come right now."

"I could have found another excuse," he said, as he swung up onto Miralys and then bent to raise her to the pillion saddle, "but I'm afraid they never would have believed me. Elidir and Mechain have been amusing themselves mightily at my expense . . . but not when Harry is there."

Elizabeth felt heat rush up over her throat and face. "Is Da angry? Is he ashamed of me for . . . for taking a lover? Does he think I have sinned? But we were together at the ball and he was perfectly happy with me, although he did ask where his little girl had gone."

"I'm afraid Harry didn't . . . ah . . . understand at the ball that we were lovers. He was too taken up with Rhoslyn, trying to make her comfortable in the Bright Court ambience. It was only after you were at Court, when I was bemoaning my miserably chaste and bereft state that he realized . . ."

"What shall I do?" Elizabeth cried.

"Nothing," Denno said, turning in the saddle to look at her. "Just be what you have always been to him, his beloved little sister. He isn't angry or ashamed, not really. He . . . he is afraid he will lose you."

"Lose me? He cannot lose me. He is my Da, my place to be when everything else is gone."

Denoriel uttered a somewhat forced laugh. "Now you are making *me* jealous."

"Do not be ridiculous, Denno," Elizabeth said sharply. "You are my beating heart, my love, my life. You share my thoughts, my troubles, my joys, and give them all meaning. Da is . . . is like a dark cave where I can rest when I can endure my struggles with life no more."

"I am appeased." Denno leaned toward her and kissed her briefly. "But do not quarrel with your poor Da if he seems a little stiff with me. He is, I am afraid, a little angry with me for turning his little girl into a grown woman."

"I . . . I think I will just not notice anything. That way there need be no explanations. I know. I will tell him about the Protector watching me and not really wanting Edward to care for me. Perhaps he will be able to suggest how I can appease him."

"Very clever, love. Very clever. Harry had plenty of experience of envy and jealousy at Court."

While Denno was speaking, Elizabeth had looked around her in surprise. In Logres or Avalon, Miralys seemed to take no more than three or four steps to bring them to Llachar Lle or the Academicia. It seemed to her that Elfhame Elder-Elf must be a very long way from the Gate. But it was not. She could see a number of small houses set around a pretty valley, just a short walk away. There was of course no sun, but somehow the houses seemed sunlit. And she could see Miralys progressing toward the valley at just about the speed a good horse would make.

Of course, as soon as Miralys sensed they were ready to join Harry and his friends, they were at Elidir's small cottage. Elizabeth sighed. It was convenient to have an elvensteed who would take you where you wanted to be almost as soon as you decided you wanted to be there, but it still struck her as making life too easy. If one did not need to struggle for anything, where did one find any spice in one's life?

One did not, Elizabeth thought, as she recalled that many of the Sidhe in Elfhame Elder-Elf had been near to drifting off into Dreaming until her clever Da had found something ugly and dangerous for them to do. She giggled and pressed her face into Denno's back. Of course, there was such a thing as too much spice, like her life too frequently had.

Still, although Underhill was a wonderful place for a short visit, like being in a pleasant dream, she had no desire to live among its easy ways permanently—aside from the delights of Denno's bed.

It did appear to agree with her Da though, Elizabeth thought, when Miralys came to a halt. He looked as young and happy as when he lived in the mortal world, and he jumped to his feet to catch her in his arms as Denno lowered her from Miralys' saddle.

He hugged her hard, then held her away from him for a long moment, searching her face. In the next moment Elizabeth put her arms around his neck and cuddled her head under his chin.

"You are my Da," she murmured. "You will always be my Da and nothing can change that . . . nothing."

"Yes," he said, and hugged her tight again. "You come first, love, because you are my little girl, no matter how grown up you get, you will always be Da's little girl."

"That is my anchor and my safety, to know you are here if I need you."

He cast a glance over her head at Denoriel, who had dismounted and was standing near. Obviously, considering Sidhe hearing, Denoriel had been aware of the exchange, but he only smiled. For a moment, Harry looked at him defiantly. Denoriel came forward and put his arms around both of them. Harry stiffened, then relaxed, shrugged, and sighed.

When the tableau broke and Harry stepped aside, Mechain and Elidir came up to greet her. Both shook their heads and remarked with smiles on how quickly she was grown from a child to a woman. Elizabeth noticed the frown that came and went on Da's face, and she said she had a problem that her dearling Denno could not help with, but she was sure that Da could. Harry was obviously surprised, but he looked eager and, Elizabeth saw with relief, smiled apologetically at Denoriel.

Food and drink appeared on a clean white table in front of the cottage, and as they ate and drank Elizabeth described Somerset's suspicion of her. "It is quite unreasonable," she ended. "I am too young to have any influence with anyone, and poor Edward is so lonely!"

"Sit for the portrait Edward wants immediately," Harry said, "and write to him. Be careful that there is nothing in your letters beyond the personal and whatever you wish to say about your lessons—as long as what you say does not reflect in any way on any political situation, does not parallel any political situation."

"But I may write my affection?"

"So long as it is phrased within the proper formality and dignity suitable to a king."

"Yes, of course," Elizabeth agreed sadly. "Poor Edward. He never did understand how to separate private friendship from public behavior. I remember when we were private that I used to hug him and kiss him and that he was surprised when I did not do so in front of his tutor or foreign visitors. I think it is possible he was openly too close to Barnaby, which is why Barnaby got sent to France."

"And how did you learn this fine art?" Harry asked, amused.

"Why from Denno!" Elizabeth said with emphasis. "I have been privately loving and publicly distanced from Denno since I was eight years old. I may slip in a glance or two, specially when something is funny to both of us, but in public there is a vast difference between us. Lord Denno is an old friend, so he wins smiles and occasionally even a touch of the hand, but I make clear he is still only a rich merchant."

Harry shuddered. "I cannot tell you how grateful I am to whatever caused my illness—no matter that it was ill-intended. I could not have endured much more of the Court."

"Well, perhaps Edward will not be so isolated forever," Denoriel said. "I made it my business to visit Denny and Cecil while Elizabeth was at Court. Denny was uneasy and William Cecil was frankly worried. Both fear that the Protector is making too many enemies. I suspect he will not last long and that Edward will make no attempt to save him."

"Nor would I," Elizabeth said, "but he is all powerful now and his dislike of me makes me uneasy. There are too many people around me all the time, servants I do not know who remain even when I dismiss my ladies." She looked at Elidir and Mechain. "That is why I hope you will be able to teach me a sleep spell and that I have power enough to use it."

Elidir and Mechain nodded.

"The trouble is," Mechain said, "that you need two different kinds. You cannot have servants or guards who are supposed to be watching you falling over asleep. The true sleep spell, *bod cyfgadur,* would be fine for the ladies who attend you at night, once they are in bed, but you need another kind also."

Elidir nodded. "The other spell, *bod oergeulo,* is not so much sleep as a blanking of the mind. The bespelled person would seem to be awake—a guard, for example, would continue to stand and watch—but actually would see, hear, and remember nothing at all until the spell is broken."

"Oh, that sounds wonderful!" Elizabeth exclaimed, bright-eyed and grinning.

"Oh no you don't!" Denoriel said, shaking his head. "No spell unless you promise to use it only in utmost need. You can get away with stickfast, *cilgwythio,* and *gwythio* because they seem like small accidents, but having a person stop like a statue . . . that could not be thought natural or, worse, it might be interpreted as some kind of disease and ruin that person's life."

"Oh." Elizabeth sighed, then added somewhat bitterly. "You are right. I never thought of that. Worse, if I should be suspected of causing the state . . . The last thing I want is to be whispered a witch as well as a whore."

"Who said such things of you?" Harry roared, rising.

Elizabeth caught his arm and kissed his cheek. "No one you can punish," she sighed. "It is Mary. Mary, who used to be so kind to me, now seems to hate me more and more. I swear I have done nothing . . ."

"There is something else," Mechain said. "You must never, never use that spell with your full power, Elizabeth."

"My full power?" Elizabeth repeated. "But whatever that is, I cannot touch it. Tangwystl tried and tried to find a way for me to tap that power."

"When you are frightened or very angry," Mechain said, squeezing Elizabeth's hand gently, "the gate to that power opens. If you cast the spell with that power, you will wipe out the mind completely and forever. So will you promise me faithfully that you will not use this spell when you are angry or frightened?"

"I do promise. I do," Elizabeth said instantly, her eyes wide and her cheeks paler than ever. "Oh, that would be terrible. I would never forgive myself if I made someone mindless. How dreadful." She swallowed. "Perhaps you had better not teach me that spell," she added reluctantly.

Elidir and Mechain consulted each other without speaking and finally Elidir said, "We did consider not mentioning this spell, but Elizabeth, my dear, in the life you will lead it would be very useful to you . . . very useful."

"We can make it harder to use," Mechain said. "We can teach you the spell so that you must say the whole thing. That would prevent you from pointing at someone and saying *fiat* when you were in a raging temper. By the time you spoke the whole spell, you would have passed the first, high fury."

"But how could I use the spell then?" Elizabeth asked, and

laughed. "I mean, no one is going to stand there and let me cast a spell on them—not to mention that I would then certainly be accused of witchcraft."

"Oh, no." Elidir smiled at her. "We are not idiots, my pet. What you would do is say the whole spell in your mind and then point your finger or, better, touch the person and say *epikaloumai*."

"That is Greek," Elizabeth said. "It means 'I invoke.'"

"So it does," Mechain agreed. "We use a lot of Greek in our spells."

"And there should not be any danger in being slow to call up this spell. It is not for defense, like tanglefoot. You will have time enough to recite the whole thing while you do something innocent, like reading or perhaps embroidering."

Elizabeth had begun to smile again. "Yes, I see that." She took a deep breath. "When do you wish to start?"

Chapter 27

It was indeed fortunate, Elizabeth thought as she reluctantly released Denno and slipped into her bed, that time Underhill could be stretched. Between learning the sleep spells—she would have to try the first one on Alice Finch tonight—and cooling the heat that her long separation from Denno had generated, she would not have had had time to close her eyes at all in a mortal night. As it was, she had had a full night's rest before returning to Seymour Place.

She smiled up at her bedcurtains as she thought it was more than sleep spells Elidir and Mechain could teach her. Before Denno could display his eagerness to whisk her back to Llachar Lle as soon as she had the spells fixed in her mind, and allow Da to think about what they would be doing there, Mechain had said she was sorry to be inhospitable but she and Elidir had to get to the Elves' Faire. And when Da had asked what they wanted there, both had looked at him as if he were losing his mind and said it was mortal Tuesday and he had told *them* he wanted to meet Rhoslyn there.

Da hadn't told them any such thing, Elizabeth thought, grinning. He had blinked with surprise; but any discomfort he might have felt about Denno taking her off to Denno's rooms had been pushed out of Da's mind. And he had gone off with them to see if they could find Rhoslyn with no more than a quick kiss on her forehead and a "Until we meet once more."

Then Elizabeth frowned. Da seemed very interested in Rhoslyn.

377

He had said he wanted to make her comfortable at the ball, but surely his dancing with her and asking her to eat with them was more than kindliness. And she thought there was a distance between Da and Mwynwen now.

But Rhoslyn was Unseleighe. Was it safe for Da to be interested in her? She would not dare harm him physically; Oberon's blue star still burned on his forehead, but she could hurt him other ways. Elizabeth drew a breath as pain flicked through her at the thought that Denno might abandon her. No. That could not happen. But what could she do to protect Da? He would laugh at her warnings—she was his little girl.

She would have to ask Denno. Da would listen to him. But was any warning necessary? Da knew Rhoslyn was Unseleighe, and Rhoslyn was . . . nice. She had really cared about Richey. Lady Alana liked her. And Da . . . well, Da was a grown man now. He wouldn't be pleased that she interfered in his life, any more than she was pleased at the thought that he might interfere in hers. Her instinct told her that Rhoslyn was no longer a threat. Perhaps she should listen to it.

Sighing and stretching, Elizabeth sat up, leaned forward to look at Eleanor Fitzalan, who was still under the spell Denno had cast, soundly asleep. Smiling, she whispered, *dihuno*, then lay down again while Eleanor began to stir.

For the following weeks Elizabeth was aware of little beside the renewed pleasures of her body and the adventures she shared with Denno, and often with Da, Underhill. It was just as well that lessons had been temporarily suspended because Master Grindal was ill. Catherine sent her own physician and Elizabeth sent what comforts she could think of. Now and again, Elizabeth felt a little guilty because she did not worry much . . .

. . . and she felt worse when Grindal died.

"I should have begged you to bring Mwynwen to him," she said to Denno and Da, tears streaking her cheeks, a few days after her tutor's death had been broken to her.

"No, love," Da said, an arm around her shoulders so her head rested against his breast. "It would have done no good. Mwynwen cannot cure most mortal diseases. She can draw off elven poisons, break curses, and heal most wounds and elven illnesses, but she could not draw off the mortal plague, which is what killed Master Grindal."

"I am sorry about him," Denno agreed, patting her hand, "and you must grieve, of course, for he served you well, but I must warn you not to grieve too long lest you find yourself with a teacher you will not like. It would behoove you to think of a man you would enjoy learning from and suggest him to Queen Catherine. If she makes an arrangement, I doubt the Protector would interfere, but if you have no tutor..."

"Master Ascham," Elizabeth said, the thought of the strict and rigid tutor Somerset or his wife might favor making her sit upright and wipe away her tears. "I know Master Ascham would like to be my tutor; he has hinted as much to me now and again. We do not agree on all subjects, but he taught me to write so beautifully and—" she found a watery smile "—I enjoy our quarrels."

"Yes, well, take your preference to Queen Catherine soon," Denno urged. "The Court has moved to Greenwich, but it cannot be very long before the news of Master Grindal's death comes to Somerset."

Ah, Elizabeth thought, so that was why she had not seen Sir Thomas recently and why Catherine had been so quiet. Thomas must be pursuing Edward at Greenwich, giving him money and hinting that Edward should appeal to the Council for a change of guardians. Edward, Elizabeth had heard Thomas say at dinner one day, would be much happier if Somerset managed the affairs of the kingdom and Thomas managed the king.

Elizabeth was not certain what she thought of Thomas' notion. Edward probably would be happier, as Thomas was far more light-hearted than his brother the Protector, but would Edward be a better king for Thomas' guardianship? She put the thought aside while Da took her and Denno to the Elves' Faire to seek out steel bolts for his gun ... and to meet Rhoslyn. Elizabeth greeted her pleasantly and pretended to be much taken with a pretty silver dagger, but she watched the Dark Sidhe and her Da as closely as she could.

She forgot all about Master Ascham until she came down to the queen's parlor after breaking her fast the next morning and found the room empty. Then she remembered that Sir Thomas had doubtless spent the day at Greenwich and either had not come back to Seymour Place at all or had come back very late. So much the better if he were out of the house, Elizabeth thought; she did not trust him not to interfere with her choice of a tutor.

Having settled herself to a new piece of embroidery, Elizabeth

sent Alice Finch to request a meeting with the queen. To her
surprise, Catherine did not at once come to the parlor nor immediately send for her. She was not refused but had to wait near
half an hour and was then shown into Catherine's bedchamber.

The queen was not yet dressed and was sitting rather limply
in a padded chair by the foot of the bed. And she did not look
well! Catherine was greenish-pale and heavy-eyed.

Lovestruck herself, the first thing that leapt into Elizabeth's mind
was Sir Thomas' absence. Simultaneous with that thought came
the memories of his flirtations with her and with the other ladies.
Catherine had always laughed at what she called Thomas' antics,
but looking at Catherine's pallid face Elizabeth could not help
wondering if the queen now feared her husband was unfaithful.

She dared not say a word that might imply she had noticed
Catherine's misery, so Elizabeth launched at once into her desire
for a new tutor that would suit her taste. Catherine seemed to
welcome the subject; they spoke of Master Aylmer, Lady Jane
Grey's tutor, but Catherine hinted that Lady Jane would not be
happy sharing Aylmer with the far more animated Lady Elizabeth.
And when Elizabeth suggested Ascham, Catherine agreed at once
that he would be ideal and that she would write to him.

That made Elizabeth feel guilty about seeming to forget Master
Grindal so quickly, and she mentioned not being so indifferent to
his loss as she seemed. Catherine was immediately sympathetic,
sighing, and saying she understood. But then she leaned back
in her chair, growing noticeably paler and her lady signed to
Elizabeth that she should go.

Only then, with the thought of Master Grindal's death foremost
in her mind, did it occur to Elizabeth that the queen might not
be grieved over her husband's behavior but seriously unwell. She
asked the lady who accompanied her back to the parlor, but
received no more than a smile and a shake of the head. Next,
Elizabeth set Blanche to ask tactful questions of Catherine's maids.
The result was that she was frightened half out of her wits by
learning that Catherine was frequently sick and had trouble keeping down her food.

Then Elizabeth herself waylaid Catherine's maid and asked
what physician had been summoned and what he had advised;
the maid was evasive. Elizabeth asked whether there was anything
she could do, offering Lord Denno's ability to obtain exotic and

expensive medications. To her surprise the maid seemed to be stifling laughter, but aloud the woman only made excuses and said she knew of nothing that would help.

If those words had not frightened Elizabeth so much, she would have understood at once from the behavior of the maids and Catherine's ladies that the queen was with child. As it was, she burst into tears when she reached her own apartment and could not eat her dinner when she regained enough calm to join the company. Fortunately she was not recovered enough to look other than terrified and miserable, and Catherine sought her out and asked what was wrong—which made Elizabeth burst into tears again and wail that she lost everyone she loved.

The queen was shocked and asked pressing questions, eventually wringing from Elizabeth the fear that her beloved stepmother was failing. Whereupon Catherine began to laugh.

"Oh my poor Bessie, it does my heart good to know that you love me so much, but you mustn't fear for me. I did not mean to frighten you. I only did not want to say too much too soon lest Tom be disappointed. I believe I am with child, my dear one. That is why I am sick."

"With child!" Elizabeth echoed, catching the queen's hands in her own. "Oh by God's sweet grace, how stupid I am!"

"Yes, well, it is only two months and one can never be certain so soon."

"I will pray it is so, madam. With all my heart, I hope it is so."

Later, of course, after the first joy of relief had passed, Elizabeth was not so completely satisfied as she had been. She added prayers for a safe delivery and a quick return to health to her prayers that the queen be truly carrying a child.

Toward the end of February, Sir Thomas left the Court. He did not seem in a terribly good mood and said nothing about what he had accomplished. He was pleased about the child Catherine was now sure she carried, but less pleased by Catherine's continued uneasy health. He suggested, and Catherine agreed with some relief, that they should return to Chelsea, where the purer air and water might do her good.

Elizabeth was equally happy with the projected move and looked forward to the greater comfort of Chelsea some time in March. Although Denno had managed a Gate in her tiny dressing room in Seymour Place, the house was much more crowded than Chelsea

Palace and exposure a greater danger. Poor Denno had needed to
use the Don't-see-me spell several times to avoid detection.

Also in Seymour Place Elizabeth's rooms were only a flight of
back stairs above those of Thomas and Catherine. Only servants
were supposed to use those stairs, but one morning Thomas,
wearing nothing but a night gown, burst into her bedchamber
"to say good morning" to her. Elizabeth sent Blanche scurrying
to Kat's chamber and remained as long as she could behind the
dressing room door.

She came out when Thomas threatened to come in; the dressing
room was so small they would have been nearly breast to breast.
He made some jest about how long it had taken her to get into
her clothing and professed to see some irregularity in the way
her points were tied. She was trying to ward him off, having a
feeling that the points, which she knew Blanche had tied, would
be soon undone and perhaps her skirt down on the floor, when
mercifully Kat entered the room.

This time Kat was not amused by Thomas' behavior. She gaped
at his naked legs and flapping gown and cried out that it was not
decent for a man to visit a maiden's bedchamber in such disarray.
All Thomas' good humor disappeared; he snapped angrily that he
intended no harm, only to please Elizabeth with early morning
cheer. In reply to which Kat said that such cheer could ruin a
maiden's reputation and that if he did not promise not to come
unclothed to Elizabeth's chamber again, she would have to beg
the queen either to accompany him or to send Elizabeth away.

He left in a temper, and Elizabeth was quite alarmed. She certainly
did not want Kat to trouble Queen Catherine, who was having a
very sickly pregnancy. However, she realized she could not take a
chance of Thomas' catching her in a nightdress so she decided to
ask Denno to return her to the mortal world fully clothed.

Denno, of course, asked why. Elizabeth sighed, but it was what
she had expected and she had deliberately chosen a time when
Da was with them to describe Thomas' flirtation, thinking Da's
presence would prevent Denno from scolding her. Oddly, it was
Da who was most upset and who lectured her on the danger
any slur on her reputation would be to the likelihood she would
come to the throne.

Elizabeth said, "Oh, Da, don't say that. Edward is so young,
younger than I, and he is healthy and clever."

"Master Grindal was healthy and clever, too, and he is dead," Harry said, shaking his head. "I do not wish Edward any ill. I will be very happy if he lives a long and fruitful life. Believe me, Bess, my love, I do *not* wish you to come to the throne. It is a hard and bitter life to rule. But if any accident should befall Edward . . . Mary is much older than you and she is in poor health. It is your duty to be ready to keep England safe, for a failure in the direct line—such as your disgrace and removal from the succession—will mean civil war."

Elizabeth stared at her half brother. Denno looked down at his hands, then squarely at Elizabeth. He did not wish to burden her either with hope or with fear, but he felt she needed to know more. This last year, living in safety with Catherine, she had become less cautious, less suspicious. Or perhaps it was just her age; halflings, as those between the age of childhood and full adulthood were called, were notoriously wild and careless, unable to believe that any ill could befall them.

"There has always been the possibility that you would rule," he said. "It is one of the futures in the Visions of the FarSeers."

"Oh," Elizabeth said, but she did not look distressed at all. Her eyes grew very bright. "Truly? Is there truly a possibility that I will come to the throne?" She drew a breath. "I will be more careful. Thomas is only boisterous and careless, but perhaps I have not discouraged him as much as I should."

"And why not?" Harry asked sharply.

Elizabeth blushed faintly. "I suppose a little because the flirting flattered me, but truly, mostly it is because Catherine becomes distressed if he is too firmly rejected."

"I have been careless, too." Denoriel sighed. "It was so . . . ah . . . convenient for you to come in a nightdress, but I see it will not do. You will need to bring some clothing to keep in my lodgings at Llachar Lle and I will make sure you are fully dressed when I bring you back to the mortal world in the morning. If you are already up and at your book, Seymour cannot talk about undone points or have any excuse to touch you."

Harry shook his head. "Grace of God, Catherine is your stepmother. Seymour is your stepfather by marriage. And to meddle with you, second in line for the throne, is treason. His behavior could ruin him, too. Why is the man such a fool?"

Suddenly Denoriel felt much better. He had been seething

with rage and, yes, jealousy since Elizabeth had begun her tale of Seymour's attentions. The blush and admission that she had been flattered twisted his gut. It had taken all his determination to maintain an attitude of indifference. He knew his Elizabeth. To expose his hurt and jealousy would only encourage her to torment him. Now Harry—blessed Harry—had given him a good reason for Elizabeth to avoid Seymour.

"A very interesting question, Harry," Denoriel said, frowning. "I hope it is because he is the kind that cannot leave any pretty girl alone. But I fear there may be a darker side to his pursuit." He turned and smiled at Elizabeth. "Not that you are not worth it, my sweet, but Seymour has always seemed to me a man first devoted to himself."

"A monster of selfishness," Harry said angrily. "Would he chance hurting his breeding wife with playing with her ladies and her stepdaughter otherwise?"

"Catherine only laughs," Elizabeth put in, looking rather shamefaced.

"Who knows what hurt that laughter could conceal," Harry said, still angry.

"I am sorry, but I am afraid there is a real reason for his carelessness, which may not be carelessness at all. Do you remember, Harry, that Oberon ordered Vidal not to do or cause any hurt to Elizabeth?"

"Of course I remember."

"Vidal fears Oberon too much to violate that order by any physical attack, but do you think he has forgotten how Elizabeth's reign would benefit the Bright Court and starve the Dark of the power of misery? Vidal is very experienced in manipulating courts and courtiers. Once Catherine brought a man who might be thought attractive to women into her household, do you think Vidal would overlook the chance of removing Elizabeth from the succession by disgrace?"

Elizabeth's lips thinned into a scarcely visible line and Denoriel had to bite his own lips to hide a smile. He recalled how her eyes glowed when he mentioned the FarSeers' Vision of her as queen. Elizabeth would be playing no more games with Sir Thomas Seymour.

"You think Vidal may have sunk his hooks into Seymour?" Harry said thoughtfully.

Denoriel shrugged. "If Edward fails, Mary's reign will be short, I think. Then, if Elizabeth has been removed from the succession ... there will be civil war. Elizabeth will have partisans who oppose whoever else is proposed to take the throne. She is the legitimate heir and the people love her. Nothing could give Vidal more pleasure than a civil war in England and that would also provide opportunities for Elizabeth to be killed by her enemies—for which Oberon could not blame Vidal."

"Civil war is not to be thought of," Harry said, mouth and chin set mulishly. Duty to his country had been drilled into Henry FitzRoy, blood and bone. There had been civil war before ... most recently, the Wars of the Roses that had been finally ended in exhaustion and compromise with the ascension of his own grandfather, Henry VII, to the throne. Harry would do anything, sacrifice anything, to prevent another such bloodbath.

But unfortunately, as he well knew, there were others who would do anything to bring such a calamity to pass.

Thus, on the following mortal Tuesday, Harry went to the Elves' Faire to find Rhoslyn. Llanelli greeted him warmly. She had seen how Rhoslyn bloomed in his presence and welcomed any diversion for her daughter, who had been deeply depressed by the loss of any hope for acceptance into the Bright Court.

In an ordinary way, Llanelli would have opposed any relationship between her daughter and a mortal, knowing that a short mortal life would only cause Rhoslyn pain. But Harry was not only marked by Oberon's protection but was a permanent resident Underhill. Mortal life was greatly extended by living Underhill and Llanelli supposed that like most Sidhe Rhoslyn would grow bored with her mortal lover and abandon him long before his life ended.

In due course, Rhoslyn arrived, her whole face lighting with her smile at Harry when he proposed that they go to the Inn of Kindly Laughter for dinner. Llanelli agreed and sent them on ahead because, she said, she still had one patient to see. Rhoslyn blushed and said, "Mother!" but Harry extended his arm for her to take and Llanelli waved them away.

"I must tell you," Harry said, as soon as they were out of hearing of Llanelli, "that I have an ulterior motive. Not that I would not come without one. I cannot tell you, Rhoslyn, how much pleasure your company gives me, but I know you are kindly disposed toward Elizabeth and there may be a threat brewing for her."

"Not from Lady Mary," Rhoslyn said defensively and then, "But she does not love Elizabeth, that is true."

"No, not from Lady Mary. I would not ask you to betray Mary in any way. I think you once told me that your brother took on the guise of a mortal sorcerer called Otstargi?"

Rhoslyn shook her head vigorously. "He has not played the role of Otstargi for many years, and he promised me he would not act against Elizabeth. He is Dark Court, but would not break his word to me."

Harry laid his hand over Rhoslyn's and squeezed it gently, hearing the pain in her voice. "No, I did not mean that your brother was doing anything to hurt Elizabeth. I just wondered whether he would do me a favor and, in the guise of Otstargi, discover whether there were any unpleasant rumors linking Elizabeth and her stepmother's husband, Sir Thomas Seymour. Seymour has been misbehaving toward her, and she told me and Denno. I want to learn whatever I can about this Seymour." Harry's mouth and eyes hardened. "He might have an accident if he is any danger to my little girl."

Rhoslyn raised anxious eyes to Harry's, eyes unshadowed by envy or jealousy because of the words "my little girl." She had heard a lot of stories about how adorable Elizabeth was as a baby, and she had seen Harry's behavior to Elizabeth at the ball. Besides it was obvious that Elizabeth wanted Denoriel's attention, and not Harry's.

Or at least, not in that way.

"Pasgen knows about Seymour. I told him because when Lady Mary learned that Seymour was married, or to be married, to Queen Catherine, she wrote to offer Elizabeth a haven in her household. Elizabeth refused, very politely, but very decidedly. Mary was hurt and said no good could come of Elizabeth living in the household of a well-known lecher." Rhoslyn bit her lip. "Lady Mary would not start any ill-natured tales about Elizabeth . . . but she would believe them."

Harry sighed. "I feared as much. Even when Elizabeth was a baby, Lady Mary was of two minds about her. Mary loves all children, and she was very kind to Elizabeth after Anne's execution, but she never forgot for a moment the pain Anne had caused her mother . . . and Elizabeth was part of that."

Rhoslyn nodded. "And Elizabeth is no longer a child. She is a young woman whose manner and appearance scream aloud that she is old King Henry's daughter. Mary cannot forgive her for that. There is little left in Mary of love or sympathy for Elizabeth." She nodded again. "I will do what I can. I cannot always reach Pasgen quickly, but I know he has been in Otstargi's household recently. I will ask him to find out what he can."

"I thank you," Harry said, and raised Rhoslyn's hand and kissed it. "Elizabeth is the daughter I will never have."

As Rhoslyn had suspected, Llanelli did not have another patient but she was very pleased with herself when she saw Rhoslyn and Harry walk off deep in conversation. Rhoslyn would have him bound fast whenever she wanted him, Llanelli thought with satisfaction, then lifted her head to look enquiringly at the brown-haired, rosy-faced maid who had come to her side.

"Lady," the maid said, "there is a Sidhe in the outer chamber who begs you to come to his companion, who was torn in a personal battle."

Llanelli shook her head. "No. Tell the Sidhe that I do not visit patients. I will wait and do what I can for his companion if he will bring that companion here or to the Goblin Market or the Bazaar of the Bizarre. However, I no longer heal in any place except the three great markets."

"I have told him that already," the maid said. "He said he wishes to explain to you the pitiable condition of his companion and says he is sure you will not be so hard of heart as to refuse him."

About to tell the maid to send the insistent Sidhe away, Llanelli realized she had to leave to join Rhoslyn and Harry anyway, and went out to the receiving room. The Sidhe waiting had the usual golden hair and light eyes but was thin to emaciation. He stretched a hand toward her, but Llanelli did not raise her hand to meet his.

"I will not come with you," she said. "You waste your time. If your companion is so much injured that he or she cannot be moved, I could not heal him or her anyway. I am a good healer but not a worker of magic. There are other healers also."

"You must come. You must. My name is Goeel. Eforian told me how you healed his arm from iron poison. Only you will be able to heal my friend."

"That healing was something special. I had a . . . an instrument that I no longer possess. It was only lent to me."

"Come." Goeel took a step forward. He did not notice Lliwglas stir from against the wall beside the entryway. "I will take you to the lender of the instrument. You can borrow it again . . ."

He leapt forward but before he could seize Llanelli's arm, Lliwglas had her long, sharp, spider-leg fingers around his neck.

"No!" Llanelli cried. "Do not harm him. I do not want you to be Removed. The market permits no violence."

Lliwglas nodded and sidled around so that her body was between the Sidhe and Llanelli. "Go away," she said quietly. "I will not let you touch her, so you are wasting your time."

"Vidal wants you," the Sidhe spat at Llanelli. "And the more of his time you waste, the worse your fate will be. Come now and he will give you all the oleander you want. He will do you no harm. He only wants you as his guest so that your stubborn, stupid children will obey him as they should."

Fear paralyzed Llanelli so completely that she lost her illusion of a red-haired, hazel-eyed, full-bodied woman. The eyes faded to dull, pale green, the hair into wispy mist-white, and the clothing hung on her emaciated frame.

"Go," Lliwglas said to the angry Sidhe. "Your master is powerless here. No one can take or touch the lady. The market cares for its own."

Without touching Goeel, Lliwglas chivvied him out of Llanelli's outer chamber, keeping her body between him and any path he wished to take, except the way out of the market. He cursed and spat, but she never touched him or lost her patience, and at last he charged straight at her and struck at her with a knife he had pulled from a hidden place. Lliwglas did not even raise her arms to protect herself . . . and the Unseleighe Sidhe was Removed. Her pursed lips pulled back, showing the wolflike teeth in a smile of satisfaction. Rhoslyn's girls were constructs, but not mindless.

By the time Lliwglas returned to Llanelli's chambers, Llanelli's illusion had been restored. She had even colored her cheeks and lips a touch more than usual so that Rhoslyn would not perceive the pallor of her terror. Despite the proof that Rhoslyn's girl could and would protect her and was clever enough, now that she was warned, to avoid Removal, Llanelli was sliding down into a pit of despair.

He would have her. She knew it. Despite what Rhoslyn or Pasgen said, Llanelli knew that they could not stand against Vidal. What was she to do? She had hoped by establishing herself in the markets where they could easily visit her, she could convince her children that they could leave the Dark Court for the Bright. But if they discovered that Vidal was pursuing her and why he was pursuing her . . . and they *would* learn. Rhoslyn's girl would tell everything if Rhoslyn asked.

Smiling cheerfully, and falsely, Llanelli said to Lliwglas, "That was simple. He has learned better. He will not come here again."

"No," Lliwglas agreed stolidly; she knew Llanelli did not like it when she smiled. "He attacked me and was Removed. He will not come again."

Llanelli's heart lifted. Removed. Then he would never report to Vidal. She would have time to think about what to do. She set out for the Inn of Kindly Laughter. Her whole attention was fixed on subjects of conversation that would keep Rhoslyn too occupied to ask Lliwglas questions. She did not see Piteka, bent over a clever device for concealing a dagger, glance swiftly once in her direction.

Pasgen was at first even more difficult than usual to find and then was simply at home, just sitting in his black and white parlor, doing nothing. He was also willing—Rhoslyn would have said eager, except that it was so unlike his usual attitude toward mortal affairs—to investigate Sir Thomas Seymour. The eagerness, the obvious need to do some external task, concerned Rhoslyn, who at last asked what was wrong. Pasgen smiled faintly and said he was just tired of research about power. These last weeks, he had been involved with Gaenor in discovering why a Bright Court Sidhe's domain had come apart, nearly killing its maker.

Rhoslyn paled and whispered, "How is that possible?" She swallowed. "Is it like . . . Did it *want* to kill him?"

"No." Pasgen sighed and then uttered a somewhat shamefaced chuckle. "Gaenor and I—I am afraid we spend too much time watching and thinking about that self-willed Chaos Land. That was the first idea that came to us and we tried and tried to find even a scrap of "thinking" mist. Finally Gaenor called in her last student, Lady Hafwen."

There was no difference in Pasgen's expression; there was no change in his voice when he said the name. Nonetheless Rhoslyn's heart squeezed and she had to look down at her hands to hide her eyes.

"She had a good laugh at our expense for seeking out mysterious horrors that did not exist," Pasgen continued, without seeming to notice Rhoslyn's reaction, "and in half a day she had found what Gaenor and I completely overlooked, a basic flaw in the construction that caused the collapse. You would like Lady Hafwen, Rhoslyn. She is a maker of some ability. She was fascinated when I told her about the not-horses and your girls, about how much self-will they have."

"If she did not disapprove of my girls," Rhoslyn said, "I know I would like her. Should we arrange to meet?"

"She is Bright Court," Pasgen said flatly.

Rhoslyn's heart sank and a hot fury rose in her. Seleighe bitch, she thought. She was all sweetness and fluttering eyelashes when she recognized Pasgen's power, and then Gaenor, the old fool, must have told her that Pasgen was Dark Court and that non-Lady Hafwen had acted as if he were meat turned putrid.

"Well." Rhoslyn shook her head. "It doesn't matter. I don't have time to spend Underhill right now. I need to be with Lady Mary to try to keep her from doing any damage to Elizabeth. And I hope you will now have time to run a spike or two into Sir Thomas' wheels. He must not, out of vanity and carelessness, ruin Elizabeth's reputation."

"I will see to him," Pasgen said. "Do not give him another thought, sister. I think you will have the far harder task in soothing Mary."

"I think I may," Rhoslyn sighed. "Mary was not at all pleased by the favor Edward showed Elizabeth during the Court visit. Truly she was furious. Edward invited Elizabeth to his side often; he called her 'Sweet Sister Temperance' because she dressed simply and let her hair fall without crimpings and curlings." Rhoslyn snorted with amusement. "Clever, that Elizabeth. Mary, Edward lectured about her religious practices and urged to conform to the 'true' form of worship."

This time it was Pasgen who shook his head. "I will never understand how mortals can get so passionate about an invisible being they cannot prove exists because it does nothing at all." He chuckled again. "I wonder what they would do if Oberon appeared and sent his Thought over them."

"Call him Satan and bring a crusade of millions to destroy him," Rhoslyn said with a shudder. "Let us not create horrors. I feel I have enough to deal with. But Pasgen, it really is important that you attend to Sir Thomas. Lady Ann, the Protector's wife, also has no love for Elizabeth. I think she speaks subtle evil of Elizabeth to Somerset, partly because she is attached to Lady Mary and partly because the people cheer whenever Elizabeth appears. And Somerset listens because he does not like Edward to be attached to anyone."

"I will. I will. I will go this very day," Pasgen said.

Which he actually did, leaving his house soon after Rhoslyn did and transporting himself to Otstargi's house. There he avoided the slack-jawed servant, who could not then betray his presence in the mortal world to Vidal. In the street, he summoned a chair to take him to Seymour Place, since he did not know where it was.

The servant who came to the door opened his mouth to say no one was home but instead backed away as Pasgen entered. It was then a matter of moments for Pasgen to extract everything he knew about his master from his mind. He was only the footman who answered the door and did not know very much, but what he did know gave Pasgen considerable food for thought.

Pasgen learned of Seymour's early morning visits to Elizabeth's chamber because they were common gossip among the servants; Seymour had used the servants' back stairs and shocked two maids by his presence and his undressed condition. Pasgen knew he was not wise in the ways of mortals, but such behavior seemed so peculiar to him that he began to wonder if Seymour was not under some compulsion to bring shame to Elizabeth.

Oddly, because he had more than once, unwillingly and against his better judgment but because it was the easiest way for him, sought to destroy Elizabeth, Pasgen now felt that he "owed" her. Resentment pricked him; it was Vidal who had set him that unwelcome task. If Vidal had tried to use him to destroy Elizabeth, was it possible that it was Vidal who had set a compulsion on Seymour?

Recalling Rhoslyn's affection for Elizabeth made Pasgen feel protective, that it was "unfair" for Vidal, practiced in evil for millennia, to so test an innocent mortal halfling. He sought deeper in the footman's mind, this time keying the man's thoughts to the name Otstargi.

That brought immediate results for the footman who answered the door was usually the one who took messages or letters delivered to the house. Two letters had been received from someone named Otstargi. The first had been discarded—the servant himself had straightened and ironed the crumpled parchment, which he then sold to a scrivner. After the second, which had a strange raised seal, Sir Thomas had ordered the footman to summon a chair to take him to visit the "sorcerer's" house.

Strange raised seal, Pasgen thought with satisfaction. *So Sir Thomas was under a compulsion.* Naturally the footman knew nothing of the actual visit of Sir Thomas to Otstargi, but the servant did remember that his master had returned from Otstargi's house very excited and had given instructions to prepare for a hurried journey to the west.

The servant assumed Seymour had gone to fulfill some duty as Lord High Admiral. Pasgen doubted that, but was interested when the servant remarked on Sir Thomas' very good temper and extra liberality when he returned. That good temper had been increased on two occasions when a special messenger had come from Bristol and had lasted until the entire household had returned to Seymour Place for a visit to Court.

Closer probing about the sources of Sir Thomas' change of disposition brought an overheard snippet of conversation between Sir Thomas and his wife. Sir Thomas was displeased because Catherine had not refused permission to Elizabeth to lodge in Whitehall at the king's invitation. He was even less pleased, the servant said a maid had told him, when Elizabeth's visit was extended. The maid was rather resentful of Sir Thomas' indifference to the fact that her work would be doubled or tripled if Elizabeth was in Seymour Place. Following the tale of ill temper, Pasgen learned that Sir Thomas turned quite sour after he had followed the Court to Greenwich.

Pasgen was not at all sure about what that meant. Sir Thomas had obviously intended to accomplish some purpose at Court and had not succeeded. It was clear enough that the purpose might have been costly and that some of the cost had been defrayed by actions Sir Thomas took in the west according to advice that Vidal had given him. That seemed to be separate from his actions toward Elizabeth.

Having removed himself from the memory of the footman and

replaced himself with a garrulous, and later apologetic, stranger to London, Pasgen returned to his waiting chair. He waved the men down the street, but when they turned toward Fleet Street and were out of sight of Seymour Place, he bade them stop.

What to do next? Pasgen had no friends at Court who could tell him what caused Sir Thomas' dissatisfaction or what profit one was likely to find in Bristol. And he did not dare try to warn Elizabeth, who could see through illusion and would know him for what he was and believe he was still her enemy. He could warn Denoriel. Yes, and Denoriel could tell him who to question about Sir Thomas' activities.

With a sigh of relief, Pasgen instructed the chairmen to carry him to Lord Denno's house on Bucklersbury.

Chapter 28

"My name is Pasgen Silverhair and I am a countryman of Lord Denno's," Pasgen said to Cropper who answered the door. "I would like a word with your master. I will not take up much of his time."

The footman smiled as he bowed. "Yes, sir, I remember. You were here last year when those men got in. You left a warning about the attack for Lord Denno and then came and helped in the fight. Master Clayborne told me that you were to be welcome at any time. Lord Denno is not at home, I am sorry to say, but Master Clayborne is here."

"Master Clayborne will do very nicely," Pasgen agreed.

The footman stood aside, holding the door for Pasgen to enter and then led the way to a closed door on which he scratched. A voice replied promptly and the footman stepped inside, shutting the door behind him. Almost at once, he came out again, this time holding the door open for Pasgen to enter the room.

"Master Silverhair," Joseph Clayborne said, bowing. "I am very glad to see you because I have long wished to thank you for the warning you left for Lord Denno and the help"—then suddenly he looked anxious—"but I do hope you do not bring another warning. The last you gave was all too accurate."

Pasgen smiled. "No, I have heard no more threats directed

at my countryman. This time I hoped to learn from him some information that might be useful to me."

"Please—" Joseph gestured toward a well-padded chair opposite his own by the worktable "—do be seated. Can I get you some wine? Any refreshment?"

"A cup of wine would be welcome, if it is no trouble." Pasgen wanted an easy atmosphere in which, he hoped, Clayborne would be willing to speak confidentially.

Clayborne smiled. "No trouble at all, sir. We are very rich in wines at the moment, a ship having come in from Spain and touched at half a dozen French ports on the way. What would you like: alicant? claret? malmsey? sack?"

"Claret, if you please."

Joseph rang the bell on the table, said "Claret" to Cropper who had opened the door, and then turned to Pasgen. "May I ask, sir, what kind of information you seek? If it is about trade, it is possible that I will be better able to inform you than Lord Denno. As I told you the last time you were here, I am his man of business and he is often away."

"Trade? Hmmm." Pasgen's lips pursed and then he nodded. "Yes, I was thinking of Lord Denno's connections with the Court, but perhaps in this case a knowledge of trade will do as well. What I would like to learn is how effective the Lord Admiral's navy has been against the pirates of the narrow sea."

"Effective? Effective?" Clayborne burst out, his face coloring with rage. "He is a pirate himself, as far as I can tell! The only reason my wine ship reached London was that we now sail in convoy. All the merchantmen are armed, and we merchants have combined to pay for at least two armed vessels to accompany our trading vessels. And that cost must be added to the loss of profit caused by filling space with armed men and guns instead of cargo."

"Is that so?" Pasgen said, smiling.

Cropper came in at that moment with a beautiful flask and two beautiful glasses. He set the tray on Clayborne's table, poured wine from the flask into both glasses, and went out. Clayborne heaved a huge sigh.

"Yes! It is so!" he said emphatically. "And he has the best naval captains and ships all at the eastern end of the narrow sea watching for a French invasion of Scotland. Who cares about a French invasion of Scotland? We need the navy to keep the narrow sea safe for trade."

"How very interesting," Pasgen murmured. "I must confess to you that for reasons of my own, I wish to . . . ah . . . make trouble for the Lord Admiral."

"Oh, bless you! And if you can see that he loses the place— although with his brother being the Protector I suppose that is not likely . . ."

Pasgen shrugged. "I do not have any connections at Court. Have you suggested arranging Seymour's downfall with Lord Denno?"

An expression of dissatisfaction, swiftly masked, passed over Clayborne's face. "Lord Denno never involves himself with politics." He sighed heavily. "Despite his friendships with those at the very head of the government, he has never requested any reduction in tariff . . ." He sighed again, then smiled. "I am growing greedy. Really it is best not to look for favors from the great. And . . . ah . . . Lord Denno has been more than usually . . . ah . . . distracted . . . of late."

"Distracted," Pasgen repeated softly, remembering what Rhoslyn had said about Elizabeth and Denoriel at the ball. "No," he said briskly and more loudly, "I suspect Lord Denno is wise to seek no favors from the Court, not when he is so much involved with the Lady Elizabeth. He would not wish to attract any notice . . ."

"Ah . . ."

Joseph did not know what to say to that. This Master Silverhair never claimed to be more than a countryman of Lord Denno's. Yet he knew a great deal about Lord Denno's affairs, he had come with a desperate warning and then had come in person to help fight off the attackers. Was that not the act of a close friend? But Joseph, accustomed to judging men's responses to each other, had felt no liking between Master Silverhair and Lord Denno. Thus when Master Silverhair frowned, as if he wanted a more specific answer, Joseph sought desperately for something neutral to say—and found it was not necessary. Master Silverhair was not, it seemed, in the least interested in Lord Denno's private affairs.

"That is Denno's business," Pasgen said, "not mine, but there is something else that I would like to know if you know it or can even guess. Is there some source of great wealth in Bristol?"

Joseph was thrown completely off stride. "Wealth?" he repeated. "In Bristol?" He considered a moment and then shrugged. "Well, Bristol is a rich and busy port, much as London is. All trade from

Spain and western France, from Afrique also, must pass no far distance from it. A merchant could grow rich there."

"I am sure, but that is not the kind of wealth I mean. I meant many coins quickly, such as a dishonest tax factor might contrive to collect."

"Coins." Clayborne nodded. "There is a mint in Bristol. But there are laws and inspections."

Pasgen drew a deep, satisfied breath. "Laws that might be overlooked or less than strictly enforced if a powerful person applied the right kind of pressure."

Joseph's eyes widened. "Do you mean to say that Sir Thomas is somehow interfering in the mint?"

"I do not know." Pasgen finished the wine in his glass in a long, deep swallow. "But I am going to find out." He rose and bowed. "I thank you, Master Clayborne." He smiled. "Who knows? The dealings with pirates would be hard to prove, but if the man is meddling with the mint . . . You may be rid of the Lord Admiral sooner than you think."

Unfortunately the move to Chelsea from Seymour Place did not have the full effect that Catherine and Elizabeth had hoped for. The fresh air and more spacious rooms were of some help. By midmorning of most days Catherine's sickness and fatigue would pass; she could dine with her ladies and take some light exercise, such as a walk in the garden. However, she still was too sick on first waking to rise early in the morning.

At first this did not trouble Elizabeth at all, except that it meant she needed to undress and get into bed, then use the sleep spell on whichever of the maids of honor was sleeping in her chamber, and then get dressed again. The process would have been burdensome, but Denno waved her nightdress off and her clothing on when he came through the Gate.

Blanche would then sit sewing by the fire in Elizabeth's bedchamber to watch the sleeping lady and to send away anyone who wanted to see Elizabeth. Such an intrusion was rare, but did occur twice. Blanche had only to say that her lady was asleep—the sight of the maid of honor sleeping in the truckle bed was evidence—and the intruder went away. When that possibility became nil, Blanche would go to bed.

By twisting time just a little, Denno would bring Elizabeth back to her chamber, fully rested, fully sated, and fully dressed. Often they would linger talking in the gallery as April warmed into May, making plans for meeting again when Elizabeth rode out or exchanging fond and lingering kisses when they would not meet again until the following night. Then Elizabeth would wake her maiden and take up whatever book Master Ascham had set for the day's lesson.

One morning Thomas again bounced into her bedchamber, calling a loud "Good morning." He was rushing toward the bed, but stopped short when he saw the curtains drawn back and the bed neatly made. And his expression was not pleasant when Elizabeth returned his "Good morning" from her writing desk, which was on the same side of the room as the door and was hidden from anyone who entered without turning his head.

"You are a very devoted scholar," he said sharply.

"My mind is clearest in the early morning," Elizabeth responded, smiling with lazy good humor.

She had had a lovely night. She and Denno had gone to a small ball at a very exotic elfhame, Csetate-Boli. She did not speak a word of either Elven or the language of the area nor they a word of English. It was most amusing to try to communicate, and the clothing had been fantastic, such full skirts, heavy with embroidery, and bodices, also embroidered, but so loose that now and again a breast peeped out. Denno had found the costume most inspiring. Elizabeth swallowed a giggle. They had ended up making love in a shadowed corner of the garden, right under the wonderful elven sky.

"And do you always wake at dawn so your mind will be fresh for your lessons?" Thomas asked, adding hopefully, "Why are you all alone?"

"I am not alone," Elizabeth responded, still smiling. "Blanche is in the dressing room with Frances—"

"Good morning, my lord," Frances Dodd said from the doorway of the dressing room. "Will you join us to break your fast?"

"Do you no longer eat in the small dining chamber?" he asked Elizabeth.

Elizabeth shook her head. "No, not for breakfast. Kat prefers to break her fast in her chamber, which gives her time to look over the household accounts or some such. And since Queen Catherine does not enjoy food in the morning, I would rather eat here where I can make up for any studying I scanted yesterday."

Thomas laughed. "You will never convince me you scanted your studies yesterday or any other day." Then he looked meaningfully at Frances and added, "Are you going to fetch Elizabeth's breakfast?"

Both Elizabeth and Frances laughed. "No, indeed," Frances said. "The last time I went to bring some cakes and wine, a disaster occurred. I will merely ring the bell in the parlor."

"But surely Lady Elizabeth must be very hungry after being awake so long. Would it not be quicker for you to fetch the breakfast yourself?" Thomas urged. "I am sure you would be more careful and no second disaster would take place."

"I am not that hungry," Elizabeth said.

Frances laughed again, as if Elizabeth was teasing her about further clumsiness. "Yes, my lady." She sketched a curtsey and started for the door. "I will just ring the bell."

As Frances left, Thomas quickly approached Elizabeth's chair. She had swung around to speak to him and Frances and she was now trapped against the writing desk when he stopped, too close, in front of her.

"I wished to bid someone a good morning," he said, looking down at Elizabeth and, she thought, trying to sound pathetic. "I am wide awake and cheerful, but my poor Catherine does not find any morning good these days."

Elizabeth made an inarticulate sound. On the one hand she had a good deal of sympathy for Thomas, who was bursting with good health and good spirits, and had no one to whom to express them. He could no longer, as he had the previous year, roar jovially and suggest such games as hoodman-blind or snatch. Catherine could not now bear the noise or the violent activity.

On the other hand, it was *his* child that was causing Catherine so much discomfort and Elizabeth knew Thomas should take his noisy high spirits elsewhere. The drawback to that was that Catherine missed him when he was gone. Suddenly Elizabeth remembered Denno sitting beside her, talking quietly, holding her hand, one month when her courses caused her a great deal of pain. Denno had not gone to seek someone else who would be merry with him when she could not be.

Just on the moment, Thomas put out his hand and stroked her cheek. Fixed in her chair, Elizabeth could do no more than try to turn her face away. Thomas smiled broadly and Elizabeth realized that her gesture had been so restricted that he thought she was rubbing her cheek against his hand.

"No," she said, just as Frances returned to the room.

Thomas took a step back and held out his hand to help her rise from her chair. He was still smiling, and Elizabeth sighed. Denno and Harry would be annoyed with her for not discouraging him but really, sometimes Catherine's weakness tried Elizabeth's spirits too. So Elizabeth took Thomas' hand and let him lead her out into the parlor where Dunstan was drawing a chair and two stools up to a small round table.

Elizabeth saw Thomas' angry glance at the stool. She knew that Catherine permitted him to sit in a chair beside her when they were in private, but Catherine had been born a poor knight's daughter and Elizabeth's father had been a king. Still, she was tempted to appease him and ask Dunstan to bring a second chair, only Frances settled onto her stool and the door opened admitting a servant with a tray.

"Oh, I am afraid I will not be able to break my fast with you after all," Sir Thomas said, looking pointedly at the stool. "There is an errand I had forgotten."

Elizabeth did not show her impulse to laugh at him for his silly pride, which would not allow a servant and Frances Dodd to see him on a stool while Henry VIII's daughter sat in a chair. Elizabeth guessed it was because she was so much younger than he; he was able to accept placement on a stool when the whole household was similarly placed in Queen Catherine's presence. *Let him go*, Elizabeth thought, *I do not need his self-importance or his suggestive gestures.*

"Very well, sir," she said cheerfully. "Thank you for your greeting and may you have a good day."

His sour expression as he turned to leave made clear that he was not pleased with Elizabeth's easy acceptance of the loss of his company. Nonetheless she held her giggle until the door had closed behind him. Frances looked rather disappointed, but on the whole Elizabeth was actually relieved. Perhaps her displayed indifference would annoy him enough to keep him away.

That hope was not long sustained. Only two days later, Thomas appeared again at about the same time, as if to confirm whether his finding her dressed and at her studies was an accident or her usual practice. He did not come in that day, merely looked in, said a rather sour "Good morrow," and went away. He also tried twice the following week to separate her from her ladies, once when he followed her down a path in the garden—Queen Catherine having stopped to rest on a bench—and a second time when she was hurrying to the stable. Lady Alana, bless her, Elizabeth thought, stuck like a burr both times, displaying a stupidity striking in its inability to take a hint to be gone.

The setbacks seemed for a while to convince Thomas that Elizabeth could no longer be counted on as a playmate to fill his idle hours. She would have been happy enough with that conclusion if he had only ignored her, but it was clear Thomas was offended. Every time she caught him looking at her it was with a scowl that said he was not satisfied with the situation.

Although Elizabeth knew she should mention his behavior to Denno, Thomas had become less and less important to her. Unless she actually saw him glowering at her, she kept forgetting about him in trying to keep straight the intricate double life she was living. In the daylight hours she was Ascham's clever student and Queen Catherine's devoted stepdaughter. At night she was whirled away Underhill into a richly satisfying love affair with Denno and a series of adventures and entertainments that boggled the mind.

To add to Elizabeth's confusion, there was some crossover between life in the mortal world and Underhill. Denno had found several Sidhe who had actually lived when Athens was queen in the world of Greek drama and they were happy to tell Elizabeth of the great dramatic festivals, the Dionysias, they had attended. The tales, combined with the Sidhe ability to create moving images of what they had seen, gave such life to Elizabeth's lessons with Master Ascham that he was nearly stunned by her brilliance and understanding.

More and more Thomas was a vague irritation in the background rather than an active danger. Totally absorbed in her own busy and satisfying life, Elizabeth was not wise enough to cover her indifference with flattery. She was polite but aloof. Naturally with Thomas' conviction that he should be the central figure around which the world revolved, the less attention Elizabeth paid to him, the more annoyed with her and indignant over her pride Thomas became. And the ruby Master Otstargi had given him flashed brighter when he thought about how Elizabeth deserved a firm humbling.

A week passed in which Thomas patted and pinched the giggling maids of honor—all except Lady Alana, who regarded him with cold, unfriendly eyes and clung even closer to Elizabeth. It would be better, Thomas thought, if Lady Alana were absent—plain-faced bitch she was too. If not for her clothes . . . He looked at his wife just rising with slow effort from her chair. Poor Catherine could certainly use some attractive clothes that would hide her bulging belly.

The week during which Thomas virtually ignored her had made Elizabeth less wary so when he left the dining parlor immediately behind Catherine, he was gone from Elizabeth's mind. Half turned just past the doorway to speak to Kat, who was rising from her seat at the table, Elizabeth did not notice that Thomas had stopped in the corridor. Elizabeth's foot caught briefly on the door sill, and Thomas caught the hand she extended to steady herself and pulled her into his arms for a kiss.

Elizabeth was too surprised to fend him off. She just stood, wide-eyed. Kat Ashley had reached the door of the dining chamber at that moment and was horrified. She pulled Elizabeth away and hurried after the queen, who was just entering her parlor. So impetuous was Kat's motion that Thomas, who had a glib explanation on his lips, had no chance to give it.

"Kissed her. Right on the mouth. Right in the corridor where the servants could see." Kat was so astonished and angry that she was almost stuttering.

"It was only a joke," Thomas said, coming into the room.

Kat pulled Elizabeth away from him so that she was between Thomas and the girl.

"Oh, Tom," the queen sighed, sinking into her chair.

"Getting stiff as a poker," Thomas growled. "Used to be a bit of fun, but I swear she's forgot how to smile. Only meant to surprise an expression onto her face," he added. "No harm done, right out in the open with her governess there."

Catherine shook her head but she spoke gently to her husband, agreeing that he meant no harm and in general his teasing would be taken as a jest. But then she mentioned Elizabeth's special circumstances, that Elizabeth was not any girl but the king's daughter and in line for the throne. Extra care must be taken to avoid any unpleasant rumor, specially now that she was past fourteen.

Thomas was furious. The more he thought about Elizabeth being in line for the throne, the angrier he became and the brighter the ruby on his finger glowed. He was making no headway in getting Edward to demand him as his Governor, and it seemed only right that Elizabeth, who had been so long his playmate, should look to him for advice and protection. Her pride needed to be broken.

Thus, two days later while the sky was barely lighting with early dawn, he crept up to Elizabeth's bedchamber. He intended to catch her asleep and with only one sleeping attendant. He would dump her naked from her bed to the floor by pulling away the bedclothes. What he would do after that, he had not quite decided. Something within urged him to throw himself atop her, steal some kisses, perhaps press himself between her legs before her sleepy maid of honor could interfere. No, that might be too much; even Catherine might not overlook that.

To be sure he would catch Elizabeth asleep, he moved with careful stealth to where he could peer in the bedchamber door. He could see the truckle bed and the dark head of Margaret Dudley soundly asleep in it, but he could not see beyond the curtains of Elizabeth's great bed. Silently he crept closer, around the truckle bed, and peered in through a gap in the curtains. For a moment he was so shocked, he stood transfixed. The bed held no sleeping body. The rich counterpane was smooth, the pillows plump and settled in their places.

Since his plan was already ruined, Thomas muttered an obscenity under his breath and turned about, expecting to see Elizabeth at her writing desk laughing at him. But Elizabeth was not where he expected to see her, preparing for her coming lesson; she was not in the room at all. He looked around wildly and to his intense shock saw, through the window of the gallery, Elizabeth wrapped in the arms of a tall man . . . kissing him avidly.

A cry of pure rage and amazement erupted out of Thomas and he charged forward. But when he leapt through the gallery door, Elizabeth alone turned to confront him.

"What do you want?" she cried. "What are you doing here?"

"Who was that man?" Thomas countered.

"What man? Are you mad?"

"I saw you! I saw you kissing a man!"

"What man?" Elizabeth repeated. She felt the feather-light touch on her arm as Denno passed her and she knew he would take the sleep spell off Margaret, so she shrieked, "Margaret! Margaret! Come here to me."

Gasping and stumbling, wrapped in her bedclothes, Margaret Dudley appeared in the doorway.

Flattened against the wall, shaking with rage and offense, Elizabeth cried, "Sir Thomas says he saw me with a man. Do you see any man on this gallery, aside from Sir Thomas himself? Is there anywhere except the bedchamber a man could have gone?"

Margaret looked around wildly, the whites showing all around the pupils of her bulging eyes. "No, my lady. This is the only door from your bedchamber to the gallery."

Thomas too stared around the gallery. There was no man there and nowhere for a man to hide. Nonetheless, he was sure of what he had seen. True, the man was in shadow and Elizabeth's arms around his neck had obscured most of his face and hair, but there *had* been a man. Only Thomas could not imagine where Elizabeth's lover could have gone. No one had rushed by him as he ran in the door.

Elizabeth's maid of honor was staring at him and her expression was not laughing and indulgent as it had been last year when he surprised Elizabeth in bed. And Elizabeth . . . her eyes were no soft brown but glittering like gold coins and her thin lips had all but disappeared, her mouth was set so hard. But there had been a man in her arms! Thomas did not know what trick she had played, but she would not get away with it. Still to accuse her would accomplish nothing, not the way her jaw was set. He must try to win her confidence, get her to confess.

"I beg your pardon, Lady Elizabeth," Thomas said, sorry now he had accused her of kissing the man he saw. "I thought I saw you struggling with a man. I was afraid some intruder had tried to seize you. Perhaps . . . perhaps it was some kind of strange reflection in the window."

Elizabeth put a hand to her throat. "You frightened me half out of my wits, Sir Thomas. And I seem to have done the same to you. Perhaps there was a strange reflection in the window. I am newly risen from my bed and I may have been stretching." Her voice was cold, her eyes glowing with fury. "But I think you had better leave now so that poor Margaret can dress."

Chapter 29

For a time Thomas' accusation that there had been a man embracing Elizabeth put an end to Thomas' expeditions into Elizabeth's apartment. Margaret whispered of what had happened to the other maidens; the whisper came to Catherine's ears. She taxed Thomas with it and he told her that he was just passing and had seen Elizabeth being embraced by a man through a window of the gallery so he had rushed in to drive the intruder out.

Catherine could not believe there had been any intruder, but for some reason Thomas' accusation made her very angry and she called Mistress Ashley to her and asked for the truth of the matter.

Kat was appalled. "Truth? There is not a word of truth! Margaret Dudley, cousin to the Protector, was in the truckle bed beside Elizabeth's bed. How could any man come into Lady Elizabeth's apartment at that hour of the morning, pass Margaret, go right through the room and out onto the gallery? No man comes to her rooms alone except for her tutor, Master Ascham, and he not to her bedchamber but to her parlor."

Catherine knew there was nothing of that sort between Elizabeth and Master Ascham. She had watched them carefully because sometimes young maidens did develop an unhealthy attachment for their teachers. There was liking and respect, and some lively differences of opinion, but no spark.

If Catherine had ever suspected a spark of that kind in Elizabeth, it had been for Lord Denno. Sometimes they had exchanged a glance that was . . . different. She had been almost relieved when Tom told her to forbid Denno's visits. No. Nonsense. Surely Lord Denno was too old, and he could not be the man in the gallery. Her servants would not admit Denno; he was not on the visitor's list for any of her houses since the day Thomas had forbidden her to invite him.

A not completely new but very unwelcome thought passed through Catherine's mind as she dismissed Mistress Ashley. What had Thomas been doing "passing" Elizabeth's apartments at that hour of the morning? Her expression must have been forbidding. Mistress Ashley looked quite shaken as she again assured Catherine that there could not have been any man in Elizabeth's gallery and bowed herself out.

Kat took the queen's warning to heart. She questioned Elizabeth sharply and got wide-eyed and furious denials. Blanche, who claimed to have helped Elizabeth dress—although actually Denoriel had spelled her clothes on as soon as they came through the Gate; he had no intention of allowing her to be caught in a nightdress by Seymour—assured Kat there had been no man. So did Margaret Dudley. The latter's word was reassuring; Kat knew nothing of sleep spells and could not imagine that Margaret would sleep through a man's arrival, whereas she was sure Blanche would tell any lie Elizabeth wanted her to tell.

It was, however, Elizabeth's soft murmur in her ear that provided an explanation for Thomas' accusation which Kat could believe. "Sir Thomas is used to getting his own way. He was angry because I refused to play with him. Perhaps he saw his own reflection in the window and it gave him an idea of how to shame me."

That was real enough, and dangerous enough in Kat's opinion, to bring her into Elizabeth's chamber at the crack of dawn. She now breakfasted with her charge and the two times Thomas came up and looked into the parlor, he found all the ladies fully dressed and at table. He did not come in.

Despite all the trouble he had caused, Kat could not find it in her heart to blame Thomas. He was certainly overindulged, especially by his wife, and she, sick as she was, could not amuse him. Kat sighed. Catherine should have checked his behavior with Elizabeth, not encouraged it by so soft a reproof. But Kat could not be totally unsympathetic to the queen's indulgence of her husband. Kat herself found Thomas' loud good humor almost irresistible, and could not believe he meant any harm. Thus, Kat advised Elizabeth to give him her best smiles and show that all was forgiven.

Elizabeth was not too happy with the solution Kat suggested, but Queen Catherine was still sick and miserable and Elizabeth could not bear to add to her troubles by being openly at odds with Thomas. She suspected, too, that Catherine was now less happy about her growing unwieldiness and feared it was making her less attractive to her husband. Twice in the week after Thomas's ill-judged invasion of her rooms, the queen had summoned Lady Alana to her, and Lady Alana's great art was dress.

It was then no great surprise to Elizabeth when, having beckoned her to a stool beside her chair, Catherine asked to "borrow" Lady Alana, whom she wished to send to London to buy gowns that would enhance her appearance.

"Of course, I am delighted to be host to my little knave, but Lady Alana says there are ways to make the change in my figure a *charming* reminder of the babe to come."

"I am sure there are," Elizabeth said, smiling, "and I am just as sure that Lady Alana will know. She does have almost a magical ability with a gown. Of course you may borrow her. And, you know, she is some kind of cousin to Lord Denno, so she has choice of anything in his warehouses."

"Lord Denno," Catherine repeated, a slight frown creasing her brow. "I hope I have not ended your long acquaintance by forbidding him to visit."

"No, of course not," Elizabeth said, smiling again. "He dandled me on his knee when I was a babe, and we have been friends since I could speak. Perhaps you do not know, but Lord Denno was very close to my D—my half brother, His Grace of Richmond, and he took me on as a legacy. When we are here at Chelsea, I ride with him two or three times a week."

Elizabeth was glad of a chance to confess what, she had a growing fear, would reach the queen's ears as a nasty rumor. Before the fiasco when Thomas caught her kissing Denno goodbye, she would not have cared if someone reported seeing her riding with him; now that Thomas had accused her of embracing a man, she wanted no suspicion that the man was Denno raised in the queen's mind.

"You ride with Lord Denno?" Catherine sounded shocked. "You never told me."

She had been right to confess, Elizabeth thought. If Catherine had heard this from some other source, she would have been very angry. As it was she was more surprised than offended. Elizabeth blinked, widening her eyes innocently.

"Not alone," she said, trying to sound shocked herself. "My guards and grooms are always with me and usually Lady Alana. The other girls say I ride too hard. But if you think I should, I will take Margaret and Agnes with me while Lady Alana is away. The other maids of honor do not ride at all."

"Do you mean you have been sending messages to Lord Denno about where and when to meet you?"

"Oh, no." Elizabeth sounded horrified. "I would never send him a message without first showing it to you, Your Highness. You know I did so when I ordered that brocade for a stomacher. But I always ride at about the same time and Lord Denno meets me somewhere along the route."

"But how could he know?"

Elizabeth giggled, thinking of the air spirits that carried word as soon as she arrived at the stable and of Miralys, who could leap from London to Chelsea in a moment.

"I think," she said, "that he set his servants to watch for me and when they told him the times and the route, he was able to come to meet me." She giggled again. "He says he is besotted with me, that I am the little daughter he will never have." Then she sobered and put out a pleading hand. "Do not be angry with me or with him, Your Highness. He is such a lonely man. He has no one in the world he cares for or thinks of as family except me."

Catherine's lips had parted to utter a stinging rebuke, but she remembered Lord Denno telling her almost the same thing when he brought the furs, that he had no one in the world to spoil and cosset except Elizabeth. And it was no ill thing, Catherine thought, to have a merchant of such wealth as a friend who would provide luxuries that otherwise would have to be foregone or paid for out of a limited income.

Nor was she in defiance of Tom's will; he had said he did not want Denno hanging around *her*. She smiled at that memory, but was aware of a sinking feeling of sadness at the same time. Tom did not seem as possessive of her now that she was carrying his child. And she could not think Lord Denno any danger to her charge. He was an old man, not likely to waken the fancy of a girl of fourteen, and never flirtatious in his manner.

"Well, it was wrong of you to meet Lord Denno without telling me," she said mildly.

"I am very sorry, madam," Elizabeth said at once. "I just never thought about it. Anyone will tell you, Kat or the guardsmen, that Lord Denno has been riding out with me for many years. It was never forbidden. We never dismount and only talk about my lessons or the strange places he has visited. It was so common to me, that I never thought of mentioning it."

"Oh well." Catherine smiled. "Now you have mentioned it, but be sure to take your ladies with you while Lady Alana is in London."

Elizabeth wrinkled her nose. "I will, madam, I promise, but they will be dull rides, all slow walks. Margaret and Agnes fear to be unseated if their mounts move any faster."

"It will only be for a few weeks, until Lady Alana returns, or I would approve a message to Lord Denno asking him not to meet you until Lady Alana returns to you."

"Perhaps that would be best," Elizabeth said easily.

She was very glad she had agreed. Catherine looked relieved, as if she were worried about Elizabeth seeing Lord Denno so often and was pleased that Elizabeth acted as if lacking his company would not matter. Since Elizabeth knew she would be with Denno every night, the fact that she would not see him during the day was not important. They always enjoyed being together and Denno had wanted her servants to remain accustomed to seeing him with her, but a few weeks' absence would not matter.

The note was duly written and sent with Ladbroke, who accompanied Lady Alana to London. Elizabeth knew that Lady Alana would explain what had happened and, of course, she could herself explain when Denno came for her that night. Note or no note, Elizabeth invited Margaret and Agnes to ride with her on the two times she went out the following week and the week after. They were witness to the fact that no one joined the riding party.

Two weeks was all Elizabeth could endure, however. Then she sent a message to the stables telling Ladbroke to exercise her horses since she could not face any more rides plodding carefully along the graveled paths at a slow walk with those two fearful slugs. To fill the time when she usually rode out, she set herself to translating *Electra* by Euripides, which Master Ascham had said was too difficult.

That was a challenge Elizabeth could not resist, and it made her quite cross to discover that Master Ascham had been correct. The translation did not flow as those he had chosen for her had done. And yet, it was not the words themselves that were the difficulty. Elizabeth knew what most of the words meant; the concepts they described did not seem to make much sense, which made her suspect that she was using the words she recognized in a mistaken context.

By the end of the week she lost patience with Blanche and sent her to the laundress and with the maids of honor, who were sitting apart from her with their sewing or embroidery and giggling about something. Earlier Alice Finch had been bemoaning the fact that Elizabeth would not go out into the garden. She had tried that the previous day and found herself distracted by sunlight dappling the grass, clouds moving across the sky, and birds flitting from tree to tree.

"Oh, go out to the garden, do," she said to the girls. "I really cannot think when you talk and laugh about such nonsense. Kat won't mind, I am sure. Just tell her that I cannot believe that Electra is trying to convince her brother to murder their mother. I must have misread something and I cannot find where I have gone wrong."

"Convince her brother to murder their mother!" Frances Dodd repeated. "Perhaps, Lady Elizabeth, Master Ascham had good reason not to want that play translated."

"Perhaps," she agreed, glancing uneasily toward the door where she would not have been surprised to see Master Ascham looming; she had thought he had asked some suspicious questions yesterday. "But," she added stubbornly, "I will never know if I do not work it out for myself. Go out, do. I will come and join you soon."

They all trooped out, *tsk*ing to each other about Lady Elizabeth's unnatural taste for learning, but closing the door behind them so that servants passing in the corridor would not disturb her. Elizabeth turned her attention to the text again, deciding to check over the early lines which had seemed straightforward. Perhaps they held a hidden meaning she had missed.

The maids of honor turned left out of the corridor that led to Elizabeth's apartment, went down the stairs, and passed the queen's parlor, talking happily about what they should do. Their voices were raised a little in reaction from trying to be quiet while Elizabeth was studying, and Eleanor Gage commented wonderingly that their lady would rather sit bent over a dull book than come out in the sun and play.

Near the door of the public parlor, which they had just entered, Thomas heard what they said. At first the remarks were meaningless to him. Catherine had wavered slightly on her feet, and her hand had tightened on his arm. He looked down at her and set his teeth. Sick again! He led Catherine toward the other end of the room and seated her in a cushioned chair. After studying her pale and sweating face for a moment, he took her hand and patted it.

"I fear you are feeling unwell again," he said, trying to make his voice soft and sympathetic, which made him feel even more irritable. "Let me fetch your maid to you, dear."

"Thank you, Tom," Catherine sighed, then added somewhat plaintively, "but don't run away. I will be better in a little while."

He bent over her and kissed her brow. "I will only give the potion a chance to work so my voice does not make you wince."

Catherine smiled and pressed his hand. "I love your voice," she assured him; well, usually she did enjoy his boisterous good humor, so she was being only slightly untruthful.

"Your woman will be with you in a brief moment," he said as he walked back to the door.

When he reached to open it wider, the ruby Otstargi had given him gleamed blood-bright on his finger. He rubbed it with his thumb, as he so often did, and suddenly he recalled what Eleanor Gage had said. The maids of honor had been sent out, so Elizabeth was alone in her rooms. Had she known that Catherine was expecting Lord Russell? Of course she did.

Alone in the corridor, Thomas chuckled. Told the maids she was preparing some lesson or other. They thought it unlikely . . . and so did he. Elizabeth must know that he would not remain with Catherine during Lord Russell's visit; Russell had had the impudence to question what he was doing about the pirates.

The ring flashed again when he pulled the door closed. Clever girl, Elizabeth. As soon as she was rid of Lady Alana—he had seen to that by having Catherine send that clinging vine to London—Elizabeth sent all the other maids of honor out into the garden where they would surely lose track of time.

Thomas smiled. No reason for him to run Catherine's errand. That was what servants were for. Yes, there was a footman. Thomas explained that the queen needed her maid immediately and turned back the way he had come. Doubtless the footman would think he had returned to his wife, but he passed the half-closed parlor door, heels clicking on the polished wood, and walked swiftly up the stairs. At the head, he turned right—a way he knew very well by now—into the corridor that led to Elizabeth's apartment.

Elizabeth frowned at what she had written, changed a word, looked another up, heard the snick of the door latch. She bit her lip and swept everything together, thinking retribution in the form of an angry Master Ascham was about to fall on her. Then she looked up, with a guilty smile on her lips . . . a smile which froze as she came to her feet and turned to face Thomas Seymour.

His smile, broad and triumphant, answered the one frozen on her face, the smile meant to appease Master Ascham.

"How clever of you to get rid of your maids after I finally got Catherine to send that Lady Alana away," he said. "How you can bear the way she hangs on you I do not know. And that face! A pudding is prettier."

Elizabeth swallowed hard. Thomas had paused while he spoke. "I thought you were Master Ascham," she said, her breath quickening as he started forward.

Thomas laughed. "Oh no you did not, you mealy-mouthed little sneak. You knew I would not stay with Catherine once Lord Russell arrived. You knew I would come up here. Lessons from Master Ascham is it? I will teach you a lesson you will greatly prefer to his."

"No. No. I was working on a Greek translation that was giving me trouble. *Electra*—"

Thomas Seymour did not love learning, but his tutor had pounded some knowledge into him. The story of Clytemnestra, who had committed adultery while her husband was away at war and murdered him when he returned, and her daughter Electra's revenge was the kind of story that would stick in his mind. He laughed.

"Enjoying the queen's love life, are you?"

"There is nothing of love in *Electra*," Elizabeth said, drawing herself up indignantly.

Thomas laughed again and started toward her. Elizabeth side-stepped to take herself out of his direct path, but Thomas was better schooled in fencing than he was in Greek literature. His body responded at once to her movement, and he was coming directly toward her again. Elizabeth again tried to dodge and he again responded. Desperately Elizabeth muttered the spell for stickfast . . . but it was too late. When his feet froze to the floor beneath them, he tipped forward, arms outstretched, and caught her tight against him.

In the public parlor, Catherine had called out for Thomas to come back a moment after he had walked out the door. The sudden wave of nausea that had made her think she might be unable to control the need to vomit had passed as quickly as it had seized her. She sighed and shook her head. She could not take the chance that she would lose her breakfast in Thomas' presence.

A little frown creased Catherine's brow. Men were the strangest creatures. They were not the least disgusted nor did they blame a drinking companion who vomited up his excess, but a woman more blamelessly nauseous became an object of revulsion. She sighed again and then smiled as the light, high voices of Elizabeth's maidens drifted from the garden through an open window.

That Elizabeth. Catherine shook her head slightly. She knew what Elizabeth was doing. It was because Master Ascham had said *Electra* was too difficult—and, of course, Elizabeth had taken that as a challenge. But she should not have sent all the maids away and remained alone.

The thought was interrupted by the click of heels on the corridor floor. Catherine smiled. Tom had sent a servant to fetch her maid and was coming back to stay with her. How good of him. She knew how much her sickness distressed him . . .

But the footsteps in the corridor did not pause at the door. They went on toward the stairway. A little shriek and laughter came from the garden. Catherine drew a hard breath. *Was* Elizabeth doing Greek translation or was she waiting for Tom to come to her? Why should she send her maids away to do a translation?

Catherine got to her feet, ran across the room, and flung open the door. When she stepped out into the corridor, she saw her maid was walking swiftly toward her. She gestured for the woman to go into the parlor and herself ran to the stairs. She needed to slow down to climb them; she was already awkward and, in addition, breathless with rage and pain, but she picked up speed along the corridor and pulled open the door to Elizabeth's parlor.

When his feet inexplicably stuck to the floor a bare step away from Elizabeth, Thomas flung out his arms for balance. The speed of his advance toward her, increased when she tried to get away, threw him forward. An instinctive need to save himself from falling wrapped his arms around her just as his feet came loose. Elizabeth's own arms were trapped under his, her face lifted to his. He was quite ready to ignore the horror in her expression; what he saw were her half-parted lips. He bent his head and pressed his mouth to hers.

"What are you doing?" Catherine shrieked.

Chapter 30

There was but one way the discovery could have ended, and Elizabeth could not be unhappy about it. She was to be sent away. Thomas Seymour's charm and bluff could avail him nothing this time. And though it was hard to see the terrible hurt in the queen's eyes, the knowledge that she would no longer have to guard herself against Seymour's unwelcome advances came as an absolute reprieve.

But Elizabeth required a guardian. And one was swiftly found in Sir Anthony Denny.

The promise Elizabeth had given Catherine was an easy one to make—and would be an easy one to keep. Elizabeth knew that Sir Anthony was a friend of Denno's and that Sir Anthony regarded Denno as his own contemporary. He would certainly think of Denno as a safe companion for Elizabeth. Sir Anthony would not object to her riding out with Denno and dearling Denno's conversation would certainly enliven the dinner table. Perhaps it would even amuse Master Ascham, who had been impolitely condescended to by Thomas Seymour and had suggested it was time for him to return to Cambridge.

Moreover, as Sir Anthony's household was much smaller than Queen Catherine's, Elizabeth could rid herself of all but two of her maids of honor. Lady Alana asked for leave, having been in close attendance for so long this was granted. Elizabeth kept Margaret

Dudley because her cousin, John Dudley the earl of Warwick, was high in the government and Denno had told her he was not totally committed to the Protector. The other girl she kept was Frances Dodd, who not only had nowhere to go but was terrified of horses and most unlikely ever to ride out with her.

Considering the benefits accruing to her, Elizabeth was hard put to look properly mournful when the time came to part. She curtsied to the ground and kissed Catherine's hands and begged her with real sincerity to take care of herself, but she stuffed Margaret and Frances into the traveling cart the queen had provided with Kat Ashley and Blanche and herself mounted her lively mare. Catherine frowned, but Elizabeth did not wait for her to ask if this behavior was careful and did not pretend she cared.

She followed Gerrit and Shaylor and behind her came Dickson and Nyle, all armored and armed to the teeth. They were followed by Dunstan, Ladbroke and Tolliver, also armed, leading her extra horses. The party was far too strong to be in any danger from the outlaws that infested the roads and attacked travelers, and Elizabeth knew that just out of sight of Chelsea, Denno would meet them. The weather was beautiful, Denno was as happy as she with her change of circumstances, and the prospect of being away from any possibility of Thomas Seymour's attempts on her seemed to promise safety.

To make up for that moment of sauciness, Elizabeth wrote to Catherine a few days after she arrived in Cheshunt, more humbly than she had been able to make herself speak: *Although I could not be plentiful in giving thanks for the manifold kindness received at Your Highness' hand at my departure, yet . . . truly I was replete with sorrow to depart from Your Highness, especially leaving you undoubtful of health: and, albeit I answered little, I weighed it more deeper, when you said you would warn me of all evils that you should hear of me; for if Your Grace had not a good opinion of me, you would not have offered friendship to me that way . . .*

The offer was important, since it was as close as Catherine could come to promising she herself would not speak of the compromising situation she had witnessed. Elizabeth was grateful, but in truth she was not sorry to be out of that household and under her gratitude was a thread of resentment over being blamed for Thomas' careless lechery.

Elizabeth settled easily into Sir Anthony's household and to

Lady Denny's infinite relief was quiet and obedient. She seemed satisfied to concentrate on her studies with Master Ascham and did not demand excursions or entertainment. She was content with Lord Denno's visits, and he did provide some entertainment, hiring players to come to Cheshunt to perform a masque or a newer form, a play. Lady Denny now and then wondered why the queen had found Elizabeth too difficult but loyally put such thoughts aside, particularly as she found Kat Ashley a most pleasant and congenial companion.

Within two weeks of Elizabeth's move, Rhoslyn was explaining to Pasgen that she did not think it necessary to bother about Thomas Seymour any longer. They were again at the Inn of Kindly Laughter waiting for Llanelli. Rhoslyn had noticed that her mother seemed more relaxed in that place than any other and met her there most often. Pasgen leaned back against the wall behind him and laughed.

"Too late," he said. "Seymour is going to come to a bad end. And he certainly deserves what will befall him. He is dishonest and derelict in his duty—more than derelict, he has perverted his duty as Lord Admiral. He is actually in league with the pirates he is supposed to hunt to make the narrow sea safe for merchant ships. Instead he has arranged for safe harbor for the pirates in the Scilly Islands and for that takes a share of their booty."

"Mary was sure there was some hidden reason for Catherine sending Elizabeth away, but she cannot find any hint of misbehavior."

Rhoslyn ran a finger around the rim of the glass in which a golden wine sparkled; a faint music just barely tickled her ear. She did not think even Pasgen could hear.

"Was there not talk of Seymour playing with all the women?"

"Yes, but always when his wife was there with them and the talk never named Elizabeth in particular. The gossip from the queen's household now, however, is all about Catherine's continued ill health. One of Catherine's ladies did say, with a touch of spite, that Elizabeth now and again showed some impatience with the queen's illness and was not properly grateful for all Catherine had done for her, but Mary could make little of that except to say it was typical."

Pasgen looked down into the mug from which he was drinking.

"Gratitude is a draught few can enjoy in any quantity," he said dryly. "But it is just as well, for whatever reason, that Elizabeth is out of that household. Seymour has done worse than consort with pirates. He and William Sharington, the vice-treasurer of the Bristol mint, have been playing games with the coinage."

"Grace of God, do you mean to say that his crimes are common knowledge?"

"The lack of his pursuit of the pirates is. There is bitter talk among the merchants, but it does not seem to have wakened any response in Bristol—who knows, perhaps collusion with the pirates is common there—and from what I could tell the tale had not spread to the Court. Of course I have no friends at Court, but I stopped and asked Denoriel's man of business—I am considered a safe friend by him after that night we helped them be rid of those attackers. Clayborne does have contact with many of the courtiers and there is currently no gossip about Seymour."

"Oh well, since Elizabeth is out of his reach, it does not matter if he escapes his crimes. And I am sorry for his wife who seems to love him. Catherine is a good person."

Pasgen shrugged indifferently. "I think he will bring catastrophe down on himself. He is the kind. But I did put the thought of Sharington's coin clipping and mixing base metals with the Church plate he melts down into the mind of the sheriff and of two knights of the shire. How or when or even whether they will move, I have no idea."

"It no longer matters," Rhoslyn said, smiling. "But how did you know who was who in Bristol?"

"There is an elfhame in the west, called Cymry."

"Oh, I know about Cymry." Rhoslyn's eyes brightened with remembered pleasure. "There was a Sidhe from Elfhame Cymry at Oberon's ball. He was attending on Aleneil. From what I heard him say, they are very different from Logres or Avalon. And even more different from the Dark Court. They value their humans and try to make them happy."

Pasgen frowned. "They are different. They use very little magic. And yet there is a great wash of power all around the elfhame. Instead of using magic, they have masses of human servants to clean and cook and even farm. Hmmm. I wonder if the power I felt can be used or whether it is like the power in the mortal world, which Denoriel says is like swallowing lightning. I wonder—"

"No, Pasgen," Rhoslyn protested. "Denoriel warned you that was dangerous and he did nearly burn out his power channels by using that human power."

"Oh, something else strange about Cymry," Pasgen said quickly, hoping to distract Rhoslyn from worrying about him and nagging at him. "Possibly because they use so little magic, they did not seem to sense that I was Dark Court and I saw Chenga there."

"Chenga?" Rhoslyn repeated. "Among a mass of humans? And doing them no harm?" Then she bit her lip. "Do you think she is taking one here and there and . . . and using them in secret?"

Pasgen frowned. "She was alone, not part of any group, but I did not see any sign of active dislike. If she is abducting some of their humans, they will discover it soon. The humans live in family groups, just as they do in the mortal world. None can disappear for long without questions being raised." The frown grew blacker. "No. I do not like that at all."

"What do you think they will do to Chenga if they learn she is harming their humans?"

"For all I care they can tear her apart or use her as a target for the fighting groups they enjoy watching so much. I don't care about Chenga, but I don't want Cymry made wary of Dark Court taint. I thought . . . I thought we might . . . *you* might consider living in Cymry. It is a pleasant place."

Several emotions showed briefly on Rhoslyn's face—a touch of interest flickering to hope which was then damped down into resignation. "No, I would not dare. With so little magic to call on, Vidal could wreak havoc in Cymry if he traced me there. Better he not know of such a rich and defenseless source of humans."

Pasgen's lips thinned but before he could speak, Llanelli came up to their table. She was looking better than she had for several past meetings. Not that she had slipped back completely to her thin, worn form; she had retained the fullness of figure and rich coloring, but there had been signs of strain in her face and a kind of wariness in her manner. This time her eyes were bright and she wore a little half smile.

"Why are you hiding back here against the wall?" she asked.

"Too much noise in the middle," Rhoslyn said quickly. "I wanted to tell Pasgen about some mortal matters."

Actually she had chosen the half-hidden table because in the recent past, at least since the empty house had been gutted, Llanelli had kept glancing around nervously when they were more in the open. She hoped Pasgen, who was sometimes impatient with their mother, would not remind her of her past fears.

"You are looking very well, Mother," Pasgen said blandly. "Have you had many interesting clients?"

"Not so many," Llanelli replied with a little laugh. "But one who is really interesting. He is Bright Court, but from Elfhame Melusine."

"He came here for a healer?" Rhoslyn asked, her voice sharp with suspicion.

"No, of course not," Llanelli said, laughing again. "He came here to try to obtain some weapon or other from some outworld source. It is made neither of our silver alloy nor of mortal iron or steel. He says it is very light and very strong and has no ill effects on Sidhe. He wants to discover whether he can ken it."

"Why not seek it in *Halle de Lutin* or *Marché de Esprit Follet*?" Pasgen asked; his voice was too bland, indifferent.

Rhoslyn's hand clenched on her knee under the table, but Llanelli did not notice Pasgen's subtle warning.

"He says it is only at the Bazaar of the Bizarre that there are so many outworld merchants. And, of course, that was what brought him to need a healer. The outworlders have no idea how dangerous iron is to us and, of course, they are protected by the warning that the buyer must beware on his own account. Fortunately Pilar *was* reasonably wary."

"He came to you to treat an injury?"

"Yes, from the stall just across the aisle from my booth. Most fairgoers know that merchants' mortal toys are gilded or silvered and that some of them are of iron. Pilar had just put the tips of his fingers around a displayed weapon. Fortunately the merchant shouted at him not to pick it up and only the tip of one finger touched it. The merchant sent him right across to me and there was only the smallest burn and no sign of poisoning. Perhaps the fact that whoever made the thing or maybe the merchant had gilded it reduced the effect."

"Did the merchant know this Pilar?" Rhoslyn asked.

Llanelli frowned at her. "I certainly did not question him about it. After all, Pilar is typically Sidhe. The merchant would know that iron was dangerous to him and not something he would buy. He lost nothing by the warning. Why are you suspicious of Pilar?"

Rhoslyn shook her head. She knew that Llanelli resented her children not seeming to trust her judgment. "I am not really suspicious, just that Melusine is so very formal and High Court. It seems odd a Sidhe from Melusine should come to the Bazaar of the Bizarre."

"One solid sign of his being from Melusine . . ." Pasgen suggested. "What did he bring to pay for his mortal or outworld toy?"

"Wine." Llanelli laughed. "That was what he offered me. It was spiced and scented, too. Rather special. He did not have it with him and had to go and come back—which he did. Does that not prove him honest?"

"And you tasted the wine?" Rhoslyn's voice was sharp again. She started to add, "After Vidal showed his hatred of us all," but she bit back the words; Llanelli faded every time she was reminded of Vidal.

"Not alone," Llanelli said coyly. "Pilar drank two goblets to my one and I assure you neither one of us suffered any inconvenience. And—since I was sure you would want to know . . ." she pulled a bottle out of the large purse she was carrying and set it on the table. "I have brought the remainder for us to finish here with our dinner. Pilar will bring more when he comes to see me again."

"He is coming from Melusine so you can look at his finger? No healer in his own domain is as effective."

Llanelli giggled softly. "Maybe that was an excuse. He said my touch was very special."

Then she turned and signaled the servitor and asked for cups for the wine. Three cups were easy for the many-fingered hand. But once they were set on the table, the server's four blue eyes blinked deliberately and a thin, high voice complained, "The inn does not rent cups. The inn sells wine. If you bring your own wine, there soon will be no inn."

"No, no," Pasgen soothed. "This is a one-time thing, I assure you. A special wine given as a gift. And we are about to order dinner."

That pacified the creature—even Rhoslyn hesitated to give it a name. It was upright and covered with a soft mauve plush, with four arms at regular intervals around the body and four eyes around the upper third of the head. A flap that moved slightly with each breath was set low on what might be called a chin between each pair of eyes, and a thin, lipless, but very toothy mouth curved down around each flap. Rhoslyn found herself thinking it was a sensible arrangement, permitting the servitor to smell anything before sticking it in its mouth.

When it turned away, Rhoslyn realized she had no idea what Pasgen had ordered to eat, but that was not important; he knew her tastes. More interesting he had uncapped the bottle and poured. Rhoslyn sniffed. So did Llanelli. Pasgen lifted the cup and waved it before his face.

"Very attractive," he said, but frowned slightly.

Rhoslyn only hmmmed and then sipped from the cup. Llanelli watched them with a smile, sipping from her own cup, her expression pleased and assured, as someone who knew and liked what she would get.

"It is very good," Rhoslyn admitted and smiled. "Why didn't you invite Pilar to join us instead of just bringing the wine?"

"Oh, I did, but he said he could not this week—I had told him we meet every week for dinner on mortal Tuesday—so he had made an appointment for this Tuesday, thinking I would not go to dinner with him as I have been doing. He said he would come next week"—she made a funny face at Pasgen—"so you needn't look as if he is afraid to meet you."

"No, it isn't that." Although to a certain extent Pasgen had wondered why Pilar was reluctant to meet Llanelli's family. "It's just that there is a familiar flavor to the wine. Something that reminds me . . . No, I don't know of what it reminds me."

"Spices are spices," Llanelli said. "It is the exact mixture that can be unique, but even in such a mixture one recognizes this or that ingredient."

"I suppose so," Pasgen said, deliberately smoothing the frown from his forehead. "And here is our dinner."

From the other side of the inn Piteka, now dark-haired and dark-eyed, watched Llanelli and her children share his wine. He bent his head over his near-raw slices of flesh cut from a living kid, hiding his sharp-toothed grin, and thought of how clever he had been to have given her that bottle of undrugged wine. Rhoslyn and Pasgen were now convinced the wine was harmless and likely that "Pilar" was harmless too.

Thought of his cleverness brought a momentary frown. He had remembered all the attributes of a Bright Court Sidhe—the golden hair and green eyes, the pale smooth skin, the high-arched brows . . . and he had almost forgotten to create the illusion of rounded rather than pointed teeth. But in the end he had remembered. Nor did it matter if any of them saw and recognized him. That would frighten Llanelli and make her even more eager to find the assurance that oleander provided.

Tomorrow he would bring wine not only spiced and scented but laced lightly with oleander. He would warn Albertus not to add so much as to bring mindless joy and obedience. This time just a touch so that Llanelli would feel comfortable in his company. The next day there would be more in the wine, enough to make her happy, and the day after there would be enough so that when the drug wore off she would begin to slide down into despair.

After that he was not sure. He could easily drug her insensible, but there was no way he could carry her out of her booth or her lodging. Those monsters that Rhoslyn had created to watch her and protect her would tear him apart if he touched her. They might tear him apart if she became unconscious sharing a drink while he was there.

He turned his head to look at the inn entrance. Yes, there they were, waiting not far from the door, their eyes fixed on their charge; no chance they could be distracted, the hulking brute like those that occasionally used to accompany Pasgen and that *thing* that looked like a skinny little girl. He would have to give Llanelli only enough of the drug to come with him, laughing and talking. If he judged the amount just right, perhaps he could convince her to dismiss the maids and guards.

Piteka sighed. He did not think he would be able to judge her capacity for the drug so closely. She would fall victim to it more quickly because she had been an addict in the past, but that might also give her an elevated resistance to the effects of the drug. If he had more time he could have experimented using more or less, but he had only the one week. She must be carried off and held by Aurilia before he was supposed to join them all for dinner.

Wait, there was one way. Since he would be pretending also to be addicted and love her all the more for sharing his vice, as soon as she was firmly in the grip of the drug again, he could just give her a generous supply of oleander. That would convince her that he was not trying to enslave her but just share a pleasure. She would know the right amount to take to make her happy and pliable.

With Llanelli in that state it would not be difficult to convince her to dismiss the guards and walk out with him. He would only need to say that he could not make love with a clutch of constructs watching. She need only come to Melusine with him where he had a beautiful domain. She need have no fears; whoever threatened her would have no power in Melusine.

Piteka pushed away the empty plate and emptied the goblet standing beside it, staring out into nothing with a beatific smile on his face. A passing kitsune shuddered.

And then, Piteka thought, he would Gate her to Aurilia in Caer Mordwyn. Or maybe he should keep her in his own hands until Prince Vidal returned. He remembered that Vidal had also ordered that she not be much damaged. Well, he would not damage her much . . . maybe break her fingers so she could not heal and certainly dole out the oleander in fits and starts so she would weep and scream for it. Piteka sighed with happy anticipation.

But he had misjudged his victim and grown careless as the drug seized her with unexpected rapidity. She was a little too happy on mortal Wednesday; "Pilar" left an extra bottle of wine so she would stay happy. She did not drink it all and had what was left to tide her over on Thursday. On mortal Friday, however, "Pilar" forgot the extra bottle. He laughed and promised to come early on mortal Saturday. But when the dose he had given her wore off and she descended with a rush from joy in having a lover from the Bright Court to utter despair, Llanelli recognized what he had done to her.

On Saturday, when he did come . . . late . . . he thought he could taste the sweet fruit of success, because she led him into a treatment room and shut the door on the maids who usually hung about her. He could tell that she was already fighting the cramping muscles and nausea of withdrawal and was glad he had come prepared when she accused him.

"No, no," he protested, smiling and taking from his purse the packet of oleander. "I only wished you to share my joy, my pleasure. I do not mean to bind you in any way. Here is enough to keep you happy for weeks and by then I am sure you will have found a source of your own or I will bring you more. In Melusine it is readily available."

For several moments, Llanelli stared down at the packet he was offering to her, then she looked up into his smiling face. The hair was still golden, the eyes bright green, the brows high arched . . . but the teeth in that smiling mouth were filed to sharp points.

"Who are you?" Llanelli whispered.

"Now, now, you know who I am, Pilar from Melusine. You are not that far gone that you are forgetting things. Here"—he held out the bottle of of wine he had brought—"take a sip of the wine and you will feel much better."

In the excitement of his success—he already had her alone, he thought, he would easily be able to convince her to come to "Melusine" without her guards—he also forgot to keep the lilting tones he had used to disguise his voice. He saw the terror in her eyes and set down the wine to take both of her hands in his.

"Llanelli," he murmured, "there is nothing to fear. I swear that you will have all you want, forever. Why do you not come with me to Melusine?"

From the deep pit of despair in which she lay, Llanelli knew that voice, knew the filed teeth, knew the false promises, knew that Vidal had found her again. This was the final proof that no one and nothing could protect her, that he would pursue her for all the remaining years of her life until he caught her and held her hostage to make Pasgen and Rhoslyn his slaves.

She had nothing left to live for. She could not heal while she was drugged and she remembered too well the agonies of trying to recover from her addiction. She remembered how Rhoslyn and Pasgen had suffered with her. Not again. Never again. And in the pit of despair a viper of poisonous rage fed on long years of hatred stirred as an unhoped for vengeance became possible at last.

Vidal had been so sure of her, so sure she would, like the fool he believed her, fall into his trap. And so she had. But he had fallen into a trap too. All she needed to do was to cry out for help and her maids and Lliwglas would rush in and tear him apart. And be Removed.

A shining icy spear of grief pierced through the black despair as she remembered the tender care Rhoslyn's servants had lavished on her. They were only constructs, but they had been her friends and companions when she had none, comforting her in her pain and listening to her troubles. She could not send them to whatever fate the market had reserved for those who were Removed.

"Llanelli!"

There was a hard note of impatience in the hated voice, the note that had always meant the withdrawal of the drug. Llanelli put her hand over the packet of oleander. "Pilar" laughed when he saw the gesture, showing those sharp teeth.

"You need not try to hold it. There is more, much more, in Melusine, enough to keep you happy forever."

"In Melusine," Llanelli repeated.

"Tell your servants to stay here and come with me. You will be safe in Melusine. You will not need them there."

Then Llanelli knew the answer, and through the dark despair red flames of joy burst upward, lifting her spirit. She fought the withdrawal-induced pain and hopelessness. She had hope now!

She would bring "Pilar," who did not realize he had exposed to her his true identity as Vidal, outside the market. Then she would scream that he was hurting her, that he had destroyed her, which was true she thought, tears filling her eyes, and the girls would rip him to pieces. Hope fought despair. With Vidal dead . . . she would be safe, free.

"They are not my servants," she said to "Pilar." "They have been bound by my daughter to watch me while I am in the market." She found a shaky laugh. "Rhoslyn never thought I would leave it, but I am sure I will be safe with you . . . in Melusine. Only we must go to a Gate outside the market. Once past the warnings, I can tell them to come back here and wait for me."

Piteka patted her shoulder gently, resisting the impulse to seize her arm. There was something in her voice, her manner, that he did not trust. However all he said was, "How clever you are." And he went to the door. She followed him docilely, relieving most of his suspicions.

When she told the servants they were going out, the male brute stepped out first and looked around, then stepped aside for Llanelli; one of the brown-haired maids and the creature with spider-leg fingers and a blue ribbon around her neck followed them.

In the crowded market lanes, Piteka did take Llanelli's arm to be sure she would not try to slip away. She shuddered, and he tightened his grip, but carefully, not so much as to hurt her. She walked beside him without protest then, but as they drew closer to the exit she began to walk faster. Piteka was surprised and almost drew back but then he thought she was thinking of endless oleander in Melusine and smiled.

He dodged right around the blank back of the BUYER BEWARE warning, holding tightly to her arm now, and then around the warning against violence. But the back of that was blank also and he did not see the threat of Removal for doing spells or violence in the market . . . until after he swung her around and said, "Send the servants away now, Llanelli."

She laughed in his face and said, "You are dead now, Vidal. You will never threaten me or my children again." And then shrieked "Help!"

As the constructs closed around them, Piteka saw the warning about Removal and realized with a shock that Llanelli had insisted on leaving the market so that her servants would not be Removed for harming him.

He cried "Wait" and dismissed the illusion of a Bright Court Sidhe that he had worn. "You fool! I am Piteka, not Vidal. You had better tell your servants not to harm me or Vidal will catch you and torture you forever. You and your stupid children too."

Horror washed over Llanelli. Instinctively she tried to pull away. Equally instinctively Piteka tightened his grip on her arm, grinding the flesh into the bone beneath. Llanelli screamed in pain. The hand that had held her arm suddenly lost its grip and then fell to the ground.

Blood spurted from the wrist where Lliwglas had severed Piteka's hand from his arm. The blood spattered Llanelli's gown. She screamed again. The brute guard seized Piteka's head and turned it all the way around. Llanelli's eyes bulged with horror. Leaping forward, the brown-haired maid caught Llanelli in her arms before she could fall to the ground.

Llanelli was in her lodging, not in her healer's chambers when she woke. One of the maids was instantly at her side, offering to help her sit up, asking if she wanted or needed anything. For a moment Llanelli could not remember how she had come to her rooms or why she felt as if the world had ended. Then she did remember and realized that, at least for her, the world *had* ended. Vidal was not dead and she was not free and never would be free.

She made her lips smile at the maid and said that she needed nothing, only to be alone for a while. The round, fresh face smiled at her and nodded. Since she had begun to heal, she had been allowed privacy if she wanted it. When the construct was gone, Llanelli rose and went to her writing desk. There would be paper and a marker that she used for writing down mixtures for medications. When she bent over the writing desk, her mist-thin white hair fell forward and brushed against her nearly transparent hand.

"My very beloved Pasgen and Rhoslyn," she began, her hand steady despite the terror and despair that made it hard to breathe.

When she told them that Vidal had tried to take her again, they would understand that she could not live any longer in a state of constant terror and despair. They would understand that she no longer had the strength to begin a new fight to escape her need for the drug. They would be glad to know that she was at peace and they were free of needing to care for her.

Chapter 31

For Elizabeth the weeks of early summer slipped by in peace and gentle pleasure. She had not realized how overwrought she had become, balancing a love affair, her exacting lessons, the visitors to Queen Catherine's palace, many of whom requested her company, and the constant if near-unconscious wariness about Thomas Seymour.

Slowly Elizabeth began to unwind. The pace at Cheshunt was slower—Sir Anthony and Lady Denny were no longer young and came to Cheshunt to escape the Court and the pressures of guiding the king and the nation. There were few visitors, and those who did come were of Sir Anthony's and Lady Denny's age. Sometimes they brought a political problem . . . but that was for Sir Anthony's ears alone. And when they asked to meet with Elizabeth, it was only to ask playfully about her studies or to be sure she was well and content with her lodging. Her maidens, with no one to compete against in matters of dress and attracting the young men who accompanied the queen's guests, became more placid, less shrill and intrusive.

Even Elizabeth's love affair with Denno became more peaceful. Although neither of them realized it, Denno had been competing with Thomas for Elizabeth's attention. He had been taking her with him to exciting places and doing exciting things and had been constantly finding places and excuses to make love so that

431

his image would be as strong and virile as that the boisterous Thomas projected.

After two weeks at Cheshunt, Elizabeth asked to be taken to the Shepherd's Paradise. Da came along and they talked, mostly about the past at first but then about the possible future. Denoriel wondered where Vidal was and what he was doing. Harry advised Elizabeth about what she should do if she were invited to Court and what to say if proposals of marriage were presented to her. Elizabeth confessed that she would fight any suggestion of marriage. She did not wish to be married . . . ever.

Four weeks passed and then six and Elizabeth discovered that there was such a thing as too much peace. Restlessness, and a nervous energy that had always been a part of her began to plague her until even Sir Anthony and Lady Denny noticed. Denno asked Sir Anthony if he could invite a troupe of players to Cheshunt to amuse the whole party. The masque they performed was a great success, great enough that the players were asked to stay and present a second piece two days later. There was extra amusement in being allowed to watch the rehearsals. The masque looked so different without scenery or costumes that it was a double wonder to see it performed.

The next week Denno suggested a picnic in the woods near a small pond. Elizabeth rode as did Sir Anthony and Denno, but a small traveling cart carried Margaret, Frances, and Lady Denny, a second brought cushions, cloths, braziers, and baskets of food and wine. Somehow the food had more savor served in the open, and a remarkable number of animals came from the woods and showed themselves on the far side of the little pond.

Elizabeth suspected Denno's Low Court servants had been sent to lead the creatures to where the picnic party could see them, but she could not speak of that . . . not that she would have if she could. She enjoyed it no less than any of the others, who held their breaths when a doe and fawn dipped their delicate muzzles into the water, and later allowed her maidens to cling to her when a bear shambled out and stood looking at them across the pond.

Denno drew his slender sword and Elizabeth's guards came forward, unlimbering their weapons, but there was no need. The bear came to the edge of the pond, but only to slash a paw through the water with amazing speed and bring out a fish.

Everyone laughed aloud in relief, and the big creature seemed startled by the sounds, as if it had not realized they were there, and hurried back into the wood.

Elizabeth noted that Denno's usually soft lips had been drawn back hard, and she rose and patted his arm. "Don't scold them," she said. "Everyone was so thrilled."

The picnic was a subject for lively conversation for several days, which was just as well because Sir Anthony disappeared and there were no visitors at all. A pall of dullness fell over Cheshunt.

When he came to take her Underhill that night Denno told Elizabeth that Sir Anthony had probably been called to London to discuss the situation with the Scots. Denno had news from William Cecil that the Scots parliament had resolved to send their little Princess Mary to France to remove any likelihood that she could be taken by English force of arms and married to Edward out of hand.

"Will the Protector bring an army into Scotland again?" Elizabeth asked.

"I do not think that is possible," Denno said. "But now we will see if Seymour's decision to send most of the naval vessels east will be vindicated. If they prevent the French from picking up the little princess, the depredations of the pirates will be forgotten."

"And if they do not?"

Denoriel shrugged. "Of course Seymour has the excuse that his wife is near her term, and Lord High Admiral or not he cannot be with the fleet. But Cecil also hinted that there are rumors of collusion . . ."

"I hope they catch the little princess. She would have a very good husband in Edward. I know he seems cold now, but I remember how quick he was to love me when he was a little boy."

"And it would save a world of trouble for Seymour, would it not?"

Elizabeth flung herself into Denoriel's arms and kissed him. "It would save a world of grief for Catherine. If not for her, I would not care if they hung Thomas."

But Thomas' naval vessels did not manage to block the French ships, and at the beginning of August, William Cecil told Denoriel that Princess Mary had been carried to France at the end of July.

At about the same time Sir Anthony gave Denno permission

to bring a different troupe of players who had a new kind of performance, a play. That was very exciting, for the story—of a forbidden love that caused two murders—was shown as it happened to real people without any fanciful wild men or interruptions of dancing and singing.

Elizabeth herself was hard pressed from time to time to keep from screaming in horror, and Margaret and Frances wept aloud and hid their faces. It was only when the "murdered" gentlemen reappeared on the platform to take their bows that the maidens would believe they had not been killed.

July and August. Elizabeth and Queen Catherine kept up a pleasant correspondence, aided and abetted by Thomas, who often wrote the letters because Catherine was by now finding it difficult to write. Elizabeth was careful, however, to have no personal communication with him; when she wrote it was asking Thomas to be *diligent to give me knowledge from time to time how his busy child doth.*

But she missed Catherine and responded warmly when Catherine *wished me with you, till I were weary of that country. Your Highness were like to be cumbered if I should not depart till I were weary of being with you; although it were the worst soil in the world, your presence would make it pleasant.*

Had Catherine lived alone, what Elizabeth wrote would have been the simple truth, but both knew they would not live together again, at best would only meet in the future for a few hours in a visit. Neither knew that they would never see each other again. Catherine survived the birth of a little daughter on the thirtieth of August, but by the fifth of September she was dead of the dreaded fever that attacked women after lying-in.

Chapter 32

The news of Catherine's death was given to Elizabeth as gently as possible by Lady Denny in the second week of September.

But for Elizabeth, the news felt like the blow of an axe. "No," Elizabeth said, shaking her head, her mouth dry and her throat closing. "No, it is not possible! I feared so much for her, but she was safely delivered. She was. We had that news only a week past. I was so happy to hear it. How can she be dead?"

"It was the fever," Lady Denny said, taking Elizabeth's hand in hers. "I am so sorry, my dear. I know you cared for the queen."

Elizabeth felt as if she was in a waking nightmare. "She took me in when no one else would give a home to me. She cared for my health and my education like a mother. I was never grateful enough. I—"

Elizabeth stopped speaking and swallowed hard. She had almost said that she had torn poor Catherine's heart by aiding and abetting a flirtation with her husband. Lady Denny patted the hand she held.

"My dear, I am sure you did express your gratitude and that Queen Catherine knew you loved and respected her. When we lose someone, we always feel that we had not said what should have been said or done what we should have done to express to that lost one how precious she was to us. You must not flay your

435

soul with regrets, which are not only vain now but very likely undeserved. Think instead of the happy times you spent together. Cherish her memory."

"Yes, madam," Elizabeth whispered, but she swallowed again and her gaze was fixed and unseeing. How could she ever think of Catherine without thinking of Thomas, of the hurt she had inflicted on the queen?

That night she refused to go Underhill with Denoriel. She did not wish to be distracted; it was wrong, when she had done Catherine so much ill. Denoriel said sharply it was Thomas who did the harm, not Elizabeth but she would not be comforted. She did not weep. She shivered as she had after her father died and she said that everyone she loved died and she had nowhere to go, no one to advise or protect her.

Denno shook her gently and then took her into his arms. "My very dear," he said, "now you are being silly. I am still here. And you know Harry is not dead. If a need great enough comes, you can live with me in Llachar Lle."

"No." Her voice rose. "I cannot leave England. I cannot. No matter what the cost or danger, I must stay here."

Both were silent for a moment and then Elizabeth shook her head. "Edward is alive and well. Long may he reign. But still, I cannot leave England."

Denoriel nodded acceptance and he said, "You must live in England, but you are no longer a child who must have a keeper. You have your own houses, your own lands, left to you by your father. You can live—"

And the door opened, and Lady Denny's voice called, "To whom are you speaking, Elizabeth? I told Frances—"

"*Bod oergeulo!*" Elizabeth whispered, pointing at the door.

Denoriel had disappeared from sight by the Don't-see-me spell before the last syllable was pronounced. The door stood a quarter open, Lady Denny's hand just visible on the edge, but it did not swing wider.

"*Dihuno,*" Elizabeth said, her eyes wide with fear that the shock Lady Denny had given her made her use too much power.

"—not to keep you awake with her chatter," Lady Denny finished coming into the room, clearly unaware that there had been any interruption in her speech.

"It wasn't Frances," Elizabeth said, and hiccupped as if she had been crying. "I was just saying to myself that I cannot believe we have lost the queen. I did not realize I was speaking so loud."

Lady Denny looked over at Frances Dodd, still solidly asleep. "It wasn't loud," she admitted softly. "I was just coming to look at you and make sure you were not weeping yourself sick and I heard . . . well, I could have sworn it was Lord Denno's voice, but that is ridiculous."

Elizabeth found a little tremulous smile. "I am very fond of Lord Denno, but I don't think I want him in my bedchamber in the middle of the night."

"No indeed. Now, since Frances is so solidly asleep and can give you no comfort, I will just sit down by you until you fall asleep."

"No, please go back to your bed. I am distressed over giving you so much trouble, my lady. I promise I won't think anymore about Queen Catherine. I will never be able to sleep if I am aware that you are sitting up and watching me."

Denoriel added the force of his will to Elizabeth's words and after another moment or two, Lady Denny agreed to go back to bed. Denoriel followed her to be sure she did not come up with any new ideas, like sending her maid with some drops or a tisane. When he returned to Elizabeth's room, he found her still shaking with shock, but she refused his offer to stay with her.

"I am too uneasy to take comfort from your company," she said. "What if Lady Denny conceives of another notion for my comfort?"

"That brings to mind what I said earlier, that you have houses of your own. I think it is time to set up your own household. If Kat stumbled upon us, I could muddle her memory and it would not matter. I cannot do so with Lady Denny."

Lady Denny unfortunately had not forgotten her guest's distraught state, and was far too eager to distract her. Actually, after the first shock of loss, Elizabeth would have mostly forgotten the queen's death. She was no longer accustomed to seeing Catherine every day and unless something specific brought the queen to mind she could forget Catherine was gone forever. But Lady Denny invited Elizabeth into her presence more often and for longer periods so that Elizabeth would not be alone and brood.

Kindly, Lady Denny spoke praise of Queen Catherine and platitudes about death, constantly reminding Elizabeth of her guilt. Then she would recommend that Elizabeth ride out or play some games with her maids of honor. Elizabeth agreed docilely, but that was not sufficient for Lady Denny who must also have spoken to the maids of honor directly. They sought and found Elizabeth wherever she tried to hide and were so cheerful and uplifting that Elizabeth very nearly used *bod oergeulo* on them.

Far worse than innocent distraction by her maids of honor was lying in wait for Elizabeth, however. Only a week after she had the news of Catherine's death, Kat had said slyly, "Your old husband that was appointed unto you after the death of the king now is free again. You may have him if you will."

"No!" Elizabeth exclaimed, drawing back.

Kat laughed and patted Elizabeth's hand. "Yes," she insisted. "You will not deny it if my Lord Protector and the Council were pleased therewith."

Rage and revulsion dyed Elizabeth's normally pale cheeks red. And to Elizabeth's horror, Kat thought she was blushing with desire and continued to talk about Thomas, how he was the noblest man unmarried in the land and thus most suitable and fitting to be Elizabeth's husband. All Elizabeth could do was refuse and refuse again even to consider the idea.

But Elizabeth was terrified that Kat would pass the notion that she would like to marry Thomas to Sir Anthony and Lady Denny. She forbade her to do so, saying it was dangerous to speculate on such matters, but though she loved Kat dearly, Elizabeth no longer had much trust in her governess' discretion.

By the end of September, despite everything Elizabeth could say, Kat was still hinting about Sir Thomas' need for a new wife and Elizabeth's suitability to fill that role. Denno then renewed his suggestion that Elizabeth would be safer in her own establishment and mentioned that Sir Anthony was feeling the weight of supporting Elizabeth and her household. The promptness with which the Dennys agreed to Elizabeth's leaving them testified to the truth of Denno's estimation of the financial burden she created, and early in October Elizabeth and her household moved to Hatfield.

Even on the journey from Cheshunt to Hatfield, Elizabeth could not escape Thomas. John Seymour, sent by the Protector to see her safe on the road, brought a message from Thomas who begged his brother to recommend him to Elizabeth and enquire "whether her great buttocks were grown any less."

Rage again colored Elizabeth's cheeks and so filled her mind that she did not dare speak at all. What message John Seymour carried back, Elizabeth did not know. She feared the worst as she settled into Hatfield but had no way to deal with the problem. She did not dare write or send a message to Thomas; that would only confirm any evil rumors. Denno tried to reach the man but could not get an audience. Thomas was too busy with schemes for ending the Protectorate and arranging for little Lady Jane Grey to marry the king, now that Princess Mary was about to be betrothed to the Dauphin of France.

In any case, Thomas was unlikely to listen to Denno when he would not heed the warnings of far more politically astute persons, such as the venerable Lord Privy Seal. Lord Russell warned Thomas that there were rumors of his hopes of marrying either Lady Mary or Lady Elizabeth and that such rumors, and even more any attempt to make suit for such a marriage, would ruin him.

At first Thomas denied any such intention, but not long afterward he was inquiring what portion could be expected with the ladies. When Lord Russell said it was no more than ten thousand pounds, Thomas protested violently that he knew Elizabeth had three thousand pounds a year and several estates. Lord Russell said that would end with her marriage, but Thomas did not believe him. When Elizabeth's cofferer, Thomas Parry, came up to London on business, Thomas took the opportunity to approach him and enquire about Elizabeth's finances and household.

One of Parry's errands in London was to secure a house in which she could stay when she came to visit her brother. Durham House, which was customarily given over to Elizabeth for her visits, was now being used as a mint. Thomas promptly offered Seymour Place but said that Elizabeth should have her own residence. He advised Parry to urge Elizabeth to appeal to the Protector's wife to get Somerset to grant her a suitable town residence.

Elizabeth, who disliked the duchess of Somerset as much as Ann of Somerset disliked her, refused to approach her although Parry insisted that Thomas had said that was the best path to solving the housing problem.

She realized that Parry was a bit too impressed with Thomas and, with some effort, maintained a studied indifference when he asked if she would be willing to marry Thomas if the Council approved. Since she did not want any hint of strong feeling to trickle back—she had cause to know that if Thomas was rejected he would only redouble his efforts to get his own way—she did not reply "when the Lord Protector hears Mass" but only that she would do what God put into her mind.

Strangely enough, the only one who was of any help to Elizabeth at all was the duchess of Somerset. For her own reasons the Protector's wife was almost as horrified as Elizabeth at the idea of a marriage with Thomas. She summoned Kat Ashley and took her severely to task over freedoms she had permitted Thomas—even though they were events that had taken place the previous December when Elizabeth was at Court.

Ann of Somerset said that Kat had failed in her duty and was not fit to be governess to so high a lady as Elizabeth; she made the attitude of the Protector clear and frightened Kat into a little common sense. To Elizabeth's considerable relief, on her return to Hatfield Kat told Elizabeth that she should not set her mind to marriage with Thomas. Likely, Kat said, Elizabeth would have to wait until the king came of age before she could get permission to take Thomas as a husband.

Although Elizabeth did not break into song and do a jig for joy, she was aware of a tremendous relief. And when she got Underhill that night, she did embrace Denno and whirl him around and around. He was even more pleased than she and sent off an air spirit to fetch Harry. They would go to Fur Hold, Denoriel said. Harry needed to have his spirits lifted. He had not been able to reach Rhoslyn for several weeks.

Unfortunately Elizabeth's care not to spark Thomas' stubborn determination to have her was not the principal influence on him. Vidal had returned to England bloated with his successes in Scotland. He had not only destroyed any chance of peace between England and Scotland with the planned betrothal of Princess Mary and the Dauphin of France, but he had set up a good chance of a civil war in Scotland between the party of Scots who wanted Mary in France against those who opposed her being raised a Catholic.

His satisfaction over the nice trickle of power from the misery caused by the raids permitted him to brush off the failure of Aurilia's plan to have Denoriel and Aleneil killed. He was somewhat more irritated by Seymour's inability to get Elizabeth into bed and quite enraged by Catherine's cleverness in preventing any scandal. Well, she would not interfere with his plans again and Seymour was now free to marry Elizabeth. Marriage was better than scandal; marriage would permanently cut Elizabeth off from the throne, whereas scandal could be covered and forgotten.

Vidal chafed at his inability to influence Elizabeth in Seymour's favor. He could not introduce any minion into the Denny household because Elizabeth still had the ability to see through illusion in the mortal world and any gift to her would be scrutinized for spells. He wasted some of Aurilia's time trying to convince her to attempt an amulet that could not be detected but before he grew desperate enough to force her compliance, an imp from the village inn brought gossip that told him no amulet would be needed.

Two maids had been gossiping about Kat Ashley, who Vidal knew had great influence over Elizabeth. Kat, it seemed, was doing his work for him, acting as Seymour's advocate without any need of Vidal's interference. Later gossip confirmed the fact, and Vidal decided he would not go near Kat Ashley or any other of Elizabeth's servants nor near Hatfield when Elizabeth moved. The last thing Vidal wanted was for Denoriel or Elizabeth to sense his influence. His best move, once Ashley's predilection for Seymour was confirmed, was to get Seymour to make an offer or even, if necessary, to abduct Elizabeth.

Having made that decision, Vidal appeared in Otstargi's house again. This time the servant's mind had nothing to tell him. Some clients had called and gone away disappointed, one very angry. Indifferent, Vidal told the servant to summon a street boy and sent the messenger with a note to Seymour. He was surprised and not pleased when the child returned with another note in reply.

It was immediately apparent that Seymour had grown very great in his own estimation. The spell in the ruby ring had barely enough control over him to send a note and agree to a meeting with Otstargi. Seymour was not a man to feel gratitude, particularly to someone so far below him in status. If he remembered that Otstargi's advice was the foundation of his new wealth and the power he intended to establish with the men that wealth had bought, he dismissed the memory.

Seymour's careless note said he had an appointment with Chancellor Rich that day. He would have an available hour for

Master Otstargi on the day after tomorrow just before the dinner hour. Vidal bared his filed teeth noting there was no invitation to join Seymour at dinner.

He would teach that fool a sharp lesson, he thought. And then he spat an oath. Until Elizabeth was married to Seymour and ruined, he could not make the man less appealing by making him ridiculous nor subject him to a political gaffe by offending Rich.

His various frustrations did not make Vidal more welcoming when Seymour arrived at Otstargi's house at the appointed time the next day. He snarled "Sit." And Seymour sat, but with a surprised expression that showed he had not been aware of setting out to see the magician. In fact, he started to rise again and Vidal had to gesture him down onto the chair.

"I am not sure I need your services any longer," Seymour said.

"But I am sure you do," Vidal snapped. "You are now free of your wife. Why have you made no effort to secure the Lady Elizabeth? She is now of an age to marry and if you do not move quickly, the stupid Council will find some foreign treaty they need confirmed with a royal marriage."

"The Council is not in favor of my marriage to Elizabeth," Seymour growled. "And besides, I learned that she will have no more than one grant of ten thousand pounds. All the lands willed to her in her father's last testament will return to the Crown."

Vidal waved a dismissive hand. "That provision was made in the case of the lady's marriage to a foreign prince. Henry was very careful about not allowing a foreign royal house to own significant lands in England. When Elizabeth's marriage to a good English subject is confirmed, it will be apparent to the Council that the lady must have an income suitable to her status as second heir to the Crown."

"Confirmed!" Seymour laughed. "The Council will not confirm our marriage. In fact, my brother has threatened to hang me if I attempt even to visit Elizabeth. Nor have I received an invitation nor a single line of writing from her since the queen's death." A shadow passed over Seymour's face when he mentioned Catherine, but it was gone in a moment and replaced by an indignant petulance. "Not even a note of condolence."

"Perhaps the lady does not want to put herself forward. You should write first to her."

Vidal sent out a spear of will but he found Seymour so armored in self-assurance and conceit that shaft did not penetrate the way it should. It did make some impression but Seymour shook his head.

"Not until I have some sign of her willingness to listen to me. Through her man, I have urged her to take certain actions to make our lands more convenient. But I do not want news of my part in her plea to exchange lands to get back to the Council . . ." He rambled on for a while, deflected from Elizabeth by his grievances against the Council.

"I would not trouble my head about the Council," Vidal urged; once Seymour had Elizabeth, Vidal would welcome the Council's disapproval. "They are a bunch of old women. Only get Lady Elizabeth before a priest and into your bed. Surely you do not believe that the king will allow your brother to punish you or to cause grief to his best beloved and most favorite sister once you are man and wife. Remember that the king made plain his approval of your marriage to Queen Catherine although your brother was opposed to it. Remember how Edward favored Lady Elizabeth when she was at Court."

Seymour nodded slowly. "You may be right about that, and I have given the king some reason to love me also. Yes, it would be well for me to have Elizabeth to wife."

Satisfied that he had accomplished his purpose, and bored with Seymour whose mortal mind was shallow and seemed to have no room for anything other than his own affairs, Vidal relaxed the mental pressure he was applying. The man shook his head again and looked around as if surprised to find himself still in Otstargi's room.

"Yes," Vidal agreed pointedly. "Once Lady Elizabeth is your wife, the way for all your other affairs will be smoother."

The phrase was meaningless to Vidal, only an opening to suggest that Seymour had other affairs to take care of and so be rid of him. Thomas, however, was sure that all that talk about Elizabeth had only been an introduction to Otstargi asking for his share of the money collected from Sharington and the pirates.

He knew that Otstargi had directed him to those profitable ventures, but he was sure he had made no commitment to give any share to the magician. No, of course he had not; why should he? He had done all the work, dealt with the pirates and with Sharington. Only the idea had been the magician's and ideas without effort do not pay in coin. In any case, he no longer had the money. It had been spent in buying support from various noblemen and in hiring armsmen.

Before Vidal could say more, Thomas got hurriedly to his feet. "You are right. My affairs are many and pressing, and I must make an accounting of them before I can ask useful questions."

Vidal was a little surprised by the sudden urgency of Seymour's move to depart, but the man's mind held only confused ideas of the Bristol mint and mercenaries. Vidal could only assume some of his own desire to be rid of Seymour had leaked out. He also stood and gestured to the door, which was opened by the servant. And as Seymour left the room, he thrust the need for Elizabeth at him one more time.

Thomas considered that need on his walk home and it seemed to him that if he wrote about Elizabeth's need for a house for her visit to Court, the Council could not accuse him of wooing her. Although Vidal's influence was already waning, his letter to Elizabeth hinted that if she came to Court for Christmas, which was now approaching, he would be more glad to see her than any other person.

Elizabeth received Thomas' letter only two days after she received one from William Cecil, who was now secretary to the Protector. Cecil's letter advised, in guarded but not obscure terms, that Elizabeth not come to Court this year. That was a bitter pill for her to swallow and she had put the letter aside without answering it, trying to convince herself that Cecil was only being overcautious.

However when Thomas' letter came, a chill ran over her. Cecil was not being cautious; he must have written with the Protector's knowledge. Elizabeth could understand why Somerset did not want to forbid her visit directly; Edward would be just as disappointed as she to be deprived of their time together. And Edward already resented many of the Protector's restrictions.

Rage again dyed Elizabeth's cheeks with color and her eyes filled with tears. Somerset must have heard the rumor that Thomas intended to woo her and wished to prevent any hint of a connection. How *could* Kat have been so foolish as to think anyone would approve the marriage of the Protector's brother to one of the heirs to the throne. Why had no one believed her when she said, over and over, that she would not have Thomas? Now the Protector suspected her, at worst of treason, of wanting to supplant Edward, at best of being too stupid to understand the political disaster of her marriage to his brother.

Chapter 33

The mortal months since Llanelli's suicide had passed as one long misery to Pasgen and Rhoslyn. When they first learned of their mother's death they had stormed into Caer Mordwyn like avenging furies, erupted into Aurilia's apartment when they found Vidal's empty, and slapped a truth spell on her.

They learned nothing to provide an outlet for their desire for vengeance. Vidal, they discovered, had been gone into Scotland since early spring. Aurilia knew nothing of any plan of Vidal's to take prisoner their mother. She had never heard of their mother in her life. She did know of a plan to attack Elizabeth in Elfhame Cymry—she struggled fruitlessly against revealing Chenga's and Albertus' roles in the plan, but to her relief Pasgen and Rhoslyn seemed to brush off her admission.

Furious and frustrated, each racked by guilt and grief, they could find no comfort in each other's company and they parted without a word at Aurilia's door. Rhoslyn went to the dreadful and bitter task of closing her mother's booths in the three markets and, most painful of all, destroying the constructs that had served and protected Llanelli.

She would have saved the constructs if she could—she did not blame them for not stopping Llanelli from killing herself; that blame she took all to herself. That Llanelli would do such a thing had never entered Rhoslyn's mind and she had not warned the constructs to guard against it. However, the shock of finding Llanelli dead had damaged them beyond repair.

They had one purpose in the half life Rhoslyn had created for them—protecting Llanelli. That task was complicated enough, requiring thought and judgment as well as obedience. Now their charge was, to them, inexplicably dead; and their minds could not continue beyond Llanelli's life. They were able to tell Rhoslyn how they had dealt with Piteka in minute detail, but their minds had closed down at the moment each had seen Llanelli's corpse.

When she had returned the poor creatures to the formless stuff of which they had been made and reabsorbed the power that had animated them, Rhoslyn was shaken to her core. Without thinking, she twisted time to her last appearance in Mary's household, when she had gone up to bed before the alarm Llanelli's maids carried screamed in her mind of disaster. She was dressed for Underhill, not the mortal world, and totally disoriented. It took some time to remember who she was and what she should be doing in this small overcrowded room. By the time she descended from her attic chamber to take up her duties, it was midmorning.

One of Mary's ladies said, rather severely, "You are late, Rosamund."

The voice held no particular censure, but the words struck Rhoslyn to the heart. Late. Too late. She had known there was something wrong with Llanelli's tale of a Bright Court Sidhe from Melusine, but Llanelli seemed so happy and she had put off any question . . . and then it was too late.

She had no idea what showed on her face but saw Lady Mary make an abrupt gesture at the maid of honor who had spoken and then ask, "Rosamund, is something wrong?"

And instead of trying to paint surprise or some other suitable emotion on her face, she found she could not hide her terrible grief and, changing one letter only told the truth. "My brother is dead, my lady."

"Oh Rosamund," Mary cried softly, and rose from her seat and took Rhoslyn in her arms. "It is a great violation of the love you bore him and suffered with him in his illness, that many would say you are both better off now that he is safe in God's arms." Tears ran down Mary's face. "But I know that for you, it is not better. There is a vast chasm where your purpose for living was."

And Rhoslyn wept aloud in Mary's warm embrace, for what Mary said was exactly true. Llanelli was better off at peace, and she and Pasgen were certainly better off without the constant drag and danger of their mother's weakness, but they did not want to be "better off." They wanted Llanelli still with them.

After a time Mary patted Rhoslyn's shoulder and drew her along. Mary sat in her chair and gestured for a cushion to be brought so Rhoslyn could sit at her feet.

"It will be too quiet for you here," Mary said softly. "You will have too much time to think of your loss, to blame yourself for not being with him, to blame yourself for all kinds of impossible things. I know. When I heard my mother was dead, I tore my heart to pieces, even though the one at fault was my father, who forbid me to go to her."

Rhoslyn sighed heavily. She had intended to try to hide her grief or to say that her brother was worsening if Mary's questioning grew too acute. Mary's sympathy had undone her, and she had lost her excuse for the freedom she sometimes needed. She could not allow Mary to believe she now had no purpose but to serve her. She sought a new excuse.

"What you say is true, my lady," she murmured, "but there is a reason why I cannot give all my time to you—glad as I would be to do so. My brother left it all to me, all, everything. And I cannot throw it away. He so loved his lands and also the people who worked the lands. He entrusted me with their welfare and I must not fail that trust."

"Of course not," Mary said. "But I hope you are not saying you will abandon me completely?"

"No, no, my lady." Rhoslyn uttered a sob but found a watery smile to go with it. "To leave you would make almost as large a hole in my heart."

Mary smiled, pleased with a mark of so much affection. And suddenly her expression lightened as if a problem had solved itself. She put a finger under Rhoslyn's chin and lifted her face.

"It has just come to me where I will find a busy place for you." Mary gestured to a stern-looking, gray-haired woman beside her. "Here is Lady Catherine returned to me and weary to her soul of struggling to attend to my interests at Court and of the constant traveling. She has begged me to find a replacement for her and I was about to tell her she would have to endure yet a month or two, but if you will pick up her heavy yoke, you will have little time for brooding."

Now Rhoslyn looked up at Mary with the most sincere gratitude in her expression. She had not been paying proper attention. Mary had been offering her the freedom she needed, but she knew she must not seem too eager to be away.

"I do not know whether I am fit for such a place."

"No, of course you are not." Mary smiled at her. "But Lady Catherine will know and she will be able to make clear what would be required of you. Why do you not go aside with her now. There will be time enough to discuss the matter, and if you are willing, for Lady Catherine to establish you in her place at Court."

Pasgen, seething with rage he could not direct at any one person or thing, fled to an Unformed land, hoping to find something that would fix his attention and give him ease. He found only echoes of his grief and rage; the mists boiled and foamed, terrifying him because he could sense nothing. For a few despairing moments he thought of ending his own life, but he knew that would be condemning Rhoslyn too. Yet he could not bear the thought of seeing or speaking to Rhoslyn now.

He turned in the Gate, blank with pain, and fell through darkness to come to rest at the simple and elegant Gate in Elfhame Elder-Elf. Gaenor was just dismounting from Nuin, her face a study of anger and anxiety.

"What have you done?" she cried.

"Everything wrong. Nothing right," Pasgen replied, in utter misery.

"Not with your life! I mean now! Did you not swear to me by the Mother that you would not go to that special Chaos Land?"

Pasgen drew in a sharp breath. "I did not," he protested, and then recalling that he had not consciously patterned for Elfhame Elder-Elf wondered whether he had, in his pain and confusion, sent himself to the place where the mist seemed to be awake and aware. But the mist he had encountered had been far from aware; they had been even more formless than usual, which was what frightened him. "No," he said more surely. "I am sure I did not."

Gaenor stared at him. "But I have a . . . a caller in the Gate there and it sounded an alarm. I have just come to Gate there to see what set off that alarm."

"I did not," Pasgen muttered helplessly, not even caring about his favorite puzzle just now.

Before the words were out, Gaenor was up on the Gate platform, had seized his wrist, and they were there. Gaenor started back a half step, catching her breath. Both of the Unformed land's creations were near the Gate, clearly visible for once. But neither of the doll-like figures looked at her. Both stared at Pasgen. Both beckoned to him and when he did not come, beckoned more eagerly. Suddenly Pasgen shuddered and shook his head violently. Then they turned together and melted into the mist.

"What did they want?" Gaenor asked, but Pasgen only shook his head and did not answer.

She then gestured and a plaque something like a patterning plaque appeared. She stared at it, touched it in several places and shook her head. "It has no record of you being here. Did you do something to my caller?"

"I did not know there was one," Pasgen said. "And I did *not* come here." He was certain now. The feeling of this domain was too distinct for him to dismiss, even as miserable as he felt.

Gaenor looked about uneasily. The mists were roiling and coiling, coming nearer to the Gate, stretching tendrils as if to enter the Gate and touch them. Gaenor quickly gestured the plaque into hiding again, grasped Pasgen's wrist, and brought them back to Elfhame Elder-Elf.

Nuin was grazing nearby but did not approach as Gaenor stepped down from the Gate, still holding Pasgen firmly by the wrist. She turned to face him.

"What is wrong? Something is terribly wrong. I can feel it boiling around you, and the mist felt it too. Pasgen, we must do something about that mist. It knew something was amiss with you—but how? I think the *mist* triggered the caller. Did the mist send you here? If you weren't there, how did it know something is wrong?"

Pasgen only heard the first three words of what Gaenor said. The rest was a dull mumble, muted by the pain he felt. The agony grew sharper as she spoke; it was important, but he could do nothing, think of nothing until he was rid of the shard of his life that pierced his heart.

"My mother is dead," Pasgen said. "She killed herself."

For a moment Gaenor stared at him, dumbfound. Then she gestured to Nuin. She mounted, held out a hand to assist Pasgen to mount the elvensteed.

Another agonizing pain, but he simply shook his head. "It will not carry me," he said.

"If Nuin did not wish to carry you, you would know it already," Gaenor snapped. "You would be trampled and she would not be standing here with a double saddle."

Pasgen blinked away the tears the expected rejection had drawn to his eyes. He had always so desired to ride the perfect beauty, perfect grace that was an elvensteed, but none, until now, had ever allowed him near. Silently, only half believing Nuin would permit it, he took Gaenor's hand and got into the saddle.

The joy that had broken through his pall of guilt and grief hardly lasted a moment. Before Pasgen could even feel relief they were at the door of a spare, white cottage. Knowing the moment of mercy had been withdrawn, Pasgen got down. Gaenor followed. Nuin simply disappeared. Wordlessly Pasgen stared at the place where the elvensteed had been.

Gaenor opened the door of the cottage and urged Pasgen inside into a large, comfortable room. "Why?" she said.

Pasgen blinked. The word made no sense. He was still thinking of the miracle of having ridden Nuin, which had somehow set the pain of Llanelli's death at a distance.

"Why did your mother kill herself?" Gaenor asked.

The grief and guilt crashed down over Pasgen again. He closed his eyes. After a moment more, he said, "It is such a very long story."

"Not so long I hope that, aged as I am, I will not survive to the end of it." Gaenor's acid tone etched an opening into the pall of grief and guilt. "When did you eat last?" she asked sharply.

"Eat?" Pasgen repeated stupidly and looked around.

Gaenor sighed and went to sit down in a chair. "I keep forgetting how young you are," she said, and gestured to another chair close to the one she had chosen.

Both chairs were old and shabby, the cushions worn enough that the pattern, whatever it had been, could not be determined. They should have scored Pasgen's tight nerves and made him furious. Instead they seemed to fit into a well established pattern that was soothing.

Beside the chair Gaenor had chosen was a small table laden

with papers and a book. A door in the back of the room opened and an old female construct stood waiting. Gaenor turned her head and addressed the construct who, Pasgen could tell, was relatively mindless, unlike most of Rhoslyn's makings.

"Bring two dinners," she ordered. And then said to Pasgen, "Well? Begin this long story."

He had to begin at the beginning, even though it cast no good light on Llanelli. "My mother," he said, "had two very strong desires. She wanted Kefni Deulwyn Siarl Silverhair and she wanted a child by him."

Pasgen expected surprise, even disbelief, but Gaenor only lifted one thick, white brow. By the time the servant brought in the dinners, he had described the means by which Llanelli had satisfied those desires. He half expected that Gaenor would silence him in disgust or say with contempt that she understood why Llanelli had killed herself; however, aside from one mild *tsk* she showed no reaction. Pasgen could only assume that the Sidhe had used stronger and more dire magics when she was young.

The rest of the story came out in bits and pieces while they ate—Kefni's failed rescue, Llanelli's struggle to protect her children and to show them something of the way of life in the Bright Court, Vidal's discovery of what she had done and his cruel punishment and revenge which resulted in Llanelli's conviction that Vidal was all-powerful. Pasgen even confessed his attempts to gain instruction from Treowth and his rejection and Rhoslyn's desire to leave the Dark Court and be accepted by the Bright.

"Somehow Mother must have learned of that, likely she listened when we did not know she was near." He sighed. "She did that often because she felt we hid from her anything that would cause her pain, but she was convinced she had to know to protect us. Her letter said that her death would free us to appeal to Oberon."

Gaenor made a sound suspiciously like a disbelieving snort which drew Pasgen's eyes to her; he had been looking off into the distance as he described his and his sister's seemingly hopeless desires. However, when he examined Gaenor's face, she looked almost as bland and blank as the construct that served her.

"This is no time to talk about how you will shape your life in the future—or lives, if as you imply, you and your sister will move together. You are too filled with rage and grief to plan a happy future. You want to kill this Vidal Dhu because you blame him for your mother's death, but you cannot convince even yourself that he was deliberately responsible for it. Worse yet, you do not *want* Vidal dead because if you kill him you might be forced to rule the Dark Court."

Gaenor laughed as Pasgen felt himself flush. "A home truth."

But then she put out a hand and patted him gently. "This is no more a time for home truths than for plans for the future. Before you can deal with those, you need enough satisfaction to calm your spirit but one that will not kill Vidal. In fact, killing him would give you little satisfaction. You would always remember how he made your mother suffer. You need to make him *suffer*, not end all his troubles and woes."

Light seemed to burst in Pasgen's head driving out the dark pall of misery. He suddenly realized that he could have his revenge of Vidal and not be in danger of being bound to the Dark Court forever.

"That is exactly right, Gaenor," he cried. "I need to make him suffer, to withhold from him all he holds dear . . ." The joyful energy drained away and he shook his head. "But there isn't anyone or anything beside himself that Vidal does hold dear."

Gaenor laughed again. "Of course there is, my young and innocent one. Vidal values his preeminence. Take away his power, reduce him in—"

"Oh, wonderful!" Pasgen interrupted, his eyes alight, his enthusiasm restored. "But I do not need to drain his personal power; that would return as he sucked misery out of the mortal world." He laughed aloud. "I will leave him as strong as ever but make sure he can barely feed himself or the monsters of his Court."

"That sounds like a suitable revenge."

"Yes." Pasgen nodded, his eyes distant again but bright now, not clouded with self-blame. "And I know just where to start. He has set his heart on the ruin of Elizabeth Tudor. I will see that his instrument for her ruin is ruined instead and that she is valued and cherished as the best heir to the realm of England."

Pasgen went west to pick up the threads he had spun almost a year earlier. Now he would weave those threads into a net that would catch and destroy Vidal's tool and had no connection to Elizabeth. He was, unfortunately, unaware of just how tangled together Thomas Seymour and Elizabeth had become.

Rhoslyn had no trouble establishing herself as a friend and companion of the duchess of Somerset. Lady Catherine introduced her and a few small twists inserted into the duchess' mind made Rhoslyn a trusted companion. By early December Rhoslyn was hearing tales she did not like. Just about the time Parry was asking Seymour about a house in London for Elizabeth's Christmas visit to the king, Rhoslyn heard rumors that Seymour was plotting political mischief.

She left a message Underhill for Aleneil that Elizabeth should avoid all contact with Seymour and should not attend Court unless she was commanded to come. Aleneil did not deliver the message herself; she had had enough of the mortal world while Elizabeth was living with Queen Catherine and was threatened by Seymour's presence. Aleneil was taking what she felt was a deserved period of rest and recreation and was now enjoying herself Underhill mostly in Ilar's company.

Aleneil passed Rhoslyn's message to Denoriel's servants at Llachar Lle. The information was too late to prevent Parry's meeting with Seymour, but together with the warning she had received from William Cecil, it was enough to make Elizabeth give up her hope of going to London and decide to stay quietly at Hatfield over Christmas.

Master Ascham gauged Elizabeth's mood and temper after this decision was made, and using the reason that no real studying would be done during the holidays, asked for leave to spend the time with his friends in Cambridge. The leave was granted, not very graciously, but Ascham felt he was well away from a storm about to break.

The celebration of the holiday was traditional but, in view of the reprimand delivered to Kat by the duchess of Somerset, subdued. Kat's anxiety spilled over onto Elizabeth. Although there was no overt threat of any kind, Elizabeth was not in the mood for merriment.

Hoping to make Elizabeth more cheerful and make up for her missing Edward's company and the celebrations in the Court, Denoriel urged her to attend a ball Underhill. She went, but it did not raise her spirits. She found herself repelled by the unthinking gaiety of the Sidhe. Despite their length of life, none of them wanted to look ahead, to prepare for the future.

She and Denno quarreled and she wept all through one long,

sleepless night, but he came with lavish New Year's gifts two days later, and she forgave him. Nonetheless she would not go Underhill again. Still, peace seemed to be restored. It was the lull before the storm.

On the sixth of January, Pasgen saw his carefully woven net catch the cony. In the guise of a minor clerk of the mint he accompanied a group of government officers who raided Laycock Abbey, Sharington's rich mansion. Small mental suggestions directed them to the evidence of Sharington's forgeries in the mint and his treasonable connection with Seymour. No one in the excited group of gentlemen who would bring about Seymour's downfall thought about the clerk, who had disappeared.

With the first step of his revenge complete and some of his self-blame soothed, Pasgen gave some grateful thought to Gaenor, which caused him to wonder how she knew to meet him at the Gate when he had not even intended to go to Elfhame Elder-Elf. He remembered then the rest of what she had said, after she asked him what was wrong. She thought the mist had *felt* his distress and done something to her caller . . . even though he had not been in that Unformed land.

Impossible. Or was it? How much did even he know about the mists of the Chaos Lands? Thoughtfully, Pasgen Gated from Bristol to Elfhame Cymry and from there to Elfhame Elder-Elf. Gaenor had said that something must be done about the mist. He definitely wanted to know what she meant. Underhill was more important than the mortal world. He could leave Seymour to hang himself.

Seymour was doing just that. Denoriel was at first merely interested since what he heard from Denny was mostly about Seymour's amassing weapons at Sudeley and trying to convince such men as Dorset, Northampton and even Wriothesley to support him. Nonetheless, because of the political tensions and rumors, Denoriel now made a practice of stopping at the house on Bucklersbury several times a week in case there were messages.

On the tenth of January, Joseph Clayborne gave him a folded and sealed note from William Cecil. Denoriel opened it with misgivings but found only an invitation to visit the house on Cannon Row. His first impulse was to rush off immediately, but on second thought he decided to present himself at the usual hour for visits.

"He is not here," Mildred said, looking harried, "but I know he wants to speak to you." She looked around as if to be sure no servant was lurking in a corner and she had signed to Denoriel to close the door when he had entered the room. "Can you come back after dinner? I am so sorry I cannot invite you to dinner, but these days . . . I don't know who will be coming home with William." She smiled wryly. "Sometimes *I* don't get invited to dinner."

Denoriel smiled at her. "Not by your husband's will, I am sure."

"Perhaps not. I think I know what he wants to speak to you about, but it would be better for you to talk to him directly."

And when he was shown into William Cecil's private closet, he understood that it was less what Cecil had to tell than what he had to ask that made their meeting imperative.

"How close tied in affection and intent is the Lady Elizabeth to Sir Thomas Seymour?" Cecil asked abruptly as soon as the door closed behind Denoriel.

"Not at all!" Denoriel exclaimed, horrified.

"Are you sure? I know you have been her friend for many years, but would she tell you if she were contemplating a secret marriage?"

"Elizabeth? With Seymour?" Denoriel gasped. "Contemplate a secret marriage? Never!"

"I have heard that Mistress Ashley was encouraging her to think of marriage to Seymour."

Denoriel muttered an angry obscenity. "Yes, the woman is a fool. But Lady Elizabeth never agreed. I know she does not wish to marry. And even Mistress Ashley only said that if the king and Council asked it of her that it would be the best marriage she could make."

"You are sure there was no secret agreement between them?"

"Yes! I am sure! Master Cecil, there has been no meeting between Seymour and Lady Elizabeth since Queen Catherine died. There are servants in Lady Elizabeth's household who know me longer than they know her. I assure you that I would know if there were secret meetings or moonlight trysts—and I would have made sure such stopped."

"No correspondence?" Cecil shook his head and waved toward a chair while he settled himself behind a handsome table laden with papers.

Denoriel sat down and said slowly, "Seymour wrote some

letters to her while the queen was heavy with child, and Lady Elizabeth did answer those in her letters to the queen, but she never wrote him a line after Catherine's death—not even a note of condolence. I know that Mistress Ashley urged her to write, but she would not."

"Nothing at all? I am afraid a thorough search will be made through Seymour's papers."

Denoriel bit his lip. "While she still hoped to come to Court to visit King Edward over Christmas, she did write to Seymour about a suitable house. You know Durham House where she was used to stay has been made into a mint. And her cofferer, Thomas Parry, went to London to speak to Seymour about it. Seymour offered her lodging in Seymour Place, and Lady Elizabeth rejected that, saying she would not stay in any house where he was."

"Seymour is lost, you know."

"Yes, I do know. Sir Anthony told me of his collusion with the pirates and his connection to Sharington and the forgeries in the mint. But what has this to do with Lady Elizabeth?"

Cecil took a deep breath and let it out in a deep sigh. "Nothing. Lady Elizabeth is not implicated in any way in Seymour's schemes in Bristol and the islands, but others are implicated who could cause some embarrassment to the government. There are those in the Council who think it would be safer and simpler to attaint Seymour for the treason of intending to marry Lady Elizabeth. You know he has boasted that he could have her—"

Cecil stopped speaking abruptly as Denoriel leapt to his feet.

"I'll kill him!" he snarled, his hand on his sword hilt.

"Sit down, man," Cecil said. "Do not be a fool. For you to attack Seymour could do Lady Elizabeth's reputation no good. Too many know you have been her friend and champion for many years."

"But why?" Denoriel protested. "Why drag her into Seymour's dirt? Surely they have reason enough to try him for treason without mentioning Lady Elizabeth."

Cecil looked more worried than he had at any other time. "I am not sure why, but I fear there is more than one cause and that the strike may be at Lady Elizabeth and Seymour just the tool. I do know that the Protector's wife has a very strong dislike of Lady Elizabeth. And there are others who, for their own safety and advancement, support the Protector's new religious practices but in their hearts long for the old faith. Those see Elizabeth as a future danger and would be rid of her. And Lady Mary has adherents that think of Lady Elizabeth as a rival to her sister, a rival to lead a civil war that favors the reformed religion . . ."

And there it was again. The terrible threat of the curse of civil war, a war that would make no one rejoice.

No one, that is, except Vidal Dhu.

Chapter 34

Vidal, sitting behind Otstargi's table, sent a light probe into Chancellor Rich's mind and smiled. It was not a mind he wished to damage so he did not tear away the surface thoughts to reach the deeper motives. In any case, Rich's mind was such a sewer that Vidal was sure of the mortal's motivation without deep probing.

Nonetheless at the moment he was not pleased with Rich. The idiot had set the hounds onto Seymour before Elizabeth was in Seymour's grasp. Now bringing about her disgrace would be much more difficult. Vidal skimmed the surface of Rich's mind again. No, there was nothing about Elizabeth in it. He did not even connect her to Seymour. The man blinked and straightened a trifle when Vidal released his mind.

"What can I do for you?" Vidal/Otstargi asked, although it was his "calling" that had brought Rich to the magician's house.

Rich frowned, bewildered momentarily because he really did not know why he had come to see the sorcerer. But before the doubt could become a solid thought, a large yellow diamond in a ring on his left hand glittered and he breathed out in a sigh, thinking he remembered.

"You can tell me whether you have foreseen any results of the exposure of Seymour's crimes."

"Why did you send in your men so soon?" Vidal asked angrily. "If your inspectors had waited six months, the case against him—"

459

"They were not my men," Rich snapped back. "One of the clerks in the mint became aware of what Sharington was doing and took fright and reported him."

Vidal uttered an obscenity—in Elven.

Rich shook his head and asked impatiently, "Well? Should I be concerned about Sharington's accusation of Seymour or is your fabled foresight useless?"

"Foresight is never useless, but now the evidence may not be strong enough. It may be needful to involve the Lady Elizabeth."

"Lady Elizabeth?" Rich's voice went flat; his face bland and blank. "Are you telling me that Lady Elizabeth is a party to Seymour's crimes?"

Vidal dared a very light probe and to his delight learned that Rich was an adherent of the old faith. He kept his convictions a deep secret; they had only been brought to the surface by the mention of Elizabeth, whom Rich wished dead as sincerely as Vidal did. The instant in which Vidal looked did not exist for Rich. To his perception, Otstargi answered his question immediately.

"She is certainly involved deeply with Seymour," Vidal said. "I doubt you will ever be able to discover whether she had any part in bilking the mint or colluding with the pirates. But by King Henry's will, would it not be treason for her to agree to marry Seymour?"

"Has she?"

Vidal wanted to say "yes" but he would lose too much influence if he made a positive statement that could be proven untrue. And he knew that Elizabeth had never agreed to marry Seymour no matter how often Mistress Ashley urged that as an end to be devoutly sought.

"That she desires it, I have seen, but probe as I will my glass does not show any piece of writing or any open statement of her preference."

"The preference is there? She did desire the marriage? And what more than marriage did she desire?"

Vidal did not smile because it would have been out of character for Otstargi, who could have no personal interest in Elizabeth, but he was deeply pleased with Rich who seemed very ready to blacken Elizabeth with every crime he could think of.

"I cannot tell you," Vidal admitted, pretending regret. "The images are much mingled and obscured. You will need to obtain this information from the lady herself and from her household. Not so much from the maidens, as she does not trust them to hold their tongues. It is Mistress Ashley who has the secrets of her heart and Master Parry who knows what she intends to do with her purse."

An expression of eager interest on Rich's face was soon succeeded briefly by one of irritation and then with one of satisfaction.

"I can do nothing yet," Rich admitted. "Seymour is not yet aware that we have Sharington and that the man is more than willing to talk and lay the blame for his crimes on someone else. Unfortunately the blame touches others than Seymour and it may be worth it to them to let him escape."

"Then you should change the chief point of Seymour's crime from the pirates and the Bristol Mint to his meddling with Lady Elizabeth."

Rich's lips twisted. "She has supporters, strong supporters among the Councilors."

"But you have the choosing of those who will question her and her household. Choose two men who are known to favor Lady Elizabeth and one who is indifferent. That way no one can say of you that you set out to do her harm. But make clear to the man who is indifferent that he must extract from Lady Elizabeth enough to send Seymour to the block. And you can promise him that if the evidence should so incriminate Lady Elizabeth that she must also be punished, no blame would attach to him for that honesty."

"That I can do—provided she does not enchant him as she does so many who visit her even briefly."

Vidal frowned. Could Denoriel or Aleneil or any of their thrice-blasted friends have taught the girl some spell that bound men to her? He looked up at Rich, who had said something about needing to return to work and was preparing to rise from his chair.

"Yes, my lord, of course. I know you are a busy man. But if you will return here tomorrow at the same hour, I will have a token for you. If you give that token to the man who is to question Lady Elizabeth, it will shield him from her unnatural attractions and remind him that his first duty is to you."

"Unnatural attractions," Rich repeated, softly, a look of intense interest coming into his face. "Do you imply that Lady Elizabeth practices witchcraft?"

"I would not go so far," Vidal replied.

"Lady Mary was once reputed to have said that her sister had called back the dead..." Rich offered hopefully

Vidal shook his head. "Such an idea would destroy me and you for consulting me. The token can do only good."

No, Vidal thought, as Rich said his somewhat disappointed farewells and left the house. It was too bad he could not go so far as to hint that Elizabeth was a witch, but that would seal his doom with Oberon. To raise the subject of witchcraft in the royal house would be far more unforgivable in Oberon's opinion than having the girl killed.

Oberon did not really care about the mortal. He had only forbidden anyone to cause her death because he wished to avoid any chance of an examination that might expose Underhill. A trial for witchcraft . . . Vidal shuddered.

That Cecil's warning was all too accurate became evident a few days later when Seymour sealed his fate with a stupid, ill-planned attempt to abduct the king. He had obtained from Edward's servant John Fowler, through whose hands he had often sent the king pocket money, forged keys to the king's rooms in Hampton Court. On the sixteenth of January, Seymour used his key and entered Edward's apartment. The boy's spaniel leapt at Seymour . . . and Seymour shot the dog dead.

The barking of the dog and the sound of the shot brought an officer of the Yeomen of the Guard. Even Seymour knew he could not seize the boy while the guard watched, and from the expression on Edward's face as he looked down at his dead pet, Seymour knew he could not get the boy to come with him willingly. It had been a mistake to shoot the dog; he should have saved the bullet for the guard.

All Seymour could do was to compliment the officer on his prompt response and say he had come to test how well the king was guarded and that he was well satisfied. The guard was afraid to arrest the Protector's brother and so he let Seymour go, but he reported the incident to the Council immediately. Early the next morning the Council met and decided to commit Thomas Seymour to the Tower to be held until further orders. He was arrested that night and in spite of earlier bluster went meekly to prison.

Despite this open act of treason, which together with his other crimes, was surely enough to convict Seymour, Rhoslyn sent Denoriel a frantic message that Elizabeth was to be implicated. The duchess had confided to her that it was Somerset's conviction Elizabeth intended to be queen. The Lord Protector had been convinced his brother had "devised and almost brought to pass a secret marriage between himself and the Lady Elizabeth." Somerset believed that Seymour intended to imprison or, perhaps, kill Edward and Mary and control the Council at his will.

Lord St. John, Sir Anthony Denny, and Sir Robert Tyrwhitt went to Hatfield on the twentieth of January to interrogate Elizabeth, but they were too late. On the night of the nineteenth, Denoriel had sleep-spelled Margaret Dudley, set Blanche Parry to watch for any other intrusion, and insisted that Elizabeth come with him to Llachar Lle.

There he told her what had happened. All she said when he told her of Seymour's incursion into Edward's apartment was first, "What a fool!" and then "Oh, poor Edward, he has so little to love. To lose the dog must have grieved him."

However, when he told her how she was implicated in Seymour's treason, the storm he had expected broke. She shrieked with rage, loud enough he feared to have penetrated the walls into her maidens' chambers or even through the spelled sleep in which Margaret lay. He was glad he had insisted on bringing her Underhill.

"Why did you not defend me?" she screamed. "Why did you not say I had no reason to desire that toad?"

"To whom should I say it? Who would listen to me? And what proof could I offer of your preference for me? And if I had proof, you know I dare not use it."

That was so obvious a truth that even in her rage Elizabeth could not argue with it. She spoke instead of those she thought were her enemies in terms that would have made her guardsmen blush. Denoriel let her rage except when she accused someone he thought secretly friendly to her. When she was exhausted, she said, "But they cannot believe it? I *love* Edward. I would never harm him in any way. I do, I do desire that he live and reign long and happily."

"I know it and you know it. The one who does not know it, or does not care if he does, is Thomas Seymour. The danger is in what he has said about you."

Elizabeth shivered. "How can I defend against that?"

"Only by ignorance. You know nothing of Seymour's ideas. You have never spoken to him except in Queen Catherine's presence or perhaps a chance meeting in passing when your maidens were with you. You have never written to him except on business. You have the letters he wrote in the queen's name from Gloucestershire?" Elizabeth nodded. "Good, be sure they are distributed among your other correspondence, not set aside as anything special."

They talked most of the night and by the time Elizabeth returned to Hatfield she was in control and able to conceal her fear. She hardly reacted to the news that Paulet, Denny, and Tyrwhitt brought. And when Tyrwhitt asked sharply if she were not surprised, she shook her head.

"No, Lord Denno rode out two days ago to tell us of Seymour's arrest."

"And why was that? Why did Lord Denno—who is this Lord Denno? It is not a title I know," Tyrwhitt snapped.

"It is not an English title," Sir Anthony said gently. "He is a very rich merchant who has been a friend of Lady Elizabeth's since her childhood."

Tyrwhitt frowned at Sir Anthony, ran his thumb over the handsome ruby ring Chancellor Rich had given him with his instructions concerning Elizabeth. For all their sakes in the Protector's government, Rich had said, Tyrwhitt must obtain enough evidence of Seymour's treasonable intention to marry Lady Elizabeth, to send Seymour to the block. He must uncover this evidence, even if Lady Elizabeth were incriminated.

Tyrwhitt turned what he knew to be an intimidating frown on Elizabeth. "And why should you care that the Admiral was arrested?" he asked.

Far from being frightened, Elizabeth cocked her head in obvious puzzlement. "He was my beloved stepmother's husband. How could I not be concerned over such evil news?"

"Surely your interest was more personal than that!" Tyrwhitt said.

"No!" Elizabeth spat, her voice rising; she drew herself up, her lips thinning to almost invisible lines. "I have not now nor ever had any *personal* interest in Sir Thomas Seymour. He was Queen Catherine's husband. Queen Catherine was my stepmother and a true mother to me. I loved her. I cannot tell you all her kindness to me. I owed to her the duty to live pleasantly with her husband."

"Now, Lady Elizabeth," Sir Anthony put in soothingly, "Sir Robert meant no harm, but we do wish to understand completely your connection with Thomas Seymour."

"You already understand it completely," Elizabeth snapped. "There was and is *no* connection. Sir Anthony, I lived with you in Cheshunt for many months. Was there any communication between me and Sir Thomas that did not concern Queen Catherine?"

"No, that is true, but in a case like this . . ." Sir Anthony turned to Tyrwhitt. "Let me speak to Lady Elizabeth in private. We are old friends."

Were *friends*, Elizabeth thought. *I dare not think of him as a friend, but I must remember what Denno said. I must speak with easy confidence. Aside from silly Kat's romantic fantasies, there* was *nothing between Tom and me. Poor Tom. The clumsy puppy has bumbled into a bog.* Cold ran down her spine. *I only hope he does not drown me with him.* She shivered as Denny gestured her ahead into her private parlor.

"Now, my dear," Denny said, "no one is blaming you. We all know that you are only a young girl. You have not been guided wisely, but that is not your fault."

No, Elizabeth thought, *Kat is not wise. She loves me too much and was too eager for what she thought would be my happiness with a strong and handsome husband. Kat knows how much I love Edward and that I would never conspire against him, so she never thought ahead to the danger of an heir to the throne marrying a strong and ambitious man already close to the seat of power.*

"Perhaps I should have been more definite in rejecting some of the advice given me," Elizabeth said, sighing, "but it was kindly meant. And only offered subject to the will of the king and the Council."

"But was not the Council's opinion spoken of as a foregone conclusion?" Denny suggested gently. "Come, tell me all that was said and done since you came here to Hatfield."

Elizabeth was ready enough to do so. Denny listened closely, eager to believe her but watching for any sign of uneasiness or concealment.

Meanwhile, Tyrwhitt had summoned the entire household

to gather in the great hall. There he announced that the Lord High Admiral, Sir Thomas Seymour, had been committed to the Tower on a charge of high treason. On pain of being judged a coconspirator, they were to answer all questions and to offer any information concerning Sir Thomas even if no question that touched that information was asked.

First he spoke to Elizabeth's maidens. They were all very excited, very horrified, by his news. They could not believe that Sir Thomas had done such dreadful things. He was such a jolly man, so amusing and playful. But though all were open and more than willing to talk, what they said was not what Tyrwhitt wanted to hear.

Item: The last time any of them had seen Sir Thomas was when they left Chelsea.

Item: While they were living in Cheshunt, before the death of the queen, letters had come from Sir Thomas and Lady Elizabeth had been glad to receive them and to answer them, but they were all about the queen and the child she carried.

Item: No communication had been received from Sir Thomas since they moved to Hatfield and he had never visited the house.

Item: All of them had heard Mistress Ashley praise the Admiral and say that he would make a wonderful husband for Lady Elizabeth. But Lady Elizabeth had always said nay by her troth, she would not have him.

Tyrwhitt had been alert for the smallest sign of guilt, when he questioned them one at a time, a fluttering eyelid, a small change of color. And when he had them all together, he watched for the briefest exchange of glances. With even a tiny hint he would have known where to prod and pry; there was nothing. The girls were all agog, but the most eager questioner could not pretend they were hiding anything.

Questioning of the guards and the grooms had no better result. No visits and no communications had ever been received at Hatfield from Sir Thomas Seymour. The servants all sang the same song. Most of them, hired when Elizabeth moved into Hatfield, had no idea who Sir Thomas was but shook their heads when he was described. No, they said, no one who looked like the description ever came. The only gentleman who was not one of Lady Elizabeth's tutors or an official of the Council or a foreign dignitary, like the ambassadors of France and Venice and Denmark who came to see Lady Elizabeth, was Lord Denno, and he never saw her in private.

By the time Sir Anthony came from Elizabeth's parlor, Sir Robert was seriously annoyed. He had thought they would have all the evidence they needed in a few hours. However, he looked up and smiled hopefully at Sir Anthony.

"Well, has she confessed?"

"To what?" Sir Anthony said. "She is innocent. Whatever the Admiral had in mind, he has not communicated it to Lady Elizabeth. He may have hinted it to her cofferer, Thomas Parry, to whom he suggested that Lady Elizabeth request that some of her lands be changed for others in the west, near his own lands. But she would have none of it and was quite cross with her man over the suggestion. Does that sound as if she planned any permanent connection with Seymour?"

Doubt flickered momentarily in Sir Robert's eyes, but the ruby ring glinted its crimson summons and his thumb rubbed its silky surface.

"She has too much support and does not yet feel the need to tell the truth and clear her conscience. Also, we will better extract the real facts from Mistress Ashley and Master Parry when they are less comfortable and secure. We must remove them from their own chambers and their own servants. Paulet has agreed that they should be arrested. He will accompany you back to London. A few days in the Tower will loosen their tongues."

Denny frowned. He thought he knew Elizabeth well and he was reasonably sure she had no agreement with Seymour. He was equally sure that she was hiding something, protecting someone. He sighed. Likely the one she was protecting was Mistress Ashley.

It was not impossible, Denny thought, that Mistress Ashley had some agreement with Seymour and that Elizabeth knew of it. If so, Tyrwhitt was greatly mistaken if he believed he could pry that knowledge out of Elizabeth. However, Mistress Ashley herself might well be brought to confess if she were lodged in the Tower and convinced that her foolishness had endangered Lady Elizabeth.

"Very well," Denny agreed. "I will take Ashley and Parry back to London with me."

Tyrwhitt waited only until he was sure Denny and Paulet were well away. Then he let himself into Elizabeth's private parlor with barely a scratch on the door. His temper was further exacerbated by finding Elizabeth in the midst of her ladies, not weeping but listening to their excited remarks while calmly working on a lovely piece of embroidery. He drew a breath as he came closer and saw that it carried the royal arms.

Silence fell as he entered the room but before anyone could say anything, he bade the maids of honor leave; he had something to tell Lady Elizabeth in private. They went reluctantly, the last girl looking over her shoulder. As the outer door closed, the one to the bedroom opened and Blanche Parry brought a stool to the doorway and sat down. She was out of hearing distance, unless Tyrwhitt or Elizabeth shouted, but she could see everything that happened.

"You may go," Tyrwhitt snapped at Blanche. "I wish to speak to your mistress in private."

Blanche did not even raise her head. Her eyes flicked up from the piece of mending she held in her lap but then went back to the sewing.

"She will not leave," Elizabeth said. "Not on the order of some strange man. She knows that I am never to be left alone. She cannot hear what you or I say, but she can be sure that you do me no hurt."

"I am an officer of the Council," Tyrwhitt said angrily. "I have their commission to question you."

Elizabeth sighed. "I have answered all of Sir Anthony's questions. Must I say the same things all over again?"

"This time you will speak without any promptings from your household. Mistress Ashley and Master Parry are arrested and on their way to the Tower, where they will be questioned and the truth will be extracted from them."

"Arrested!" Elizabeth cried, dropping her embroidery and clasping her hands. "No," she gasped and burst into tears. "No! No! Oh, no. Not Kat! Oh, I beg you, Sir Robert, please bring them back to me. They have done no wrong. Truly they have not. Their only crime is to wish me happy. Please set them free. I will bid them to answer anything you ask, anything."

"They are long gone and I would not bring them back even if it was within my power, which it is not."

"Please, Sir Robert," Elizabeth sobbed, "please. I will tell you anything you want. Only bring Kat back to me."

"Certainly you will tell me anything I want to know. That is your duty and your own path to safety. Mistress Ashley and Master Parry have led you sadly astray and put you in great danger. Think on that. I will speak to you again when you have considered and calmed yourself."

Chapter 35

The decision Sir Robert made to allow Elizabeth to stew in her own juice of fear was the end, although he did not know it, of his purpose of wringing a terrified confession from her. He compounded his error by summoning the household again to forbid her maidens to return to her. No one was to disturb Lady Elizabeth for any purpose, he commanded.

"Will you starve the lady?" Dunstan asked, loudly enough for the whole assembly to hear. "I do not think the other commissioners would be glad to hear of that."

"No, no, of course not," Tyrwhitt snapped, looking hard at the middle-aged man who had spoken. "And who are you?"

The question usually caused anyone who had addressed him in less than servile tones to shrink away. This man gave back as hard a glance as Tyrwhitt's own, making Sir Robert suspect that he was more dangerous than he looked.

"My name is Sander Dunstan, and I have been Lady Elizabeth's majordomo since she was three years old. I am naturally concerned for her well-being." He spoke in a clear voice that drew heads toward him.

"Well, of course an evening meal will be carried to Lady Elizabeth's chamber," Tyrwhitt said coldly, aware of the appalled expressions on the faces turned to him.

Some of those faces, the maids of honor and the few gentlemen of the chamber were well connected to high families. There was no way he could silence them all and word of his depriving Elizabeth of food would surely spread. Tyrwhitt was furious. He had intended Elizabeth to be hungry and to believe her entire entourage had deserted her.

"But," Sir Robert added, "she is not to be troubled by her ladies or anyone else. She has much to consider and needs time and privacy to do so."

Only Sir Robert's plan was already in shambles. As soon as the door to the parlor closed, Blanche rushed to Elizabeth and took her in her arms. She had, while seemingly being totally absorbed in her mending, heard every word, since she was far from either deaf or uninterested.

"Never you mind, love, never you mind," Blanche said to the weeping, trembling girl. "Mistress Ashley may not have been very wise about praising Sir Thomas to you, but she must realize now what a mistake that was. She won't say anything, and Master Parry, he doesn't know anything, except what you've already told Sir Anthony. And anyhow, Lord Denno . . . he'll get into the Tower and set everything right, you'll see."

That assurance was enough to lift Elizabeth out of the pit of panic and despair. Next she demanded an immediate rescue and deplored the fact that her life had been so pleasant and uneventful over the past few months that no air spirit was in attendance to bring Denno to her at once.

Blanche shook her head. "No, lovey, he can't come now. What if that cream-faced loon should walk in on us."

Elizabeth showed her teeth in what was not a smile. "I'd freeze him where he stood, Blanche. I'd freeze him so well, so truly, he would remain as a statue for the rest of his days." She could never speak of Underhill, but there were many mortal ways to "freeze" an enemy. So as long as Elizabeth did not imply use of a spell, the words would come.

"No you wouldn't," Blanche said, laughing and snorting disdain. "What'd we do with him? Surely you wouldn't want him standing about as a most unlovely ornament in your apartment."

Elizabeth uttered a half-hysterical giggle. "No. He isn't that decorative."

But then she sobered and acknowledged that she would need to wait until Denno thought it safe to come. At least there would be no maiden to weave into a sleep spell. She tried for a little while to read, but the words made no sense to her and she took up her embroidery instead, idly asking Blanche why Tyrwhitt should have stared at it as if he had never seen embroidery before.

Blanche frowned. "I'm sorry he saw that piece." And when Elizabeth raised a questioning brow at her, added, "It's got the royal arms on it."

"Well, of course it has," Elizabeth replied, mildly irritated. "I am doing it for Edward."

"Yes, only Sir Robert doesn't know that. You'd better find a way to tell him or, better, get one of the ladies to tell him."

Elizabeth's eyes widened and grew dark. "You mean he thought I was doing it for myself? As if I should soon be . . . be . . . No." She swallowed and blinked back rising tears. "Edward is young and strong. He will be a good king and for a long, happy reign."

"We all hope so," Blanche agreed.

"I am not so stupid as to embroider anything with the royal arms on it for myself." Elizabeth was again indignant.

"No, of course not," Blanche said. "And I hope you will not be so stupid as to ask the impossible from Lord Denno."

Elizabeth started to reply, but there was a scratch on the door. Blanche scurried out of sight as soon as they heard the scratch, and Elizabeth herself went to let the groom in. She should have been annoyed over her need to do a servant's duty, but she was too absorbed by her worry over what Blanche had last said to do more than nod civilly at the young man. Absently she looked at the meal he carried to her, gestured for him to set the tray on a table, and actually begin to eat before she waved him away.

Thus he carried back a very unsatisfactory report to Sir Robert. No, Lady Elizabeth had not rejected the food, she had begun to eat at once. No, he had not told Lady Elizabeth he was forbidden to speak to her because she had never spoken to him. No, she was not weeping. No, she did not seem distressed by the fact that she was all alone and had to open the door herself, like a servant. No, she did not look at all frightened. And then, at last, Sir Robert got a yes. Yes, Lady Elizabeth seemed as if she was thinking deeply and seriously.

Elizabeth ate her meal, indeed thinking deeply and seriously. Once she was calm enough not to become hysterical, Blanche had pointed out that even Denno could not wave his hand and waft prisoners out of the Tower of London. And even if he could, it would not be very sensible because a hue and cry would be raised for the missing prisoners. That would mean the end of their lives for Kat and Parry.

"But they would *be* alive," Elizabeth protested.

"Would they?" Blanch asked, brows raised. "Parry would lose the work he so dearly loves. He would have nothing to manage, no plans to make, no friends to impress. Kat would lose you and Ashley, the loves of her life. She would be empty with no one to care for, no one to love."

"But the Tower . . ." Elizabeth's voice trembled.

"Many come out and resume their lives."

Elizabeth shuddered. "Many do not."

She was thinking of her mother, but she never spoke of Anne, had not mentioned her name since she was a child of three. She was thinking of all those who, although innocent, died with Anne and of Catherine Howard and her lovers. Elizabeth shivered again. They were all dead already and it was useless to worry about them. She had better think of herself. If she went to the Tower, she would never come out alive.

So when Denno stepped through his Gate, she flung herself into his arms and burst into a storm of weeping. "He has arrested Kat and Parry," she sobbed, "and sent them to the Tower. You must save them. Blanche says you cannot, but you must be able to do something!"

The truth was that he could not, but he did not want to try to reason with her when she was in this state. He stroked her hair. "Elizabeth, come with me where it will be safe to talk."

"No." She shook her head vehemently, gulping. "I cannot leave. He comes in without warning and he doesn't care a bit about things like invading my bedchamber. I don't dare not be here."

Denoriel's hand dropped to his sword hilt. "He? Who is this he?"

"Sir Robert Tyrwhitt. He came with Paulet and Denny. Sir Anthony asked me about what I knew of Tom's doings since Catherine died and I told him everything, even about asking Tom about houses for my visit to Edward." She sniffed and swallowed. "I thought that was the end of it, but then this Tyrwhitt came in and told me that Kat and Parry had been arrested and taken to the Tower. I begged him to let them go. I told him I would order them to tell him anything he wanted to know and that I would tell him anything he wanted to know..." She sobbed for a moment. "But he would not."

He could be rid of Tyrwhitt in two minutes, Denoriel thought, his free hand tightening on the sword hilt while he held Elizabeth close with the other arm. Then he sighed. No he could not. Killing Tyrwhitt, who was questioning Elizabeth, would only fix an impression that her guilt was so deep that murder was necessary to hide it.

Rhoslyn's warning had been all too true. The Council already had evidence enough to execute Seymour, but they did not want to use it. They wanted to find another cause... likely because some of them were involved in Seymour's schemes. But it was also possible that Seymour was only an excuse to implicate Elizabeth in some crime large enough to remove her from the succession... or destroy her.

Denoriel pulled out the truckle bed that the maiden on duty slept on and seated himself and Elizabeth on it. It was low, and they could not be seen from the doorway. He hugged her hard, once, and kissed her hard on the lips, but did not let the kiss linger. Elizabeth sighed, and he felt her tension ease.

"Blanche says you cannot do anything for Kat and Parry," she said softly, tears streaking her cheeks.

"I can see that they do not die," Denoriel replied, "but that would be the end for all of us in the mortal world." He forced a smile. "And it is a danger far away. There is no present threat to Kat's life or Parry's... unless they have done the unthinkable and conspired with Seymour to force you into marriage with him."

"Of course they have not!" Elizabeth wiped away the tears and sat up straighter.

"Are you sure?" Elizabeth nodded and Denoriel said, "Then they are in no danger. They will eventually be released from imprisonment."

Denoriel was not nearly as sure as he sounded, but he needed Elizabeth to be calm and able to think. She was in as much danger as her servants, but she could save herself and them as long as she did not panic and "confess" a willingness to marry Seymour.

First, Denoriel thought, he needed to be sure from where the threat came. If it was solely an attempt to hide the peculations of members of the Council, he could make sure that they were either dead or exposed and the attempt to involve Elizabeth would end. If the threat came from Vidal's attempts to remove Elizabeth from the succession, he would need to identify Vidal's agent and deal with him. For that he would need Elizabeth's help.

Fortunately, although it was silly, Elizabeth was far less afraid of plots against her by the Unseleighe Sidhe than of threats from the mortal government. Perhaps, Denoriel thought, because she had triumphed over her Sidhe opponents whereas her mother and cousin had died. He was briefly reminded of the sorcerer with the caved-in chest, but pushed the memory away. It was far safer to remove the threat in the mortal world.

"No," he said, "I cannot do anything for Mistress Ashley and Master Parry. I have no way to reach them."

"You can make a Gate—"

"How could I know where to make one open? Neither of them has a token. And I dare not bribe my way in to visit them to provide a token. Think what could be assumed against you for me to pay a gaoler in the Tower to allow me to see either Parry or Mistress Ashley. Would it not be believed that there was some dangerous secret between you?"

Elizabeth swallowed. "I knew Blanche was right, but I . . . I cannot bear to think of them alone and afraid and perhaps cold and wet and starving in the dark."

"Now, Elizabeth, do not be so foolish. No one likes to be a prisoner, but I assure you ladies and gentlemen like Mistress Ashley and Master Parry are housed in comfortable enough chambers with lights and fires. They have to pay for those, but Master Ashley can make sure of that and I can make sure no one is short of money."

Elizabeth sighed and rested her head on his shoulder. "I am sorry I have been so silly. But it was such a shock to me that they should arrest Kat and Parry. I suppose I should not be surprised that some of the Council had their fingers dipped in Tom's pie and now wish to hide that. But why use me to prove his guilt? I am second heir to the throne. Surely they should wish to shield me, not to smirch someone so close to the crown."

"Yes. That is a most interesting question. There are those who do not like the reforms the Protector has made, who think you approve of those reforms and who secretly long for the old faith." Denoriel stared at her purposefully for a while and then asked,

"Have you felt anything strange about Tyrwhitt or those who came with him? You know what I mean."

"No," Elizabeth said, "but that doesn't mean much. I haven't seen anyone close except Sir Anthony, and he was just himself. Sir Robert?" She thought, then shook her head. "He is certainly just an ordinary man. Now that I bring my mind to it, perhaps there was a faint aura, like a smoke or mist around one of his hands . . . But it is as likely that I am now feeling that because of what you said more than because he did carry some amulet."

"True enough, but watch keenly because Rhoslyn has passed a rumor likely from the duchess of Somerset that the attack is more at you than at Seymour. The Council will take Seymour down—after that attempt to seize the king they must—but it is you they want ruined more than him."

"Rhoslyn!" Elizabeth repeated. She could say the name because it carried no implications concerning Underhill. Anyone might be named Rhoslyn. She sat up, her lips tight but her eyes bright. "So that is where the trouble falling upon me started."

"I am beginning to think so, but I have no way to prove it and, worse, no way to stop it. Remember, your best defense is ignorance and a total submission to the king and Council regarding your marriage. Not that you should imply you will marry anyone they choose, but that you will *never* consider marriage to anyone without the express spoken, and *written*, consent of both the king and the Council."

"No matter what they say or who says it—if Tyrwhitt is not successful with you they may send back Denny or Paulet—you cling to that line. No one without the consent of the Council, and Parry and Mistress Ashley counseled the same."

Elizabeth found her next interview with Tyrwhitt easier. Partly that was because she and Denoriel took the chance of blocking the bedroom door and Denoriel spent the night. Since he had no way to twist time in the mortal world, Elizabeth was sadly short of sleep the following morning and her pale cheeks and blue-ringed eyes made Tyrwhitt confident.

She admitted that she had remembered certain matters she had forgotten to tell Sir Anthony. Sir Robert leaned forward eagerly and Elizabeth found her eyes drawn to the magnificent ruby ring he wore. She told him of two more letters she had written to

Seymour . . . but both were about totally mundane things, such as soliciting his help to regain possession of Durham House.

She also confessed that Mistress Ashley had written to Seymour to advise him not to visit Elizabeth "for fear of suspicion." Elizabeth snorted angrily. "Suspicion of what?" she hissed. "There was nothing of which to be suspicious. Oh, I was very cross with Kat for using such language, although I agreed that I did not want Sir Thomas visiting me."

Tyrwhitt lectured her on the need to be more open lest there be peril that her honor be smirched. He offered her again the out that Denny had first suggested—that she was young, inexperienced, and innocent and that any agreement she had with the Lord Admiral could be ascribed to the bad advice of Kat and Parry. But she only opened her eyes as wide as they would go and said that there was never any agreement of any kind, not even to rent Seymour Place, with Sir Thomas.

The next day Tyrwhitt used what he called "gentle persuasion" and he progressed so far that Elizabeth admitted that Master Parry had once told her he believed the Admiral leaned toward marriage, which was why he wanted her to exchange her present properties for others in the west nearer his own. And Master Parry had asked how she would receive such an offer if the Council agreed to it.

"But it did not sit well with me," Elizabeth said, with a superior wrinkling of her nose. "He had been married to my stepmother and it seemed close to incest. Still, I did not want to shame Master Parry so I only said that if the king and Council suggested such a marriage I would then do as God put into my mind."

It began to dawn on Tyrwhitt that he was being outwitted by a very clever young woman. He changed his tune and changed it again, but Elizabeth—bolstered by most satisfying visits from her dearling Denno—remained impervious to threats, persuasion, blandishments, or any other device Tyrwhitt tried.

The only time her sober self-control was broken was when Tyrwhitt told her rumors were abroad that said she was also in the Tower pregnant with Seymour's child.

"These are shameful slanders!" Elizabeth cried, jumping up and smoothing her gown down around her body so that her slim figure showed. "You see me as I am. And I can prove that I have never laid eyes upon Sir Thomas since we parted in Chelsea in July.

How then could he get me with child? Liar! You have spread these foul rumors! I will tell the world you have misspoken me."

"Lady Elizabeth! I have done no such thing, I swear."

Tyrwhitt was shocked and thoroughly dismayed also. Although he was completely convinced that she had agreed to marry Seymour and that Seymour had been her lover, it had become a growing possibility that he would get no confession from Elizabeth no matter what he did. Her reaction to the rumor he related was not shame and fear but rage. She did have supporters and should she somehow extricate herself from the situation, she could do him much harm.

"How not you?" she spat. "You are the one who sees me daily and knows I am as I am. If you did not say these shameful lies, who did?"

It was perhaps not the best time for it, but Tyrwhitt then produced a letter written about Elizabeth by Somerset. Tyrwhitt had hoped to give it to her when she was in a softened, melancholy mood, beaten down by the slanders on her, so that she would be overawed and respond to the Protector's offers. Now, however, he hoped it would distract her from her rage or direct it where it belonged.

At first he thought that too had failed when she read the letter with a lip curled with scorn, but then she read it a second time and in a slightly more pleasant tone of voice agreed to reply to the suggestions in the letter. Tyrwhitt promptly offered to help her phrase her reply but she just looked at him, and he wrote to the Protector that she would in no wise follow his advice but writ her own fantasy.

That fantasy was to proclaim her innocence, to repeat that she had not laid eyes on the Admiral since she left Chelsea in July, and that she should be summoned to Court so all could see her as she was. The Protector ignored this plea and others in which she begged him to issue a proclamation that the rumors about her were slanders. He did not do that either . . . and Elizabeth did not forget.

The stalemate continued until the beginning of February when confessions concerning the antics at Chelsea were wrenched first from Parry and then from Kat. On the fifth of February the signed confessions were shown to Elizabeth. She was terrified beyond reason, convinced that being kissed by Tom would brand her as a whore, was tantamount to treason, and that she would die under the axe like her mother. Fortunately she was so frightened she was unable to catch her breath, so unable to speak that Tyrwhitt repeated his first error and left her to recover, commanding her to save herself by making a full confession of her own.

Blanche was almost as terrified as her mistress. Their combined distress alarmed the air spirit, which fled, gabbling of treason, first Underhill and then to the house on Bucklersbury. It was never possible to get too much sense from an air spirit, but the word treason frightened Denoriel. He knew nothing of English law on the level of treason but the heir to King Henry VIII had been drilled in every aspect of that crime. Denoriel arrived Underhill to disperse an army of air spirits to find Harry.

Thus, not only Denoriel but Harry came through the Gate in response to the air spirit's frantic message. And amidst all the terror and the great regret that Elizabeth would not be able to bring in the age of glory that the Bright Court so desired, Denoriel's heart leapt with joy because it was into his arms rather than her Da's that she flung herself.

Denoriel asked no questions. He took Elizabeth into his embrace and assured her over and over that no one would hurt her, that she would be safe with him. And then he said she need not worry. He would just go and rid the mortal world of Tyrwhitt as he did not think the loss would be noticed.

"No," Harry said. "If this is a case of treason, killing the inquisitor would convince the whole Council that there *was* treason. Elizabeth, in the name of God, what did you do?"

Elizabeth was still crying too hard to make sense, and she showed Harry the depositions that Tyrwhitt had left with her. He read the confessions of Parry and Kat. Then he read them again. And then a third time, studying each word.

"Bess," he said, reaching across Denoriel's arm to shake her shoulder. "What has happened to your head? There is no treason here. Neither yours, nor theirs, nor even that jackass Seymour's. This all happened before Queen Catherine died."

Elizabeth lifted a ravaged face from Denoriel's breast. "Yes," she whispered, then sniffed. "I never saw Tom again after Catherine's death."

Harry made a disgusted noise. "Well, then no matter whether he kissed you or fondled you—and really, Bess, that was stupid and in the worst taste! I am ashamed of you."

"I knew it was wrong," Elizabeth sobbed, "but Catherine was there and I was afraid if I pushed him away that she would be offended."

"Catherine was there," Harry echoed, looked down at the papers he held, and shook his head. "Yes, I see that it says *Queen Catherine was there*! Silly goose. You cannot agree to marry a man whose wife is standing in the room with you. And the only act of treason you could have performed with Thomas Seymour is to agree to marry him. Even bedding him would not be treason if his wife was there."

"Is that true, Harry?" Denoriel asked.

"Oh, well, there are a mort of ways to commit treason, and Seymour seems to have tried all of them. However, there is only one way—at least in the situation in which she is—that Elizabeth could have committed treason and that is to have married or to have agreed to marry Seymour without the consent of king or Council."

There was a silence into which came the sound of Blanche Parry's heartfelt sigh of relief. Elizabeth freed herself from Denoriel's embrace and turned to face Harry, sniffing and wiping her eyes.

"Then I can admit this is true without danger?" she said.

Harry frowned, wearing an expression of distaste. "Yes, without danger, but I hope with appropriate blushes. How could you so demean yourself, Bess?"

"For the Mother's sweet sake, Harry," Denoriel put in, hugging Elizabeth, who had hidden her face in his breast again, "she was fourteen years old. Her stepmother was taking part in the 'games.' What did you want her to do?"

"Well, it wasn't very clever," Elizabeth admitted with a sigh, "but I can't make too much of a pother about my age because it will make Kat look even more careless than she is. What am I to tell that toad Tyrwhitt?"

"Exactly what I told you," Harry said. "That you should have known better, but that while Catherine was there, you were not committing treason. In fact, if anyone committed a crime it was Catherine, who should surely have stopped her husband from behaving in such a way."

"She loved him so much," Elizabeth murmured. "She could deny him nothing. Now, looking back, I think her laughter at his antics covered much hurt. But I did not know it then. I wish—"

The latch clicked and then there was a mild thud as someone

applied pressure to the door. Denoriel whispered, "Tonight," as the outer wall yawned blackly and he and Harry disappeared. Elizabeth saw him gesture as the Gate closed, and the door burst open.

"Why was the door locked?" Tyrwhitt snarled.

Elizabeth blinked. "It was not locked, Sir Robert. If it had been and I had unlocked it, the door would have struck me when you opened it. I suppose it stuck."

"The latch would not move," Tyrwhitt insisted.

Elizabeth shrugged but said nothing. She had contributed all that was safe to the accusation. If she said more, she might slip in some way.

"To whom were you talking?" Tyrwhitt asked next, looking around suspiciously.

"To Blanche." Elizabeth blinked again.

"I hope she advised you to confess all! All!"

"Blanche is my servant, the maid who cares for my jewels and my clothing. I trust her with such things. I do not seek advice from a maid, though I have been told that you have sought information from her."

Although the truth was that Elizabeth did frequently ask Blanche for advice, she was sure that Tyrwhitt would try to remove the maid if he thought she was important. Thus, there was a wealth of scorn in Elizabeth's voice when she spoke, and Tyrwhitt looked embarrassed for a moment. He reminded himself that it was his duty to seek information and he frowned awfully at Elizabeth.

"So then, what were you saying to your maid?"

Elizabeth managed not to grin as she said, "I had not finished my remark. But I intended to say that I wished that you would go away and leave me in peace."

"That would be easily obtained if you would only tell the truth about what passed between you and Seymour."

"Nothing passed between us."

"Now that is an open lie. Under your hand are the depositions of your servants who have confessed to a great deal that passed between you and Seymour—his invading your very bedchamber and his treasonous behavior—"

"There was no treason!" Elizabeth cut him off, her voice high and indignant. "Nor could there have been. You seek to prove that he planned marriage with me and thus committed treason . . . *while his wife was in the chamber with us*? You make a lie of what may well have been foolish but was also innocent as Queen Catherine's presence proves. And as I have said, and my servants have said, I have never seen Sir Thomas since Queen Catherine died."

"You have sent Seymour messages since the queen died."

"Yes, and you have seen my copies of the letters sent and seen his replies. All of them were about a house in London for me."

"Seymour made proposals that you exchange the lands your father willed for your upkeep for lands that adjoined his."

"And I thought it a foolish notion and told Parry so. You must know that I have *not* requested any change in the properties assigned to me."

"But Parry did tell you that he believed Seymour to be leaning toward a proposal of marriage."

"Yes, and he asked me if the Council and the king would approve it whether I would agree. You know that. We all told you about it. Never. Never have Mistress Ashley or Master Parry suggested that I marry anyone without the full consent of the king and the Council. It is not treason to talk of possibilities so long as all are agreed that nothing is possible outside of my father's last will."

That was not the end of the questioning, but the sharper and more accusatory Tyrwhitt's statements, the calmer and more sure were Elizabeth's replies. Indeed, Tyrwhitt's anger and frustration brought assurance that her Da had understood the case. What Parry and Kat confessed was not treasonous. She and Tyrwhitt were both weary and scarcely civil by the time Sir Robert rose to his feet.

"You are to write your own confession," he snarled. "It is to be complete. Very complete. This is your last chance to clear your conscience and escape the consequences of your folly."

Elizabeth doubted that; she was certain that Sir Robert would continue his persecution until the Council recalled him or she confessed to treason, but she had been distracted from that depressing idea. She had noticed a curious circumstance during the long questioning. It seemed to her that before each strong accusation or demand a ruby ring on Tyrwhitt's hand flashed brighter.

She told herself that the change in light might well be owing to a movement of Sir Robert's hand. Perhaps he had a tremor so slight she could not see it, but it was the hand about which she sensed the faint aura of magic. She remembered the amulet she had touched which had brought her near death and swallowed to ease a suddenly dry throat. Had he ever touched her with that ring?

Although she thought about it all through the evening meal, which made her very silent and seemed to give Tyrwhitt much satisfaction, she could not remember his ever touching her at all. What could she do to protect herself? The iron cross she wore protected her from being seized by the Unseleighe, but it had done her no good against the evil amulet. For now, she resolved, she would stay well away from Tyrwhitt so he could not touch her.

On the sixth of February, Elizabeth obediently confirmed in writing the evidence Kat and Parry had given, but not in a way that could give Tyrwhitt any satisfaction. *As concerning Mistress Ashley,* she wrote, *she never advised me unto it, but said always (when any talked of my marriage) that she would never have me marry, neither in England or out of England, without the consent of the King's Majesty, Your Grace's, and the Council's.* Nor did she forget to take the chance to complain again about the malicious rumors of her pregnancy and to ask that the rumors be publicly denied.

Needless to say Tyrwhitt was infuriated. He wrote his own letter, pointing out that *They all sing one song. And so I think they would not do unless they set the note before.* The one situation he did not consider was that what they said happened to be the truth, but he could not really contemplate that while Chancellor Rich's diamond shone so brightly on his finger.

Two more weeks passed in fruitless attempts to break Elizabeth's resistance, and then Tyrwhitt announced that the Council had decided Mistress Ashley had shown herself unfit to be Elizabeth's governess. Lady Tyrwhitt, Sir Robert's wife, would supply that place. If he hoped that in her loneliness Elizabeth would transfer her affection from Kat to his wife, he showed he had learned nothing about Elizabeth's nature.

Elizabeth Tyrwhitt was herself not at all happy with the appointment and it soon seemed to be a foretaste of hell. Not only would Elizabeth scarcely speak to her—in fact Elizabeth addressed all her remarks to her maids of honor, whom Tyrwhitt had restored to her in an effort to pave his wife's way with favor—but poor Lady Tyrwhitt seemed to be reduced to bumbling adolescence in Elizabeth's presence. She constantly tripped over her own feet, caught her shoes in the rug so that she nearly pitched forward on her face, and most destructive to her dignity, exploded into and out of rooms as if she were being pushed or pulled through the doors.

Elizabeth kept her mischief a secret because she knew how opposed Denno was to any use of magic except in dire emergency. But this was, in her opinion, a dire emergency; if she did not have some way to express her frustration and rage, she felt she would have yielded to despair despite Denno's love and support and confessed to anything, hoping to die and be free of torment.

First she had intended to tell him, thinking how he would laugh at her cleverness in providing relief and revenge for herself, but then she had second thoughts. He was her one great comfort, and might not think tripping poor Lady Tyrwhitt was funny. She did not want him to scold her for being petty and mean to someone who was helpless against her.

Each time she thought of Denno, she let Lady Tyrwhitt walk in peace, but thinking about spells brought her mind back to the ring on Tyrwhitt's finger. Was he also a helpless victim of the hatred the Unseleighe bore her? It was significant, Elizabeth thought, that he was efficient and fair about running her household; he did not persecute her servants. For example when his wife was foisted on her to replace Kat she had begged him not to appoint anyone in Parry's place, and he had sighed but assigned one of his own clerks to keep her accounts. An honest clerk, too, who saved her a hundred pounds a year.

But if Sir Robert was under an Unseleighe spell, what could she do? She knew no spells for breaking other spells, aside from the one-word commands that reversed spells she herself had cast. She did try all of those, staring at the ring while Tyrwhitt lectured her on the benefits of confession. To stare was safe enough. Sir Robert doubtless thought she had lowered her eyes in shame or to hide her thoughts.

None of the commands she gave worked. Perhaps it would be necessary to touch the ring . . . but she was afraid to do that. And Denno would murder her for taking such a chance, even if no harm came of it. Yet she could not ask his advice. He knew she could see through illusion, yet she could not see any real evidence of a spell on the ring. She remembered the crawling lights on the evil amulet; she had seen that clearly enough though she did not then know what it meant.

Thus she was reluctant to tell Denno about the faint aura and the possible flashes of light in the ring. She did not want him to take away the possibly foolish hope that the enmity came from the Dark Sidhe rather than from people she knew and thought liked her. Also from what she had heard from Denno and Lady Alana it was far more difficult to remove a spell cast by another. That was work for a healer or a magus.

Still as Tyrwhitt continued to nag at her to confess when she knew any sane man would have accepted that there was nothing to confess, she became more desperate. On the twenty-first of February, she wrote to the Protector again, gritting her teeth as Tyrwhitt sat opposite her urging phrasing that would make her sound shamed and guilty. The ring was very bright. She did not dare touch it with her own hand, but was there not something else she could use? Something that would carry her essence but protect her.

Later when Elizabeth was changing her morning gown for one more suitable for dinner, she by habit touched her iron cross to be sure the black chain was hidden and the cross lay flat and would not be seen. The metal was warm from her body. Surely, she thought, that warmth carried her essence, and the black cross protected her from the creatures from Underhill, even the Sidhe. She could touch the ring with the cross. Maybe the iron would break the spell.

How? What excuse could she give for taking Sir Robert's hand? What excuse could she have for pressing a black iron cross to his ring? Elizabeth had an active and inventive mind but even she could not think of any rational reasons for such actions. She was quiet and thoughtful during dinner until a swinging door caught a servant unaware. The servant cried out in alarm and a tray of serving dishes, all of them fortunately metal and not breakable, crashed to the floor.

The ear-splitting crash and the servant's scream shocked everyone into a momentary paralysis. Elizabeth recovered a heartbeat before the others and revelation swept through her. She didn't need to explain why she wanted to touch Tyrwhitt's hand and there was no reason that he needed to know she had touched his ring with her cross. All she needed was to be alone with Sir Robert, except for Blanche, for five minutes.

Usually that was no problem. Almost every day in the past,

Tyrwhitt sent her maidens away so there would be no witnesses to complain that he pressed her too hard. As soon as her maidens had withdrawn to the other end of the room, Elizabeth intended to use *bod oergeulo* on him. While he was frozen, she could pull out her cross and press it against the ring. Elizabeth trembled with expectation, one moment with hope and the next with fear that it would not work.

For spite it seemed Tyrwhitt did not come near her all the next day. He was waiting, in fact, for news that the Council had formally accused Seymour of high treason. There were thirty-three Articles, one of which included plotting to marry "the Lady Elizabeth by secret and crafty means, to the danger of the King's person." If Seymour confessed that he had done so and that Elizabeth had agreed, Tyrwhitt would have evidence against her at last and force a confession from her.

Sir Robert licked his lips, but he was aware of a kind of discomfort within his triumph. On the twenty-third, the charges were read aloud to Seymour but he refused to answer them, demanding that his accusers come before him and that he be given an open trial where he might make his declaration before all the world. But Seymour was to have no trial. Parliament passed an Act of Attainder against him.

On the third of March, Seymour was informed there was to be no trial, and he did speak out. He denied that he had ever meant to usurp his brother's position as Protector or abduct the king. He denied all the serious charges, only confessing to sending the king pocket money. And he never once mentioned Lady Elizabeth, as if she was not part of his plans.

That news came to Hatfield in the evening. It was a disappointment. Tyrwhitt's finger itched and he rubbed the ruby ring. Well, but only he knew that Seymour had denied everything. He swallowed down a slight queasiness, for in general he was an honest man and decided to try one last time to wring a confession from Elizabeth. It was for her own good after all. He would tell her that Seymour had confessed he intended to marry her so she need no longer lie to protect him. To save herself she should speak the truth.

She had been reading when he came in. To his surprise, she laid the book down on a small table and waved away the attendant maidens. Lady Tyrwhitt sighed but went with them to be sure that their conversation would cover any words between her husband and Elizabeth.

"I bring you sad news about the Lord High Admiral. The Council has evidence of many crimes and has brought against him thirty-three Articles—"

Elizabeth lifted her head. "*Bod oergeulo.*"

Her voice was just above a murmur. If any sound carried to the women across the room, it would seem that she answered something Tyrwhitt had said. Hurriedly, trembling with hope, she brought out the cross that she had been carrying in her pocket for days and touched it to the ruby ring.

Nothing seemed to happen. Tears rose in Elizabeth's eyes and she swallowed hard and muttered, "*Dihuno*" because she did not dare keep Sir Robert frozen. Someone might notice.

"—of which the Admiral denied all except that of giving pocket money to the king," Tyrwhitt continued, with no sign he knew a few minutes had been carved out of his life. "This gives you one more chance to state your own case to the Protector before any confession by Sir Thomas involves you."

Elizabeth blinked away her tears of disappointment. "I have told you a thousand times that there is nothing on my part to confess, no matter what Sir Thomas says. Yes, there were rumors in my household that the Admiral wished to marry me, but I did not agree, and no one urged me to accept him unless the offer was made with the permission of the king and Council."

Tyrwhitt stared at her with a rather puzzled expression. "So you have," he said. "So you have."

Chapter 36

Thomas Seymour was executed on the twentieth of March but he made no confession and he never mentioned Elizabeth's name. Vidal exploded and killed every weak creature that was not well shielded for half a day. Nothing he had done had saved his tool or damaged the red-haired bitch. However, Vidal had learned several frustrating lessons about working with humans between the time the accusations against Seymour were first made and his death. He learned that Chancellor Rich's self-interest was strong enough to override the subtle compulsions Vidal had set upon him to save Seymour.

First Vidal hoped to prevent the Council from acting against Seymour by having Rich convince the young king that he should show mercy. However when Rich came with the rest of the Council to request permission to go forward with the proceedings, he saw from Edward's expression that an appeal would be useless. Rich remembered the tale told by the guardsman and thought Seymour should have shot the guard instead of the dog. Edward had loved the dog.

In the face of the hard evidence about Seymour's crimes, Rich fought the urges he felt to defend Seymour. He did once speak to the Protector, implying that Seymour's ambition had been fed by favorable suggestions from Lady Elizabeth, but the earl of Warwick challenged his implication of Elizabeth. Warwick pointed out that after more than a month of questioning, Rich's own choice of investigator had failed to find a single sign of Elizabeth's favor toward Seymour.

Rich suppressed Vidal's subtle compulsions, which he thought of as a stupid sentimentality toward Seymour, and withdrew to neutrality. About the only effect Vidal's yellow diamond had was that Rich did make sure the plan to marry Elizabeth was one of the Articles charged against Sir Thomas. Vidal growled and spat, but Rich was simply so intent on his own self-interest that subtle magic could not influence him. Well, Vidal decided, if Rich would not serve his purpose willingly, he would do so unwillingly.

Vidal drew Rich to Otstargi's house a week before the Bill of Attainder had been presented in Parliament and set a compulsion that would force Rich to speak against the bill. Rich's knowledge of the Parliament and what was politically possible fought so hard against the spell that the result was a waxwork figure. Even Vidal recognized no one could for a moment believe the bespelled creature was natural. It would be clear to every man in the Parliament either that the person speaking was not Rich or that Rich was under a spell.

So furious that his hands dripped power and burn spots appeared on the floor of Otstargi's chamber, Vidal suddenly began to tremble with weakness. The power he had expended in calling Rich to him, bespelling Rich, and then expended in his futile rage was not being renewed in the mortal world.

Vidal drew back everything he could as he removed the compulsion from Rich, but he saved no power because he then had to wipe out Rich's memory of his visit to Otstargi. Barely restraining himself from killing the man—he knew Rich would be useful in the future—Vidal sent Rich on his way.

Then he sat down and gathered his rage-scattered wits to plan his next move. The door to disgracing Elizabeth and thus removing her from the succession quietly in a way that would not incur vengeance from Oberon was closed and would not open again. Even if Elizabeth was too stupid to learn and Vidal could find another man to tempt her, Denoriel and Aleneil would make sure she had no more chances to misbehave.

Time was growing short, too. Vidal knew from looking into Rich's mind that the first signs of Edward's illness were appearing. The king's human physicians had not yet noticed, but Vidal knew what that look of health and blooming cheeks presaged. In a year or two the boy would begin to cough and have trouble with his breathing. Then he would die.

Vidal hissed with irritation. That poisoned thorn had been meant for Elizabeth. Curse her. That it touched Edward had been her fault. Curse Denoriel and Aleneil, and Rhoslyn and Pasgen, too, for being traitors. Once Edward was known to be failing, Elizabeth would be Mary's heir presumptive.

The whole Bright Court would have its eyes on the red-haired monster in eager anticipation of the feast of joy and song and art her reign would bring to them. Vidal ground his teeth. She would be watched and guarded both in the mortal world and Underhill. He had no more time to waste on elaborate schemes that he could not control in the mortal world. Elizabeth must die before she gained greater importance, before anyone realized that Edward would not reign long.

By the beginning of March, Elizabeth had high hopes that her cross had broken the evil spell on Tyrwhitt's ruby ring. The ruby was still very beautiful, but it only caught the light from beams of sunlight or from a flickering candle. And what she had felt, faint as it had been, was now gone completely.

Certainly Sir Robert no longer pressed her to confess her plans to marry Seymour. He even remarked to his wife in their bedchamber that he wondered why he had been so certain of her guilt.

Lady Tyrwhitt still felt unwelcome and was aware of Elizabeth's coldness, but at least most of her clumsiness had abated. She seldom tripped or caught her feet in things now. And although she knew Elizabeth would never accept her, only indifference, not hate, looked out of the girl's dark eyes.

"Perhaps," she replied rather frigidly, "your accusations frightened her into avoidance of all mention of Sir Thomas, which you took as guilt. She does not seem guilty to me. When Sir Thomas and his fate is mentioned, she shakes her head over what he has done. She calls him brash and foolish, with that high-nosed look of contempt she has—not a look a girl wears when speaking of a lover in mortal peril—and she says openly she hopes he will escape the full penalty."

The truth was that Elizabeth had realized she was no longer in any personal danger, and the wariness that did give an impression she was hiding guilt was gone . . . but she could not rejoice. Her dearling Kat, not wise but unconditionally loving, and dear Parry, again not terribly wise or even a good cofferer but *hers*, were still in the Tower. They had not committed treason, but it could be said that they had not fulfilled their duty and they might be kept in prison or punished. And Denno could not or would not help them.

Elizabeth bent the full power of her mind to saving her servants and her reputation, which had been damaged by the slanderous rumors of her pregnancy. She wrote with and without permission to the Protector, trusting that William Cecil would see her letters got to him. She was not sure why, but she was very glad indeed, that William Cecil was committed to her interests.

Once the Bill of Attainder had been rushed through Parliament and it was clear that Elizabeth was not involved, the Protector began to feel there was little point in holding her servants. The imprisonment of a couple of servants was a very unimportant matter when compared with the fact that he would soon need to decide whether his own brother lived or died.

Choosing his moment carefully, Cecil presented still another letter pleading for the release of Mistress Ashley and Master Parry. This one contained a strong and reasoned argument for Elizabeth's insistence on the freedom of her servants, ending with the cogent point that *it shall and doth make men think I am not clear of the deed myself but that it is pardoned to me because of my youth, because she that I loved so well is in such a place.*

"And if you do plan to make a proclamation of the Lady Elizabeth's virtue and innocence," Cecil pointed out, "it would be well her servants were released."

By mid March, Kat and Parry were freed, but Elizabeth's spirits would not rise. Kat and Parry were forbidden to return to Elizabeth's service. Sir Robert and Lady Tyrwhitt remained in charge of her household. When Denoriel suggested that Lady Alana return to service as an antidote to Lady Tyrwhitt, Elizabeth flew into a rage. It was Kat she wanted and if he could not think of a way to get her Kat, she didn't want Lady Alana or him either.

Seymour was executed on the twentieth of March, still without admitting to any crime or mentioning Elizabeth. When Tyrwhitt brought her the news, she said only, "This day died a man with much wit and very little judgment." And she returned to the translation Master Ascham had set for her.

April passed, May and June. By the end of July, as if she felt she had been indifferent long enough that her collapse would not be associated with Seymour's death, Elizabeth fell ill. She had violent headaches and painful indigestion, she lost weight until she was no more than skin and bones and even developed jaundice for a time. Sir Robert and Lady Tyrwhitt offered every comfort and consolation they could think of but they made little of the illness for fear they would be blamed.

Terrified, Blanche acted on her own and, although Elizabeth forbade her to tell Denno, sent Reeve Tolliver, the undergroom, to the house on Bucklersbury. Denoriel came that night, but Elizabeth would not listen to his near frantic pleas that she let him bring a healer. In fact, she reviled him furiously and sent him away. She wanted Kat, she wept. She wanted Kat.

Denoriel sought an appointment with William Cecil very early the next day, before it was really decent to call. Nor did he make any attempt to conceal his anxiety when he confessed that Elizabeth's maid had sent him a message. Her lady was very ill. Because of the recent trouble, Denoriel said, he did not feel that Lord Denno should call on the lady, but the maid knew Elizabeth well and if she were frightened something serious must be wrong.

Later that afternoon, William Cecil mentioned to the Protector that there were rumors that Lady Elizabeth was very ill. Rumor also had it that she was not well attended, there being only a coarse local doctor to see to her. Cecil sighed and shook his head.

"Alas, some blame is likely to reflect on Your Grace, which is why I mention the matter at all. It is said Lady Elizabeth was cruelly questioned and is being kept like a prisoner in Tyrwhitt's hands and that her illness is being deliberately ignored so that she may die."

That was enough to raise real anxiety in Somerset. He knew he was being called unnatural because of allowing his own brother to be executed. He needed no rumors about this. The scandalous rumors he had permitted to spread were now lashing back at him. His own proclamation had declared her innocent and she had regained much of her popularity. Now, according to Cecil, who was rarely wrong, the public was prepared to make a holy martyr of her with him as her demon opponent.

Somerset promptly arranged to send Dr. Thomas Bill, the king's own physician, to attend Elizabeth. Bill was actually a skilled physician, a practitioner at St. Bartholomew's Hospital rather than a panderer to noblemen's imaginary ills. He also was no fool and knew that a deep disturbance of the spirit could ravage the body.

Having listened to Elizabeth's symptoms and watched how she trembled and could not work at her lessons, although she tried, how she pushed food away, he sought more information. First he questioned her ladies but soon realized that she did not confide in them. At last he turned to her maid.

"My lady was all alone with no one to help her," Blanche said resentfully, "and they badgered her day and night and told her she must tell them what was not true to save herself from being accused of treason. And even when it is proven that she was not guilty of anything at all, those who tormented her are set to rule her. She can find no peace, no assurance of safety. In her sleep she cries out for Mistress Ashley, who raised her from a child of three."

Bill made an indeterminate noise.

Encouraged, Blanche continued. "Mistress Ashley was the only mother my lady ever knew. Queen Catherine also cared for her, but Queen Catherine is dead. My lady is exhausted and afraid because she is still under the domination of Sir Robert and Lady Tyrwhitt. I do not say that they are not kind and civil to her now but . . . but she cannot trust them."

So the doctor prescribed palliative medication and strongly recommended to Somerset that Mistress Ashley be restored to her position. His letter was naturally enough opened by the Protector's secretary. William Cecil grinned privately. He knew just how and when to present the idea to Somerset. Mistress Ashley and Parry would be reinstated, the Tyrwhitts dismissed. William Cecil would not be sorry to see Tyrwhitt gone from Elizabeth's household. He had nothing against Tyrwhitt except that now that his duty as examiner was finished he might insinuate himself into the lady's regard.

William Cecil tended to look at all the paths into the future. He was already known to the young king as a good public servant. If Edward lived and reigned, Cecil could expect advancement. If he did not . . . that was not as hopeful, for Mary would come to the throne and Cecil favored the reformed religion. But Mary was not young and not well. The chances were her reign would be short. Then Elizabeth would rule. William Cecil had every intention of being the principal man of her reign.

In August Elizabeth was able to fling herself into her dear Kat's arms and they sat up for a week's nights running, telling each other about all the terrible things that had happened. Kat wept over her foolishness and swore that she would never, never again consider any man worthy to urge on her lady. Elizabeth said no more in blame than that she wished Kat had believed her when she said she would not have Seymour. Parry, too, was restored to his duties—except that now Elizabeth read over the accounts and initialed every page.

Before the end of the month, the Tyrwhitts were gone. They parted from Elizabeth on reasonably pleasant terms, Lady Tyrwhitt giving her a small volume of morning and evening prayers, *Divers Hymns and Meditations*. Then it was over, truly over. The nightmare was ended. Life returned to a placid round of lessons and musical practice and cozy chats with Kat—in which Elizabeth made sure her maidens took part so they could report on what was said if that ever became necessary.

In September Elizabeth received a courtesy visit from the Venetian ambassador, a sure sign that she had been restored to favor in the Court. By then she was in blooming health and took him hunting. He was utterly amazed at her skill in riding, the fact that she spoke Italian as if it were English, and at her modesty and elegant manner.

Kat, of course, did not accompany the party on the hunt but after the ambassador had gone and they were sitting over spiced wine and small cakes in the evening, she said in a troubled way, "Where is Lord Denno?"

"You mean the old gentleman with white hair, the rich merchant?" Margaret Dudley said. "He never appeared again as soon as the Council threatened my lady."

"No!" Elizabeth exclaimed.

"No, Margaret," Kat said. "That is impossible. Lord Denno has been a faithful friend to Lady Elizabeth for more years than you are alive. And he does not desert his friends when they are in trouble. He still visits the duke of Norfolk in the Tower."

"Well, he didn't visit you," Frances Dodd said.

"Because he did not want the appearance that I was in contact with my lady," Kat said. "That was considerate and wise. And I know that some comforts were given me which the gaolers pretended not to see and for which no one had any explanation. I was sure those came somehow through Lord Denno's hands."

She glanced up and saw the sudden tears in Elizabeth's eyes. "Oh, well," she said, closing the discussion. "It is likely he is away on a trading voyage."

But the next day when they were walking in the garden and the path narrowed so that she and Elizabeth were side by side and the maidens straggling along behind—Elizabeth did tend to set a quick pace—she asked again about Denno.

"I sent him away," Elizabeth muttered. "I wanted him to get you out of prison and he would not."

"Elizabeth!" Kat exclaimed, but keeping her voice too low to be heard by the maidens behind them. "The very worst thing that could have befallen you—even worse than my betraying Sir Thomas' behavior—would have been for me and Tom to escape. Child, I would not have gone if he did arrange it. My fleeing would have declared you guilty before all the world. You must write to him. You must tell him you are sorry and beg him to visit again."

Elizabeth's lips trembled and then thinned with pride. "No. I said he could come back when you were restored to me and . . . and he has not come."

"No, nor would I." Kat said, more sharply than she usually spoke to Elizabeth and then lowering her voice again. "How could you be so unkind and so ungracious after the years he has been so faithful a friend and the rich favors he has given you?"

"I—I wanted you. I was afraid for you."

Kat took her hand and kissed it. "You are so forgiving to me, can you not forgive him? More especially when what he did was for your good . . . and he was right to do it."

"He is always right," Elizabeth grumbled.

But her heart was leaping with hope and joy. Her breasts were filling, the nipples pressing hard against her bodice, and her nether lips were full and moist. All the time she had been questioned, the memory she needed to conceal, of Tom's crude fondlings and loud kisses, had turned her body to ice. Any sexual touch and anyone associated with lovemaking had seemed disgusting. And then, after she had been cleared, she felt worse yet, but the spying Tyrwhitts were still watching her and she could not even let herself crawl into the dark and weep for fear it would be said she wept for Tom.

Then Kat had been given back to her and her illnesses had mostly passed and her restoration to Court favor had been signaled by a visit from a foreign ambassador. Elizabeth had been dreaming about Denno, about the big, soft bed in the chamber of Llachar Lle, about the fantastic gowns in the closet of her own bedchamber, about singing and dancing and laughing aloud with her hair streaming loose like a common trollop on the stage in Fur Hold. But she could not think of any way to draw him back that would not bend her stiff pride.

"Shall I write to him?" Kat asked. "I can say that it is possible you will be invited to Court for this coming Christmas and that you will need new gowns, furs, and trimmings. I can write as if it is my own idea..."

Elizabeth did not answer. She was thrilled by the hope that she would see Denno again but frightened that this time he really was too angry to want her anymore. He had come when Blanche sent for him and he had done his best to arrange she be cured, but aside from begging her to let him bring a Sidhe healer he had hardly spoken to her. He had not begged her pardon for not obeying her or tried to explain himself.

She had been too self-absorbed during her trial and her illness to think of anyone else, but now she remembered how he had looked, standing beside her bed, then kneeling beside it and begging her to let him bring Mwynwen. He had looked old and tired, his green eyes dull and his hair flat white rather than shining silver. Elizabeth swallowed hard. Surely he had suffered as much as she, possibly more because he had so much power... and could not use it.

"Yes, write to Lord Denno," she said as the path widened and two of her ladies caught up. "He always has the most elegant goods and gives me the best prices."

She laughed as she said that and blinked away tears too, because Denno never charged her at all. She wrote a reasonable cost into her expense books, but the coins came into her own hands for her to distribute as largesse.

Rhoslyn was sitting quietly with a group of the duchess of Somerset's lesser ladies apart from her inner circle of confidants. Rhoslyn was holding a book of meditations in her hands. Now and again she turned a page, but she was really listening intently. No one guessed the keenness of Sidhe hearing. She should not have been able to detect a word the duchess spoke from where she sat, but that was how she had heard enough of the duchess' animosity to Elizabeth to be able to pass warnings to Denoriel.

The duchess' ladies had been talking about the possibility of Lady Mary coming to the Court for Christmas this year. And one said that a friend on the Council told her that Lady Elizabeth would be invited. The name caught Rhoslyn's ear and she listened more closely.

"She is not only a whore like her mother but a witch like her mother, too." The duchess' voice grated.

There was a slight, appalled silence. "Your Grace?" one of the women said faintly.

"She was the guilty one! And she somehow witched my poor brother-by-marriage not only into her plans but into silence about her guilt, even to the moment of his death. So she escapes all blame."

No one spoke and the duchess went on bitterly, "And now she is to be brought to Court and received by the king who is so eager to see her that he has been heard several times to speak of pleasures to be enjoyed 'when Elizabeth comes.' She will be honored by all, whore and witch though she is."

Rhoslyn turned another page of her book and breathed a quiet sigh. For now, Elizabeth had won. Ann of Somerset would not have been so vicious if she had not realized that further persecution of Elizabeth would only do her husband greater damage. And Rhoslyn suspected from a thought or two she had garnered here and there among the courtiers that Somerset was in trouble. He had been too high-handed in his treatment of the nobles, the country was seething with religious discontent because he had pushed reform too hard, and there were economic problems which had caused major unemployment and higher prices for food.

Whether the Protector could hold on to his position was now a growing question. But if he was unseated, Rhoslyn thought, the man who would do it and replace him was the earl of Warwick. And the earl of Warwick had sometimes tried to protect Elizabeth. Rhoslyn sighed again and shut her book. There was little more she could do for Elizabeth for a while. If Somerset weathered the storm about to descend on him, she might try active meddling with the duchess' mind, but for now what she wanted and needed was to be free of the mortal world. She needed to see Pasgen, to be sure he was recovering from their mother's death . . . as she was, Rhoslyn realized.

After the first shock of loss wore off, she had begun to recognize the truth of Llanelli's bitter claim in her death letter that when she was gone her children would be freed from the chains of her transgression. The first time the idea had crossed Rhoslyn's mind, she had been thrown back into a morass of guilt and despair. However, that had been just when the most determined assault was being made on Elizabeth. Rhoslyn had needed to direct most of her will and attention at the duchess to prevent her from sending a personal clerk to make a few alterations in Ashley's confession that would imply Elizabeth had eagerly agreed to marry Seymour and then to stop other schemes to discredit Elizabeth.

With no other choice, Rhoslyn had tampered with the duchess' mind, planting in it pictures of what would happen when her meddling was discovered and making her certain it would be discovered because the clerk she planned to use was dishonest and untrustworthy and would betray her. It cost the man his position, but the scheme was not put into effect. Seymour's indifference to Elizabeth was decisive. Despite the duchess' efforts to make her husband see Elizabeth as an enemy the case against Elizabeth collapsed.

When Rhoslyn had leisure to think again about Llanelli's death, the pain was not so acute. She remembered what Lady Mary had said about blaming herself, although she was utterly blameless, when her mother had died. Llanelli had made her own troubles as had Mary's mother, who could have lived out her life in honored, comfortable retirement in a convent if she had not been so pigheaded. So could Llanelli have lived safely if she had not believed Vidal was all-powerful.

For some weeks longer Rhoslyn had needed to be alert to divert the duchess from any new stratagems to make Elizabeth look guilty but now, with Seymour dead, the woman had recognized, if not accepted, defeat. Rhoslyn's duty with regard to helping Elizabeth was temporarily done. And suddenly she had an urgent need to be with Pasgen, to speak to him of how she had come out of the vale of shadows of guilt. Now was a good time, the best time, to ask for leave. The bad harvests and other economic troubles were the ideal reason for her to need to attend to her brother's lands.

The duchess parted with Rosamund Scott readily, scarcely knowing who she was, but Rhoslyn took the precaution of going to take her leave of Mary also before she went Underhill. She was kindly greeted and told that in case of any trouble at Court, she would be more than welcome to return to Mary's service. She was sorry to see that Mary looked ill and exhausted and as soon as she could get to her in private, she asked Susan Clarencieux what was wrong.

"She—" Susan whispered, shrugging "—I know it is silly, but she is afraid of her sister."

"Afraid of Elizabeth?" Rhoslyn murmured, opening her eyes wide. "But I think Elizabeth loves Mary and always speaks of how kind her sister has been to her."

Susan sighed and shook her head. "Oh do not repeat this, I beg you. She thinks that Elizabeth is a witch. She recalls years ago when she swears she saw Elizabeth talking to her dead half brother in the garden at Hampton Court at night."

"I remember that." Rhoslyn widened her eyes again. "I remember that we all tried to convince her it was not so. And she is so short of sight . . ."

"Yes." Susan sighed again. "She is also distressed by the Act of Uniformity, which forbids the Mass she loves. She believes that if anything happens to the king, she will not survive him by so much as a week, that the reformists will have her killed and set Elizabeth on the throne."

"Oh no," Rhoslyn whispered. "Elizabeth is little more than a child and to tell the truth, I do not think that Elizabeth cares that much about the new extreme form of the service. After what has happened with Seymour, she simply does whatever the Council orders."

She fixed that idea firmly into Susan's mind and hoped it would be transferred to Mary but she did not really care. She wanted urgently to be Underhill and refused Lady Mary's offer of a few days lodging so she could rest and set out for London that very afternoon. There she dismissed the hired coach, paid her maid for a month and sent the girl home to wait for her, and Gated to the Elves' Faire.

For a little time Rhoslyn wandered the Faire just enjoying the ambience and absorbing the flow of power. Only as it flowed in to her did she realize that although she did very little magic in the mortal world she had been greatly depleted. Soon, however, she began to wonder where to go next.

Home, was her first thought, but she froze where she stood,

causing someone to bump her from behind. She thought of her own domain and swallowed hard. It was no longer home. Too much of it had been designed with Llanelli's help and to Llanelli's taste. The reminders would be too acute.

She began to walk again, found an inn, found a table, and sat, swallowing panic. She had nowhere to go, she thought, shivering. After a while she told herself firmly not to be a fool. She could go to Pasgen's domain. Tears stung her eyes; it was so comfortless and cold. She could not stay there if he was not there, his presence subtly warm and reassuring despite the rigid, frigid setting.

Well, there was the empty house. Rhoslyn thought that over, remembering Llanelli's fear, remembering Vidal's invasion of the place. Yes, she could wait for Pasgen there but she could not live in the empty house. It was designed to be empty, a place only to take and transmit messages. Rhoslyn drew a deep breath. What a fool she was. There might be a message from Pasgen for her.

Going to the empty house was a wise decision. Not only was there a message from Pasgen telling her the best way to reach him was through Gaenor in Elfhame Elder-Elf but there was a sheaf of messages from Harry FitzRoy.

Rhoslyn smiled and arranged them in order. The first was very ordinary, simply asking her whether she would be willing to attend a private ball to be given by a friend with him. He would come to fetch her on Lady Aeron when and where she set. The second said only that he was sorry she did not wish to attend the ball with him; he was sorry, too, if he had offended her by asking for a private meeting. Would she be willing to meet him, as they had in the past, in the Inn of Kindly Laughter?

There was a longer period between that message and the following one. This asked whether he had somehow angered her and how he could amend his offense. Another long stretch and then a note saying he was very sorry if he seemed to be invading her privacy but he was frightened. He had looked for her in the empty house and the servants there had told him it was a very long time since they had seen her. Please, he begged, send him a message, even if it is only to tell him to cease from pursuing her.

Rhoslyn suddenly felt very much better. She had a vivid image of Harry FitzRoy. Compared to elven men he was not at all handsome. Plain fine brown hair, soft brown eyes, an undistinguished nose, little stubby round ears . . . but his smile, ah, that was different. He had the sweetest smile, the merriest laugh, with no cruel or bitter undertones, and he was brave and kind. She remembered how he had fought them to save Elizabeth and tales Pasgen had told her about his routing out of the evil infesting Alhambra and El Dorado.

Without delay she dispatched three messages: the first went to Gaenor's house in Elfhame Elder-Elf in which she told Pasgen she was going to meet Harry at the Inn of Kindly Laughter and that he should try to join them there. If not, she said, she would come to his domain. The second and third messages were dispatched to Mwynwen's house and to Denoriel's rooms in Llachar Lle and they were identical, begging Harry's forgiveness for seeming to ignore him. She had not meant to do that. If he was still willing, she would meet him in the Inn of Kindly Laughter and explain.

She stayed a while in the empty house, checking on the structure itself and on the servants. She had never had much feeling for the place and it did not affect her as she feared her own domain would affect her. Two of the servants were becoming fragile. Without really thinking about it, she drew in Dark Court power, hating the sour, bitter feel of it.

Still, she was relieved that she could use it, and redirected the power to the servants, glad to be rid of it. Fleetingly, but with only sadness, not wrenching pain, she thought of the wing that had been added for Llanelli. That was no longer there. She had destroyed it, directing the power that had been used into the rest of the house, after she had destroyed the constructs that served Llanelli.

Duty done, with a strong lifting of spirits, she set out for the Bazaar of the Bizarre and the Inn of Kindly Laughter. She wondered how long she would have to wait before one of her menfolk . . . *her* menfolk? Pasgen possibly was hers, though she would probably get her ears burned off if he heard her say so, but Harry? Harry was Mwynwen's. He had been hers for many years.

Rhoslyn paused and cocked her head. Mwynwen was Sidhe. Was it possible that she no longer found the mortal very interesting? Was that why Harry was so eager to find her . . . as a balm to a wounded heart? But at the ball he had not seemed hurt when Mwynwen left them. Was Harry bored too?

She began walking again somewhat more quickly. Had Mwynwen cast Harry out? Did he also have no home? Not that he would need a place to live; he could always live with Denoriel, but that was not the same as a home of one's own. Her steps hesitated as she thought of Harry in her domain and then quickened again. But the man who rose from his chair as she approached the Inn of Kindly Laughter was Pasgen.

They met with almost identical expressions of anxiety. Both realized it and they both began to laugh. It was an acknowledgment that they could laugh, that they could take each other's hands, but neither mentioned Llanelli.

Pasgen directed Rhoslyn back toward the table at which he had been sitting, saying, "I hope you have not summoned me for more business in the mortal world. I have made enough trouble for that Seymour person, so he will be no further danger to your Elizabeth and—"

"Made enough trouble!" Rhoslyn repeated, stunned. "He is dead. Executed for treason."

"Oh, good." Pasgen lifted a hand to summon a service being. "Then he will certainly no longer be attractive to Elizabeth."

"Pasgen!" Rhoslyn exclaimed, exasperated. "Was it you who exposed Seymour's dealings with Sharington and the pirates?"

Something striped in bright blue and yellow slithered up to the table and lifted its upper portion enquiringly. Pasgen ordered "the ordinary" and a bottle of blond wine. The creature slithered away. Rhoslyn looked after it, wondering how it would carry the dishes of food and the wine and glasses. Pasgen paid it no more attention.

"Yes, of course," he said. "You told me that Vidal had this plan to use Seymour to entrap Elizabeth, so I set up the exposure to remove him. But then he and his wife went to that manor of his in the west, so I let the matter lie. When the wife died, you said he was growing dangerous to the girl again, and besides I knew that Vidal was trying to use him as a tool. I intend to strip Vidal of every tool, so I set the wheels of his exposure rolling again."

"And just left them to roll wherever they happened to go? Oh, Pasgen. You very nearly pulled Elizabeth down with that idiot Seymour."

He made an irritated gesture. "I thought I knew where the wheels would roll. I do intend to see Elizabeth on the throne because that will best torment Vidal Dhu, but the mortal world is a nuisance. How could I guess she would be involved? I made very sure that she had no connection whatsoever with the pirates or the forgeries at the mint. How did she get dragged into Seymour's disgrace?"

Rhoslyn sighed. "Because there were others in high places that were touched with that pitch, they tried instead to convict Seymour of arranging to marry Lady Elizabeth. That, without the consent of king and Council, would be treason and there would be no need to expose crimes in which they could be involved."

Pasgen's golden brows very nearly touched the fringe of golden hair on his forehead. "I had no idea that so many of them were dishonest. Mortals are all mad. How was I supposed to know that? And I cannot for the life of me see how Seymour's evil intentions could involve Elizabeth anyway."

He started to say something more and the food arrived, the tray that carried the dishes supported on several sturdy arms seemingly extruded from the body of the servitor. Pasgen moved the tray to the table and deposited several bright tokens, which he had had the forethought to obtain when he first arrived. He poured wine for them both. Rhoslyn speared a well-browned segment of something from the dish nearest her.

"Because," she said, "it is not treason if it is only a thought in a man's mind. They had to prove that it was a real plan, that he had proposed marriage to her and that she had agreed."

Pasgen uttered a disgusted snort and then also began to eat. "But you assured me that she wanted no part of him." He shook his head. "It does not matter. Since he is dead and Elizabeth is all right—I am sure you would have told me at once if harm had befallen her—I do not see what more there is to say."

Rhoslyn just stared at him for a moment and then smiled with exasperated affection. Pasgen was very powerful and willing, even in his way eager, to make sure Elizabeth would be queen of England; nonetheless he still did not understand the mortal world and did not find it interesting enough, because it was devoid of magic, to learn. Perhaps it would be best if she only asked for him to do very specific things, like making Gates.

"You are quite right, Pasgen," she said. "One of the reasons I am here is because I think the mortals most opposed to Elizabeth will not trouble her for some time and I have come Underhill to refresh myself . . . and to think of the future."

She stopped speaking and took a sip of wine. Pasgen raised his eyes from his food.

"I . . . I think I need to change my domain," Rhoslyn said.

There was a silence. Rhoslyn looked away and Pasgen drew a

quiet breath, nodded, and said, "It is too much tied to Llanelli. I understand. I will help in any way I can. Where will you go?"

Rhoslyn poured more wine and sipped it. Her mother's name no longer buried her in an agony of depression. That Pasgen was able to say it, not easily, but it did not choke him either, made her feel even better.

"I thought . . . before I chose an Unformed land that we should both go . . . to the Bright Court."

Another silence in which Pasgen looked down at his hands on the table. Then he said slowly, "That . . . that might be possible. But I would like to wait a little while." He sighed. "Where is your Harry FitzRoy? I would like to speak to him. Gaenor told me that he has an interesting project to reclaim two elfhames overrun by evil in which he has involved a number of the Sidhe who were near Dreaming. She thought my skills might be of use to them."

"They are all Bright Court?" Rhoslyn asked eagerly.

"They are all very old. I think Bright Court and Dark were not well distinguished in their youth. But the ones who work with FitzRoy are all awake and alive and I think if they spoke for us their voices would be heard."

"I do not know if my message reached him, but I am sure if he does not soon arrive here that he will send another message to the empty house. I can wait there, I suppose."

"Good enough. I will wait with you."

Rhoslyn smiled gratefully at her brother and both of them addressed themselves to the food and wine. It was a relief to both that they could. At the time of Llanelli's death neither had much appetite and they could take no comfort in being together. That both continued to eat and drink and occasionally exchanged glances and smiles was an enormous relief, a sign that they had both put aside guilt and were dealing with their grief.

Pasgen had just pushed aside his nearly empty plate, when a man's voice said, "Rhoslyn!" and then, "Oh, I beg your pardon. I did not mean to intrude."

"Harry!" Rhoslyn said, getting up. "You aren't intruding at all. This is my brother, Pasgen."

"Your brother." The stricken look on Harry's face changed to a broad smile. "I am very glad to meet you."

Pasgen gestured to another chair and Harry drew it out, waited for Rhoslyn to sit down, and then seated himself while Pasgen said, "And I to meet you. Gaenor told me that I might be of use to you and I wanted to talk to you about the cursed elfhames."

"Yes, Alhambra and El Dorado," Harry said, but he was not looking at Pasgen; he was looking at Rhoslyn.

Pasgen glanced at Rhoslyn's face, at the way she was pushing the remnants of her meal around her plate and looking sidelong at Harry. He never used to care much about what Rhoslyn wanted. Maybe, he thought, no one had cared about what Llanelli wanted. Foolish guilt, he thought, but right now he wanted Rhoslyn to be happy. His interest in Harry's project could wait. He sighed.

"Unfortunately I cannot stay longer just now. Can we meet somewhere to discuss whether I might be a help against what you are fighting?"

There was a little silence. Harry was looking at Rhoslyn and Pasgen had to clear his throat before the young man turned to him and said, "Oh yes, of course. Or you could speak to Mechain or Elidir at Elfhame Elder-Elf. Gaenor will know where they live and they will know where I am. I am a little rootless these days. Sometimes Mwynwen asks me to stay, but often I am at Denoriel's lodging in Llachar Lle."

"Until soon, then," Pasgen said, smiling, and to Rhoslyn, "I will check at the empty house for word from you."

Rhoslyn stood up as he stood, ready to leave, and stretched a hand to touch his sleeve. "Thank you, Pasgen."

Harry had risen when Rhoslyn did. "I was so worried about you," he said, his voice tight and anxious, not even waiting for Pasgen to step away. "First I thought I had somehow offended you, but when you never sent a word, not even to tell me to leave you alone or mind my own business . . ." He shook his head and lowered his voice. "I know the Dark Court can be a dangerous place. I was afraid some ill had befallen you."

"Some ill did," Rhoslyn said softly. "My mother killed herself."

"Oh Rhoslyn!" Harry breathed, and opened his arms.

He did not draw her into his embrace, having learned that most Sidhe do not like to be touched, but he made the offer, and she stepped forward and leaned so that her head rested on his shoulder. His arms closed around her. And it felt to both of them like coming home.

Chapter 37

Kat's note to Lord Denno was delivered by Reeve Tolliver on Tuesday afternoon, making an appointment for Thursday after dinner. Elizabeth had nearly asked Kat to invite him to dinner, but then she had grown afraid. What if he was angry? What if he showed it? What if he did not come? What if he did come?

It would be impossible for her to soothe him in the formal atmosphere of the dining parlor. On the other hand it would be equally impossible for her to see him alone. The maids of honor, who all had experience of Lord Denno's generosity, were bubbling with excitement. They could not wait to appeal to his good nature for assistance with their wardrobes.

Thus on Thursday afternoon, Denoriel found Elizabeth seated among her maidens. They all called greetings as he crossed the room—all except Elizabeth. Kat greeted him very kindly, even squeezed his hand, and signaled for one of the footmen to bring a stool like those on which the maidens sat.

"I am sorry we have been so long parted," Elizabeth said. Her voice froze in her throat for a moment when she heard the formal tone, and she swallowed hard. "But I am sure you know I have been in some trouble."

"Through no fault of her own," Frances Dodd said.

"I knew, of course," Denoriel said. "I came once and was turned away rather harshly by the order of Sir Robert. I did not try to visit again because Sir Anthony Denny . . . ah . . . warned me away."

"We were not allowed to be with Lady Elizabeth either," Margaret Dudley said. "At least not until Lady Tyrwhitt came." She pursed her lips and shook her head. "You would not believe what a clumsy cow she was, forever tripping on her own feet and catching her shoes in the rugs so that she almost fell."

Elizabeth uttered a little gasp and quickly said, "I think perhaps she was aware of being unwelcome—" She saw Denoriel roll his eyes and gasped again, adding hurriedly, "Perhaps that made her awkward."

"That is enough, girls," Kat said, aware there was some significance in Elizabeth's rather desperate remark. "I am certain that we will be meeting Lady Tyrwhitt again if we do go to Court. Remember she was doing what may have been to her an unwelcome duty."

While Kat spoke, Elizabeth had reached out to the small table near her chair that held a book, some sheets of paper, and a pen and ink. She drew the paper to her, moistened the pen, and biting her lip began to write. Denoriel glanced at her and glanced away. She never liked to be corrected, but this ostentatious withdrawal was too much.

Margaret Dudley sniffed but seemed to take a warning from Elizabeth's withdrawal and did not make the remark on the tip of her tongue. Instead she smiled and said, "We are greedy little pigs, Lord Denno, and all have hopes of seizing this and that tidbit from your warehouses. I hope the weather has been mild enough that your ships have made safe harbor and carried handsome cargoes."

"They are greedy little pigs," Kat agreed. "But I did warn you that we have hopes of Elizabeth's full restoration to favor by an invitation to spend Christmas at Court. She has had nothing new because we did not attend Court last year and what with the extra charges on the household because of Sir Robert's presence . . ."

Denoriel laughed, although he was more disturbed than ever. He had hoped that small break in Elizabeth's formal facade when Mistress Dudley had betrayed her use of magic to torment Lady Tyrwhitt, would herald an easier manner toward him, but she now seemed to want to ignore him altogether. She did not even seem interested when he began to describe the stock he had on hand. It was so unlike Elizabeth, who loved elaborate clothing, to take no part in the eager talk about gold tissue and silk brocade. Finally he suggested that everyone come to London and let Joseph Clayborne show them what was available.

The maids of honor all squealed with pleasure and bubbled with thanks. Elizabeth said only, "Kat can certainly take the girls into London next week, but I do not know if it would be wise for me to go. Actually, considering my brother's convictions, I think it best to dress simply and there is little I need. I have prepared a list for you, Lord Denno. Master Clayborne could give what you have to Kat to bring home with her." And then, her eyes almost black with some emotion he could not read, she rose, handed him the note, and left the room.

"Oh, dear," Alice Finch sighed. "We have had so few visitors. I hope our chatter was not too much for her."

"Nonsense," Eleanor Gage said, "she was strong enough to hunt with the Venetian ambassador only last week, and talked all through dinner and the afternoon with him."

Denoriel rose and bowed. "I will look forward to seeing all of you next week. You need only send a note to Joseph, Mistress Ashley, and he will make all ready for you on any day that suits you."

Kat got up too and came to take his hand and walk with him to the door. "Forgive her, Lord Denno. She gets these terrible headaches, sometimes from excitement. Perhaps she will change her mind and come with us to London."

"Whatever is best for her is best for me," he said, and walked off toward the stable.

She had not forgiven him, he thought, unconsciously tightening his grip on the note so that the paper crackled. He stopped, about to toss it away, and then realized he would have to provide whatever she asked for so the break between them would not be so visible. He unfolded the paper, hoping the items would not be difficult to ken. The longer he had to work on them, the longer she would be in his mind, and the sharper his pain of loss would be.

"I cannot bear to look at you without touching you," the note said. "Come to me, my love."

Denoriel just stared down at it, at first so suffused with joy that he thought he could fly and then moments later almost as furious as he had been joyful. That little red-haired devil! No apology. No explanation. Just "come to me" as if he had nothing else to do in life but attend on her.

The rage faded as swiftly as it had come. After all what else *did* he have to do? Denoriel continued on his way toward the stable, chuckling softly. Doubt began to creep past his amusement when Miralys had brought him to the sheltered copse where he had hidden the Gate that permitted him to ride to Hatfield like an ordinary visitor. Elizabeth was not given to so open an exposure of her feelings. Could that message be designed to distract him from something else?

Denoriel was still wavering between doubt and desire when he stepped into the Gate he had had Treowth create from Logres to the dressing room in Elizabeth's apartment. He could now build Gates himself, for he had been industriously studying magic, but he could not take the chance that his less than perfect construction would permit tampering and allow an enemy to reach Elizabeth. Treowth's Gate would not operate for any person but Denoriel himself.

Doubt was all but dismissed when Elizabeth came rushing from her bedchamber when the Gate opened and flung herself into his arms. "Let us go," she whispered urgently, letting go of the nightdress she had been clutching around her. "I have put Eleanor asleep and Blanche is watching by the door to say I am abed and keep out any visitors."

"Where?" he asked with a tinge of bitterness. "Where shall I take you? You told me the last time we went to Llachar Lle that you never wanted to see the place again."

Elizabeth laughed. "Then I did not. Now I do." She stood with her arms around his neck looking up into his face and slowly the smile faded from her lips. "Do not be angry with me, Denno. I cannot explain what went wrong between us. When Tyrwhitt was sniffing everything I had done and felt, just as a dog sniffs for other dogs' leavings, when I was terrified of even thinking about how Tom had touched me, anything to do with coupling became disgusting. And everything that had ever meant pleasure became a danger."

"Poor love," Denoriel said, putting an arm around her waist. "I never guessed that. I thought *you* were angry because I would not extract Kat from the Tower. And I could not, Elizabeth. It would only have convinced the Council that she had made a criminal agreement with Seymour and . . ."

She rested her head on his shoulder and said softly, "I know that. I am sorry I hurt you, Denno, but even when I had Kat back, for a long time I only wanted to be innocent again. I wished I had never met you, never loved you. I knew too much and it all had become horrible to me."

He bent his head to kiss her brow. "Well, let us go to Llachar Lle. And if you are not easy there, say so at once. I will find somewhere else . . . somewhere not for making love. Somewhere where you can feel innocent again."

"No, I want—" Elizabeth started to say, but the doubt in Denoriel's voice woke new doubts in Elizabeth.

She had been waiting for him eagerly, actually thinking about taking him into her bed because she was so eager to enjoy his body again. Now she was one moment hot and the next cold. Fortunately Miralys was waiting at the Gate and seemed to arrive at the palace in one bound.

Elizabeth tried not to think at all as they went up the white marble stairs and through the small open door beside the great closed brass doors. Oddly the huge, ornate great corridor made her more comfortable, reviving the familiar feeling of admiration and exasperation Underhill woke in her. And the more ordinary corridor, in which the door to Denno's rooms were, was as known and welcome as the hallways of Hatfield, as was the illusion of a distant manor house which hid Denno's door.

She was keenly aware of Denno a few steps behind her, that he was following her in tense expectation that she would turn and reject him, but Elizabeth did not hesitate. She was warm all through now and she stretched her hand back to him and pulled him with her up the stairs, turning to face him in the bedchamber.

"It's all right," she said, pulling his head down so their lips could meet. "It's all right now."

Albertus had been given a token that would make any Gate take him to Caer Mordwyn. He sat staring at it now in the darkest corner of what had been the garden of Chenga's house. The house no longer existed . . . nor did Chenga. The Sidhe of Elfhame Cymry had dissolved its substance into power and dissipated that power. What they had done to Chenga . . . Albertus shivered.

That was not important except that he would have to tell Aurilia what had happened and she would have to tell Vidal.

Albertus shivered again. Surely she would not make him tell Prince Vidal—that would be his death warrant. Surely he was still of enough value to her . . . He looked at the token in his hand again. If only he could use a Gate to take him anywhere but Caer Mordwyn. But there was nowhere for him to go, except back to the mortal world and without the gold Aurilia furnished and the lodging in Otstargi's house, he would barely scrape out an existence in squalor and misery.

Suddenly Albertus rose to his feet. It was not far to the Gate that Vidal had constructed for Chenga and he stepped into it with a kind of desperate courage, knowing that his token would at least bring him into the palace. Aurilia knew he could never have survived making his way from the outer Gates past the monsters that Vidal let roam loose in his domain. He had no shields; he had no weapons; and his body was soft and mortal.

The courage lasted until he came to the door of Aurilia's apartment. There he hesitated, swamped by an abject impulse to run past and try to seek sanctuary in his own room. But Aurilia's door opened on its own and her voice, sweet and soft as it always was before she did something truly dreadful, called out to him.

He took a step and then another and then, weeping, fell to his knees. "Chenga is gone," he whimpered.

Aurilia's eyes were bright, her hair, piled high on her head in an elaborate creation of curls and thin braids except for a thick fringe across her forehead that hid the scars, was bright gold. She lifted a delicate hand and gestured with a pink-tipped finger. Albertus slid across the floor, shaking with fear.

"What do you mean . . . gone?" she asked.

"It was not my fault," Albertus gasped.

"What was not your fault?" The voice was not so sweet.

"Chenga caught a child—it was only a mortal child, but the Cymry Sidhe . . . they value their mortals." He covered his face with his hands and wept. "She—she partially skinned it and . . . and did other things. She used magic to keep it alive and a Sidhe heard it screaming and . . . and caught her."

Aurilia's lips thinned. "Vidal will not be pleased. He had planned for her to start a disturbance in which Elizabeth could be caught." She sighed. "You said 'gone' so I assume you know to where she fled when they drove her out."

"They didn't drive her out." Albertus' voice was little above a tremulous whisper. "I thought they had little magic, but I was wrong. They have it when they want it, especially when they are angry." He shuddered and shuddered, clutching his arms around himself. "They did to her everything that she had done to the child, and it healed . . . and then it happened all over again . . . and again . . . and again. She screamed her voice away. And then they said they would take her to a place called Wormgay Hold. They all agreed that she could never get free, that Wormgay would drain all her power from her."

"Wormgay!" Aurilia sat more upright and her teeth set. "By all the Powers! Vidal could perhaps have brought her out of Cymry, but he will not go to Wormgay. And besides, bearing the wounds you spoke of, something would likely have eaten her by now."

She gestured and a blow from an unseen force knocked Albertus flat. He lay, sobbing, until several hard kicks forced him upright again. He shrieked as another harder blow knocked him down once more and began to scream for mercy and to try to crawl away from more brutal kicks. Aurilia's frown lessened and she leaned forward and sucked in his terror and agony. Human misery did provide the best power; she really understood why Chenga had been overwhelmed by temptation.

"It was not my fault," Albertus yelled. "She always stayed in the house if I was not with her so she would not be tempted." He got out the words between gasps and groans of pain from the blows rained on him. "How could I guess that a child would come to the door with an announcement about the Great Tournament?"

"Why were you not in the house with Chenga?" Aurilia snarled. She was the one who recommended to Vidal that using Albertus as a human servant would make Chenga look more like the other Sidhe of Cymry and Vidal would blame her for the new damage to his plans. "You were supposed to watch her and see that she did their mortals no harm!"

A new blow, harder than the others, rendered Albertus incapable of responding to the kicks on his sides and belly. A lifted finger suspended the beating momentarily. Aurilia did not want to kill him; she intended to let Vidal do that to assuage his temper. If Albertus died under the punishment she meted out, she would need to break to Vidal the news that his last plan for being rid of Elizabeth had just fallen apart and she would have no scape-goat to hand to him.

Albertus assumed the cessation of blows was to provide him breath to answer. "I had gone to Lady Ilamar's house to make a potion for calming her—her lover is looking elsewhere—"

Aurilia had forgotten the question. Her mind had been on Vidal and his plans. Suddenly a few of the words Albertus had said developed meaning. She pointed and a violent kick wrenched a new shriek from Albertus and sent him skidding sideways. Her finger lifted again, and Albertus lay gasping.

"The Great Tournament. You said the child came with an announcement about the Great Tournament. I know Vidal had plans for getting Elizabeth to the Great Tournament and dealing with her there. What was the announcement?"

"That it would be held in a mortal week's time in Elfhame Cymry, that the Sidhe would contribute music and dancing. That the mortals would present all their skills for judgment, all variety of physical combat, cooking, art, needlework and so on, the judgment to be by two High Court Sidhe, Prince Denoriel Siencyn Macreth Silverhair and the FarSeer, Princess Aleneil Arwyddion Ysfael Silverhair."

"Ah," Aurilia breathed, her rage suddenly assuaged. "So at least Chenga was successful in convincing someone in Cymry that their Tournament would be accorded a higher place in Sidhe amusements if they themselves were not the judges. Yes, Chenga could be quite cunning and even charming when she did not allow her lust for pain to overpower her common sense." She nodded slightly. "Come over here." She grew impatient as Albertus started to crawl painfully toward her, and a force shoved him rapidly to the foot of her chair. "So you did not always stay with Chenga but went out and about among the Cymry Sidhe and their mortals?"

"You did not forbid me," Albertus whined, crouching in on himself in fearful expectation of being beaten again.

However, no blow fell, and Aurilia stared at him for a little while as if assessing him. Then she asked, "Have you learned Cymry customs? How their mortals behave? Can you explain about these contests?"

"Yes, my lady."

Her brows went up. "Well then, you might survive telling Vidal what happened to Chenga. I will go so far as to provide you with a shield that will turn away a levin bolt or two. And I will suggest that he not kill you so that you can guide him in Elfhame Cymry."

"No," Albertus pleaded, beginning to weep. "No, please."

A force lifted him to his feet and turned him toward the door, at which point his bowels released and terror deprived him of his senses. When he became aware again, he was lying on the floor once more but in Vidal's chamber and he could hear Aurilia's voice.

"What I am trying to tell you, before you turn Albertus into minced meat, is that you can use him so that not all is lost. Chenga somehow managed to get the prince of Elfhame Cymry to invite Denoriel and Aleneil to judge their stupid mortal contests. That will almost certainly guarantee that Elizabeth will come to the Tournament *and* that her two guardians will be thoroughly occupied."

"And how am I to get invited to the Tournament? Chenga would have arranged that and—"

"My dear prince," Aurilia said, smiling, "you will go as a mortal. After what Chenga did, I am afraid that anyone not strongly vouched for as a long-time friend will be regarded with suspicion. What is more, Albertus tells me that the Cymry Sidhe have more magic than they show. Who knows whether they can detect Bright Court or Dark. However, there are so many mortals that no one will notice one more. Especially when that extra mortal behaves as if it has always lived in Cymry."

Vidal's mouth had opened to make a blistering reply, but he did not speak and now he first stared at Aurilia and then glanced at Albertus, obviously having second thoughts. Those second thoughts seemed satisfactory. A faint smile touched his lips as he said, "You may be right about that, my dear. A strange Sidhe with a Sidhe's power would be noted, perhaps even watched after Chenga's stupidity, but a mortal . . . mortals are harmless."

"Yes," Aurilia agreed. "You can be sure that Elizabeth would be careful, likely would flee to one of her protectors if any strange Sidhe approached her, but she would not fear a mortal."

Elizabeth and Denoriel were a long time about their reconciliation. They made love, dozed, made love again. Denno's invisible servants brought food, a small table, soft-padded chairs to the bedchamber. They ate, went back to bed. Elizabeth could feel tight bands inside herself unwinding.

She had thought that having Kat back and being assured that she would be received into favor once more had drained away her tension, but life in the mortal world was never like this. There she had lessons, she had the maids of honor to deal with, she always had to watch what she said and how she acted because she knew there were spies for the Council in her household. And everything had to be done with strict attention to the time.

Underhill, time was of no account at all. As far as she knew they had no way to tell the hours and longer stretches were measured in mortal time. Often that annoyed Elizabeth, who liked the feeling of having accomplished specific tasks according to schedule, but today was different.

After a little doze to recover from the strenuous exercise of lovemaking, Elizabeth bounced out of bed. When Denno only groaned and turned over, she trotted into the adjoining bedchamber and opened the wardrobe. The clothes were all there. She admired the magnificent Court dress with its wide sleeve cuffs of squirrel fur, but she was too full of energy today to move with the studied grace that dress required.

Which then? One of the modest day gowns? Those were best for the market. Or should she put on the long leggings and tunic, most comfortable for sitting astride if one were going adventuring. She remembered how horrified she had been when Tangwystl magicked that type of garment onto her, but she had learned to value the freedom when long, clinging skirts were banished.

A tiny chill touched her and she reached for one of the morning gowns. She did not want to be adventurous today; she wanted to be safe and happy. She would ask Denno to take her to the market—the Bazaar of the Bizarre today; they had the oddest things there—and she would ask Denno to buy her something she could take back to the mortal world to remind her of this day's joy.

The thought saddened her because it foretold of troubles to come, times when even Denno could not solve her problems because solving them would create worse problems. But not now, she told herself, and ran to wake him so he could make her happy.

He succeeded so well that Denno had to twist time very hard to get Elizabeth back to her bed in Hatfield at dawn in the morning after she left. She lifted the sleep spell she had put on Eleanor and when the girl woke naturally and in turn woke Elizabeth, she came from the bed rosy and smiling.

"What a bad mood I was in yesterday," she said, as soon as Kat came to break her fast with them. "Poor Lord Denno. I wonder why I bit off his nose that way. Oh well, he is used to me. I know he said once that he could not do without having his blood boiled once or twice a week."

"He never minded quarreling with you, Elizabeth," Kat said, frowning. "But I have never seen you turn him away so coldly. He was hurt."

"I will amend it," Elizabeth said lightly, thinking she had amended her coldness some four or five times already. "I will write him a note and . . . and say I am sorry."

"Well, if that does not amend the hurt, it may not matter," Margaret Dudley said, laughing. "The shock of seeing you say you are sorry for something might kill the old man."

"Margaret!" Kat protested.

But Elizabeth only laughed and went to the writing desk to write Denno a note that Tolliver would deliver to the house at Bucklersbury. The note naturally enough brought Denoriel to Hatfield the next day, where his meeting with Elizabeth was much less strained so that Kat sighed with relief and the maids of honor giggled among themselves and planned raids on Lord Denno's warehouse.

For several days Elizabeth tasted the joys of Underhill as if they were new. She got to wear her grand Court dress at a formal ball given by Lord Ffrancon to welcome and entertain Prince Idres Gawr of Elfhame Cymry. He was a beautiful Sidhe, dark-haired, pale-skinned, with piercing gray eyes rather than green, and the Elven he spoke was more like singing.

He stopped when Elizabeth was presented to him and said, "The red-haired queen. I give you greeting, lady."

"Your Highness," Elizabeth breathed, startled by what he had said and with her heart leaping in exultation. "You do me great honor."

"And you will bring us great joy in the future," the prince said. Then he nodded, smiled, and gestured as if to dismiss formality. "May I hope you will accompany Lord Denoriel and Lady Aleneil when they come to judge the mortal Tournament?"

"Mortal Tournament," Elizabeth repeated, paling and casting a reproachful glance at Denno as she thought of the blood and death a tournament of mortals to amuse Sidhe too often meant. "I . . . I . . ."

He put out a graceful, long-fingered hand and took hers. "Ah, you fear for your fellow mortals. No, no. We of Cymry value our mortals. There will be no worse hurts than a few bruises from the bouts of wrestling. Swordplay is always with blunted weapons, and our healers are there and ready."

Elizabeth sank into a Court curtsey. "Then I will come with a very glad heart."

The prince moved on and Elizabeth looked up at Denoriel. "He said I would be queen . . . and red-haired. Does that mean soon, Denno?" Her eyes lit, then darkened. Yes, the idea that she *would* be queen was intoxicating but—what that meant—

Was appalling.

There was only one way she could become queen. Her heart chilled with anticipated sorrow, and the image of a big-eyed child, eyes gone blank and glazed in death, swept across her mind. "Grace of God, Denno, but that means Edward must die and Mary too." But it was not of Mary that she thought, as she looked up, stricken, into Denoriel's face, and faltered. "Grace of God—I do not want Edward to die."

Chapter 38

Elizabeth was enchanted by Elfhame Cymry. It seemed to be a bright, fertile cup guarded round about by towering mountains. To Elizabeth, who had never seen mountains, only the low, rolling hills of Hertfordshire, the view of the gray craggy cliffs crowned by snow-covered peaks was breathtaking.

There was a palace; it seemed to be set up on the side of the tallest mountain, with a pale road winding up from the village in which they had arrived. One could just make out the tower of the keep behind the great walls of gray stone. Elizabeth thought it must imitate the huge castles Edward the First had built in an attempt to suppress Welsh revolutions.

"I hope," she said to Denno, who was looking about with almost as much surprise as she felt, "that the castle here is warmer and more convenient than the ones in mortal Wales."

"If it is not," Denoriel replied, laughing, "I will be sadly disappointed in Prince Idres Gawr. But this does look like a Welsh village . . . only much larger and neater and cleaner. I think—ah, here are Ilar and Aleneil."

"Come along. Come along," Ilar said. "I will show you where the combat will take place and then we can go look at the pavilions set up for displaying the crafts."

"The items are all mortal-made," Denoriel said quietly in

517

Elizabeth's ear, "so if you see something you like and it is for sale, I will buy it for you to take back with you."

Elizabeth nodded happily; she loved bringing home odd and sometimes valuable items for which she had to find a background. Her explanations of how she obtained them needed considerable inventiveness not to be repetitious and yet to satisfy Kat.

There was another thing about Cymry she noticed. No one looked at her with any special interest. In Avalon and Logres and even more in other elfhames, the Sidhe always looked her over most carefully. Occasionally one would approach Denno to ask if he would be willing to part with her. That always made her a little anxious, not that she thought Denno was likely to trade her for some favor or valuable item but that a quarrel might ensue. The explanation that she did not belong to Denno but was Underhill by the special permission of Queen Titania had always settled the matter, but it still made her uncomfortable.

She realized almost immediately why the Sidhe were not interested in her. Here she was not anything unusual. The village teemed with mortals. Indeed there were comparatively few Sidhe. Elizabeth could pick them out because they usually stood a head taller than the mortals.

There, she thought, I have drawn the notice of at least one. And then realized she was wrong. It was one of the mortals who was staring at her, not a Sidhe, although this mortal was easily as tall as the Sidhe. Elizabeth stepped a little closer to Denno. That mortal was not only staring at her, he looked as if he would like to eat her. But then his face warmed with a broad smile.

Elizabeth's breath sighed out in relief, and in the next moment she had forgotten him because Denno said, "Look there. Ilar and Aleneil are waving at us."

"Come along. Come along," Ilar said. "I will show you around. We still have a little time before Denoriel must get up on the judge's seat to watch the trials."

Denoriel sighed and shook his head. "Why in the world did your prince decide that I would make a good judge?"

"It was the mortals. There was some talk among them that Cymry Sidhe would favor the mortals from their own domains and when Idres Gawr thought it over, he felt that perhaps it was not wise that the judges should know the contestants too well."

"I understand that," Denoriel said ruefully, "but why me?"

Ilar frowned slightly. "That was partly because one of the mortals—I do not know to whom he is bound, but he is a good healer—raised the point that the Sidhe who judged the events should not only not be from Cymry but should know mortals and their abilities. The rest you can blame on Aleneil. She was complaining to me about how much time you and she had to spend in the mortal world, so I brought that information to Prince Idres Gawr—" Ilar grinned "—and he was suitably grateful."

Denoriel groaned and looked reproachfully at Aleneil. "How could you!"

She laughed heartily. "I am trapped in my own net. I am judging a host of crafts."

They parted soon afterward, the judges to their duties and Ilar to his own, which currently was confirming the registration of contestants. Elizabeth wanted to listen to the elven music and Denoriel somewhat reluctantly agreed that she could go with Lady Ilamar, Prince Idres's sister, if she would wear her shields. Elizabeth promptly called them up and went off to the concert.

This, too, was a contest, unfortunately, and the same piece was presented by several groups and also by individual performers. It was indeed very interesting to hear how different the music sounded, although she knew it was the same. It also took quite a long time to get through each piece.

Elizabeth listened through two sets, but she was starting to get hungry and the novelty of hearing different versions of the same basic music had worn off. When the preparations were being made for a third presentation, with two more to get through, she was ready for something new. If she went to part of the Tournament that was like a fair, she thought, she was sure she could find food and drink as well as something interesting to buy. And Denno had given her plenty of tokens.

She patted the purse tied around her waist under her skirt and asked Lady Ilamar if it would be possible for her to get something to eat and to look at the crafts that were being presented.

Lady Ilamar, accustomed to the short patience and eager appetite of young mortals, smiled and nodded, gesturing to a pair of mortal women who had accompanied her. "Go with Lady Elizabeth to the serving pavilion and then let her look at the fairings." She looked down at Elizabeth. "Do you need tokens, child?"

Elizabeth shook her head and rose suddenly as she heard the

new group begin to tune their instruments. She dropped Lady Ilamar a curtsey and hurried away before they could start to play; the two ladies, startled by her movement, were left behind.

Someone else, another mortal Elizabeth saw, her lips curving in amusement, felt the same as she and was hurrying from the pavilion. The first notes of the new piece sounded, and Elizabeth lost interest in everything but escape. She quickened her pace even more and stepped through the flap of the pavilion. As it fell closed behind her, she felt a violent blow on her back, a blow strong enough to drive her forward several steps to keep from falling down.

"Ow!" she exclaimed, turning as soon as she could to see who had banged into her; but by the time she had caught her balance and looked there was no one there.

It was just as well she had been shielded, she thought, wanting to rub the spot but unable because of the shield. A blow she could feel through the shield that way and that thrust her forward so hard might have hurt her. It was odd that she had not seen anyone, not even anyone running away. But this was Underhill, she reminded herself, and she could not see through illusion here. Likely someone bent on mischief had a Don't-see-me spell.

Just then the two ladies who were supposed to accompany her came out of the pavilion. "Oh, my lady," the shorter of the two said, "I am so sorry. Ellis tripped just as you went up the aisle and it took us a moment to catch up."

Ellis tripped? Elizabeth thought. Of course, Ellis was human, not Sidhe, and might be a bit clumsy, but there was also tanglefoot. Elizabeth renewed the power to her shields and resolved to stay with her companions at all costs.

Vidal looked down incredulously at the blade in his hand. It was bent. His arm throbbed with the shock of the blow he had landed. The little red-haired bitch was shielded and so thoroughly shielded that most of the strength of his blow had reverberated up his own arm. Who would have believed it? He thought his problem was solved when Denoriel had abandoned her to a less careful guardian and that Sidhe had let her go with only two mortal servants.

He slipped around the end of the next pavilion, pulled on the binding he had attached to Albertus, and reappeared in his mortal guise.

"Where is she?" he snarled at Albertus.

"Just ahead with the two women, my lord."

Vidal slapped Albertus so hard he fell to his knees. "Do not call me 'my lord' you fool. Go, follow them. She saw me, I think, but not you."

Albertus had no trouble following. Elizabeth's red hair was easy to see and the three women were moving in a leisurely way toward the serving pavilion. When they entered and sat down, Albertus hurried back and told Vidal.

"Good," Vidal muttered.

He fingered his pouch, then decided against poison. It was too uncertain. He *really* wanted to see Elizabeth die. She would need to drop the shield in order to eat. He drew Albertus to the side and pressed a thin-bladed poniard into his hand.

"While she is eating, just pass by behind her and slip this knife in. A healer knows best where to put the blade."

Albertus went wall-eyed with terror. Vidal hissed between his teeth. He could not trust the mortal to do it right, but he could follow concealed by the Don't-see-me spell and . . .

Only it was almost immediately apparent that there would be no opportunity to be rid of Elizabeth so simply. The women with Elizabeth were well known and popular and it seemed as if every friend they had rushed over to greet them and to be introduced to Elizabeth.

At least they were talking about what dishes to choose. Vidal waited for Elizabeth to rise. She would have to drop the shield to carry the food, but she continued to sit and talk with those around her. One of the women Ilamar had sent with her went to fetch the food.

Turning away, Vidal tried to work his way to the food counter to try poison after all; he would not care if the others got poisoned too. In fact that would work out well, concealing the fact that Elizabeth was the target. But a tall Sidhe monitor told him he must wait his turn and forced him away toward the end of the line. He almost struck the Sidhe down, but that would have marked him as Sidhe himself, after which he could not have tried to take Elizabeth and blame her death on the mortals.

He gave up and returned to the table at the back where Albertus sat, shaking. The creature was useless, but the group had closed around Elizabeth again and Vidal knew it would be impossible to approach her. Each woman wanted to speak with her or touch her; they stood all around her while she ate, quite close. He would not have cared if Albertus had been caught doing the murder, but there was no chance for striking. Elizabeth's back was never exposed.

As the women ate, laughing and talking, Vidal put aside his disappointment over not being able to be rid of Elizabeth quickly and easily. Once the meal was over, she would call up the shields again. He would have no trouble stripping those shields away, he thought, but for that he would need time. Vidal began to be pleased again. It would be very amusing to peel off her shields and drink in the powerful energy of her terror as she realized she was being exposed to anything he wanted to do to her.

He took back the knife he had given Albertus and whispered a new plan. Elizabeth must be led to the end of the area set aside for the Tournament. There were Gates there—Vidal had come through one of them—built specially for the convenience of anyone coming to the Tournament. And those Gates would be destroyed when the Tournament was over, Vidal thought with considerable satisfaction, closing any trail behind him.

The whole party left the serving pavilion together; Vidal was annoyed and was about to set Albertus on them, but the women soon began to separate. Some went back to the stalls at which they were working; others stopped at craft booths while Elizabeth went on, still others continued on while Elizabeth and her companions stopped. Vidal began to follow closer, smiling. They were going straight down one aisle of booths, coming nearer and nearer to one of the Gates, all of which were marked with golden posts and a banner bearing a red dragon.

Almost at the end of the row of booths there was a stall that sold shawls. A hurried instruction to Albertus made him walk quickly ahead to that booth and begin to examine the shawls minutely. For his wife, he said to the woman who worked the booth. His wife loved shawls and would be thrilled if he could bring her a new one. The trouble was that she had so many. Yes, she had one like this, and one that color with a design only very slightly different. Was there something truly unusual?

The woman bent to look through her baskets. Elizabeth came nearer and nearer. Behind her and the two ladies, Vidal strolled along, not close enough make them conscious of him, but close enough with a magic lift to get behind Elizabeth. He knew he could not grasp her, but if he could push her into the Gate he could take her anywhere.

The woman rose, holding out a shawl with a most peculiar design and unusual colors. Albertus knew that if he said his wife had one like that, the woman would know he was just trying to take up her time. He whistled through his teeth and held up the shawl, spreading it out. The movement attracted Elizabeth's eye.

"Mistress," Albertus called, when he saw her head turn, "could you give me a moment and look at this shawl?"

Elizabeth hesitated, the two women stopping alongside.

Albertus began on the tale of his wife and the many shawls. "And this one is truly unusual," he said, his breath coming a little short as he saw Vidal right behind the group, his hands reaching toward the tops of the two ladies' heads. "But do you think it ugly?"

He held the shawl out to Elizabeth. It was a fascinating pattern in odd shades of green and violet and orange. Truly she could not decide whether she thought it ugly. She took a step closer, not noticing that the ladies were no longer right alongside.

Denoriel rose gratefully from the seat on the dais on which he had judged the wrestling matches, the cudgel work, and the quarterstaff bouts. He had been highly amused by the cudgel fights. He had wondered how Prince Idres Gawr would fulfill his promise that no one would be seriously hurt if the bouts were to be fought in earnest.

He learned that the Cymry Sidhe, or, at least, Idres Gawr, were indeed clever users of magic. Each cudgel was bespelled to weigh and feel exactly like the true weapon, and when it landed, to cause such pain as a stroke from a cudgel would. If it struck a vulnerable place, like the head, the blow would seem to render the victim unconscious; however, the cudgels were actually nothing but a hollow tube that squirted colored dye each time they struck an opponent with sufficient force and did no real harm at all.

The same was true of the quarterstaffs and would be true during the afternoon matches with swords and javelins. Only the bows and arrows were perfectly natural, since the targets of stuffed leather could not be hurt. He had enjoyed himself and hoped Elizabeth had also enjoyed herself, but he was now ready for a nuncheon and he wanted to eat it with Elizabeth.

He went directly to the pavilion where music was playing and immediately saw Lady Ilamar . . . but Elizabeth was not with her. His heart in his throat, he made his way to Ilamar and asked anxiously for Elizabeth.

"Now, now, there is nothing to fly into a pelter about," the lady said, smiling. "Cymry is a safe place. Elizabeth got hungry and impatient with sitting still so long. You know what mortals, especially young ones, are. I sent her off with two of my ladies to the serving pavilion. You will find her there or looking at the fairings. The child said she had tokens enough."

"Yes, thank you." Denoriel gave a sketchy bow and rushed out.

His entry into the serving pavilion was so precipitous that he ran into two Sidhe, who had paused in the entryway to look around. He began to dodge past and was caught.

"Don't you bother to say— Denoriel, what's wrong?" Aleneil asked.

"Elizabeth's gone," he said, pushing past her to look around the pavilion. "Lady Ilamar let her go with just two mortal serving women."

"Cymry is a safe place," Ilar said, lips thinning. "We only recently conducted a sharp lesson on what befalls those who transgress. Let us ask the serving women before you imagine horrors."

The report from those who provided the food was soothing. They all remembered Elizabeth, because of her red hair and because their FarSeers, like those of Avalon, had seen the possible future if she became queen. They all agreed that she had been surrounded by women who were eager to meet her, that she had eaten soup and bread and cheese and fruit with the others, and that they had all gone out together.

"She will be looking through the booths," Ilar said. "Come and eat something. Then we will find her. After all she has just eaten. She will not want to join us."

"No," Denoriel said. "I must find her first." And he started down the most direct aisle of booths.

"What—" Ilar began.

Aleneil had turned toward the aisle of booths to the right. "The Dark Court want her dead," she said to him.

Ilar hurried after her. "There are no Dark Court Sidhe in Cymry. We did have one, but she was caught in a filthy act and we punished her and set her in Wormgay, from where she will not ever trouble anyone again."

"I hope you are right," Aleneil said over her shoulder, "but Denoriel will not rest a moment until—"

"Here!" Denoriel called, waving to his sister. "She went this way with her two ladies."

The boothkeeper to whom he had spoken was one of the women introduced to Elizabeth in the serving pavilion. She told him Elizabeth was just intending to walk down to the end of the aisle and then over to the next aisle. Denoriel swallowed and went along. Two booths down, another man had seen Elizabeth. There were only four or five women together he said, but the red hair was unmistakable. The mortals in Cymry were nearly all dark-haired.

"Did anyone seem very interested in her?" Aleneil asked. "Did anyone seem to be watching her?"

"No." The man seemed rather surprised. "We all looked at the red hair, of course, but no one seemed to be trying to stop her or speak to her."

Denoriel let out a relieved sigh, but when Ilar urged him again to return to the serving pavilion, he shook his head. "I must see her and be sure," he said, and continued down the aisle until a sharp cry made him break into a run.

"My shawl!" a boothkeeper was shouting. "He took my shawl."

However it was not her accusation that turned Denoriel's guts to ice. It was seeing two women standing not far from the booth, who did not turn their heads toward the cries, who did not move, who did not seem even to breathe.

"Where did he go? Was he alone?" Denoriel asked trying to project calm despite his panic. "What happened?"

"He wanted a special shawl, one that was like no other," the woman said, rather breathlessly. "I had one. I do not know what possessed me to make it. It was all swirls and then sudden breaks and hard edges—"

"Yes, yes," Denoriel interrupted. "But the one who took it? A man? A woman? Was he alone?"

"He called to a red-haired girl who was walking by and asked her if the shawl was ugly. He held it out. The girl came toward him. Then, suddenly, he wrapped the shawl around her and someone rushed by—I didn't see much of him, just a big man . . . and they were gone. Gone with my shawl. But none of them were Sidhe. None could do magic, so how were they suddenly gone?"

Aleneil had stopped near the frozen women while Denoriel

went to question the woman who had lost her shawl. Ignoring Ilar's expression, which had become horrified when he saw the women were in stasis, she released the two waiting women from Vidal's spell.

"Lady Eliz—" one of them said, starting forward and peering around. "She's gone again," she said to her companion. "I swear I just blinked, and she is gone."

"I think it was more than a blink," the second woman said, her eyes resting on Aleneil.

"You were put in stasis," Aleneil said quickly. "What did you see before you 'blinked.'"

"There was a man—"

"Sidhe?" Aleneil asked.

"Oh, no," the second woman said. "He was assuredly mortal. Old. With gray hair and lines on his face, and his hands shook as if he were frightened."

Frightened. Aleneil swallowed. One of the mortals who had been forced to help to take Elizabeth. "So, this man?"

"He was looking at shawls," the first woman put in quickly. "There must have been a hand and a half full of them lying on the counter. And he had the most outré-looking one in his hands, all violet and green and orange. He called out to Lady Elizabeth and she looked toward him, and . . ."

She stopped speaking, her eyes going wide. The other woman said, "And then I don't remember anything until you—"

"Go back to Lady Ilamar and stay with her," Ilar said severely. "Do not wander around the fairings alone anymore."

The women made frightened exclamations, clasped hands, and hurried away together. Ilar and Aleneil rushed forward to join Denoriel just in time to hear the booth-keeper say that none of the people who had taken her shawl were Sidhe, so how could they disappear.

"The ladies sent with Elizabeth were in stasis!" Ilar exclaimed. "Mother watch over the child. There must have been a Sidhe involved, a Sidhe disguised as mortal. I fear your Elizabeth has been abducted. I will go and tell Prince Idres Gawr—"

If Denoriel heard him he gave no sign; he was staring at the booth woman. "They disappeared," he repeated, "Did you hear anything, anything at all? See anything? You were staring at the place where they disappeared . . ."

"Gate," the woman said. "Someone said 'Gate' just as they winked out."

"Gate?" Ilar repeated, looking ahead and then right and left. "Where is the Gate?"

"What do you mean, where is the Gate?" Aleneil asked.

"There should be a Gate at the end of this aisle of booths. See, look down there, you can just make out the Gate at the next aisle—"

"Dear Mother, help," Denoriel breathed. "Let it be a concealment spell."

He began to mutter and gesture, and sure enough the Gate reappeared.

"He did the quickest thing," Aleneil sighed. "He was afraid Elizabeth would break the Don't-see-me spell or he was distracted. She must have been fighting him—them. But how could she fight two strong men?"

Denoriel let out his held breath and started toward the Gate. "She had her shields up. I warned her before she went off with Lady Ilamar to put up her shields. Whoever tried to seize her would not be able to get a grip on her."

"Good shields?" Ilar asked anxiously hurrying after him.

"Tangwystl's shields," Denoriel said. "There are no better."

"But where are you going?" Ilar cried, catching at Denoriel's arm. "Come with me to Idres Gawr. He will be able to trace them, I hope . . . But the Gates are all open Gates to accommodate visitors from all over . . ."

"I think I know where they will arrive," Denoriel said, his eyes fixed and staring as they stepped into the Gate. "If Elizabeth was really frightened and angry, there is one place they are almost certain to go . . ."

What Elizabeth felt when the shawl went around her and she felt herself propelled forward, was sheer rage. Perhaps under the rage was a flicker of fear, but her shields were up and at full strength and she knew no one could hurt her physically.

She did not know who was trying to seize her, but she did know that they had ruined not only the happy day she had been enjoying but probably other free and happy times in the future. Now she would be watched and guarded ten times more closely. She loved Denno, loved him dearly, but she did not love to have him breathing down her neck whenever they were doing anything outside of his bedchamber in Llachar Lle.

She heard a man's deep voice cry "To the Gate" or "In the Gate" and sheer vicious pleasure drew back her lips as she fixed her mind on the mist. On the lovely friendly mist that had made her a kitten once and then made her a lion to save her.

Mist! She demanded with every fiber of her anger fueled by that oily spray of fear. Mist! Come for me, mist! And something black/red and hot fountained up inside her and strange little symbols floated atop the boiling of her rage and her fear.

"Where are we?" a second man's voice cried, thinner and tremulous.

"Stickfast! *Fiat!*" Elizabeth yelled and lurched forward, freeing herself from the shawl, and tumbling off the Gate platform.

Fortunately it was not much of a fall and the shields protected her from any bruise. The fall was fortunate too because she felt a hand, inhumanly swift, grab for her. He would have caught her if she had jumped off the platform standing. Now she did not rise but crawled away as fast as she could in the few moments before the stronger voice roared a counterspell to her stickfast.

Around her the mist was thick as wool, impenetrably white. Elizabeth rolled over and sat up. "Greetings, mist," she said. "I'm sorry I only seem to come here when I'm in trouble but I haven't been Underhill much until a few weeks ago. I was in trouble in the mortal world."

A faint frisson of remembered panic passed over her. The mist billowed around her and in the distance she heard a faint roar.

"Oh no, mist. No more lions, please. That one did save me but it was too hungry and too mean. We are going to have to think of something else so I can get away from these people. I don't know who they are or what they want, but—"

Her voice—she had been speaking in normal tones—cut off suddenly as the mist began to thin between her and the Gate. Elizabeth heard the strong man's voice chanting and she drew in a sharp breath and got to her feet.

"Please, mist," she whispered, "don't let them find me. I hope they are not hurting you, but . . . but . . ."

She ran off at an angle where the mist seemed to be thicker and then heard the thinner voice cry out, "Prince Vidal, beware—"

That voice cut off suddenly as if the speaker had been silenced and she heard Denno call her name. She looked around wildly, saw another thicker patch of mist and yelled. "Denno! I am here! I am unharmed, but Vidal is causing the mist to thin. If he finds me—I must flee, Denno, to some place further so he cannot follow my voice!"

"Elizabeth, be careful. You'll get lost in the mist. Come back toward our voices, toward the Gate. There are three of us here to protect you."

Elizabeth wondered why he thought she would get lost; she always knew where the Gates were. But fortunately the thicker patch of mist was in the direction of the Gate and she darted off that way, looking anxiously through the thinning mist behind her for a shadow. She was afraid she would run right into the arms of her attacker.

"Let her alone, Vidal," Aleneil called. "Let us take Elizabeth back safely and I will not go to Titania and tell her you were trying to harm Elizabeth."

"Done is done," the strong voice snarled. "When she's dead the Dark Court will be stronger than the Bright. Whatever Titania thinks she will do to me will fail."

Elizabeth gasped with fear and shrank back into the small curdling patch of safety as the mist in the whole area between the Gate and Vidal's voice faded. Beyond, the mist was thicker. A hint of red hair shone through it, perhaps coming toward the Gate. Suddenly Vidal plunged out into the open area and rushed toward the glint of red.

Aleneil screamed.

Denoriel leapt after Vidal, his drawn sword in his hand, crying out in terror because he knew he would be too late.

He was. Vidal's long knife plunged. Plunged again. Ripped upward and downward.

Out of the mutilated body came long streamers of mist, not thin and fragile, but glinting in the twilight like liquid silver. Before Denoriel could plunge his sword into Vidal, the bands had bound him round and round and round. Vidal's voice, high and thin with terror, shrieked to be let loose, to be set free, but the streamers of mist rising from the torn body seemed endless and continued to entangle him in a strangling cocoon of—what?

"Elizabeth . . ." Denoriel sobbed, down on his knees beside the body.

"That isn't Elizabeth," Aleneil breathed, shaking so hard that the tremors moved Denoriel's tense shoulder. "Look at the face. It isn't . . . It isn't even a bad making."

Then Elizabeth's hand joined Aleneil's on Denoriel's shoulder, but she didn't look down at him, she looked away into the mist. "Oh, mist," she said, tears in her voice, "was that your girl? Oh, I am so sorry. So sorry. Is there anything I can do to help?"

Did she feel a little tugging at her mind? Elizabeth almost called up her inner shield, but it was such a small tugging away, not a pushing in. She didn't fight it.

A moment later, Denoriel gasped. A vaguely familiar male figure with blond hair, but no better defined than the red-haired creature, had stepped out of the mist. It bent and lifted the fragile, paper-thin remainder, almost unrecognizable except for the red hair, and carried it away. One streamer of mist was still attached to whatever-it-was and Vidal was drawn after it, screaming for help.

Epilogue

They had all gathered in Gaenor's house because Oberon did not generally send his Thought over Elfhame Elder-Elf. The eldest of his children were the least likely to bring disaster Underhill. Oberon Knew that the mortal Harry FitzRoy had wakened many of the eldest, but they had more wisdom, enough to keep FitzRoy in check, and Oberon was pleased with the foresight that had made him mark Harry with the blue star. Fortunately Elizabeth's bright aura was masked by those of the Sidhe around her and did not draw Oberon's attention. As a centerpoint for disaster, Elizabeth was high on Oberon's list.

Gaenor's house was small, but it obligingly stretched itself to accommodate the whole party. Sitting on the floor at Rhoslyn's feet, Harry shook his head.

"Oh, no," he said. "This is way beyond me, unless you want me to go into the mist, find Vidal, and shoot him with this." He tapped the holstered gun that shot iron bolts.

"Go right ahead," Elizabeth said. "I'm tired of being Vidal Dhu's favorite target."

"No," Pasgen protested. "If you shoot him, Oberon will make me rule the Dark Court, and I've never done anything evil enough to merit that kind of punishment."

"No," Denoriel said, almost simultaneously. Then he waited

courteously for Pasgen to finish and added. "Harry can't go into the mist. He'll be lost in it."

"We will be wary for him," Mechain said, smiling.

"And I do not think Vidal Dhu will be easy to kill, even with a steel bolt," Elidir remarked. "Nor will he be easy to find if the mist wishes to hide him."

"He recovered the last time I shot him," Harry said, making a face.

"In any case, I cannot think it wise to kill the prince of the Dark Court," Gaenor said. "Oberon has his reasons for what he permits and what he punishes. If you desire Prince Vidal punished more than what the mist has done, Elizabeth should complain to Oberon."

"But then Oberon would know about the mist," Elizabeth said, looking distressed. "He will . . . end it. That wouldn't be fair! The mist is like a baby, just learning. One doesn't kill a baby for making a mistake."

"That is a large and very dangerous baby," Rhoslyn pointed out. "It has learned to make. The lion it made killed two mortals."

"That was me," Elizabeth said anxiously. "I asked it to make a hungry lion that would eat the men who had abducted me. It wasn't the mist's idea."

"And the mist didn't like the lion," Pasgen said thoughtfully. "The lion attacked the male . . . ah . . . doll. The one that looks something like me. And when I struck it, the lion I mean, with my sword, the mist dissipated it."

"It hasn't made anything dangerous on its own," Elizabeth put in eagerly. "The red-haired doll and the gold-haired doll did no harm to anyone. They were gentle things."

"But it took the kitten and the lion from your mind, Elizabeth," Denoriel said. "The Mother knows what it will pick out of Vidal Dhu's mind."

"It won't take anything from him because he won't ask it nicely," Elizabeth said firmly. "He'll yell at it and threaten it."

"So far it does not seem to want to kill," Mechain said. "It must have been aware of what Vidal did to its construct. Could it not have fashioned a knife—think how strong those bands in which it wrapped Vidal were—and stabbed him?"

"Hmmm." Elidir bit his lower lip. "Vidal could live a long time wrapped in those bands. There is power in plenty, in great plenty, in that Unformed land. He can draw that in to sustain his life."

"Then likely he will not die at all," Pasgen said, a note of relief in his voice. "He is a very good mage once he sets his mind to magic rather than rage. Once he recovers from his shock and initial fear, he will soon devise a spell to release himself."

Elizabeth sighed. "Then no harm at all will have been done," Elizabeth said. "And there will be no need to tell Oberon about the mist."

Gaenor looked around at her guests. Elizabeth looked hopeful. Pasgen, Mechain, and Elidir looked brightly interested. Harry and Denoriel both had the same expression of concern, their eyes on Elizabeth. When Vidal was free he would try again to be rid of Elizabeth. Rhoslyn alone looked worried and undecided. Gaenor nodded. Rhoslyn had "made" fearsome things and feared the damage such constructs could do if the mist created them out of Vidal's mind.

"Then, for the present, we will do nothing," Gaenor said. "Pasgen and I, and perhaps my student Hafwen, who seems able to 'smell' evil constructs, will keep watch. Unless the mist does create something monstrous"—her lips quirked into a smile—"we will let the baby grow."